MICHELLE BETHAM

I'm an ex-media technician turned rock-music-loving author of hot, sexy romance and chick lit with a kick! My love of books began the second I could read, and some of my happiest memories are of me curled up in bed as a child devouring every Malory Towers and Famous Five book I could get my hands on. As the years progressed I read everything from horror to Harry Potter, Jackie Collins to Jilly Cooper, but I always knew that I wanted to write romance. I love the idea of escapism – of creating a world in which readers can lose themselves, and characters they'll want to spend time with. And thanks to inspiration from the aforementioned Ms. Collins, I always knew that I wanted to write romance of the more racy variety, and to be able to do that every day is a dream come true for me.

After a spell living on the beautiful Canarian island of Tenerife, I'm now back in the UK and settled in County Durham with my wonderful husband and my gorgeous West Highland Terrier, Archie. A proud Geordie girl, I adore the north east of England, but I also love the odd glass of wine, Keanu Reeves, a decent TV drama, Peter Kay… and darts!

You can follow me on Twitter @michellebetham, find me on Facebook www.facebook.com/AuthorMichelleBetham or chat to me on my blog http://michellebethamwriter.blogspot.co.uk/.

EXTRA TIME

MICHELLE BETHAM

A division of HarperCollins*Publishers*
www.harpercollins.co.uk

Harper*Impulse* an imprint of
HarperCollins*Publishers Ltd*
77–85 Fulham Palace Road
Hammersmith, London W6 8JB

www.harpercollins.co.uk

A Paperback Original 2014

First published in Great Britain in ebook format by HarperImpulse 2014

Cover Images © Shutterstock.com

A catalogue record for this book
is available from the British Library

ISBN: 978-0-00-810502-0

Automatically produced by Atomik ePublisher from Easypress

This book is dedicated to all those who love The Beautiful Game... especially my husband Ian, who loves it more than most!

Chapter One

Jim Allen threw open the white shutters that covered the huge French doors, taking in the view of the cobalt-blue sea in front of him. The palm trees surrounding the small and private oval-shaped pool outside on the terrace swayed slightly in the gentle breeze, the sky cloudless and clear, heralding another beautiful day in paradise.

Shoving his hands in his pockets he turned away from the window, walking back over to the huge king-size bed in the centre of the room. She was still asleep, still oblivious to this new day, but he didn't want to wake her, not yet. He just wanted to look at her for a few more minutes.

He leaned against the wall, closing his eyes for a second or two before opening them, directing his gaze at her as she lay on her back, one arm slung high above her head. And what he wanted to do more than anything right now was reach out and move the thin sheet that was covering her, just enough so he could see all of her, because he knew she was naked. He knew that, because they'd made love just an hour ago, before he'd had to leave her to go and join the Newcastle Red Star squad for a team breakfast. Even though he'd much rather have stayed there, with her.

He watched as she moaned quietly in her sleep, shifting slightly so the sheet fell down below her perfect breasts and he couldn't help but react. She had that effect on him; she'd always had that effect on him. He'd loved this woman for over twenty years, yet they'd only been together – properly together, not like the last time – for a matter of months. At the age of forty-nine Jim Allen felt as though his life was only just beginning, and he couldn't be happier.

She gave another, longer moan, shifting again, becoming more restless, and for him that was enough. He couldn't watch her any longer without wanting to touch her, and as the sheet moved further down her body, falling just below her hips, low enough to give him a tantalising glimpse of heaven, he could feel himself growing harder.

'Jesus… what you do to me…' he groaned, pushing a hand through his slightly greying hair, watching as she drew one leg up, an action which caused the sheet to fall down even further, her nakedness now revealed in all its tanned and beautiful glory. 'Shit, Amber. I've got so much work to do, honey, yet I'm gonna have to fuck you so hard first before I can get any of it done.'

'Get on with it then,' she murmured, without opening her eyes, a slight smile on her face.

He couldn't help smiling, too. 'You want more, huh?'

She opened her eyes, pushing herself up onto her elbows. 'I always want more, Jim. I'm never satisfied.'

'Yeah, tell me about it,' he laughed.

'Just get undressed, come on. We haven't got all day.'

He shrugged off his shirt, letting it fall to the floor as he walked over to the bed. 'We've got a few minutes.'

She looked up at him as he leaned over her, her eyes slowly closing as he kissed her gently. 'We can do a lot in a few minutes, Mr. Allen.'

'We sure can, Mrs. Allen,' he whispered, sitting down on the edge of the bed, pulling the sheet away from her body, letting his fingers trail lazily over her stomach before finally resting on her hip. 'I love you, Amber. You do know that, don't you?'

She reached out and gently touched his face, smiling at him. 'Yeah. I know that. Now.'

'Everything else is in the past, baby. It's all in the past.' Although even as he said the words he knew that could never really be the case. How could everything be in the past when the past was still there? Right there, with them, on this stunning island.

She said nothing, just leaned forward and kissed him, her slightly open mouth covering his in a painfully beautiful kiss, every movement her lips made against his making him want her more.

'These past few months, they've been incredible, Amber. Finally having you here, beside me, with me, after everything we've been through…'

She put a finger to his lips, stopping him from saying any more. 'You just said the past is gone, Jim. So let's not go there, okay? We don't need to go there.'

He gently took hold of her wrist, pushing her back onto the bed, nudging her legs open with his knee. 'No. We don't.'

She smiled again as she closed her eyes, putting up no fight, despite the fact he was holding her wrists quite tightly now. In fact, if anything, it seemed to be turning her on more, which in turn made him twice as eager to go back to that safe, secret place he'd visited just an hour earlier.

She arched her back, pushing herself up against him, inviting him inside, and he wasn't going to hang about. He wasn't even going to waste time removing the rest of his clothes, there was no need. He was hard and he was ready, so why wait any longer?

Keeping that tight grip on her wrists, her arms up at either side of her head, he carefully pushed inside her, taking his time, loving the way she felt, all soft and wet and warm. And then he was there, buried deep within her.

Finally letting go of her wrists, he placed his hands on her knees, pushing her legs back up against her stomach, enabling him to go deeper, her moans urging him to push harder, making it difficult for him to hold back any longer. And as she thrust her hips up against his again, he felt that burning release begin to build until he had no option left but to let go, spilling out inside of her, holding onto her as she wrapped her legs around him, keeping him there, holding him in.

But that wasn't the end. It wasn't over. It would have been selfish of him to assume that, so slipping an arm around her waist, he pulled her over in one swift movement, groaning loudly as she climbed astride him, naked and beautiful and yet to come. But she was going to do it now, just for him, and he had a front row seat.

He watched as she threw her head back, reaching down to touch herself and it was almost crazy how quickly he felt himself grow hard all over again. With his hands on either side of her thighs, he carefully moved her forward, lifting her up slightly before lowering her back down, sliding into her once more with an ease only those who'd made love so often possessed.

With him firmly back inside her, she quickly resumed the journey to her own climax, closing her eyes and pushing her breasts out, her hand taking position back where it had been before, and Jim watched as she continued those slow, circular motions, every move her fingers made against herself bringing him closer to another crashing finale. Jesus, he never wanted this to end! Never. And he'd come so close to this not happening at all, to losing her, so he had to bring out his A-game this time. To make sure he didn't lose her again.

'Amber, baby…' he groaned, not taking his eyes off her hand as those once-gentle circular motions became more frantic, signalling her imminent arrival at her own endgame, but he wasn't to be outdone. As that familiar, beautiful tingle started creeping its way up his body he knew they were going to come together this time. And they did, almost simultaneously, their bodies shuddering to that blissful halt as one, leaving them both spent and breathless. 'Jesus, that was good. That was so fucking good!' Jim sighed as Amber collapsed on top of him, her head on his chest.

'Yeah.' She smiled, a more-than-satisfied smile, her eyes still closed. 'It was.'

He kissed the top of her head, burying his fingers in her dark red hair. 'I've really got to go in a minute, honey. We've got a game to prepare for, and if I'm not on top of it all…'

She raised her head slightly, finally opening her eyes. 'I'd much rather you stayed here, on top of *me*.'

He returned her smile, kissing her long and slow. 'Yeah. And there's no place I'd rather be, beautiful. But, unfortunately, I'm here to work. And so are you.'

She groaned, throwing her head back down on his chest. 'I know, I know.' She closed her eyes again, making the most of those final, few precious seconds together before reality returned and took over. 'I just wish I didn't have to.'

Reluctantly pushing herself up and off him, Amber got up and walked over to the French doors, looking out at the stunning view of the pool and the palm trees and the sea that stretched out ahead of them like a never-ending blue blanket.

Jim couldn't take his eyes off her. His beautiful wife of just five months. The woman he'd never thought he'd get close to again, after everything that had happened. Their past history was complicated, but from the second he'd walked back into her life he'd had no intention of losing the fight, not this time. Even though there'd been days when he'd thought he was going to have to concede defeat.

'Isn't Ronnie coming over to the island today?' Jim asked, hauling himself off the bed and joining her at the French doors, slipping his arms around her from behind, pulling her naked body back against him.

'His flight lands at lunchtime. I said I'd go pick him up. They were going to send a car for him, but…' She stopped talking and turned round in his arms, running her fingers lightly over his rough jawline, '… he's my friend, and I want to… You don't mind, do you?'

'Why would I mind?' Jim laughed, his hand gently stroking the base of her spine.

'I don't know.' Amber shrugged, pulling away from him, suddenly realising what a stupid question that had been. *Why* would Jim mind? She and Ronnie were good friends, best friends, and now they were work colleagues, too, but that was all. Okay, so they'd once had a brief relationship, back in the days when he'd been a professional footballer and she'd been the Sports Editor at News North East, a popular regional TV news programme based in her native North East England. But that had been years ago. All forgotten. She didn't feel that way about Ronnie, and he didn't feel that way about her. Not anymore. 'I just didn't know if we were meeting up later, that's all.'

He followed her into the bathroom, watching as she switched on the shower, shaking out her hair before throwing him a look over her shoulder, smiling knowingly at him.

'Want to join me?'

Fuck it! Everything else could wait.

'Do you miss her?' Gary looked at Ryan out the corner of his eye as they finished up the last of their coffee over what had been an unusually long and somewhat more leisurely than expected breakfast. This pre-season trip to Spain and the Canary Islands was turning out to be a more relaxed affair than anyone could have anticipated, but that was mainly because Newcastle Red Star's recently-married manager, Jim Allen, was still very much in the 'honeymoon period'. And because of that, he was being far more lenient with his rules than was the norm.

'Miss who?' Ryan asked. A purely rhetorical question, of course, because he knew exactly who Gary was talking about.

'You know who,' Gary said, leaning back in his seat and stretching out his legs.

Ryan looked at him. He knew what he was trying to do, but it wouldn't work. He wasn't going to give anyone the satisfaction of knowing how he was really feeling. He was stronger now; there was no time to be weak, not anymore. Being weak had cost him big in the past, and he wasn't going there again. 'Why would I miss her, Gary? I'm with Ellen now, aren't I? And she understands the kind of relationship I need; a relationship that doesn't involve any kind of commitment.'

Ryan Fisher was twenty-seven years old, tall, dark and indecently handsome, in a rough-and-ready sort of way. With his multitude of tattoos adorning both highly-toned arms, and most of his back, constant stubble that sometimes materialised into a beard when he was feeling particularly lazy, unruly, dark brown, messed-up hair and a smile that seemed to give him the ability to attract any girl he wanted, he was the kind of man that a lot of women fantasised over. A bad boy, a troublemaker, that was Ryan Fisher. Or, at least, it had been.

A highly talented, ridiculously well-paid professional footballer with Newcastle Red Star – one of the biggest and most successful teams in the top flight of the English game, and current league champions – Ryan was lusted after by a never-ending succession of wannabe WAGs, and envied by those men who would do anything to have his life, to be who he was. But Ryan's life hadn't always been perfect; it still wasn't. It probably never would be. But the outside world didn't need to know that. His past had had enough of an airing over the last few months. It was time to leave all that crap behind him now and concentrate on the forthcoming season; it was time to show them all that Ryan Fisher was back, bigger and better than he'd ever been.

'So?' Gary persisted, standing up and pushing his chair back under the table.

'So, what?' Ryan sighed, following suit.

'You're telling me you're really over her now? Amber, I mean.'

'Yeah, I know who you mean, thanks, Gary.'

'And it can't be easy at the minute, can it? Having her around all the time.'

'She isn't around *all the time*, Gary,' Ryan said, shoving his hands in the pockets of his combat pants.

'Yeah, but she's *here*, isn't she?' Gary went on, obviously not taking the hint to drop a subject that Ryan really didn't want to talk about. 'In fact, she's *right* here. Look.'

Ryan turned his head slightly as Gary nudged him, catching sight of Amber as she walked into the breakfast room, all flowing dark red hair and tanned skin, her incredible long legs shown off to perfection in a short white dress and wedge-heeled sandals. Amber Allen. Beautiful, crazy, ice-queen Amber Allen. Or, at least, she'd been a bit of an ice-queen when he'd first met her a year ago, on his return to the North East of England. Back then he'd been Red Star's multi-million-pound new signing, their star striker, and she'd been Amber Sullivan, a beautiful, feisty sports reporter with too much attitude and a smile that had floored him the minute he'd set eyes on her.

But their first meeting hadn't exactly been all sweetness and light. Far from it. There'd been no flirting, no secret smiles or furtive touches. They'd practically hated each other on sight, even though he'd known he wanted to fuck her the second she'd walked into the room. But that was Ryan Fisher. He was used to getting what he wanted when he wanted it, and Amber Sullivan – as she'd been back then – had proved to be a challenge he hadn't been able to ignore. He'd almost won, too. Almost. He'd fallen in love, for the first time in his life. Once he'd thawed the ice-queen, knocked down those barriers she'd built around herself, the ones that had stopped her from finding the love she really deserved to find, he'd honestly thought his life had changed for the better. He'd thought he could finally put his playboy past behind him and settle down. But he hadn't banked on *her* past catching up with her. And he certainly hadn't banked on that past being his boss. Jim Allen was a hurdle he just couldn't get over, and he'd let that get to him, just a little too much – with almost career-ending consequences. But he'd fought back; he'd come through it all, everything that had happened. He'd come through it all. But nobody had promised him it would be easy from now on. Ryan had loved Amber. He'd loved her, simple as that, and even *he* wasn't deluded enough to think that that was going to change any time soon, even if she *was* now Amber Allen, wife of one of the most successful football managers ever to grace the Premier League. She was his boss's wife. And he just had to deal with that. Somehow.

'She's looking good,' Gary whistled as Amber bent down to pick up something she'd pulled from her pocket and promptly dropped on the floor. Ryan continued to watch her as she slowly stood back up, laughing at something Jim whispered to her on his arrival by her side, his arm snaking around her hips in a protective, almost proprietorial manner. Ryan felt his heart shudder in his chest, unable to tear his eyes away from a scene he didn't really want to witness. His ex-fiancée and her new husband – his manager – acting all loved-up right there in front of him, even if they had no idea he was watching. He didn't think they cared, anyway. It had been like that for the past couple of days, ever since they'd all arrived here in Tenerife for the last leg of their pre-season tour. So far all they'd done was chill out and relax before they played their match against one of the island's local teams tomorrow evening. But relaxing had been difficult for Ryan. He couldn't ignore Amber and Jim, couldn't ignore their stolen kisses and not-so-subtle attempts at touching each other when they thought nobody else was watching. And Amber had looked so hot as she lay round the pool in a tiny black bikini – no wonder their boss couldn't keep his hands off her. After all, Ryan knew exactly what Jim was getting once he got his new wife back inside the privacy of their hotel room. That thought alone depressed him more than anything, despite the fact he had a beautiful woman of his own back in Newcastle, just waiting for him to come home. It was nothing serious, of course, because Ryan didn't do serious, not anymore. He'd tried it once and look what had happened. But he had someone there if he needed her. And he did need her, or he needed a distraction, anyway, and Ellen was proving to be just that

– a beautiful distraction. A role she was rapidly making her own.

'You okay, mate?' Gary asked, squeezing Ryan's shoulder.

Ryan nodded, finally tearing his eyes away from Amber. Although he hadn't missed Jim's hand slipping down onto her perfect backside, giving it a sly squeeze. Shit! He'd been such a fucking idiot to let her go.

'You never stood a chance, Ryan,' Gary said, as if reading his mind. 'Not with the past those two had.'

'Yeah,' Ryan sighed, following Gary out of the room, a headache starting to form right behind his eyes that he could well do without, especially with a training session in 30 degree heat looming. 'So everyone keeps telling me.'

Amber swung the car into a parking bay and quickly jumped out, recoiling slightly as the midday heat almost knocked her backwards. Twenty minutes in a lovely, cool, air-conditioned car made you forget how incredibly hot it was outside.

Sliding her sunglasses down over her eyes, she walked quickly out of the car park, almost jogging across the small road that led onto the busy coach park at Reina Sofia Airport as she made her way towards the arrivals entrance.

Walking into the busy airport, she pushed her sunglasses back up onto her head and stood still for a second, breathing a sigh of relief. She was just glad to be out of the heat for a little while. It was so hot on the island right now, so stifling, that any shade or escape was welcome, no matter how brief.

Looking up at the huge screens that hung from the ceiling, she scanned the list of arrivals to see if Ronnie's plane had landed on time. It had. Five minutes early, to be precise, so she quickly headed over to the arrivals gate, joining a handful of other people who were waiting for friends/relatives/clients to arrive on this beautiful Spanish island.

Amber Allen was living a life she hadn't expected to be living. But she was more than grateful that her life had turned out the way it had. Just a year ago she'd been the Sports Editor for News North East. It was a job she'd loved, a job she'd been good at. And she'd honestly thought she'd always be there, that she'd never leave. Because she hadn't wanted to, not really. But a lot had happened over the past year. She hadn't banked on becoming involved with one of the most high-profile, most talked-about footballers in the game – Ryan Fisher. She hadn't banked on that, and she certainly hadn't banked on everything that had come with that relationship. She hadn't expected to let it get so far, to care so deeply about a man who had so many problems. A man so much younger than her. A man who had caused her to break her strict, self-enforced no-footballer rule. She hadn't expected any of it. And she certainly hadn't banked on Jim Allen – the love of her life; a man who'd hurt her so badly in the past, not once but twice. A man she hadn't really thought she'd ever see again. She hadn't banked on him walking back into her life. But from the second he'd taken the manager's job at Newcastle Red Star a year ago she should have known that everything would eventually come to a head. Still, she certainly hadn't expected – less than twelve months on – to be Jim's wife. Mrs. Amber Allen. Something she'd dreamed of being since the age of sixteen. Just thinking about that made her stomach flip over in a barrage of glorious somersaults, and she couldn't help but smile to herself, staring down at the ground for a brief second in case people thought she was slightly crazy, grinning away like some demented idiot.

But marriage to the Premiership's hottest – in more ways than one – manager wasn't the only change in Amber's life. She'd finally bitten the bullet and left News North East for pastures new. Top footballing agent, Max Mandell, had been on her case for months, telling her she could easily become the female face of football on national TV, bombarding her with texts and phone calls, job offers that just seemed too good to be true. She'd never been someone who enjoyed being the centre of attention, never been one to court publicity or feel that urge to become a celebrity of any description – despite her father being a famous ex-professional footballer himself, and her husband being about as high-profile as you could get in the world of football right now. But Max had worn her down with his almost dogged persistence, and with Jim's encouragement she'd joined Max in London a few weeks ago for a series of interviews and meetings, which had culminated in her landing the job of presenter/reporter for Cloud Sports, a major satellite TV sports channel. She had, indeed, become their new face of football, and the fact it now meant that she also got to work alongside Ronnie – her best friend – well, that just made it all the more perfect. Of course, it was going to mean working in London a lot more, and long periods away from Jim loomed on the horizon, which she wasn't particularly looking forward to, but she was enjoying the challenge. Football was her world. The people involved in the sport were her life. It was where she wanted to be.

As bodies started to stream out of the arrivals exit, Amber craned her neck to see if she could spot Ronnie. She knew he'd be travelling light, just hand luggage, so he wouldn't have to hang around by the baggage carousel. He should be one of the first out of there.

Ronnie White. Her best friend. An ex-professional footballer-turned-TV pundit, they'd known each other for years, slept together a few times, and remained as close as two people could be, on a purely platonic level. He'd just remarried his ex-wife Karen, and as far as Amber was aware that was all going well, second time around. She couldn't be happier for him. But the summer break had meant they hadn't really seen all that much of each other since his wedding, and she couldn't wait to see him now. To start working with him. It was just another amazing chapter of this dream-come-true life she'd suddenly found herself living.

She checked her watch. Jim would have the squad out training now, despite the fierce lunchtime heat. He wanted them to be ready, to be used to the temperatures this island could throw at them, even though all their games would be evening kick-offs, when the temperatures were cooler – but only just, at this time of year.

She smiled again at the thought of Jim. Jim Allen, her handsome, beautiful, all-American man. With his grey-flecked hair and that low, deep accent of his, she didn't think it was possible to be more in love with anyone than she was with him. In some shape or form he'd been her world for over twenty years, made love to her when she'd been just sixteen years old and a star-struck teenager, and he'd been a twenty-seven-year-old teammate of her dad's at Newcastle Red Star.

Their history had been chequered, to say the least. There'd been a lot of pain, a lot of heartache; people had got hurt – Ryan had got hurt, her father had got hurt, and that was something she really hadn't wanted to happen. Telling him that one of his oldest friends had slept with her when she was still a teenager was a memory Amber couldn't erase. The look on his face when he'd found out about her and Jim, it still made her flinch. But all that mattered now was that Ryan seemed to be okay, her dad was slowly coming to terms with everything, and Jim was finally where he belonged. With her. The way it always should have been.

She felt her stomach give another flip as she remembered Jim touching her that morning, waking her up with a kiss before pulling her against him, stroking her breasts and kissing her neck as he'd gently pushed inside her from behind. Oh, Jesus, why had she started thinking about that now? She could feel the tingling between her legs already taking effect and it really wasn't the time or the place for that to be happening.

She shook out her hair, taking a deep breath at the same time, looking up again at the trickle of people still filtering out of arrivals. And then she saw him – all tall, dark and handsome, dressed casually in a pair of dark trousers and a white shirt, the sleeves rolled up to his elbows, his hand-luggage holdall slung over one shoulder, his sunglasses perched in his short, dark hair.

He saw her almost immediately, his face breaking into a wide grin, his pace quickening as he approached her. Amber couldn't stop her heart from beating faster as he got closer, dropping his bag on the floor as he scooped her up in his arms and hugged her tight, kissing her quickly on the mouth.

'Hey, gorgeous! How's my beautiful new work colleague doing?'

Amber repositioned her sunglasses on the top of her head as she smiled at him. He'd picked up a bit of a tan since they'd last seen each other, and it suited him. 'I'm doing just fine, thanks. You?'

'Yeah, things are okay. They're okay.'

Amber frowned slightly as she watched him pick up his bag and sling it back over his shoulder.

'Been looking forward to heading out here, though,' he went on, shoving his hands in his pockets, his eyes now fixed firmly on hers. 'Kind of itching to get back to work.'

She raised a questioning eyebrow. 'Really?'

'Yeah,' he laughed, following her as she headed out of the airport, bracing herself for the wall of heat that was going to hit them the second they stepped outside. 'Really. How's it all going over here, anyway?'

They were both due to cover the Newcastle Red Star match in Tenerife, although Amber had a feeling her new employers were easing her into her new job gently by giving her this particular trip to cover. Her best friend had just joined her to give her a bit more support, and she'd had her husband by her side all the way. But she didn't need 'easing' into anything. She'd managed fine so far. Still, she wasn't complaining. She was going to be apart from Jim a lot more than she really wanted to be once the new season kicked off, so any time she could spend with him, no matter what the circumstances, was precious. She wasn't going to knock it.

'It's all good, Ronnie. Jim's incredibly relaxed, which means the squad is relaxed, so the atmosphere is really nice. Oh, and the hotel is amazing!'

Ronnie smiled as they crossed the road and headed back towards the car park. 'So married life's suiting you, then?'

She looked at him as they walked, throwing him a sideways

smile. 'Yeah. It is.'

He arched an eyebrow and she couldn't help but laugh.

'Here we are,' she said, pressing the key fob to open the doors of the small white Citroen hire car. 'Climb in and I'll take you to the hotel.'

'Do you fancy stopping off for some lunch first?' Ronnie asked, throwing his bag onto the back seat of the car. 'I'm starving, and we don't have to go back to the hotel straightaway, do we? And, we're not technically at work again until tomorrow.'

She looked at him over the roof of the car. 'Yeah. Okay. It can't do any harm, I suppose.'

'Of course it can't do any harm, what are you talking about? Come on. You've been here a couple of days now, you must know somewhere decent to grab something to eat.'

She smiled at him before climbing into the driver's seat. 'Yeah. I do.'

He climbed in beside her and shut the door, sitting back and letting out a huge sigh as the air-con kicked in almost immediately. 'Then take me there, beautiful. I'm gasping for a pint.'

Chapter Two

The last of the evening sun beat down on the balcony as Ryan stepped outside, pushing a hand through his dark hair as he stared at the stunning view that greeted him, at the island of La Gomera out in the distance. The sun was just beginning to set, and the colours it created as it began to dip below the island were just beautiful, turning the sky a mixture of red and gold as the light changed at the rapid pace that was common in the Canary Islands.

He was really starting to appreciate shit like this now, after everything that had happened, everything he'd been through. It had opened his eyes to what was important in life – to a point, anyway, because Ryan Fisher hadn't turned into a saint. He still liked a drink, still loved the women – and the women still loved him, and being here, on this holiday island, well, it was like being in some kind of human sweet shop where he could have access to anything he wanted at any time. He only had to step outside the hotel and women of all ages were suddenly surrounding him. Once upon a time that would have been a dream come true, but there were times now when it just felt like something he had to do in order to keep up an image he was slowly becoming tired of. But even though he had someone back home who would quite happily help him to settle down – he only had to say the word – he just couldn't bring himself to take that step forward.

He just couldn't seem to let it all go, not yet. He'd tried it once and it hadn't worked, so why put himself through all that again?

No, he was quite happy just to let things tick along the way they were. Commitment wasn't something he was thinking about right now. Serious relationships had been put very much on the back-burner. He was going to start living again, start enjoying himself, start making the most of this new beginning he'd been lucky enough to salvage from what could have been one hell of a mess. A mess the old Ryan had created. And despite the old Ryan being someone he couldn't completely say goodbye to just yet, he wasn't altogether sure he was that person anymore – the one who partied 'til all hours, slept with as many women as he could before breaking their hearts as he told them goodbye without a second thought to anyone's feelings but his own. He couldn't say he wanted to leave *all* of that behind him, but it wasn't as exciting as it had once been, because it had been that lifestyle that had pushed Amber away. The old Ryan had made her leave and he regretted that every single minute of every single day.

The phone ringing back inside his room made him jump slightly, pulling him back from his thoughts of a life he hadn't realised he'd wanted, until it was way too late. A more settled life. A life with Amber.

He wondered whether he should answer it – he wasn't in the mood to talk to anyone right now. He'd been looking forward to a bit of time alone before they all met for another squad night out – Jim had organised dinner for them in a sea-front restaurant not far from their hotel in another of his pre-season 'team-bonding' sessions, and Ryan needed time to prepare himself for the fact that Amber would be there, with Jim, doubtless looking beautiful and elegant and sexy as hell. And she wasn't his anymore. His own fault.

Whoever was calling him was certainly persistent, and he turned and walked back into the room with a heavy sigh, closing the door behind him to keep the air-conditioning working. He sat down on the edge of the bed and picked up the phone.

'Yep.'

'Ryan, it's me.'

He didn't know whether he was glad to hear her voice, or slightly angry at her for bothering him when he'd really wanted to use this time away from her to grab a bit of space. 'Hey, babe. How you doing?'

'I miss you.'

He closed his eyes, the pause he left adding nerves to her voice. 'Ryan? You don't mind me calling you, do you? Only...'

'No,' he sighed, opening his eyes and staring out at the beautiful sunset that was happening right there in front of him. 'No, of course I don't mind. It's good to hear your voice. Everything okay back home?'

It was her turn to pause, and when she spoke again the nerves were back. 'I wouldn't know. I'm not *at* home.'

Ryan frowned, running a hand along the back of his neck as he continued to stare out at the now rapidly setting sun. 'Huh? Where are you, then?'

'I'm here. I'm in Tenerife.'

The cool water lapped around Amber's thighs as she waded into the small but private pool on the terrace of their plush and rather spacious hotel suite. The sun was about to set and the sky carried the most incredible rust-coloured glow as the island got ready to turn from another hot and sticky day into a warm and balmy evening.

Despite the darkness that was about to descend, the pool was lit up by the terrace's low lighting, making it seem all the more ethereal, almost. Peaceful. Perfect for a swim before she had to shower, change and get ready for Jim's team dinner. It'd be the first time she and Jim had gone out with the rest of the Newcastle Red Star squad since they'd arrived in Tenerife, and she'd be lying if she said she wasn't apprehensive about being so close to Ryan. He wasn't somebody she deliberately made a point of being around, not if she didn't have to be, and so far, on the whole, she'd managed to avoid it. What they'd shared and the things they'd gone through, it all still felt quite raw sometimes, but Amber knew their relationship had been one that could never have worked. So many obstacles had stood in their way, making it impossible to move anywhere or go any further forward. But she still cared about him, still loved him, in some strange kind of way.

Shaking all thoughts of Ryan Fisher from her mind, she ran her hands through her hair, pushing it back off her face as she stared out ahead at the sun falling rapidly behind the island of La Gomera. Everything felt so calm here, so serene, with nothing but the sound of the sea and the muffled noise way off in the distance of a holiday island getting ready for another night of fun.

She loved the fact it was still so warm, even with darkness descending. There was no air to speak of, the humidity was seeing to that, but the coolness of the water felt good as she finally dipped under for a few seconds before pushing back up to the surface, shaking the water off her barely-clothed body.

'You have no idea how incredibly sexy that looked.'

The sound of that low American accent caused her to swing round as fast as she could waist-deep in water. Jim was crouched down beside the edge of the pool, ready to join her in just his beach shorts, his tanned and toned body exposed. For a man of forty-nine he was extremely fit, and even now he still took Amber's breath away. Her beautiful American man. Her wonderful husband. The man she'd waited to be with for over twenty years.

She smiled at him, pushing her hands through her hair again, watching as he slid into the pool, joining her in the water. Her heart was already beating out of her chest, anticipation flooding her body. Sometimes it felt like he only had to look at her and she wanted him like crazy, but she guessed that's what being away from him for so long had done to her. All those years of missing him, wanting him, it was bound to build up, wasn't it? All that frustration, that sexual tension. They had all that missed time to catch up on.

She backed up against the pool wall as he swam over to her, stopping right in front of her, their eyes locked together as he reached out to gently push a stray strand of wet hair from her face.

'You look hot,' he whispered, his mouth almost touching hers and she could feel her heart beating even faster now, pounding away like some out-of-control drum as his fingers slowly moved down from her cheek, running lightly over her collarbone. 'So – fucking – hot.'

She threw her head back as he kissed the base of her throat, his fingers running down over her arm, his touch so feather-light it caused a million goose bumps to appear out of nowhere, despite the heat and the temperature outside.

'Jim…'

He shut her up with a kiss, and Amber had no choice but to respond, sliding a hand round the back of his neck as his mouth pressed harder against hers, their tongues touching, moving around each other in some kind of erotic dance. What this man did to her she just couldn't explain. And to think she'd almost lost him; that she'd tried to fight these feelings, push him away, when it was only ever going to end up with them being together. It was their fate. She truly believed that.

The kiss left her breathless, and she pulled away slightly, flinching just a touch as she felt his fingers start to snake up her spine, gently tugging at her bikini top until he'd loosened it completely, pulling it away from her and discarding it on the poolside. It was quite a liberating feeling, to be slowly stripped naked, outside, on this humid night, and even though neither of them were totally aware of exactly how private their terrace was, they didn't really care. Amber certainly didn't. They weren't hiding anymore. Nothing was a secret.

'Oh, Jesus, Jim…' she gasped, throwing her head back again, pushing her breasts hard against his hands as he cupped them before slowly rubbing his thumbs over her nipples, causing them to harden immediately. That's what his touch did to her. And it felt so good!

'Let's take this one step further.' He slid both hands down under the water, loosening the tie-sides on her bikini bottoms, pulling them away from her in an instant. 'Let's face it, honey, they were so small you might as well not have been wearing them in the first place.'

A shiver ran right through her as he kissed her again, a kiss so deep and beautiful; a kiss that turned her on so much she thought she might come before he'd even touched her, before he'd had a chance to make love to her. And she ached to feel him inside her, so she had to hold back, had to let him take the lead.

His hands were on her hips now, gently lifting her out of the water, sitting her down on the very edge of the poolside, and Amber knew exactly what was coming next. She knew, and her entire body tingled with the anticipation.

He pushed her legs apart, touching her first with his fingers, stroking, probing, running them through a wetness that wasn't caused by the water alone. She closed her eyes, her hands palm-down behind her to steady her as his fingers probed harder, deeper, before slipping inside her for just a matter of seconds, but long enough to make her cry out loud with a mixture of pleasure and pain. He was touching her, inside and out, and it felt amazing!

She kept her eyes closed as his fingers slid out of her, her stomach clenching as another wave of anticipation flooded her. And then she felt his mouth replace his fingers, his tongue taking over where they'd left off. He was touching her, tasting her, drinking her in, and Amber felt as though she was going to explode. Oh God, what he could do to her! He was gently easing her wider apart with his fingers, his tongue covering every inch of her down there, and it was the most intense, incredible experience. She could already feel those beautiful pins and needles start to creep up her body, that release beginning its attempt to break free, and he must have sensed that, too, because he pushed harder, probed deeper, and she pushed against him, giving him everything she had as it all came to a crashing end, her body shaking in spasms of ecstasy. But he stayed right where he was, taking everything she was giving him, drinking her dry until she could do nothing but collapse around him. Her legs were weak, her body tingling, yet she knew it wasn't over. She knew he needed more, and so did she. She still ached to feel him inside her, despite the fact she'd just experienced one of the most glorious orgasms of her entire life. She still wanted to feel him, hard and ready, deep, deep inside of her.

He pulled her back into the water, stroking her cheek with his thumb as his mouth lowered down onto hers. She could taste herself on him, his lips salty and damp, and it only served to heighten everything she was already feeling. Every nerve ending was on red alert, just waiting for the next instalment of this erotic ride.

He was naked now, too. He was naked and he was hard, his erection pressing into her thigh, and she honestly thought she was going to pass out with the intensity of it all. Had she missed out on all of this for over twenty years? Or was it only like this *because* of those years apart? It didn't matter now, not anymore. They were together, and that was all that mattered. They were together. Finally.

Lifting her up again, but keeping her in the water this time, he pushed her back against the pool wall as she wrapped her legs around his hips, her arms around his neck, burying her face in his grey-flecked hair as he finally pushed inside her. And he pushed hard, fast, sliding in and out of her in a beautiful, perfect rhythm, his hands underneath her bottom, keeping her firmly on him as he continued to fuck her in the most incredible way. And maybe it was the water that was helping to intensify everything, she had no idea; all she knew was that, when the climax finally came, she'd never felt anything like it. When he exploded inside her, she felt every drop of him spill out, every shudder and jolt sending her further over the precipice into a heaven she'd had no idea existed.

She had to bury her face in his shoulder to muffle the screams, to silence the moans, and he held onto her so tight she almost couldn't breathe, waiting until it was over, until she'd experienced every last, heart-stopping second of it all before he finally loosened his grip. She almost fell against him when he did, and he had to grab onto her quickly to hold her up, her legs were so weak. She felt drained, almost; all energy had been sapped out of her.

'Hey, beautiful,' he whispered, tilting her chin up so her eyes met his. 'You okay there?'

She smiled, nodding slowly, slipping a hand round the back of his neck, playing with his damp hair. 'Where'd you learn to do all that?'

He laughed, that low, sexy laugh that made her stomach flip and her heart race. She was falling in love with this man all over again, although she doubted whether she'd ever fallen out of love with him. From the age of sixteen he'd been all she'd ever wanted, all she'd ever dreamed of, even if she'd only just realised that now. No other man could ever match up to him. Ever. 'When I'm with you, baby, it all comes naturally, believe me.' He buried his face in her hair, his fingers gently stroking her breasts, their bodies still pressed together. 'You taste so good, Amber. So fucking good.'

She shivered slightly as he spoke, remembering the feel of his tongue as it had touched her, brought her to that crashing climax. He was the only man who'd ever managed to do that, and he always would be – now. The only man she'd ever need. 'Remind me to repay the compliment one day.' She smiled, reaching down to take him in her hand. She was surprised to find he was still hard, and she couldn't stop that small shiver from turning into another huge tingle. 'Mr. Allen, surely you must be done by now?'

'Never.' He returned her smile, nuzzling her neck, covering that space just below her ear in hundreds of tiny kisses.

'Then you'll have to let me repay that favour the second we get back from dinner. We can't have you in any way dissatisfied now, can we?'

He looked at her, smiling that smile, and she felt her stomach dip and dive again. Oh Jesus, she loved this man so much. So, so much. 'I'll hold you to that.'

She closed her eyes as he kissed her again; a beautiful, slow and languid kiss that caused her to melt against him, never wanting to leave his arms, but knowing she had to. They couldn't stay here all night, even if that was where they both wanted to be.

'Later.' He smiled, stroking the damp hair from her face before climbing out of the pool. Amber watched him walk back into their hotel suite, naked and handsome and still as sexy as he had been when she'd first met him over two decades ago.

'Later,' she whispered, looking back out at the view in front of her, the resort below now shrouded in a blanket of darkness, the lights of the bars and hotels twinkling away like a myriad of coloured fairy lights. And she just wished later would come sooner than it was going to.

'I could do without this,' Ryan muttered, sitting back in his seat, pushing it backwards until it rested on its rear legs, kicking the table leg in front of him like some petulant, bored child.

'Jesus, you're not still moping over Amber, are you?' Gary sighed, sitting down beside Ryan, handing him a pint of lager. 'Get over it, mate. It's been months now. And I thought, after everything you've been through recently…' He stopped talking as Ryan threw him a look, and Gary turned away, taking a quick sip of his lager. 'I thought you were over it, that's all. You can't have her anymore. She's married to the boss. Deal with it.'

Ryan said nothing, just swung back on his chair again, resting his hands on his toned and taut stomach as he watched everything going on around him on the dimly lit, fairy-light-strewed terrace of the restaurant Jim had told them all to meet up in. Colin Bailey – Red Star's head coach and assistant manager – had made sure all the guys in the squad had got there on time, but there was still no sign of Amber or Jim. Ryan could only guess at what they were doing that was making them so late. And it hurt.

'It's got nothing to do with Amber.'

'Oh really?' Gary asked, raising a cynical eyebrow. 'You sure about that?'

'Ellen's here.'

'Eh? What do you mean, Ellen's here? Ellen's where?'

'For fuck's sake… she's here, in frigging Tenerife. What do you think I mean?'

'Okay, okay. Chill out, will you? When did that happen? I thought partners weren't allowed on this trip? Otherwise I'd doubt-less have had Debbie hanging off me arm 24/7, which I can well do without. I can have me pick of women here, but not if the wife's around.'

Ryan looked at Gary. 'You finished? Partners *aren't* supposed to be here, but Ellen's taken it upon herself to have what she's calling a "girly weekend" with her mates – here, in Tenerife. She's staying at a hotel in Torviscas, wants to know if I can meet her tomorrow. I've told her it's match day, that it's not a good idea, but then she puts that voice on, you know? That little-girl-lost voice, like I've physically wounded her or something… What am I supposed to do, Gaz? Ignore her?'

Gary just shrugged.

'You're no fucking help, do you know that?'

'Well, what do you want me to say? You can't really ignore her, can you? Not after she's come all this way. But it might be a good idea to make sure the boss doesn't find out. The last thing you need is him on your back.'

'She should've asked me first, Gary. I mean, we have fun, don't get me wrong, and she's a frigging stunner but… this was supposed to be a break, a chance for me to kick back and let loose for a bit.'

'She's spoilt your fun, huh?' Gary grinned. Ryan didn't return it. In fact, he didn't say anything. He just watched as more figures stepped up onto the terrace, and all of a sudden he felt his heart start to beat harder. In anticipation? Of what? Of Amber walking in, taking one look at him and realising that she'd chosen the wrong man? That *he* was the one she should have stayed with? Yeah, because she'd been acting as though that was the way she'd been thinking ever since this pre-season tour had started. She'd barely looked in his direction. What the hell was he doing? After what he'd done to her, the way he'd behaved…

He felt his stomach literally sink when he saw Ronnie White arrive, because he was alone. Still no Amber and Jim.

'I'm going for some fresh air,' Ryan sighed, standing up.

Gary looked at him. 'Fresh air? We're outside, Ryan.'

'I need some space…' He was stopped from going anywhere as more people arrived, and this time he saw her – Amber. His ex-fiancée and his boss had finally put in an appearance.

He couldn't take his eyes off her. There was something different about her now; about the way she looked, the way she acted. She was slimmer, more beautiful, that ice-queen image she'd once given off now seemed nothing but a distant memory as she smiled at everyone who looked in her direction – everyone except him. Because, when his eyes finally locked with hers, that smile disappeared, just for a few seconds, until she turned away, back to look at her new husband, and then the smile returned. Ryan felt his heart ache as he watched her stand up on tiptoe to kiss Jim Allen. He watched as their lips met in a long kiss, one that was met with whoops and whistles from the rest of the squad as Jim's arm snaked around her waist, his hand resting on her hip.

'I really need that space now,' Ryan muttered, standing up and almost kicking his chair back. 'I won't be long.'

'Ryan…' Gary started, but thought better of it. He knew that, sometimes, it was best just to let Ryan get on with things the way he saw fit. As long as you didn't let him out of your sight for too long. He may have come through that latest round of rehab with no problems, but he was still quite volatile, still likely to do something he shouldn't if pushed far enough. And Gary knew that better than anyone.

Quickly making his way out onto the beautifully-paved walkway that separated their restaurant from the beach in front of them, Ryan stopped only when he finally found the space he needed, walking over to the low wall that overlooked the beach, placing his hands palm-down on it and leaning forward, closing his eyes, breathing in deeply before exhaling loudly. He hadn't thought it would be this hard. Was that incredibly naive of him? Since coming out of rehab, regaining his form as one of the greatest footballers of his generation, being given the captaincy at Newcastle Red Star and then taking them to that historic Premier League win, he'd felt fine about it all. He was back in the game, free of his demons – or so he'd thought. But maybe the summer break had given him some kind of false sense of security as far as thinking his feelings for Amber had changed. This pre-season trip was the first time he'd seen her since the end of last season. The first time he'd had a chance to properly face those feelings he'd had for her head-on. The first time he'd really faced up to the fact that she was actually married now, that she'd spent the summer break on a honeymoon that should have been the honeymoon *he'd* shared with her, not his boss. But he'd fucked that one up good and proper, hadn't he? Thrown it all away in one night of utter stupidity that just thinking about it brought with it a stabbing pain of regret he couldn't seem to shift.

Taking another deep breath, he exhaled again, opening his eyes and staring out ahead at the view of the beach, which was shrouded in darkness, almost eerie in its feel as the sound of the waves lapping slowly against the sand echoed in the distance.

Maybe Ellen turning up was the best thing that could have happened. With her around he'd have less chance to think about Amber. Less chance to think about what he'd lost. Instead he could focus on what he had now, and that didn't just include his career being back on track. It also included a beautiful young woman he should be happy to have by his side.

Maybe it really was time for Ryan Fisher to start thinking about settling down. With Ellen? That wasn't something he wanted to think about just yet. He just knew that over the past couple of months he'd finally started to become the man he really wanted to be, and he also knew that if he tried really hard he could deal with his feelings for Amber. He just had to be stronger, and he could do it. He could. He could do it. He had no other choice.

'You look different,' Ronnie said, leaning back against the bar. 'I meant to tell you that earlier, over lunch. But you do. You look different.'

'Different, how?' Amber laughed, taking a small sip of cava.

'Well – and don't smack me for saying this, because I know what you're like – but, for starters, you look like you've lost a bit of weight, which I'm assuming is down to all the sex you're having.' He grinned at her, sticking his hands in his pockets and throwing her a wink.

Amber couldn't help smiling, looking at her best friend out the corner of her eye. 'Yeah,' she said dryly. 'That'll be it. Is that all?'

Ronnie watched as the large group of footballers that had taken over the greater part of the restaurant for the night laughed and joked with each other in a less than subtle manner, shouting loudly before being told to keep it down by Colin, whose booming Glaswegian voice was far louder on its own than the whole squad's put together. 'You just seem, different.' He shrugged. 'I don't know… more confident… no, that's not true, because you've *always* been confident. It just seems as though you marrying Jim – it seems as though marrying him has changed you, somehow.'

She looked straight at him, narrowing her eyes. 'In a good way? Or are you about to accuse my new husband of changing my entire personality?'

'No, Amber, that's not what I'm saying…' Ronnie pushed a hand through his hair, wishing he hadn't started this conversation now. She *did* seem different to the last time he'd seen her, which had been at his wedding only a matter of weeks ago, but he just couldn't seem to explain what he meant by that. Yes, she *had* lost weight, or maybe she'd just toned up a bit more. Not that she'd been big in the first place, but the change in that respect was quite noticeable. Her hair was the same – she'd decided to keep that dark red colour which suited her so well – long and layered, falling in loose waves down her back. But there was something about her that felt like the Amber he'd once known – well, she wasn't quite there anymore.

'What *are* you trying to say, then?' Amber asked, taking another sip of cava, her eyes not leaving his.

Ronnie watched as she sipped her drink, her nude-coloured lips leaving a small mark on the side of her glass. She really was an exceptionally beautiful woman, and maybe that's what he was trying to say. Maybe that's what had changed about her – she'd always been beautiful, yes, but somehow, after all the events of the last few months, despite all the crap that had happened, throughout all of that she'd only grown even more stunning. So much so that he had to look away for a second. Was this what marriage had done to her? Had Jim Allen managed to finally bring something out in her that made her realise just how beautiful she really was? Because Ronnie had never been altogether sure that Amber had ever known that.

'Ronnie?' Amber asked, touching his arm gently. 'You all right?'

He slowly turned back round to face her, pushing a hand though his hair again. 'Yeah. Yeah, I'm fine. I think I just sat out in the sun a bit too long this afternoon.'

She reached out and stroked his cheek with her fingertips, smiling at him. 'You feel a bit hot, actually. You need to pace your-self, mister. Don't want you flaking out on me, you're supposed to be helping me through my first proper work assignment. Not sure how it's going so far and I'm bricking it here, wondering if I'm doing okay.'

Ronnie laughed as a glimmer of the old Amber reappeared. He gently placed his hand over hers, bringing it to his lips and kissing it quickly. 'You're doing great, kiddo. You're gonna be one hell of a hit, I know you are. We'll have men tuning in just to watch you, and fuck the football.'

She laughed, too, pulling her hand away from his and tucking a strand of hair behind her ear, looking down into her drink. 'Yeah, well, I'd quite like to be taken seriously, Ronnie. I don't just want to be seen as some sort of bimbo-style presenter, only there to get the viewers in. I want to be good at what I do.'

'You *are* good at what you do, otherwise you wouldn't have got this job, I promise you that. I know the way they work over there at Cloud Sports. They don't just employ anyone.'

'They employed you, didn't they?' She smirked, taking another sip of cava.

'Yeah. You're funny. You adding comedian to your list of talents now, are you?'

She stuck her tongue out at him and he pulled a face, making her laugh out loud.

'Anyway,' Ronnie continued, '… the fact you're beautiful is a bonus, of course it is…'

She looked at him, right at him, her eyes boring deep into his, and Ronnie had to swallow hard before he spoke again.

'It's a bonus, Amber. That's all. But you've got to start realising just how beautiful you really are, kiddo. You have to start realising that, because you are. You really are beautiful.'

'If you say so.'

'I say so.'

Amber smiled, planting a light kiss on his cheek. 'Get the drinks in, okay? I'll be back in a minute.'

Jim stood at the back of the restaurant and watched, his hands in his pockets, his expression stoic. He watched as Ronnie White smiled at his wife; *his* wife. He watched as he said something then turned away from her, watched as he looked at her again, watched as she reached out and stroked his cheek before Ronnie took her hand and kissed it, and all the while Jim felt a pull in the pit of his stomach that he knew he'd have to get under control. She was with *him* now. She was finally his; she'd married him, for God's sake! How much more connected to him could she be? And Ronnie White was no threat. Those two had been friends for over a decade now, they were bound to be close. Okay, so they'd once been a couple, but that had been years ago. They were friends. That was all.

Looking down at the ground for a second, he quickly composed himself before taking another look across at the bar, but Amber had gone, and Ronnie was now talking to one of the Red Star players. Jim looked around the restaurant, trying to find Amber, but he couldn't see her anywhere. He made a mental note not to let her out of his sight again for the rest of the evening. Looking the way she did right now, with that crazy red hair and those long, tanned legs of hers in that short yellow dress she was wearing, she was bound to attract attention, and he wasn't altogether sure how he felt about that.

He turned around as Ryan walked past, his head down, his hands shoved deep in the pockets of his jeans.

'You all right?' Jim asked, fixing his young striker with a look that told him he expected an answer, and not just the usual grunt or shrug that was sometimes thrown his way whenever he spoke to Ryan Fisher. Yes, he understood that things were complicated, given the kid's past relationship with Amber, but he was still his boss, and that demanded a certain level of respect, no matter what.

Ryan stopped walking and turned to face Jim, although the manner in which he did so came across as slightly begrudging. 'I'm fine. Why?'

'You don't look fine. You look distracted.'

'Listen, boss, no disrespect or anything, but we're not at work now, are we? We're on a night out…'

Jim moved a step nearer, his face close to Ryan's as he spoke. 'Whilst we are here, Ryan, on this island, on this pre-season tour, we're constantly at work. You got that?'

Ryan just stared at his boss, laughing quietly before walking away, saying nothing. Jim threw his head back and sighed heavily. Shit! That had actually been really unnecessary. Ryan hadn't been doing anything, he wasn't causing any trouble, and there'd been no word of his past antics coming back to the forefront during the summer break, when he'd had plenty of chances to relapse. Since his stint in rehab he'd turned into the kind of player every big club in the country dreamed of signing, which is why Jim had given him the captaincy, given him that incentive to stay on track, because, despite everything, he believed in Ryan Fisher. He was one of the game's brightest stars, a true talent, and nobody wanted to see that go to waste. So why was he starting on him now, for no good reason? What good would *that* do? Jesus, he had to find Amber.

'You seen my wife?' Jim asked Gary as he passed him on his way to the bar.

Gary looked at his manager. 'Amber? Yeah. She's out there.' He indicated the walkway outside. 'Everything okay, boss?'

'Everything's fine, Gary, thank you,' Jim said, turning and making his way out of the restaurant.

Amber was sitting on the low wall opposite, just staring out ahead of her.

'Amber?' Jim waited until she turned her head to look at him, a small smile appearing on her beautiful face. 'Everything all right, honey? What you doing out here?'

She turned to look out at the beach again, the sound of the waves crashing against the shore the only sound that could be heard, bar the hum of chatter and noise coming from the other restaurants and bars situated along this pretty walkway.

'I just wanted some air, and yes, I know the restaurant is, to all intents and purposes, outside, but you know what I mean. It's still a bit claustrophobic over there.'

Jim sat down beside her, reaching out to take her hand. 'It's all still taking a bit of getting used to, isn't it?'

She looked at him, her smile growing wider this time, which in turn made him smile, too. She looked twice as beautiful when she smiled.

'This time last year I was a single woman, and determined to stay that way. I had a job I loved, my own little house… Things were quite happily ticking along, and now look at me. I'm embarking on a whole new TV career with a major satellite channel, and I'm married to the Premier League's most high-profile manager. How the hell did that happen, Jim?'

'Do you regret it?'

She shook her head, suddenly realising that tears were now slowly running down her cheeks and she wiped them away with the back of her hand, quite shocked and surprised to find them there in the first place. What was wrong with her these days? Over emotional had never been something she was known for – quite the opposite, in fact. But hadn't that only been the case because she'd been holding back, keeping all those feelings under lock and key because she hadn't wanted to feel them for anyone but Jim? Had it taken until he'd walked back into her life to make her feel human again?

'No, Jesus! No. I don't regret it, of course I don't.' She reached out to touch his face, and just that one tiny touch was enough to send her stomach on another dip-and-dive session, making her breathless almost. 'You know how much I love you, Jim. I mean, I had my career, I had my house, I had a life – but I also had nothing, because I didn't have you. And you were all I ever wanted, you know that. For all those years, you were all I ever wanted. And now I've finally got that future I've always dreamed of…' She trailed off, staring out ahead of her again. 'It's just a lot to take in sometimes, that's all. Everything's happened so fast, and all of a sudden I'm feeling things I didn't know I could feel, wanting things I never thought I wanted and…' She left that sentence hanging in the air. Now wasn't the time to start *that* conversation.

He reached out and gently touched the side of her face, her cheek resting in the palm of his hand as her eyes met his. 'I love you so much, Amber Allen. And you have no idea how good it feels to finally be able to say that.'

She smiled, too, looking down for a second, breaking the stare. 'I used to write that, a lot, when I was at school – *Amber Allen*. I used to write it over and over, scribbling it down on anything I could find, just to see how it looked.' Her eyes met his again. 'How I got through the Sixth Form I don't know. You were such a bloody distraction.' Her stomach did another jolt as she remembered how incredibly handsome he'd been back then, in his professional playing days. How young and striking he'd looked. Every girl in her class had fancied him, all of them wanting to be close to her because they knew her dad was best friends with Jim Allen. If only they'd known how close she'd been to their football fantasy. If only they'd known what he'd done to her back then – both physically and emotionally. If only they'd known. 'And then…' She stopped talking, looking away briefly. 'I like it. Being Mrs. Allen, I mean.' She looked at him again, and for a few seconds she forgot where she was as his mouth lowered down onto hers, kissing her in that beautiful, heart-stopping way that only he could. A slow kiss, a deep kiss, a kiss that sent shivers running right through her and caused those goose bumps to cover her skin, despite the humid night air. 'Things feel different, Jim. And that scares me. It just… it just feels as if everything is suddenly hitting home – all the changes that have happened, all the things we've been through…'

Again, she let that sentence hang in the air, pulling away from him slightly. Jim frowned. What did she mean by that? Things felt different – how? 'Amber… Do you… do you feel like we rushed into things, is that what you're trying to say?'

She stood up, facing the beach with its dark, eerie feel, folding her arms against her. She didn't think they'd rushed into things. How could you rush into something you'd wanted for almost your entire life? But things *did* feel different. *She* felt different. The

things she wanted now, they were different. And she knew she'd
have to talk to him but, not yet. Not here. Now wasn't the time.

'Amber? Honey?'

'I love you, Jim.' She turned to face him, smiling, and he felt a
rush of relief wash over him. 'And I know you love me, so that's
all that matters in the end. Isn't it?'

He pulled her against him, his hand firmly in the small of her
back, their foreheads touching as he leaned in towards her. 'Yeah,
it is, baby. That's all that matters.'

Amber snuggled into him, enjoying the feeling of safety and
comfort being in his arms brought. He was the love of her life,
her world; he was everything she'd ever wanted and she loved him
beyond any words. She loved him. As simple as that.

'This is going to work this time, Jim. Isn't it?' she whispered,
staring up into his eyes.

He smiled, gently tucking a strand of hair behind her ear,
nodding slowly before kissing her gently, not wanting to pull away,
she tasted so good, felt so perfect in his arms. Why had he waited
so long to come back to her? Why had he done that? But the thing
was, he knew why. He knew exactly why. And he only hoped, with
all of his heart, that when Amber found out, she'd understand.

Chapter Three

Ryan walked into the small, almost secluded tapas bar which was tucked away up a narrow side street in the small fishing village of Poris de Abona, about twenty miles or so from the main Tenerife tourist resorts of Los Cristianos and Playa de las Americas. He'd driven there after managing to escape any major interrogation from his teammates as to where he was sneaking off to during their morning off from training. He wanted to explore, that had been his excuse. And although a few of the lads had looked at him as though he was mad – surely any free time they had should be spent by the pool or playing golf? – after what Ryan had been through, nobody questioned him. Not even Jim. But then, he had other distractions, didn't he?

Looking around the dimly lit bar, Ryan saw her sitting in the corner, her blonde hair piled up on top of her head, her eyes down, concentrating on her mobile phone. He walked over to the small, square wooden table, pulling out the chair opposite her and throwing himself down onto it, switching on the Ryan Fisher charm in an instant. Now he'd seen her, seen how hot she looked in that pale pink dress, her skin already lightly tanned, he was glad she'd turned up here, unannounced. He quite liked surprises, and surprises that would guarantee him a shedload of sex were the best ones of all.

'Hey, babe.'

She looked up from her phone, placing it down on the table as she smiled the biggest smile. 'Hey, back.'

'So, you thought you'd surprise me, huh?'

'I needed a break, and this is the last chance I've got to take one before the new season starts. It's already getting busy back at work.' She looked right into his eyes. 'And I missed you. I didn't realise how much I was going to until you'd gone.'

He felt a small twinge of guilt as he realised he hadn't really missed her at all since he'd been here. He'd been way too busy to even think about her. Busy doing stuff she didn't really need to know about. 'I missed you, too.' Jesus! The lies still came so easily to him. But at least he felt guilty about reeling them off these days, unlike before, when his lies had driven away the woman he should have been married to by now. But instead she was married to his boss. How frigging wrong was that?

'Really?' Ellen gasped, her voice shaking him out of his thoughts of Amber. He had to learn to stop doing that, drifting back to memories of someone he was never going to have. No matter how much he still thought he wanted her. 'Oh, Ryan… I was so worried about telling you I was here, because I know partners aren't allowed on this trip, and what with me working for the club and everything… That's why I chose this place to meet, it's out of the way…'

He shut her up by leaning over the table and planting a kiss on her unsuspecting mouth. She tasted good – a mixture of coconut lip balm and sun cream.

'Was I going on a bit too much?' she asked, her voice quiet, her eyes carrying an almost worried expression. 'I know I can talk for England once I get started but…'

'Ellen, it's okay. Really. I'm happy you're here, and hey, I like a woman who's willing to break the rules now and again.' He grinned, turning the Ryan Fisher charm up a notch, and he could see her relax instantly. Her pretty shoulders sagged, and her face almost lit up as she looked at him. But somewhere inside, a very small, very quiet alarm bell started ringing in Ryan's head – he liked being with her, but was she starting to become just a little too attached to him? They'd spent a lot of time together over the summer break, and he'd tried really hard not to give her any mixed signals, because the last thing he wanted to do was mislead her. The last thing he wanted to do was hurt her.

'Ryan… you and Amber…'

This was a conversation he really didn't want to get into, not with her, so he was happy when a striking-looking dark-haired woman materialised at their table with two more bottles of beer, smiling at them both before retreating back to her post behind the bar. She provided a short but welcome distraction, and Ryan couldn't help but watch her as she began serving another customer, smiling and laughing with a group of people at the bar whom Ryan guessed were regulars. It was that kind of place.

'Ryan?'

He waited a second before turning to look at Ellen, that famous Fisher smile now firmly back in place. 'Let's finish these beers and go back to your hotel. Then you can show me just how much you've missed me. Okay?'

She smiled back, relief once more quite evident on her face. 'Yeah. Okay.'

There was nothing like sex for taking Ryan's mind off things. Nothing like it at all.

Amber closed her eyes and let the burning sun wash over her skin. Sighing contentedly, she settled back on her sun lounger by the huge circular pool at the team's hotel. It was the day of Newcastle Red Star's final match in their pre-season tour of Spain and the Canary Islands but, thankfully, Amber didn't have to start work until later, when she and Ronnie would be at the match, talking to some of the players and interacting with the guys back in the studio, live from the game itself, a game which was being televised in the U.K. that evening on one of the Cloud Sports channels.

So, for now, all she had to do was relax. She couldn't deny the nerves weren't still there, though. This was a huge deal for her. She was the new face of football on a major satellite TV channel – for Amber it didn't get much bigger than that. Cloud Sports had put a lot of faith in her, and she didn't want to let anyone down, that was all. So far she'd been getting some great feedback, but those nerves were still going to take a while to settle down.

'You look a bit apprehensive,' Ronnie said, sitting himself down on the edge of the lounger next to her.

She opened her eyes, pushing her sunglasses up onto her head. 'Yeah. Thanks for that, Ronnie.'

He smiled at her. Amber pushed her sunglasses down over her eyes and lay back again.

'You're doing great, Amber. Everyone back home is loving you, believe me.'

'You're not just saying that, are you? To placate me. I know what you're like.'

'As if. Anyway, you've done live TV before, haven't you? Loads of times. Why should this be any different?'

'I used to be on *local* TV, Ronnie. *This* is a whole different ball game.'

'No it's not. Where's Jim?'

'Team talk. They're off to the ground for a training session in a little while.' She sat up again, propping herself up on her elbows. 'Why didn't you bring Karen with you?'

Ronnie looked away for a second, staring out at the sea view in front of him. 'I'm working, Amber.'

'Yeah, and so am I. But I'm here with my husband.'

Ronnie looked at her. 'Your husband is the manager of the team we're following.'

'So?'

He laughed slightly. 'Come on, kiddo. Karen doesn't want to hang around while I'm working. She'd only get bored.'

Amber sat up properly, pulling her knees up to her chest and hugging them to her. 'She'd get bored? Here? Look at it, Ronnie. It's beautiful! She could have...'

'Leave it, Amber, okay? Just – just leave it.'

She widened her eyes as she looked at him, slightly taken aback by his tone. 'All right. I'm sorry. Look, is everything okay?'

He sighed, pushing a hand through his hair. 'No, and it's me who should be sorry. Things are just a bit... a bit weird at the minute, that's all.'

Amber cocked her head, desperate to know what he meant by that but getting the feeling that, whatever it was, he wasn't in the mood to talk about it. But she couldn't leave the subject alone altogether. 'All the more reason to bring her with you, then, surely?'

'No, Amber. Don't you see? If I'd brought her with me, if I'd insisted she come here, wouldn't that just have looked as though I wanted to keep an eye on her? Keep tabs on her? Make sure she wasn't...' He stopped talking, looking out at the sea view again.

'If it was me, I wouldn't have seen it that way.'

'Well, Karen's not you, all right?'

Amber frowned. 'You're happy though, aren't you? I mean, you don't regret marrying her again, do you?'

Ronnie continued to look out over the stunning clear-blue sea that was dotted with the odd jet ski and a catamaran way off in the distance, no doubt out on a whale and dolphin sightseeing trip.

'I'm happy, yeah. I'm happy.'

Amber rested her chin on her knees as she looked at him. 'Really?'

He finally turned to face her again. 'What is this, Amber? I came over for a chat not a frigging interrogation. Things are fine and I'm happy, end of story.' He closed his eyes for a second, taking a deep breath, and although Amber badly wanted to continue grilling him over his slightly erratic moods, she thought better of it. Whatever was on his mind he quite obviously didn't want to go into it here. Not yet, anyway. But she'd get it out of him, eventually. She always did.

'Right,' he sighed, leaning over to quickly kiss her forehead, giving her hand a small squeeze before standing up, shoving both his hands in his pockets. 'I'll see you later.'

'Where are you going?'

'For a walk. Clear my head before we set off for the match.'

Amber watched as he headed back into the hotel, still frowning slightly. Something didn't seem right, but she wasn't going to push it.

Grabbing a short, bright pink kaftan from the table by her side, she pulled it over her head and stood up, smoothing it down over her white bikini. She was tired of sitting out in the sun now. Being out here on her own was only giving her far too much time to think about things, to dwell on stuff that she shouldn't really be dwelling on, stuff that wasn't important. Stuff that didn't matter. And some stuff that did.

She was missing Debbie, too. She'd never really had a close female friend before, not until she'd met Debbie Hogan – part-time glamour model, North East socialite, gossip columnist, and new wife of Gary Blandford, Newcastle Red Star's top defender and Ryan Fisher's best friend. When she'd first met Debbie just a few months ago, Amber had thought there was no way the two of them could, or would, ever get on – Debbie was, more or less, your 'typical' WAG, if there really was such a thing, because Amber was beginning to think there wasn't. Not really. Her attitude towards the women who shared the lives of these sometimes overpaid, cosseted, egotistical men had certainly changed after everything she'd been through with Ryan. And Debbie had become a friend Amber loved like a sister now. There were things she could talk to her about that she couldn't share with anyone else, not even Ronnie, and especially not Jim. And right now, Amber missed her. Right now, Amber needed her.

Breathing an inner sigh of relief as the cool, air-conditioned interior of the hotel hit her, Amber strode towards the elevator, hoping with all her heart that Jim was in their room. She really wanted to spend just a little bit more time with him, on their own, before work took over once again, because sometimes she felt a little bit like she was still living in that glorious honeymoon period, and she was scared to let that feeling go. Scared to let reality back in.

Sliding her key card into the lock on the door of the hotel suite that had been their home for the past few days, she closed it behind her and walked inside, throwing her beach bag down onto the floor and pulling off her kaftan, casting it aside as she continued to walk through into the bedroom.

He was sitting on the edge of the bed, her handsome husband, flicking through a pile of papers, his mobile phone close beside him, a frown covering his face.

'You okay?' Amber asked, watching as he lifted his head, his frown quickly turning into a smile.

'I am now.'

She smiled back, climbing onto the bed and kneeling up behind him, sliding her arms around his shoulders, kissing the back of his neck. 'You look tired,' she said, slowly beginning to massage his shoulders, feeling the knot of tension below her fingers as she kneaded deep. 'And you feel so tense.'

He threw his head back, still holding onto the papers he'd been flicking through. 'I'm fine, honey.'

She continued to knead his shoulders, listening to his quiet moans as her fingers pressed harder. 'What are you looking at?' she asked, resting her chin on the top of his head. He quickly turned the papers over, placing them on the bed beside him, his hand palm-down on top of them.

'Just work stuff. Nothing important.'

It was Amber's turn to frown at the way he'd quickly hidden those papers from her view. But maybe he just didn't want to talk about work anymore. That would be understandable. 'Anyway,' she said, shrugging it off. 'How about trying to ease that tension just a little bit more, huh?'

'What you got in mind?' He smiled, closing his eyes as her thumbs stroked the back of his neck in small, circular motions.

She stopped what she was doing for a second, untying her bikini top and throwing it onto the floor before pressing her naked breasts against his back, running her hands up and down his arms as she rested her chin on his shoulder. 'Oh, I don't know. You got any ideas?'

He gave a low, sexy laugh. 'Get over here. I need to look at you.'

She slid round in front of him, climbing astride him, pushing her breasts out as an invitation for him to touch her because, oh God, she wanted to be touched. She wanted him to touch her so badly.

'Jesus, Amber,' he groaned, running his fingers ever-so-lightly over her nipples, his eyes watching their every movement. 'I don't think I'd have got through this trip without you here.'

'Yeah, you would,' she breathed, throwing her head back as his fingers pressed harder against her naked breasts before travelling slowly down her body, trailing over her stomach, stroking her hips. 'You'd have managed.'

'You know that for sure, do you?' he whispered, his lips lightly brushing the base of her throat as he began slowly untying the sides of her bikini bottoms, pulling them away from her so she was completely naked.

'You'd have found some way of relieving the tension.' She smiled, burying her fingers in his hair as his mouth covered one of her breasts, his tongue flicking over her nipple, sending her stomach on another major somersaulting session.

The time for talking was over. They both knew where this was heading now.

She could feel his erection hard against her, ready and waiting to fill her up, and she reached down to free him, taking him in her hand, gasping as her fingers wrapped themselves around him. His groans turned her on even more, her need to have him inside her growing by the second, so when he lifted her up slightly, she made no attempt to fight the inevitable, lowering herself back down onto him, guiding him in with her hand.

'Oh Jesus, Amber…' he groaned as he slipped inside her. She was so wet it took no force at all, no effort to push his way in. 'You have no idea how much I need this right now.'

She threw her head back again as she rode him hard and fast, feeling him slip in and out of her in a beautiful, almost painful rhythm, her fingers buried in his hair as he thrust deep into her. She really couldn't live without this man. She'd tried – for nearly two decades she'd tried – but despite thinking she'd put him to the back of her mind, laid all those ghosts to rest, she'd only really been kidding herself. He'd taken her at such a young age, and his hold had never loosened its grip. She was caught in his trap, entangled in his web, and there was no place else she'd rather be.

Within minutes she could feel that tingle begin to appear, start its climb, slowly turning from a delicious shiver into a tidal wave of exquisite pins and needles as he pushed deeper, taking her to that beautiful precipice before tipping her over the edge in a wave of pleasure and pain that engulfed her completely, making her cry out loud.

Oh God, she loved this man. She loved him so much. They had so many lost years to catch up on, and Amber wanted to make sure that, this time, nothing was wasted. No opportunities were overlooked or lost. She couldn't afford for that to happen. She wanted to be with this man forever. And she wanted everything he could give her. Everything.

'I love you so much, Jim,' she whispered, her face buried in his hair as their bodies shuddered to a halt, his arms falling around her. He was still inside her, and Amber wanted him to stay there, just for a little while. Just for a little bit longer. 'I love you so much.'

'Hey, I love you, too, baby,' he said, gently stroking the small of her back in slow, rhythmic movements. 'You drive me fucking crazy, I can't begin to tell you…'

She pulled away slightly, closing her eyes as his mouth touched hers, kissing her in the most beautiful way – slowly and carefully, his mouth slightly open, his tongue touching hers. But she knew that if she didn't make a move soon, didn't leave this little bubble of theirs behind, she was never going to be able to concentrate on work. And that's where she needed her head to be now.

'I'd better go grab a shower.' She smiled at him, running her fingers lightly over his cheek as she felt him finally leave her body, and the sudden wave of emptiness that one small action caused her to feel was quite shocking.

'We're gonna be okay, Amber. Me and you. We're gonna be okay.'

She just smiled at him again as she stood up, running her fingers through her hair, and Jim watched as she walked into the bathroom, naked and beautiful, and his. She was all his. Finally. And he loved her so much it hurt like hell when she was out of his sight, when she wasn't near. It had always been that way. All those years apart, out of her life; he'd always felt that way. And nothing he'd done to try and forget her had worked. Nothing.

Looking down at the pile of papers by his side, he picked them up and turned them back over, scanning the pages again, his stomach turning, making him feel slightly sick at the realisation of just how close Amber had come to seeing them.

He stood up and walked over to his briefcase that was lying next to the dressing table, lifting it up and flicking the catches to open it, throwing the papers inside and slamming the case shut, locking it quickly. He was married to the woman of his dreams; the only woman he'd ever really loved – the only woman he'd allowed himself to love – and that meant there should be no secrets, not anymore. In fact, he'd promised her there'd be no more secrets. He'd promised her that, even though she'd asked him never to promise her anything ever again, after what he'd done to her all those years ago. So maybe it would have been better if he'd let her see the papers. It would have brought forward a situation he was dreading having to face; but it had to happen. And soon. He couldn't avoid it. He had to tell her, she had to know. He had no choice now anyway. Events and circumstances had seen to that. Circumstances he'd known had been coming, but he'd chosen to bury his head in the sand and delay the inevitable.

But here, in Tenerife, it just wasn't the time or the place to tell Amber everything. He'd wait until they were back home. He'd waited this long, another few days wasn't going to make any difference. It wasn't going to change the situation.

It was almost time to get everything out in the open once and for all; to prove to her that he had nothing left to hide. But he *had* been hiding something. And how she reacted to that was something Jim didn't even want to think about.

'Have I been doing okay?' Amber asked, her heart beating ten to the dozen as she called Debbie back home in Newcastle after the game, which Newcastle Red Star had won 4-0, despite the humid evening and still relatively high temperatures. But even though they were on foreign soil, Tenerife was a holiday destination, and they were playing in the south of the island, which was a Mecca for British tourists. So the crowd had largely been made up of British supporters – holiday-makers and ex-pats, mainly – which had helped with the atmosphere. At times it had almost felt like a home game. 'I've been so nervous, Debbie. I swear I was almost sick just before I went live to the studio for the first time last week, it's ridiculous! I mean, like Ronnie said, it's not as though I haven't done this before. I've been working in TV for years now...'

'Amber, chick, slow down, will you? Take a deep breath and slow down. You've been more than okay, do you hear me? I've watched all the games, and you've been doing great. Me and the girls, we're all over at Tanya's place tonight because she's just had a brand new Smart TV fitted on the living room wall, you should see the size of it... anyway, everybody said the same – you're a natural!'

Amber breathed out a long, loud sigh of relief, closing her eyes as she leaned back against the wall. 'Really? You're not just saying that because you're my friend?'

'No. I'm not just saying it. You're so good at what you do, hon. You put the rest of us to shame, I mean, you're the only one of us with a proper job, for starters.'

Amber couldn't help but smile. '*You've* got a "proper" job, as you put it, Debbie.'

'What? Writing a small column for a celebrity gossip magazine?'

'Not just *any* celebrity gossip magazine though, Debs. *The* most *popular* celebrity gossip magazine there is. And you've got your modelling. You work just as hard as me, in different ways, that's all.'

Debbie laughed, and Amber wished she could just pop over to her place right now, open a bottle of something white and sparkling and settle down for a good, long chat. Because Amber really needed to talk to her about something. Something that had been preying on her mind for a few weeks now, and she couldn't shake it, couldn't stop thinking about it. And it wasn't something she wanted to bring up with Jim. Not yet, anyway.

'You know what I mean,' Debbie said. 'And, at the risk of sounding shallow – but this is a very valid point, I think – you looked fabulous! Whoever did your hair and make-up is a true artist. Those eyes… And did you pick your own outfit?'

'Debbie, I work for a sports channel, not E! Entertainment. Of course I picked my own outfit. You don't think Ronnie and the guys have stylists, do you?'

'I don't know, do I? They should do. The state of them sometimes.'

Now it was Amber's turn to laugh. She knew that calling Debbie straight after the game would be a good idea. She always had a knack of cheering her up, or taking her mind off things, and now was no exception.

'So, those black, leather-look skinny jeans are yours, then?'

'Yes,' Amber laughed, unable to keep the surprised tone out of her voice. 'What are you trying to say, missy?'

'My influence must be rubbing off on you.'

Amber just knew she would have had the biggest smirk on her face when she'd said that.

'What you up to now?' Debbie asked. 'Are you finished for the night?'

'Yeah, thankfully. I'm shattered! I think Jim and I are off out for dinner somewhere. Alone, hopefully.'

'How are things with you and Ryan? Have you spoken to him much since you've been over there?'

'Bar the interviews I've done with him whilst we've been here, no. I've hardly said two words to him to be honest. It's not that I've been avoiding him or anything, the opportunity just hasn't been there, that's all.' There was just the tiniest hint of a little white lie, but there was no need for Debbie to know that.

'And there's no awkwardness?'

'No. Why should there be? It's been months since me and him… since it all happened, Debbie. It's in the past now. We've both moved forward.'

'Yeah. Yeah, you have.'

Amber was slightly distracted by the sound of voices – Ryan's being one of them – getting closer. 'I'm gonna have to go now, Debs.'

'Okay, chick. I'll see you in a couple of days.'

'Yeah. And I can't wait. I'm dying for a girly catch-up.'

'Me too, hon. See you soon!'

Amber quickly ended the call but wasn't fast enough to make her escape before Ryan and Gary pushed their way through the double doors she'd been standing beside. She couldn't really run away now, could she?

'Hey, Amber.' Gary smiled at her, and she returned it.

'I've just been talking to your wife.'

'She okay?' Gary asked. 'Behaving herself, I hope.'

'She's at Tanya's, with the rest of the girls. They've been watching the match.'

'Yeah, sure,' Gary laughed. 'Since when were any of that lot interested in what we do? They're just interested in the money we make.'

'You need to give them a bit more credit, Gary.' Amber tucked her phone into the back pocket of her jeans. 'They're not quite as superficial as you all seem to think they are.'

Gary just let out a derisive snort, said something to Ryan that Amber didn't catch, and walked away, throwing Amber a wink over his shoulder. Amber narrowed her eyes and glared at him, slowly shaking her head.

'You avoiding me?' Ryan asked. An afternoon spent sampling the delights of the gorgeous Ellen still hadn't managed to stop him from hoping he'd bump into Amber after the match. Okay, so he'd spoken to her in a professional capacity over the past few days, in a couple of interviews for TV, but he'd wanted to catch her alone. And right now, as he looked at her, all crazy red hair and piercing pale blue eyes, every memory all those hours with Ellen had managed to erase came flooding back tenfold.

Amber swung round, her eyes instantly meeting his. 'No. No, of course I'm not avoiding you.'

'It feels like you are.'

'What do you want me to do, Ryan? Actively seek you out for regular get-togethers?'

He stuck his hands in his pockets, turning away from her for a second. 'It just feels…' He looked at her again. 'I don't know… It just feels as though, what we had… it feels like it never happened sometimes, that's all.'

'Yeah, well, there's been a lot of water under the bridge since then,' Amber said quietly. It was hard to forget what she'd once felt for this man, and maybe she didn't really want to. 'So much has happened.'

'Tell me about it,' Ryan sighed, pushing a hand through his hair. He really didn't want to still be feeling this way, but he couldn't help it, couldn't push those feelings down, no matter how hard he tried.

'Are you… is everything okay, Ryan?' Despite everything, she'd never stopped caring about him. She couldn't do that, couldn't just switch those feelings off, even after all these months.

'Everything's fine,' he replied, his eyes meeting hers again. 'It would just be nice to talk to you sometimes, without it having to be under the guise of a TV interview.'

'That's my job, Ryan.'

He just looked at her, and she stared back at him. He was so handsome, so young. So dangerous. She only hoped he'd learned enough lessons to allow him not to let history repeat itself. Again.

'I'm married now, Ryan. You do understand that, don't you?'

'Don't treat me like a kid, Amber. Yeah, I know you're married. It's bloody hard to ignore that fact when all you do is wrap yourself around the boss twenty-four-seven…' Now he was thinking aloud. Not the best idea.

'Do you know how childish you sound? If you can't act like a grown-up…' She turned to walk away but he grabbed her wrist, swinging her back round.

'I'm sorry. I'm sorry, okay?'

'Yeah. You should be.' She pulled her arm free of his grip, rubbing her wrist. 'Look, I know things are still a bit weird…'

'I just want us to be friends, Amber. That's all. I want us to be able to talk to each other and forget the past; put it behind us.'

She looked into his eyes. Kind eyes. Yeah, he really had changed over these past few months. Or that was the impression he was giving off, anyway. 'And you think we can do that, do you?' she said quietly, suddenly realising that this was the first time she'd really spoken to him – properly spoken to him – in weeks. He was right. All that time and the only talking she'd ever done with him had been because she'd had to – to interview him. Professional purposes only. Had that been deliberate on her part? All those months and this was the first real conversation she'd had with him. That thought flooded her with guilt, because he really hadn't deserved that.

'I think we can try,' he replied, his eyes still fixed firmly on hers.

'Ryan… I am so sorry. I am so, so sorry. I just…' She sighed, leaning back against the wall, pushing a hand through her hair. 'Maybe I just didn't know how to handle it all. How to handle being around you. I mean, it's still so complicated…'

'It doesn't have to be.'

'Doesn't it?'

He smiled, and Amber felt her stomach give a small but noticeable jolt. 'I just want us to be friends. Nothing more, no ulterior motive. I promise.'

'Yeah, well, you know how I feel about promises.' She was aware of Jim's voice somewhere nearby, and despite what Ryan had just told her, she still didn't want Jim to think Ryan may be playing some kind of game. She wasn't altogether sure how much Jim trusted Ryan. They'd never really talked about him – about what he and Amber had shared. And maybe that had been a mistake, too. Maybe they should have been more open, about everything. 'Look, I've got to go, Ryan. I'll see you later, okay?'

He nodded. 'Yeah. Okay. Oh, and Amber?'

She turned round to look at him.

'I'm happy for you. Really.'

If he said that out loud enough times then he might actually start to believe he meant it because, right now, he wasn't altogether sure that he did. Of course he wanted her to be happy – after what he'd put her through it was the least she deserved. But it still hurt to think that, had it not been for his sheer stupidity, they could have been happy together. They'd come so close, so fucking close.

'Why did you do it?' Ryan whispered to himself as he watched her walk down the corridor, over to her husband. He watched as his boss smiled at her, kissing her quickly, sliding an arm around her waist as they talked, both of them totally unashamed of showing how much in love they were. 'Why?'

But Ryan knew the answer to that. And as much as he would have liked to turn the clock back and rewrite history, he couldn't.

He just had to get on with his life, the way she was getting on with hers, and he would. He'd start doing just that.

Making his way down the corridor to join the rest of the team as they celebrated their win over CD Adeje, one of Spain's most popular clubs, despite not being in the very top flight of Spanish football, he recalled a short and totally unexpected conversation he'd had just before the game. A conversation he'd thought nothing of, in fact, he'd just laughed it off as something flattering but highly unlikely to ever happen. However, seeing Amber just now, it made him think again. Maybe it wasn't such a stupid idea after all. Maybe it was exactly what he needed. Maybe he shouldn't dismiss it out of hand altogether.

Decision made. He just hoped it was the right one.

Chapter Four

'Jim?'

He looked up as Amber walked into the kitchen of their home in the small, North East coastal village of Tynemouth. Her arms were folded against her, and she had a slightly unsettled expression on her face. He took a sip of coffee and continued to watch her as she fiddled with the strap of her watch, a tell-tale nervous reaction of hers. What did she have to be nervous about?

'Is everything okay, honey? You look like you've got something on your mind.' A small but noticeable chill ran up his spine as he continued to look at her, her eyes refusing to meet his.

'Can I ask you something, Jim?'

He took another sip of coffee before putting his mug down and folding his arms, smiling slightly as she finally met his gaze.

'Of course you can. Come on, Amber, you can ask me anything, baby. I'm your husband.'

She looked away again, down at the ground, her fingers once more fiddling with her watch. She hadn't wanted to bring this up whilst they'd been over in the Canaries – it hadn't really been the time or the place – and now they were back home, she still wasn't sure the time was right, but then, she wasn't sure the time would ever be right, not really. So the only thing she could think of to do was to bite the bullet and just talk to him, before it started to become an obsession that took over her life.

'Amber? Sweetheart?'

She took a deep breath. 'What do you think about...?' She slowly lifted her head, her eyes meeting his again, and he couldn't help but notice a touch of sadness in them, something which did nothing to ease that chill. 'What do you think about... about us starting a family?'

He felt relief sweep over him, followed by confusion, which was swiftly replaced by the return of that chill. This was totally unexpected, and it had thrown him slightly. He narrowed his eyes as he looked at her. 'Sorry, I... Starting a family...? Amber, I...'

'A baby, Jim. I want a baby. I want *our* baby.'

'Jesus, honey, where's this come from?' The day had hardly got off the ground and his head was already spinning. This had come completely out of the blue, something he'd never expected to hear from her. Not Amber. Not from a woman who'd shown no inclination to ever have a baby, none whatsoever. She'd only just come round to the idea of marriage, for heaven's sake, and now she was talking babies?

'I'm thirty-eight years old, Jim. In terms of motherhood I'm right at the business end of things now. I haven't got much time left to waste.'

He walked over to her, aware that his somewhat surprised expression had caused that frown to appear, clouding her pretty features. 'I just... We've never really talked about starting a family, have we? I wasn't even aware it was something you were thinking about, I mean, you've never even hinted at it being...'

'I'm talking about it now, Jim,' Amber said quietly, allowing herself to fall against him as he took her in his arms. She loved it there, in his arms. She felt safe. She felt as though nothing could touch her when she was there. When he was holding her. She felt as if all the confusion she was suddenly feeling was something she could keep under control when, in reality, she didn't think she could.

He kissed the top of her head, rubbing her back gently. She picked her times to start conversations like this, he'd give her that. He was due to leave for the training ground soon, and this wasn't really the kind of conversation he wanted hanging over his head all day. It wasn't really the kind of conversation he wanted, full stop, if he was completely honest. Not right now. The timing was way off. 'What's brought this on, Amber? Huh?'

She pulled away slightly, looking into his eyes, stroking his face with her fingertips. 'I love you, so much, Jim. And I guess marrying you, finally being with you, the way I always wanted to be, I guess it's suddenly made me want all those things I… all those things I thought I didn't want. When all the time it was… it was just that I couldn't have them with you. I didn't want them if I couldn't have you. And to have them with anyone else, it wouldn't have felt right, none of it felt right. But it feels right *now*. Now I can't stop thinking about all those things and… I can't stop thinking about *us*, about how right that feels.'

Jim took her hand in his and squeezed it gently, leaning forward to kiss her. She tasted so good, her lips so soft against his, her mouth opening in response to him as he kissed her harder, pulling her against him.

He loved her like he'd never loved anyone before – to the point of obsession sometimes. But it was an obsession he could handle, because he knew how she felt about him. And for her to want this, for her to want a baby – *his* baby – it spoke volumes. And maybe he wanted that, too. Maybe he wanted that family, that security. Something to soften the blow when she found out the truth about him? About what he'd been hiding from her? From everyone? He didn't want to think about that right now. Although the longer he kept putting it off, the worse the situation was going to become, he knew that. But she'd kind of put paid to any likelihood that he was going to tell her anything today. Now *really* wasn't the time. 'You want a baby? Really?'

She smiled at him, resting her forehead against his. 'I know this sounds crazy, Jim. I know it sounds as though it's come completely out of the blue, but… I haven't been able to stop thinking about it. For weeks now it's been on my mind and… and since coming off the Pill I…'

He shut her up with another kiss, a slower kiss, a longer kiss, because he needed time to think about this. He didn't want to lose her, not now, not ever, not after everything it had taken to win her back. But was this *really* what he wanted? What he needed? Was it really the right way to be going? Under the circumstances? Circumstances she was completely unaware of. But it couldn't stay that way. It wasn't *going* to stay that way, that was out of his hands now. And he didn't have long before it was all going to come out, regardless of whether he'd found the time to tell her or not. And it really would be better off coming from him.

'Look, Amber, honey, you've just got this brand new job and… How's it going to look if you suddenly need time off to…?'

She cut him off mid-sentence with one of her trademark withering looks, and Jim couldn't help but smile. That's what he loved about Amber. His beautiful wife, the woman who could cut you down with a stare or shut you up with one smart remark. 'You're really going down the sexist route, Jim? Hmm? Is that where you're going?'

He was still smiling, he couldn't help it as he backed away from her with his hands held up in mock surrender. 'Amber, baby, I'm sorry. I'm sorry. But this is so crazy, sweetheart, you have to see that. The Amber I knew, she didn't want to be a mom. She didn't want any of that, and I'm just finding it strange…'

'And you think I'm not? You… you think this is something I'm handling okay, do you? This fucking weird and sudden alien need inside me to…' She looked at him, pushing both hands through her hair. 'I don't have a lot of time left, Jim. I don't have time to sit and think about this, to weigh up every pro and con a million times over until I'm 100 per cent certain that this is what I really, truly want. I don't have that luxury. I've got to make that decision soon – *we've* got to make that decision soon. Before it's too late. Because…' She stopped talking, looking away for a second.

He walked back over to her, tilting her chin up so she was looking straight at him. 'Because, what?'

'It doesn't matter,' she sighed, letting him pull her closer.

'You really want this, huh? Me and you, making babies?'

'Only you could make that sound like the most erotic thing in the world.' She smiled, her breathing suddenly starting to speed up for some reason.

'And, isn't it?' he whispered, his mouth almost touching hers now. 'I mean, surely, the act of making babies *is* one of the most erotic things in the world.' She felt her stomach flip over what felt like a thousand times as the warmth of his body engulfed hers, the heat between them palpable. 'I don't know,' she said quietly, quite surprised that she could actually string a sentence together right now.

'Do you want to see just how erotic it can be?' He smiled, his mouth still not quite touching hers as he spoke, but almost. Maybe this *was* the right way to go. Yeah, he was definitely coming round to the idea. After all, giving Amber a baby might mean she was distracted from anything else that was going on, and that, as far as Jim was concerned, wouldn't be a bad thing. He loved her beyond words, he loved her more than he could ever explain, and that's why he needed to protect her. He needed to do that. And anyway, why wouldn't he want a baby with the most beautiful woman he'd ever set eyes on? Why wouldn't he want to make her happy? Anything she wanted – if he could give it to her, then he would. He would do that in a heartbeat.

She could feel his breath on her face, his hand stroking the small of her back, pulling at her dress, and already her heart was beating out of her chest, hammering hard inside her. This was crazy! What had started out as a sensible conversation about starting a family had suddenly turned into a sex-fuelled encounter that was only ever going to end one way.

She closed her eyes as she felt his hand slide her dress up over her legs and she couldn't help but take an almost involuntary sharp intake of breath as his fingers began stroking her inner thigh. Already she could feel that familiar tingle between her legs, and a part of her just wanted him to take her there and then, to do it quickly, because she was finding it hard to control herself. Her skin was breaking out in tiny goose bumps, her head was starting to spin, her legs growing weaker by the second as his mouth finally covered hers in the lightest, most beautiful of kisses.

Oh God, she wasn't sure how much more she could take of this. She wanted to strip off her own underwear and just make him take her now, right now, because she was physically aching for him. Were these intense, crazy feelings she had for this man ever going to fade? Yeah, of course they were. In time. Which is why she should be making the most of them while she was still feeling this way, feeling this excited, this turned on. Because nobody knew how long it was all going to last.

'You sure this is the way you want it to go?' he whispered, his hand on her cheek, his mouth still close to hers as he spoke. 'No protection. No barriers. Nothing to stop it from happening. You're really sure this is what you want?'

She looked into his eyes, searching his face, wanting, needing to know that he was serious, that he felt the same way about this as she did. 'Are *you*?'

He kissed her gently, his thumb lightly stroking her cheek, his other hand still stroking her inner thigh, which, in turn – combined with his kiss – was making her breathing quite unsteady.

'Oh, I think we'd make a rather good mommy and daddy, don't you?'

Just the way he'd said that, in that wonderful accent of his, his voice dirty and deep, he'd made it sound like the sexiest thing she'd ever heard.

'Yes,' she breathed. It was all she could manage to get out before his fingers slid underneath the thin material of her panties, touching the sudden wetness, making her gasp out loud. She threw her head back as his lips brushed over the base of her neck, his fingers still probing, touching her, burying themselves in her, and it was all she could do to stop the loudest cry of pleasure from escaping. She could feel it all building up inside her, amassing itself into one huge ball of ecstasy, just waiting for its chance to be set free.

'Jim…' she groaned, gripping the counter top behind her, opening her legs wider to give him easier access.

'It's okay, honey. It's okay,' he said quietly, pushing her dress farther up over her thighs, sinking to his haunches as he slowly and carefully peeled her panties down her legs in an action that Amber thought might make her come there and then. She stepped out of them, the freedom she now felt turning her on to the point of no return – almost. 'You are so beautiful,' Jim whispered, letting his hands run back up the length of her legs as he stood up, finally resting them on her hips. 'So beautiful…'

Their eyes locked together, and for a second Amber thought her heart had literally stopped. It was almost that same feeling she'd experienced the very first time she'd set eyes on him, when he'd walked into her mum and dad's house all those years ago as a twenty-seven-year-old professional footballer, and she'd been a fifteen-year-old teenager in the middle of planning her sixteenth birthday party. But the effect him walking into their living room that day had had on her had been life-changing. Literally. Just as this could be now, what they were about to do here.

He gently pushed her back against the counter, her dress now up around her waist, and she closed her eyes as his lips once more brushed the base of her neck, his hands resting on her hips, keeping her steady as he carefully pushed into her.

Throwing her head back, Amber groaned out loud as he pushed hard, rocking her back against the counter, and she buried her fingers in his hair as his mouth finally met hers. The feel of his body inside her, his mouth kissing her slowly and sensually as he held onto her hips, keeping her steady, it was all so overwhelming, still so hard to get used to at times; him being there, the fact they were married. Sometimes she'd wake up in the morning and for those first few seconds she'd forget that he was her husband, that he was right there beside her. Sometimes she'd forget that he really was hers.

'Are you still sure, honey?' he whispered, his mouth resting on hers as he spoke. 'Because I'm so close to coming, baby, and if you want I can just…' She shook her head, silencing him with a kiss, and he smiled, gently stroking a stray strand of hair from her eyes. 'I love you, Amber.'

'I love you, too,' she said quietly, slowly closing her eyes as he kissed her long and deep, pulling away only when she felt his body tense up, signalling his impending release, and she too prepared herself for one of her own as those familiar tingles started creeping across her body. 'Jim…' she moaned quietly as he buried his head in her shoulder, his body shaking and shuddering in her arms as she felt him explode, spilling out into her, and she luxuriated in the warmth that feeling created. It was as if he was filling up every inch of her, taking her over, and she didn't want to open her eyes because she felt that if she did, then this would all just be some kind of dream. Over too soon.

'Jesus, Amber…' Jim groaned, his hands still on her hips as his own movements slowed down, his own journey coming to an end. But she had yet to reach that summit, and he knew that, reaching down to gently touch her as he slowly withdrew. 'You feel so good…'

She gripped the countertop behind her tighter as his fingers stroked her so carefully, touching her right where she needed to be touched and with just the right amount of pressure. The feel of his hand was enough to start the beginning of the end, to send those tingles spreading through her at a rapid rate, taking her over until she could hold out no longer. His fingers speeded up their action, pressing against her, his lips covering her neck in quick, feather-light kisses as she came in a crashing climax of cries and moans, pushing down against his hand, the feel of him there heightening every last, tiny sensation. And then it was over, done. Time for reality to make itself known again. Just like that.

'Two seconds.' Jim smiled, finally pulling away from her. She watched as he left the kitchen, trying hard to catch her breath. She felt drained, but also invigorated, and slightly confused. What had they just done? Had she really just told him she wanted to start a family? Had she really said all that out loud? Just like that? When she knew, deep down inside, that it wasn't going to be quite as simple as she made it out to be. But, yeah, they really had just gone through with it. They'd taken that first step. But the journey wasn't going to be an easy one.

She bent down and retrieved her panties, pulling them on and repositioning her dress, shaking her hair out as she tried to compose herself. Spontaneous sex wasn't exactly an unusual occurrence, considering they were still very much in the 'honeymoon' period of their marriage, but what had just happened there had sobered her up; to the point where she felt a little disorientated. What the hell was wrong with her today?

'You okay?'

She swung round at the sound of his voice. 'Yeah. Yeah, I'm fine.'

'You sure?' he asked, frowning slightly as he walked over to her, slipping an arm around her waist and pulling her against him. 'Because you look as though you've still got something on your mind. Is there anything else you want to talk about?'

She smiled, running her hands up and down his strong arms, the soft material of his shirt smooth beneath her fingers. 'I'm sorry, Jim, if this all feels a bit surreal, my sudden need to have a baby, but…' She looked into his eyes. Her heart still skipped that proverbial beat when she did that, and she never wanted that feeling to go away, ever. She wanted to cling onto it for as long as she could. 'I really have been thinking about it, seriously, for a while now.'

'So why didn't you talk to me? Did you think I wouldn't listen? That it was something I wouldn't want?'

'Well, to be fair, Jim, the look on your face when I mentioned it just now wasn't that of a man who was expecting those words to come out of my mouth.'

'No, I suppose it wasn't. But only because you never seemed to be the type of woman who…'

She shut him up with a kiss, standing on tiptoe, holding onto his upper arms to steady herself as her lips touched his, ever-so-lightly.

'The type of woman who, what?' she asked, a slight smirk appearing on her face. 'Who never showed any maternal inclinations whatsoever? Then you really don't know me at all, Jim. My mum was the best mum a girl could have asked for. She was funny and smart and beautiful…'

'Just like her daughter.'

She stopped talking and looked at him, cocking her head.

'I knew your mom, Amber. Remember? I knew what an amazing woman she was.'

She said nothing for a few seconds as she let memories of her late Spanish mother fill her head, her heart aching all over again with a loss that still hurt. Because there were times when she really needed her mum. And now was certainly one of those times.

'What I'm trying to say is that I always wanted to be like her. She was so beautiful, so kind and funny and strong, she was so strong. Right to the end she kept on fighting, until there was nothing more anyone could do. She didn't give up until she had to. She had this… this aura about her, you know? She would walk into a room and it would just light up. I loved her so much, Jim. So much. We were so close, never a day went by when I didn't speak to her. And she was so supportive, always there for me no matter what. She was my rock. My best friend, and when she died… I miss her so much, all the time, that never goes away. Ever. And I… I always wanted to be the kind of mum to a child of my own that she was to me, and just because I didn't go round shouting about the fact

I would love a baby one day…' She broke off, walking over to the window, folding her arms as she looked outside, the late-summer sunshine making their large, walled garden look gloriously pretty with its multitude of coloured flowers and fruit trees. 'Deep down inside, I'm scared I'll never get the chance.'

She closed her eyes as she felt his arms wrap around her from behind, pulling her back against him, and she rested her head against his shoulder, just letting him hold her. She wanted to tell him. She really wanted to tell him. But she couldn't, not yet. Not just yet. Not until she was sure.

'I want you to have everything you ever dreamed of, Amber,' he said quietly. 'Everything. And I will try my hardest to make sure you get it all, believe me.'

She turned round in his arms, opening her eyes and shaking her hair out again, changing the mood in an instant. There were some things she knew he may never be able to give her, it was just that now wasn't the time to think about that.

'Anyway, come on,' she said, straightening the collar of his shirt. 'You're going to be late if you don't get a move on.'

He frowned slightly. He wasn't sure he wanted to leave this conversation still hanging, but she was right. He was supposed to be at the training ground in half an hour and it took nearly as long as that to drive there from their home at the coast.

'So, what are you up to today?' he asked, reluctantly letting her go, grabbing his jacket from the back of a chair.

'Well, I'm not due in London until the end of the week, so I thought I'd go and see Debbie. Maybe do a little bit of shopping. She's still training me in the ways of the WAG.'

Jim smiled, shoving his hands in his pockets. 'Really?' He arched an eyebrow and Amber laughed, suddenly relaxing. Yeah, every-thing was fine. She hadn't ruined it all by laying this on him the way she had. He was fine. She just wished she'd had the nerve to tell him everything, because she knew she'd have to, at some point.

'Yeah. Really.'

'So,' he went on, picking his phone up from the table and quickly checking for messages. 'You nervous about making your live studio debut for Cloud Sports on Friday?'

'Yeah, a little bit,' she sighed. 'But…' She smiled at him, pulling her hair back into a loose ponytail, '… at least it means you can watch me on TV when I'm not here, and then maybe you won't miss me quite so much.'

He quickly pulled her into his arms again, stealing another kiss. 'Ah, yes, but, the excellent timing of it all means that because Red Star's first game of the season is down in the capital, I don't really have to miss you at all, do I? In fact, beautiful, I can be with you the second you come off air on Friday night. I'll leave Colin in charge of the squad at the hotel, and I'll come and spend some time with you, if that's what you want.'

Why would she want anything else? 'You'd better be there, handsome, or I'll be extremely disappointed.'

'And we can't have that, now, can we?'

She shook her head as his mouth moved closer to hers. 'No. We can't.'

One more kiss then he'd have to go, even if he'd much rather stay where he was. How he was going to cope when she wasn't there, when she was away, working, he didn't know, but at least she was right in one respect – he could watch her, there on TV, knowing she was his. Knowing that beautiful woman was finally his, after all those years of waiting, wishing and hoping. All those years of getting everything so wrong. But wasn't he still getting it wrong now? Knowing what he knew – what she had yet to find out.

'If you want to come down to the training ground…' Jim began, pushing those thoughts firmly to the back of his mind.

'I think I'll stick to shopping with Debbie, if you don't mind.'

As much as he would have loved to have seen her later, he'd all but known she would have declined that offer. Anywhere Ryan Fisher was, Amber tried to avoid. Jim just hoped it was for all the right reasons. He trusted Amber, but as far as his feelings towards his star striker went, that was a different matter. He rested his forehead against hers, smiling slightly. 'So, I guess I'll see you tonight.'

'Yeah. You will. And play your cards right, mister, and you can see as much of me as you want.'

'Jesus, Ryan, come on,' Gary groaned as Ryan miskicked another shot at goal, the ball flying high over the crossbar. 'What the hell is wrong with you this morning? The boss is gonna go ape shit if he sees the way you're playing today.'

Ryan dropped to his haunches, his head in his hands. 'Nothing's wrong with me, Gary. I'm just a bit off form, that's all.'

'Well, your timing's crap, mate. You know, it being just a couple of days away from the beginning of a brand new season. Our first game isn't exactly an easy one...'

Ryan stood up, looking at Gary, his hands on his hips. 'We're fucking league champions, Gary. Right now, at this moment in time, *we* are the fucking best, so we should be frightened of no one. We should be able to go out there on Saturday and show them that *they* should be intimidated by *us*, not the other way around. We should be able to win that match easy.'

'Not if you play the way you've been playing this morning we won't. You letting yourself get a bit too distracted by the new lady in your life?' Gary winked.

'Fuck off,' Ryan sighed, turning away and walking over to the touchline, his head down.

'Going somewhere, Fisher?'

Ryan looked up. Jim Allen stood right there in front of him dressed – unusually for him – for the training ground rather than the office, sporting tracksuit bottoms, football boots, and a white t-shirt that clung to a physique most forty-nine-year-old men would kill for. Lately he'd been involving himself more and more in the physical aspects of training, and Ryan wondered if this need to keep in shape had anything to do with the fact he was now married to a younger woman – a very beautiful younger woman.

A woman Ryan didn't really want to think about for too long, because it still hurt. No matter how much he pretended it didn't.

'No. Just taking a break, boss.'

Jim continued to stare at him, raising an eyebrow, but he said nothing. He just let him go, and Ryan didn't stop to argue. He needed five minutes away from it all, just to get his head together.

Things with Ellen had started moving way faster than he'd wanted them to, even though he'd tried his hardest not to give her any signals that could easily be interpreted the wrong way. He was determined to try and put his old ways behind him, but he was beginning to realise that going cold turkey wasn't the best idea. Baby steps – that was the way to go about a change he had a feeling was going to take a lot of getting used to. Little by little, step by step, and he'd get there. But the fact Ellen had started talking about staying over at his place, leaving some of her things there so she didn't have to keep bringing stuff over – that was the thin end of the wedge as far as Ryan was concerned. And no way was he anywhere near ready enough to have her move in with him, even though it was more than obvious that that was what she was hinting at. His life was in no state to welcome a serious relationship. Not the way things stood at the minute.

Everything was so much harder than he'd ever thought it would be. Something that should be so simple was proving to be the most difficult thing Ryan had ever had to face, but the past year had changed him in so many ways. And maybe the one thing he'd tried not to think about over the past few days was the only option left open to him now. He certainly had to open his mind to the idea that it could be a possibility.

His head was spinning with everything that was going on in there, and now, more than ever, Ryan wished he had someone he could talk to. He wished he had Amber.

'I can't believe I did that, Debbie, I really can't,' Amber sighed, sinking into the soft cushions of the sofa in the bar they'd ducked into for a glass or two of wine after a particularly busy morning's shopping.

'You said Jim's fine about it.' Debbie sat down on the chair opposite Amber. 'In fact, you said he's more than fine.'

'He is,' Amber went on, crossing her legs and wishing she could kick off her shoes. She was still getting used to walking in these new heels, never mind shopping in them, and her feet were killing her. Why she'd let Debbie talk her into wearing them today she had no idea. She wasn't usually swayed so easily. 'But still… I must have sounded like some crazed, hormonal, pre-menopausal madwoman. The poor bugger was only trying to get ready for work and I walk in and start demanding a baby! I still can't believe those words came out of my own mouth.'

Debbie briefly turned her attention to the young man who'd just turned up at their table with an ice bucket and a bottle of something white and sparkling. She smiled at him as he placed it down in front of them, and Amber couldn't help but be slightly amused at his flustered expression. Debbie could be quite intimidating when she wanted to be, with her striking white-blonde hair and glamorous exterior. 'I envy you sometimes, Amber,' Debbie sighed, winking at the young man as he beat a hasty retreat back behind the bar.

'Envy *me*? Why? Look at the life *you've* got.'

'Hmmm,' Debbie said, leaning forward to pour two glasses of champagne. 'It's not quite as fabulous as I make it out to be, chick. Gary hasn't changed all that much since we got married, although, to be honest, after what happened with Ryan, he *is* trying to rein it in a little bit, and for that I should be eternally grateful, I suppose. But you and Jim… oh, what I wouldn't give to have a man like that.'

'Yeah, well, hands off. He's mine.' Amber threw Debbie a small smile as she took the glass she held out for her, indulging in a long and very welcome sip of the cold, bubbly liquid.

'And you two will make such beautiful babies,' Debbie sighed, leaning back in her seat as she sipped her own champagne.

Amber couldn't help smiling again, even though that smile was accompanied by a brief and unwelcome jolt of reality. A reality that was starting to bite hard. 'I'd like to think so… Christ, listen to me! This is mad, Debbie. I mean, marriage, babies, a career that takes me out of the North East way more than I'd like it to – all things I never thought I wanted. Well, okay, at the back of my mind I suppose I did always wonder what it would be like to have kids, but I never really *wanted* them. Not at the time. Does that make sense?'

'Sort of.' Debbie frowned, crossing and uncrossing her long, tanned legs, giving the men sitting across the bar from them more than they'd bargained for. She was wearing a short, lemon-yellow sundress and Amber could only pray that she was wearing under-wear. You never could tell with Debbie.

Amber took another sip of champagne, and for a second she had to stop and think about where her life had taken her over the past few months. Yes, it had all happened so fast – sometimes it took her breath away to think of how quickly her life had been turned on its head, to the point where she was now sitting in one of the most upmarket bars on Newcastle's Quayside, drinking champagne in the middle of the afternoon. Who'd have thought?

'Earth calling Amber.'

Debbie's voice pulled Amber back to reality and she turned to look at her friend.

'You were miles away, chick. Everything okay?'

Amber looked down for a second, focusing on the beautifully understated but perfect wedding ring on the third finger of her left hand. A never-ending band of white gold that signified perfectly her love for Jim Allen. Never-ending. It always had been and it always would be. She couldn't see that ever changing now. So maybe she owed it to him to be honest. Once she knew the facts.

'I don't know.' She looked back up at Debbie's slightly confused expression. 'I don't know if everything's okay.'

'Has something happened, hon? Are you and Jim okay?'

'Oh God, yes. We're fine, I don't mean that… Me and Jim, we're good, we're more than good. It's just… me becoming a mum it's… it may not be quite as simple as I might have made it out to be.'

Debbie put her glass down, leaning further forward, her expression still confused. 'How do you mean, chick?'

Amber drained her glass of champagne and placed it down on the table in front of her, pushing a hand through her hair. It was time to face up to this now. It wasn't something she could block out and put to the back of her mind anymore, because that's what she'd been doing. For a very long time. And she'd been able to do that purely because there'd been no need to confront it, no need to even think about it. Until now.

'When I was young, very young – I think I was about seven or eight when it happened – my appendix ruptured. It was pretty serious, apparently, although I don't remember all that much about it. But, according to my dad, it was serious. Anyway, the upshot of all this was, because of the ruptured appendix and the subsequent peritonitis…' She stared down at her wedding ring again, twisting it round and round her finger. 'My fallopian tubes are scarred to hell, Debbie. At the time, the doctors told my mum and dad that I may have trouble conceiving when I was older and they never hid the truth from me so… so I've always known there's a chance that… that it may not be all that easy, but… I've got to cling onto hope, haven't I? I never really gave it much thought before because I'd always resigned myself to the fact that I was never going to be a mum. I didn't think I'd ever find the right man anyway, that one man who could… who…' She felt tears start to prick the back of her eyes and she rummaged round in her bag for a handkerchief, desperate not to cry. She didn't want to start crying. Jesus, this was so wrong! Amber Sullivan hadn't wanted kids. Amber Sullivan hadn't felt these ridiculous feelings; this sudden, aching need. But Amber Allen did. 'But then he came back. Jim. He came back.' She looked at Debbie, whose face was now a mask of genuine concern, which only made Amber's tears fall faster. 'And everything changed, Debbie. Everything.'

Debbie jumped up and sat down next to Amber, taking her hand and squeezing it tight. 'You don't know anything for definite though, do you?'

Amber looked at her. 'I know the worst case scenario.'

'But that might not be the case for *you*, chick. Have you seen a doctor?'

Amber shook her head. 'I'm scared, Debbie. I'm scared of what they're gonna tell me, of having to face up to something I thought I'd be able to handle, but now I'm not so sure that I can.'

Debbie got up and went over to retrieve her handbag, sitting back down next to Amber as she started scrolling down the contact list on her phone. 'I'll get you an appointment sorted with an amazing specialist I know. He runs a private fertility clinic in Jesmond.'

Amber frowned. 'A fertility clinic? How do you...?'

Debbie looked at her. 'Oh, don't worry. I've never actually needed his services. I've got enough on my plate looking after Gary. He's a big enough kid. But Dr. Lowry, he's a very good friend of my plastic surgeon who told me that if I ever needed advice in that department then Dr. Lowry was my man. I met him at a party once. We got on really well. He's a real looker, too, I have to say; very Pierce Brosnan, but don't let that intimidate you... There it is! I knew I had his number.'

Amber felt her head suddenly start to spin. Things had started moving way too fast again. Shouldn't she talk to Jim first? Before she did anything? Shouldn't she tell him everything she'd just told Debbie? Didn't he have a right to know?

'Debbie, I... I'm not sure about...'

Debbie threw her a stern yet sympathetic expression. 'So what are you going to do, Amber? Sit and stress about everything? Is that the best plan of action? Surely you need to know what you're dealing with, chick. Then we can move forward.'

'But what if…' Amber swallowed hard, finally realising that she *did* have to face up to this, sooner or later. If having a baby was what she really wanted. And it was. It really was. 'What if it's bad news, Debbie? What if… if I can't…'

'Hey, now, come on.' Debbie's tone was sympathetically scolding as she took Amber's hand again. 'Let's promise ourselves that we won't think that way, okay? Let's just wait and see what Dr. Lowry has to say.'

Amber swallowed again, suddenly feeling as though she'd been thrust into some kind of alien situation that just didn't seem real. She couldn't relax as she watched Debbie get up and walk over to a quieter corner of the bar to make the call; a million things had started running through her head and none of them made any sense. Sometimes she wished things could go back to the way they'd been a year ago, when her life had been uncomplicated, well ordered, and she'd been in complete control of everything. But a year ago Jim hadn't been around. A year ago her life still hadn't been complete, no matter how well organised and controlled it might have been. So, if having Jim meant that she had to live with this chaos and lack of control, then she'd take that. Every time.

She looked up as Debbie came back over, her heart beating ten to the dozen. 'How soon before he can fit me in?'

'How soon?' Debbie asked, sliding her phone back into her handbag. 'Grab your things, chick. We're going over there right now.'

Chapter Five

'You're a natural, do you know that?' Ronnie said, leaning back against the edge of the desk. It was coming up to a quarter-past eleven in the evening and they'd just finished a six-hour stint in front of the cameras, scrutinising the twists and turns of the summer transfer market so far, and with just a couple of weeks until the window closed, it was shaping up to be an exciting time. There'd been some interesting moves happening, some surprise transfers, and some exciting rumours. It brought back so many memories for Amber as she remembered last August, when all the rumours flying around back then had concerned Ryan Fisher's move from a top London club to Newcastle Red Star, a move that had signalled the start of a life-changing journey for both of them. A journey she'd never forget.

She'd co-hosted the live broadcast alongside Cloud Sports' popular and extremely likeable football anchorman, Steve Summers, who'd gone out of his way since Amber had started working at the channel to make her feel one of the team. Ronnie had been there as part of a panel of pundits made up of ex-footballers and managers, past and present, there to assess every move that was being made as players changed hands – and clubs – for copious amounts of money. Speculation about how the coming season could now go had begun in earnest, and Amber loved being a part of it all. She'd forgotten how exciting it could be, being right there in the thick of things.

She loved her new job, even if did take her away from Jim, and her beloved North East England, for short periods of time. But to make sure that she still felt at home even when she wasn't *at* home, she and Jim had bought a small but comfortable semi-detached house not far from the £200 million pound purpose-built Cloud Television studio complex that was Amber's new workplace. If she had to be away from where she would always consider home to be, then she at least wanted a place to stay that was theirs. Somewhere that *felt* like home.

But what made up for the fact that she'd be spending long periods of time away from the North East was the excitement of live TV. It was something she loved, something that gave her such an adrenalin rush. She'd spent years working in regional television so she wasn't exactly a novice in that department, but this was a whole different ball game, what she was doing now. But it was where she belonged, where she felt comfortable, and, of course, it meant she continued to be surrounded by people who felt as strongly about the beautiful game as she did.

It also meant she was being kept extremely busy, and, right now, she wanted to be busy. The past couple of days had allowed her mind to focus on other things, and that was exactly what she'd needed.

'A natural, huh?' Amber smiled, leaning back in her chair and stretching her legs out in front of her, pushing both hands through her long, dark red hair.

'A natural.' Ronnie grinned, folding his arms. 'You were amazing. No way would anyone have thought that was your first time behind that desk. You handled this lot like a pro.'

Amber laughed as she mouthed *goodnight* to one of Ronnie's fellow pundits as he made his way out of the studio. 'Yeah, well, keeping you lot in line is easy really. You just need to know what you're doing.' She threw Ronnie a wink before finally, and reluctantly, getting up out of her seat. She'd grown quite comfortable in that chair over the past few hours, and she couldn't wait to sit in it again tomorrow when she was due to co-host the channel's regular Saturday afternoon Soccer Special – the first of the new season – alongside Steve.

'Have you ever thought about having kids, Amber? I reckon you'd make a great mum. If you can keep this rabble in line then babies'll be a breeze!'

It was a comment that had come out of nowhere, but it was a throw-away comment none-the-less and Amber knew that, because Ronnie had no idea what was going on in her life right now. But it still hit her hard. It still touched a nerve.

'Yeah,' she sighed, looking around for her phone. She'd thrown it down on the desk during one of the ad breaks and now she couldn't find it anywhere. 'Maybe.'

Ronnie frowned, sensing her change of mood immediately. 'Everything all right?'

She looked at him. 'Hmm? Sorry? Did you say something?'

'Is everything okay? Only, you've gone a bit quiet. Is it something I've said?'

He'd said that with his tongue firmly in his cheek, it was obvious, and Amber couldn't help but smile. 'Funnily enough, yes.'

Ronnie's expression changed instantly. 'Huh? What… what *have* I said?'

Amber suddenly wished she hadn't said anything now. She'd just inadvertently opened up floodgates she'd intended to keep very firmly shut until she had some answers. Until she'd spoken to Jim.

'Nothing,' she mumbled, finally finding her phone underneath an old running order. 'Forget it.'

'Erm, no. Can't do that, sorry. Come on, what's up? What have I said?'

Amber checked her phone for messages and saw that she had one from Jim, telling her he was on his way to the studios to pick her up and take her home.

'I shouldn't really be telling anyone else this, Ronnie.'

'Not even your best friend?'

She looked at him. He was concerned now, worried. She couldn't exactly leave him hanging, could she? She knew what he was like. If she didn't give him some kind of plausible explanation he'd only be ringing her at all hours of the night, just to make sure she was okay.

She sighed, probably a touch too heavily, throwing her head back. 'You said I'd make a great mum, right?'

'Yeah. So…' His eyes widened. 'You're not, are you?'

Oh, how she wished she could just nod and tell him yes, she was. How she wished she could do that. But instead she just shook her head, and quickly told him everything that had happened over the past couple of days. Things she should probably have told him before, considering he was her very best friend, the closest person to her, bar her father. So maybe she shouldn't have shut him out, but thanks to Debbie's fast-tracking of the whole situation there hadn't really been time to fill him in on all the details.

'So, I'm just waiting to see what Dr. Lowry has to say,' Amber said, fiddling with her watch strap, her eyes looking down at the desk. 'Waiting to find out the truth.'

Ronnie said nothing for a few seconds. He was too stunned. 'Jesus, Amber, sweetheart. Why didn't you… why didn't you talk to me?'

'Come on, Ronnie. You've just got married. You've got Karen to think of now, you don't need me and my problems.'

He walked over to her, tilting her chin up so their eyes met. 'Hey, now, listen. You listen to me. I will *always* need you, we're a team, you and me. You're my best friend, Amber, and your problems, they're my problems too, kiddo, so don't ever shut me out again, do you hear me?' He smiled at her, and she couldn't help but smile back, even though she could feel those stupid tears starting to well up behind her eyes again. 'So I take it you haven't spoken to Jim about any of this?'

She shook her head. 'He knows I want a baby, he just doesn't know how much. Or how difficult it might be for it to happen at all. Oh God, Ronnie, I really should have talked to him, shouldn't I?'

Ronnie sighed, pulling her against him for a hug. 'I don't know, babe. I really don't know. I mean, he *is* your husband, and this does concern him...'

She pulled away from him, tucking a strand of hair behind her ear. 'I've done everything back to bloody front again, haven't I? What happened to the organised, controlled Amber I used to be?'

'Hey, hang on, kiddo.' Ronnie almost had to run to keep up with her as she made a fast exit out of the studio, heading towards the Green Room. 'Hang on! Look, maybe it *is* best to wait and see exactly what it is you're dealing with, but then you do need to talk to him.'

'Yeah, I know that, Ronnie.' She stopped walking and turned to face him. 'I don't even know if he really wants a baby. I don't even know that.'

'I thought you said he was fine about it?'

'He could just be humouring me.'

'And why would he do that? He loves you.'

'Doesn't mean to say he has to agree with everything I want, does it?'

'You're being slightly paranoid now.'

'Am I?'

'Yeah. You are. Why *wouldn't* he want a baby?'

'Because he's almost fifty years old?'

'And looks about fifteen years younger, the bastard... Look, you're just throwing ridiculous excuses around now. I'm sure that whatever Jim's told you, he means it. And these tests... if they...' He stopped talking, looking down at the ground, pushing a hand through his hair.

'You can say it, Ronnie. If I don't get the answers I want to hear – is that what you were going to say?'

'Amber, babe, just talk to him. And talk to *me*, okay? You know

I'm always here. Just because some things have changed for both of us, it doesn't mean to say our friendship has to. Does it?'

She shook her head. 'No. No, it doesn't.' She looked up into his eyes, trying desperately not to let the tears that were threatening run free. Jesus, she was turning into some kind of hormonal wreck! 'I'm scared, Ronnie. I'm scared because… because if these results come back and… and they're not what I want to hear… I don't know how I'm going to be able to handle that. I don't know if I *can* handle that.'

Ronnie pulled her into his arms again, holding her tight, kissing the top of her head as he held her against him. 'You can handle anything, Amber. But let's just wait and see what happens, okay?' He held her away from him slightly, smiling at her, gently stroking her cheek with the palm of his hand.

She nodded. 'Okay.' Her phone beeped again, and she pulled it out of her jeans pocket, looking at the message on the screen. 'Jim's here. I'd better go.' She stood on tiptoe and kissed him quickly on the mouth. 'Thanks, Ronnie. For being there. For putting up with me.'

'That's what I'm here for, kiddo.' He winked at her, making her smile again. 'I wouldn't have it any other way.'

She mouthed *'I love you'* at him, before she turned and ran off in the direction of the Green Room, trying desperately to get her head together before she saw Jim. She'd already made the decision not to tell him anything until she knew exactly what she was dealing with, and maybe that was the wrong decision, maybe she *should* talk to him about what was happening, but she couldn't. She didn't want to. She didn't want to spend the night talking about 'what ifs', especially not the night before the first game of the new season. When she had something concrete to tell him, when she knew the facts, that's when she'd talk to him. Because she might have no other choice.

Pushing open the Green Room door, she felt her stomach give that wonderful jolt it always gave the second she saw him, all handsome and tall, that smile of his making him look twice as sexy.

'Hey, beautiful.' He grinned, turning round as she walked into the room, that deep voice of his combined with that soft American accent making her stomach jolt again. 'How's the sexiest TV presenter this side of the Atlantic?'

'She's fine, thank you.' Amber smiled, walking over to him and grabbing the collar of his dark shirt, pulling him towards her, kissing him quickly. 'But she's all the better for seeing her handsome husband. I have missed you so much, Jim.'

'I've missed you, too, baby. Like you wouldn't believe.'

She closed her eyes as his mouth lowered down onto hers again, kissing her longer and slower, their bodies almost melting together in the, thankfully, otherwise empty Green Room.

'I need to get you home,' he said quietly, his hand gently rubbing the small of her back. 'Because I'm a little bit tired of playing by myself.'

She felt her stomach lurch again as his thumb ran lightly over her slightly parted lips, his eyes boring deep into hers. 'I've been doing a bit of that, too,' she whispered, conscious of his growing erection pressing into her, but she was unable to stop herself.

'Did you think of me?' He smiled, sliding a hand inside her shirt, and Amber couldn't help but let out a sharp intake of breath as his thumb grazed her nipple, his hand cupping her breast as his mouth briefly touched hers again. 'When you touched yourself. Did you think of me?'

'Who else would I be thinking about?' she breathed, closing her eyes as his lips brushed lightly over her collarbone.

'It was thinking about you, touching yourself, that kept me going.' His eyes met hers again, sending her stomach into overdrive. 'Maybe we need to make some private movies, huh? So I don't just have to imagine you doing those things – I can actually watch you.'

'Jesus, Jim,' Amber groaned, finally pushing him away, straightening her shirt. 'We really have to get home. The last thing I need to be found doing is fucking the Premier League's most successful manager in the Green Room at Cloud Sports half an hour after I've just done my first live TV stint for the channel.'

'I love it when you talk dirty.' He grinned, grabbing her round the waist again and pulling her against him for a longer, deeper kiss. A kiss that signalled, once and for all, their need to escape this place and retire somewhere a little more private.

'Well, take me home then, handsome, and I'll show you what *real* talking dirty sounds like.'

He arched an eyebrow. 'Is that a promise?'

'Oh yeah. That's a promise.'

Ryan couldn't sleep. He had a million and one things going round in his head and none of them were what he *should* be focusing his attention on. His mind should be on tomorrow's game, and it was, to a point. His mind was certainly on football that was for sure. Amongst other things.

Hauling himself up off the bed, he walked over to the window, leaning forward, his hands placed on the windowsill as he stared out ahead of him. It was dark outside, the summer sun now long gone, but he could still hear the sound of people out and about, the sound of a normal Friday night, and what he wouldn't give to be sitting in a bar somewhere, downing vodka shots and forgetting everything he didn't want to think about right now. But he'd made himself think about it. He'd made sure the idea had stayed there in his head, because he needed to think it over. He had to be sure he wasn't just making some snap decision that he might regret somewhere along the line.

He lowered his head, closing his eyes as memories of the past few months washed over him in a wave of unwelcome reminders. He couldn't go down that road again, he had to be strong. But that was easier said than done when all he really wanted to do was escape.

Opening his eyes, he pulled his phone out of his back pocket and scrolled down his contact list, stopping at a number near the bottom. If he called that number he could very well be putting into motion wheels that he may not be able to stop from turning, and he had no idea what the consequences of that could be. He was taking a huge risk, so he had to be sure.

He hesitated for a second. Maybe he should wait until he'd spoken to Max. He was his agent, after all. Wouldn't he be able to guide him in the right direction? Or would he just tell him he was being rash. Stupid. Would he tell him he was just running away again, like he had done in the past? Like he was capable of doing again.

Looking back up and out of the window, Ryan's finger hovered over the touchscreen. One press, that's all it would take to give him the space he really needed. One press…

'You're setting a dangerous precedent, aren't you?' Amber said, stretching out in their wonderfully luxurious bed in their small but comfortable north London home.

'What's that, honey?' Jim shouted out from the en-suite.

'You're setting a dangerous precedent, not staying at the hotel with the rest of the squad the night before the match.' Amber turned over onto her stomach, grabbing her phone from the bedside table and checking for any messages. There was just one, from Ronnie, asking if she was okay. 'I mean, it's *your* rule, and you've just broken it.' She quickly tapped out a reply to Ronnie, pressed **send**, then threw her phone onto the table, turning back over. 'Big time.'

Jim closed the en-suite door behind him, smiling as he watched her lying there, naked and beautiful. She looked even more beautiful post-sex. Almost like making love gave her some kind of ethereal glow. 'My rules to break, Amber. Anyway, Colin's way more forceful than I am at making sure that lot stay put.'

'Oh yeah? Have I turned you into some kind of soft touch?' Amber smirked as Jim slid back into bed beside her.

'Me? A soft touch? I doubt that very much.' He placed a hand

on her hip, turning her onto her side so she faced him. 'I can be
a real monster when I want to be.' He lunged forward, playfully
biting her neck, causing her to giggle out loud, suddenly forgetting all the tension and the worry she'd been feeling previously.
Oh God, she loved this man so much. So, so much. 'Hey, listen.'
Jim smiled, pulling her against him, running his hand lightly over
the curve of her waist, resting it on her hip. 'I've been thinking.
Why don't we move?'

'Move?' she asked, frowning slightly. 'Move where? Away from
Tynemouth? I thought you loved that house?'

'I do. I do, it's a great house. But, if we're gonna start a family…'

Amber felt her stomach lurch as he spoke, and everything she'd
been trying so hard to forget, even if it was just for a few hours,
suddenly invaded her head all over again.

'… I think we need a bigger place, don't you?'

'I… Jim, I…'

'I don't want to leave Tynemouth, Amber. I really like it there,
I love being by the sea. And if we *do* have kids then what better
place to bring them up, huh? By the sea, with the beach on our
doorstep? I just think that, well, it would be nice to buy a place
together. A place that's ours, something we chose as a couple.
What do you say?'

She wanted to say a lot of things. She wanted to tell him how
she wished everything was going to be as simple as he was now
making it sound, when it was going to be anything but that. And
part of her wished she hadn't brought the subject of babies up
at all, not until she knew what she was dealing with. But she'd
let herself get carried away with thoughts of her dream life with
Jim, making her forget, for a brief amount of time, that none of
it was going to be plain sailing.

She smiled, hoping it was a smile that had reached her eyes,
because the last thing she wanted was for him to think she was
hiding something. Even if she was.

'We don't need to rush into anything, do we?'

He frowned slightly, stroking her cheek with his thumb. 'You don't like the idea?'

'I didn't say that, Jim, I just… Do we have to make a decision right now?' She knew just how to take his mind off moving house, how to steer the conversation away from anything that allowed her to think about something that only made her feel on edge. 'I mean, while we're here, together, shouldn't we be making the most of our time *doing* things, rather than talking? Before we're separated again?'

He returned her smile, and Amber felt her heart literally melt. He'd turned her into some kind of simpering, lovesick idiot at times, but he was all she'd ever wanted. Despite their shaky start, all those years of missing him, hating him, trying to keep him at bay, all she'd ever really wanted was to have him – totally. To be with him forever. Despite everything.

'What you got in mind then, beautiful? You wanna show me some of your diversion tactics?'

She reached down and took him in her hand, closing her eyes as she kissed him, slowly.

'Oh, baby, I can see you know exactly what you're doing,' Jim groaned, burying his fingers in her tousled hair as she stroked him harder, faster.

She felt him grow in her hand, excitement rising inside her as the tension built, their bodies warm and waiting.

'Turn around,' he whispered, his lips resting on hers as he spoke.

She looked at him, half of her not wanting to turn around because she liked to see him when they made love, liked to know he was really there, really hers. But the other half of her wanted to experience sex this way again; that wonderfully sensual experience of leaving it all up to him. So she slowly turned around, closing her eyes as he gently pulled her back against him, his hand running over her thigh, her waist, moving slowly around to touch her, to make sure she was ready for him – which she was, she was more than ready. And as his fingers plunged into that warm, wet place between her legs she cried out loud, gripping the pillow tight as he opened her up, preparing her for what was about to happen. Oh Jesus, what he could do to her with just one touch.

She gasped as his fingers entered her briefly, biting down on her lip as they moved around inside her, his groans sending her stomach into a barrage of continuous somersaults as he pushed deeper, causing her to cry out again.

As his lips kissed that space just below her ear, he gently pulled his fingers out of her, her body relaxing slightly as his hand ran back up and over her stomach, carefully cupping one of her breasts as he slowly pushed into her from behind. Amber groaned loudly, pushing herself back against him, wanting him to go deep, to push harder. She could feel him fully inside her now, his lips brushing the back of her neck, her shoulder, shivers rocketing up and down her spine like some constant, crazy electric shock as he whispered things in her ear that turned her on like crazy. She was so in love with this man that when she was with him, when they were this close, nothing else mattered. Nothing. Because this was all she'd ever wanted. He was everything, and he had been for over twenty years. That was never going to change.

'It's okay, baby,' he whispered, his hand sliding between her legs again, touching her, helping her on her way to what she knew was going to be one sweet climax. And when that release came, it came fast and hard, an intense wave of white-hot pleasure flowing rapidly through her body, coming in short, sharp spasms as he held her tight against him, his lips kissing her neck, whispering to her until he came, too, just as fast and just as hard. 'Jesus, Amber…'

She smiled, closing her eyes, lying back against him, his hand closing over hers as it rested on her stomach. 'I needed that like you wouldn't believe,' she moaned, just wanting to lie there until she fell asleep, not wanting to leave his arms. 'I missed you so much.'

'I missed you, too,' he said, his mouth covering her shoulder in tiny kisses. 'I missed you, too.'

Opening her eyes, she stayed facing away from him, staring at a picture of them both on the bedside table. A picture of them on their honeymoon. They looked happy, relaxed, Jim as handsome as ever, despite his eyes being covered by his trademark aviator sunglasses. Sometimes it all still felt like one big dream, a life she was living from the side lines because she couldn't quite get her head around the reality. But she knew now, more than ever, that reality had to be faced, head-on. She'd always thought she'd been prepared for the eventuality that she may never have children – she'd always, always thought that she'd be fine with that outcome. It wasn't like she'd ever fooled herself into thinking some miraculous recovery was going to happen the second she found the right man. But now, more than ever, she only wished that were the case.

Chapter Six

'I need to see you, Max.'

'What? Now? You do know what time it is, don't you? And what are you doing on the phone at this time on a match day? I know Jim Allen's softened up slightly since he married your ex but I wasn't aware he'd given you lot carte blanche to break every rule he'd ever imposed.'

'Shut up, Max, will you?'

'Oh, that's a nice way to speak to the man who made you what you are.'

Ryan knew he'd said that with his tongue firmly in his cheek, and he sighed, leaning back against the wall as he tried to block out the sounds of a football stadium on a match day – the noise of the crowd outside, the chatter of voices coming from what seemed like every corner of the ground.

'Can you come and see me or not, Max?'

'What you up to?'

'I'm not up to anything... Jesus... I just need to talk to you about something, okay?'

There was a pause, and Ryan knew now that he shouldn't have said anything. Max was bound to think the worst, and with good reason. Given Ryan's past, what else was he supposed to think?

'You sure you're not...'

'Everything's fine, Max. I just need to talk to you, as my agent. Is that okay?'

Another pause. 'Okay. You're back in the North East tonight, aren't you? Give me a ring when you're home and I'll come to your apartment tomorrow. Luckily for you I'm up north for the next couple of days anyway. Just promise me…'

'I promise you, Max.'

'All right. I believe you. Have a good match, and I'll see you soon.'

Ryan quickly ended the call, throwing his head back and closing his eyes. He was doing the right thing, he was sure he was. He just needed someone else to tell him that.

'Do you want to give that to me?'

His eyes sprang open as he heard Jim Allen's voice. He was standing right beside him, eyeing him suspiciously.

'It was an emergency call, boss.'

'Really,' Jim said dryly, arching an eyebrow as he held out his hand. 'I don't want to start treating you like a child, Ryan, but if you insist on acting like one…'

'For Christ's sake, it was one lousy phone call. One I needed to make to put my mind at rest.'

'You're distracted?' Jim asked, that eyebrow still arched as he stared at his young, talented, but extremely unpredictable striker. 'Something on your mind?'

'Not anymore.' Ryan reluctantly placed his phone in Jim's still-outstretched hand.

'Glad to hear it.' Jim slipped Ryan's phone into his jacket pocket before returning both hands to the pockets of his immaculately cut suit trousers. 'I'd hate to think you had anything on your mind other than helping us win this game.' Jim's eyes stayed fixed on Ryan's for a few seconds longer than Ryan felt comfortable with. 'Back to the dressing room. And no more escape acts. You got that?'

Jim watched him walk back off in the direction of the away team dressing room, not entirely convinced that everything was as it should be, but then, Ryan Fisher was never going to be a player he could totally trust. He just had to make sure that Ryan did what was required of him and didn't stray too far off those rails he'd once been so fond of veering from.

He was stirred from his doubts over Ryan Fisher's concentration by his own phone ringing. He answered it quickly. He should be setting an example to his players, not flouting his own rules, but right now he had no other choice. He needed to be near a phone; he couldn't risk messages being left with just anyone.

He listened carefully as the voice on the other end of the line spoke before finally speaking himself. 'Not yet, no… Jesus, I thought we'd talked about this.' He sighed, leaning forward so his forehead rested against the wall, closing his eyes as the voice continued to speak. 'Soon, I promise… it's just that… No. It isn't like that, and you know it isn't, I… Look, I've got to go. This is a really bad time and I'm sure you shouldn't be… Yeah. I know. I know that.' He turned round, leaning back against the wall, checking to make sure nobody was within earshot. 'I've really got to go. We'll talk later.' Ending the call, he slipped the phone back into the inside pocket of his jacket and closed his eyes again, just for a second or two, as he tried to compose himself. Tried to get his focus back. Life should be great right now – he'd just married the woman of his dreams, and they were making plans for a future he'd always wanted. He just hadn't banked on that future turning complicated. But he should have seen it coming. He should have. For once in his life Jim Allen had been naive, and now he had a very real fear that that could be his downfall.

'Oh, that feels *fabulous*!' Amber sighed as Ronnie gently massaged her shoulders during a commercial break. 'I was so tense!'

'Tell me about it.' Ronnie dug his thumbs harder into the space between her shoulder blades, eliciting a small groan from Amber. 'You're all tight around the back of the neck. You need to learn to chill out more.'

Amber threw her head back and Ronnie stopped what he was

doing, moving round in front of her, leaning back against the desk.

'Is everything all right?' he asked, folding his arms as he watched her rub the side of her neck.

'I've got to go and see Dr. Lowry as soon as I get back to Newcastle.' She sat up straight, looking over at the floor manager to see how long they had left before they were back live on air.

'Test results?' Ronnie asked, trying to read Amber's mood. She seemed fine, and she'd been as professional as ever as she'd joined in with the banter and comments that flew around the studio during these live Soccer Specials, but underneath he knew how she'd really be feeling. She'd always been good at hiding her true emotions.

Amber said nothing as she quickly checked through the papers on the desk in front of her, making sure she was ready to go the second they were back on air.

'Couldn't they tell you over the phone?' Ronnie went on, still watching her.

She looked up at him. 'I don't want them to tell me anything over the phone, Ronnie. It's not news I want to have to deal with whilst I'm at work. And they didn't say it had anything to do with test results anyway. They just said to make an appointment and come and see Dr. Lowry when I'm back in Newcastle.'

'Do you want me to come with you?'

She frowned slightly. 'Why would you want to do that?'

'Because I'm your best friend and I care about you.'

She looked back over at the floor manager, who mouthed something at her and held up ten fingers. She shook out her hair, composing herself before they went live again. 'I'll be fine. You'd better get back in your seat, we're on in ten.'

Ronnie resumed his position in the chair to Amber's left, not entirely convinced she was fine about any of this, but he wasn't going to push it. He'd known her long enough to know that was never a good idea. And as he watched her mood change in an instant the second they were back on air, shifting automatically to that of professional presenter, he knew she'd still like to think that she could handle all of this on her own, because she thought she could handle everything on her own. But if the past year had taught her anything – if it had taught Ronnie anything – it was that she couldn't. Not really. And she didn't have to. She'd never had to. Now all he had to do was make her realise that.

Jim shook the hand of the opposing team's manager, smiling a smile of sheer relief as he made his way down the tunnel behind his team after a tense match that had seen Newcastle Red Star tested until the very last second of injury time, when they'd managed to snatch a fourth goal in those dying minutes that saw them finish the afternoon the winning team. But it hadn't been easy, and Jim was under no illusion that this forthcoming season was going to be a walk in the park. He really needed to focus if he was going to make sure they kept their place at the top of the Premier League. A focus that he knew, at some point very soon, was going to be severely tested. He felt sick at the thought of what he was going to have to tell Amber, but time had run out. She needed to know. She needed to know now. And it was nobody's fault but his own that it had got this far.

He felt drained, almost as if he'd been playing the 90-plus minutes out there on the pitch himself, and all he wanted was to go and see Amber. All he wanted was to spend the evening with her, drinking wine and watching TV. But that wasn't going to happen. Not tonight, anyway. He was due to fly back to the North East with the rest of the squad in an hour or so – no staying over in London for any of them; he wasn't taking that risk – whilst she wouldn't be returning home until tomorrow. He was beginning to hate being away from her more and more. Every second he wasn't with her right now he was nervous that, because of the job she was in, somebody would find out, someone else would tell her what he had to tell her himself, and if that happened it could quite possibly be game over for him. No chance of extra time.

His phone rang and he reached into his inside jacket pocket

to retrieve it, walking as he talked. 'Jim Allen…' The voice on the other end of the line made him realise the need to check the caller ID before he answered. It wasn't that he didn't want to speak to them, it was just the timing wasn't great. And they knew that, they knew this wasn't a good time, just as they'd known calling him before the match hadn't been a great idea either. They knew that better than anyone. And that's what aggravated Jim more than anything. 'Can this wait?' Jim lowered his voice, quickly darting into a quiet corner before any reporters could get hold of him for the required post-match interview. 'Everything I said before… Look, I'll be home later on this evening. Call me after nine, okay? We can talk properly… Yeah, thanks. It was a tough game. This is a tough league, but you'll find that out for yourself soon enough.' He quickly ended the call, looking up as he heard his name being called. There were certain things managers were required to do after a game, regardless of the mood they were in, and the post-match TV interview was one of them. So, fixing a smile on his face, he walked over to the beckoning reporter, ready to tell them whatever they wanted to hear. The Jim Allen charm was about to go into overdrive, whether he felt like turning it on or not.

Chapter Seven

'Do you know much about Wearside Spartans' latest signing?' Amber asked Ronnie as she gently nudged the front door open with her shoulder. She'd felt like some company, and Ronnie didn't seem in any hurry to go back to his empty flat, so it seemed only natural that they should end the evening together with a takeaway and a bottle of wine.

'Brandon Palmer?' Ronnie followed Amber into the kitchen, placing the bag of Indian food on the counter and taking a couple of plates out of the cupboard.

'Yeah. Their new striker. Young American guy. That was a signing that came out of nowhere. Who did he play for over in the States?'

Ronnie started pulling cartons of food out of the brown paper carrier bag. 'A team based in Brooklyn, I think. To be honest, I don't know all that much about him. But he's quite a talent, apparently. Do you want some of this lamb madras?'

Amber nodded, opening the fridge and taking out two bottles of lager. 'I was talking to Steve about him earlier. Brandon Palmer, I mean. It's a signing that's come completely out of the blue, and it seems to have taken everyone a bit by surprise. But Spartans wouldn't just sign anyone for the hell of it. They're aiming for a European place this season, and everyone knows they're in desperate need of a decent striker. So they must rate him or they wouldn't have spent all that money on him. Is he playing tomorrow do you know?'

'Well, as far as I'm aware, he's had the medical, and his paper-work's through, so I can't see Spartans not playing him if he's available. I think the home crowd'll give him a pretty decent North East welcome, too, don't you? And, as it happens, I'm on the pundit panel for that match, so… Hang on, isn't Jim going to check the new Spartans squad out? See what the local opposition has to offer this season? Why don't you tag along with him? Get a look at their new signing for yourself?'

'Yeah,' Amber sighed. 'I might just do that. I'm interested to see Brandon Palmer in action, see what all the fuss is about.'

'He's a bit of a looker, too, don't you think?' Ronnie grinned, carrying plates piled high with wonderful-smelling curry over to the dining table.

'And he's young enough to be my son.' Amber smiled, sitting down and taking a swig of lager, mainly to hide the sudden jolt of – of something she couldn't really explain. As she'd said those words, the realisation that she had a visit to Dr. Lowry scheduled for Monday morning suddenly hit her. She'd forgotten all about it. Almost.

'Well, it's not like you haven't gone down the toy boy route before.' Ronnie smirked, thankfully unaware of Amber's brief wobble.

She couldn't help smiling back. 'Yeah, well, let's not go over old ground, okay? Shut up and eat your curry. Here, have a piece of naan bread.'

Neither of them said anything for a few seconds, enjoying each other's company without the need to speak too much. But after a lot more small talk, Amber couldn't stop herself from asking Ronnie something she'd been wanting to ask him ever since Tenerife. She'd just never found the right time, and what better time than now, when they were relaxed and alone?

'Ronnie, is everything okay between you and Karen?'

Ronnie put down his fork and looked at Amber. 'Everything's fine.'

'Is it? Really? Only…'

He scooped up the last of his curry and ate it, looking down at his now-empty plate. 'I don't want to talk about it, Amber.'

She said nothing for a second, finishing off her own meal before she spoke again. 'So, there *is* something to talk about, then?'

He almost threw his fork down on the plate, the rattle of steel hitting china making Amber jump slightly. 'Just… just don't, Amber. All right?'

'Don't what, Ronnie? Don't be concerned about my best friend? Don't care about how he might be feeling? Don't care that something might be wrong?'

Ronnie sat back in his chair and picked up his lager, taking a long swig before banging the bottle back down on the table. 'Nothing's wrong.'

'Well, I think it is. Every time I ask you anything about Karen you become, well, evasive, almost. As if you don't want to talk about her.'

'That's because I don't.'

Amber stared at him, his words taking her aback slightly. She hadn't actually expected that. 'Why?' Her voice was quieter now, less confrontational.

Ronnie said nothing, just threw his head back and closed his eyes, letting out a heavy sigh. 'I said I didn't want to talk about it.'

Suddenly Amber noticed something she couldn't believe she hadn't noticed before. 'You're not wearing your wedding ring.'

He opened his eyes and sat up, looking down at his left hand. 'No. I'm not.'

'Why?'

'You're asking a lot of questions tonight.'

'With good reason, it would appear. What's going on, Ronnie?'

He sat forward, putting his head in his hands. 'It's complicated, Amber.'

'Okay.' She got up and went back over to the fridge, taking out a couple more bottles of lager before sitting back down at the table. 'Looks like we're gonna be here for a while so we might as well have another drink.'

'Should you be indulging in too much alcohol? I thought you were trying for a baby,' Ronnie said, twisting the cap off his second bottle.

'Not right this second I'm not, so shut up, drink up, and tell me what's going on.'

He took a small swig and sat back again, looking down into his bottle as he spoke. 'Karen and I… we aren't married anymore.'

Amber frowned, trying to take in what he was telling her. What did he mean, they weren't married anymore? She'd seen them get married with her own eyes, just a few weeks ago. 'I… don't understand.'

He looked at her, his eyes meeting hers as he carried on speaking. 'I knew it was a mistake the second I saw her standing there, in the register office. I knew it, I felt it, Amber, right there in the pit of my stomach. It was all-consuming, screaming at me to stop it from happening but I… I couldn't do it. I wasn't strong enough to go with my convictions, to listen to my heart because there was no…'

'No what, Ronnie?'

He looked back down into his bottle for a few seconds. 'I thought it was just nerves; I thought they'd disappear and that everything would be all right once the ceremony was out of the way and we were finally married again. I thought everything would just click right back into place, but I was wrong.'

'I still don't understand. I mean, you seemed fine on the day; you seemed to enjoy the reception… Ronnie, I don't understand…'

'I guess I'm better at hiding my feelings than I thought I was.' He looked at her again. 'Mind you, I've learned from the best on that score, haven't I?'

Amber ignored that comment and took a swig of her own beer. 'So… so what's…?' She stopped talking, because she didn't actually know what to say. She'd been expecting him to say that he and Karen had had a big row or something, that their second attempt at marriage was just going through a few teething troubles. She hadn't expected this. 'You said... you said you weren't married anymore, Ronnie. What... what do you mean by that? How can you not be married anymore?'

He leaned forward, putting his bottle of lager down and resting his elbows on the table, his hands sliding round the back of his neck. 'The marriage has been annulled, Amber. It's over. Finished.'

Amber's frown deepened. 'Annulled?' Now she was really confused. Surely it wasn't that easy to end a marriage so quickly, just like that?

Ronnie looked at her. 'We had this huge row on our wedding night. It was a killer, a real battle of words, and believe me, kiddo, it appeared she hadn't really wanted to marry me again, either... Jesus, what a fucking mess...'

Amber didn't know what to say. What *could* you say in a situation like this? When you didn't really understand exactly what was going on.

'She's pregnant, Amber.'

Amber's head shot up as she stared at him, every hidden, pushed-aside feeling she was trying to keep buried flooding through her at breakneck speed. 'Pregnant?' Even saying the word was hard.

'It's not my baby.' Ronnie's voice was quiet, resigned, almost. Sad. And that in itself made Amber sad, too.

'Ronnie... Oh, Jesus, I'm... I don't know what to say.'

'There are only a handful of reasons why you can get a marriage annulled so quickly,' Ronnie went on, his eyes back on his lager bottle, '... and it would appear that being pregnant with a baby that isn't your husband's is one of them. Otherwise I'd have been waiting for yet another divorce to come through. She's made a right fool of me this time, Amber. And I can't believe I let her. Again.'

Amber was speechless. She really didn't know what to say. 'I...

why didn't you say something, Ronnie? I'm your best friend; I would have been there for you.'

'You'd just married Jim, and you were so happy. You were so, so happy, Amber, and I didn't want to throw cold water over your happiness by bothering you with my problems.'

'Bothering me? Ronnie, Jesus, come on! What happened to my problems are your problems? It works both ways, you know.'

He got up, walking over to the kitchen window, looking out over the small back garden, which was nothing more than a decked patio area decorated with a few potted shrubs. The sun was just beginning to set, casting a warm orange glow over the cream countertops.

'I should never have let it happen,' Ronnie said, staring straight ahead, his hands in his pockets. Amber walked up behind him, her arms circling his waist, her chin resting on his shoulder.

'I really thought you were happy, being back with Karen.'

'She lied to me, Amber. She lied in the worst possible way.' He turned round sharply, causing Amber to quickly let go of him. 'I mean, what exactly did she think she was going to gain by lying like that? Huh?' He leaned back against the counter, pushing a hand through his hair. 'It's not like you can hide a pregnancy forever, is it? What the hell was she playing at, letting things get that far?'

Amber hated seeing him like this. She wanted him to be as happy as she was, to have finally found that one person you know you're going to grow old with. But even she had to admit that, in the back of her mind, she'd had her doubts about Ronnie and Karen getting back together. She hadn't said anything at the time because she'd thought Ronnie was happy, and that was all that mattered. His happiness. However, if she'd had even the tiniest inkling that he'd been feeling this way she would have voiced those doubts. She would have voiced them in a heartbeat.

'Have you talked to her? Properly, I mean,' Amber asked, folding her arms as she watched him stare down at the ground, his hands back in his pockets.

'Of course I've talked to her.' He sighed heavily, throwing his head back and closing his eyes. 'I'm asking myself rhetorical questions because I still can't get my head around it all, not really. Sometimes it just feels so surreal…'

'I'm assuming the baby… It's Frankie Greenham's?' Frankie Greenham was the man Karen had left Ronnie for the first time round. He was another big-name footballer, a goalkeeper for Kenway Town, one of the league's biggest North West-based clubs.

Ronnie nodded, his eyes meeting Amber's again.

'But… I thought that was all over between them?'

'So did I.' Ronnie sighed again. 'Obviously, I was wrong.'

'I really don't know what to say, Ronnie.'

He gave her a wan smile. 'Well, I'm sure plenty of others will have a lot to say once the press get hold of it. I can't believe they haven't already, to be honest. But then, neither of us is really proud of the way things have turned out, so we've both tried to keep quiet about the truth. That can't last forever though, can it? Not once the pregnancy becomes obvious.'

'Is she… is she living with Frankie now?'

Ronnie nodded again. 'She moved into his place in Southport just before I flew over to Tenerife. So that's it. I've got nothing more to say to her. She's got her own life to get on with now, same as I've got mine.'

'Oh, Ronnie…' Amber wrapped her arms around his waist and hugged him tight, feeling a knot of sadness in her chest for this man she loved like the brother she'd never had. She hated seeing him unhappy, hated to think he was alone again when he deserved so much more.

'It's fine, kiddo,' Ronnie said, kissing the top of her head. 'It's a relief, if I'm being honest. Like I said, before I even knew about her being pregnant I was having doubts; I knew it was wrong. And I've been proved right.'

Amber let go of him, walking over to the table to begin tidying away the remnants of their finished supper. 'Was it because you had a feeling her and Frankie weren't over? The reason why you had doubts?' Amber asked, placing a pile of plates noisily down on the counter before opening the dishwasher door.

Ronnie shrugged. 'I don't know, exactly. Everything's such a blur. And I guess I'm just trying to put it behind me now, forget it ever happened.'

Amber began loading the dishwasher, saying nothing. She was still too stunned by Ronnie's revelations to take it all in.

'I mean, as far as I knew she never even wanted to have a kid,' Ronnie went on, before realising what he'd said, and his expression changed in an instant as he noticed the look on Amber's face. 'Oh Jesus, Amber. I'm sorry, babe. I'm really sorry. How bloody insensitive of me.'

'No, it's fine. It's fine.' Amber smiled, shutting the dishwasher door and wiping her hands on a nearby tea towel. 'Really.'

'I didn't even think…'

'Ronnie, it's fine.'

He walked over to her, tilting her chin up with his thumb and forefinger, kissing her forehead quickly. 'Maybe I should go, huh? It's been a long day and we've got that early flight back to the North East tomorrow.'

'No. I want you to stay. Will you stay? Please?' The words had come out of her mouth before she'd even had time to think about what she'd said. 'I… I don't really feel much like being on my own and… and I don't think you do either, do you?'

He smiled, shaking his head. 'No. I don't. Do you want me to go make up the spare bedroom?'

She smiled, too, nodding.

'Okay then. You finish up in here, I'll sort out the spare bed, and I'll meet you back in the living room for a nightcap, all right?'

'Yeah. All right.' And as she watched him walk out of the kitchen, heard him almost running up the stairs, she couldn't help but think how their lives – lives they'd thought were finally getting back on track – had suddenly become complicated all over again. And she had no idea how it was all going to turn out. For either of them.

Jim opened the front door, his eyes immediately meeting those of the young man standing on the doorstep. Tall, with short dark hair and piercing green eyes set in a handsome face, he reminded Jim of himself twenty years ago.

'Well, you gonna let me in or leave me standing out here all night?'

Jim stood aside, indicating to his visitor to come in. 'Go through to the living room.'

Closing the door, Jim leaned back against it, closing his eyes and taking a long, deep breath. He needed a couple of seconds to gather his thoughts, compose himself, because what was happening here was something he should have sorted out a long time ago. But he'd let it go too far, left it so late that he didn't really know how to handle it all now. Even though he'd known it had only been a matter of time before it all came to a head. He'd had twenty years to prepare for this, so why did he feel so out of control?

He walked into the living room, looking up to see his young visitor standing by the large bay window, looking out at the view of the North Sea. 'Nice place you've got here,' he said, shoving his hands in his pockets, turning round to face Jim. 'I like it. I wouldn't mind a place like this one day.'

'Work hard and you'll get there.'

'I intend to work hard. That's why I'm here.'

Jim walked over to the sideboard, pouring himself a small measure of brandy. 'Do you want one?' he asked, out of politeness more than anything, because the last thing he should be offering this man tonight was alcohol.

'No, thanks. Not supposed to touch that stuff the night before, you know how it is.'

Jim said nothing, turning his back for a second as he took a sip of the warm, dark liquid. Yeah, he knew exactly how it was.

He turned round, having taken a couple more seconds to

compose himself again. 'So, how come you were allowed out?'

'We don't have the same stringent rules that you do at your club. The boss lets us stay home the night before a game. Well, the night before a home game, anyway. I guess my new club places a lot more trust in us than you do your guys.'

'It's not a matter of trust,' Jim said, looking the young man straight in the eyes. 'It's a matter of making sure everyone is focused. Are *you* focused on tomorrow?'

The young man shrugged. 'I guess so. I'm excited, I know that much. And glad that all the paperwork came through in time to allow me to play tomorrow, because it was hit and miss for a while there.'

Jim took another sip of brandy, his eyes still fixed on his visitor. 'It's good to see you. I really mean that. With everything that's happened over the past year or so it's been difficult for me to get away, to get back over to the States, and… Look, I know things are complicated, and I know we've still got a lot to talk about, but…'

'Mom said you'd freak out if I signed for an English club.'

'I'm not freaking out, Brandon…'

'You still haven't told her about me, though, have you? Your new wife. She still has no idea who I am. And in her line of work I would have thought it was only a matter of time before the truth came out. Surely you'd prefer to tell her yourself?'

Jim sat down on the arm of a nearby chair, draining his glass of the remaining brandy. 'It's not that simple…'

'*Why* isn't it that simple? Huh? You see, I don't get it. Not really. Everyone has baggage, everyone has a past. So what if you've got a son? Is she really gonna think that's such big news?'

Jim sighed heavily, pushing a hand through his hair. 'Listen, Brandon. When I say it isn't that simple, I really mean that. Amber and I… yeah, we've both got baggage, we've both got a past, but the thing is, that past, it… both of us… I had an affair with her, Brandon. With Amber. When she was just sixteen years old, and I was a player at Newcastle Red Star.'

Brandon raised his eyebrows in surprise, leaning back against the windowsill, folding his arms. 'You did, huh? So the reputation you had back then as a player was true, was it?'

Jim looked at his son – his twenty-year-old, professional football-playing son. The son nobody but a handful of people knew about, and one of those wasn't Amber. He was a secret Jim really shouldn't have kept, but he had. He'd never mentioned Brandon to anyone, and he didn't even know why, he'd just assumed it would be better that way. Better for who, though? Better for him? Had he let his own selfishness jeopardise everything, again?

'Amber and I, our relationship – our past relationship, it's complicated…'

'You're telling me. She was sixteen years old, Dad.'

'She's the only woman…' Jim paused for a second as memories of a past he couldn't seem to escape from invaded his head. 'I love her, Brandon. I love her so much it physically hurts sometimes.'

'Then doesn't she deserve to know the truth? Didn't she deserve to know the truth from the start?'

Jim pushed both hands through his hair, looking down at the ground for a second or two. 'Like I said, Brandon – it's complicated.'

'I just don't get it, Dad. If you love her half as much as you say you do – if you care about her, then why did you hide my existence from her? Or is it just that you've let the lie grow so big that you're now scared she's going to freak out big time? Is that it? Because you can't hide this any longer, you do know that, don't you?'

Jim said nothing. What *could* he say? This was a mess *he'd* created, something he'd let get this far out of hand. And now it was up to him to try and limit the inevitable fallout.

'Maybe if you'd been completely honest with her from the start then you wouldn't be in this mess,' Brandon said.

'Yes, thanks, I'm aware of that.' Jim sighed again. 'But…' He looked over at Brandon. 'Look, I… I didn't just walk straight back into her life and pick up where we'd left off all those years ago. It wasn't that simple. When I came back up here, back up north, she didn't even want to be in the same room as me to begin with, so believe me when I say this, I had to fight to get her to love me again, and I had to fight real hard, Brandon. I had to fight real hard to get her to trust me…'

'But she'd be right, wouldn't she? She'd be right *not* to trust you.'

'I never meant for it all to get this far, you have to believe me. That's the truth. I was always gonna tell her about you, at some point, but when I got word through that you'd signed for Wearside Spartans, I panicked. I know you'd mentioned you were in talks with an English club, and I should have been more prepared, but… I wasn't ready, I just wasn't. And I couldn't just come out with it, could I? After all this time. I couldn't just suddenly tell her that I had a twenty-year-old son.'

'Why not? Because that's exactly what you're gonna have to do now. I'm tired of being your dirty little secret, Dad. I'm tired of denying who I really am, who I want to be. I want to be your son, don't you get that?'

'You're not my "dirty little secret", Brandon, come on…'

'You should have told her.'

'I know that. I know… Jesus…' Jim stood up, walking back over to the sideboard to pour himself another drink. 'The timing, it's… it's not good. We're trying for a baby of our own right now and…'

'Then I would've thought this was the perfect time to let her know that daddy duties aren't exactly something you're new to.'

Jim sat back down on the arm of the chair, clutching his drink. 'Look, I know I haven't exactly been the best dad in the world, but I've always tried to do what I think is best for you, Brandon, even though I've been so far away from you for most of your life. I've tried to do what I thought was right…'

'She needs to know, Dad. And she needs to know now. The time for pretending is up, it's over. I did as you asked for twenty years and I think that was long enough, don't you? I don't want to do it anymore, and I don't think I should have to. I'm proud to be your son, and I'm only here, doing what I love, playing soccer for a living, because of you. Because I inherited your talent, I got that from *you* and I want to let everyone know that. I don't want to hide away in the shadows and lie anymore. And it isn't my fault that you can't tell the truth. That isn't my fault.'

What could Jim say? Brandon was right. He was this bright young talent from America, someone everyone was talking about right now, and it didn't take a genius to work out that, no matter how much Jim wanted it to remain a secret – that Brandon Palmer was his son – it couldn't stay that way. Brandon was right, none of this was his fault and if he wanted to tell the world who he really was, then he had every right to do that. But it was up to Jim to make sure that Amber heard the truth from him – she'd found out enough bad news through the press in the past, he didn't want to put her through that again.

'You can't hide me away forever,' Brandon went on. 'Look, I want this to be a new start for us, don't you see? This is why I came here, to England. Why I chose to play for Wearside Spartans. I did that because I wanted to be nearer to you. Because I want a new start for both of us.'

'And I want that, too, Brandon. More than anything. But… can't you just give me a little more time? Please? Just a little more time.'

Brandon leaned back against the windowsill, letting out a frustrated sigh. 'You've got to tell her, Dad. Before she finds out for herself. Because, after what you've just told me, that would be nothing short of worst-case scenario. And if you love her half as much as you say you do, then I'm sure you don't want that to happen.'

Once again, Jim knew Brandon was right. Of course he was right. And yes, he should have told Amber about him from the start, he should have looked for the right time a lot harder than he actually had. But he'd been so terrified of losing her that he'd pushed it all to the back of his mind. Yes, he'd always had every intention of telling her, but he'd kept putting it off and putting it off until it had just seemed easier to live with the lie. Because he'd never really expected a future with Amber. He'd just assumed that would never happen. But when he'd heard about Brandon's move to Wearside Spartans the panic had set in. The truth had caught up with him, and now he was beginning to regret being so weak in the first place, because he had no idea how he was going to break the news to Amber without it sounding like he'd deliberately tried to hide it from her. Which he had. That was the reality of the situation, and he couldn't change that.

'You haven't told anyone yet, have you? And Max, he's been making sure nothing gets out? I've had a word with Wearside Spartans' Chairman and he's agreed to…'

'I know what they've all agreed to, Dad. And I know how powerful a man you are in soccer circles, but I'm kinda tired of you pulling all these strings in order to keep our relationship a secret until the time is right for *you* to reveal the truth. That's not really fair, and it's putting extra pressure on me, pressure I don't need right now, don't you see that? So just tell Amber, all right? And tell her soon, because by the time you get to the stadium tomorrow everyone will know just who I am, and just who my famous father really is. I'm tired of pretending, Dad. So tell her. Because I don't think you want her to find out any other way, do you?'

Chapter Eight

'Is something wrong?' Ellen turned over onto her side, reaching out to gently stroke Ryan's rough chin, running her fingers lightly over stubble that was fast turning back into a beard. 'You look – distracted.'

'I'm just tired,' he sighed, taking her hand in his and bringing it up to his lips, kissing it quickly, throwing her the famous Fisher grin. He *was* distracted, but she didn't need to know that. The last thing he needed was for her to get even a whiff of anything he was up to. The fewer people who were involved in all of this the better. For now. 'It was a tough match yesterday.' He also had a slight hangover due to the glasses of Jack Daniels he'd downed last night once he'd got home from London, before he'd called her and asked her to come over. Something he hoped hadn't sent out the wrong message. He'd just needed to be with someone, that was all. He'd come home to an empty apartment and hadn't fancied his own company all that much. End of story. No other reason.

'Yeah, but Newcastle Red Star won, didn't they? Thanks to you.'

He smiled at her. His beautiful Ellen. He'd met her just minutes before he'd set eyes on Amber, just over twelve months ago. She worked in the PR department at Tynebridge and she'd been the one who'd taken him to his first ever interview as a Newcastle Red Star player inside the ground that day – the day that had started the whole crazy journey this past year had taken him on. She'd known exactly what he was like back then, and even after his almost catastrophic breakdown, she was still there. Still willing to give him another chance, despite his sketchy past. Didn't she deserve something from him to let her know he was grateful? That he was glad she was around? Because he was. Deep down inside, he was grateful she was there – beautiful, tolerant, and red hot in bed. His perfect woman. Almost. But the thought of taking that one step further towards a second stab at commitment still scared him. Especially with what might lie ahead.

'So, what are you up to today?' Ryan asked, quickly moving the subject away from his slightly sombre mood. He had a lot on his mind, but nothing he needed to share with her just yet.

'Well, I thought I'd nip into town, meet the girls, do a little bit of shopping, then…' She smiled, letting her hand move down until her fingers were touching him, wrapping themselves around him, '… then I thought I'd come back here and see if you wanted to play out tonight. Or stay in. It's up to you.'

He couldn't help smiling, too. She had her hand wrapped around his dick, what else was he supposed to do? He wasn't going to piss her off, that was for sure. Despite the fact he was more than enjoying her company right now, he had plans for tonight, and they didn't involve her. But she didn't have to know that. Not yet, anyway. He could let her down gently later, and not face-to-face. That was the beauty of text messaging.

'Maybe you'd like to show me what you have in mind.' He grinned, stroking her blonde hair away from her face. 'You up for that?' Because *he* certainly was. Literally.

'Oh, absolutely,' she whispered, her mouth almost touching his. 'I'm up for anything.'

And all that was left for Ryan to do was close his eyes and let her take him some place where his problems didn't exist.

'You look worried,' Amber said, sitting down opposite Jim at the kitchen table. She'd only been home half an hour after an early, and thankfully quick, flight back up north from London. 'Has something happened I don't know about?'

Jim looked up sharply. Did she know already? How could she? As far as he was aware there'd been nothing leaked publicly yet about his son's debut for Wearside Spartans that afternoon. But he knew he couldn't keep it a secret any longer. Time was up. He'd been embarrassingly naive over all of this, burying his head in the sand over something that was never going to go away or disappear, so he deserved everything that Amber could quite possibly throw at him. And he felt sick at the thought.

'Amber, I… I really need to talk to you.'

She took a sip of her tea, looking at him over the rim of her favourite pink mug. For a girl who'd grown up very much a tomboy she really did have the most contradictory taste as far as some things were concerned. 'Oh yeah? What about?'

He swallowed hard, turning away for a second. He couldn't do this right now. He just couldn't. He needed a little more time, just a half hour more. He needed time to get his head together. 'I missed you last night.' His eyes met hers again and she smiled at him.

'Are you all right? Only, you seem a bit weird. A bit distracted.'

'Did you miss *me*?'

'Of course I missed you. But I only saw you on Friday. Jim, what's going on?'

'Come here,' he whispered.

She frowned, putting her mug down and walking over to him. He held out his hand, pulling her down so she was sitting astride him.

'You know how much I love you, don't you?'

'Of course I do. Jim…'

He stopped her from talking by kissing her slowly, his hands resting in the small of her back, his fingers snaking up under her shirt, touching naked skin. She flinched slightly, but she didn't pull away. All it took was one kiss and she was under his spell once more, but she wasn't complaining. She loved this – kissing him, feeling his fingers on her skin as those wonderfully familiar tiny tingles shot through her. And who was she kidding anyway? She'd dreamt about this happening from the second she'd woken up that morning; dreamt about him welcoming her home with his deep and dirty kisses, and a whole lot more. They had time, before they headed out to watch Wearside Spartans' first game of the season. They had plenty of time.

'I love you, too.' She smiled at him, her thumb gently stroking his cheek. 'So, have you got me over here for anything in particular, or was that it? Just a kiss?'

'What do *you* think?'

'I think you're not the kind of man to do anything half-heartedly. So I probably need to get naked, am I right?' She hoped she was right.

He felt his heart start to race faster, and he tried to push the feelings of guilt to the back of his mind so that he could enjoy this delaying tactic – because that's all it was. A delaying tactic. Once they'd made love he still had to tell her. Did he think that by having sex first she'd be less likely to be shocked or angry? Less likely to hate him for lying to her again? He didn't really know what to think, he just knew that he wanted to be with her for one more uncomplicated fuck before the shit hit the fan.

'You are so right.' He smiled at her. 'But let *me* do it, okay? Let me help you get naked.'

She felt her stomach dip and her skin break out in those all-familiar goose bumps as she climbed off him, backing up against the breakfast bar as he stood up and moved closer, running his fingers gently along her collarbone, round to the back of her neck, pulling her forward for another, harder kiss. He began slowly unbuttoning her shirt, his mouth still on hers as he pushed it back off her shoulders, his lips moving down to lightly kiss the base of her throat, and she kept her eyes closed, enjoying every single touch, every second of him being this close. She was still making up for all those lost years, and she wasn't done catching up yet. She wasn't sure she ever would be.

Biting down on her lip to stifle a groan, she felt him unhook her bra and toss it aside, his mouth moving ever lower. It was now touching her breasts, covering them in kisses until she thought she was going to explode, but he wasn't even close to being done yet. As he moved even lower, she buried her fingers in his hair as he crouched down, sliding her jeans down over her long legs. She stepped out of them, kicking them aside, throwing her head back and letting that groan finally escape as he hooked his fingers into her panties, pulling them down so slowly she thought she was going to orgasm right there and then.

She was so ready now. Ready to take him, hard and fast, the only way she wanted him this morning. Even the shortest of time away from him made her want him like crazy, so much so that sometimes she felt like a teenager who'd just discovered sex for the very first time and now couldn't get enough of it. Jim Allen had turned her from a woman who'd once been quite indifferent to sex into someone who was now bordering on obsessed. And she was going to enjoy it while it lasted because she wasn't naive enough to think these feelings would last forever. Things would settle, they'd calm down. But she wasn't ready to let that happen just yet.

In one swift movement he'd lifted her up onto the breakfast bar, quickly freeing himself before spreading her legs wide, pushing inside her as though he hadn't been there in ages. She could almost feel the desperation flooding out of him and into her as he thrust hard, rocking her whole body. And with every thrust she remembered how it had all started, this almost lifelong need she had for Jim Allen. How from the second he'd first touched her she'd known he was the only man she'd ever want, and even when he'd hurt her, when he'd taken everything from her and thrown it all back in her face, still she couldn't let him go. So now she finally had him, now he was finally hers, she was going to enjoy him.

Now she could remember those early days, the way he'd used to make love to her, the way he'd touched her, kissed her, she could remember those days now without it tearing her apart inside.

It was over in minutes, the inevitable full-on finale complete with cries of pain and pleasure and the requisite white-hot climax that brought with it an endgame that Amber couldn't live without, not now. If this was all suddenly to go away she really didn't think she'd be able to cope. So she let the sensations take over, let the feeling of him still inside her last for as long as it possibly could, and he didn't seem in any hurry to withdraw, resting his forehead against hers as they waited for their breathing to slow down.

'I love you so much, Amber,' he whispered, the palm of his hand resting gently against her cheek.

'I know you do.' She smiled, running her fingertips lightly over his slightly open mouth. 'I know you do.'

He pulled away from her, and she felt a ridiculous wave of emptiness wash over her as he finally left her body. Slipping down from the breakfast bar, she quickly retrieved her clothes, pulling them on as she watched his whole demeanour change, just like that. Something was wrong, and although she didn't want it to happen, she couldn't stop a feeling of uneasiness taking over from that emptiness.

'Jim?'

He had his back to her, his head down, and this did nothing to ease the growing nerves inside her.

'Jim, will you look at me, please?'

He slowly turned around, raising his head so his eyes met hers. 'There's something I need to tell you, Amber. And I need to tell you now before it becomes public knowledge… because that's exactly what it'll be. Soon.'

She felt her stomach turn, sinking like a lead weight as the uneasiness doubled, making her feel slightly nauseous. She'd been here before with him, she recognised the signs. He was about to tell her something that she knew was going to break her heart, she could feel it, she could sense it coming. She'd really thought all that was over now. She'd thought he'd changed. She'd hoped he'd changed. 'Just say it.' She folded her arms, leaning back against the breakfast bar, willing herself not to freak out. Whatever it was he was going to tell her, she'd stay calm. She'd try, anyway.

'I have a son.'

She'd heard him say the words, but she wasn't entirely sure she'd taken in exactly *what* he'd just told her. 'I'm… sorry? You… you have a… a *son*?' Saying the words out loud didn't make it any easier to take in. And another feeling washed over her now – one of disgust, almost. Why had he made love to her right before telling her this? Why had he done that? Why?

'Amber, please, believe me, honey, I never meant for it to get this far. I never meant for it to be this big secret, I… I should have told you from the start but I didn't want to lose you, and I… I thought that if I…'

'If you'd what, Jim? If you'd told me the truth? Huh? Is that what you were going to say? But, hey, hang on, that's something you find so fucking hard to do, isn't it?'

'Baby, please… Listen to me.' He walked over to her, and as much as she wanted to get away from him, she had nowhere to go. She'd backed herself right up against the breakfast bar, so her only option was to stay rooted to the spot. But after wanting nothing more than to be touched by him in the most intimate way possible just seconds ago, now she didn't know if she could stand to be touched by him at all. 'I know I've been stupid…'

'Stupid?' She couldn't help laughing. This whole situation was just too surreal for words. 'Jesus, Jim…' She pushed a hand through her hair, turning away from him. 'Is it too much to ask that you could be honest with me? Just for once? For me? After everything you've done, I really thought you'd changed.'

'Baby, I have. I promise you, I *have* changed, and keeping this from you, it was… it was stupid and naive and I know I've acted like an idiot, because all of this… none of it has been fair on him, either…'

She looked at him, her eyes meeting his. Did he look sorry? Did he regret doing this to her yet again? 'This isn't just some silly little secret, Jim. This is… this is pretty big, as far as secrets go. And you… you just coming out with it like this, at this time, when…' She stopped talking, the nauseous feeling in the pit of her stomach now rising as the reality of what he'd just told her started to sink in. 'How old is he?' she asked, her voice almost a whisper. There was her, just a day away from finding out whether she herself could have kids or not, and now her husband had just sprung it on her that he was already a dad. The irony was almost too heart-wrenching to bear. All she'd wanted was to have this man's baby, and now she'd just been told that someone else had got there first. That role had already been taken. And it hurt.

Jim looked down at the ground, his stomach turning over and over, every nerve ending in his body on red alert. 'He's twenty.'

Amber couldn't stop the gasp from escaping. 'Twenty? Jesus, Jim, you've kept him a secret for twenty years?' She couldn't believe what she was hearing now. And then it suddenly dawned on her – if he'd fathered a son twenty years ago, then it meant that this was a secret he'd been keeping from her for decades. When they'd been together all those years ago, he'd known then, but he'd chosen not to tell her. He'd lied so many times about so many things and she'd forgiven him, but this was another matter. This was messing with her head big time.

'It happened after me and you… after we split up, the first time,' Jim began, his heart almost breaking as he watched the expression on her face change instantly. 'I… I went back to the States during the summer break, and I… I met someone. She was a lawyer, just out of a messy relationship, and I guess we were both looking for some kind of escape…'

'You had a girlfriend back home in the U.K., Jim,' Amber said quietly, her brain still trying to piece together all the bits of information she was being told. 'I mean, that's why you left me in the first place, wasn't it? Because you'd found somebody else?'

'And you know as well as I do that that relationship didn't mean all that much.'

She looked up sharply, her eyes meeting his. 'Oh, well, that's all right then, isn't it?'

'Amber…'

'No, Jim. Do you understand how hard this all is for me? Have you got any idea how difficult this is to take in? I've been home less than an hour, and so far, to say you've messed with my emotions would be a bloody understatement! First you make love to me, then you tell me you've got a twenty-year-old son! What the hell made you think *that* sequence of events would work? Why would you do that? Huh? Why now, Jim? Why tell me this now?'

'Because in a couple of hours' time, the secret's going to be out, that's why.'

Amber frowned, confusion well and truly setting in now. 'What the fuck is going on here?'

'Brandon Palmer, Wearside Spartans' new signing…' Jim looked down at the ground, pushing a hand through his hair. '*He's* my son.'

Amber couldn't take her eyes off him. His words had rendered her unable to move, her stomach now knotted so tight she felt sick. Really sick. 'Brandon… Brandon Palmer? Oh Jesus, this is crazy… this is fucking crazy…'

He tried to take her hand but she pulled it away, finally pushing past him and walking out of the room, running upstairs.

'Amber, baby, please… Let me explain…' Jim ran after her, taking the stairs two at a time to catch up with her, following her into their bedroom.

'I don't know if I want to hear it, Jim. I really need to get my head around this.'

'Of course you do. Jesus, I'm so sorry. I can't believe I've been so stupid…'

She sat down on the edge of the bed, suddenly feeling as though every emotion had just been sucked out of her. She felt devoid of any feeling. And she really didn't know what to do next. She just couldn't think straight.

'I should have told you, Amber.'

'Yes. You should.' She clasped her hands together in her lap, her head spinning from events that had happened so fast she felt dizzy, even though she was sitting down.

'Me and his mom, it didn't work out. It never even went beyond that one night, but...'

'You were with her long enough to father a child.'

'Amber...'

'Which is something you might never get the chance to do with me.'

It was Jim's turn to look confused. 'What... what do you mean? Amber?'

'I don't know if I can have kids, Jim. That's what I mean.'

Jim was still confused, his heart beating like a drum as he watched her wring her hands, her eyes staring straight ahead. 'Amber? Honey? I don't understand...'

'I guess you're not the only one who's been keeping secrets.'

This whole day was turning out to be one big mind-fuck. For both of them. What the hell was she talking about?

He sat down next to her, trying once more to take her hand but she wasn't giving in, even though, right now, she needed her husband more than she'd ever needed him before. But she needed the husband she'd had ten minutes ago, not the one sitting beside her now.

'Ever since I was young – very young – I've known that there's a chance I might not be able to conceive a child of my own,' Amber began, surprised to find that no tears were ready to fall, even though she felt like crying. She really, really felt like crying. 'A ruptured appendix and a nice dose of peritonitis saw to that. But I clung to hope, you know? Tried to look on the positive side of things because I hate being a pessimist. It's such hard work.'

Jim couldn't help a small smile appearing as traces of the Amber he knew and loved tried to show themselves. But, at the same time, what she was telling him was quite hard to take in.

'But there comes a time when you've just got to face up to the truth.' She looked straight at him, her eyes boring into his. 'Even if it isn't something you want to face up to at all.'

'Amber, baby…'

She turned away from him again, her hands still clasped in her lap, although she'd stopped wringing them now and had started fiddling with her wedding ring instead. 'When you walked back into my life I fell in love so hard, Jim. If I'd ever fallen out of love with you in the first place, that is. Which I don't think I ever did. And this might surprise you, but I've always wanted that happy family kind of thing – marriage, domesticity, husband… two-point-four kids. I've always wanted that. It just had to be with the right man, that's all.' She looked at him, and this time he was sure he felt his heart breaking. There was so much sadness in her eyes and he'd added to that – again. '*You* were that right man, Jim. You always have been. I married my dream guy, don't you see?' She let out a slightly cynical laugh, once more diverting her eyes away from his.

'Why didn't you talk to me, Amber? When you said you wanted a baby I had no idea…'

'For a few days I just wanted to believe that everything would be simple. That we'd go to bed, make love, and hey presto, I'd fall pregnant. You have no idea how many times I've dreamt about that scenario.'

'Amber, honey, look at me. Please, baby, look at me.'

She slowly turned her head, tears now threatening big time, stinging her eyes. 'But that scenario is probably never going to happen now.'

'You don't know that,' Jim said quietly, trying to reach for her hand yet again, but still she resisted.

'I've seen a doctor. He's a specialist in this field and… Debbie got me an appointment.'

'Debbie? Why… why didn't you talk to *me*, Amber? Jesus, you told *Debbie*?'

'She's my friend, Jim. And I had to talk to someone.'

'I'm your husband…'

'And I didn't see the need to tell you until I knew what I was dealing with.'

He looked down at his own hands, also clasped tightly in his lap. 'Shit, Amber…' He looked back up at her, his stomach turning over and over so many times, he couldn't seem to stop it. 'And… and what *are* we dealing with?'

She shrugged, pushing a hand through her hair. 'I don't know. Well, I mean, I don't know for sure, but… I've got to go and see Dr. Lowry – the specialist – tomorrow. I guess I'll find out then.'

'Tomorrow? You… you mean you've gone through all of this on your own?'

'I've had Debbie with me. She's been amazing.'

Jim stood up, pacing the floor. He'd thought all he'd have to face today would be the aftermath of Amber finding out about Brandon, but this was crazy. This was something else. He'd had no idea she'd been going through all that. He'd had no idea just how much she wanted a baby. His baby. Why the hell hadn't she just talked to him?

'I'm coming with you. Tomorrow,' Jim said, sitting back down beside her. 'I want to be there, I want to be with you.'

Amber shook her head. 'No, Jim, I… I'm still trying to get my head around the bombshell that you're Brandon Palmer's dad, and that's enough to deal with right now. So I'm not sure I…' Not sure she was what? What wasn't she sure of? She couldn't even think straight right now let alone make any real decisions. 'I just don't know if I want you there.'

'Amber, honey, I'm your husband, and I love you…'

She stared at him. 'Do you? Do you really? Only, you keep doing this to me, Jim. You keep throwing shit at me and then expect me to deal with it just like that, and I really don't know if I've got the energy to deal with any of it anymore.'

He gave one last attempt to take her hand, and this time she relented, letting his fingers wrap around hers. She was right. She didn't have the energy to deal with it, but she also knew she had no other choice left now but to try.

'I want to make this right, Amber. And I don't even know how to start explaining things to you because there's no excuse for keeping something so big from you… there's no excuse.'

She threw her head back and sighed, closing her eyes for a second as though that short space of time would give her some clarity on this situation. Like that was going to happen any time soon. 'I take it he's using his first game for Wearside Spartans to announce the family link, am I right?'

Jim nodded, gently rubbing his thumb over her knuckles.

'Why, Jim? Why keep him a secret all this time? Because you're right, that hasn't been fair on him, never mind me.'

'I don't know, Amber,' Jim sighed, looking down at their joined hands. 'I don't know why I do half the things I do sometimes. All I know is that having you back in my life… I didn't want anything to jeopardise that.'

'We're talking about your son here, Jim. A real-life human being…' The phone ringing stopped her from going on and she reached over to the bedside table, picking up the receiver and answering the call immediately. 'Hey, Ronnie.' She'd recognised his mobile number flashing up on the screen.

'Did you know about this?' he asked, his voice full of something she could only assume was surprise. 'Did you know Brandon Palmer is…?'

'I know,' she said, interrupting him before he could finish the sentence. 'Jim's told me.'

'Oh, so *now* he's decided to tell you? I'm assuming you had no idea about any of this before?'

'No,' Amber replied, her voice quiet but steady, despite the somewhat surreal events surrounding her. 'No, I didn't. But that's not the impression we're going to give everybody else, okay?'

Jim's expression changed to one of confusion again as she spoke, an emotion that also seemed to have taken over Ronnie's tone on the other end of the line.

'Huh? What the hell are you talking about?'

'If it comes out that I had no idea Brandon Palmer was Jim's son, how's that gonna look?'

'It's gonna look like the truth.'

'I don't want to start another media frenzy on top of the one that's already going to happen now everyone knows who Brandon's father really is. We can all do without that, especially now. I've got enough to deal with.'

'Amber, babe, are you sure about this? I mean… *when* did he tell you? Jim, I mean.'

'Just now.'

'Just *now*?'

'Yes. Just now. Look, Ronnie, we're right in the middle of something, as you can imagine, so all I'm going to say is, if anyone asks you whether I knew about Brandon, the answer is yes. Okay? And I know everyone at Cloud Sports is going to think this is all a bit weird, that I didn't say anything about this, but… well, I'll deal with all that later.'

'Amber…'

'Can you just do that for me? Please? You know more than anyone that I've got a lot on my mind right now and I really don't want this to become something bigger than it needs to be.' She looked at Jim, his hand still holding tightly onto hers. 'Jim knows what he's done. He knows.'

'Well, you're more forgiving than I would be.'

'Can you just do that for me, Ronnie? Please?'

She heard him sigh heavily down the line. 'Are you okay?'

'I'm fine. Really, I'm okay.'

'Well, you know where I am if…'

'If I need you, yeah, I know. I'll see you later.' She put the phone down and looked at Jim. 'He won't be the only one ringing, you know that, don't you? My Dad'll be next, and Christ knows what *he'll* have to say. He's only just got used to the idea that you slept with me when I was sixteen years old.'

'Did you mean that?' Jim asked, squeezing her hand, probably tighter than was necessary but he was anxious. More anxious than he'd ever felt in his life. 'About letting everyone think that you knew about Brandon all along?'

She let go of his hand, standing up and walking over to the wardrobe. 'You heard what I said to Ronnie. I really haven't got the energy to deal with this right now, so yeah, I'll play the happy step-mum and pretend this is such a proud day for all of us.' She pushed a hand through her hair, her eyes meeting his. 'I suggest you call Brandon's agent and let him know what's going on before we get to the stadium.'

'I'll call Max in a minute, but...'

Amber frowned. 'Max? Max Mandell? *He's* Brandon's agent? Jesus Christ, this day just gets better...'

'Amber...'

'What? Is there anything else you want to add to the crap you're piling on me today? Got something else you want to throw at me? Any more secrets you'd like to get off your chest?'

Jim flinched slightly, taking a deep breath before he spoke again. 'Does Ronnie know that you... Did you tell him about...?'

She let out another cynical laugh, turning away from him. 'You not happy with that? Does that make you feel just a little bit angry that I confide in another man about something that involves you? Does that bother you?'

'Yes, actually, it does.'

She swung round to stare at him. 'Well fucking tough, Jim. Deal with it. Secrets can really fucking hurt, can't they?'

'Amber... Look, I'm sorry, okay? I'm sorry.'

'That word is so overused by you, Jim.'

'What you're doing today... I really appreciate...'

The expression on her face made him flinch again. 'I'm not doing this for you, and I'm not even doing it for Brandon, although God knows he didn't deserve to have to keep your secrets, too. I'm doing it because I really don't need the drama. Not today. I can't think about anything else except what I'm going to be told tomorrow, and this… this is just…' It was almost as if everything had all of a sudden come crashing down on top of her, all at once. Everything he'd told her, the reality of what that now meant, and the fact that she might never be able to have a child of her own – something she really, truly hadn't realised she'd wanted quite as badly as she did right now. And after what he'd just told her, the pain of never being able to carry his baby was going to hurt twice as much, she knew that. If that was what she was told tomorrow, if her worst fears were confirmed, she knew she was going to feel things she'd never experienced before, emotions she was going to find hard to keep in check, and the thought of that brought with it an all-consuming sadness that just took over, causing her to sink to her knees, the tears finally falling, her whole body shaking with sobs she couldn't control.

'Oh Jesus, Amber…' Jim ran over to her, crouching down beside her, pulling her into his arms and, despite everything, she let him hold her. She needed to be held, needed to be close to someone. And she loved him. Even after everything that had happened, she still loved him with every inch of her being, every beat of her breaking heart, and she didn't know if she could do this without him. She didn't know if she wanted to. 'Baby, I am so sorry. I'm so fucking sorry.'

She took a deep breath, willing the tears to slow down, to give her a second to try and be strong. 'Just call Max, Jim. Please. Let's at least try and keep this thing under some kind of control, okay? That's the best thing you can do for me right now.' Letting go of him, the tears still streaming down her face, she stood up, pushing both hands through her hair as she took another deep breath. 'I'm going to get ready. Just make sure everyone over there at Spartans knows the score, okay?'

'Amber… You really don't have to do this.'

She looked at him as he stood there, hands in his pockets, his handsome face sporting an expression that told her he probably was truly sorry for what he'd just done. For what he'd been doing for over twenty years. She just didn't know if that was enough anymore. 'No. I know I don't.'

'Let me come with you tomorrow, please. I don't want you to go through this on your own.'

'I'm used to it, Jim.' She looked up at him, part of her wanting to slap him for hurting her yet again, but another part of her just wanting things to be normal. She wanted the clock to rewind and this day to begin again, without the surprises and the drama. 'You've put me in a really uncomfortable position at work, too. I mean, people are going to ask why I didn't let on about you being Brandon Palmer's dad, that's a given because of the job I do. For Christ's sake, we were only talking about him yesterday in the studio, and now this has all come out… I'm going to have some explaining to do.'

'You're a professional, Amber. We both are, and we'll get through this, I promise.'

She threw him another look that caused that flinch to return. 'You and promises, Jim – they don't go together, so don't make them, okay? Just, don't.'

She turned to walk into the bathroom but he quickly stopped her, gently grabbing her arm and swinging her round. 'Amber… I love you, and you need to know that. You need to know just how much I love you, how much I really need you and I know you hate me doing this, but I promise you, baby, I will never, ever hurt you again. There are no more secrets, no more lies, no more skeletons in any closet, I promise you that.' He looked into her eyes, eyes that were red and damp from the tears she was still crying, although they were falling silently now, running slowly down her beautiful face. He loved her so much, and the thought that this could push her away scared the hell out of him. 'I love you, Amber. It's as simple as that. I love you.'

She stared up at him, wanting to believe him, needing to believe him, because she didn't want to lose him. Not again, she couldn't face that. She couldn't, she wasn't strong enough, not anymore. 'Yeah. I know you do. And despite everything, Jim, I love you, too. God help me, I love you, too.'

Chapter Nine

Ryan hung his head, watching out of the window as Ellen practically skipped down the road, away from his apartment building, off to enjoy a day with her friends in town, unaware that he wasn't going to be around later like she hoped he was going to be. He had plans. The last thing he wanted her to think was that he was available at her beck and call whenever she wanted him. That was *his* territory.

Moving away from the window, he pushed a hand through his messed-up hair as he walked over to the kitchen. His head was still banging, that self-inflicted hangover making its appearance felt once again now the morning sex was over and reality was back. He needed some kind of quick-fix relief, especially as Max was due any minute now. He really didn't want or need his agent to see him looking like shit, even if that's exactly how he felt. But he'd needed last night, needed that chance to escape, even if it had only been for a few hours. He'd needed to be with someone, to do something that took his mind off everything that was going on, but he also knew he had to make a decision soon. He had to grow up and face things head-on, or he knew he could be in danger of losing it all – and he wasn't willing to go there again.

Pouring himself a glass of orange juice, he sat down in a chair by the window, bowing his head, focusing on his blue and yellow trainers – one of the many freebies he'd been given over the course of his career. He'd lost count of how many others he'd received, everything from holidays to flat-screen TVs, even a car. And yet, right now, he'd give it all away if it meant he could just turn the clock back and make everything right. Turn his future into something he wanted, rather than something he needed to do.

Knocking back what he hoped would be a miraculous cure for his headache from hell, he wondered if a nice greasy fry-up would have been a better option, but he didn't have the energy to crack an egg, never mind cook up the full works. Maybe he should have asked Ellen to make him breakfast before she'd left. He was sure she'd have done so gladly, but letting her take control in his kitchen might have sent off more of those wrong signals he really didn't want her to pick up on. So a glass of orange juice would have to do.

He'd no sooner drained his glass, putting it down on the table in front of him, pushing it away with his foot, when he heard the front door of his riverside apartment open, causing him to look up sharply, which he soon realised had been a really bad idea, given his condition.

'Jesus Christ. What happened to this being a secure building?'

Max Mandell, Ryan's agent, kicked the front door shut behind him and walked into the large, open-plan living area, his hands shoved deep in the pockets of his no-doubt extremely expensive dark grey suit. 'What's wrong?' he asked, looking briefly at Ryan before going straight into the kitchen and flicking on the kettle.

'Huh?' Ryan frowned, getting up and following Max. 'What the fuck are you talking about?'

'You look shifty,' Max said, leaning back against the counter and folding his arms. 'Like you're up to something.'

'What the…? Why do you always think the worst of me?'

Max just raised an eyebrow. Max Mandell was one of the most respected and revered football agents around, not to mention one of the shrewdest. He'd been Ryan's agent for almost eight years and he knew him better than anybody, having been with him through the many highs and lows that Ryan's career had experienced. His client list was short, but the names he had on that list were big names, names that brought the money in, and because of who he was and what he could do for his clients, the waiting list to get on his books was growing longer by the day.

'Jesus…' Ryan said, turning to look out over the view of the River Tyne, the hustle and bustle of Newcastle City Centre just minutes away from his doorstep. He loved this city, he loved the life he had. But he just wasn't sure things could stay the way they were when he still felt the way that he did.

'You promise me you're not up to anything?' Max asked, pouring boiling water into a mug he'd retrieved from the cupboard.

Ryan turned back around. 'Is this how it's gonna be from now on? You always two steps behind me, keeping an eye on me? Making sure I'm not lapsing back into my old ways?'

Max shrugged. 'I don't know, Ryan. Do I need to be two steps behind you?'

Ryan averted his eyes away from Max's, rubbing a hand up and down his tattooed arm. 'No. You don't.'

'You sure?' Max asked, looking at Ryan over the rim of his mug as he sipped his coffee. 'Because, judging by the state of you, I don't think you came home last night and went straight to bed. Not on your own, anyway.'

'For Christ's sake,' Ryan sighed, finding it hard to keep the irritation out of his voice. 'I told you I wasn't going back there, okay? And I mean it this time.'

'Well, let's hope you do. Anyway, I thought you might like to come with me to the Wearside Spartans match this afternoon. My newest client's playing and I want to be there to support him.'

'Newest client?' Ryan frowned, rubbing a hand along the back of his neck.

'Brandon Palmer,' Max said, looking at Ryan as though he should be aware of this fact. 'Managed to snare his signature before he'd even set foot on British soil. I mean, the fact he's Jim Allen's son should mean there's some talent in there somewhere, not to mention the fact that his family links alone will have the sponsorship deals flooding in. And he's a good-looking kid, so that's a bonus…'

'Whoa, hang on…' Ryan interrupted, confusion now setting in big time. 'Can you rewind a bit there? Did you say Brandon Palmer was Jim Allen's *son*?'

Max looked at Ryan with that same expression that said he really should know all this. 'Yes. Christ, have you not been listening to any news at all this morning? It's been kept a bit of a secret, granted, which hasn't made my job any easier, but I guess the kid wanted to get noticed on his own merits rather than because of who his famous father is. Anyway, whatever the reason, it's worked. He had about half a dozen clubs after him, but he wanted to go to Spartans.'

'You *knew* he was Jim Allen's son?'

'Of course I knew,' Max said, taking another sip of coffee. 'There's not much I don't know about any of my clients, Ryan, you should know that by now. I can't deal with people's shit if I don't know anything about it.'

'And… does Amber know about this?'

'No, she doesn't. Well, she didn't, but apparently Jim broke the news to her this morning, although Christ knows why he hasn't told her before. The kid's twenty-years-old for heaven's sake. But who am I to question what kind of relationships these people have?' He took another sip of coffee as Ryan continued to stare at him in disbelief. 'Anyway, thank heavens Amber's playing ball and acting the role of the proud stepmother. It's a wise move. It won't cause any added or unwanted media attention, which I know she hates. We're trying to keep the focus on Brandon here. She's a good girl is Amber. Sensible. She knows the score. No pun intended there by the way.'

Listening to Max talk about Amber so candidly made Ryan

flinch slightly.

'But…' Max went on, oblivious to Ryan's feelings, '… as far as I'm concerned it's going to make great headlines. And it won't do her new career any harm either. Married to the Premier League's most successful manager, step-mum to his extremely talented son – and an extremely beautiful step-mum at that. Actually, that's just reminded me, I've got a few men's magazines chomping at the bit to have her featured on their covers wearing nothing but a Newcastle Red Star scarf and a smile.'

'Jesus fucking Christ, Max…'

'What? What have I said?'

'Have you heard yourself? Jim Allen has only *now* told Amber that he has a twenty-year-old son? And she's okay with that?'

'I have no idea whether she's okay with that or not, Ryan. What happens between her and Jim behind closed doors is none of my business.'

'Shit! This is fucking crazy.'

'All I know is I've now got half the Allen family on my books, and that equals big bucks. For everyone concerned.' Max didn't usually represent TV presenters, or any other kind of entertainment-based celebrities – he was a football agent. That's what he specialised in. But he'd seen something in Amber, and he wanted to be the one to guide her to exactly where she needed to be. As far as he was concerned she'd been wasted in regional TV. She deserved a bigger platform, and he'd gotten her exactly that. And the fact he now represented her stepson, too, well, Max couldn't be happier. 'The money is gonna come rolling in, I can feel it.'

'And fuck how people may be feeling, is that it?' Ryan sneered, his mind now on something other than his own problems.

Max arched an eyebrow again. 'Sorry? And who are you? Mr. I-give-everything-I-earn-away? This is what I do, Ryan. I'm an agent.' He put his now-empty mug down on the counter behind him. 'Anyway, what did you want to speak to me about?'

Ryan leaned back against the wall, pushing a hand through his hair. He'd almost forgotten that it was him who'd asked Max to come over. 'It doesn't matter.'

Max looked at him through slightly narrowed eyes. 'Well, it sounded like it mattered when you called me yesterday.'

'It can wait,' Ryan sighed, his headache now a thing of the past. 'It's not important.'

'You sure?' Max asked, his expression conveying that he didn't entirely believe what Ryan was telling him. 'Look, Ryan, if there's something going on…'

'I'd tell you, Max. All right? I'd tell you. I promise.'

That seemed to placate Max, but for how long Ryan had no idea. And it wasn't that he'd changed his mind about what he was going to do, it was just that, after what Max had told him, he wasn't really in the mood to talk about it right now.

'Okay,' Max said, keeping his eyes on Ryan. 'Well, come on, then. Let's get going. I want to have a word with Brandon before kick-off.'

There were people Ryan wanted a word with, too. But Brandon Palmer wasn't one of them.

'Everything all right?' Ronnie asked as Amber joined him up in the makeshift TV studio in the corner of the ground.

'Everything's fine. Why wouldn't it be?'

Ronnie diverted his attention away from what was happening on the pitch outside to look at her. 'Sorry, am I missing something here? Didn't your husband just inform you, not an hour ago, that he has a secret son? A son who just happens to be making his debut as a Premiership player for a rival local club this afternoon?'

'I'm dealing with it.'

Ronnie turned back to look outside. Some of the players from both teams were warming up on the pitch, but there was no sign of Brandon Palmer. 'Yeah, well, maybe you need to stop "dealing" with things in your usual way.'

'And what way would that be?'

'Burying your head in the sand and trying to pretend that things don't exist, or that the problem will just go away if you leave it alone for long enough.'

'Jesus, Ronnie, credit me with a little bit of intelligence, will you? We're talking about a human being here, so he isn't just going to "go away", is he?'

'No. He isn't.' He turned round and leaned back against the huge plate-glass window that looked out over the pitch. 'So, have you met him yet?'

'No. Not yet.'

'And, are you going to?'

'In a minute, yes. Jim's just talking to him.'

'Telling him what to say, huh?'

'What is wrong with you?'

Ronnie let out a cynical laugh, folding his arms. 'Well, forgive me, Amber, but it would appear that Jim's spent twenty years making sure that kid was kept a secret so...'

'Can we stop this now, please?'

'Stop what? Me telling you how it really is?'

'I don't need this, Ronnie. I've got enough on my mind...'

'He lied to you, Amber. Again.'

'I'm aware of that.' She looked at him, reaching out to take his hand, squeezing it gently. 'And I'm also aware that you're only looking out for me, that you care about me...'

'Yeah. I do. And never forget that.'

She couldn't help smiling, squeezing his hand again. 'You never give me a chance to. Look, I know it sounds as though I'm... as though I'm just turning a blind eye to what he's done, but what's the point in going off on one, huh?'

'To let him know how you feel?'

'He knows how I feel.'

'Does he?'

'Yes. He does. But I love him, Ronnie. I can't help it, okay? I love him, and this isn't going to change that. I won't let it. Because I won't lose him, not again. Yes, I'm angry. Yes, I'm upset that he didn't tell me and yes, I still don't know how this is all going to pan out, but… but I need him right now, you know? I really need my husband.'

Ronnie pulled her into his arms, hugging her tight, kissing the top of her head. 'I know, kiddo. But you've always got me, you know that, don't you?'

She pulled away from him slightly. 'Yeah. I know.'

He kissed her forehead, stroking her fringe away from her eyes. 'You've been crying.'

'I got tired of trying to be Superwoman. Sue me.'

He smiled at her, reaching out to gently stroke her cheek. 'Sometimes it's good to just let go of those emotions. You should try it more often.'

She stood on tiptoe and kissed him quickly on the mouth before letting him go, throwing herself down into one of the chairs that surrounded the small glass coffee table which Ronnie and his fellow pundits – her new work colleagues – would soon be sitting around to discuss the match, both on and off-air. Part of her wished she was joining them. If she was working she wouldn't have time to think about everything that was going on.

'So, tomorrow…'

'What about it?' Amber asked, crossing her legs and looking straight at Ronnie.

He returned her stare through slightly narrowed eyes. 'They're coming back up, aren't they?'

'What are?'

'Those barriers. I can almost hear the crashing of steel as they fall right back into place.'

She said nothing, just looked down at her wedding ring, twisting it round her finger.

'Have you told him? About…' Ronnie stopped talking, not quite sure how to put it.

'Told him what? That I might be barren?'

'Jesus, Amber, come on…'

She threw her head back, closing her eyes for a second. 'Well, that's what it comes down to, doesn't it?' She looked at Ronnie again. He was staring back at her with a somewhat despondent expression on his face. 'If I can't have kids, then that's exactly what I am.' She felt hot tears start to threaten again and she quickly rummaged round in her pocket for a tissue, dabbing at her eyes before anything had a chance to fall.

'Are you sure you're okay to be here?' Ronnie asked, his voice softer now. 'I mean, today's been one hell of a mind-fuck, Amber. Maybe you just need some time to…'

'To what? To sit and dwell on everything? To over think it all? Yeah, because that's what I really need, isn't it?'

Ronnie said nothing. Those barriers really were well and truly back up now and there was a part of him that couldn't blame her for resurrecting them. Not today, anyway. This situation between her and Jim, it wasn't anything new. His lies, the way he'd treated her in the past, the way he'd broken her heart so many times Ronnie could never understand why she kept running back to him, that was the reason why she'd always closed herself off to relationships. Especially relationships involving footballers. She'd erected those barriers around herself because of what Jim had done to her. Because she hadn't wanted to be hurt again. But he *had* hurt her again, and now those barriers were back up, and there was every chance that, after tomorrow, she may well leave them there for quite some time yet. Ronnie could only hope that he was wrong – about the barriers, and about what was going to happen tomorrow.

'I'm better off keeping busy,' Amber sighed, hauling herself up out of the chair, pushing both hands through her hair. 'Better off facing up to things and getting on with it. So, I guess I'd better go meet my stepson.'

Ronnie indicated with his head for her to come over to him, which she did, stepping into his arms and letting him hug her again. 'Take it easy, okay? And if you need me you know where I am.'

She smiled, gently placing the palm of her hand against his cheek, looking into his dark eyes. Honest eyes. Loyal eyes. Eyes that had never hurt her, ever. She loved those eyes. 'I'll see you later, Ronnie.'

Ronnie watched her walk out the door, exhaling loudly as she pulled it shut behind her. 'Yeah,' he whispered, still staring at the door. 'Later.'

'Looks like everyone thinks this whole keeping me a secret ploy was just that – a ploy, to gain maximum publicity. And it's working!' Brandon beamed, receiving an encouraging slap on the back from Max.

'It sure is, kiddo. It's working like a dream. You, this bright young player from across the pond with the successful manager for a father and the beautiful TV presenter step-mum – it's publicity you couldn't buy! Not for any amount of money.'

Jim watched his son as he engaged in conversation with his agent. Looking at him he was surprised nobody had guessed the connection earlier because Brandon's resemblance to him was quite unmistakeable. He had the same mouth, the same eyes, and Jim knew he possessed that same talent for this game that he'd once had. But the one big regret he couldn't shake was that he should have gone about things very differently. He should have handled this situation a lot less selfishly, for Amber's sake. And for Brandon's.

'You should be very proud of this one, Jim,' Max said, his voice shaking Jim back to reality. 'He's going to be one hell of a player, I can feel it.'

Jim managed a small smile, although inside he still felt a little uneasy. Amber had yet to meet Brandon, and he had no idea how that eventual meeting, when it happened, would pan out. She was vulnerable, to say the least, right now, and even though the official line was that Amber had always known about Brandon, it was also common knowledge that she had yet to meet him in the flesh. So it stood to reason that reporters and photographers would be lurking somewhere, just waiting for that money shot of the three of them together.

'I *am* proud of him, Max. I'm very proud of him.'

'Good. So you should be.' Max gave Brandon another friendly slap on the shoulder. 'Right then, kiddo, I'll see you after the match, okay? You have a good game now. Show them what you're made of.'

Brandon watched Max leave the dressing room before turning his attention back to his dad. 'Are you? Proud of me, I mean.'

'Of course I am,' Jim replied, surprised that he should even begin to think otherwise. 'Just because I haven't been there constantly it doesn't mean to say that I haven't followed your career or kept up with what you've been doing, it's just that...'

'Hey, I understand, Dad.' Brandon smiled, reaching out to gently touch his father's arm. 'Really, I do.'

Jim smiled, too, a small wave of relief flooding over him. But that relief wouldn't be complete until Amber had met his son. Maybe then, with that hurdle cleared, they could concentrate on creating a family of their own. And he could only hope they'd be lucky enough to be given that chance.

'Jesus, Ryan, what are *you* doing here?' Amber gasped, turning a corner to find him standing there, finishing a call on his mobile phone.

'Nice to see you, too,' Ryan muttered, sliding his phone into the back pocket of his jeans. 'I'm here with Max. I've come to watch the game.' He looked straight at her. 'Is that a crime?'

'Okay. What side of the bed did *you* get out of this morning? Sounds like you've been taking lessons from me on how to give attitude.'

'Guess I learnt from the best.' He grinned, and Amber couldn't stop the smile from spreading across her face, the atmosphere changing in an instant.

'Yeah, you did, and don't you forget that.'

'So, how *is* the ice-queen today, then?' he asked, sticking his hands in his pockets as he leaned back against the wall, one foot up against it.

'She's fine, thank you.'

He looked at her again, and she frowned slightly.

'What's the matter?'

'Hmm? Oh, nothing. Just wondering why, all of a sudden, Jim Allen's chosen now to unveil his secret son to the world. Oh, and to his wife.'

Amber shifted from foot to foot, desperately hoping her expression didn't convey what she was feeling inside.

'When did he tell you?' Ryan went on, asking a question he already knew the answer to. But he just wanted to see how honest she could be with him.

'Ryan…'

'When did he tell you, Amber? When you were a teenager, lying in his bed, giving him exactly what he wanted whenever he wanted it? When he came back to the North East all those years later? Did he tell you then? Huh?'

'This has got nothing to do with you,' Amber said, starting to walk away, not in the mood to get into anything this personal with him.

Ryan reached out and grabbed her arm, stopping her in her tracks. 'I care about you, Amber. That didn't stop. Those feelings, they haven't gone away.'

She looked at him, right into those deep, dark blue eyes of his. 'He told me about Brandon, okay? *When* he chose to tell me has got nothing to do with anyone…'

'I care about you, Amber.'

'So you said. Can you let go of me now, please?'

Ryan loosened his grip on her elbow, shoving his hand back in his pocket. 'And this is the first chance you've had to meet him, is it? Seems a bit strange, to be honest.'

'Look, Ryan, Brandon has been living in New York, okay? He's been living in New York, playing his football in New York…'

'And you didn't think going over there to meet him, in private, would have been a better idea than doing it now? In the middle of a Premiership football ground on the day of his first match for one of the biggest clubs in the league?'

She didn't reply. What could she say? Everything he was pointing out was true. People probably *were* going to find it hard to believe if she'd known about Brandon before, that meeting him here, amidst all this publicity and media frenzy, was a great idea. It was a terrible idea, but what else could she do? It was the only option she had left. Thanks to Jim.

'It's complicated.' Her voice was quiet, tired of trying to protect her husband yet again. He *had* lied to her, of course he had. But she didn't really want to give Ryan the pleasure of knowing he was right. Even if he was.

'Isn't it always, Amber.' It wasn't a question.

'I've got to go. Jim and Brandon are waiting.'

Ryan looked at her through slightly narrowed eyes. He knew she wasn't telling him the whole truth, but maybe pushing it wasn't the best idea. Not here, anyway. 'And you're okay with that, are you? You don't mind that your first meeting with your stepson is going to be in front of the waiting media? You know they're queuing up to get that first shot of you together, don't you?'

Amber looked briefly down at the ground, sticking her own hands in her pockets to stop them from indulging in some nervous fiddling with something. Anything.

Ryan saved her from answering his question by asking her another one, his voice slightly less confrontational this time. 'Are you okay? Only, you look a bit…'

'Ryan, listen, we might share an agent now but that's about as far as our relationship goes, all right? And sharing an agent doesn't give you the right to… to…'

'To, what? To ask how you are? Is that forbidden now?' He moved closer, his breath warm on her cheek as he spoke. 'We used to fuck, Amber. Me and you. Do you remember? We used to do things to each other that, if I remember rightly, you couldn't get enough of. We were close, we were really close, so I think that gives me some small right to ask how you are, don't you?'

She stared at him as she backed off, shaking her head as she walked away. Shit! Why had she reacted like that? With Ryan, of all people.

'Hey, there she is! Great timing.' Jim smiled as he came out of the Wearside Spartans home team dressing room. 'I was just about to come looking for you.'

'I was talking to Ronnie,' Amber said, trying desperately to regain the composure she'd lost just now. That encounter with Ryan hadn't exactly been a welcome one.

Jim frowned as he looked at her. 'You all right?'

'Can people just stop asking me that? I'm getting really tired of it.'

Jim raised his eyebrows, smiling slightly. Sometimes the old Amber found it hard to lie down and retreat. 'Okay. No more asking how you are, I…' He knew better than to utter the word 'promise' after the day she'd had, so he stopped himself from saying it. It was safer that way.

'Is he in there?' she asked, indicating the home team dressing room door.

Jim nodded. 'He's dying to meet you. He's heard a lot about you.'

She said nothing for a second, silently composing herself to meet this man her husband had kept from her for all this time. This man he'd kept secret from the world, come to think of it, not just her. Another small stab of, she wasn't sure she'd call it anger, but it was certainly something close to that, washed over her but she suppressed it, readying herself to do what she knew she had to do. For whose sake, though, she couldn't quite work out. 'Come on, then,' she said, shaking out her hair and running her fingers through it. 'There's not long until kick-off and he's gonna need to be out there soon, warming up with the rest of them.'

'Listen to a manager in the making.' Jim grinned, holding out his hand for her to take, which she ignored. Instead she pushed straight past him, walking into the dressing room.

'Right then, I hope anyone left in here is decent, although it wouldn't be anything I haven't seen before.' She turned her smile up full, quickly hugging Wearside Spartans' manager Billy Bishop – another old friend of her father's from his playing days – before she finally looked over at the young man who was now officially her stepson. And that first sight of him there, in the flesh, almost took her breath away, because she just hadn't been ready to face what she was seeing in front of her. The pictures she'd seen of him, the images on TV, none of them had done him justice. How had nobody noticed the quite obvious resemblance between Brandon Palmer and his father? It was like looking at Jim twenty years ago and Amber could literally feel her heart start to hammer hard against her ribs as she tried to turn away, but she couldn't. She couldn't break the stare. In front of her stood a man with the same mouth, the same beautiful eyes, the same short dark hair her husband had once had before the flecks of grey had taken over. And nobody had noticed that?

'Hi, Amber.'

The same soft American accent. He even said her name the same way his father did.

'I...' *Jesus, come on, Amber! String a bloody sentence together!* She let her eyes meet his, the warm smile he was giving her making her feel slightly more relaxed now. 'I... it's... it's good to finally meet you, Brandon.' She held out her hand but he bypassed that and pulled her into his arms, enveloping her in a hug that sent a million memories rushing through her head like some kind of super-fast-forwarding replay. Memories of his father holding her all those years ago, looking just like Brandon looked now – young and handsome and full of attitude. Her all-American beautiful boy.

'It's good to meet you, too.' Brandon grinned, folding his arms as she took a couple of steps back, reaching out for Jim's hand in a reflex action she couldn't control. 'Dad never told me you were quite so beautiful.'

'Jesus, Brandon, enough of the flannel,' Billy sighed, quickly checking his watch. 'You remind me of your dad when he was a player.'

Jim smiled, looking down at the ground, his hand gently squeezing Amber's. Yeah, Billy was right, Amber thought. He reminded *her* of Jim, too. And she should know, she'd fallen for that flannel all those years ago, hadn't she?

'I'm being serious!' Brandon laughed, pushing a hand through his dark hair. 'Amber, I'm sorry. Am I outta line here?'

She shook her head. 'No. No, of course you're not.'

'Dad's a very lucky guy. I hope he realises that.' His eyes met Amber's again, only this time they held the stare just that little bit longer, making sure Amber was the first one to break it.

'I realise it,' Jim said, squeezing Amber's hand again. 'I know just how lucky I am, Brandon, believe me.' He looked at Amber, reaching out to gently touch her cheek in a way so intimate it was almost as if he'd forgotten where they were. 'You okay, baby?'

'I'm fine.' She smiled, turning back to face Brandon, inwardly composing herself, letting go of Jim's hand as the professional inside her took over. 'So, we have another star striker in the family, then?'

Brandon's grin showed no sign of subsiding. 'Well, I've got a way to go before I can live up to what my father achieved, but I'm certainly gonna try.'

'He's selling himself short,' Billy said, checking his watch again. 'He's hot property is this kid. And it's time you were out there with the rest of them, Brandon. Go on, get out and warm up. Go on.'

Brandon threw Amber one more smile before walking out of the dressing room, leaving her with the strangest feeling. A feeling she couldn't explain. A feeling that just added to the confusion and anxiety she was already experiencing.

'You sure you're okay?' Jim asked, gently pulling her round to look at him.

She stared at him for a second. She was still as angry as hell with him for putting her in this situation, and that alone was making her feel uncomfortable. Confused.

'Can we… can we get out of here? Just for a few minutes? We'll come back, but… but I just need to get out of here for a little while. Is that… is that all right?'

Jim nodded. 'Yeah. Of course it is. Come on.'

'Do you want to use my office?' Billy asked, sensing Amber needed a bit of time to get her head around something even he knew must be quite overwhelming to take in, and having it happen in a setting that wasn't exactly private couldn't be making it any easier. 'You can grab some privacy in there.'

'That'd be great, thanks.' Jim smiled at Billy, catching the set of keys he threw at him. 'We won't be long.'

'Take as long as you need,' Billy said, now engrossed in the notes his assistant manager had handed him.

Jim looked at Amber again, catching the silent message she was sending him, giving her a small, reassuring smile. 'Come on,' he whispered. 'Let's go.'

Ryan stood on the touchline, hands in his pockets, watching closely as Brandon Palmer ran out onto the pitch. He was met with a rapturous round of applause from those supporters who were already in their seats, eagerly awaiting their first glimpse of their club's new, young signing, hoping that he was going to be the one to lift them from the mediocre into the top six. It reminded him of his own arrival back in the North East just twelve months ago. The Red Star supporters had shared that same sense of anticipation, that same feeling of hope that he could give them the success they felt they deserved, and he'd certainly helped them gain just that. Along with Jim Allen. Could his son be about to do the same for Wearside Spartans?

Ryan watched closely as Brandon took the ball from a fellow

teammate, dribbling it a short distance along the touchline not far from where Ryan was standing before inching it up onto the top of his foot, flicking it onto his knee. He could indulge in a bit of showmanship with the best of them, quite obviously, and Ryan smiled to himself as he watched him play to the crowd, nudging the ball up onto his head to a rousing round of cheers and applause. The kid had talent, there was no doubting that. But how was his appearance in Jim's life going to affect his relationship with Amber? Ryan couldn't help a fleeting but still slightly selfish feeling of hope wash over him – hope that it would drive a wedge between his ex-fiancée and her new husband? Yeah, why lie about it? Of course he'd love that to happen. His feelings for Amber were still strong, still very much there, and if anything happened between her and Jim then Ryan couldn't lie and say he wouldn't be the first in line to help her through the aftermath. And if that happened then everything he'd been planning to do, those wheels he was about to set in motion, that could all change. All of it.

'Remind you of anyone?'

Ryan almost jumped out of his skin as Max appeared beside him. 'Shit, Max! Where'd you spring from?'

'The tunnel, where'd you think I came from? Daydreaming again were we? Not about the new Mrs. Allen, I hope.'

Ryan said nothing, turning his attention back to Brandon, who was now running up and down the touchline, stopping intermittently to do a few stretches.

'He likes the limelight,' Ryan pointed out.

'Yeah, well, he's young, isn't he? He's in a new country, he's just signed to a top-flight English club, not to mention the fact he's a good-looking kid, with a famous father, who's probably going to have his pick of the women.'

Ryan looked at Max. 'You don't think he's going to…?'

'I've got my eye on him, Ryan. And I'm hoping the fact his dad's only nine miles down the road will stop him from indulging too much in that stereotypical footballers' lifestyle.'

'It wouldn't stop me,' Ryan muttered, turning away again.

'Hmm? Sorry, did you say something?' Max asked, sliding his phone back into his pocket.

Ryan shook his head. 'No. Didn't say a thing.'

'Are you sure you're all right?' Max asked, frowning slightly, shielding his eyes from the bright, late-summer sunshine. 'You seem a bit distant. Are you sure there's nothing you want to talk to me about? I know you said it could wait, but...'

'I'm fine,' Ryan sighed, pushing a hand through his hair. 'Just a bit tired, that's all. I'm going back inside to grab a drink before kick-off.'

'Ryan... Promise me you aren't...'

'Everything's fine, Max. Okay? Everything's fine.' If he said that out loud enough times, might he just start to kid himself it was true? No harm in trying because, right now, that's all he could really do.

Kicking the door of Billy's office shut behind her, Amber backed up against it, grabbing Jim's shirt and pulling him towards her.

'Like old times.' She smiled, her breathing growing more laboured as the need to just do this grew more urgent.

Jim laughed, a low, almost dirty laugh and even though Amber's head was trying to tell her she was still angry at this man because he'd lied to her yet again – big time – her heart, and her body, needed him. Needed this. Needed something to take her mind off the surreal and confusing events of the day – by making everything just that little bit more surreal and confusing? Yeah, that was just what she needed, wasn't it? But right now she didn't care. All she cared about was feeling him inside her, knowing he was there. Whatever else was going on in her head, she'd deal with it later.

'Old times, huh?' Jim whispered, his mouth almost touching hers now, his breath warm on her cheek. 'I can go for that.'

'Good. That's good,' she breathed, sliding her hands inside his shirt, her fingers sprawling out over his naked chest, his skin warm underneath them. 'That's really good.' Closing her eyes, she felt her body almost sag as his mouth lowered down onto hers, kissing her slowly, gently, his tongue sliding in between her slightly parted lips to touch hers, an action that sent her stomach dipping and her heart into overdrive.

'Fuck me,' she whispered, pulling away just a little bit, enough to create the space she needed to undress. 'I really, really need you to fuck me.'

'Here?' Jim asked, somewhat surprised by her request. They'd never been averse to a match-day fuck in his own office over the other side of the river at Tynebridge, but another manager – a rival manager's office? Shit! That was actually one hell of a turn-on.

'Yeah.' Amber smiled, pulling her t-shirt off over her head. 'Right here.'

Who was he to say no? Within seconds the necessary clothes had been discarded and there was no going back. He was hard and ready, she was wet and waiting. There was only one way this was going.

Amber closed her eyes as he lifted her up, pushing her back against the door again as she wrapped her legs around his hips, moaning quietly as he pushed into her with a force that almost winded her; it literally took her breath away. But, in some weird and twisted kind-of way, it was almost cathartic. The last thing she'd wanted to do not ten minutes ago was even hold his hand, yet here she was, allowing him to touch her like this, allowing him deep inside her. Why was that? Why couldn't she tell him how she really felt? How all of this had messed with her head, confused the shit out of her; made her love him even more. Yeah, go figure *that* one out!

Burying her face in his hair, she clung onto him as he thrust into her, over and over again until, finally, she felt his release, felt that beautiful warmth spread out inside her as he came hard and fast, sending her body into a spasm of beautiful pain and pleasure all of her own. Jesus, he was good!

But then, almost like the curtain coming down on one incredible encore, she felt a finality flood her body that instilled nothing but a feeling of sheer emptiness. The confusion was returning, along with the fear of what Dr. Lowry was going to tell her in the morning. It all seemed to build up within a few rushed seconds and she couldn't stop the tears from spilling down her cheeks.

'Amber, baby...' Jim felt that pull on his heart again as he looked at her. All he wanted to do was make everything right, but how could he do that? How could he?

'I'm fine,' Amber sniffed, wiping her eyes with the back of her hand, composing herself as quickly as she'd let that lapse of strength happen. 'I'm fine.'

'Amber...'

She pulled away from him and quickly got dressed. 'Come on. We need to get out of here. It's gone 4 o'clock; they'll have kicked off already.' She turned to open the office door, not looking at Jim as she reached out to grab the handle. Not until his hand covered hers, leaving her with no choice but to turn back around and face him. 'What the hell happened today, Jim?'

He closed his eyes for a second, throwing his head back. 'I will do anything I can to make sure...'

'What, Jim? To make sure you don't lie to me again? To make sure that you hide any more skeletons still left in your closet a little better than you hid this one?'

'Brandon was never a skeleton in a closet, Amber.'

'Wasn't he? So why didn't you just tell me about him? Why couldn't you just do that? Twenty fucking years, Jim... I mean, it's not like you didn't have plenty of chances.'

'Amber, honey...'

'Look, just... just back off for a second, okay? I can't fucking breathe right now and you standing there, telling me you want to make everything right, that you're sorry, that it'll never happen again...' She looked up at him, the anger returning in spades. 'I've heard it all before, don't you see? Everything you're doing, everything you're saying – I've heard it all before.'

'Baby, please, this time it's…'

'Different? This time it's different? Is that what you were going to say?' She let out a small, cynical laugh, turning away for a second. 'But it isn't different. It'll never be different, will it? And I should have known that the second you walked back into my life. I should have known that.'

'Amber, I promise…'

'No, Jesus… No. I told you never to promise me anything, Jim. Don't ever promise me anything.'

He looked at her, her face now hard, cold, those barriers of old that she'd kept around her for so long, they were right back up now, and he'd helped put them there. His fault.

'But… do you know what? Despite everything…' Her eyes met his and once more he felt that almost painful pull on his heart. 'Despite everything, I need you so fucking much right now, you have no idea.'

'I do, Amber. I know…'

'No, you don't. You *don't* know. You have no idea, trust me.'

She leaned back against the wall, pushing a hand through her hair again, sighing heavily. 'I really don't know what to do. This day, it's just been – it's been crazy. And we haven't even begun to face the press and the media that are all waiting outside, something I really don't think I've got the strength to cope with today. Not today.'

He took a tentative step forward, reaching out to gently place a hand on her cheek, his thumb stroking away the remnants of the tears that were still there, damp beneath his fingers. 'We'll get through this,' he whispered. 'We've gotten through worse.'

She looked at him, her stomach flipping over as she stared deep into his eyes. 'We shouldn't have to, though, should we? We shouldn't have to get through anything. You could have prevented all of this from happening.'

'I know. I know, and I'm…'

She shook her head, bringing her hand up to cover his as it rested against her cheek. 'I'm tired of hearing you say you're sorry, Jim. I just want to move on now and deal with this as best we can. I just want to get to tomorrow, do you understand?'

He nodded, leaning forward to gently kiss her, the taste of salt from her tears evident on her lips. 'Let me come with you tomorrow, Amber. Please.'

She reached out and slipped a hand round the back of his neck, pulling him down for another, longer kiss, losing herself in dreams and memories of times when all she'd known was this man. When her life had revolved around him – had anything really changed? Was this the way it was always going to be?

'Is that a yes?' Jim asked, wishing they could just stay there all afternoon, alone. Together. All of a sudden they had so much to talk about.

It was her turn to nod, her forehead resting against his. What else could she do? She needed him. No matter what else had happened, she needed him. Simple as that.

Chapter Ten

'You should have told me, Max.'

'Client confidentiality, Amber. You know how it is.'

Amber stared at her agent, her head already messed up with thoughts of what else she might have to face today, without everything else that was going on. 'I don't even know what to say to that.'

'Look, Amber, I know this is a really crazy time for you, what with your new job, and then Brandon appearing on the scene, but it's all good, kiddo.'

She raised her eyebrows in surprise, folding her arms as she leaned back against the windowsill, the cool air blowing in from the slightly open window ruffling her hair. 'It is? How do you work that one out?'

'All this publicity, it never does anyone any harm. Oh, by the way, Cloud Sports want you to cover this weekend's Soccer Specials with Steve. Viewing figures were up over forty percent last time you were on screen, so it stands to reason they want you on air as much as possible.'

'Saturday *and* Sunday?' Amber asked.

'Yep. You okay with that?'

'Do I have a choice?'

'Not really.'

'Will Ronnie be in the studio, or is he out covering games this weekend?'

'No idea. You'll have to ask him yourself, sweetheart.'

She closed her eyes for a second, rubbing the bridge of her nose with her thumb and forefinger. Newcastle Red Star's match that weekend was a home game at Tynebridge, which meant she'd be spending days away from Jim, at a time when she wasn't entirely sure that was a good thing. Or maybe it was, given everything that had gone on.

'Oh, and I meant to tell you, Ice Magazine have been on the phone. They want you to do a cover shoot, an interview, and an accompanying five-page photo spread inside. And they haven't been the only men's magazine to get in touch with me about you, but they were the ones who offered the best deal.'

Amber opened her eyes and stared at Max. 'You *are* kidding me, aren't you?'

He stared back at her with a slightly incredulous expression. 'Why would I be kidding?'

She couldn't help but let out a little laugh. An almost disbelieving laugh. 'Me? On the cover of Ice? You know what kind of magazine that is, don't you?'

'I'm well aware of its content, Amber, yes.'

'I'm thirty-eight years old, Max.'

'And your point is?'

'You want me to get my tits out on the cover of a men's magazine? Seriously?'

'It'll all be very tastefully done, and you don't have to show anything, not if you don't want to. It's up to you.'

She couldn't help but laugh out loud again.

'You *don't* want to, I take it.'

'You can take it and shove it, Max. Come on…'

'Come on, what? Have you any idea what kind of a stir you're making out there right now, kiddo? Those paparazzi pictures of you by the pool in Tenerife, almost wearing that bikini, they were all over the tabloids. I'm telling you, Amber, you are hot property at the minute. You should be capitalising on that.'

She stared at him again, unable to believe what she was hearing. 'Sorry, have I just entered the Twilight Zone or something? Exactly what is going on here? I thought you'd come round to apologise for the fact you knew my husband was Brandon Palmer's father long before *I* did – something which I'm still extremely angry about, I'd like to add – and yet it appears you're only really here to let me know I'm working over the weekend and you want me to get my kit off for a men's magazine!'

'Who's getting their kit off for a men's magazine?' Jim asked, walking into the living room.

'Nobody,' Amber replied, throwing Max a look. Which he ignored.

'Ice want your wife to be a cover girl.'

Jim raised an eyebrow. 'Really?'

Amber turned her stare on him. 'Is that so hard to believe?'

'No. No, that's not what I meant… You're not, though, are you?'

'No. I'm not.'

'She's thinking about it,' Max said, causing Amber to throw him yet another look. 'What? Come on, Amber. You're the new face of football on a major satellite sports channel. Everybody's talking about you right now, everybody wants to see more of you, and I mean *more* of you.'

'Okay, now you're just being offensive.'

'Jim, help me out here. Is she or is she not stunning enough to be an Ice cover girl?'

Jim looked from Max to Amber, not really wanting to get caught in the middle of this one. Amber was his wife, and yeah, of course she was stunning enough to be on the cover of Ice. He just wasn't altogether sure he wanted the world to see her like that.

'It's up to Amber.' He shrugged, deciding to sit very firmly on the fence.

Max sighed. 'Just what I need. A diplomatic husband. Right, I'd better get off. I've got a meeting with your son in an hour.'

Jim didn't miss the expression on Amber's face as it changed instantly, her arms still folded defensively against her as she watched Max leave. Jim followed him out into the hallway, stopping him before he let himself out.

'Max, listen… Thanks.'

'For what?' Max asked, turning to look at Jim.

'For keeping quiet about Brandon.'

'Yeah, well, I can't say I was happy about it. I mean, look at the position you've put me in with Amber. She's pissed off with me, to say the least, and I can do without the hassle of one of my number one clients giving me shit. Especially when there's work flooding in for her that I really need to talk to her about. I need her onside, Jim.'

'I know. And I'm sorry, but you understand…'

'No, I'm not sure I do, to be honest. For someone who claims to love that woman as much as you say you do, you've got a really weird way of making sure you don't lose her.' Max turned away, opening the door and stepping outside before turning back to look at Jim. 'Do me a favour, okay? Talk to her, make her see that getting her face – amongst other things – on the cover of Ice is a great opportunity for her.'

Jim took a deep breath. 'All right. But I can't say I'm happy…'

'No. Neither can I, Jim. Neither can I. I'll talk to you later.'

Jim kicked the front door shut and leaned back against the wall, his hands in his pockets, staring down at the dark wooden floor. Just a few weeks ago everything had seemed so perfect. He'd married the woman he loved, his career was very much in the ascendant – he'd felt as though he'd had it all. But his inability to be honest made it feel as though everything was now slipping away from him, and that was nobody's fault but his own.

'We should be going soon.'

He looked up to see Amber standing in the doorway, her arms still folded. 'You okay?' he asked, before realising it was probably the most stupid question he could possibly have asked her today.

'Not really.'

His eyes met hers, holding her gaze. 'I'm so sorry, Amber. For everything.'

She shrugged, pushing a hand through her hair. 'Yeah, well, it's done now, isn't it?'

'I don't want this to change anything…'

She stopped him from going any further by throwing him a look that dared him to say another word. 'Right at this moment in time, Jim, everything's changed.'

'Don't say that, Amber. Please.'

'You lied to me. You had a son, and for all those years you lied to me. Can you really not understand how hard it is for me to get my head around that?'

He looked down at the floor, just for a split second, before meeting her gaze again. 'I just thought that…'

'That, what? That because I let you fuck me yesterday everything was going to be all right? I don't believe for one second you're that naive, Jim.'

'I just thought that we could talk about it. That you could at least let me try and make things right. You said you loved me…'

'And I do. That's what makes this all the more difficult for me to cope with. I love you so much, but I just… I can't understand why you keep doing this to me. Why you keep lying, hiding things from me, making me feel like…' She threw her head back and let out a deep sigh. 'Forget it. Come on. We need to go.'

She closed the living room door behind her and walked out into the hall, making her way over to the coat rack, but Jim grabbed her wrist before she had a chance to do anything else. 'This is a mess, I know that. I get that. And I get that it was me who caused it all. But this – what's happening today – I need you to know that I love you, and I'm here for you, and believe me, I will do anything I can to…'

She shook her head, but let him pull her into his arms, too tired to fight him anymore. She hadn't slept much, and she was angry at herself for letting Max get away without giving him the big tirade she'd had planned in her head. And on top of all of that she felt sick at the prospect of what she was going to be told when she saw Dr. Lowry, even though half of her already had a feeling that the outcome wasn't going to be the one she wanted to hear.

'Don't promise me the impossible, Jim.'

He rested his forehead against hers, sliding an arm protectively around her waist as he gently pulled her against him. 'I'm not promising you anything, Amber. You told me never to make you promises, remember? I'm just telling you that I'll try to make it all okay, because all I want is to see you happy.'

'Then stop lying to me. Stop hiding things from me because, right now, I just don't know if I can trust you. And I really need to be able to trust you, Jim.'

'I know. Baby, I know.' He lightly stroked her cheek with his thumb, kissing her slightly open mouth, his stomach flipping over 360 degrees as she responded, kissing him back, her hand on the back of his neck pushing him down. 'I'll make it all okay again, I really will.'

Her fingers absentmindedly played with the hair at the nape of his neck as she searched his face for anything that would tell her he was being honest. Anything that would let her know he was telling her the truth, because she needed to feel that, needed to at least feel that he was being honest this time.

'What if you can't make it okay, Jim? What if we get news today that we just can't fight?'

Stroking her fringe from her eyes, he kissed her long and slow, his hand fanning out in the small of her back, pushing her against him, and once again her body responded, moulding itself against his as the kiss deepened. 'Then we give it our best shot. We try to prove them all wrong. That's all we can do.'

Against every better judgement she was feeling, she smiled at him. The exhaustion of everything the past twenty-four hours had thrown at her was beginning to kick in and all she really wanted to do was forget any of it had happened, take Jim back up to bed, and make love for hours. That's what she really wanted to do. But reality was making its unwelcome presence felt and she just had to go with that. Everything else could wait, for now.

'Do you have any idea how beautiful you are when you smile?' Jim whispered, gently tucking a strand of hair behind her ear.

'Come on,' she said, finally pulling away from him. 'We really have to go now. I don't want to be late.'

'Amber…'

She swung round to look at him, wishing with all her heart that everything was different. Everything.

'We *will* get through this, baby.'

She could only hope he was right.

'That one,' Ellen smiled, pointing at the delicate gold tennis bracelet. Her arm was tight around Ryan's waist as she snuggled in against him, her face glowing as she stared in awe at the expensive array of jewellery spread out in the window in front of them.

'You sure?' Ryan asked, watching as her pretty face lit up. 'Like I said, you can have anything you want.' Well, almost anything. He was drawing the line at rings of any description. That left the door wide open for all kinds of misinterpretation.

'No. That's the one,' she said with an air of finality. 'Definitely.'

'Okay then.' Ryan grinned, giving her shoulders a quick squeeze, planting a light kiss on her forehead before they went inside the rather upmarket city centre jewellery store. And even though he knew he *should* be feeling guilty, Ryan just couldn't let that emotion through. He wasn't feeling it. Did that make him a bad person? Probably. Did it bother him? Not really. Ellen knew the score. She probably had every idea that he'd taken her into Newcastle today to buy her off, to placate her; he'd spent so little time with her lately, cancelling nights out with her in favour of nights out on the town with his teammates because he'd much rather be making sure Ryan Fisher still had what it took to have the women falling at his feet, even if, once they fell, he couldn't really be bothered to make use of them.

'I can't believe you're doing this,' Ellen squealed as the slightly-over-made-up but exquisitely dressed woman behind the counter unlocked the tray of beautiful and extremely expensive bracelets that contained the one Ellen had fallen in love with.

'You deserve it,' Ryan said, throwing the sales assistant one of his famous grins, which she reciprocated, accompanied by a rather coy glance from beneath a set of perfectly fitted false eyelashes, '... for putting up with me.'

Ellen was oblivious to the now quite-obvious flirting going on between her boyfriend and the sales assistant. Her focus was fixed entirely on the gold bracelet that was now fastened around her wrist, turning her arm first one way then the other, letting the bracelet fall delicately with each turn, watching the way it glistened and shone against her lightly tanned skin. 'Oh, Ryan, it's beautiful!' she gasped, letting go of him so she could touch the bracelet, taking it gently between her fingers as she looked at it more closely. 'But it's so expensive!' Her eyes met his, and this time he couldn't stop that familiar pang of guilt from pricking his conscience.

'You're worth it.' Even he had to cringe at that cheesy line. But it was true. She *was* worth it. She was worth every penny. And even though this *was* a gift to keep her happy, it was also a gift to let her know how much she meant to him, how she was keeping him sane as a million and one confusing emotions were partying on inside his head, oblivious to the fact he just wanted to get on with his life. But he couldn't do that, could he? He couldn't just get on with his life, not yet. Not until he was ready to forget, ready to move on, and he was nowhere near that.

'Oh, Ryan.' Ellen smiled, leaning forward to kiss him quickly before letting him go, her eyes back on the bracelet, but not before she'd thrown the sales assistant a very brief but nonethe-less noticeable look that said *Back off, sister!* And Ryan couldn't help but smile, too. She might look all pretty and innocent, but underneath that soft exterior was a woman after his own heart. 'Thank you so much!'

'We'll take it,' Ryan said, turning the Fisher grin back up full pelt and directing it at the woman behind the counter. Her expression was a little less friendly than it had been a second ago, when she'd thought she might have stood a chance with this famous footballer, but that was before she'd realised his girlfriend wasn't quite as oblivious to her less-than-subtle flirting than she'd first thought she was. She'd got the 'off-limits' message loud and clear. Once upon a time that would have bothered Ryan, but not now. He just didn't have the energy anymore. It was nice to know he still had what it took to make the women want him, but, at the same time, he couldn't be bothered to take all of them up on their sometimes quite-blatant offers. Not as bothered as he'd used to be, anyway. 'Do you want to keep it on?' he asked Ellen, who looked at him with excited eyes, nodding wildly. He handed over one of his many debit cards and watched with slight amusement as the sales assistant made the transaction, leaving him with one last renewed attempt to gain his attention. But fluttering eyelashes and a sexy smile didn't always cut it with him these days. He was looking for more than that. He was looking for a relationship that was going to change his life, and he'd found that. Once. Whether he could do that again remained to be seen.

'Come on.' He smiled at Ellen, slipping his hand into hers, leaving the rejected sales assistant with one final blast of the Ryan Fisher grin before they left the shop. 'Today's *your* day so you decide what we do next. Whatever you want. Anything.'

'Well,' she said, turning to face him, standing on tiptoe to plant a kiss on his mouth. 'I really fancy lunch somewhere, maybe in Durham, down by the river. Then how about a drive into Sunderland and a walk along the beach? It's such a lovely day and I feel like being out in the fresh air.'

'Really?' Ryan grinned, snaking an arm around her waist, pulling her closer. 'You mean, you don't want to spend the afternoon indulging in the many delights *I've* got to offer?'

She giggled, nuzzling her nose against his neck. 'There's plenty of time for that later, isn't there?'

'Yeah,' he whispered, kissing the top of her head. 'There's plenty of time for that later.'

There was plenty of time for everything, wasn't there? But he knew there wasn't. Not really. If he was going to do what he was seriously thinking about doing, then he needed to make a decision quick. But that really all depended on Amber. Everything depended on Amber. Everything.

Amber turned the cup round and round on its saucer, staring straight ahead of her. She couldn't really describe what she was feeling right now, because she just felt empty, devoid of any emotion, Dr. Lowry's words still ringing loud and clear in her ears – *'It's extremely unlikely that you'll ever have a child of your own, Amber. I'm really very sorry…'*

They kept playing over and over in her head like some cruel mantra, taunting her, telling her what she'd already known, deep down inside. But hearing the words hadn't made facing the truth any easier. It just finally made it real.

'Amber?'

She looked up at the sound of his voice. 'I'm fine, so don't ask, okay?'

Jim sat down opposite her, wishing there was something he could do, something he could say to make it all right, but what *could* he do? All he could really do was be there for her, if she wanted him to be. And the way things had gone lately he wasn't altogether sure that was going to be the case. 'I was thinking…'

She looked at him again, finally pushing her untouched coffee away. She just didn't feel like drinking it.

'How about I take some time off…'

'Jim, come on. How the hell are you going to be able to do that, huh? The new season's only just started, you're in the process of defending the league title, and you know as well as I do that you can't just take time off whenever you feel like it. You don't have that kind of job.'

'I can if I need to, Amber. I'm not indispensable. Colin can take over for a couple of weeks if there's something I need to deal with…'

'Something you need to *deal* with? This isn't some situation that can be sorted out with a week away in Magaluf.' She sat back, sighing heavily as she stared up at the ceiling. 'This is something *I* have to deal with, Jim.' She looked at him, his expression one she really couldn't read. 'Me. I have to live with this, and I will. I'll get used to it. It's not like I've been told I'm dying or anything.'

'*You* have to deal with it?'

'Yes. Me. I'm the one…'

'And you don't think that news affected me, too, huh? You don't think that maybe it's killing *me*, too? This isn't something *you* have to deal with, Amber. It's something *we* have to deal with. Together.'

She held his gaze, her head beginning to thump with the stress of the day, and it was only lunchtime. 'You already have a son, Jim. You know what it's like to be a parent, and that's something I'll never get the chance to experience now. So… so yes, this is something *I* have to deal with. Because you have no idea how I'm feeling right now. No idea.'

'Do you know how selfish that sounds?'

She said nothing for a second before letting out a small laugh. 'Sorry, you're going to sit there and lecture *me* about being selfish? You, the man who…' She stood up, pushing her chair back away from the table and walking over to the French windows. 'You kept Brandon a secret from me for all those years, Jim. When I… when I came home from university, all those years ago… when I let you back into my life, despite what you'd already done to me, you knew you were a father and yet you chose to keep that from me. You chose to shut me out, to lie to me – to everyone – so don't sit there and tell me *I'm* being selfish.'

'I did that for *you*, Amber. Everything, all of it, I did it for you.'

She swung round to face him as he walked over to her, but she put her hand out to stop him from coming any closer. 'No you didn't, Jim. You didn't do it for me, not really. You did it because you knew that telling me the truth could mean you lost everything *you* wanted. And even after all those years apart you still couldn't do it, could you? You still couldn't bring yourself to tell me the truth, so instead you made sure I fell so deep in love with you that once I *did* eventually find out there was no way I could walk away from you, no matter how I was really feeling. That isn't doing it for me.'

'Amber…'

She took a deep breath, exhaling slowly as she threw her head back again in an attempt to keep the tears that had been threatening all morning from falling, because she didn't want to cry. Crying wouldn't do anyone any good.

'I can't do this right now, Jim.'

'Amber, come on, honey, please…'

But she'd pushed past him before he had a chance to stop her, running out of the house and into her car. She had no idea where she was going, she just knew that she needed to get out for a while, she needed to get away from Jim. She needed time to think, to get her head straight. Time to think about what she was going to do now, because she really didn't know. In just a matter of days her world had been turned upside down – again – and where she went from here was anybody's guess.

Ryan pressed **send** and sat back in his seat, placing both hands behind his head as he exhaled deep and loud. Had he done the right thing? Without saying a word to Max? He didn't know. He didn't really know anything anymore, all he knew was that he had to do something. He'd wanted to wait, wanted to see if Jim Allen's out-of-the-blue revelation that Brandon Palmer was his son was going to have some kind of effect on his and Amber's marriage, but who was he kidding? He was living in some kind of fantasy world where he wished things would happen with no real concrete evidence that they would ever turn out in his favour.

No, he needed to move on and he needed to make sure things were put in place to make that happen, sooner rather than later. For the sake of his own future.

Slipping his phone back into his pocket, he smiled as Ellen returned to the bench he was sitting on, carrying two polystyrene cups of coffee she'd bought from a nearby snack van. They'd just spent a pleasant half an hour walking along the coast at Seaburn, enjoying the sunshine, and for a few blissful minutes he'd almost forgotten he had anything else going on in his life other than an incredible career and a beautiful woman by his side. A beautiful woman that he could quite possibly be lining up for heartache at some point soon, even though that was the last thing he wanted.

'Here you go.' She smiled, handing him a coffee as she sat down beside him. 'Isn't it lovely here? I used to come down to this beach all the time when I was younger.'

'Did you grow up around here?' Ryan asked, taking a sip of extremely strong and incredibly hot coffee. Just the way he liked it.

She nodded, putting her coffee down for a second while she pulled her blonde hair back into a ponytail. 'I was born in Newcastle, but we moved to Sunderland when I was a baby. My dad's originally from this side of the river – Durham born and bred. And he's a staunch Wearside Spartans fan.'

'Whoa, I bet he was over the moon when his daughter started working at Tynebridge, then. Or did he see it more as you infiltrating enemy lines?'

She laughed, picking her coffee back up and swirling it round in the cup before taking a sip. 'Well, he wasn't overcome with excitement, let's put it that way, but the fact I can get him decent seats for the local derby always makes up for the fact his only child's working for the opposition.'

Ryan watched as she smiled at a small boy who ran past their bench into the arms of his mother, screaming with excitement as she held out an ice cream for him. He'd had a great day with Ellen, he couldn't deny that. A long and lazy lunch in a riverside restaurant in Durham followed by this slow walk along the Sunderland seafront – he'd felt the most relaxed he'd felt in a long time. So why had he still felt the need to send that email? Why couldn't he just give what was happening here a chance? Give Ellen a chance, a real chance. Because he knew, deep down inside, that he couldn't really give anyone or anything a chance until he got his own head sorted. Properly sorted. Until he could move on from the one thing that was stopping him from believing he could finally make that new start.

'You look miles away.'

Ellen's soft voice shook him back to reality and he quickly pulled himself together, smiling at her. 'Sorry. I guess the fresh air is making me drift off.'

'I haven't worn you out too much, have I?' she smirked, and he couldn't help laughing.

'Sweetheart, you couldn't wear me out if you tried.'

'Want to prove that?'

'You setting me some kind of challenge?' He grinned, enjoying the flirtatious sparring that had started up.

'I thought Ryan Fisher liked challenges?' Her eyes met his over the rim of her coffee cup.

'Oh, he's real big on challenges, beautiful. Real big.'

And none was bigger than the challenge he'd just set himself. But whether he got the chance to play it all out was something he had yet to find out.

'I think you know my feelings on Jim Allen, Amber.' Freddie Sullivan leaned back against the windowsill, folding his arms as Amber settled herself into the corner of her father's new and extremely comfortable sofa. An ex-professional footballer, and now manager of a local First Division team, Freddie had once been best friends with Jim. But to say that his relationship with his former friend and teammate had been severely strained after the revelations of Amber's teenage affair with him was somewhat of an understatement. For Amber's sake Freddie had tried to get on with Jim, tried to forgive him for what he'd done to her all those years ago. And he'd tried, really hard, to understand why she still loved him so much after everything that had happened, but he still found it difficult. Jim had joined Newcastle Red Star as a twenty-seven-year-old player just as Freddie was reaching the end of his playing career there, but Freddie had still taken him under his wing, brought him into his family. And to think that he'd abused that trust by turning Amber's then-very-young head was something Freddie found very hard to deal with. 'For all those years he hid that kid from everyone… doesn't that tell you what kind of a man he is?'

Amber pushed a hand through her hair, curling her legs up underneath her as she sank further down into the sofa. Part of her just wanted to snuggle up and sleep, try to forget the day she'd just had, but life wasn't that simple anymore. True, she'd run to daddy in the hope that he could give her some kind of comfort, but she'd only been kidding herself really. She should have known that coming here was only going to mean that she had to listen to her father reeling off a list of '*I told you sos*' until she just switched off and tried to think about something else.

'I'm over it, Dad. Really.'

Freddie looked at his daughter with a somewhat incredulous expression. 'You're over it? What? You mean, he suddenly unveils his secret son to the world, gets you to pretend you knew about him all along, and you sit there and tell me you're over it?'

'He didn't get me to pretend anything, Dad. Okay? That was my idea. And I think it was the best idea in the long run. I can do without the added media storm it would cause if people got wind of the fact Jim had kept Brandon a secret from his wife.'

'People should know what he's really like,' Freddie muttered. 'All those years, we trusted him, me and your mam. We took him into our home, into our family…'

'All right, Dad. Enough. I've heard it all before. I know how you feel, and I understand, I really do. It's hard for others to see him the same way I do, I get that. But he never meant to hurt me, and I truly believe that. He just… he just doesn't think, that's all.'

'That's all?' Freddie asked, arching a sceptical eyebrow. 'You know, the man is truly brilliant at managing football teams, but when it comes to managing his own personal life he's got no bloody idea.'

Amber rolled her eyes, letting out a heavy sigh. Her father's opinion of her husband wasn't going to change anytime soon, and the appearance of Brandon had only served to strengthen his resolve that Jim Allen wasn't right for her. 'Anyway, I've got more important things to worry about now.'

Freddie looked at his daughter, his arms still folded. 'Like what?'

She proceeded to tell him about her visit to Dr. Lowry that morning, a visit borne out of some sudden and desperate need to have a child of her own, to be the kind of mum her own mother had been to her. And Freddie listened, his eyes never leaving hers as she spoke.

'Oh, Amber, sweetheart. Why didn't you talk to me? I had no idea…'

'Well, to be fair, Dad, nobody had any idea, did they? I mean, how could they? I've never exactly shown myself to be the maternal type. Nobody ever really expected me to be mummy material. And even *I* was surprised at the strength of these ridiculously unexpected feelings that just swept over me all of a sudden. So I had to know, that's all. And I think I always knew the truth, deep down. You and mum never sugar-coated anything, you never hid the facts from me, so it wasn't like I had all that much hope of it turning out to be the miracle I would have liked it to be. I was realistic enough to know that the truth wasn't going to be perfect.

But hearing those words – hearing someone actually tell you that you're probably never going to have a child of your own…' She stopped talking, looking away for a second as a stray tear rolled slowly down her cheek. She quickly wiped it away before turning back to look at her father. 'Anyway, now I know the facts I guess it's time to move on. Draw a line under things I can't achieve and concentrate on those things I can.'

'There's no shame in talking about how you're really feeling, Amber. This isn't something you can just get over in an hour and forget about.'

'Yes, it is,' she said, hauling herself up off the sofa. 'It is. I've got a brand new career to concentrate on, and a marriage that needs a lot of work…'

'Your marriage is in trouble?'

She looked up. 'That isn't what I said, Dad. So you can wipe that hopeful look off your face. I said it needs work. The revelation that my husband has a secret son coming out the day before I find out I can't have his baby has thrown us a bit of a curveball, that's all. We'll get over it. I just need some time to think about things.'

'And running away from Jim is the best way to go about that, is it?'

'I haven't run away. I'm not five. Am I not allowed to come and see my dad now?'

Freddie threw her a look that told her he wasn't convinced, but he said nothing, just watched as she walked out of the living room and into the kitchen.

Amber was beginning to wonder whether it would have been a better idea to drive into the countryside, take a walk, stop for a pot of tea somewhere and just people-watch for a while rather than spend time with a man she loved more than anything, but he was her dad, so he was bound to crowd her, want to know what was wrong. But she was fast beginning to realise that she didn't really want to talk about it. Any of it. She just wanted to escape from it all, just for a little while. She wanted to think about something else other than secret kids and babies she couldn't have. Maybe going down to London early would be a good idea. There was nothing like throwing yourself into work to take your mind off things.

'Hey, you.'

She swung round at the sound of Ronnie's voice. 'What are *you* doing here?'

'Yeah, I'm pleased to see you, too.'

'Shut up and get over here. I really need a hug.'

He walked over to her, pulling her into his arms and holding her close, kissing the top of her head. 'Your dad's just told me, about what happened at the clinic this morning.'

She pulled away slightly, pushing both hands through her hair. 'Well, it wasn't a complete surprise really, was it?'

'There's the sound of those barriers coming right back up again.'

'Come on, Ronnie, what else am I supposed to do? I'm trying to pretend it's all okay, that I'm dealing with the fact Jim's son is Brandon Palmer, that I can live with never having a baby of my own. I'm trying really hard to pretend it's all okay but I'm struggling here. I'm really, really struggling.' She couldn't fight the tears any longer and all Ronnie could do was pull her back into his arms as she cried them all out.

'Hey, come on. Come on, kiddo. Nobody expects you to be strong all the time you know. Especially with what you've had to deal with over the past couple of days.'

She pulled away from him again, wiping her eyes and blowing her nose. 'But I want to be strong, Ronnie. Don't you see? I hate feeling like this, I hate feeling weak and vulnerable and tired. I hate it. I don't want to be upset or angry or… it's such a fucking waste of time!'

'Okay then. Just push it all to one side and let it build up to the point where it starts to eat you up inside. That'll work.'

She looked at him. 'I hate *you* when you start spouting sense.'

He leaned back against the counter, folding his arms as he watched her. 'So, you and Jim. What's going on there, then?'

'Nothing's going on.'

'So why are you here and not with him? I mean, surely he's feeling a little shell-shocked by today's events, too.'

Amber said nothing, she just let a small and brief pang of guilt wash over her before she met Ronnie's gaze again. 'He says he is.'

'And you don't believe him?'

Amber stood next to Ronnie, her hands gripping the countertop behind her. 'I don't know what to think if I'm honest. He said I was selfish for saying that this was something *I* had to deal with, rather than something we had to go through together…'

'And he's probably right.'

She looked at him. 'Whose side are *you* on?'

'I'm not on anyone's side, Amber. I'm just trying to play devil's advocate, that's all.'

She stared straight ahead of her, watching as a large blackbird landed in the centre of her dad's patio and began pecking at a pot full of lavender. 'Maybe I shouldn't have run out on him like I did. But I just needed some space, some time away.'

'From Jim?'

She looked back at Ronnie. 'From everything. I'm thinking of going down to London early. It might be for the best. It'll give both me and Jim a bit of time to get our heads straight.'

'You really don't think you should be together at a time like this?'

'I've only been told I can't have kids, Ronnie. I haven't been told I'm ill.'

'And those barriers come crashing up once more.'

She said nothing to that as she turned away from him, her attention back on the blackbird who was now hopping between the potted plants and shrubs like they were some kind of avian obstacle course. 'Nobody's marriage is perfect, Ronnie. You should know that better than anyone.'

'Whoa, that was a low blow there, missy.'

She threw her head back and sighed heavily. 'Ronnie, I'm sorry.' She looked at him. 'I'm really sorry, I didn't mean that, I shouldn't have said that.'

'I know… Look, of course no marriage is perfect, Amber. But you and Jim, you've only been married five minutes.'

'Yeah. And maybe we shouldn't have got married at all.' The words were out before she'd had time to realise she was saying them. She'd been thinking out loud, she hadn't meant for anyone to hear that.

'Amber, look at me.'

Her eyes met Ronnie's, and for a few seconds neither of them said anything.

'Did you mean that?' he asked, breaking the silence. 'Are you saying you regret marrying Jim?'

'I don't know what I'm saying, Ronnie. Right now, my head is a mess. Which is why I'm leaving for London tomorrow.' She looked up at him, right into his eyes. 'You coming with me?'

Chapter Eleven

'Am I talking to myself this morning?' Jim Allen's voice boomed out across the training pitch as he, unusually for him, let everyone know that his mood wasn't a good one. Even Colin was looking at him as though he was slightly wary of what he might say or do next.

'Looks like the honeymoon period's over,' Gary muttered as he kicked the ball over to Ryan.

'Any reason why he's exhibiting the mood from hell this morning?' Ryan asked, flicking the ball up onto first one knee then the other.

'Fisher! We're not here to play fucking games, you got that? Get the ball back down on the fucking ground and get on with what you're supposed to be doing!'

Ryan kicked the ball at Gary, pulling a face. 'Jesus. What's eating him?'

'Well, I'm going to hazard a guess here, but I'd say it wasn't the beautiful Amber.'

Ryan stood still. 'Huh? You reckon him and Amber have had a row?' He couldn't stop another one of those fleeting waves of hope from washing over him. And it would appear it was written all over his face, too.

'Hey, mate, reel it in, will you? I don't think they're heading for the divorce courts or anything. But ever since Brandon Palmer came on the scene, I've heard rumours that Amber hasn't exactly been jumping for joy.'

'Rumours?' Ryan frowned.

Gary looked at him. 'Debbie.'

'Okay…'

'You do know she's gone down to London days earlier than she needed to.'

'Who? Debbie?'

'No, Christ, keep up. Amber. According to Debbie she didn't need to be down there until Friday but she wanted to go early. Doesn't that tell you something? I mean, why would she head down there now if something wasn't going on? Ever since they got together, her and the boss have been like a couple of lovesick teenagers and yet now she's travelling down to the other end of the country for absolutely no reason rather than staying here with him.'

'How do you know she's gone down there for no reason? We don't know that, do we?'

'Come on, Ryan. Something's up, I can tell.'

Gary wasn't exactly the world's oracle when it came to relationship advice, but that didn't stop Ryan from hoping that, this time, he was right. He wanted Amber to be happy, he really did, but if she and Jim *were* having problems then that would be nothing short of music to his ears.

'Anyway,' Gary went on, quickly passing the ball back to Ryan, '… Debbie reckons it's not just the appearance of Brandon Palmer that's causing problems. There's something else going on, and she knows what it is, I know she does, but she won't tell me anything.'

'Probably because it's got nothing to do with you.' But Gary's words were filling Ryan with a feeling of hope he hadn't felt in a long while. Had his boss pushed Amber too far this time? Had the revelation of one final secret been too much for Amber to take? He quickly looked over at Jim Allen, who was throwing himself right into that morning's training session, dribbling the ball through a line of cones like he was the new kid on the block rather than a forty-nine-year-old ex-player. He still had it. But did he still have Amber?

'Hey, Ryan, snap out of it,' Gary said, gently nudging his shoulder. 'Whatever it is, they'll work it out, so stop imagining she's gonna come running straight back to you. It ain't gonna happen.'

'Who says?' Ryan could have bitten his own tongue off. He really hadn't meant to say that out loud.

'I wouldn't, Ryan.' Gary's voice carried more than a hint of warning. 'Don't piss the boss off, not when he's put all that trust in you, I mean, he made you captain and… You owe him, big time, mate. After everything that happened.'

'Yeah,' Ryan sighed. 'Yeah, I know.'

'Come on. Sort yourself out before the boss catches you slacking.' Gary threw the ball at Ryan, who caught it square in the chest. 'Look, how about we go out tonight? We'll go down the Quayside, maybe pop into the casino for a couple of hours. What do you say? It'll be like old times.'

'Is that a good idea?' Ryan asked, finding it hard to tear his eyes away from Jim Allen as he continued his kick-about on the pitch, a couple of the younger and newer members of the squad looking on in awe. 'I mean, it was those old times that got me into all that shit before, wasn't it?'

'You know what I mean. Come on. You can handle nights out like a grown-up now, can't you?' Gary smirked at him, but Ryan just threw him a look that told him he wasn't funny. 'You up for it or not?'

Ryan sighed, throwing the ball into the air and heading it in Gary's direction. 'Yeah. Why not?' He had nothing to lose. Except everything.

'Max, I'm not doing it, all right?'

'Come on, Amber. You're down there in London anyway, you could meet the guys from Ice Magazine, have a chat with them

– what's the problem?'

Amber looked up as Ronnie walked onto the studio floor and she smiled at him, mouthing *'Give me a minute'*. 'The problem, Max, is that I don't want to get naked for all and sundry to see. That'll do my reputation no end of good.'

Ronnie frowned as he sat on the arm of the sofa Amber was sitting on.

'It'll do your reputation the world of good, in my opinion,' Max said.

Amber rolled her eyes and mouthed *'Max'* at Ronnie, crossing her legs and drumming her fingers on her knee.

'And I know what I'm talking about, kiddo. You've seen what similar publicity has done for some of the players on my books, including your ex. Ryan's had his shirt off in many a magazine.'

'This is completely different, Max.'

'How? Oh, hang on, you're not going all feminist on me, are you? You're not gonna start spouting off about how sexist and demeaning it all is?'

'I might, if you carry on the way you are.'

'You're presenting *Scoreline* tonight, aren't you?' Max decided it was probably best to change the subject. The last thing he wanted was to piss her off more than she already was.

'Yes, and you know I am. They said you asked if I could present it tonight because of Brandon's interview.'

'I just want the kid to feel comfortable, Amber. I really wanted to be there with him myself, but I've got a meeting with a player in Munich tonight, so the next best thing is to have you there to keep an eye on him. You don't mind, do you? I thought with you being down there anyway you might as well do something.'

'No, I don't mind. It's not like I've got anything else to do. And there's no harm in showing a bit of enthusiasm, is there? Seeing as I'm still very much the new girl.'

'Amber – there's nothing wrong, is there?'

Amber stopped drumming her fingers and stared down at her

wedding ring. 'Why would anything be wrong?'

'No reason. Just checking. I'm your agent, it's what I do. I make sure everything's okay.'

'For whose benefit?' She hadn't meant that to sound quite as cynical as it had done.

'Yours, Amber. Just think about the Ice shoot, will you? Please? I'll talk to you later.'

Amber threw her mobile down next to her and sat back against the cushions of the cobalt-blue sofa, closing her eyes and sighing heavily.

'That's all I've heard you do these days,' Ronnie said.

She opened one eye and looked at him. 'What?'

'Sigh. And are you working tonight or something?'

'I'm presenting *Scoreline*.'

'Since when? I thought Steve was doing that?'

Amber sat up, clasping her hands between her knees. 'Well, he isn't now, is he? I am. That's why I'm here this afternoon, checking things over. There's a lot to talk about in tonight's show, including that interview with my new stepson. That should get the viewers in.' She'd let the cynicism take over again, but she couldn't help it. She was in a cynical mood.

Ronnie watched as she stood up, shaking out her long, dark red hair. 'Brandon's coming here? Into the studio?'

'Yeah. Wearside Spartans' match at the weekend is in north London, as you know, and the squad are already here, so…'

'And they asked *you* to interview him?'

'Well, Max asked them if I could interview him, actually.'

'And you're all right with that?'

'Why wouldn't I be?' Amber got up and walked over to the long, semi-circular-shaped desk at the rear of the studio. 'It's what I do.'

Ronnie followed her, perching himself on the edge of the desk as she started rifling through a pile of papers. 'Your behaviour, Amber…'

She looked up sharply. 'What about it?'

'It's pretty erratic, to say the least.'

She didn't reply, just resumed the sorting through of those papers.

'Amber?'

She looked up again. 'What? What do you want me to say, Ronnie?'

'I know these past few days have thrown up a few things that can't have been easy to deal with…'

She raised her eyebrows at that comment.

'But…' Ronnie continued, '… I just think… I think… You need to be with Jim.'

'And that's your considered opinion, is it, Dr. White?'

'Quit with the flippancy, Amber.'

'I need to be *here*, Ronnie. Okay? I need to be here, and I need to be busy. Anyway, Debbie's coming down tomorrow. We're going shopping.'

'That'll be nice.'

'Now who's being flippant?'

'And you really think that you, sitting there interviewing his son on live TV – you think that's gonna make Jim feel any better about things? Because if *I* was married to you that would be confusing the hell out of me.'

She looked down at that pile of papers again. 'Yeah, well, you're *not* married to me, are you? So it's not your problem.'

'Oh, it's very much my problem, Amber. I'm making it my problem.'

'Well don't.' She stared at him, her eyes telling him to back off. 'I'm fine. Really, I'm fine. I just need to face things head-on, and that includes getting to know my stepson.'

'By interviewing him live on TV? Why not just take him for a drink or out to dinner, or something? But this… And why are you doing this without Jim?'

'Will you stop bringing Jim into this, Ronnie, please?'

'Look, Amber, I'm not the guy's biggest fan – not on a personal level, anyway – but is it fair to leave him back home, alone, dealing with the fact you're Christ knows where feeling Christ knows what?'

'He knows where I am. And can we just stop this now. Just… just, stop it.'

'Why? Am I hitting a few nerves?'

'You're not being fair.'

Ronnie said nothing for a second, just looked at her, holding her gaze. 'Well, that'd make two of us, then. Wouldn't it?'

'Jesus. I'd forgotten how loud this place can be,' Ryan shouted, throwing himself down into a seat in what he hoped was going to be a quieter corner of the VIP area in one of the city's more exclusive Quayside bars.

'Here, get this down you.' Gary grinned as he handed Ryan a vodka shot.

Ryan eyed it warily. He'd once spent nights knocking these back, setting up rounds of them in all different flavours just so he could impress the ever-present crowds of women who flocked around him before picking out those he quite fancied spending a bit more time with. That life seemed like such a long time ago, yet it had only been a matter of months since those nights of partying to excess with women whose names he could barely remember the next day. He couldn't lie and say he didn't miss the adrenalin rush that lifestyle gave him; the high knowing every woman in the room wanted you was something he still craved from time to time. But when he remembered what he'd almost lost – what he actually *had* lost – through living the way he had done, it didn't always feel so glamorous.

'One isn't going to hurt,' Gary said, noticing Ryan's reluctance to take the shot. 'And you know your limits now, don't you?'

Ryan took the drink and knocked it back, placing the empty glass down on the table in front of him. 'Yeah. I do. But doubtless you'll be keeping an eye on my alcohol intake anyway.'

'Don't be so frigging cynical, Ryan. I'm not your babysitter. I'm your friend, and I care about you, you dozy sod.'

Ryan looked at him, throwing him the famous Fisher grin.

'And that doesn't work on me,' Gary said, rolling his eyes. 'I'll go get us a couple of beers. Don't want to put you in temptation's way by letting you go to the bar yourself, do we?'

Ryan sat back on the comfortable black suede sofa, watching as the VIP area filled up with local celebrities, footballers, and what seemed like an abundance of glamorous women in figure-hugging short dresses that showed off an array of never-ending legs. For a brief second he felt as though he was back in heaven, that kid in a metaphorical candy store, because he could, if he wanted, have any one of those women. He knew he could. Just because he was in the process of trying to clean up his act it didn't mean to say he had to start living like a monk. He was only human. And famous. And incredibly good-looking. Not to mention loaded.

'Well, long time no see, Ryan.'

Ryan's head turned quickly to his right to see a very beautiful, very blonde young woman sitting beside him. With her smoky grey eyes and pale pink pout, she seemed vaguely familiar to him, but he couldn't quite place where he'd seen her last. But that was no surprise. Over the course of his years as a professional footballer he'd had more women than he could keep track of, the majority of which had never stayed in his life for more than a couple of days. Most of them were lucky to last a few hours. As yet, he wasn't sure which category this woman here in front of him fitted into.

'I haven't seen you since that incredible night in The Goldman last September,' she purred, her hand resting lightly on his leg.

The Goldman Hotel was one of the most upmarket hotels in the North East, and, despite its reputation as a top-class riverside establishment, it was the venue of choice for celebrities, rock stars and footballers when they needed to 'let off steam', as it were, with people they'd rather not be seen with. The hotel offered a very discreet service to its celebrity clients, and any member of staff found offering information of any kind to reporters or photographers – no matter how tiny a titbit – knew they could face instant dismissal. As a one-time regular Ryan knew this, and he'd made use of The Goldman's discreetness on many an occasion. Too many to remember, if truth be told.

Ryan grinned as recognition slowly began to take over. She'd been a 'few days' girl – starting off in The Goldman after a night in the casino, and ending in The Goldman just a couple of days later. For no reason other than he'd become bored of her. 'Paula, isn't it?'

She nodded, running a finger gently along his thigh. 'You remember me, then?'

'It's pretty hard to forget you, sweetheart, considering some of the things you did to me in that hotel room. I'm not even sure half of them were legal.'

She laughed a low, throaty laugh that was actually incredibly sexy, stirring up something in Ryan he hadn't felt in a while – that urge to indulge in no-strings, no-questions-asked sex with a woman who didn't want anything from him other than his body.

'You haven't been out and about for a while,' Paula went on, her hand now stroking his arm, and he watched as she uncrossed and crossed her legs slowly, letting her skirt deliberately ride up her thighs. 'And after everything that happened I wasn't sure if we'd ever see you back here again.'

'I went into rehab, Paula, that's all. For a number of reasons. And they're all sorted now.' Were they? Really?

'Still…' She smiled, edging closer to him, '… it's good to see you again.'

He looked over towards the bar where Gary was deep in conversation with one of their teammates, and suddenly a night of sitting exchanging small talk about Debbie's latest ideas for interior design seemed like something Ryan really couldn't be bothered to face. He wanted some fun. He *needed* some fun, before he made a decision that could change his life. For a little while, anyway.

'You here with anyone?' Ryan asked, turning his attention back to Paula.

'Nobody I mind leaving.' She smiled. 'Not if *you're* after some company.'

'Oh, it's more than company I'm after.' He grinned, grabbing her hand and pulling her up off the sofa. 'Come on. Me and you, we're gonna relive some old times.'

Jim stood in the kitchen, facing the TV on the wall, sipping a small glass of whisky as he watched Amber's *Scoreline* interview with Brandon. His handsome son and his beautiful wife. Together. What a mind-fuck *that* was turning out to be! He'd only found out she was going to be talking to him when Brandon had called him earlier, and it hurt more than Jim cared to admit that Amber couldn't have told him herself. Especially as she'd finally answered one of his frequent calls just half an hour ago, only minutes before she'd gone live on air. She could have easily told him about the interview with Brandon then. But, at the same time, just hearing her voice had been enough to calm him slightly. She wasn't blanking him completely, although it had been obvious to him that she was still upset. But she'd told him she loved him, and he couldn't begin to describe the relief he'd felt when he'd heard her say that. She loved him. That didn't mean everything was suddenly going to be okay; it didn't mean that once the weekend was over and she was back in the North East – if she came back to the North East, that is, because she hadn't exactly told him *when* she'd be back – it didn't mean that she was going to forget everything and it would all go back to normal. He'd just told her he had a twenty-year-old son, and she'd just been told she may never be able to have kids of her own. How could anything ever really go back to normal after that?

He turned his attention back to the TV, watching as Amber laughed and joked with Brandon, putting him instantly at ease, because that was what she did. She was good at her job, the best. She conducted interviews like they were the most natural thing in the world to her, making every person she spoke to want to stay there and chat longer than their allotted time slot. And it didn't seem to matter what else was going on in her life, she never displayed anything other than total professionalism. She never gave anything away, and even though he knew how she still felt about the revelation that Brandon was his son, all he could see there on the screen was a woman who was giving this young footballer the airtime he deserved in order to let football fans across the country get to know him.

Of course, it was inevitable that the interview wasn't going to pass without some mention of the family ties involved, and Jim couldn't help but flinch as she mentioned his name, because her face showed nothing. There was no emotion, not even a flicker of something he could grab onto that could make him think she'd had the space and time she needed and was now ready to come home and let him explain. Not that he could explain much, really. He'd lied to her. Again. What on earth had made him think she was just going to take that? Didn't he know her well enough after all this time?

Swallowing the last of his whisky, he switched off the TV and headed upstairs. The house was too empty without Amber in it. The silence was giving him way too much time to think about things. An early night seemed a much better option. When he was asleep he didn't have to think about what he might have done, what he might have lost. What he might have to fight twice as hard to keep now. But if he had to fight, he would. Whatever it took.

Chapter Twelve

'Thanks, Amber. For doing this.'

She looked up at Brandon. The show was now over but he'd hung around for a while after they'd come off air to chat with some of the *Scoreline* team. It was still quite unnerving to see how closely he resembled his dad, and although she'd managed to put it to the back of her mind during the interview, all it was doing now was reminding her of Jim. And right now she didn't really want to be reminded of him.

She smiled, pulling her jacket on and running her fingers through her hair. 'You've got nothing to thank me for. It was the guys here at *Scoreline* that wanted to interview you, I was just doing my job.'

'Yeah, but I'm still pretty new to all this. I didn't have anything like the level of publicity I'm getting here in the U.K. over in the States. It's a whole different game over there, and this – this is just crazy sometimes.'

'Tell me about it.'

He smiled at her, a smile so like his father's it sent Amber's heart skipping beats all over the place. 'You made me feel, I dunno… comfortable. You know all about the way this works, the way this should be done – that's why I want to say thank you.'

She looked at him again, all handsome and young and just

starting out on this – as he'd so rightly put it – crazy journey. 'You're very welcome.'

She started walking out of the studio, and he fell into step beside her, his hands in his pockets. 'Look, I know this is probably none of my business, but… you and my dad. Is… is everything okay? Only, I know he kept my existence from you for…'

She stopped walking and turned to look at him. 'You're right, Brandon. It *is* none of your business.' She hung her head, closed her eyes and let out a deep sigh before looking back up at him. 'I'm sorry. I suppose it *is* your business really, isn't it?'

He smiled at her again, and she couldn't help but notice the way that smile lit up his handsome face. Just like his dad's smile did. 'Listen, you can say no, but do you fancy joining me for a drink? I mean, it wouldn't be a bad thing if we tried to get to know one another a little better, would it? Away from any TV cameras.'

She hesitated for a second, trying to answer that question for herself. Would it be a bad thing? How *could* it be a bad thing? Pretending he didn't exist wasn't going to work, so what other option did she have, when she was married to his dad?

'Yeah. Okay. I guess one won't hurt.'

Ten minutes and a small-talk-filled walk later they were ensconced in a fairly quiet corner of the bar within the purpose-built studios at Cloud Sports.

'When your dad asked you to keep your family connection a secret, were you happy about that?' Amber looked straight into Brandon's eyes, watching to see if there was a flicker of something that told her he was covering for Jim, telling her what he thought she wanted to hear rather than what he really felt.

'No. I wasn't.'

It seemed as though Brandon was quite happy to let his real feelings be known.

'But…' Brandon shrugged, sitting back and taking a small swig from his bottle of beer. 'Well, nobody back home really knows who my dad is anyway. A few people in the soccer world know of him, and I know one of the big L.A.-based clubs even asked him to come over and be their manager a few years back, but he turned their offer down.'

'Did that bother you?'

Brandon looked at her. 'You're very direct.'

'I just ask straight questions. It's my job. You don't have to answer them.'

He said nothing for a second, just continued to look at her, his eyes never leaving hers until she looked away, down at the table. 'Yeah. At the time it *did* bother me. I was fourteen years old, and the thought that my dad might actually come home was…' It was his turn to look down at the table. 'I missed him, that's all. Missed having him around. He did what he could, came over for visits whenever his job allowed, but he made it clear the U.K. was his home.'

'But you would have liked him to come back to America?'

He looked at her again. 'Of course. No doubt about it. But, thinking back, that was never gonna happen. When he was approached by the L.A. team he was managing a big club in London, winning silverware regularly, bagging manager of the month awards like they were going out of fashion. He was never gonna give that up to come back home and manage a team that may well be big on the West Coast of America, but they're practically unknown everywhere else.' His eyes met hers again. 'And, from what he's told me recently, he was never gonna give up *you.*'

Amber felt slightly uncomfortable and she looked away again, focusing on a group of her new work colleagues over at the bar. 'For a lot of years me and your dad were never really together,' she said quietly, shifting her focus back to Brandon just as Ronnie walked in. 'So I had nothing to do with any decisions he made back then.'

'No. I guess you didn't.'

'Why did you do it, Brandon? Why did you agree to keep your connection a secret?'

He shrugged, taking another sip of beer. 'I don't know, and that's the honest truth. I suppose I had my own life over in New York, I had a career that had nothing to do with my dad, so there was no need to bring him into it. And me and my mom, we had a good life. She made sure I didn't want for anything; she made sure that me not having my real dad around all the time wasn't the worst thing in the world. I had – I *have* a great stepdad. He's been there for me for most of my life, and he'll continue to be there for me. I'll always love him like a father. Always.'

Amber paused for a second before asking another question. 'You joining Wearside Spartans – was there some method in your madness there?'

He looked at her, frowning slightly.

'Did you deliberately choose to play for a North East club because you wanted to be closer to Jim?'

He laughed a small, low laugh. 'You really can't switch that reporter mode off sometimes, can you?'

She smiled, finally taking a swig of her own beer. 'I'm just curious, that's all. You had clubs much bigger than Spartans putting in bids for you, but most of those were down here in London. And, let's face it, most young players from abroad like the idea of playing for one of the big London clubs. I know you turned two of those clubs down. So I can only assume that your decision to play for a northern club was because you wanted to be nearer to your dad.'

'You got me. Yeah, that's the reason.' He leaned forward, resting his elbows on the table, his hands clasped in front of him. 'For all those years I never really knew him, Amber. Growing up, he was never really there. And that wasn't his fault, I know he did his best, but I missed having my dad around. And then along came this chance to move over to the U.K., to play the game I love in the same country as my father. It felt like, I dunno, fate, or something. It felt like I finally had a chance – a real chance – to get to know him. To tell the world where I got this talent from, to let them all know who my father is. And it's something I need to do. For me. It wasn't my fault he chose to keep me a secret from you. I had no idea of your past with my dad, Amber, believe me. I had no idea, because, if I had…'

'It's okay. Really. None of this is your fault, and I completely understand everything you've just told me. My dad is the most important person in my life, and if I didn't have him around…' She looked up into Brandon's piercing green eyes. Eyes that reminded her so much of a young Jim. Eyes that, once again, sparked a myriad of memories. 'He should be very, very proud of you, Brandon. Very proud.'

He smiled, reaching out to quickly squeeze her hand. 'My dad's one very lucky guy.'

She looked down at her wedding ring, twisting it round her finger.

'Amber?'

She looked up, still twisting her wedding ring round and round.

'Tell me to mind my own business, but I don't think I'm the only problem between you and my dad right now, am I?'

'You're not a problem, Brandon. The fact Jim kept you a secret from me is the problem, but…'

'There's something else, isn't there?'

She took another quick sip of beer before hurriedly gathering her things together. This get-to-know-you drink had been very nice but she really needed to leave now. 'I should be going. I've got a long day at the studio tomorrow.'

He gently put a hand over her wrist, stopping her from getting up. 'This is complicated, Amber, I know that. And I know how confusing it must be…'

'For a man so young you're extremely perceptive, aren't you?'

'I had to grow up fast, believe me.'

She sat back down, closing her eyes for a second, letting out another deep sigh. 'Things *are* complicated, Brandon. And they're complicated for a number of reasons. Everything just seems to be happening all at once and… Look, we'll work it out, me and your dad. It's just really hard at the minute, given how busy we both are and the jobs we do. We don't seem to get all that much time together these days.'

'He loves you, Amber.'

'You know that, do you? I mean, you've been here all of five minutes and you think you know the way his mind works?'

'My dad can be quite transparent when he wants to be. It's a weakness he never displays in a professional capacity, but you take him out of the dressing room and he just can't seem to help himself.'

'I know he loves me,' Amber sighed, her eyes catching Ronnie's over at the bar. 'And I love him, too. So we'll work it out. Eventually.'

Brandon frowned. 'There *is* something else, isn't there?'

She looked at him. 'Yeah. There is. But it's between me and your dad, okay? It's nothing for you to worry about. You just concentrate on Saturday's game. Do your job. Billy's putting a lot of faith in you to go out there and start scoring, and you're playing for a North East team now, so take it from one who grew up around North East football – those fans will be expecting a lot from you, too. Let them down and you'll know about it.'

He gave her another smile. 'I don't intend to let anyone down.'

She smiled back. 'Make sure you don't. I'll speak to you soon, okay?'

'Okay. And, thanks again, Amber. I mean that.'

She gave him one more smile before making her way out of the bar. All she wanted to do now was curl up in bed with a glass of wine and something rubbish and mind-numbing on the TV. But someone else had other ideas.

'What was all that about?'

She turned to look at Ronnie as she continued to walk towards her car. 'What was all what about?'

'You and Brandon Palmer?'

'We were just talking. I told you, it's about time I started to get to know my stepson. And you have no idea how weird it sounds saying that.'

'Are you okay?'

She finally reached her car, stopping to look at Ronnie properly. 'I'm fine. Why?'

'Amber, come on. These past few days have been nothing short of crazy…'

'Yeah, they have. But I'm dealing with them, in my own way.'

'Really?'

She looked at him over the roof of her car. 'Do you want a lift?'

He just looked at her, raising his eyebrows. 'Seriously?'

'What?'

'You're doing it again. Pretending your head isn't all over the place and putting this cold front up that just pushes everyone away. Well, those closest to you, anyway.'

'Do you want this lift or not?'

'Jesus, you frustrate the hell out of me sometimes!'

'Just get in.'

He slid into the passenger seat, slamming the door shut as Amber started the engine.

'Do you want to come back to mine?' she asked, reversing slowly out of her reserved space in the Cloud Sports car park. 'For a nightcap. I've only had a couple of sips of beer, seeing as I'm driving, and I could really do with an alcohol hit.'

'You're not the only one,' Ronnie muttered. 'How any man puts up with you is beyond me.'

She looked at him out the corner of her eye, smiling slightly but saying nothing.

'See what I mean?' he said, but he couldn't help laughing. 'I'm going to make you call Jim in the morning.'

'Yeah, we'll see how that works out then, shall we?'

'You hungry?'

'Starving.'

'We'll get some Chinese on the way home, help soak up that

nightcap. What do you say?'

'Good idea. And you're paying.'

It felt like old times as Ryan lay back and listened to the sound of the shower coming from the en-suite, imagining Paula's deliciously naked body stepping under the water as she soaped herself all over. He could feel his hard-on reappearing already, but he wasn't in the mood to go solo. Not when he had a beautiful woman on hand to take care of all that. He'd wait until she was out of the shower, then he'd make sure she got down and dirty all over again. Jesus, sometimes he loved his old life so much.

The Goldman had come up trumps once again, giving him one of their best rooms, and the kind of service they reserved especially for those who tipped generously. And Ryan was having one hell of a night. *Just like old times*, Gary had said. It certainly was! It was a night Ryan was in no hurry to see end, despite training starting at 7a.m. the next day. He'd be fine. He could do this shit and still be there on the training pitch kicking balls like the professional he was. He was Ryan Fisher, wasn't he? Nobody could do this crap like he could.

Smiling to himself, he flicked on the TV and immediately turned to the Cloud Sports News Channel. He liked to catch *Scoreline* whenever he could. Keeping up with what was happening in the football world was something he enjoyed, especially at the minute with the transfer window still yet to close, and anyway, there might be something happening out there that could be useful to know.

Settling back against the ridiculously over-stuffed but unbeliev-ably comfortable pillows, he watched as the commercial break finished and *Scoreline* started. But the second he saw her, sitting there on the familiar cobalt-blue sofa that graced the *Scoreline* studio set, looking hot and crazy-beautiful in skinny jeans and a black open-necked shirt, her red hair falling loosely over her shoulders, he felt his stomach dip. That all-too-familiar feeling that always crept up on him whenever he saw her. He just hadn't expected to see her tonight, there on the TV. He hadn't expected that. Sometimes he forgot she wasn't Amber Sullivan – local news reporter – anymore. Sometimes he forgot she was now Amber Allen – sports presenter, TV celebrity, and wife of one of the country's top football managers.

Grabbing the remote, he quickly switched to a rolling news channel, sitting up and pulling his knees to his chest, hanging his head in his hands. Already he could feel the beginnings of a dull ache behind his eyes, his head spinning. He'd come here tonight to escape all of this, yet here it was, right there with him. Because there *was* no escape. Not here. He'd tried to kid himself he could do it, that it was all getting better, that he was coping. But he wasn't. And he knew that, now.

Throwing the covers off, he slid out of bed and started pulling on his clothes. As far as he was concerned it was game over tonight. It was game over – full stop.

'You're miles away.'

Amber turned to look at Ronnie. He was standing in the kitchen doorway, hands in his pockets, a concerned look on his face.

'Metaphorically, and literally,' she whispered.

Ronnie frowned. 'Are you really okay?'

She shook her head, feeling tears start to well up again as he came over, gently pulling her into his arms. 'It *is* all right to cry, you know. You don't have to be hard-faced all your life.'

She couldn't help smiling. 'You always do this to me.'

'What? Try to cheer you up?'

She pulled away from him, tearing off a sheet of kitchen roll to wipe her eyes with as she leaned back against the counter. 'Oh God, Ronnie, it's all such a mess.'

'It doesn't have to be,' he said, his hands back in his pockets. 'Maybe you just need to talk to…'

She shut him up with one of her looks, shaking her head. 'No. Not yet. Look, I don't even want to talk *about* him right now, let alone talk *to* him. I can't even explain these bloody feelings going round in my head, and that's what's so confusing.'

'You really should…'

'Just leave it, Ronnie, please.'

He looked down at the ground, scuffing the heel of his shoe against the bottom of the kitchen cupboards. 'Then talk to *me*, Amber.' He looked up at her, his eyes locking onto hers. 'Please. Just talk to someone, because you're bottling stuff up, I know you. And you don't do that.'

'Oh, yes, I do,' she said, letting out a small, ironic laugh. 'I so do. For almost twenty years I bottled up how I really felt for Jim. I battered those feelings down until I almost began to convince myself that they weren't real.' She stared at Ronnie. 'But they were. They were very real, and I just wish I'd acted on them sooner.'

'You think that would have made this situation any different?'

She shrugged, wiping her eyes again before throwing the crumpled sheet of kitchen roll into a nearby bin. 'Probably not. But it might have meant that at least, by now, I'd be used to it all. I'd have accepted that Jim was a father, and that I won't ever be a mum.' Just saying the words out loud felt like someone had thrust something sharp and jagged right into her chest. The pain was so real she actually flinched, and Ronnie had to step forward to catch her in his arms as she fell forward.

'Okay, that's it. Come on. I think it's time you got some sleep. You look worn out.'

'I'm not a child, Ronnie.' She pulled away from him, continuing to tidy up the remnants of their takeaway supper. 'I'm fine. It was just a wobble, and I'm sure I'm going to have quite a few more of those before…'

Ronnie grabbed the plates she was holding, pulling them out of her hands, instantly shutting her up. 'Leave those. They'll still be there in the morning.'

'Yeah. I know. That's why I'm clearing them away now.'

'Jesus, will you just do as you're told! I know you think you're some strong-minded northern woman who can tackle anything, no matter what the situation, but you're wrong, okay?'

She turned to look at him, narrowing her eyes. 'I'm wrong?'

'Yeah. You're wrong. You're weak, Amber. Deal with it. And, more importantly, just let it happen. It isn't a fucking crime to show a little weakness now and again, especially when you've spent most of your life trying to portray yourself as someone who doesn't feel anything.'

'That's not what I...'

'It was. Look, what's happening to you right now, most people would expect you to feel a little bit confused, a little bit upset. What you've been told, that's big, Amber. It's life-changing.'

She felt fresh tears start to fall, and she knew that if she looked at Ronnie she was only going to start crying – really crying – all over again. And she was tired of doing that now. She'd spent the past few nights crying herself to sleep – not that she'd slept all that much. And she wanted to sleep, wanted to go some place where the pain wouldn't get to her, but she wasn't even allowed that luxury of escape.

'I just feel so empty, Ronnie.'

He reached out and took her hand, squeezing it gently as her tear-filled eyes stared into his. 'I know, sweetheart. I know. But pushing people away isn't going to help.'

'Will you stay tonight? Please. If you go and I'm on my own again I know I'm just going to be awake all night going over and over everything until it makes even less sense than it already does. And I really don't want to be alone.'

He smiled, resting his forehead against hers, stroking her cheek with his thumb. 'You want me to stay, I'll stay. But only if you promise you'll talk to me. Do we have a deal?'

She couldn't help smiling, too. 'Yeah. We have a deal.'

'Good. Okay, you head on upstairs, run yourself a bath and try and relax. I'll tidy up down here.'

She leaned forward, kissing his cheek. 'Thank you.'

'I'll bring you up that nightcap once I'm done.'

Half an hour later she eased herself out of the bath, feeling slightly more relaxed than she had done before she'd got in it. With the wonderful sound of Joe Bonamassa's rock/blues voice and incredible guitar playing having taken her to a place where she felt a touch calmer, she actually thought she might have a chance of some sleep tonight. To get more than a couple of hours in a row would be like heaven, after the past few nights.

'I brought you that drink.'

She turned round to see Ronnie, his white shirtsleeves now rolled up to his elbows, his dark hair slightly dishevelled.

'Feeling any better?' he asked as he hovered in the doorway.

Amber nodded. 'Yeah. A bit. You can come in you know.'

'I just thought you might… I thought you might be tired. I'll go get the spare room ready…'

'Ronnie, please. Just come in, will you?' She sat down on the edge of the bed, pulling her bathrobe tighter around her.

He sat down next to her, clasping his hands between his knees.

'Brandon is a really nice guy,' she began, staring straight ahead of her as she spoke. 'But sitting there tonight, talking to him, knowing who he was… it was so hard. So, so hard. None of it is his fault, all of this…' She broke off, saying nothing for a few seconds. 'He represents a lie, Ronnie. And I know that sounds like a really selfish thing to say because I've just said none of this is his fault, but, to me, when I look at him, all I see is this secret that Jim kept from me and… I don't know… it's all still so confusing.'

Ronnie reached out to take her hand and she closed her eyes as his fingers wrapped around hers.

'But he doesn't just represent a lie. He's also going to be this constant reminder of something I can't ever have, and something my husband will have forever – a son. And again, I know this sounds selfish, but I don't know if I can be around him, Ronnie. I really don't know if I can do that, and if I can't be around him, then I can't be around Jim, can I?'

'Amber...'

She shook her head, pulling her hand away from his. 'No. It's okay. I can't expect you to answer that. It's just me voicing all these mixed-up, crazy, painful thoughts that are just spinning round and round and round inside my head...' She sighed, heavy and deep, throwing her head back, pushing both hands through her hair. 'Oh Jesus, Ronnie...'

'Hey, come on. Come on. It's okay...'

'But it's not okay, is it?' She looked straight at him. 'How can it be okay? If I can't accept Brandon as Jim's son purely because it's too painful for me to... This is getting us nowhere. I don't know what I'm saying, not really. Everything's still too messed up right now.'

'You should get some sleep,' Ronnie said quietly, gently brushing her hair back off her shoulders. 'We've got a busy day tomorrow.'

She looked at him. 'I don't want to be selfish, Ronnie. I really don't want that. I just need to face up to my own reality before I can start to accept Jim's. Does that make any sense?'

He gave her a small smile. 'Yeah. I think it does.'

'It's just that... I feel like I'm so far away from accepting anything right now. And I know that I shouldn't be acting like this. I shouldn't have run away from everything by coming down here, I should have stayed in Newcastle and talked this out with Jim, but... after everything we've been through, after everything that happened between us in the past...' She looked down at her clasped hands. 'It's hard. For me to know that he kept a secret so big from me. From everyone. Why did he do that, Ronnie?' She looked at her best friend. 'Why? I just... I just don't understand.'

'Do you love him, Amber?'

She stared into his eyes, feeling something in the pit of her stomach that she couldn't explain. 'Yes, I love him. I just don't want to be with him right now. It's too hard. It's just too hard, and some people might find that difficult to understand, and that word selfish may be thrown around again, but... but I have to deal with this in my own way, I have to…'

'Amber, it's okay. You don't have to explain anything to me, all right? I understand.'

'I'm not sure I understand what I'm feeling myself, Ronnie.'

He tucked a strand of hair behind her ear, his hand lightly brushing her neck as he did so, an action that caused a strange sensation to pass through her, like a forbidden shiver, something she shouldn't be feeling, but she was.

'It *will* be okay, Amber. I promise you.'

She smiled at him. 'I believe your promises.'

He smiled, too, his hand absentmindedly resting on her bare knee. 'Then believe that this *will* all be okay. Eventually. No one expects you to have it all worked out overnight.'

'It's going to take time, I know that. So I guess I've just got to be patient.'

He was so close now that Amber could feel his breath on her cheek, his hand still resting on her knee, but she made no attempt to move it.

'There are a lot of strange feelings happening right now but… but I guess I've just got to run with them.' She looked right into his eyes, a sensation akin to a tiny electric shock shooting right across her chest, rendering her breathless for a split second. 'Haven't I?'

'Only if you feel comfortable with whatever those feelings are,' he whispered, his hand slowly sliding up her leg, underneath her robe to touch her thigh. And something inside him told him he shouldn't be doing this, that she was vulnerable and tired and not thinking straight, but she felt so warm and soft, her skin still damp from the bath she'd just had. And he couldn't pull away, couldn't stop himself.

Amber closed her eyes, knowing in the very small but still-present rational part of her brain that this was wrong. This was really wrong. But, at the same time, this was her chance for an escape, a chance to forget everything that was making her feel so confused – by embarking on something that would only serve to confuse the situation even further? Just more proof that she wasn't thinking straight.

'I should go,' Ronnie said, sensing her reluctance, and he wasn't going to push it. He cared too much about her for that. She didn't need him playing with her already messed-up emotions, that wasn't fair. 'You need to sleep.'

She said nothing as he got up off the bed, just watched as he walked towards the door, his head down. And it was only when that all-consuming feeling of emptiness washed over her once more that she stood up and ran over to him.

'Ronnie, no! Wait. Please.'

He swung round to look at her, her pretty face now devoid of those tear stains that had covered it not that long ago. She looked younger than she was, but her eyes were sad. Lost, almost, and he wasn't used to seeing her that way. It hurt him like he couldn't explain and all he wanted to do – with every inch of his being – was make everything better. He wanted to make it all better. By doing what he so badly wanted to do? Was that going to help anyone? Really?

'It's not fair, Amber.'

'On either of us – on Jim. I know. I know it isn't fair, but… Jesus, Ronnie, sometimes life isn't fucking fair, is it?'

'You're not thinking straight. It's wrong. I mean, I want to, don't get me wrong, Christ, I want to. So much you wouldn't believe…'

She slowly undid the robe she was wearing, leaving it loose but not allowing it to fall open.

He couldn't take his eyes off her. 'We're both so confused about things right now, Amber. I don't think we…' He turned his head away for a second, pushing a hand through his hair as he tried to get some sort of clarity on a situation that was fast getting out of hand. And he wasn't sure either of them had the strength to stop it.

'No. You're right,' Amber said, tying the robe back up. 'You're right.'

He watched as she walked over to the bed, and the pain he felt cut across his chest was quite shocking in its intensity. Almost as if someone was putting some kind of invisible pressure on him that he couldn't stop. Yes, he was right. Of course he was right. But sometimes, just sometimes he wanted to be wrong, and fuck the consequences.

She still had her back to him, busying herself folding up the towel she'd had wrapped around her wet hair, and he just stood and watched her for a few seconds, waiting to see if she would turn around and tell him she was ready to make the mistake he so badly wanted to make with her. A big, beautiful, heart-wrenching mistake. But she stayed facing away from him. Because she knew that if she turned around she'd have no choice?

Looking briefly up at the ceiling, letting out a deep but quiet sigh, he walked slowly over to her until he was right behind her, reaching out to gently push her damp hair away from the back of her neck, kissing it lightly.

'Don't turn around,' he whispered. Was this the coward's way of making his move? If she didn't look at him, if he couldn't see her face, would it mean he felt less guilty?

He could hear her breathing begin to speed up, become more shallow, and he ached to feel her skin beneath his fingers. He ached to touch her, to see her naked, to make love to her. It was like a million pent-up feelings had come rushing to the surface after years of being pushed down and ignored. Even though they'd always been there. So, was opening this Pandora's Box really a fair thing to be doing? To her? But especially to himself? When he knew she'd never leave Jim, she'd never do that. So could he cope with just being her escape? If that's what she really wanted?

Amber closed her eyes as his lips brushed the back of her neck, sending tiny little tingles up her spine that made her physically shiver. It felt like hundreds of invisible fingers were running up and down her back, and she couldn't stop a small groan from escaping, it felt so good.

It was as if she was working on autopilot now as she untied the robe again, this time letting it fall open, keeping her eyes closed as she felt him slowly pull it back off her shoulders, letting it slip to the floor. She kicked it away, putting up no fight as he pulled her back against him, his hands resting on her hips, his mouth kissing her shoulder. It felt like the worst thing in the world she could possibly be doing, yet, at the same time, it felt like the only place in the world she wanted to be. With every touch of his lips, the pain and confusion of the past few days was being washed away, and that was a feeling she was eager to cling onto. Sweeping everything under the carpet and pretending it wasn't happening wasn't a long-term option, she knew that. But pushing it aside for a little while was.

Leaning back against him, her head resting against his shoulder, she bit down on her lip as his hands moved up her body, stroking the curve of her waist, touching her breasts, eliciting small and quiet moans from her as they worked their way back down. She was filled with something she really couldn't explain – a mixture of overwhelming guilt mixed with an impossible amount of lust. Her whole body felt on fire, burning up with all the conflicting emotion, every right and wrong feeling it was trying to fight clashing head-on in some crazy, erotic battle she couldn't control. Even though the bigger part of her wanted to. The bigger part of her still couldn't stop thinking about Jim; the love of her life, the man she would always go back to, she knew that. What had happened between them, was that really something so bad it could actually tear them apart?

She groaned quietly again as Ronnie stroked her inner thigh, his fingers deliberately staying close to but-not-quite-touching a place she now wasn't sure she wanted him to touch anymore. But hadn't they come too far to turn back now? Hadn't that line already been crossed?

'You need to get naked, too,' she said, suddenly breaking the spell that had only just started, turning round to face him, something Ronnie hadn't been expecting. What *had* he been expecting? A cold reality hit him, although it wasn't cold enough to make him want her any less. She was standing there in front of him, naked and beautiful and what was he supposed to do with that image? Go back to the spare room and wank himself to sleep? 'Because, if you don't get naked, this isn't going to work.'

He pushed a hand through his hair, unable to take his eyes off her. 'Amber, are you… Jesus, I don't think I can do this…' What was he saying? Of course he could do this. What was the matter with him?

'You don't have to do anything you don't want to,' she whispered, slowly unbuttoning his shirt, pushing it back off his shoulders until it fell to the floor, a small but sharp intake of breath escaping as she caught sight of his toned chest and stomach. He was still such an attractive man. Karen really had been a fool to let him go.

'I think you know I want to,' Ronnie said, closing his eyes for a second as she loosened his belt, sliding it off and throwing it down next to his discarded shirt. 'But what *I* want doesn't really come into it.'

She stood on tiptoe, her mouth resting on his as she spoke, a small smile playing on her lips. 'Just forget all that, and come into *me*.'

'Jesus, Amber…' Ronnie sighed, sliding a hand around her waist, pulling her against him, his erection now straining to be set free.

'It's too late to stop this now,' she said, taking a few steps back from him. 'Isn't it?'

He shook his head, his erection now verging on the painful as he watched her touch herself between her legs, a small, quick but deliberate action that told him she was right. It really was too late to stop this now. Or was it? He could just turn and walk away, go back to the spare room and give himself the relief he was going to get somehow tonight, that was the only thing he was certain of right now. That relief was coming, and he would be, too. One way or another.

'Amber, don't. Don't, please. I need to… I need to think about this. I need to…'

She looked at him for a second before opening the drawer of the sideboard beside her, pulling out a short, black negligee, slipping it on over her naked body. Not that it covered much. Ronnie could still see every inch of her through the sheer material. 'I'm going to the loo,' she said, her voice purposeful and a little cold. It was up to him to bring her back round, to see this through to the end because, whatever happened tonight, they'd crossed a line. They were over it, it had happened.

'Want me to come with you?'

She turned around and smiled at him, backing up against the wall. 'Well, that all depends, doesn't it?'

He walked over to her, sliding his hands up under the thin material that was doing little to cover up a body that Ronnie knew could, in the words of the Rolling Stones, make a dead man come. 'On what?'

'On whether we're taking this to the next level or not.'

'Is that what you want?'

She looked at him. Was it? Not forever. But she figured he already knew that. 'I don't think it matters what *I* want, Ronnie. You need to be sure…'

He shut her up with a kiss; a long, deep, languid kiss that, at first, surprised her, but then it began to fill her with a warmth and an exuding feeling of calm that she couldn't get enough of. It was exactly what she needed.

'I'm going to kiss you, okay?' Ronnie said, divesting her body of the unnecessary negligee, slipping first one thin spaghetti-strap down over her shoulder, then the other, until it fell to the floor. 'I'm probably going to kiss you for most of the night. I might even touch you, just quickly, because I need to feel you, right here…' He slid a hand between her legs, causing Amber to groan out loud as he pushed up against her and she opened her legs wider to give him more room. 'But no sex, do you understand?'

She looked into his eyes, a sharp flood of disappointment filling her as he moved his hand away. 'Why? I mean, we're just one small step away from fucking each other anyway so why stop now?'

'No sex, Amber. I just want it to be that way. For now.'

She smiled, sliding a hand round the back of his neck, pulling him down closer so her mouth was almost resting on his. 'For now?'

'For now,' he whispered. 'I know it's stupid, and probably pointless seeing as I've just had my hand between those incredible legs, and you are so fucking wet… Shit!' He pushed a hand through his hair, backing away, just a couple of centimetres, but he'd needed to back off, just for a second. The confusion was absolutely overwhelming. 'This is killing me…' He looked at her, moving closer again, resting his hand on her hip. 'But it just feels right. To stop it here.'

There was nothing right about this situation. Nothing at all. But somehow Amber understood his somewhat warped logic.

'Okay.' She nodded, resting the palm of her hand on his cheek. 'Okay. But… will you stay with me? Please. I want you to stay with me.'

He smiled, running his thumb lightly over her nipple, the hardening of which did nothing to abate his now-painful hard-on. 'Yeah. I'll stay with you.'

'So, what are we going to do about this, then?' She smiled back, her hand briefly resting on his erection.

'I guess I'll just have to fly solo.'

'Same here,' she whispered, her mouth touching his as she spoke. 'You don't have the monopoly on frustration.'

He kissed her gently, the feel of her naked breasts against his chest sending a million and one mixed emotions flying round his brain. 'Can I watch?'

'Oh, so that's okay then, is it? That's allowed?'

'I'm making this up as I go along, Amber. Humour me.'

'So, you want to watch me touch myself?'

'Jesus, yes, I want to watch.'

She smiled, all thoughts of Jim, Brandon, and babies she would never have suddenly disappearing from her mind, albeit for a brief amount of time, she knew that. They'd be back. But what little respite she could take she was grabbing with both hands. 'Okay. But no helping, all right? Look, but don't touch. Two can play at rule-making, Ronnie.'

Two could play at lots of things. But once the playing was over, just what would the consequences be?

<h1>Chapter Thirteen</h1>

'Sorry, you want *what*?' Jim asked, pushing his chair back slightly and staring at Ryan as though he'd just started speaking in a foreign language.

'I want to put in a loan request.'

'You want to put in a loan request,' Jim repeated, getting up and walking round the front of his desk, causing Ryan to take a couple of steps back. 'Do you want to tell me why?' He leaned back against his desk, folding his arms, not taking his eyes off his striker. 'Because I can see no reason why you would want to leave a club that has shown you the kind of support Newcastle Red Star has shown you over the past year.'

'It's personal.'

Jim laughed – a short, sharp laugh, looking briefly down at the floor before meeting Ryan's eyes again. 'It's personal. This wouldn't have anything to do with my wife now, would it?'

What was Ryan supposed to do? Deny it? Putting in a request to be voluntarily loaned out to another club meant that the reasons had to be good, and they had to be valid. And even then there was no guarantee that any request would be granted. But Ryan had to try. He had no other choice now.

'Things are complicated, boss. I'm sure you understand…'

'Oh, I understand plenty, Fisher. I understand plenty.' Jim

walked back behind his desk, but he didn't sit down. 'I understand that this club has shown you nothing but respect, despite
everything that's happened. And you want to throw that back in
its face? Back in *my* face? I put my trust in you, Ryan. I gave you
the captaincy, and I did that because I believed you could change,
that you deserved a chance to show everyone what you could do,
and as far as your football's concerned you've been worth that
risk. Although, looking at you today, I'm not sure how long that's
gonna last. You look like crap. Were you out last night?'

Ryan pushed a hand through his hair, looking away for a second.
'Yeah, but…'

'You knew it was an early morning start for training, yet you
still went out the night before.'

'I needed a bit of downtime, boss.'

'Oh, *you* needed a bit of downtime? Life a bit tough for you
right now, is it?' Jim knew he was taking his own mood out on
Ryan, which wasn't completely fair. Or professional. But then, given
their past and their shared connection to Amber, those lines were
already quite blurred.

'I just need some time away,' Ryan said, acutely aware that his
manager's mood wasn't a good one. Did that have anything to do
with the fact Amber had been down in London for most of the
week? When she hadn't really needed to be?

'Why?' Jim asked, folding his arms and staring straight at Ryan.
'Why do you need some time away? You've just had a couple of
months off, which should have been more than enough time to
take any breaks you needed, so coming to me when we've played
just one game of the new season, informing me that you're not
happy here is really crap timing. So, I'll ask you again, has this
got anything to do with my wife?'

Ryan returned his manager's stare, standing his ground. He'd
put the wheels in motion now, what was the point in lying? 'I
loved her, Jim.'

'When we're at work, Ryan, you call me boss. You got that? And

I know you loved her.' Jim didn't really want to talk about Amber, not with Ryan. He didn't like to acknowledge the fact they'd once been together. It wasn't something he'd ever really thought about. But, at the same time, he needed to know if Amber had spoken to Ryan since she'd walked out on him. And was that what she'd really done? Walked out on him? He still didn't know. He didn't know anything much, and that's what was killing him. He was in the middle of something he couldn't control, and that wasn't a situation he was familiar with.

He closed his eyes for the briefest of seconds and quickly composed himself. To show any sign of weakness – no matter how small – in front of Ryan Fisher would not be a wise move. 'I'm rejecting your request, Ryan.'

'What? Hang on, you haven't even…'

'That's the end of it, Fisher.' Jim fixed him with a look that told him he was shutting this conversation down. 'You owe this club, and whatever you're feeling, whatever you think you can't cope with, you suck it up and move on. Do you hear me? Newcastle Red Star need you and we need you at the top of your game, so you grow up and get back out on that training pitch. We'll say nothing more about this matter. Okay?'

Ryan looked at his boss, letting his words sink in. Jim's reaction wasn't exactly a surprise. He was under no illusion that this request was going to be one that was accepted easily, but it was one he was going to push for.

'I wouldn't have come to you if I didn't feel…'

'If you didn't feel what, Ryan?' Jim's eyes bored right into him, but Ryan was determined to fight for this decision. To some it might display a certain level of weakness, the fact he felt the need to run away, almost, because he couldn't bear to be around a woman he still loved too much to admit. But to him it was a necessary move he had to make. For the sake of his own sanity. For the sake of his career. 'If you didn't still feel something for Amber?' Jim's voice shook him back to reality. 'If you didn't still love my wife? Is that what this is all about? Huh? You can't bear to see her with me so you thought you'd just stick in a random loan request and take yourself out of the picture for a while? And what's that going to achieve? You think a few months away from here will change things?'

'I really need to do this, boss…'

'And I really need to have this team working at full strength, so having my star striker distracted by ridiculous ideas of being loaned out when we're fighting to regain the league title isn't something I'm going to waste my time even considering. Just because you're not adult enough to deal with a situation…'

'You have no idea how I'm feeling. No fucking idea.'

Jim leaned forward, resting his hands palm-down on his desk, his eyes still staring straight into Ryan's. He wasn't in the mood for this, not this week. He really wasn't in the mood. 'This conversation is over, Fisher. Get out of here, go on. And if I get just one whiff of your behaviour changing as a result of this meeting, there *will* be consequences. So don't think that refusing to play will get you what you want, do you hear me? I'm well aware of that tactic. I've been faced with players trying that one before and it doesn't work with me.'

'You can't just refuse me. You have to listen…'

'Oh, I think you'll find I can *just* refuse you. You've been in this game long enough to know the rules.' Jim sat back down, his body language telling Ryan, in no uncertain terms, that he was done.

'Jesus…' Ryan sighed, before reluctantly walking out. What the hell was he supposed to do now?

'You all right, mate?' Gary asked, almost bumping into Ryan as he left Jim's office.

'What are *you* doing up here?' It wasn't all that often that players ventured into the administration block, not unless they were seeing the manager or had some paperwork to sort out.

'Just needed to check something over on my new contract. You been in to see the boss?'

Ryan leaned back against the wall, throwing his head back and letting out another heavy sigh. Had he just made the biggest mistake of his life by letting Jim Allen know how he was really feeling? But what other choice did he have? Jim was his manager. Who else was he supposed to go to? 'I've asked if I can be loaned out to another club for a few months. Maybe for the rest of the season.'

Gary said nothing for a second, letting Ryan's words sink in. 'You've *what*? Why? What the fuck's happened?'

Ryan dropped his head in his hands, his fingers pressing into his forehead in an attempt to ease the tension that was slowly building up. 'What do you think, Gary?'

'I don't know… I mean… Oh, hang on. This isn't about Amber, is it? Jesus, Ryan, come on! I thought you were over her, mate. I thought you were past all that. What about Ellen?'

'What about her?'

'I thought things were good between you two?'

'They are,' he sighed, throwing his head back again. He suddenly felt as if he could just close his eyes and sleep for a week. That'd teach him to stay out late the night before an early morning training session. He'd thought he could handle it, but it didn't feel that way right now. 'Things are great. She's an incredible woman, it's just…' He looked at Gary. 'I can't get past it, Gaz. I can't get past *her*. Amber. Every time I see her I see that life we could have had, if I hadn't pissed it up the fucking wall. I remember how weak I was, how I just couldn't give her what she needed and I regret that so much. So fucking much. Because I still love her, I can't help it. And I can't cope, being here, knowing she's so close and I can't do anything about it. I blew it, and I still can't believe I did that.'

Gary reached out to gently touch his friend's arm. 'Hey, I know this has been hard for you, Ryan, but can't you see what you're doing? If you don't pull yourself together you're gonna let history repeat itself, and you really don't want to go down that road again, mate.'

'Right now, it's the only place I want to be,' Ryan said quietly, wishing he could just go home and sleep, because he hadn't managed to do much of that last night.

'You don't mean that. Come on. You went through so much and came out the other side a much stronger person – do you really want to throw all of that away because you're still fixated with some woman?'

'Amber isn't *some woman*, Gary. She was the one, I know she was.'

'You're sounding like some lovesick teenager now. Come on, get changed and get outside. Colin's got us playing practice matches this morning, so that'll blow the cobwebs away.'

Ryan just looked at Gary. 'You reckon?'

'It *will* get easier, Ryan. I'm sure it will.'

Ryan wished he could share in his friend's optimism, but he was still adamant that the only way he was going to be able to get any kind of handle on this situation was to move well away from it. Just for a while. And Jim was right, Newcastle Red Star *had* been good to him; they'd given him a second chance when other clubs may not have been quite so forgiving. So he did owe them. But he also owed himself a chance to do what he felt was right. Jim may think the conversation was over, that the matter was dealt with, but he was wrong. Ryan was nowhere near giving up. On anything.

Jim moved away from the door, having heard every word of Ryan and Gary's conversation. They really should be more careful where they had their little chats, and outside the manager's office wasn't the wisest of places, especially when that chat involved his wife.

Sitting down on the edge of his desk, he picked up the phone and punched in a number, looking at a picture of him and Amber that took pride of place on his desk as he waited for the person on the other end of the line to pick up and answer. Which they did, after half a dozen rings. 'Max, hello, it's Jim. Jim Allen.'

'Jim! How are things? You spoken to Amber lately? Any news

on her thoughts regarding the Ice Magazine shoot?'

'You'll have to speak to her about that one yourself, Max. I'm calling about Ryan.'

'Ryan?' Max's tone of voice changed immediately. 'What's up?'

'He's just been in to see me, at the training ground, looking like he spent most of last night out partying.'

'Oh, Jesus…' Max sighed. 'What's he done now?'

Jim paused for a second before answering. 'He's put in a loan request. Ryan Fisher wants to leave Newcastle Red Star.'

'We need to talk,' Ronnie said, catching Amber as she made her way to the Cloud Sports News studio. 'What happened last night… ?'

'Ronnie, I'm sorry.' She stopped walking and leaned back against the wall, clutching the pile of newspapers she was holding tight against her chest. 'I don't know what came over me, or why I acted that way. It was selfish, and it was wrong. My head's just…' She turned away from him for a second, exhaling loudly. 'No. That's no excuse, there *is* no excuse for what I did.'

'I think you'll find I played a part in it, too, kiddo.'

She looked at him. 'What did we do, Ronnie?'

He leaned against the wall beside her. 'I don't know. And that's the truth. I don't know.'

'I'm sorry… for leaving early this morning but I… I didn't know what to say to you, what to do. You're my best friend, Ronnie, and what happened last night really shouldn't have happened.'

He turned sideways so he was facing her, resting his shoulder on the wall, his hands in his pockets. 'We're both to blame. We're both going through… well, let's just say relationships aren't exactly our strong point right now, are they?'

'That's still no excuse. Look, I'm late, I've got to go.'

'Hang on, Amber!' He reached out to grab her arm, stopping her from walking away. 'We need to talk.'

'About what? If I hurt you, I'm sorry…'

'Jesus, you haven't hurt me, how could you hurt me? I just want to know you're okay, that's all.'

She looked right into his eyes, trying hard to at least make some sense of what was going on inside her head, but that was hard with the overwhelming barrage of emotions that were fighting against each other in there. 'I really need to see Jim and yet, at the same time, I don't know if I can face him. I don't even know if I want to. I just can't… I can't think straight, Ronnie. And last night was probably just some kind of knee-jerk reaction that I really should have controlled because… because it didn't help matters.'

Neither of them said anything for what felt like minutes but it was really only a second or two. 'It was a mistake.' Ronnie's voice was quiet, an almost resigned tone to it. 'Let's try and forget it happened, okay?'

She nodded, finally allowing herself a smile as she stood on tiptoe and quickly kissed his cheek. 'Thanks, Ronnie. The last thing I need is to lose you as my friend.'

'That's never gonna happen.' He smiled back. 'Go on. I'll see you later.'

She threw him one more smile and walked away, still clutching the newspapers to her chest. Had last night really been a mistake? It wasn't like she'd been drunk or anything, she'd been fully aware of everything she'd done. And there'd been plenty of chances for her to walk away, to leave it alone before it had got as far as it had.

They'd slept together, but there'd been no sex. All they'd done was hold each other. But that didn't make it okay, it didn't make her feel any less guilty, because it was a situation she should have controlled. She'd handled everything like a child rather than the grown-up she was supposed to be, but, for some reason, nothing felt right anymore. Nothing.

Her phone ringing knocked her back to reality and she stopped walking to answer it, leaning back beside the huge double doors that led into the Cloud Sports News studio. 'Amber Allen.'

'This can't go on, Amber.'

She closed her eyes, the sound of his voice both calming her and making her feel incredibly sad, all at the same time. 'I know,' she whispered.

'I never promised you our life would be perfect…'

'You never promised me anything, Jim.'

'Because you won't let me.'

She opened her eyes and stared up at the ceiling, the noise coming from inside the studio telling her that this really wasn't the time or the place to be having this conversation. 'I'm sorry.' Her voice was quiet, waves of guilt washing over her as she remembered last night, remembered Ronnie touching her, kissing her, and more waves of guilt hit as she felt her stomach flip involuntarily. For what reason? Because she was talking to the one man who would always be there in her life, whether she liked it or not? Or because of what had happened last night?

'You have got nothing to be sorry for, baby. Nothing.'

Hadn't she? How had her life got so complicated all of a sudden?

'I just needed to hear your voice, Amber. I miss you.'

She felt tears start to prick the back of her eyes, which was the last thing she needed. She had work to do, a long day ahead, and she didn't want to be falling apart in front of her colleagues. She wasn't some weak, needy woman, she was Amber Sullivan – strong, feisty and ambitious. Except, she wasn't, was she? Not anymore. Now she was Amber Allen – weak, tired, and confused. And she couldn't allow that person to take over.

Taking a deep breath, she closed her eyes again as she composed herself, willing the woman she'd used to be back to the surface. Because she needed her now more than ever.

'I've got to go, Jim. I'm really busy…'

'Did you know Ryan Fisher's put in a loan request?'

That almost stopped her in her tracks and her eyes sprang open, her heart starting to beat faster all of a sudden. 'Why would I know anything about that?'

'I dunno. You tell me.'

She walked away from the studio doors, sensing the change in his tone. 'Are you accusing me of something here, Jim?'

'Like I said, I don't know, Amber. All I know is that you upped and left without us having any time to talk about things – things we really need to talk about – and the next thing I know I've got your ex walking into my office asking for a loan request because he claims he's still in love with you.'

'What?' She stopped walking, sitting down on a sofa in a quiet alcove. Her head was starting to spin. What the hell was going on now? 'I… Did he actually say that? Or are you just assuming… are you…? I mean, there could be other reasons why…'

'Oh, come on, Amber. What other reasons could there possibly be? You know as well as I do how he still feels about you. Have you seen him lately?'

'Of course I haven't. Why would I have seen him?'

'You're down there, miles away from me, and for all I know he could have…'

'Could have what, Jim? What could he have done?'

There was silence for a few seconds as any sign of those tears that had been threatening before disappeared, to be replaced by something very close to anger.

'Has he been to see you? In London?'

'You're just being ridiculous now. When has he had time to come and see me? You've got them training all hours of the day…'

'He's had plenty of time, Amber.'

She said nothing, just let his words and his accusations sink in. In one breath he was telling her he missed her, and in the next he was accusing her of seeing Ryan behind his back. How wrong could he be? She felt another wave of guilt wash back over her as memories of Ronnie's fingers stroking her skin, his lips on the back of her neck, flooded her brain. None of this was right. None of it. It was so fucked-up it was unbelievable.

'I don't believe you,' she hissed, hanging up on him before he had a chance to say anything else. Is that what he really thought she was doing while she was down here? That she was seeing Ryan behind his back? That he could think she'd even contemplate going back there again made her feel both sick and sad. If Ryan Fisher really did want to leave Newcastle Red Star then it wasn't her fault. She didn't know he still felt that way about her. Did she?

Picking up her phone again, she scrolled down her contact list and pressed dial, sitting back against the sofa cushions as she waited for the recipient of her call to answer.

'Hey, Amber. Have you heard about Ryan?'

'I'm not here to talk about Ryan, Max.'

'But you've heard, haven't you?'

'Yes,' she sighed. 'I've heard. Look, do you want to hear what I've got to say or not?'

'Fire away. I'm all ears.'

'The Ice Magazine shoot – I'll do it.'

Jim threw the phone down and dropped his head into his hands. Why the hell had he done that? He'd all but accused her of seeing Ryan behind his back when that was probably the last thing she'd been doing. And he was almost certain Ryan hadn't left the North East all week. Taking his own frustrations out on those closest to him wasn't a personality trait Jim was proud of, but right now it was coming to the fore much more than he was comfortable with.

He needed Amber back home. He needed to see her, to talk to her, to tell her that everything was going to be okay. He'd make sure of that. He just had no idea how right now. But knowing Ryan Fisher still felt that way about his wife – well, it had hit a nerve.

Pushing both hands through his hair, he sat back in his chair, letting out a heavy sigh as he stared up at the ceiling. Maybe moving Ryan Fisher out of the picture for a while wasn't such a bad idea, although it was an idea he was going to have to be able to sell pretty hard if the club were going to go for it. But if it meant one less problem in his life, he was willing to put his job on the line to give Ryan what he wanted. Because the one thing he wasn't willing to lose was Amber.

Chapter Fourteen

'You know, I'm your agent for a reason,' Max said, watching Ryan as he paced up and down the floor of his riverside apartment, hands stuffed deep in the pockets of his battered jeans. 'And that means you're supposed to come to me before you make any stupid, rash decisions. It's my job to nip them in the bud before they get out of hand.'

Ryan stopped pacing and looked at Max. 'I'm serious, Max. That wasn't some idle threat I made last week, I didn't just go in there to make some kind of statement. I want to be loaned out. I need to get away, just for a bit.'

'Really?' Max raised an eyebrow, watching Ryan's expression. Not a glimmer of anything. What was up with this kid? Usually he could read him like a book but lately it would seem the pages weren't giving all that much away.

'Really. I can't hack it here anymore, Max.'

'Of course you can. Look at what you faced last year, and you came through all of that.'

'That was different.'

'Was it? That was a damn sight harder than anything you're professing to be unable to face now, son. This is nothing. You just need to pull yourself together, concentrate on your football and put women to the back of your mind. I'll get in touch with Jim

209

and tell him you didn't mean what you said. I'll tell him you had a small crisis of confidence or something…'

'But I *did* mean it, Max. I meant every word. I want out. Just give me the rest of the season away from here, and I'll be fine.'

'You think? You think that'll solve anything, do you? A bit of time away from her will change everything?'

'Yes.'

'Then you need to grow up. I'll be telling Jim to forget any more loan requests you might continue to throw at him, because you aren't going anywhere, Ryan. You're going to stay here and learn how to face up to things like an adult. Jesus, we're talking about a woman, for Christ's sake! Just move on, forget about her.'

'How can I do that when she's fucking everywhere, Max? How can I do that?'

'By realising what's important in your life. And right now your job is the most important thing. Remember that, and make sure you *keep* remembering that, because carry on the way you are right now and you won't fucking have one. I know Jim Allen, I know how powerful he can be in the football world, and you really, really don't want to piss him off. He could end your career like that, Ryan. Just like that. So be very careful.'

'He can't threaten me, Max. He has to work within the rules…'

'Jesus, Ryan, how long have you been doing this? What rules? People make their own rules, they find ways to make them look legitimate, and no matter how great a player you are, no matter how much fucking money you earn, you will not win against a man like Jim Allen.'

'A man who didn't even know his own son was signing to a club just nine miles down the road from his own? He's *that* powerful, is he?'

'Oh, he knew Brandon was coming, Ryan, believe me. He knew.'

'So why…?'

'Not your business.'

Ryan narrowed his eyes as he stared at his agent. 'Do you…?'

'Be careful, Ryan. That's all I'm saying.'

'I want out, Max. You're the best agent there is, so if anyone can help me…'

'You're going nowhere. I'll go and see Jim, sort this mess out, and you – you can start dealing with things like a grown-up. You can't afford to mess things up a third time, Ryan. You've had your second chance. There's no extra time left on the clock now, kiddo.'

'I'm not interrupting anything, am I?'

Jim looked up from his laptop, and just the sight of her, standing there, it took his breath away. It had been a week since he'd last seen her, a week since she'd walked out on him, and to see her there in front of him, he hardly dared believe she was back.

'I thought you were mad at me. I mean, the last time we spoke you seemed… Look, I'm sorry. What I said about Ryan, what I insinuated…'

She shrugged, throwing her bag down on the sofa next to his office door. 'It doesn't matter. Not right now, anyway.'

He frowned slightly, watching as she started to untie the thin, wrap-over coat she was wearing. 'Not right now…?'

'I'm still mad at you, Jim. I'm still confused and I'm still angry; a week away hasn't eased much of that, believe me. But, right now…' She finally opened her coat, letting it drop to the floor, and as Jim watched it fall his stomach dipped so low it felt as though it was on some kind of crazy rollercoaster ride. She was naked – completely and totally naked – except for a pair of knee-high, spike-heeled boots. 'I just really need you to fuck me.'

He stood up, not taking his eyes off her, rubbing a hand along the back of his neck as he walked over to her. 'Jesus, Amber. You sure know how to make an entrance, honey.'

'Being mad at you became something of a turn-on,' she whispered, her eyes locking with his as he finally reached her. 'It was all I could think of, on the flight home. Seeing you, wanting you… And I know we should be sitting down and talking, I know that.

But talking is probably going to mean we end up fighting and I don't want that. Right now, I just want you to fuck me.'

'You're not giving me much of a choice, are you?'

She smiled, reaching out to touch his mouth, her fingers trailing along the stubble on his chin. 'Everyone's busy outside. Colin's got training well under control, and I've told your secretary you're not to be disturbed while I'm here, because I think you deserve something special after taking Newcastle Red Star to the top of the league table over the weekend. You've done very well, Mr. Allen. Very, very well. You should be congratulated.'

'Amber…'

'No. No talking. Like I said, talking is only going to end up in a fight, believe me.'

'You're still that mad at me, huh?'

'Oh yes.'

He threw his head back, groaning slightly as she reached down to touch his growing erection, her hand already closing in around him.

'So enjoy yourself while you can, before I start yelling at you.'

'You're gonna yell at me?'

'More than likely.' She smiled, pressing her body against his, feeling his hard-on digging into her hip, his hand now resting in the small of her back. 'But I can't yell at you if you're kissing me, can I?'

'No. No, you can't.'

She closed her eyes as his mouth finally lowered down onto hers, the taste of him overwhelming her. Because, despite everything, she'd missed him. So much. But at the same time she knew she couldn't just let things go back to normal – how *could* they be normal? She was still dealing with his secret son and the revelation that she would probably never have children of her own. All of that meant things couldn't be normal, not yet, anyway.

'I need you inside me,' she whispered. 'Now.'

'Can't I just look at you first, baby? I feel as though you've been away from me for so long and I…'

In one swift movement she'd pushed him down onto the sofa, climbing astride him like the woman on a mission she was.

'You're not hanging about, are you?' He grinned, slightly taken aback by her behaviour, but he wasn't going to put up a fight. Not when he needed her so badly.

'I'm too turned on to hang about, Jim.'

'Yeah.' His eyes looked down to where she was straddling him, his hand automatically reaching out to touch her. She was so wet it almost made him come there and then. 'I can see that.'

'So make use of it,' she whispered, throwing him a smile before leaning over to kiss him, deep and slow, positioning herself over him so he slid effortlessly inside her. 'It's just like old times, isn't it?' She smiled again, alluding to the many encounters they'd shared in his offices at both Tynebridge and here at the training ground. The times they'd had sex on his desk, or when he'd pushed her up against the door to stop anyone from coming in while he fucked her hard and fast. Those spontaneous, sexually-charged encounters that had made her realise she could never leave this man alone.

'Oh, baby…' he groaned, pushing her down onto him, his hands firmly on her hips, keeping her in place because she was so wet he felt as though he was going to slip out at any given second. And he wasn't ready to do that just yet. But it didn't take long for the endgame to arrive, a crashing conclusion that she helped herself reach by touching herself, which only served to drive him even more crazy. Watching her fingers bring herself to climax was almost hypnotic, and he couldn't take his eyes off her as she arched her back, pushing her breasts out, crying out loud as he came first, so fast it made his head spin, but he was unable to slow down an action that seemed to drain him of anything he had left to give – both in the physical and emotional sense.

'That…' Amber smiled, leaning forward, her hands on his chest, '… was good. That was very, *very* good.'

'Glad to have been of service,' Jim breathed, his heart beating so fast he thought he might pass out. When he'd got up this morning and headed over to the training ground, he certainly hadn't expected this to be part of his schedule.

She climbed off him, and still he kept his eyes on her, watching as she leaned over to retrieve her bag from the sofa beside him. She was totally unashamed of her body, and he could see why. Over the past few months she'd toned up, her waist had become smaller, her thighs harder, but she still had those ridiculously sexy rounded hips, and breasts he could happily stare at forever.

'Have you been home yet?' he asked, sitting up, his heart finally beginning to slow down a touch.

'I dropped my case off, got changed…' She looked at him and he had to smile, pushing a hand through his hair, '… then I came straight here.'

He felt almost disappointed as she began pulling clothes from her bag, slipping a short black dress on over her naked body, shaking out her hair, something he found incredibly sexy to watch. He found *her* incredibly sexy. His beautiful, beautiful wife.

'Well, I'm glad you did. Amber…'

She pulled her hair back into a high ponytail. 'We'll talk later. Back at home. Okay?'

He frowned, standing up and walking over to her. He was still reeling from what had just happened, yet she seemed to have turned the temperature from hot to decidedly cool.

'You're leaving?'

'You've got work to do.'

'I haven't seen you for almost seven days, Amber. I mean, come on, honey, do you actually remember what happened this time last week?'

She stared at him, right into those green eyes of his. Eyes she wasn't entirely sure she trusted anymore. If she ever had done. 'I can't believe you even thought about asking that question, Jim.'

'Jesus… Amber! Baby, come on…'

But she was out of the room before he had a chance to say

anything else, striding through the outer office that led off from Jim's, aware that his secretary was watching her – trying to put two and two together, probably. Once word of their relationship had hit the headlines a few months ago it had become common knowledge that they'd shared more than just coffees and cosy chats behind the closed doors of his offices, so it was only natural that people would assume something which was, in all honesty, more than likely pretty close to the truth. And she *had* told her not to disturb Jim while she was in there with him. What were people *supposed* to think?

'Amber! You're home I see.'

Amber looked up as Max Mandell held the door of the training ground administration block open for her. 'Your powers of perception are quite remarkable, Max.'

'And I see sarcasm is something you still do very well. You been to see Jim?'

'You could say that. What are *you* here for? Something up with Ryan?'

'You know very well there's something up with Ryan. The kid's behaving like an idiot. Can you go and tell him, Amber? Please?'

'Tell him what?'

'That you're never going back to him.'

'And you think that'll help, do you?'

'It can't hurt.'

'I think it's best I just avoid him as much as I possibly can, don't you? He knows the score, he knows what we had is over, so… Why am I even having this discussion? I've got more than enough to worry about without having Ryan Fisher on my conscience, too.'

Max stayed silent for a second or two, sticking his hands in his pockets as he stared down at the ground. 'Amber, I'm sorry.'

'About what?' She really wanted to leave now. She just wanted to go home, sink into a hot bath and forget about anything and everything until Jim got home. Then maybe they could begin to start working this whole mess out.

He looked at her, his expression one of genuine concern. 'About… well, you not… not…'

'So I'll never be a mum.' She shrugged, sliding her bag back up onto her shoulder. 'It just means I can use this body for other things, doesn't it? Oh, talking of which, the shoot for Ice Magazine is confirmed now. And they're coming up to Newcastle to do it. They've just got the go-ahead this morning to shoot the pictures in Tynebridge.'

'Does Jim know? That you're doing the shoot, I mean?'

She shrugged again. 'No idea. *I* haven't told him yet, but it's more than likely word might get out about the pictures being shot in the stadium, now it's official. They also said something about maybe getting Jim in on one or two of the pictures…'

'Whoa, I hadn't thought of that angle. What a great idea! Do you think he'll go for it?'

'I'll try putting it to him after we have the conversation about the son he kept secret from me for twenty years and our childless marriage, shall I?'

Max looked at her, aware this was a subject he should handle with care. She was doing the shoot, and that was a step in the right direction as far as he was concerned.

She turned away for a brief second, looking over at the training pitch where Ryan and the other Red Star players were busy doing laps. 'So, *are* you here because of Ryan?'

'I'm here to tell Jim to ignore any loan request that idiot may have put forward.'

'He's serious, then?'

'Of course he's not serious. He doesn't know what he's doing, he's just being childish. He can't have what he wants so he decides the only other course of action is to throw his toys out of the pram. Typical footballer behaviour.'

Amber raised her eyebrows as she looked at Max. '*I* think he's serious.'

Max fixed her with a questioning look. 'You do?'

'I know Ryan. I got close to him, Max. Remember?'

'Yeah, well, serious or not, it isn't happening. He's going nowhere. Besides, Red Star aren't going to let him go, not when they're chasing a second league title, European glory *and* the FA Cup. What club in their position would let a striker of Ryan's ability go elsewhere? He's an idiot, and an extremely naive idiot at that, to even think this was going to happen.'

'Are you going to spend the rest of your life sorting his out?' Amber asked, quickly checking her watch.

'Probably,' Max sighed. 'You off home?'

She nodded. 'It's been a tough few days. I think I deserve an hour in the bath and an afternoon in front of daytime TV, don't you?'

'Amber, listen. Cloud Sports – they're unbelievably happy with you, they want you to know that. Ratings for their shows are up, and that episode of *Scoreline* you did with Brandon Palmer had a record amount of viewers. There's even a rumour going round that subscriptions to the Cloud Sports channels are up since you joined the team. And you were brilliant over the weekend, kiddo. Especially considering the amount of crap you've had on your mind.'

She looked down at the ground before turning her attention back to the training pitch, watching as Ryan dribbled a ball past half a dozen other players, finally slamming it into the back of the net before punching the air and shouting out loud. 'Well, you'd be surprised how much work takes your mind off things.' She smiled at Max, a smile she wasn't entirely sure had reached her eyes. 'And I had Ronnie there for support, didn't I?'

'You sure you're okay?' Max asked. He cared a lot about this woman. She'd been – and still was, whether she knew it or not – a big part of Ryan's life, and Ryan was like a son to him. Which was why he needed to make sure he didn't do anything stupid. That neither of them did anything stupid.

'I'm fine, Max. I'm just tired. I'll talk to you later.'

'Yeah, sure. Later.'

He watched her walk off in the direction of the car park, an air of something he couldn't quite put his finger on surrounding her. Whatever it was, he just hoped everything turned out okay for her, because she was a talent that was only going to get bigger, and he'd discovered her. How bloody good was he?

Walking inside the administration block, he smiled at the receptionist, throwing her a wink as he sauntered past the front desk to the elevator. He just had this little matter of Ryan's loan request to sort out then he could go and meet another potential new client for lunch. Max Mandell's star was still rising, mainly because nobody could do it like him. Nobody.

Ryan stopped what he was doing and turned to see what had grabbed the attention of most of his teammates. It was the wolf-whistles that had distracted him, meaning it was probably the arrival of one of the more celebrated WAGs turning up unannounced that had caused this sudden rush of schoolboy behaviour. But then, some of the lads *were* attached to women that positively courted this kind of reaction.

Stopping the ball with the heel of his boot, he stood on it to keep it still, turning to see just which WAG it was that had stopped training in its tracks. And his stomach dropped the second he saw her. In a short black dress and knee-high boots, her long, dark red hair tied back in a high ponytail, she looked incredible. There'd once been a time when she'd come here to the training ground to see him, and he couldn't help remembering the heart-stopping sex they'd had in the showers of the dressing room, or the way she'd stood on the touchline, watching him train, promising him so much with just one look. No matter how hard he tried to push all those thoughts away, they were going nowhere, because he knew why she'd been there this morning. And it had nothing to do with him. She'd been there to see Jim. And considering they'd been apart for almost a week it seemed highly unlikely she'd just popped in to say hello. He'd caught them once, over at Tynebridge, having sex in the boss's office – had she come to see her husband for a repeat performance?

'When did she get so frigging sexy?' Gary whistled, his hands on his hips as he stood watching Amber disappear into the car park.

'When she married the boss,' Ryan replied, kicking the ball he'd had underneath his foot so hard it almost reached the other end of the pitch.

Gary turned to look at him. 'Like I said, mate, you need to reel that in, get it under control. Yeah, she's hot, but she's not yours anymore. She is well and truly off-limits now.'

'You know, it's a good job you're here to remind me of that fact, Gaz. I'd hate to think I'd ever forget it.'

'Okay, okay. Chill out. Come on, let's get back to the game otherwise we'll have Colin on our backs, and that's the last thing I want today. I've got enough to deal with thanks to Debbie's obsession with redecorating the house from top to bottom. I can't move for frigging wallpaper samples and colour charts. I've got no idea what's wrong with her at the minute, but it's doing my head in.'

Ryan retrieved another ball from a net on the touchline. 'Yeah, but it's not like you've got to go home and get the paintbrush out. She'll get a man in, won't she?'

'I have no doubt she'll be getting several men in, and I suspect more than one of them will be wielding more than a fucking paintbrush in her direction.'

'And you're all right with that, are you?'

Gary folded his arms as he fixed Ryan with a look. 'As long as it means I don't have to get involved in what colour the bloody kitchen ends up, I'm fine with it, mate. Gives me more time to please meself.'

'Fisher! Blandford! Less frigging chat and more football, you got that?' Colin Bailey yelled over. Gary held a hand up in reply and nodded at their coach, running backwards, away from Ryan.

'Come on, let's move it before he starts getting agitated.' Gary indicated with his head to where Colin was standing watching them, arms folded, a stern expression on his face, and Ryan couldn't help but laugh. Once training was over he'd give Ellen a call, see if she was free, although he had no doubt she would be. He only had to click his fingers and she'd be there, ready to give him whatever he needed. Yeah, when all was said and done he may not have the woman he really wanted, but he had one that would certainly do for now.

'If he wants to go, I'll try my best to sort it out for him.'

Max looked at Jim, trying to take in just what he was telling him. 'Hang on… are you saying you'll *accept* Ryan's request to be loaned out? Only Ryan told me you'd rejected it. Which is what you *should* do.'

Jim looked up from his laptop, staring at Max as though he'd just asked the most ridiculous question possible. 'Well, I've been thinking. And if that's what he wants, then maybe it's for the best.'

'No.' Max shook his head. 'No, this isn't happening. Forget he even asked, Jim, come on. There's no way the board of directors will go for it anyway. Your season can't survive without him.'

'One man doesn't make a team, Max. You should know that.'

'Jim, most of the players on my frigging books think their teams would fall apart without them. I'm surprised half of them can get through the door, the size of their egos. And like I said, the board of directors here at Red Star aren't going to let you loan Ryan Fisher out, are they? Not without a damn good reason.'

Jim looked at Max again, his expression oozing cool. 'I consider one of my players still being in love with my wife a damn good reason. Don't you?' He turned his attention back to his laptop. 'However, I want Fisher's reasons for needing a break from Red Star brought out into the open less than anyone around here, so this won't be happening immediately, even though, technically, we still have a few days of the August transfer window left. If he wants to join another club that badly he can wait until I've worked out a way to make it happen. I need to talk to a few people first, see if it's possible, because I'm assuming – if he really is serious about this – that he doesn't have the patience to wait until the January transfer window opens.'

Max sat down on the arm of the sofa opposite Jim's desk, folding his arms. 'How the hell are you going to get everyone here to agree to this? Providing it all goes ahead, which it isn't going to, because I'm going to do all I can to make sure of that.'

'They listen to me,' Jim said, ignoring Max's comments. 'Persuading them to lose Fisher for a few months will be easy.'

'Oh, you think so, do you?'

Jim looked up, staring right at Max with an expression of determination Max wasn't sure he'd ever seen before. On anyone. 'I know so. Look, Max, you know as well as I do that the August transfer deadline means nothing, not really. I could still make sure he leaves this club within a matter of days, at any point in time. If I wanted to.'

'But you don't want to.'

'No. Not yet. And anyway, it isn't a matter of what *I* want, is it?' He fixed Max with another look. 'It all depends on Ryan.'

'Jim, come on. The kid hasn't got a clue what he's doing. We don't even know if there's a club out there interested in him…'

Jim just looked at Max, raising an eyebrow.

Max stood up, walking towards the door. 'Unless he comes to you again, Jim, can we consider this something that we're talking about on a purely hypothetical basis?'

'If that's what you want.'

'It's what I want. I'm his agent, and it's my job to make sure he doesn't piss his career away by making stupid decisions.'

'Then we'll say no more about it.'

'Okay. Good. I'll talk to you soon.'

Jim didn't even look up as Max left his office, closing the door behind him. So Max wanted to make sure Ryan didn't put his career in jeopardy with stupid decisions. Fair enough. He was Ryan's agent, that was his job. But the thing was, what may have started out as a stupid decision, even in Jim's eyes, now really didn't seem all that stupid anymore.

Amber ran down the stairs, tying her bathrobe tight around her, her damp hair flying out behind her.

Flinging the front door open, forgetting for a second that she'd literally just climbed out of the bath and probably wasn't looking her best, she smiled at the person standing on her doorstep, relieved that it wasn't a total stranger there in front of her.

'You should have called, Ronnie. I was in the bath.'

'I wanted to surprise you.' He grinned, holding up a bottle of sparkling wine.

'Yeah, well, you've certainly done that.'

'You gonna let me in or what?'

She stood aside to let him through into the hall, closing the door behind her and following him into the living room. 'You've only brought one bottle?'

He turned to look at her, still grinning. 'Well, I assumed you'd have at least one more in the house. Am I right?'

'Of course you're right. What kind of person do you think I am?' she laughed. 'Give me five minutes, okay? I'll just go throw some clothes on.'

She ran upstairs, ridiculously happy to see him, despite the fact she'd only left him at Newcastle Airport a few hours ago. It was just nice to have some company. Jim had called to say he was going to be late home due to a meeting with the club's sponsors, and she hadn't really been looking forward to spending yet more hours alone, dwelling on what she was going to say to him once he did get home. Ronnie would be a nice distraction. And a couple of drinks wouldn't hurt. A bit of Dutch courage was never a bad thing.

Slipping on denim shorts and a sleeveless white t-shirt, she ran back downstairs to find Ronnie already settled on the sofa, two glasses of wine poured and waiting on the table.

'I could get used to this, being waited on hand and foot.' She smiled, sitting down next to him, curling her legs up underneath her before reaching for her glass of wine.

'Well, just to let you know, I don't do washing up.'

'Neither do I. That's what dishwashers are for.'

'When's Jim gonna be home?'

'Not until this evening now. He's got a meeting with the club's sponsors and after that he has to take a couple of them out for drinks, so it could be a late one, on a day when I really needed him to be home, too.'

'You haven't had a chance to talk to him yet, then?'

'Well, I went to see him this morning at the training ground, but I guess turning up wearing nothing but a raincoat and high-heeled boots and then ordering him to have sex with me meant we didn't really get round to doing much talking.'

'Jesus, Amber,' Ronnie spluttered, almost choking on his drink. 'Are you kidding me? You really turned up at the training ground naked? Except for your *coat*?'

She shrugged, taking another gulp of wine. Not very ladylike, but she wasn't exactly feeling very ladylike right now. 'A bit clichéd, I know, but I wanted to give him no choice other than to fuck me, so what else was I supposed to do?'

'I'm assuming he took you up on the offer,' Ronnie said, feeling a stab of something he could only describe as envy pierce his heart. It was a strange feeling, but not a completely unfamiliar one. He was learning to control it better, that was all. It just wasn't always that easy.

'Of course he did.' Amber smiled, refilling her already-empty glass. 'All I had to do was open my legs and he was putty in my hands. Well, actually, he was anything *but* putty, in fact, he was rock hard within seconds of me dropping the coat... Oh, sorry, Ronnie, you really didn't need to know all of that.'

He looked at her. She seemed different. It was like she was changing every time he saw her, letting every little thing that was going on in her life affect her in ways he was finding hard to understand. Was this her way of coping? Bringing the barriers back up and turning herself into somebody she'd never really been before?

'Are you okay, Amber? I mean, with everything that's going on…'

'I'm fine. Honestly, I'm good. It's pointless dwelling on things you can't change, isn't it? So, I might as well focus my attention elsewhere.'

'And by that you mean…?'

'Well, Max seems to think I should be turning myself into some kind of celebrity, now I'm on a major satellite TV channel, so where's the harm in seeing where that leads?'

'You know where it leads, Amber.'

'It didn't do *you* any harm.'

'I wasn't using it as a distraction from my problems.'

'That's not what I'm doing, Ronnie.'

He raised a cynical eyebrow. 'Oh, Really?'

She took another sip of wine, looking at him over the rim of her glass. 'Really. Look, my life's changed so much in such a short space of time, and yes, okay, some of those changes have been hard to get my head around…'

'Because you haven't given yourself any bloody time to… to deal with stuff…'

'I don't need any more time, Ronnie. When Jim gets home, I'll get everything I'm feeling off my chest, we'll probably argue, it may get quite heated, but once that's out of the way we can move on, can't we? Because that's what we need to do now. We need to move on.'

'So you've accepted the fact he lied to you about Brandon?'

'I didn't say I'd accepted anything. I just don't want to waste any more time dwelling on things I can't change, things that are out of my control. Like I said before, it's pointless. I'm going to get that other bottle of wine.'

Ronnie watched her leave the room, throwing his head back

against the cushions of the sofa, sighing heavily. He wasn't altogether sure that his being there was such a good idea, given the confusion flying round inside his head right now. More than anything he wanted her to be happy, and given the events of the past week he wasn't entirely sure that she was, despite what she told him. He knew she was only trying to tell him what she thought he wanted to hear, but what he really wanted to hear was something in her voice that told him she was being completely honest with him. And with herself.

'Here we go,' she said, throwing herself back down on the sofa beside him. 'More wine. I knew we had a bottle lying around somewhere.'

'Amber...'

'No, Ronnie. I'm not getting into anything deep and meaningful, all right?'

'You know what, Amber? You've spent your whole frigging life sweeping your feelings under the carpet; you pretend they're not happening, and I really don't think that's the way to handle things anymore. Do you?'

'No. And I've told you, when Jim gets home I'll talk to him.'

'Does he make you happy?' Ronnie could have kicked himself. He really hadn't intended to say that out loud, it was just a thought that had been going round and round inside his head for a while now, and somehow it had just slipped out.

Amber looked at him. 'I'm always going to be in love with him, Ronnie. You know that.'

'That isn't what I asked.'

'It's what I'm telling you.'

She turned her head away from him, staring out of the window.

'What happened in London, Amber. Between us...'

'Nothing happened, Ronnie. We've been over this.'

'But we haven't, have we? Not really. And something *did* happen. Just because we didn't have sex that doesn't mean...'

She climbed off the sofa again. 'Do you fancy something to

eat? There's got to be stuff in the cupboards I can make use of.'

'Amber…'

He watched her walk out of the room again, but this time he got up and followed her into the kitchen. 'I'm not hungry, Amber.'

She stopped what she was doing, closing the cupboard door she'd yanked open, almost pulling it off its hinges in the process. 'No. Neither am I.' She kept her back to him, looking down at her hands gripping the edge of the countertop in front of her, the sun glinting off her wedding ring, causing her to blink a couple of times as the glare hit her eyes. 'Is something happening here, Ronnie?'

He said nothing for a second, keeping his hands in his pockets, despite every inch of his being crying out to touch her. 'I don't know.'

'Maybe you should go.'

'Is that what you want?'

She closed her eyes, exhaling loudly before she finally turned around. 'I think we both need another drink.'

He looked at her, right at her. Her face was devoid of make-up, which only made her seem more vulnerable, somehow. There was no mask to hide behind. 'Is that a good idea?'

'I can't think of a better one, can you?'

He walked over to her, stopping just in front of her, reaching out to push a strand of damp hair from her shoulder. 'I want to break so many rules here, Amber, you have no idea. Mainly because I don't think Jim Allen is good for you, but it isn't my place to say that, really, is it?'

'You just have.'

'Then I guess I've already broken rule number one.'

'You've got a list?'

'As long as your arm, kiddo.'

She looked up into his eyes, not really knowing what she was feeling. She'd known this man for so long – briefly as a lover, but mainly as her friend – and she didn't want to lose the closeness they'd built up over the years. The thought of him not being around anymore scared her more than anything right now, because she needed him.

'We've already crossed a line,' he whispered, his fingers lightly stroking her neck, and she closed her eyes, tilting her head so it rested on his hand, enjoying the feeling of calm his touch was giving her. 'Maybe it's too late to take that step back now.'

She reached up and put her hand over his, keeping her eyes closed as his fingers slipped between hers, feeling him move closer, his body almost touching hers now.

'This is wrong,' she said, finally opening her eyes and looking into his. 'This shouldn't be happening.'

'I know what I'm doing.'

'Do you? We don't know what consequences this is going to have, me and you…'

'Then walk away. I won't stop you, if that's what you want to do.'

'I don't know what I want, Ronnie.'

'Do you want to escape?'

She looked at him again, her body suddenly tingling with an anticipation she couldn't describe. Was it the danger? Was it because this whole situation was so wrong? Or was it the fact that, yes, she did want to escape. From so many things.

'I don't know…'

Her heart was beating out of her chest, her stomach tied up in so many knots she wasn't sure she'd ever lose the nervous feeling it was giving her. She loved Jim, with all of her heart she loved him. Did she trust him? Did she even *like* him right now? Those were two questions she couldn't really answer.

She closed her eyes again, the palm of his hand resting on her cheek now, his thumb running lightly over her mouth until she couldn't take it anymore. She couldn't fight the feelings that were quite obviously trying to claw their way to the surface. It was wrong, on so many levels, but he was right. They'd already crossed that line. All they were doing now was finishing the job.

'I'm still your best friend, Amber,' Ronnie whispered, his mouth almost touching hers as he spoke. 'That will never, ever change. It's just that, well, maybe I come with a few more benefits now, that's all.'

She couldn't help smiling, not even trying to stop him as he unzipped her shorts, nudging them down until they fell to the floor, and whilst half of her still didn't think she should even be contemplating doing this, the other half was too far down that wrong and dangerous road to turn back. She needed a fantasy, some kind of escape, and who better to take her there than a man she trusted beyond anyone else, even her own father. A man she cared deeply about. A man who would never hurt her.

'This is so wrong,' she moaned, her eyes still closed as his lips brushed the base of her throat, his hands pushing her t-shirt up over her breasts, exposing them, touching them, sending her heartbeat racing through the roof. 'So, so wrong.'

'Which makes it all the more exciting.' He smiled, pushing her back against the counter. 'Don't you think?'

She didn't know what to think anymore. She was about to step into a world she'd never entered before – one of deception and betrayal; a world of charged emotions and endless confusion, where friendship and sex merged together and lines were crossed, causing actions that could never be erased. She was married. She had a husband – but her husband was a man who'd deceived her, a man who'd betrayed her in the past. So was this nothing more than some kind of payback? A revenge he'd never know about? Something to make her feel better? Whatever it was, it was too late to stop it. It was way too late.

She opened her eyes and looked straight at Ronnie, all those doubts and feelings of guilt now pushed aside to be replaced by a feeling of freedom, of laid-bare lust; of escape.

'Our secret,' she whispered, pulling her t-shirt off over her head before pulling him against her by his shirt.

'Our secret,' he repeated, quickly freeing himself before lifting her up onto the countertop, her legs wrapping themselves around his hips as he pushed into her, taking her hard, almost as if he was desperate to make that move before she changed her mind. And it hurt, both physically and emotionally. But it was a beautiful pain, so different to anything she'd felt before. Another reminder of how this man could make her feel, if she let him.

Burying her face in his hair, she clung onto him tightly, wishing it wasn't going to be over with as quickly as she knew it was going to be, because she could already feel his body tensing up, his thrusts becoming harder and faster. But maybe that was for the best. Jim could still come home at any minute, for any reason, and things were complicated enough without this adding to it.

'Oh, Jesus…' she groaned as he finally exploded inside her, filling her with a warmth and a calm and feelings of guilt that she couldn't push down. It felt so beautiful, so right, but it was the wrong thing to have done. It was wrong. She might have been able to kid herself that they'd done nothing to be worried about before, but now she'd lost that luxury.

'Are you okay?' Ronnie whispered, easing himself out of her slowly before gently lifting her down from the counter.

She nodded, pulling her shorts back on, unable to meet his eyes for a few seconds. Her thighs were still tingling from where he'd been between them, her skin still sensitive to the touch, her head a mess of confusion. 'I'm fine.'

'Amber…'

His hand fell onto her hip, sliding down her still-open shorts and she closed her eyes, welcoming the kiss he gave her, not stopping him as his hand wandered round to rest on her bottom, pushing her half-naked body back against his.

In that instant she felt something hit her – like a bolt from the blue, and it did nothing to ease the confusion or the guilt or the huge, complicated mess that was about to ensue. But she wanted it. She needed him. Her best friend. He'd let her be the person she needed to be; when she was with him she'd be able to escape the confusion and the guilt and the problems she should be working through with her husband, and she would. She *would* work through them. When she was ready. But, right now, she didn't really know who she was anymore. She'd wanted to be Mrs. Jim Allen – wife, sports reporter; working mum. But she wasn't, was she? Because two out of three just wasn't cutting it when the most important piece of the puzzle would always be missing. Always.

'I really need you right now, Ronnie.' She looked up into his eyes, wishing they were back in London, alone, without any of the problems being back up north brought with it. 'But I really don't want to hurt you, and if this…'

'Sshh…' He pressed his fingers against her mouth, shaking his head. 'I know what I'm doing, Amber. I told you that.'

'I feel so guilty,' she whispered, closing her eyes as he kissed her neck, his thumb stroking her cheek. 'I shouldn't be… There's Jim, and…'

'Just promise me one thing, Amber,' Ronnie said, burying his fingers in her hair as he stared deep into her eyes. 'We don't talk about him when we're fucking, okay?'

She couldn't help smiling. 'Can you promise me one thing, too? Promise me we can have fun. Because I really need to have some fun. That's all I really want right now. Do you understand, Ronnie?'

'I can give you fun. I can give you any kind of fun you like.' He smiled, too, before bending his head to cover one of her breasts with his mouth, the feel of his tongue as it circled her nipple sending her stomach flipping over a million times as she pushed her breasts up at him, wanting him to touch her some more, needing to feel him on her – in her. She wanted this man in so many ways; all of a sudden she needed to experience things she'd never really wanted to try before, because she'd never needed to. Jim had been enough. But he wasn't what she needed right now. He wasn't. He was what she *wanted*, she couldn't deny that. Jim Allen was the only man she'd ever really been in love with, despite what she'd once thought she'd felt for Ryan. But she *needed* Ronnie. She needed this.

'You should go.' She finally found the strength to push him away, reaching down to pick her t-shirt up off the floor, pulling it down over her head, bringing to an end whatever had just happened. 'Jim could be home any minute.'

'I thought he had a meeting with the club sponsors,' Ronnie said, pushing both hands through his hair.

'He does. But that doesn't mean he couldn't come home any second. What if he's forgotten something? What if he pops home before the meeting?'

Ronnie frowned slightly, sticking his hands in his pockets. 'You trying to get rid of me? I mean, it's not unusual for Jim to come home and find me here with you, is it? I'm your friend...'

'We've just had sex, Ronnie.' She walked over to him, taking his hand and sliding it up underneath her t-shirt, placing it on her breast. 'Wonderful, incredible sex.' Her mouth was almost touching his as she spoke, her heart beating hard and fast again. How could she suddenly want to be so close to this man? So close his body was deep inside hers, and just thinking about that had started a tingle in her thighs she knew she'd have to sort out on her own once he was gone. 'Sex I want to experience again, and again.'

'Jesus-fucking-Christ, Amber...' Ronnie groaned, unable to stop his erection from returning – how could he? He had his hand on her breast, her mouth was touching his, and he knew that if he could just feel between her legs she'd still be soaking wet. And he wanted her, in ways he just couldn't explain. 'This is crazy...'

'I know. I know it's crazy, but we've started something now, haven't we? We've opened the floodgates and I can't shut them, Ronnie. Not yet. I don't want to.'

'Are you sure?' he whispered. 'Really sure? Because...'

'I'm as sure as I can be, given the circumstances.'

He took her hand, his fingers sliding between hers as their mouths touched, moving against the others in a slow, gentle rhythm, tongues touching, hearts racing. 'That'll do for me.'

'Can I see you tomorrow?'

'You've never bothered to ask permission before.' He smiled, wanting so much to pull those shorts of hers down again and spend some more time inside her. He wanted to touch her, to taste her, to do things he'd never even thought of before. Because he'd never had the chance to? Whatever the reason, he hoped he was going to have that chance now. For however long it might last.

'Well, I don't just want to come round and help you organise your DVD collection, do I?'

'So, I've lost you as my unpaid slave, is that it?'

She smiled, too, her heart still beating out of control, leaving her almost breathless. 'I can still be your slave,' she whispered. 'If you want me to be.'

'For fuck's sake, Amber… Where the hell did you learn to talk like that? I'll be lucky if this fucking hard-on goes down before bedtime.'

She smiled again, every inch of her just wanting to get naked with him and fuck to forget, because that's what she was doing – what they were *both* doing. Fucking to forget the shit that was happening in their lives. His ex-wife was having another man's baby, and she couldn't have the baby she so desperately wanted with the man she loved. It was one huge, hot mess that was only going to get bigger. *She* knew that, *he* knew that. And it didn't seem as though either of them were ready to do anything about it.

Chapter Fifteen

'Do you fancy eating out tonight?' Ellen watched Ryan as he tapped out yet another message on his mobile phone.

'Hmm? Sorry? Did you say something?' Ryan looked up, totally unaware that she'd been talking to him. He didn't even know how long she'd been there. He'd thought she was in the bath.

'I really can't be bothered to cook anything, Ryan, so are we going out to eat? Or shall I just ring for a takeaway?'

Ryan frowned slightly, turning his attention back to his phone. The way she was talking you'd think she'd moved herself in. Mind you, he was almost sure that was her intention. If she hung around long enough would he finally get the message and ask her to live with him? Is that what she was trying to do? Was she trying to wear him down? That was never going to happen. Not just yet, anyway. Who knew how he'd feel after a few months away from the North East, because, despite what Max and Jim might think, he was serious about taking a break from Newcastle Red Star. But he might as well keep his options open as far as Ellen was concerned. She'd put up with everything he'd thrown at her up to now, all he needed to do was make sure he didn't push her too far. He never knew when he might need her.

'Ryan? Are you gonna answer me?'

'Jesus, all right! Yes, okay, we'll go out. Happy now?' He threw his phone down on the sofa beside him and stood up, looking at her. 'Well? Are you coming or not?'

She stared back at him, and he immediately changed tack. He could see how upset she was and he didn't want to do that to her. She didn't deserve that. Just because *he* wasn't feeling on top of the world didn't mean he had to drag her down with him.

He sat down next to her, taking her hand, leaning forward to quickly kiss her. She didn't respond, so he tried again, kissing her a little harder and a little longer, running his fingers lightly up and down her arm until she couldn't help but smile at him. 'I'm sorry, babe. Okay? I'm just a bit… a bit stressed, that's all.'

'Anything I can help with?' she asked, running her fingers through his unruly dark hair.

'Oh, I'm sure you can help with plenty, gorgeous. But I thought you were hungry.'

'I can wait.' She smiled, starting to unfasten the belt on his jeans, sliding it off and throwing it down on the floor. 'Why don't we get the starters out of the way first, huh?'

He grinned, all thoughts of Amber, Max, and his surprise loan request suddenly fading into the background. He really should start treating Ellen a lot better, considering how good she was for him. Without her, he'd have gone crazy these past couple of months. 'Ellen…'

'Yes?'

Maybe he hadn't been able to put everything to the back of his mind quite as easily as he'd thought he had, because now he had a ridiculous urge to tell her everything. 'Nothing. It doesn't matter,' he said, shaking his head, pulling himself back from the brink of involving her in something she didn't need to know anything about just yet. Why let her think he could be leaving her behind when he didn't even know if it would happen? Wanting it to, and knowing it definitely was were two completely different things at the minute, so maybe it was best to leave her out of it until he knew what was going on.

'You sure? You looked like you were going to tell me something there.'

He felt his heart sink as he caught the expression on her face – one of hope and excitement. Had she thought he'd been going to ask her to move in with him? Shit! He really wasn't helping matters.

'It can wait,' he said, looking down at his hand holding hers, feeling her loosen her grip the second those words had come out of his mouth.

'Come on, then.' She let go of him, her mood turning almost business-like as she stood up, grabbing her handbag from the table beside the sofa. 'Let's go and get something to eat, before I lose my appetite.'

Ryan watched her walk out into the hall, throwing himself back against the sofa cushions, closing his eyes and sighing heavily. Yeah. He *really* had to get out of here for a while. There was way too much going on for him to even begin to get his head around any of it.

Reaching over to grab his phone, he sat up, leaning forward as he scrolled through his contact list, stopping at a number he'd called regularly over the past few weeks.

'Ryan!' Ellen shouted through from the hall, her voice carrying more than a hint of impatience now. Did he really need this shit?

'Two minutes, babe! Just got to make a phone call!' It made no sense to aggravate her any more tonight.

'I'll wait for you outside. Don't be long.'

'Yeah, okay...' He'd be as long as it took. This needed sorting, soon, before he lost his chance. 'Oh, hi. Can I speak to Bennie, please?' He closed his eyes as he listened to the voice on the other end of the line. 'Yeah... Tell him it's Ryan – Ryan Fisher. I'm returning his call.'

The wheels were well and truly in motion now, and he had no intention of slowing them down.

Amber heard the front door shut downstairs and she tried to stop the feeling of nausea rising up in her, the guilt she felt still overwhelming her. Yet she wasn't sorry it had happened. Every time she thought about Ronnie touching her, his body filling hers with a feeling she really couldn't explain, she felt something inside her almost cut loose, relax. She felt a happiness she hadn't felt in a while. Although she wasn't stupid or naive to think it was anything other than actions undertook to mask everything else she was really feeling but didn't have the strength to face up to just yet.

She sat up on the bed, crossing her legs underneath her as Jim ran up the stairs. It was late, far later than she'd expected him to be home and she wondered whether he was just as unwilling to open discussions on everything they needed to talk about as much as she was. Had he deliberately stayed out rather than come home to her?

Looking up as he finally walked into their bedroom, she couldn't help but notice the slightly agitated expression on his face.

'I see you've decided to do the photo shoot for Ice Magazine after all,' he said, throwing his jacket over the chair by the door.

She continued to watch him as he moved around the room, taking his watch off and placing it down on the chest of drawers. She didn't say anything.

'And then I find out from the PR Department that the photo shoot is actually taking place inside Tynebridge.' He turned to look at her. 'My place of work, Amber. And you didn't think to tell me any of this?'

Still she said nothing.

'You know, it really would be nice if I could try and not be the last person to know what's going on in your life.'

She stared at him, her eyes never wavering from his. 'Ditto, Jim.'

He held her gaze for a few seconds longer before turning away, walking into the en-suite, closing the door behind him. Amber lay back on the bed, flinging her arms up above her head as she stared at the ceiling. There were so many things they needed to say to each other, but it didn't look like any of them were going to be said tonight. It was late, he was obviously in a mood, and she had so many things on her mind she couldn't think straight. Maybe it would be better just to close her eyes and let sleep take over, start a new day tomorrow and see what that might bring, although she knew it would bring her more time with Ronnie, which, in reality, wasn't unusual. They always spent time together when they were in the same part of the country. But things had changed slightly. Their relationship had shifted somewhat, taken a wrong turn and ended up on the sexual side of the tracks, and even though she didn't want to feel the things she was feeling now, they were there. Those feelings were there, and fighting them wasn't something she was prepared to do just yet.

As her fingers gripped the pillows under her head, she smiled to herself, loving the tingling feeling that swept across her body as she remembered Ronnie's touch; his fingers on her skin, his lips brushing over her neck, kissing her breasts. It was all she could do to stop the moans from escaping, so vivid were the memories.

'I'm sorry.'

She quickly opened her eyes as the spell was broken, sitting up and hugging her knees to her chest as she looked at her husband – handsome and tired, and all of a sudden a whole new rush of feelings overtook her. All the guilt and the confusion and the emptiness she felt inside just overwhelmed her and this time it was tears that threatened to escape as the weak and needy Amber returned.

'Me too,' she whispered, allowing him to pull her against him, enveloping her in a hug she badly needed. 'Things are just so crazy right now, Jim. I don't even know where to start.'

He tilted her chin up so she had no choice but to look at him, kissing her quickly. A familiar kiss. A kiss that, in its own way, induced a feeling of calm.

'I just wish you'd talk to me, Amber,' Jim said, his thumb gently stroking her knuckles, his eyes watching as it did so. 'When you walked out on me…'

'I didn't walk out on you, Jim.'

'That's what it felt like.'

She pulled free from him, getting up and walking over to the window, looking out, even though it was dark now. The window was slightly open, so she could still hear the sea, and that in itself proved to be yet another one of those necessary calming influences. 'I guess I'm not as strong as I always thought I was,' she said quietly, her eyes focusing on a light way off in the distance that probably belonged to a faraway ship out in the North Sea. It was somewhere she quite fancied being now – far away, from everything she was still too weak, too scared to face up to.

'You're still acting like this is something you have to go through alone.' Jim walked up behind her, his arms circling her waist and she let herself fall back against him. 'We'll get through it together, baby. You and me.'

She closed her eyes, trying to block out those thoughts of Ronnie as Jim's fingers gently stroked her hips in a slow, rhythmic motion. And all of a sudden that raw and burning pain of knowing she would never be a mum to this man's child crept up out of that dark hiding place she'd put it in, all hopes that it would stay quiet and forgotten dashed as just feeling him this close to her in this situation tore into her heart like a jagged dagger. She knew they weren't rational feelings, she knew that. She knew that she was making everything so much worse than it needed to be, but that was how she was feeling right now. Those were the feelings that had taken over and suddenly it felt as though she was back in that clinic, listening to those words all over again. Words that had changed her life and ended her perfect dream.

'It hurts so bad, Jim,' she whispered, turning round to face him, tears streaming down her face.

'I know, honey.' He reached out to gently stroke those tears away, his lips moving over her damp cheek until they finally reached her mouth. And what else could she do but lose herself in him? Lose herself in the moment. She just wanted to be held, that was all. She didn't want him to make love to her, or touch her in any way that involved anything that could lead to sex. She didn't want that, not tonight. He was her husband, and she just wanted him to hold her. But it seemed he had other ideas.

'No, Jim. Not tonight.' She pulled away from him, backing off towards the bed. 'I'm really tired. It's been a long day.'

He looked at her, not missing the slightly defensive stance she was giving off, her arms folded tight across her chest. 'Is something wrong, Amber? I mean, what am I supposed to think when this morning you walk into my office and demand sex like we're in some kind of cheap porn movie…'

'Is that what you really think of me, Jim? Is that really how this morning felt to you?'

'No, I didn't… Amber, listen…'

She laughed, her eyes staring straight at him. 'Seriously?'

'No… Look, sweetheart, what am I supposed to think, huh? One minute you're devastated because you can't have kids and the next you're opening your legs and acting like that shit never happened.'

'That *shit*? Jesus…'

'And this Ice Magazine shoot… What the fuck is *that* all about? You didn't want to do it, I heard you talking to Max. You were adamant. What the hell changed your mind?'

'Do you care?'

'I'm a respected man, Amber. Do you honestly think I want to see my wife on the front of some men's magazine with her tits out? Do you think I want everyone looking at you like that? Act like you care, Amber. Act like you want all this crap to get sorted, because I don't think you *do* care right now, honey. Act like you give a shit about everything we have and then maybe, just maybe, we can start to work out where we go from here.'

She said nothing, letting his words sink in for a few seconds. 'Act like I care…' she repeated, speaking the words slowly, her eyes still on his. 'You… you think I don't care? Is that it?'

'It's how it seems to me, Amber. Because you haven't been here. Do you have any idea how selfish that was? Just upping and leave me like that? That news fucked with *my* head, too, you know. It fucked with my head, too.'

She continued to stare at him, feeling the mess that had already started to evolve unravel even further, gathering speed as it went. 'I think *you* need to realise that your secrets helped a situation already teetering on the edge move closer to freefall. Did you ever think about that, Jim?'

'For Christ's sake... I sat and watched you interview him, Amber. My son. You sat there on live TV and you interviewed him, so why are you standing there telling me you still can't get your head around his existence?'

'Oh, my head is fine with the fact he exists, Jim. I don't have a problem with the fact he's here. I spent a bit of time with him after that interview and he's a good kid. No, he's a *great* kid. What I have the problem with is that *you* saw fit to hide his existence *from* me – from everyone. *That's* where my problem lies. And then, just a day later, to find out that not only will I never be the first woman to have your child, but that child will never actually exist. *Our* child will never exist. Now, hearing that news alone would have been bad enough, but to hear it just one day after finding out my husband already *has* a son was something my head is still trying to get around, so don't you dare stand there and tell me I don't care. Don't you fucking dare.'

'Amber...'

'No, Jim. I've had enough for one night.'

'We need to talk...'

'And like I predicted this morning, talking has only ended up in us fighting. And I'm too tired to fight.'

'Is this the way it's gonna be from now on? Everything on *your* terms? We talk about it only when *you* feel like it? You don't think *I* might want to talk about it now? You're being incredibly selfish again, Amber...'

'Selfish?' She let out another cynical laugh, turning away from him to grab an overnight bag from the bottom of the wardrobe.

'Well, I guess that makes us two of a kind, then, doesn't it?'

'Jesus, Amber, come on. This is stupid. Where the hell are you gonna go at this time of night?'

'Does it matter?'

'Of course it fucking matters. Will you stop acting like a child and just calm down?'

She swung round to face him, throwing her robe off and pulling on jeans and a shirt, running her fingers through her hair. 'This is not going to get any better if I stay here tonight, Jim. And you know that.'

'I don't want you to go, Amber. Walking away again isn't going to solve anything, this is ridiculous.'

She sat down on the bed, dropping her head into her hands as tiredness swept through her, taking over her whole body so fast it was as if someone had just waved a magic wand and cast some sort of spell over her. All she wanted to do now was close her eyes and let sleep take over.

'Amber?'

She opened her eyes to see him crouched down in front of her, watching as his fingers slid between hers, and she didn't pull away. She didn't think she had the strength left to even try.

'We *will* work this out, baby.'

All she could do was nod. She was too tired, too emotional to even think about speaking. All she wanted to do was sleep, and tomorrow she'd let Ronnie take away all the pain. Tomorrow. A day that couldn't come quick enough.

Chapter Sixteen

'What the hell is the matter with you?'

Jim looked up as Max stormed into his office at Tynebridge. Sitting back in his chair, he folded his arms, smiling slightly, not in the least bit taken aback by Max's unannounced and rather loud entrance. 'Something I can help you with, Max?'

'You've been talking to CD Adeje, is that right?'

Jim sat even further back in his chair, swinging his feet up onto the desk. 'I may have spoken to their Director of Football in a brief conversation, yes.'

'About Ryan?'

'He's a very determined young man, Max, I'll give him that.'

'And you're actually thinking about letting him go? Seriously?'

'I'm thinking about loaning him out. He isn't going anywhere on a permanent basis, and he knows that.'

'You're letting personal feelings get in the way of your professional life, Jim. And that's a dangerous thing to be doing.'

Jim sat up straight, staring at Max. 'If I don't hear him out, Max, he is going to go above my head, and what then, huh?'

'He gets knocked back. Jesus Christ, Jim, come on! You're better than this. You're really going to do what he wants? You're going to let him get away with that?'

'I'm not letting him get away with anything. I'm simply sorting out a situation that will only get worse if I don't listen to him. He wants to do this and...'

'You're letting personal feelings get in the way, Jim.'

Jim just stared at Max, saying nothing.

'And you really think you can get the board of directors here to agree to loaning Ryan out?' Max already knew the answer to that. Jim Allen could do anything he set his mind to, if he wanted it badly enough.

'A lot of players would give their eye teeth to have a spell playing in the Spanish league. It's one of the best football leagues in the world, so think of it as an unexpected chance for him to showcase his talents. After all, who knows what the future might hold for him.'

'I don't believe you...'

Jim stood up, walking round the front of his desk. 'Look, Max, all I know is that he wants to go, for whatever reason. And I'm not entirely sure it's all to do with my wife. I think he's unsettled, that's all. After everything he went through last season I suspect he just needs some time to get his head around everything. And being here, in the North East, it isn't helping him do that.'

'You sound almost sympathetic towards him.'

'He's an incredible footballer. And I'd hate to see that talent go to waste.'

'And that's your real motive for wanting him out of the picture for a while, is it?'

Jim narrowed his eyes as he looked at Max. 'I don't want him *out of the picture*, as you put it. As manager of this club I don't want him to go anywhere. Why would I want that?'

'Because of Amber.'

Jim said nothing, just fixed Max with a look before walking back behind his desk.

'He's trying to sort himself out, Max, that's obvious. But he's still a loose cannon, although I'm sure I don't have to tell *you* that. I don't want him going off the rails again.'

'You think there's a risk of that?'

'I don't know,' Jim replied, looking straight at Max. 'Do *you*?'

Max sat down on the arm of the sofa. 'I thought he was getting back on track, I really did. But he's obviously decided he doesn't want to share these latest plans of his with me.'

'Because he knows you're against it.'

'With good reason. This is completely out of character for him.'

'You think so?' Jim asked, raising an eyebrow. 'I'd say it was typical Ryan Fisher. Acting without really thinking things through.'

Max looked at Jim as he sat back down. 'I know you, Jim. I know what you're capable of, and I know the contacts you have. I just didn't think you'd ever use them to the detriment of your own club.'

Once again, Jim said nothing, turning his attention back to whatever was on his laptop screen.

'Jesus, Jim… You're playing a very dangerous game here.'

'I'm playing by the rules, Max.'

'You sure about that? Because, unless something's changed that I haven't been made aware of, emergency loans don't apply to Premiership teams.'

'There are always exceptions to every rule, Max. Anyway…' Jim got up and walked out in front of his desk again, leaning back against it, folding his arms, '… as you know, CD Adeje aren't in La Liga's First Division – if they were, then yes, things would be slightly more complicated than they are now.'

'So he's quite willing to step down a level, just to feed this stupid need he *thinks* he has to… Jesus, Jim, I can't believe I'm hearing this crap.'

'The kid's confused, that's all. He's had way too much far too young and he can't handle it anymore. When he couldn't have Amber it was like a sudden realisation that all his money, all the fame and the attitude, it really *couldn't* get him everything he wanted, and I think he just needs more time to deal with that.'

'And you really think leaving Newcastle Red Star for a few

months will help him?'

Jim shrugged. 'Who knows?'

'But if this is all because he still has feelings for Amber…'

'He *thinks* he does. I told you, Max. I'm not entirely sure everything he's feeling is to do with Amber. She's just the obvious excuse.'

'Jim, I'm confused. I don't…'

'I've got more important things to think about than Ryan Fisher's feelings, Max. If he wants to be loaned out, I'll let him go. I'm not going to waste time fighting him.'

'And that really is the end of the matter now, is it?'

Jim walked back behind his desk, sitting down and slipping his reading glasses on, resuming whatever it was he'd been doing before Max had walked in, dismissing the conversation within seconds. 'That's really the end of the matter.'

'So when is this shoot for Ice Magazine happening?' Debbie asked, crossing her long, spray-tanned legs as they settled themselves at a table in a central Newcastle coffee bar.

'Soon,' Amber replied, checking her watch.

'You got to be somewhere, chick?'

Amber looked at her friend, smiling slightly. 'No. Not really.'

'Not really?' Debbie questioned, raising an eyebrow. 'My company not good enough anymore?'

'I'm sorry, Debs.'

'What for? What have you done?' Debbie grinned, and even though it was a perfectly innocent question, with no hidden meaning at all, Amber felt a huge rush of guilt hit her. What *had* she done? She'd been having an affair with her best friend, that's what she'd been doing. An affair that she knew should end, but she just couldn't do it because those hours she spent with Ronnie were the only time she didn't think about those things she couldn't have, and the pain that still caused. All she'd wanted was the perfect marriage – or as perfect as it could be – yet she was doing everything in her power to prevent that marriage from moving forward. She and Jim were stuck in a world of things unsaid, pretending everything was healing itself and that she was slowly getting over it all, but she wasn't. Not really. Or else, why would she be running to Ronnie?

'I wanted to be able to deal with this, Debbie. I really wanted to be able to deal with this.'

Debbie leaned forward, reaching out to take Amber's hand, and all Amber could do was focus on her friend's perfectly manicured pink nails in an attempt to stop yet more tears from falling. 'I'm sure there are things you could do, babe. What about IVF? Have you looked into that? I'm sure…'

Amber shook her head. 'No, Debbie. No. We've already talked about that, but I can't do it. I can't… I don't want to put us through all of that when there's still no guarantee that anything will happen. All that stress, all that time and money and…'

'Yeah, but money's not a problem, is it? You could go private, get things moving almost immediately. Amber, chick, if you really want a baby so badly surely it couldn't hurt to just think about it?'

'It's not happening, Debbie. Besides, me and Jim are fragile enough right now without putting any more pressure on an already fractured marriage.'

'Are things really that bad?'

Amber let go of Debbie's hand, sitting back in her seat as she looked out of the window. All around her, life went on, the busy Newcastle streets full of people going about their business, and somewhere out there, there were women just like her, other women who couldn't have the one thing they so badly wanted. Did they feel like she felt right now? Empty inside?

'I hate the way I feel,' she said quietly, still looking out of the window, watching as a couple of young mums walked past pushing their babies in the autumn sunshine. A simple act, but one Amber would probably never experience and that thought brought with it a rush of sadness that almost overwhelmed her, so much so that she had to swallow hard before speaking again just to stop herself from crying. 'It scares me, Debbie, because I didn't want this. This is alien and strange and it isn't me. Or, it wasn't me. Just a few months ago this wasn't me. I was somebody else, a completely different person, and it wasn't until Jim…' She stopped talking, taking a second to compose herself as she looked down at her wedding ring. 'He changed everything. When he walked back into my life, he changed everything. And I just don't know if I want to be that person I became when… I don't know anymore.'

'Nobody expects you to be able to deal with this in such a short space of time, Amber. It's going to take a while, but Jim, he…'

'He loves me, I know that. I know he loves me, and I love him, too. I always have, and I always will. No matter what happens. But he changed me, and that's what scares me. All of this – marriage, babies, being in the public eye more than I really feel comfortable with – it's weird, you know?'

'You said yourself that you'd always just been waiting for Jim to come back to you. Wasn't that what you'd always wanted?'

'Well, maybe I should have been more careful what I wished for… Oh, I don't know, Debbie. I'm just thinking out loud, trying to make sense of it all, all these feelings going round and round in my head. I love Jim, I do, it's just… when he walked back into my life I didn't know he'd be bringing with him more lies, more secrets. I thought we were past all of that. I'd begun to trust him because I really thought he'd changed. And even if he'd told me about Brandon back when he'd first taken the job at Red Star, it might have been okay. But keeping him a secret, deceiving me for all those years, making his own son keep quiet about who his dad really was… Maybe I don't know him at all, Debbie. And maybe he hasn't really changed.'

'Have you talked to him? Really talked to him, I mean? About everything you're feeling?'

'It's all we do, Debbie,' Amber sighed. 'Every day, to the point where I don't even want to go home some nights because I can't face another discussion, another night of him trying to put suggestions forward, things I just can't get my head around and… I actually look forward to having to go to London. I look forward to going to work, to not having to talk about everything over and over again.'

'Look, I know what he did upset you, and I understand that, I really do. But I'm sure he just wants you to be happy.'

'I'm not denying that. Of course he wants me to be happy, but he can't just buy me a baby, Debbie. It doesn't work like that. It isn't that simple.'

Debbie looked at Amber, frowning slightly. 'Is there something else you're not telling me?'

'Like what?' Amber asked, almost kicking herself for the over-defensive tone she'd used just then.

'I don't know. You tell me, chick.'

'I'm just tired, that's all. I'm not sleeping much.'

'Amber… you and Jim…'

She looked straight at Debbie, aware that her phone was ringing in her bag, and it was a call she really wanted to take. 'What about us?'

'You *will* work things out, won't you?'

Amber looked down at her wedding ring again. 'I don't know, Debbie. And that's the truth.'

'What you're feeling, Amber… is it really *all* to do with the fact you can't have Jim's baby? That he kept Brandon a secret from you? Or are those just catalysts for something else? For other feelings you don't really want to think about?'

Amber looked up, fixing Debbie with a tough stare. 'When did you turn amateur psychologist?'

'I just care about you, that's all. You *and* Jim. And I can't help thinking that, well, if you really wanted his baby that badly you'd try everything in your power to make that happen, because surely there are things…'

'Why do you care so much, Debbie? Why are you so desperate for me to find a way to have that baby you assume I want more than anything?'

'I'm not desperate…'

'Yeah, you are. You can't seem to keep off the subject, when you know it's not something I really want to talk about…'

'I'm pregnant, Amber.'

Amber felt like she'd been sideswiped. She really hadn't been expecting that. 'You… you're… you're pregnant?'

Debbie nodded. 'We haven't told anyone yet, because it's still very early days and we don't want to jinx it, but… I wanted you to find out from me, hon. I didn't want you to read about it in the papers or find out via the gossip grapevine, so… I wanted you to hear it from me.'

'Because you thought it would tip me over the edge and you wanted to be there when I fell?' Amber was aware she was being slightly sarcastic, but she could feel that emptiness beginning to sweep over her once again and this time it stung twice as hard because the one thing she would never experience was now happening to one of her closest friends. And that meant she was going to have to find a whole new way of dealing with things.

'No, Amber. I just didn't want it to…'

'Debbie, I'm fine, okay?' Amber smiled, reaching out to take Debbie's hand, squeezing it tight. 'And I'm really, really happy for you. Honestly. It's fantastic news.'

'Is it?' Debbie asked, still unsure that what Amber was telling her was the truth. 'Really?'

Amber nodded, squeezing her hand again. 'Really. Bit of a shock, though, I have to admit.'

'Tell me about it,' Debbie sighed, absentmindedly placing a hand on her still very-flat stomach. 'But nobody was more shocked than Gary, believe me. It was that last-minute trip to Marbella that did it.'

'Maybe this will be the making of him, huh?'

Debbie let out a little snort of derision. 'Well, that remains to be seen. Amber, are you really okay with this?'

What was she supposed to say to that? No, she wasn't okay with this? That it felt like one massive kick in the teeth? Some cruel twist of fate? What was she supposed to say? If any of her friends got pregnant they were to avoid her like the plague? She didn't want that. She didn't want people to feel sorry for her or avoid her just because something was happening to them that could never happen to her. She didn't want pity. That in itself made her feel sick to her stomach. She didn't want to be that woman.

'If *I* can't have kids, Debbie, then the next best thing is having a friend who can.'

Debbie smiled a smile that exuded relief. 'Oh, I am so glad you feel that way, chick, because Gary and I want to ask you something – we want you to be the baby's godmother. You're the obvious choice, hon, and I know you'll be a wonderful influence on him, or her. Far better than their own father, probably… Sorry, I'm rambling, aren't I?' She fixed Amber with a hopeful look. 'So will you? Be the baby's godmother? Please?'

'You're not just doing this out of some sort of pity, are you?'

'I'm not that kind of person, Amber.'

'I know. I know, I'm sorry, I just…' She smiled, squeezing Debbie's hand again. 'I'd love to be the baby's godmother.'

'You would?' Debbie squealed, almost throwing herself over the table to hug Amber. 'Oh, that's fantastic! You've made my day, chick. Now, we need cake to celebrate. I'll go find us something nice, sticky and gooey – won't be a sec.'

Amber watched her totter off in her four-inch heels in the direction of the dessert chiller, waiting until she was deep in conversation with the young woman behind the counter before taking out her phone and ringing the number of the missed call she'd ignored earlier.

'Hey. I thought you were avoiding me.'

'I'm with Debbie. She was in the middle of telling me some… Ronnie, I really need to see you.'

'Are you okay? You sound a bit, I dunno, upset.'

'I'm fine. It's just been one of those days.'

'Do you want to come over? I'm not doing anything this

afternoon. Except you – if that's what you want.'

She knew he'd be saying that with a smile on his face and she felt her stomach flip over at the prospect of an afternoon of doing whatever it would take to escape from a reality she was becoming less and less keen to spend time in.

'Never mind what I want. It's what I *need*.'

'Good. That's good. Because I've got plans for you.'

'Oh, really?' Amber smiled. She was starting to feel better already as her mind began to filter out everything she didn't want to think about – including the guilt – and replace it with thoughts that made her feel calmer. A false calm, maybe, but that didn't matter.

'Really. What time will you be over?'

'Well, I'm still with Debbie, so about an hour and a half? I can't just up and leave her. She's buying cake.'

Ronnie laughed and she felt her stomach give another ridiculous leap. How could she be feeling this way about a man she thought of as the brother she'd never had? A man she called her very best friend. How could it have happened so suddenly? If it really *had* happened suddenly, but she wasn't even going there. 'In that case, I'll see you when I see you.'

'Don't start without me.'

'As if.'

She ended the call and slid her phone back into her bag, turning to look out of the window again. Just a few short months ago she really had thought she'd found her happy ending. And even though the prospect of never being a mum had always been there in the back of her mind, she'd always thought she'd be able to handle it, that she'd be able to deal with it purely because it was news she'd been expecting to hear for most of her life. But what the past few months had taught her was that you can never be fully prepared for anything, no matter how much forewarning you have. They'd taught her that, yes, dreams *can* come true, but those dreams never stay the same. The reality doesn't always live up to the fantasy, and rushing into things just because you assumed it was all you'd ever wanted could sometimes be the biggest mistake of your life.

Chapter Seventeen

'That's Brandon Palmer, isn't it?' Gary asked, nudging Ryan as they walked into the Players' Lounge at Tynebridge.

'Looks like it,' Ryan replied, not really taking a great interest. He was more concerned with finding out where Ellen had got to. He hadn't exactly been good to her lately, and he felt guilty about that. After everything he'd promised himself about treating her better, about keeping her onside until he found out whether a loan to CD Adeje was on the cards or not, after all of that, all he'd succeeded in doing was alienating her further by playing it cool. Too cool, sometimes. He'd started going out more, spending evenings with his mates or just giving her some excuse not to come over because he wanted to be on his own. But now he felt like he needed to try and reel her back in, get her back onside. Back in his bed. That should do the trick. If nothing else, she was a sucker for a night between the sheets with England's sexiest striker. 'You seen Ellen?'

'No. But Amber's here.'

Ryan's head swung round, almost as if it was on autopilot. She was talking to Ronnie White in the corner of the room, looking beautiful in a simple outfit of jeans and a black shirt, her dark red hair falling loose over her shoulders. Shit! He really could have done without seeing her tonight, but he should have known there would be a chance she'd be there. It had been a midweek game for

Newcastle Red Star, and because she now worked most weekends for Cloud Sports, she didn't get to as many Red Star matches as she used to. So the odd midweek fixture was a chance for her to come to Tynebridge and support her dad's old club. Just like old times. Times when she'd been his. Times he wished he could get back.

'Can I have a word, Fisher?'

Ryan turned around to see Jim standing there dressed, as always, in his trademark match-day dark suit and white shirt. 'Yeah. Yeah, sure. In your office?'

'Five minutes.'

Before Jim left, Ryan couldn't help but notice him throw a quick glance over at Amber and Ronnie, although his expression gave nothing away.

'What was *that* all about?' Gary asked as Jim exited the Players' Lounge as quickly as he'd appeared.

'The boss wants to see me.'

'I got that much, you div. I meant, that look he just gave his missus.'

'What look?'

'You didn't see that?'

'Didn't see what?'

'Forget it… I'm off to find Rob. He owes me 250 quid from that night out at the casino last week. Catch you later.'

'Yeah. Later,' Ryan mumbled, frowning as he watched Amber lean in close to Ronnie, resting her head on his shoulder as she laughed at something he said.

'You really can't let her go, can you?'

He swung round again at the sound of another voice, and this time it belonged to someone he *did* want to talk to. 'Ellen, babe, I've been looking for you…'

'Really? Because from the way you're ogling your ex, I'd say you weren't looking all that hard.'

'I'm not "ogling" anyone, Ellen. I didn't even know she'd be here, and just because…'

'Just because what? Just because I happen to catch you staring at her, it doesn't mean I should assume you still want her?'

'She's married, in case you hadn't noticed. To the boss.'

'That means nothing in your world, Ryan.'

He grabbed her gently by the wrist and led her out of the Players' Lounge, back through into the main reception area. 'And what's *that* supposed to mean?'

'It means, I can't compete with her, can I?' Ellen replied, shaking him off. 'How can I, when she's still here, and you still feel the way you do about her.'

'What the… Ellen, Jesus, I don't feel *any*thing for her. I don't…'

'Then why can't you move forward, Ryan? Why can't you *let* yourself move forward?'

He took her hand and led her outside, finding a quiet corner away from the post-match crowds of people still milling about in front of the main entrance. 'What are you talking about?'

'Me and you, Ryan. I'm talking about me and you.'

'You really do pick your fucking times to start a conversation, babe, I'll give you that much. And this really isn't the time or the place. I've got to go talk to the boss in a minute, so…' He looked at her. She was this beautiful, kind, loyal woman. She was everything he needed, and he was lucky to have her in his life, he knew that. But she just wasn't Amber. And that's where all his problems lay.

'I love you, Ryan.'

Her words hit him like a bolt from the blue; he felt as though someone had just kicked him hard in the stomach, knocking every breath out of him. He really, really didn't need this. Not now.

'Doesn't that mean anything to you?'

'I don't deserve you,' he whispered, leaning back against the wall, his eyes staring down at the ground.

'Yeah. You do.' Ellen smiled, quickly kissing his mouth, her hands sliding up under his t-shirt.

He looked at her again – right into her eyes. Was he taking the coward's way out? Pinning all his hopes on a loan request that may never happen in the hope that it stopped him regretting actions he could never take back? Shouldn't he just be strong and deal with things like an adult? Isn't that what Amber would tell him to do?

'I think it's about time we made things a bit more permanent, don't you?' he said, trying to batter down a brief feeling of – was that fear? – over what he was about to do next. Knee-jerk reactions never had worked for him in the past, but he had to try something. Anything.

'Yes?' Ellen breathed, her eyes wide with hope.

'Why… why don't you move in with me? Let's try and make a proper go of things. What do you say?' What was he doing? The only thing he could do, really. Carry on with the life he had, because he couldn't have the one he wanted.

'I say yes! Of course I say yes!' she squealed, jumping into his arms and hugging him tight. 'Oh my God! I'm so excited!'

Ryan wished he felt the same, but all he was getting was the feeling that he'd just made a huge mistake, and one he couldn't exactly take back now, could he?

'Can I bring my stuff over tomorrow?' Ellen asked, already tapping out a message on her phone.

'Yeah, sure… Look, Ellen, can we keep this kind of low-key? For now? Just until we both get used to the idea.'

She looked up at him, and he wished he hadn't had to do that because this was obviously something she'd wanted for a while, in fact, he knew it was. And to finally hear those words from him had probably made her day, even if he did say so himself. But he just didn't want his private life being made public knowledge – for a change. And whilst that might not be able to be the case forever, he could try and keep it quiet for as long as he possibly could.

'Yeah. Okay. If that's what you want.' She couldn't hide the disappointment in her voice, and Ryan felt another sharp stab of guilt.

'Just for a little while, babe. I don't want to jinx anything, you know?' He might have been lucky enough to have pulled that one back from the brink, as the smile she'd worn before quickly replaced the frown.

'That makes sense,' she said, dropping her phone back into her bag.

He breathed a silent sigh of relief. 'Okay, listen, I've got to run. The boss wants a word and I'm already late, but I'll see you later, all right?'

She nodded, and he left her still smiling as he ran back inside, the relief he felt at being out of that situation – even for just a few minutes – palpable. Whatever he'd done, he was going to have to see it through now. Until such a time when an opportunity arose to get him out of it.

'Do you know how hard it's been tonight?' Ronnie whispered.

Amber tried not to look directly into his eyes, because she knew exactly how hard it had been.

'There must be some place we can go? I just need to touch you, Amber. To see you naked, feel how ready you are…'

'Will you shut up!' she hissed.

Ronnie grinned, and she couldn't help but smile back. 'You are so easy to wind up,' he laughed.

'Bastard,' Amber said, laughing too, despite herself. 'But I don't even think we should be joking about it, Ronnie, not in here. Everything's just a bit too close, you know?' She looked at him, which only served to kick-start a barrage of mixed emotions she couldn't control. Part of her wanted to do nothing more than go home with him and let him temporarily erase all the guilt, whilst the other half wanted to find Jim and get out of there as soon as she could, before temptation led her into something else she could stick on her list of regrets. And she knew which part of her was losing the fight. 'I need some fresh air, okay? I won't be long.'

'Amber…'

'It's nothing you've said, Ronnie. I just can't deal with this when we're here, all right?'

She threw him a smile before pushing her way through the

crowded post-match Players' Lounge, not stopping until she was outside. The affair with Ronnie had been going on for weeks now, and whilst she knew it was wrong, she couldn't stop herself. When she was with him she felt different; she didn't feel pressured or confused – she felt free. She felt as though she could do anything, and she liked that feeling. It was a feeling she could get used to.

Her relationship with Jim was still strained, but they were talking things through; they were trying to move forward, but how could that happen when she was doing what she was doing with Ronnie? How could anything ever get better when she was stuck in a cycle of cheating and deceit? Something she'd accused Jim of so many times in the past, so the hypocrisy of what she was doing didn't escape her.

'You all right?'

She opened her eyes to see Brandon Palmer standing next to her, his young and handsome face once again bringing back a million memories of a past with his father. And a future she was almost single-handedly wrecking.

'I'm fine. Thank you.'

'You don't look it.'

Amber didn't really want to get into this conversation with him, so she quickly changed the subject. 'It was good of you to come tonight. Jim was really pleased to see you.'

'Well, considering I only live a stone's throw away from Tynebridge, it wasn't exactly a chore to get here. And I like to check out the opposition, what with the local derby just a few weeks away.'

Amber couldn't help smiling. 'You've never experienced a local North East derby, have you?'

He shook his head, leaning back against the wall beside her, his hands in his pockets. 'Dad tells me they're something else, though.'

'Oh, they're that all right,' Amber laughed, suddenly glad he'd turned up. He made her smile, despite him being – albeit indirectly – one of the causes of her and Jim's problems. But it wasn't *his* fault. Whatever was going on between her and Jim, none of it was Brandon's fault. But it *was* his father's.

'Are you and my dad okay, Amber? I mean, I don't want to pry or anything, but…'

'Then don't.'

'I'm sorry. I guess it's none of my business. I just don't want my being here to get in the way, I don't want to cause any trouble…'

'I've told you before, Brandon, you're not in the way. And you're certainly not causing any trouble. Me and your dad, we're just going through a tough time right now, that's all. And I know we've only been married a few months, and it normally takes a lot longer for tough times to manifest themselves in marriages, but… well, things are never straightforward, are they? And mine and your dad's relationship is nothing if not complicated.'

He looked down at the ground, his hands still firmly in his pockets. 'Did my dad tell you I've been called up for the England squad? For the match against Portugal next week at Wembley?'

Amber frowned as Brandon's words slowly sunk in. 'England? How can you…? You're American. How can you be called up for the England squad?'

He looked at her with a slightly confused expression. 'I've got dual nationality, so I got to choose whether I played for the USA or England. And even though I'm American through and through – I love my country – but as far as getting noticed on the international soccer stage is concerned, I had to pick England, really… Didn't my dad tell you? My mom's English. He met her over here, in the North East… Amber…'

She'd heard enough. More lies, and once again it would appear she was the last to know.

'You spoken to Max yet?' Jim asked, not looking up as Ryan closed the office door behind him.

'About what?'

This time Jim did look up. 'About your loan request. Don't get smart with me, Ryan. It won't work.'

'I wasn't trying to… No. I haven't spoken to him. I mean, I've mentioned it, but… I haven't spoken to him properly about it. Not yet.'

'How serious are you about all of this?' Jim asked, standing up and walking round the front of his desk, perching himself on the edge of it, his eyes never leaving Ryan's.

'I'm… I…'

'What you've asked for, Ryan, it's big. You're not a player this club will want to lose, even for just a few months, so if you're just playing some sort of game…'

'I'm not playing a game, boss. I really do think it would be best for me – and my future here at Red Star – if I took some time away.'

'Because of Amber?'

Ryan looked down at the floor, aware that Jim's eyes were still on him.

'Okay,' Jim sighed, thankfully allowing Ryan no time to answer his question. 'So you want to experience what it's like to play soccer over in Spain? Even if it's with a lower division club?'

Ryan looked up, although he didn't meet Jim's eyes. Instead he focused on a wall full of framed Manager of the Month awards. Jim Allen obviously liked to display his success. 'I didn't want to go to another English club. What would be the point of that?'

'Not far enough away from your problems, huh?'

This time Ryan's eyes met Jim's, holding his stare, even though the strength of it was slightly intimidating, even for him. 'I just need some time away, boss.' Especially now. He'd just done something he wasn't proud of, asking Ellen to move in with him when he really didn't feel that strongly about her – not enough to be less than a few steps away from an engagement, anyway. So if ever he needed to get out of there and get himself back to square one before it was too late, it was now.

'Why? I mean, I sort of know why, but I really want to hear you say it.'

'I'm not in love with her, if that's what you think.' Wasn't he? If he was completely honest with himself, he didn't know what he felt anymore. For anyone. Which was why he needed that space.

Jim raised an eyebrow, not making any attempt to break that stare, his arms folded across his chest. 'I don't *think* anything, Ryan. I just need to know how serious you are about that loan request because there's going to come a day soon when I have to go into that boardroom and convince the directors of this club that loaning you out during one of the most important seasons in Newcastle Red Star's history is a good idea. And, right now, I have no clue how that's going to pan out. I mean, what do I tell them?'

'They're personal reasons, boss. Isn't that all they need to know?'

Jim laughed, finally breaking the stare as he looked down at the floor, shaking his head. 'You have a lot to learn, kiddo. They need to know a lot more than that, believe me. So you tell me, right now, how serious *are* you?'

This time it was Ryan's turn to throw out the determined stare. 'I'm serious.'

'And if Amber wasn't around? Would you still be serious?'

Ryan frowned. He was thrown slightly by that question. But given what had just happened with Ellen, maybe Amber wasn't the only reason he needed some time away from the North East. He didn't seem to be handling anything very well at the minute. 'Yes. I would.'

Jim said nothing for a few seconds, just continued to stare at Ryan. 'And if it became possible for you to make that move *before* the January transfer window opens? Would you be quite happy to leave Newcastle Red Star at a moment's notice? I've been talking to Bennie Felipe, CD Adeje's manager, and he's quite keen for you to go over there for a few months, if that's what you really want. They've had a great season so far but they need a replacement striker while their main guy recovers from injury, and he tells me you two have spoken since our pre-season tour, is that right?'

Ryan nodded. 'Yeah. Yeah, I spoke to him when we were out

there in Tenerife, and I've been in contact a couple of times over the past few weeks.' He frowned again, his head starting to spin. Suddenly everything seemed to be happening at a speed he hadn't been prepared for. 'But I… I didn't think it would be possible to leave Red Star before January, not without one hell of a valid reason.'

Jim walked over to the sideboard and poured himself a small glass of whisky. 'Want one?' he asked, lifting up his glass and looking at Ryan.

'No. No, thank you. I thought…'

'Nothing is impossible, Ryan.' Jim took a sip of his whisky. 'Not if you know the right people.'

'And you know the right people, do you?'

Jim looked straight at Ryan, but he didn't answer his question. Finishing off his drink in one more mouthful, almost slamming the glass back down on the sideboard, he walked back behind his desk. 'I just needed to know how serious you were, Ryan.'

'And I've told you – I'm serious.'

'Then you'd better talk to your agent. And make it sooner rather than later. Okay?'

Amber pushed the door of Jim's office open, taken aback slightly by Ryan's presence.

Jim looked up, not even the tiniest flicker of surprise crossing his face at her unexpected entrance.

'Is he leaving?' she asked, looking briefly over at Ryan, who immediately looked away.

'I'll speak to you later, Fisher,' Jim said, dismissing him instantly. 'Let me know when you've spoken to Max.'

Amber waited until Ryan had closed the door behind him before she turned to face Jim. 'Brandon has dual nationality?'

Jim looked at her, and his silence did nothing but anger Amber even more.

'He's been called up for the England squad, Jim. Just how long did you think you'd be able to keep *that* one a secret? Given that I'm covering that international match for Cloud Sports next week? Jesus Christ, how do I not know these things?'

'It's no big deal, Amber. I never said his mom was American, did I? Her nationality is of no consequence. I only said I met her in America…'

'But you didn't, did you? Because I've just been talking to Brandon, and he told me you met her in England. That you met here, in the North East. So why the big secret, Jim? What else have you got to hide?'

'There's no secret, Amber. Honey, believe me, it doesn't matter. It really doesn't matter.'

'It matters to *me*, Jim. Don't you see? Because it's one more lie, one more secret, one more thing you didn't tell me, and if it really doesn't matter then why didn't you just tell me the truth? Why did you tell me you met her in the U.S.? Why did you do that?'

Jim pushed a hand through his hair, walking over to her, but she backed away. 'Amber, I really didn't think it was important, I mean, she moved over to New York before Brandon was born, and we were never really together as a couple. Not for long, anyway…'

Amber narrowed her eyes as she looked at him. 'You told me you were never together as a couple at all. You told me it was one night, that was all. Just one night. You told me it meant nothing… Why the hell do you find it so fucking hard to be honest with me, Jim? Why? I just don't get it. It's like… it's like you're trying everything you can to push me further away.'

'It isn't like that, Amber.'

'Then why lie to me? Again? You told me we weren't even together when this happened, so I don't understand why you couldn't just tell me you met her over here? What difference would it have made?'

'I don't… Look, I got so much shit wrong, okay?'

'You think?'

'And I didn't tell you about Brandon's mom because… because

I didn't think you needed to know… I didn't think…'

'No. You didn't. You never do. Oh, do you know what? I've had enough of this. I don't even want to think about it anymore, I'm out of here.'

'We were married, Amber. Me and Brandon's mom. We were married.'

She stopped dead in her tracks, keeping her back to him.

'But it was a marriage of convenience, I swear to you…'

Amber didn't want to hang around and listen to any more. She was tired, of so much more than just Jim's lies.

'Amber, baby, please…'

She just shook her head as she walked out of his office, closing the door quietly behind her.

'Everything all right?'

She looked up at the sound of Ryan's voice. He was standing out in the corridor, hands in his pockets as he leaned back against the wall.

'Everything's fine.'

'Really?' he asked, raising an eyebrow.

'It's none of your business, Ryan.'

'I still care about you, Amber. I told you, those feelings haven't gone away.'

'Then maybe you need to make sure they leave soon, because the last thing I need is…' She sighed, leaning back against the wall beside him. 'I'm so tired.'

'Of what?'

'Everything.'

'Do you want to talk about it?'

She turned to look at him, smiling slightly. 'What? With you?'

'Why not? I'm not the guy I used to be, Amber. I'm a grown-up now.'

'Haven't you got a girlfriend you need to take out somewhere?' She was still smiling. She couldn't help it.

'Not tonight. I'm going home alone tonight.' *For the last time,* he thought. And that thought was something that made him feel quite sick inside. He didn't always like being alone, but sometimes it had its perks.

'Well, I'm sure you could quite easily change that, if you wanted to,' Amber said, quickly looking back at Jim's closed office door. How had things got so bad between them? When all she really wanted, deep down inside, despite everything, was to be with him. So why was she pushing him away? Why wasn't she giving him a chance to explain things? Because she was tired of listening to his excuses, that's why. 'I'll see you later, Ryan.' She started walking away but stopped briefly to look over her shoulder, smiling a bigger smile this time. 'Oh, and congratulations on the England call-up, by the way. Captain, too, huh? You must be doing something right.'

She practically ran the short distance back to the Players' Lounge, finding Ronnie chatting to a couple of fellow TV football pundits at the bar.

'You all right?' he asked, frowning slightly as he looked at her.

'Yeah. Yeah, I'm fine. I just need a word, that's all.'

'Oh. Okay. Now?'

'Please.'

He quickly said his goodbyes, and followed Amber out of the lounge.

'Get enough fresh air, did you?' he asked, almost running to keep up with her as she strode quickly out into the main reception area, heading for the exit. 'Amber, hang on, will you? What's the rush? Where are we going?'

She stopped briefly at the top of the steps outside, turning to look at him. 'We're going home. *Your* home.'

'My…? What about Jim? Amber, what's going on?'

'Do you want to fuck me, Ronnie?'

'You know I do.'

'Then shut up, stop asking questions, and let's go home.'

Ryan pushed a hand through his hair and closed his eyes. Every time he thought he might just be over her, something happened to make him realise he wasn't. He wasn't over her. He wasn't over that life they could have had together, that future he'd ruined. He wasn't over the fact they'd been just a matter of weeks away from a wedding – *their* wedding. He wasn't over any of it, and he needed to be. He wanted to be. He wanted to be able to look at her and not feel the regret and the guilt. He wanted to be able to hold down another relationship without her always intruding into his thoughts, affecting his life. And if that meant leaving Newcastle Red Star, just for a while, in order for that to have any chance of happening, then that was the way it had to be. Even though, in his heart of hearts, he knew he was only using it as some kind of personal rehab attempt that had no guarantee of working. But he had to give it a try. He had no other choice. Because he knew he had no chance of moving forward if he stayed in Newcastle.

'You still hanging around, Fisher?' Jim said, finally coming out of his office. 'I would have thought you had better things to do than loiter round the corridors here when there are women out there just waiting to be entertained by your very presence.'

'Are you condoning me going out on a bender, boss?'

'I'm sure those weren't my words, Ryan. And I'm sure you know how to enjoy yourself without resorting to the kind of behaviour we saw from you last season.'

Ryan said nothing for a second, not until Jim started walking away. 'How soon do you think it could be, boss? Before any kind of loan could be sorted out?'

Jim slowly turned around, fixing his star striker with a firm stare. 'I can't work miracles, Ryan. But I've got a few people at the F.A. I can have a quiet word with.'

'Thanks.'

'You seem slightly more desperate than you were when I spoke to you not twenty minutes ago. Something happened?'

Ryan looked down at the floor, scuffing the heel of his trainer against the red skirting boards.

'You been talking to Amber?' Jim didn't miss the change in Ryan's body language when he asked that question. 'Ryan. Is something going on between you and my wife?'

Ryan looked up, the words spilling from his mouth before he could stop them. 'I don't think it's me you should be keeping an eye on, boss. I think you need to be looking closer to home on that score.'

'Just lie still, and I promise you, you'll enjoy this,' Ronnie said, lightly running his fingers over Amber's back, up and down, slowly and gently.

'Oh, that feels so good,' Amber groaned, closing her eyes and letting him do all the work. 'My shoulders were so tense.'

'They still are,' he whispered, leaning over so his mouth was close to her ear. 'But I can change that.'

She smiled, letting out another low moan as his fingers started to knead the space between her shoulder blades, digging deep, a beautiful pain that sent shivers right through her.

'Just yell if I'm pushing too hard.'

Amber couldn't help but smile again. 'You could never push too hard, Ronnie.'

He laughed, leaning over again until his lips were touching the back of her neck, his fingers moving down, his thumbs stroking the edges of her spine as his mouth followed in their wake.

Amber gripped the pillow, keeping her eyes closed as his hands reached her lower back, stroking her hips, moving down to her thighs and around to caress her bottom. It was all she could do to stop herself from crying out loud; it felt incredible!

'Jesus, Ronnie… Why wasn't it like this when we were together?'

'Because *you* always took the lead, missy. Remember?'

She smiled again, her stomach dipping and diving as he gently parted her legs, his hands now back on her bottom, pushing her up onto her knees.

'But I think you'll find that, this time, *I'm* in charge.'

'I'm all yours,' she moaned, gripping the pillow tighter as he spread her legs wider, kneeling up behind her. And before she had a chance to catch her breath he'd pushed into her, gently and slowly, pulling her back against him until he was deep, deep inside her.

Pushing herself harder against him, she screamed out as each thrust he gave brought with it an exquisite pain, his hands on her hips keeping her in position, her fingers still gripping the pillows. She clung onto them, tighter and tighter with every move he made, until the inevitable crashing climax swept over them both, his body jarring and shuddering behind her first, before her own gave in to those beautiful waves of pleasure, and she couldn't help but scream even louder as it did so.

'You are killing me, kiddo,' Ronnie breathed, rolling over onto his back, throwing his arms up above his head.

'You just need to get back in shape.' She collapsed onto her stomach, letting the last of those delicious post-sex tingles shudder through her.

'I'm in perfect shape, I'll have you know.' He grinned, reaching out to gently stroke her thoroughly messed-up hair away from her face.

'You keep telling yourself that.' Amber smirked, closing her eyes as he kissed her, slow and deep, causing one or two final, lingering tingles to make themselves felt. 'Ronnie…'

'Uh oh. That doesn't sound like the beginning of a sentence I want to hear the end of.' He sat up, and Amber followed, pulling the sheet up over her naked body, although quite why she was doing that she had no idea, considering he'd seen all of her and so much more not a few seconds ago. 'Come on. What's up?'

'What are we doing?' Her voice was quiet, almost as if the realisation of how wrong this was had finally hit home.

'Well, unless I'm very much mistaken, I'd say we were conducting a very steamy…' He leaned over, kissing her again, '… very, *very* sexy affair. What do *you* think we're doing?'

She hung her head, her fingers fiddling with the white cotton sheet. 'I think we're playing a very dangerous game.'

Ronnie sighed, pushing a hand through his hair. 'I guess play-time's over.'

She looked at him. She hadn't been sure what she'd wanted before, but looking at him now, she knew what she had to do. What they *both* had to do.

'I don't *want* to end it, Ronnie. I just think we should. Before it goes too far.'

He leaned forward again, gently pulling the sheet away from her. 'Whatever you think is best, kiddo. We never said this was gonna be forever.'

'No,' she whispered, closing her eyes again as his mouth rested against hers, his breath warm on her face. 'No. We didn't.'

'But I really hate ending things just like that, don't you?'

She couldn't help smiling, sliding an arm around his neck as he pulled her astride him. 'Are you trying to say you want one more ride before we forget this ever happened?'

'Well, a guy's gotta try, hasn't he?'

'And sometimes he'll get what he wants.' She wrapped her legs around him, her forehead resting against his. 'One last time, anyway.'

He let his fingers run lightly up her arm, an almost absent-minded action, as he looked right into her pale blue eyes. 'Why now, Amber? Why decide to do this now? Today? Did something happen tonight?'

She said nothing for a second, before climbing off him, grabbing his shirt up off the floor and slipping it on. 'Jim's been married before.'

Ronnie frowned. 'Huh?'

She turned to look at him. 'He's been married before.'

'He told you that? Tonight?'

She nodded, leaning back against the wall. 'Brandon told me earlier that he's been called up for the England squad, and obvi-ously, because he's American, I asked him why he was playing for

England. Jim told me he met Brandon's mum in the States, so I just assumed she was American, but… but Brandon told me he met her in Britain. Here, in the North East. She's English.'

'More lies?' Ronnie asked, getting up out of bed, pulling on his jeans before walking over to her.

'More lies,' Amber whispered.

Ronnie leaned back against the wall beside her, his hands in his pockets. 'So, what's the story, then?'

'I don't know,' Amber shrugged. 'I didn't give him a chance to explain. At the time I didn't even want him to. I just wanted to get out of there, wanted to get away from the lies and the secrets and… I don't know, Ronnie. It just feels like one thing after another right now.'

'But you want to know the truth, don't you?'

She nodded, looking down at the floor.

'I knew something had happened. Amber, babe, why do you let him do this to you?'

'Because I love him, Ronnie.' She looked at him. 'It's as simple as that. I love him. Always have, always will. Nothing can change that. Not even you.'

'And what if he tells you something you really don't want to hear?'

She looked down at the floor again, her fingers fiddling with the bottom of the shirt she was wearing. 'I said nothing can change the fact I love him, Ronnie. I didn't say it meant everything would be all right.'

Ronnie threw his head back, closing his eyes for a second. 'What happened to escaping, Amber?'

'I can't run away from things forever, can I? There are so many questions to ask, so many things to face up to, and I don't think I can do any of that while I'm hiding from the truth, do you?'

'That's very grown-up of you.'

'If there was ever a time to be grown-up about things, it's now. Don't you think?'

He looked at her, reaching out to take her hand, squeezing it gently. 'I guess that one last time isn't gonna happen now, huh?'

She shook her head, gripping his hand tighter.

'Well, it was fun while it lasted.' Ronnie smiled. 'Playing out, I mean.'

'Yeah. Yeah, it was,' she whispered, looking into his eyes and hoping he understood. Hoping this didn't mean their friendship had changed, because the last thing she wanted was for that relationship to be damaged in any way.

But being with Ronnie, having spent the time she had with him – especially tonight – it had brought her a strange feeling of calm, and a moment of clarity she wasn't sure she'd felt in a long time. The only man she should ever be this close to was Jim. Her husband. It was time to stop escaping and head back to a reality she may not feel much like facing, but it was *her* reality. Whether she liked it or not.

Chapter Eighteen

Jim paced the floor, looking up at the clock on the living room wall for what felt like the millionth time, Ryan's words still playing on his mind – '*...you need to be looking closer to home on that score.*'

It didn't take a genius to work out what he meant by that. But was he really telling Jim something he ought to be taking notice of? Or was he just trying to cause a diversion so that his own behaviour could be overlooked? Whatever the reason, it involved Amber. It involved his wife, the woman he loved more than he could even begin to explain. And if something *was* going on, then *he* was the one who'd handed her every excuse she'd needed. Who else could he blame?

He stopped pacing the second he heard the front door close, staying rooted to the spot, waiting until she walked into the room.

'Where've you been?' he asked, wondering if she was going to tell him the truth –whatever that truth was, because he didn't really know – or whether she was just going to spin him some excuse. Would he even know which answer it was she gave him? 'It's late.'

'I've been at Ronnie's,' Amber replied, throwing her bag down on the sofa by the door. 'I needed to get away from you, Jim. Just for a couple of hours, to get my head straight.' She looked at him, right into his eyes, and it was at that second that he knew. He could tell. She'd been with another man. It was written all over her face – the guilt, the anxiety, it was all there. Almost as if she couldn't be bothered to hide it. Like she wanted him to find out.

'Is it straight now?' He continued to watch her as she moved around the room, sliding off a black scarf she'd had tied round her neck, letting it waft slowly to the floor as she shrugged off her jacket.

She said nothing, just nodded as she walked over to the sideboard to fix herself a drink.

'When did you get divorced?' She finally broke the brief silence that had ensued, taking a sip of brandy as she slowly turned back around to face him.

'Two years after we married.'

'Was it ever serious?' She took another sip, shuddering slightly as the dark liquid slipped down her throat.

He shook his head. 'No. No, it was never serious. It was never anything, Amber.'

'So why did you marry her? Because she was pregnant? If that was the case, then why not follow through and help her bring up the baby?'

'We were never a couple, Amber. I've tried to tell you all of this…'

'I don't understand any of it, Jim.'

His eyes locked with hers. 'Is that why you've been sleeping with Ronnie?'

Amber felt her stomach give a dip so harsh she felt physically sick. Had he known all along? Had he always suspected? Was this his way of trying to trick her into some kind of confession?

'Did I push you that far away, Amber?' His voice was quiet, no anger evident at all, which only served to confuse her even more. 'Was it my fault?'

She closed her eyes for a second, taking a deep breath before opening them and facing him. 'It's all such a mess, Jim. Everything. And I don't even know how we got to this, how it became so fucked up and complicated. I don't know.'

'She was a prostitute.'

Amber blinked a couple of times to make sure she was actually awake and this wasn't just some crazy, disjointed dream she was having. What was he talking about? *Who* was a prostitute?

'Brandon's mom. Well, she was a prostitute at the time I met her, anyway.'

She couldn't help but stare at him, trying to take in exactly what he was telling her. How had they got from the subject of her sleeping with Ronnie to him telling her his ex-wife was a prostitute? How? What messed-up route were they on here?

'I… Jim, I… Does Brandon know?'

'Of course he doesn't know,' Jim said, pushing a hand through his hair as he sat down on the arm of the sofa. 'And he never *will* know. That was the whole point of me marrying Heather – his mom. To give Brandon a better life than the one he could have ended up with.'

Amber poured herself another drink – one she very much needed now. 'Do you want one?' she asked, looking over at Jim as a multitude of mixed feelings washed over her at a pace so rapid she felt dizzy.

He nodded, grateful that everything was finally coming out in the open. All the years of pretending hadn't been easy. Or necessary. It wasn't as if the world needed to know every detail about his past, but Amber should have known everything. He knew that now. Would it have prevented this whole mess from happening? He couldn't answer that. He didn't even know if getting past everything that had gone on was an option anymore, all he knew was that it all had to come out. Or most if it, anyway. And then the truth of what Amber had done had to be faced.

'Me and you, we weren't together when I met her,' Jim began, taking the drink Amber held out for him. 'We'd just split up and I was with…' He looked down at the floor, closing his eyes as he took a quick sip of brandy. 'Well, you know who I was with at the time.'

Amber leaned back against the wall. She didn't want to sit down. She didn't want to get comfortable. 'Where did you meet her?'

'The Goldman Hotel.'

Amber threw her head back, sighing quietly. 'Jesus Christ, Jim…'

'I know. I know I was stupid, and I know it could have ended up a whole lot worse…'

She stared at him, arching an eyebrow. 'Oh, you think so?'

He closed his eyes again. This was harder than he'd ever thought it could be, because Amber had almost certainly erected those barriers around herself again – to protect him from her, as well as the other way around? And if that was the case, could they ever really get back to where they'd once been? To a time when they'd been happy. But that had been a time when the lies and the secrets and the painful inevitabilities of their marriage had still existed, so was what was happening here a situation they were never really going to be able to avoid? Was it always going to have happened, no matter what? He took another drink, draining his glass. 'It really was just one night, Amber. That was the one and only time we ever slept together, I…' He looked at her. He was going to say '*I promise you*', but knowing the way she felt about him saying those words, he thought better of it.

'You married her,' Amber pointed out, walking over to him and retrieving his empty glass, giving him a refill without asking if he wanted one.

Jim took a deep breath before speaking again. 'It was about – I dunno – about three months later, maybe more, when she contacted me again, when she told me she was pregnant. And given her line of work I wasn't convinced, you know? I wasn't convinced the baby was mine.'

'Understandable,' Amber said, resuming her position by the fireplace.

'But she was insistent. She said I was the only guy she'd slept with who hadn't used any protection…'

Amber looked down at the floor, not sure she really wanted to hear anymore, but at the same time she knew she had to.

'I'd been careless, reckless. I had to take responsibility.'

'So you married her? Just like that?'

'She was… she was a student. Studying law. She'd been in her final year at university and… and even though she'd only done what she'd done to make some extra money, she… it was never gonna be a way of life for her. She'd made mistakes – and we all do that, don't we?'

His eyes locked onto hers and Amber felt a shiver run right through her. But she said nothing, just let him continue.

'I couldn't know for definite that it was my baby, not until it was born but… I trusted her.'

'You trusted a prostitute? Who worked The Goldman?'

He looked at her again, his eyes almost begging her to believe him. But getting her to believe anything he said wasn't an easy thing to do anymore. If it ever had been. 'I trusted her, Amber. And that's when I realised – if that baby *was* mine then I didn't want him being brought up in a life where his mom had to struggle to survive, where he couldn't have the simplest of things. I wanted him to have a safe life. To have a roof over his head and food on the table.'

'And you thought marrying her was the way to go about all of that, did you?'

He looked down into his drink. 'She graduated just a couple of months before Brandon was born. She wanted to be a lawyer…'

'We all want a lot of things we can't have, Jim.'

His eyes met hers again, a silent, almost painful message passing between them. 'I just wanted my baby to be happy and settled, Amber. That's all. And it was something I could afford to do.'

'So, you thought it would all work out much better for you if she was out of the country, am I on the right track here?'

He hung his head, because that was the truth, in reality. He couldn't deny that. It was the truth. And the beginning of decades of secrets and lies. 'If it had all come out, yes, it could have damaged my career, maybe, possibly. I can't... I can't lie.'

Amber almost flinched at the irony of those last few words.

'There were opportunities for her over in the States,' Jim went on, taking a small sip of his second drink.

'Is that what your agent told you?'

He looked up at her. 'You don't flinch from asking the hard questions, do you?'

'It's my job.'

He turned his head away for a second, trying to compose himself, because he knew this could turn out to be one long night. 'We got married in Brooklyn. A very quiet, very quick ceremony – just us, my agent, and my manager. All very hush-hush. The way it had to be...' He trailed off for a second, taking another sip of brandy. 'I set her up in a nice, comfortable house in a quiet neighbourhood, somewhere perfect for bringing up kids... Brandon was born just days after the wedding.'

'Were you there? At Brandon's birth?' Just asking that question almost broke Amber's heart, because the thought of him being there, being a part of something he could never be a part of with her, it hurt like nothing had ever hurt before.

He shook his head, and a selfish wave of relief flooded Amber's body. 'She didn't want me there. We meant nothing to each other, Amber, and that's the truth. Everything I did, I did it for Brandon. I did it for him. But I... I did see him, not long after he was born.'

Amber closed her eyes, every crazy, mixed-up emotion, every messed-up, painful feeling she'd gone through in the past few weeks all colliding inside her like the most insensitive party ever thrown, taunting her until she found it hard to keep the tears at bay.

'By the time I had to go back to the U.K. Heather had a place at law school lined up, childcare was sorted, and a DNA test had proved Brandon was mine. But I guess you only have to look at him now to know that.'

Amber said nothing, but he was right, Brandon had so much of Jim in him it was ridiculous.

'I only married her to make sure she could stay in the U.S., Amber. To make sure my name was on that birth certificate, to make sure my son was going to be okay. No other reason. And you can stand there and tell me you don't want me to say these words, but I promise you that. I promise you. We divorced as soon as was legally possible, and I guess I was lucky, in reality. Heather never placed any unnecessary demands on me, she understood the way things worked. She still does. She let me get on with my life, and I let her get on with hers. All I ever asked for was the chance to visit my son whenever I could.'

Amber looked down into her almost-empty glass of brandy. 'I'm assuming she never went back to…'

'No. She's worked as a lawyer for years now. And she's a good one. She met her husband just days after joining the firm she's worked for since she left Law School. They've been happily married ever since. Both of them have been made partners now, so, all in all, it's worked out for the best.'

Amber looked up at him. 'Really?'

His eyes stayed locked on hers. 'Maybe everything could have been handled a lot better, Amber, but in the long run nobody got hurt.'

'Nobody got hurt…' she repeated, finishing the last of her brandy before walking over to the sideboard, placing the empty glass down on it, her hand hovering over the bottle as she contemplated a third drink. 'Is that how you really see it, Jim?' She decided against the drink and turned back round to face him. 'Nobody got hurt?'

'Heather got a new life over there in the U.S., a life she loved – still loves. Brandon was well looked after, and I tried to visit him as much as I could, but…'

'Nobody got hurt.'

He walked over to her, his eyes on hers all the time, never breaking the stare. 'How could I know it would all end up like this?'

'You could have tried being honest from the start, Jim. That could have changed everything.'

'Would it have changed the fact you slept with your best friend?'

She kept her eyes on his, knowing that to break the stare would make her look weak, and yes, she felt guilty, but she wasn't alone in being in the wrong here. 'I slept with Ronnie to escape the shit that was going on around me, Jim. And I know that sounds like the most pathetic, over-used excuse, but it's the truth. There *is* no excuse for what I did, and I'm sorry, I truly am, because I shouldn't have acted so childishly. It was a rash and stupid decision, in hindsight, but do you not see what you do to me? How you push me away? With the lies and the secrets and the fact I just don't know if I can trust you anymore. Can you not see that?'

'You slept with another man, Amber. We're married, and you slept with another man. So if we're playing the blame game here, how can I ever trust *you* again, knowing what you've done?'

She stared at him, narrowing her eyes slightly. 'Then walk away.' She hadn't even realised the words had slipped out, that she'd said them out loud, but there they were, hanging in the air like some dark, unwanted storm cloud.

'Is that what you want?'

'Don't make *me* the one who decides where we go from here, Jim. Don't make *me* the one who has to make that decision.'

'Someone else touched you, Amber. In the most intimate of ways. Someone else touched you. He's been inside you, he saw things only I should be seeing…'

'And isn't that exactly what *you* were doing when I was with Ryan? Wasn't that you? Weren't *you* the one who'd turn up on my doorstep, smiling that smile and making me want you?'

'That doesn't make it okay.'

'I never said it did.'

'You weren't married to Ryan.'

She looked into his eyes, once again holding the stare. 'I almost was.'

He paused for a second before speaking. 'But you weren't,

Amber.' He paused again, their eyes still locked together, the air heavy with the intensity that surrounded them. 'Do you wish you *had* married him?'

She couldn't help laughing a short, cynical laugh. 'Jesus, what the hell is that supposed to mean? No, I don't wish I'd married him.'

'You slept with another man, Amber.'

She shook her head, backing out of the room and running upstairs. What happened now she had no idea, all she knew was that everything was still as messed up and complicated as it had been before. Nothing was sorted, nothing felt any better or nearer to any kind of conclusion. She didn't even know how she felt anymore. About anyone, or anything.

'Are you in love with me, Amber?'

She turned to face him, even though a part of her just wanted to curl up and go to sleep, to forget any of this was happening. He stood in the doorway of their bedroom, leaning against the doorpost, watching her with those piercing green eyes of his. Her handsome husband. A man she didn't feel as if she knew anymore – if she'd ever really known him at all.

'You know I am.'

He shook his head slowly, his hands in his pockets. 'I don't think I do.'

'Then you've just got to believe me.'

He hung his head, pushing a hand through his hair. 'Ronnie White – a best friend with benefits, huh?'

'It isn't like that, Jim.'

He looked up at her. 'Isn't it? I thought it would have been *exactly* like that. I mean, why else turn to him? You didn't go running into Ryan's arms, did you? You didn't end up in *his* bed.'

'And why would I have done that? Ryan doesn't even want me anymore.'

'Oh, doesn't he?' Jim fixed Amber with a look that sent her stomach dipping as low as it could go. 'Why do you think he's put in this loan request, Amber? Why do *you* think he's putting

Newcastle Red Star's season in jeopardy just so he can run away? Why do you think that is, huh? Just what is it he can't deal with? It's you, baby. He can't deal with *you*.'

'That isn't my fault,' Amber said quietly. 'I can't help the way he feels, I can't…' She looked straight at Jim, wishing with all of her heart that none of this had happened. None of it. 'You thought me and him…? You really thought…'

'I trusted you, Amber. But I had my doubts about him. Seems I should have had that the other way around though, doesn't it? Oh, I know he wants you. He's told me as much himself. But the thing is, he hasn't acted on that, has he? And that's why he wants to get away, because he's scared that he will. He's scared that he might do something he eventually regrets. And the reason why I was reluctant to let him go? Why, up until this evening, I was *still* reluctant to let him go? Because even though I knew, deep down, that he would never really try to do anything stupid, not after what he went through last season, there was always this irrational fear in the back of my mind that he might try something – Ryan Fisher is a law unto himself, after all. But there was also the rational part of my brain that said he wouldn't dare. Not now. Not right under my nose. However, knowing what I know now, Amber; knowing how easily you just give up and run to others when you need some time out – knowing all of that, well, it's *you* I don't trust. Just one small move on his part and you could just crumble, couldn't you, honey? You could just give in and give him what he wants and I can't risk that, especially now. Right up until tonight I was still uncertain that letting him go was the right thing to do, even though I could have him on his way within weeks, if that's what he really wanted. Days, even, if I can talk the right people round. But now – now I'll do anything in my power to make sure he leaves the North East for as long as it takes him to forget what he had with you.'

'You really think that low of me? After everything you've done, you really think that low of *me*?'

He walked over to her, tilting her chin up with the back of his hand so she had no option but to look into his eyes. 'I love you, Amber. And I'm doing it for you, as much as for him.'

'You really believe that, don't you?' she said quietly, shaking her head. 'You know, maybe we really do need some time apart.'

As she made to turn around, he reached out and grabbed her wrist, swinging her back round to face him. 'You still want me, Amber. Despite all of this, despite everything I've just told you, you still want me. I can feel it, I can see it in your eyes.'

What could she say to that? A part of her probably did, it was just a part of her that was keeping very quiet right now.

'And even though I know another man's touched you in ways he really shouldn't have, I still want you, too, because I am crazy in love with you, Amber.'

'You got the crazy bit right,' Amber said, pulling her wrist free from his grip, but he was too quick for her, grabbing her again, this time round the waist.

'This is what you do to me,' he whispered, his mouth close to her ear, his hand on her hip keeping her against him. 'In some strange way, the thought of you with another man is actually turning me on.'

He began kissing her neck, and against everything she wanted to feel, she felt herself giving in to him. She felt those familiar tingles, that deep ache in the pit of her stomach that signalled something incredible was about to happen.

'Jim...'

'It's okay, baby... Everything's gonna be okay.'

Was it? Really? After everything that had happened?

'Lie down,' he whispered, pulling back slightly so she could see his face.

It felt as though she'd suddenly been hypnotised by some invisible force as she lay back on the bed, closing her eyes as he slowly stripped the clothes from her body. Bit by bit she could feel herself becoming exposed, creating an almost warped sense of liberty, given the circumstances. Part of her didn't really want this, yet another part of her wanted it more than she could explain, and as his lips began touching her naked skin, she knew which side of her had won out. Despite herself.

'Put your hands above your head,' Jim ordered, taking something out of his back pocket.

Amber recognised it as the scarf she'd taken off downstairs, and once again her stomach did that flip, sending out a message to her to get ready for something she wasn't going to forget. 'Jim… I don't…'

He just smiled at her, gently pulling her wrists together above her head, tying one end of the scarf loosely around them before fastening the other end to the headboard. 'I won't hurt you, Amber. In fact, I guarantee, you're gonna love this.'

'Shouldn't we…?'

'I don't want to argue any more, baby. I just want to be with you.'

She was about to say something, to put up some kind of fight, when she felt his hand slide between her legs, parting them gently, and just that one touch sent her heart racing, her body breaking out in a million tiny goose bumps. Arching her back, she gave in to it all, surrendering to whatever it was this was going to turn out to be, because, all of a sudden, *this* was the way she wanted it– for him to be in total control, to take over everything. She was too tired, too exhausted for it to be any other way.

'Oh Jesus, Jim…' she groaned, her hips bucking as his mouth replaced his hand, his tongue slowly exploring a place he knew only too well. His hands were pushing her legs wider apart, his mouth taking in every inch of her – Amber had never felt anything like it. She was burning up, turned on by the fact she couldn't touch him, her stomach dipping and diving on a constant loop as he continued to probe harder and faster, taking her right to the edge before pulling her right back again.

She wanted to come – she could feel it about to happen, feel that rush about to take hold, and he must have felt it, too, because he pulled away, kneeling up for a second to look at her. It was both the strangest and the most erotic experience of her life, just watching him, staring at her, his eyes scanning her naked body in a way that almost brought her to orgasm without him laying another finger on her. It felt as though he'd cast some kind of spell over her, like he was working invisible strings as her legs opened wider, her back arched more so her breasts were pushed right out, willing him to touch her, to take her, to put anything he wanted inside of her because, right now, she didn't care what, she just wanted to feel a part of him there.

The throbbing between her legs was becoming almost too much for her to bear, knowing she couldn't reach down and touch herself, knowing that everything was up to him. He controlled the outcome of this, and that only served to send her stomach flipping again, her head starting to spin with the painful anticipation.

'Jim, please, this is killing me,' she groaned, feeling the sheet beneath her growing damp.

'All in good time,' he whispered, leaning over her, letting his fingers trail lazily over her stomach. She could feel his erection rock-hard against her thigh and that just made her want him more; she needed to feel him inside her before this pushed her over the edge. She'd never felt so turned on, so out of control of a situation, and that lack of power only heightened everything, whether she wanted it to or not. Her body was ruling her head here, and there wasn't a thing she could do about it.

'Oh… Oh, Jesus, you have got to do something,' she moaned, closing her eyes as she felt his fingers move down again, touching her, teasing her, hitting that spot for a glorious second, delving inside her for a few seconds more before pulling away again. It was almost cruel. And how he was managing to hold out himself was beyond her because she could feel him throbbing hard against her. 'Jim, please… I'm begging you…' Is that what he wanted? Was that was this was all about? Did he *want* her to beg him? Did he want her to want him so much that she would do anything to make sure that happened? Even if that was the case, she was in no position to fight it. He'd pushed her too far, taken her too close to the edge now and without the endgame she needed, she couldn't leave. Wouldn't leave.

Totally unexpected tears started to fall down her cheeks which, for just the briefest of seconds, took her mind off the frustratingly beautiful pain she was feeling. And when he started to kiss them away, his hands either side of her hips, she finally began to feel a sense of this all coming to an end, even though she wasn't entirely sure she wanted it to. What she did know for sure was that she wanted him to take her hard, to push his way into her so fast and so rough that it physically hurt, and she had no idea *why* she wanted it that way, she just did. She wanted it to be painful, she needed it to be that way for a reason she couldn't explain. And when he finally did push his way into her, it was every bit as beautiful as she'd wanted it to be. Every thrust hurt, his hips thudding against hers as he pushed harder, making her cry out. It was the most incredible, the most intense, the most erotic sex she'd ever had, and a part of her never wanted it to end. It was making her feel things she hadn't felt in weeks – it made her feel alive, made her feel strangely empowered, despite the fact he was the one holding all the cards.

Closing her eyes and arching her back once more, pushing her hips up against his as their rhythm got faster and faster, she bit down on her lip as she got ready for the impending finale, waiting for it to take over for those few, beautiful seconds it took to end whatever this had been. And when it came, it hit her with an intensity she just hadn't been prepared for, washing over her like a tidal wave of pure pleasure, a violent assault on every feeling she'd ever experienced that made the tears fall and the anger build. When she felt him explode inside her it was as though he'd taken over every inch of her body, filling her up with something she wasn't altogether sure she wanted, but it was taking her anyway, engulfing her, making her scream out loud and cry with pain until that wave subsided – until she could feel him moving no more. Until she felt him slowly leave her body.

She kept her eyes closed as he untied her wrists, pulling the scarf away, letting her body take the final few seconds it needed to feel like hers again before she sat up, pulling her knees to her chest. For a couple of seconds she just looked at him, before slapping him so hard she felt her hand sting with the force. 'Don't you *ever* do that to me again,' she hissed, getting up and throwing her clothes back on as quickly as she could.

'Amber…'

'No, Jim. Something… something's changed. Somewhere along the line something's changed between us, and I can't explain what that is. I can't, and I want to, but… I really think we need that time apart. Don't you?'

He shook his head, getting up and walking over to her, but she backed away, putting up a hand to stop him coming any closer. 'No, Amber, I don't. What happened here…?'

'I wanted it, Jim. What you just did to me, yeah, I wanted it. But we can't carry on like this, not knowing what the hell is going on, because that's how I feel now. That's exactly how I feel.' She felt the tears return, streaming down her face, and she didn't even try to wipe them away. What would be the point? They weren't going to stop. 'All I wanted was to be your wife. To have your baby. That was all I wanted, and yet, somehow, that problem's got lost amongst all the other crap, and I can't even think straight because I love you, so much it fucking hurts, but I can't be with you anymore.'

He looked down at the floor, his hands in his pockets. 'Maybe you're right.'

Despite everything she'd just said, Amber was surprised at her own reaction to his words.

'Maybe we *do* need some time out.'

She couldn't say anything. The words wouldn't come.

'I love you, Amber. I want you to know that – I *need* you to know that. But if we stay together, this could destroy us. I mean, look at what's happened tonight. I don't know what came over me, but… it was like I wanted to hurt you. Physically, emotionally, feelings I had no control over were there, flooding my brain, making me do that to you and…'

Amber made her way over to the walk-in wardrobe in the corner of the room, silently looking for her small, pink carry-on suitcase.

'This doesn't mean it's over, does it? It doesn't have to be over.'

Amber turned to look at him. He was leaning against the archway that led into the wardrobe, his expression conveying everything she was feeling. 'I don't know.'

'We could just try sitting down and talking. Something we probably should have done a long time ago. Surely that wouldn't hurt?'

Amber shook her head. 'It's too late, Jim. And I think you know that, too.' She didn't think she could bear delaying what seemed to be the inevitable any longer. For the past few months she'd been the happiest she'd been since Jim had walked into her life two decades ago. Yet now, knowing what she knew, knowing how all those years had panned out, she wished he'd never walked into it at all. 'I think we just need to draw a line under everything and admit that we were never really meant to be together.'

'Is that what you think?'

'Look at our history, Jim. Look at our relationship. It was never straightforward, never conventional…'

'And that's a bad thing?'

She looked at him again, holding his stare for a few seconds longer. 'Yeah. When I remember how I felt a lot of that time, then, yeah. It was.'

He looked down at the rust-coloured carpet. 'I'm sorry. For the way things have turned out.'

'Me too,' she whispered, turning away from him as she began throwing a few things into her case, stopping only when she felt his hands on her hips, slowly turning her round to face him. 'Jim…' He was kissing her before she'd had time to register what was happening, his thumb stroking her cheek, his mouth moving slowly and gently against hers. It felt like a kiss goodbye; a heart breaking kiss. A kiss that made Amber feel as though she was bidding farewell to a chapter in her life she hadn't yet finished reading. A chapter that had to end before its time or this story just wouldn't work out, because, sometimes, the story doesn't always have the ending you want, no matter how much you're rooting for it. And there isn't a thing you can do to change that.

Chapter Nineteen

'Oh, my God! It's kicking!' Amber laughed, placing her hand on Debbie's swollen stomach. She had the most perfect baby bump, rounded and small, and not much extra weight gain either, despite her eating – as Debbie put it – like a horse!

'Yeah. It would appear we have another footballer in the making, or that's what Gary's saying anyway,' Debbie sighed, rubbing her lower back.

'Did you not want to know the sex of the baby?' Amber asked, watching as Debbie continued to rub her back.

'Well, *I* did, but for some reason Gary wants to keep it a surprise. God knows why, but I'm humouring him.'

'You okay? Is your back giving you trouble?'

'No, I'm fine, chick. Just getting used to my new shape, that's all. And even though I'm only five months gone I still can't keep off the loo! Back in a tick.'

Amber smiled as she watched her friend almost jog out of the room to the downstairs bathroom. So far she was having a fairly easy pregnancy, and Amber was slowly getting used to being around all the baby talk and the excitement a prospective new arrival generated without it tearing her up inside. She couldn't say she didn't still get fleeting moments when the sadness would just wash over her, making her mourn the baby she would never have.

Because that happened. It happened a lot. But she could handle it now. She had to, she had no other choice. It was the way her life had panned out, and she just had to accept it.

Sitting back in her chair at the dining table, she took a long sip of coffee as she looked around Debbie's newly-decorated kitchen. To say her and Gary's house was typical 'footballer' probably wasn't too far from the truth, because if there was one thing Debbie loved it was her bling. And even here, in the kitchen, that was evident. A huge, elaborate, crystal chandelier hung from the stark white ceiling above a granite-topped island; the units were also white, sporting grey-black diamante-flecked work surfaces that shimmered when the light from the many huge windows dotted around the room hit them. There were two large Gaggenau cookers – although quite why there were two Amber couldn't really fathom, considering she'd never seen Debbie cook a thing in all the time she'd known her – a massive double-sized dishwasher and various other appliances Amber had yet to work out the purpose of. At the other end of the room, where she was sitting, was an enormous, white, glass-topped dining table around which eight silver and white chairs were placed. Professionally taken black and white framed photos of Debbie and Gary hung from the walls, as well as a TV so big it could almost pass for a small cinema screen, and music was filtering into the room through hidden speakers and a central sound system, the whereabouts of which Amber had no idea. The whole house was a little too much for her, but Debbie had just spent months painstakingly redecorating it, and to her it was her palace. Although Amber couldn't help thinking that she hadn't really factored in the arrival of a baby. There was so much white around the place – from the walls to the sofas, and even the stair carpet – that the thought of cleaning it all once that baby reached toddler age made Amber nervous, and she didn't even live there.

It was all a far cry from her own new home – a modest but beautiful house on the outskirts of Newcastle, not far from the airport, so it was handy for all those trips to London she had to make. Detached, and fairly private with a gated driveway, it had a small back garden, a double garage, and inside she'd had it decorated in colours ranging from a yellow hallway to a red kitchen. It was almost bohemian in its feel – lived in and comfortable. She may have been married to an ex-footballer, and was best friends with the ultimate WAG, but she was never going to become one herself. She just didn't do chandeliers and swimming pools. She did squishy sofas and wooden coffee tables with magazines and DVDs lying around all over the place. She liked being surrounded by her own kind of mess. She liked having her own space. Most of the time. There were even days when she quite liked being on her own again. Although Jim was never far from her thoughts, and sometimes the feelings of sadness and regret would hit her out of the blue, physically winding her. But she was getting used to them. She was getting used to a lot of things.

'Hey, you okay?' Debbie asked, sitting back down and swinging her legs up onto the chair beside her.

'Yeah.' Amber smiled, shaking those thoughts she didn't want to think about from her mind. 'I'm fine.'

'You sure?'

'Debbie, I'm okay. Honestly.'

'Well, I'll try and believe you, but you're not convincing me.'

Amber took another sip of coffee, looking briefly out of the French windows onto Debbie and Gary's ridiculously huge back garden with its landscaped lawn, outdoor swimming pool, separate pool-house and guest bungalow. And today there was also the addition of a massive marquee next to the pool, set up ready for the party Debbie was throwing for Gary's birthday.

'It's only been a couple of months since you and Jim split up, chick. That's no time, and, let's face it, it isn't even like you can completely walk away from it all, can you? Given your line of work.'

Amber turned to look at Debbie. 'I can handle all of that, Debs. Really. I've seen him loads of times since we separated and we're fine. We're getting on okay.'

Debbie just raised an eyebrow, placing a hand on her baby bump, which didn't escape Amber's notice. Somehow, that one, tiny, innocent action, along with the mention of Jim's name, had brought back all that pain and heartache she'd felt when she'd been told she could never have children. That she could never have *Jim's* children.

'You *are* going to stay for this party, aren't you?' Debbie's voice broke into Amber's thoughts, jolting her back to a reality very different to the one she'd thought she'd be living.

'Hmm? Oh, yes. Why wouldn't I be staying? I said I was, didn't I?'

'Yeah, well, I know you, missy. If you start dwelling on things too much, your whole mood changes, then you claim all you want to do is go off and be alone.'

'I do not,' Amber laughed, even though that *was* actually true. She did do that. Sometimes. 'Well, okay, maybe I do. Now and again. But I won't do it tonight, I promise.'

'Good. Because the girls are dying to see you again, and I'm looking forward to having your company for more than a couple of hours. You always seem to be rushing about these days.'

'It's the nature of my work, Debbie. I need to be down in London a lot more than I used to be because of this TV show I seem to have got myself attached to… I could kill Max sometimes. It's almost like he can talk me into something without me actually realising it's happening.'

She'd just been made a regular panel member on *Back of the Net*, a Cloud Sports-produced football-themed game show, alongside Ronnie, who was one of the team captains. It was a lot of fun, very tongue-in-cheek most of the time, and she loved doing it, but it only added to her already packed workload.

As Max had predicted, her Ice photo shoot had propelled her profile through the roof and she was currently enjoying being courted by several big-name beauty products wanting her to be their new 'face'. At the age of thirty-eight she had offers of modelling contracts – which was crazy, in Amber's eyes – invitations to parties and events she couldn't keep up with, and a life that left her permanently exhausted. But that was the way things needed to be. If she was constantly busy then she had no time to sit and think about things. No time to miss him. No time to dwell on what they could have had but lost because neither of them could face up to the truth.

'Yeah, but you're having fun, aren't you?' Debbie said, dunking a chocolate chip cookie into her coffee. 'You know, I never used to touch these things before I got pregnant but now I can't stop eating them.'

Amber smiled, reaching over to grab a cookie herself. 'Well, let me take a couple of those off your hands. Then, if you don't mind, I'll nip upstairs and finish getting ready for this party of yours. Where *is* the birthday boy anyway?'

'Gone to help the DJ sort out the music for tonight, God help us. I've told him, if he doesn't make sure there are some J-Lo tracks, a bit of 70s disco, and some early 90s dance music in there then he's a dead man, birthday or no birthday. He and his mates aren't the only ones at this party.'

Amber quickly shoved the last of her cookie into her mouth and stood up. 'Right, I'd better go and start making myself look presentable. How long have I got? When does it all kick off? No pun intended there.'

'You seem to have cheered up incredibly quickly,' Debbie pointed out, taking the last chocolate chip cookie from the plate.

'I wasn't *not* cheerful.'

'Yeah. You were. It's all starting around seven-ish, so you've got a good hour or so before people start turning up. Actually, I'd better go and do some tidying up of my own before the catering company arrives with the food. They'll be here in ten minutes… I tell you, since I became a mummy-to-be my hair just won't do anything it's supposed to.'

'That's because most of it isn't your own.' Amber grinned,

winking at Debbie over her shoulder as she made her way out of the kitchen.

'Cheeky cow,' Debbie laughed, throwing a zebra-print cushion at Amber, and missing. 'And don't touch my champagne body wash. It's the only thing that doesn't bring me out in a rash at the minute.'

Amber practically skipped up the stairs, glad she'd decided to make a day – and a night – of it with Debbie. It had really cheered her up. And the fact she was also sleeping over in one of their many spare rooms meant she didn't have to go home to an empty house tonight, which was a bonus. She may have told Debbie she was handling things okay, but sometimes, just being in the same part of the country as Jim hurt more than she cared to admit. And tomorrow she'd be seeing him again, although it was purely on a professional basis. Just a few hours ago he'd called a press conference for the following morning at Tynebridge, without giving any clue as to what it was all about. But Amber had an inkling of just what was about to happen. And she wasn't quite sure how she felt about it. All she knew was that she was going to enjoy tonight, and deal with whatever announcement Jim had to make in the morning.

A quick shower and hair wash later and she was ready to step into the baby-pink wrap-over dress she'd bought especially for the party, with the help of Debbie and a more-than-attentive shop assistant in a small, exclusive, and way-too-expensive boutique in town. Despite earning quite a bit more than she used to when she'd worked at News North East, throwing money away on dresses, handbags, shoes and nails still wasn't something Amber felt comfortable doing – it just wasn't her. But as a special treat to herself, thanks to the Ice photo shoot and the money she was getting for being a regular panellist on *Back of the Net*, she'd thrown caution to the wind for once and splashed out on a new dress, and heels that were probably going to have her feet aching after five minutes, but what the hell. She actually felt incredibly sexy as she stood in front of the mirror in just her underwear, admiring those new shoes, pulling her hair away from her shoulders as she turned first one way, then the other.

'Very nice!'

Amber quickly swung round to see Ronnie standing in the doorway, a huge grin on his face.

'Debbie said you were up here.'

'You could have knocked first.' Amber hurriedly tried to locate the whereabouts of her recently discarded bathrobe.

'Come on, Amber. It's not like I haven't seen it all before. What's the point in being shy now?'

She looked at him, raising her eyebrows. 'Because our relationship isn't like that anymore?'

He walked into the room, gently closing the door behind him. 'It *could* be. If you want it to be. I know *I* certainly won't be complaining if you decide you need some more sympathy sex.'

'Sympathy sex?' Amber raised her eyebrows again.

'Yeah. You know, a little bit of a release from all the stress. I mean, there's…'

'There's what, Ronnie? There's nothing standing in our way now? Seeing as my marriage is all but over?'

'That isn't what I meant, Amber.'

Abandoning the hunt for the bathrobe, Amber pulled her dress up off the bed and slipped it on, turning back to look in the mirror.

'You look beautiful,' Ronnie whispered, coming up behind her, gently pushing her hair away from her neck, leaning over to kiss it.

Amber squirmed slightly, pulling away from him. 'Don't, Ronnie.'

'What's the matter?'

She turned to face him. 'I'm really not in the mood for any of this.'

He held his hands up and backed away, sitting down on the huge king-size bed in the centre of the room. 'You seen Jim lately?' Ronnie asked, swiftly changing the subject.

'I saw him yesterday. I was at the training ground recording a piece for Saturday's show, about Red Star's match against Daventry United. He was actually taking the training session, for a change.'

'He doesn't usually do that.'

'No. I know he doesn't. But Gary says he's been a lot more involved in that side of things this season. Don't ask me why.'

Ronnie watched her as she began running her fingers through her hair, ruffling it up at the roots to give it a touch more volume. 'Did you talk to him?'

'No, I just blanked him. What do you *think* I did? I *had* to talk to him – I was working.' She turned around, satisfied that that was as good as her hair was going to get. 'We didn't really break up on bad terms, Ronnie, I told you that. And, to be honest, I don't really want to go over it all again.'

'I don't know why you don't just try and work things out, if you're getting on that well.'

'Have you come up here to deliberately try and wind me up?'

'No,' Ronnie sighed, throwing himself back on the bed, flinging his arms up above his head. 'No, I haven't. You just confuse the hell out of me sometimes, Amber.'

'Think what I do to myself, then,' she said, turning back to the mirror to double-check her make-up.

'I meant what I said, though.' Ronnie hauled himself up off the bed, walking back over to Amber. 'About being there, if you need me. For any reason. But especially if you need me for sex.'

'Will you stop that,' Amber laughed, playfully thumping his arm. 'Anyway, I'm abstaining from sex for the foreseeable future. It's safer that way.'

Ronnie arched a surprised eyebrow. 'Yeah. Whatever.'

'Get out of here, go on,' Amber said, still smiling as she pushed him gently out of the room. 'Go get me a drink. Anything pink and sparkling'll do.'

'That's all Debbie's serving by the looks of things.'

'Go on, out! I'll be down in a few minutes.'

'Nice to see bossy Amber back.' Ronnie winked at her before practically running down the long, winding staircase to the party.

Amber closed the door, leaning back against it and closing her eyes. Sometimes she felt as though her whole life was running on autopilot. On the surface she seemed cool and calm, but underneath she was frantically trying to keep it all together. And how long she could keep going like that was anybody's guess. All she knew right now was that she was going to enjoy tonight, and try and forget about everything else, even if it was just for a few hours.

The sound of people arriving downstairs, and music thumping from the marquee outside in the garden, told Amber the party had started now. It was time to go and show her face, show everybody that the past couple of months hadn't got her down half as much as everyone might have thought they had. She could put on a good act if she needed to.

Taking a deep breath, she opened the door, ran her fingers through her hair one more time and walked downstairs, fixing a smile on her face that she was determined was going to stay there all night. She'd make sure of that. After all, she was good at hiding the truth, wasn't she?

'Where's Ellen?' Gary asked as Ryan wandered into the conservatory, his hands in the pockets of his dark jeans.

'She's gone out with her mates. There's some gig on at the arena she's had tickets for since January, then they're off clubbing.'

'You don't look too fed up to be here on your own,' Gary said, handing him a bottle of lager.

Ryan shrugged, taking a swig from the bottle. 'She's got her life, I've got mine.'

'That's a strange way to talk about your relationship when you've been living together for months.'

Ryan said nothing, turning to look outside at the garden decorated with fairy lights hanging from the trees and fences, the huge marquee which was acting as a makeshift nightclub, and a patio area surrounded by heaters and more fairy lights that had been set up as an outdoor bar area. People were swarming everywhere, all fake tan and high heels, designer gear and bright-white smiles, laughing and drinking and enjoying the party. Which was exactly what Ryan intended to do – enjoy himself. He had a reason to now, didn't he?

'You look shifty,' Gary pointed out, flicking the top off a new bottle of lager. 'What's the matter?'

'Nothing's the matter,' Ryan protested, looking outside again. 'How's Debs? Everything going okay with the baby?'

'Everything's fine, apart from the fact I still can't get me head around the fact I'm gonna be a dad. But stop changing the subject. You were in with the boss for hours this morning, and I know Max was with you, too. And the only reason you *and* Max would be in with the boss together, especially for that amount of time, is if something's going on. You gonna tell me what?'

Ryan took another drink, turning back to face Gary. 'I'm leaving, Gaz. Temporarily. But I'm leaving. Soon.'

Gary frowned. 'Leaving? You mean…?'

'The loan's been agreed with CD Adeje. I'm off to Tenerife at the end of the month. It's all sorted. But keep it quiet, all right? The boss has called a press conference at Tynebridge tomorrow morning, he's going to make the official announcement then. You're the only one I've told so far.'

Gary let out a low whistle. 'Wow. You've kept that one quiet. I just assumed it'd all died down because you hadn't mentioned anything for a while, but…'

'To be honest, for a time it did look as though it was all going to fall through. The boss had a job persuading the board to let me go, and then there's been his own personal problems to deal with…' Ryan stopped talking, staring down at the ground as he remembered how he'd felt the day he'd heard that Amber and Jim had separated. A trial separation. That was the official line. No divorce, no word from either of them publicly about how long that trial was going to last, and even though, just for one brief second, it had almost been enough to make Ryan think twice about what he was doing, the rational side of him told him that changing his plans wasn't an option. He couldn't let what had happened between Jim and Amber sink him deeper into some make-believe happy ending that lived only in his head. They were having problems – the world knew that now. But they hadn't said their separation was forever. Amber and Jim Allen would never be over, no matter how much they might think they were. 'But, Newcastle Red Star are doing well,' Ryan sighed, wishing he felt happier than he did, '…and anyway, I've been out with this ankle injury for a couple of weeks and you've managed fine without me, haven't you? You don't need me.'

'*I* need you, mate,' Gary said, leaning back against the window. 'Jesus, Ryan, I never actually thought you were serious. I thought you were handling everything okay, that you and Ellen were…' He looked at Ryan. 'What are you gonna do about Ellen?'

Ryan didn't know. He really didn't know. She was obviously going to find out about his imminent loan spell now, and he assumed that she'd more than likely want to come with him. But he didn't want her to. He wanted to do this alone. That was the whole point of this move in the first place, to forget all the crap he'd got himself into and try and make a new start, away from it all, before returning home the Ryan Fisher he *really* wanted to be. Someone who didn't spend every waking minute of every day wanting something he could never have.

'Ryan?'

Gary's voice shook him back to reality. 'What? Sorry, mate, I…' He trailed off again, looking up just as Amber walked into the kitchen. He couldn't take his eyes off her. For a woman who was going through a difficult time in her very short marriage, and going through it all very much in the public eye, she looked as though she didn't have a care in the world. She looked incredible. With her dark red hair hanging loose over her shoulders, her make-up minimal, and those perfect legs of hers on show, accentuated by the sexiest heels he'd ever seen her wear, she looked stunning. 'Jesus Christ,' Ryan gasped, his hand gripping the bottle he was holding as he watched her float around the kitchen, smiling at everyone, hugging her friends, exuding that air of celebrity she seemed to have honed to a fine art lately. 'I thought that shoot she did in Ice magazine was hot, but...'

'As hot as you can get without showing anything,' Gary mumbled, not altogether comfortable with the way Ryan was looking at his ex. 'I mean, come on. I thought we might at least have got a glimpse of those tits of hers, but she went down the tasteful route, didn't she? Take it all off, but show nowt.'

Ryan looked at him. 'Are you for real?'

Gary raised an eyebrow. 'Oh, yeah. I forgot. It wouldn't have bothered you, would it? You've seen it all before.'

Ryan ignored him, turning back to watch Amber, their eyes briefly meeting as she turned to take the glass of pink champagne Ronnie held out for her. 'She looks amazing,' he whispered, unwilling to take his eyes off her just yet, waiting for her to break the stare first. Which she did, as she turned and made her way out of the kitchen.

'You're walking a dangerous road there, mate,' Gary warned. 'Her and the boss, they'll never split up, not for good. We all know the problems they went through, or we do now, anyway, but... You know, maybe this loan period will do you the world of good.'

'Yeah. Maybe.' Ryan put his drink down on the table beside him, an idea forming that he was determined to see through, before he lost his nerve.

'Ryan... where you going?'

'I'll see you later.' He almost ran out of the conservatory, determined not to lose sight of her, pushing his way through the crowded kitchen, following her into the slightly quieter back room.

'Are you stalking me?' Amber asked as she turned round to face him, her hands in the pockets of her pale pink dress.

He stopped dead in his tracks, grinning at her. 'I could do, if you want me to.' His eyes dropped down to her cleavage, although there wasn't a great deal of it on show. But he knew what lay beneath the thin material of that dress. He knew only too well.

Amber couldn't help smiling. 'Yeah. Still the same old Ryan. You on your own? No Ellen?'

'Why's everyone asking me where Ellen is tonight?'

'Because she's your girlfriend?' Amber pointed out.

'Yeah, well…' He stopped himself from saying anything else, not sure how much information he should give her just yet.

'Yeah, well – what?' Amber asked, cocking her head.

'Nothing,' Ryan sighed.

'Okay… Do you want to go check out the nightclub?'

'You mean that big tent in the back garden?'

Amber smiled again. 'You know, sometimes you're quite rubbish at this footballer lark.'

He grinned again, giving her the full-on Ryan Fisher charm. 'I can kill 'em on the pitch, but I don't always get it right off it, huh?'

'Something like that. Come on. It might be a bit livelier outside.'

Ryan couldn't move for a second, it was like he was rooted to the spot, unable to get his head around the fact she was being so friendly. So forthcoming. And it felt good, talking to her like this. It felt like old times. Was he reading too much into it? Probably. He wasn't naive enough to think she was giving him any kind of green light. But, then again, the night was young, and he'd be stupid to ignore any signs she *might* just give off later. If he played his cards right.

'I wouldn't.'

Ryan swung round to see Ronnie standing there, his hands in his pockets, his expression serious.

'Wouldn't, what?' Ryan asked, his eyes meeting Ronnie's.

'She's incredibly vulnerable right now, and you know that, so I'd be very careful if I were you.'

'You warning me off?'

'I'm just letting you know that Amber doesn't need any more mess in her life, okay?'

Ryan narrowed his eyes, smirking slightly. 'You waiting for your own chance to get back in there, huh? Literally. She feels good, doesn't she?'

Ronnie looked down at the ground for a split second before looking back at Ryan, his face still darkly serious. 'I'll pretend I didn't hear that.'

'But you and her – you *were* sleeping together, right? Just before she split from Jim?'

Ronnie ignored him, walking away from him without another glance. Ryan pushed a hand through his hair and laughed quietly to himself. Nobody knew for sure that Ronnie White and Amber Allen *had* been having an affair, but it was quite obvious to Ryan that, at some point, they'd become best friends with benefits, even if that time had been brief. It had happened, Ryan was sure of it, and that, combined with everything else that the public *did* know about – her and Jim's baby battle, the revelation that Brandon Palmer was Jim Allen's son – it had all added to the reasons why Amber and Jim had separated. But no matter how much he wanted to believe that this could mean a re-entry back into her life – and he wanted that so much he could almost taste it – he knew that was exactly the reason why he needed to leave here for a while. Still, it didn't mean to say he couldn't enjoy tonight, before the big official announcement at Tynebridge tomorrow.

Ryan Fisher had never really said goodbye to Amber, not properly. And, as far as he was concerned, the time had come for him to put that right.

'Sorry, I… Brandon, hi!' Amber smiled, looking behind her at the man whose shoulder she'd just connected with as she'd made her way through the crowded marquee. 'It's… it's good to see you. You okay?'

'I'm fine. I'm doing great, thanks. How are you? I mean, I know you and my dad are…'

He trailed off, and Amber briefly looked away. To meet his eyes when she was thinking about Jim was such a bad idea. Brandon reminded her so much of those early days with his father – he reminded her of how ridiculously handsome Jim had been back then, how he'd managed to draw her into his world with a grip so strong she'd never been able to sever it. And look at the consequences. But, once again, she had to remember that none of that was Brandon's fault. He was just another innocent victim in Jim's web of secrets and lies.

'Me and your dad, we'll work something out,' she said, forcing that smile back onto her face. 'Our relationship's never been straightforward so…' She shrugged, '… this is just another hurdle we have to get over, that's all.'

He looked at her for a few long seconds; right into her eyes. 'And do you think you *will* get over it?'

She broke the stare, looking over at the marquee entrance. Ryan had just made an appearance, a small flock of women instantly surrounding him. 'I don't know,' she whispered, turning her attention back to a slightly confused Brandon. 'Yes. Yes, we… we'll work something out. We'll be fine.'

'You okay?' Brandon asked, frowning slightly.

'I'm fine. My mind's just preoccupied with work, that's all. Your dad's announced a press conference at Tynebridge tomorrow and I'm just curious as to what that's all about. He hasn't said anything to you, has he?'

He looked at her, raising an eyebrow. 'You think he shares anything work-related with me? I play for the enemy, remember?'

She smiled, looking down at her far-too-high heels. Sometimes she wondered what she was doing wearing stuff like that when it had never really been her. Debbie's influence must be sinking in far more than she thought it had. 'You're getting used to the local rivalry between Wearside Spartans and Newcastle Red Star, then?'

'I've been doing my homework, yeah.' He grinned, and Amber

felt her stomach give a tiny leap. He had so much of Jim in him it hurt to even look at him sometimes. 'Do you want me to pass any messages onto my dad?'

She looked right at him, his voice shaking her back to reality. 'Hmm, sorry? Oh, no. No, I mean, I only saw him yesterday, so… Anyway, I'll be at Tynebridge tomorrow for the press conference. I'll see him then.'

Brandon held her stare, a more serious look on his face. 'If he knew how beautiful you look tonight…'

'You're your father's son all right.' Amber smiled, desperately trying to push all thoughts of Jim from her mind. She didn't really want to think about him tonight. She wanted some time off from all the confusion that still reigned heavy over their relationship. 'You have a good time tonight, okay?'

He smiled, that smile that was so like Jim's it made her heart skip that familiar beat. 'Amber?'

She turned round to look at him.

'He loves you. Whatever's happened between you two – and I only know what everyone else knows – he loves you. He's told me that much.'

She stood still for a second, letting her stomach settle and her breathing slow down. 'Yeah. I know he does.'

She gave him one last smile before continuing to push her way through the crowd, heading for the bar at the far end of the marquee, grabbing the first glass that came to hand, downing the cool liquid inside in a couple of mouthfuls. She didn't even know what it was, she just hoped it was alcoholic.

'That is such a fucking turn-on, you have no idea.'

She opened her eyes and looked at Ryan, smiling slightly. 'Yeah. Of course it is.'

He took the empty glass from her hand and replaced it with a glass of something white and bubbly. 'Mind you…' he whispered, his mouth close to her ear, his fingers brushing hers for just a moment too long as she took the glass from him, '… I know what

I'd rather be doing with that champagne.'

Amber felt a shiver she really shouldn't be feeling, and quickly pulled her hand away from his. 'Don't, Ryan. Tonight I just want to get drunk, have a good time, and forget.'

He stuck his hands in his pockets, the famous Fisher grin still there on his handsome face. 'Want some company?'

Amber couldn't help smiling, too. Whatever she'd drunk just now, it was obviously going straight to her head. 'You going to behave yourself?'

'Can't promise, no.'

She looked at him for a second, wondering whether spending time with him tonight was such a good idea, given the circumstances. But she really did need to kick back and relax. She needed to forget, just for a few hours.

'You'd better go get yourself a drink.' She smiled, taking a sip of her own, her eyes meeting his over the rim of her glass. 'Not gonna be much of a party if you don't at least drink something. Although I'm not condoning you reverting back to the Ryan Fisher I used to know.'

'Just as well you're here to keep an eye on me, then, isn't it?' he said, holding her gaze for a fraction longer than was necessary, but long enough to send the briefest of messages her way. Whether she responded or not was completely up to her.

'You're drunk,' Ronnie hissed, grabbing Amber's arm as she walked into the kitchen.

'And your point is?' Amber asked, looking him straight in the eye.

'You're hanging about with Ryan Fisher, knocking back the booze like it's going out of fashion… What are you playing at?'

She shook her arm free of his grip, leaning back against the centre island. 'I'm not playing at anything, Ronnie. I'm just trying to have a good time. You going to deny me that now, are you?'

'No, of course I'm not,' he sighed, leaning back against the island, too, folding his arms. 'I'm just trying to look out for you. The way things are at the minute…'

'Ronnie, I'm a big girl now. I don't need looking after. What I need is just a few hours off from all the thinking I have to do, all the decisions I have to make, because sometimes… sometimes it all just gets a bit too much, you know?'

'No. I'm not sure I *do* know, actually.'

She said nothing, just stared straight ahead, out of the huge window in front of her at the party going on outside. Ryan was talking to an extremely pretty brunette, his body close to hers as they spoke, her eyes looking adoringly up at him. She didn't look a day over twenty – another beautiful young woman so easily sucked in by the Ryan Fisher charm offensive. And she should know. Although she was also old enough to know better.

'Be careful, Amber.'

She turned sharply to look back at Ronnie. 'I'm not some infatuated teenager, Ronnie. I've been around the block and back again as far as Ryan Fisher's concerned. If anyone knows how to handle him, it's me. So don't even start with the lectures. Okay?'

'You're not thinking straight tonight, though, are you? I saw you talking to Brandon earlier…'

'What's that got to do with anything?'

'Jesus… Grow up, Amber. You're still head over fucking heels in love with Jim and talking to his son is only going to bring those feelings to the fore, isn't it?'

She turned away from him again, focusing on Ryan, who was still talking to the brunette, her hand now resting on his arm as he said something to her that made her throw her head back and laugh. 'I need another drink.'

'Amber, come on…'

She almost ran back outside, picking up a drink from the tray of a passing waiter on her way. All of a sudden she wanted to be alone, just for a few minutes. To get her head together. To grab a bit of time to sort herself out, because maybe Ronnie was right.

Maybe she did need to slow down and take it easy tonight. She didn't drink like this often, so when she did it almost always went straight to her head, and she could do without a hangover from hell tomorrow.

'You okay?'

She looked up as Ryan approached. 'Yeah. I just needed a bit of time on my own, that's all.'

'Do you… do you want me to go?'

She paused for a second before shaking her head, leaning back against the tree, the fairy lights hanging from its branches casting a multi-coloured glow over them both.

'Okay.' He moved a step closer. 'Amber, I…'

'This press conference tomorrow – it's to announce that you're leaving, isn't it?'

He looked down at the ground, shoving his hands in his pockets.

'Ryan? The fact you can't even look at me, never mind say anything, speaks volumes. Are you leaving Newcastle Red Star? Is that what my husband is going to announce tomorrow morning?'

Ryan looked up, moving another step closer. 'I'm not going for good. It's only temporary, and I'll be on a rolling monthly contract so… I… I need to do this, Amber. I need to do this.'

'Why?' She felt her stomach give an unwanted jolt, something she tried to ignore.

He looked at her, right into her eyes, and she tried to ignore another jolt from inside. 'Because I'm still in love with you, Amber. And I can't fucking deal with it anymore.'

'No,' she whispered, shaking her head again. 'No, Ryan, you're not. You just *think* you are, but you're not in love with me. You're with Ellen now, you love her.'

'Jesus fucking Christ!' he sighed, pushing a hand through his hair. 'I'm not, okay? I'm not in love with her, I've *never* been in love with her.'

'Have you told Ellen that?' Amber asked, finishing her drink and crouching down to place the empty glass at the foot of the tree.

Ryan watched as she stood back up, watched the way her dress fell slightly open, giving him a quick glimpse of those incredible thighs. 'Ellen knows we're not forever.'

'Oh, really?' Amber raised her eyebrows in surprise. 'So you're not aware of the fact she's been telling people at work about how she hopes you're going to ask her to marry you soon, preferably on her birthday? It's all over Tynebridge... Do you even know when her birthday is, Ryan?'

'For fuck's sake...' He threw his head back, sighing again, only heavier this time.

'You asked her to move in with you. You know how she feels about you, you know all that, and yet, you know nothing. Because you've got your head stuck in the fucking sand again.'

'Well, you'd know all about that, wouldn't you?'

She looked at him. 'We're not talking about *me*, Ryan.'

'But we are, Amber. We *are* talking about you, about how you get under people's skin, right underneath so nobody can forget you're there...'

'That isn't my fault,' she hissed, her eyes boring right into his. 'I'm not to blame for the fact you can't move on.'

He laughed – a small laugh, a slightly cynical laugh – turning away from her for just a second before catching her completely by surprise. His mouth was on hers before she had time to even realise what he was doing, his hand on her thigh, his body pressed close against hers, and to her horror, she felt herself responding to a kiss the like of which she hadn't experienced in a long time. A kiss she hadn't forgotten. A kiss full of passion and heat, a full-on, deep, deep kiss that she couldn't break free from. She felt like a rag doll as he pushed her back against the tree, her arms hanging limp at her sides as he held onto her hips. It was a cold November evening yet she was burning up. Even when he finally pulled away, she could still feel the heat between them.

'*That's* why I have to get out of here,' Ryan whispered, his thumb gently stroking her cheek as their eyes met. Something

Amber couldn't quite work out was happening here, but then, her judgement was clouded by too much alcohol and thoughts of a man she loved beyond anything else, but should never be with. And that man was at home, planning how to tell the waiting football world that this man here in front of her was leaving the North East, albeit temporarily, for reasons too personal to make public. Everything was such a mess, and if she did what her heart was telling her to do now, that mess was only going to get bigger. 'I need to say goodbye, Amber. I never got to say goodbye, and I need to do that.'

'No,' she whispered, shaking her head but making no attempt to move away from him. 'No. Do you realise how stupid that would be?'

'I don't care.' His breath was warm against her skin as he kissed her neck – tiny, soft, lingering kisses that were sending her stomach into a whirlwind of somersaults, flipping so fast she couldn't catch her breath, couldn't speak. 'I really don't care.'

She couldn't stop a small moan from escaping as his hand slipped inside the top of her dress, his fingers gently running over the curve of her breast as his mouth lightly brushed her collarbone, and she closed her eyes, desperately trying to summon up the strength to push him away, to end this now. She was drunk, she wasn't thinking straight. Jim had been on her mind way too much tonight and she was torn between a weird kind of excitement at the thought of seeing him tomorrow, and wishing she didn't have to think about him at all.

'No!' A moment of clarity finally surfaced and she pushed Ryan away, repositioning her dress. 'I'm going back inside. This is crazy…'

She started to walk away, picking up as much speed as she could in heels she could barely walk in, but she knew he'd follow her. So maybe the wisest thing would be to find Ronnie. She doubted very much that Ryan would approach her if she was with him.

'Debbie, have you seen Ronnie?' Amber asked, finding her friend in an unusually empty kitchen, for a party night.

'Ronnie? No. I haven't seen him for a while, chick. You okay? You look a bit flustered.'

Amber pushed a hand through her hair before grabbing a glass from the draining board and filling it with water. 'I've just had a bit too much to drink. You know how it is. You drink nothing for days, then you have a few too many one night and it all goes straight to your head. Not the most sensible thing for me to be doing considering I've got that press conference at Tynebridge first thing in the morning.'

Debbie leaned back against the sink, folding her arms and resting them over her baby bump. 'Brandon's here. Have you seen him?'

Amber nodded, catching sight of Ryan outside on the patio. He'd been cornered by that pretty brunette again, and Amber watched as she grabbed his arm and took him over to meet her friends at the bar.

'Oh, what the hell,' she sighed, walking over to the huge table that was littered with bottles of various wines, spirits and champagnes, glasses of every shape and description all lined up beside them. She grabbed a large wine glass and filled it with an Italian Prosecco. 'It's still early.'

'I'm so jealous,' Debbie groaned, rubbing her bump. 'I miss my bubbles so much.'

'More for me, then.' Amber smiled, throwing Debbie a wink as she walked back over to the window. But Ryan was nowhere to be seen. Neither was his female companion. That figured.

'Oh, for God's sake…' Debbie sighed, her hands still on her bump. 'I only went to the loo ten minutes ago… Back in a tic.'

Amber smiled at her friend as she practically ran out of the kitchen, before another wave of envy – an emotion she kept well hidden from Debbie – washed over her. Jealousy wasn't something she liked feeling. It wasn't nice, and she wasn't proud of it. But there were times when she would quite gladly give up everything just to go through what Debbie was experiencing.

Knocking back a large mouthful of wine, and then refilling her glass, she walked out into the hall. The thumping beat of dance music seemed to fill the whole house, no matter what room you were in, and for a second Amber just stood there, watching everyone all around her enjoying the party. Whether you were indoors or outdoors you couldn't escape it, but all of a sudden she didn't feel much like being part of the crowd anymore. She wanted to be alone. So, taking her glass of bubbly with her, she ran upstairs, heading towards the spare room that was hers for the night. As far as she was concerned, the party was over. But as she nudged the door open with her shoulder, she almost dropped the glass she was holding when she realised the room wasn't empty. Someone else was already in there.

'Beat you to it.'

He stood there in the centre of the room, cocky as the day she'd first met him, his jacket now discarded over a nearby chair. Looked like he'd made himself more than comfortable. 'How…?'

'There's more than one staircase up to this floor, Amber.'

'How did you know I was coming up here?'

'Because *you* want *me* as much as *I* want *you*.'

She couldn't help laughing. 'You think a lot of yourself, don't you?'

'You already knew that.'

She stood still for a second as the room started to spin. Maybe drinking that glass of fizz she'd brought up with her wouldn't be such a good idea after all. She reached over and placed it on the dressing table beside her, trying to steady herself at the same time.

'Whoa, there you go. I've got you.' Ryan stepped forward, gently grabbing her arm as she swayed slightly in her ridiculously high heels.

'I should take these off,' she said, closing her eyes for the briefest of seconds as she tried to get her somewhat frazzled head together.

'Leave them on,' he whispered, leaning forward so his mouth

brushed over her neck, his fingers trailing lightly up her arm. 'But take everything else off.'

She inhaled deep as she tried to control her breathing, but everything was so muddled up, her thinking hazy, her judgement blurred. 'Ryan… We are not having sex, so… so… Come on…'

He carefully untied her dress, letting it fall open, watching as it revealed tanned skin in the briefest and sexiest plum-coloured underwear – barely-there panties and a bra that pushed her breasts right up, making him want nothing more than to see them in all their incredible glory, to run his tongue over her nipples, to hear her moan out loud and make him crazy. 'Goodbye sex, Amber. That's all it'll be. I just want to say goodbye.'

She shook her head, finding enough sense in her clouded brain to quickly pull her dress back around herself, walking away from him into the en-suite.

'You need to go,' she said, turning round to face him. 'Go on. Get out of here. I need to pee and I don't need an audience.'

'Why not?' He smiled, keeping his eyes locked on hers as he pulled off his t-shirt, revealing a washboard stomach so toned it made Amber almost gasp out loud. It looked like he'd been spending the short time he'd been out with injury making sure his fitness levels hadn't suffered. The gym had certainly been *his* best friend for the past couple of weeks. 'You know better than anyone that I actually find that a turn-on.'

'Jesus, Ryan…'

'You're not shy all of a sudden, are you? Come on, Amber. Remember how we used to be with each other – how intimate we used to be, the things we used to do…'

'That was then, Ryan. Things have changed.'

He stuck his hands in his pockets, staring down at the ground for a second before looking back up, back into her pale blue eyes. 'Look, Amber, I walk out of this room and that's it, I lose my chance to say goodbye. Again.'

'You've already said goodbye.' Her voice was barely a whisper.

'Not the way I really want to.'

'Ryan, please… I'm married…'

'In name only, at the minute.'

'That doesn't make any of this right. I've already hurt him so much when I did what I did with…' She stopped herself from saying any more, but it was quite obvious Ryan had already put two and two together. Damn! She could only blame the alcohol, again. It was turning out to be a handy excuse tonight.

'So you and Ronnie White *did* sleep together.' It wasn't really a question. He'd just had confirmed what he'd already guessed.

'Shit!' Amber sighed, leaning back against the wall, pushing a hand through her hair. The room was spinning again and suddenly she just wanted to lie down and go to sleep. She wanted to forget this night had ever happened. And she needed to stop whatever was happening here.

'Your secret's safe with me,' Ryan said, walking over to her. 'Although I suspect Jim already knows, doesn't he?'

She opened her eyes and looked into his. She was one small step away from doing something incredibly stupid and she had to make sure she kept enough already dwindling wits about her to enable her to stop it from going any further. 'You need to go,' she repeated, hoping her voice sounded more determined than she felt.

'Why?'

'Because I want you to.'

'Do you?'

She paused for a second. Big mistake.

He reached out and untied her dress again, this time helping it to fall open, pushing it back off her shoulders until it fell to the floor. She made no attempt to kick it away, her eyes not leaving his as he slipped an arm around her waist, pulling her against him, and it wasn't until her almost naked skin touched his that she felt herself give in totally, even though there was still a part of her that knew this was the worst idea in the world. She hadn't had sex in weeks, but that was because she only really wanted sex with one man – her husband. She only wanted Jim. So why was she here with Ryan? Yeah. The worst idea in the world.

'If it means I can have just one more minute inside you, Amber, then pretend I'm him,' Ryan whispered, his mouth almost touching hers, his fingers sliding the straps of her bra down over her shoulders. 'If that's what it takes, I can live with that.'

She closed her eyes, throwing her head back as his mouth kissed the base of her throat, so lightly it made her heart jump and her stomach leap around like it was on some kind of internal trampoline. It sent waves of forbidden pleasure she didn't really want to feel coursing through her at a speed that left her breathless. The room was still spinning, and this time she wasn't entirely sure it had everything to do with the alcohol.

What was she supposed to do? Was she too far over the line to step back now? Or could she, quite easily – if she really wanted to – just walk away? She knew she could. Of course she could. She just wasn't sure she had the energy or the will to fight this now.

'I don't want you to love me, Ryan.'

'You don't get to make that decision.' His hands were now back on her hips, his fingers playing with the sides of her panties as his lips touched hers ever so lightly, barely kissing her, but touching them enough to send a bolt of electricity through her that almost sobered her up immediately. 'Just one more time, Amber. Then I promise, I promise you, baby, I'll leave you alone. I won't be here, will I? You don't need to see me, because I won't be here.'

'It shouldn't be like this,' she groaned, keeping her eyes closed as she felt him sink to his haunches, slowly pulling her panties down until she had no option left but to step out of them, guilt hitting her head-on like an express train at full speed. 'It shouldn't be like this.'

'Keep your eyes closed,' he whispered, his mouth back resting on hers, his fingers finally unclipping her bra, tossing it aside before lowering his head to kiss her naked breasts – first one, then the other. 'It's too late now, Amber. We're here, we're at that point of no return so just close your eyes and pretend I'm him.'

She shook her head, trying to cling onto a strength she didn't really have anymore. She was too tired, too drunk, too confused to fight it. It was wrong, but it was happening. Another mistake to add to the growing pile she was fast accumulating. 'Ryan, I can't...' But she could. She could do anything she wanted, and right now, she wanted this. She didn't want *him*, not really. She hadn't wanted Ryan Fisher back in her life for a long time. But she wanted this, this release, those few minutes of letting nothing else matter except what was happening inside her. She'd deal with the fallout in the morning. 'I can't...' she whispered, before finally giving in, letting her body fall against him, familiar feelings rushing forward, overwhelming her, taking over, whether she wanted them to or not.

He felt so different to Jim. That was the one thing she remembered more than anything – how different he was to Jim. His touch, his kiss, the way he held her, it was all so different. And she couldn't shake those thoughts of her husband from her mind as Ryan lifted her up, her legs automatically wrapping themselves around his hips as he held onto her so tight. She wanted Jim, she needed Jim, but she was here, with Ryan, about to cross another forbidden boundary that she was only going to regret in a few hours' time, but what could she do? He was pushing inside her now, she could feel him, hard and ready, and she hadn't exactly put up much of a fight, had she? She'd let him in, given him that permission he'd needed to take another piece of her away with him, and leave her with – what? Regret? Guilt? Hope?

And then, before she'd even had a chance to get her head around what was happening, he withdrew, gently putting her down.

'Ryan? What's...?'

'You're right. It shouldn't be like this.' He rested his forehead against hers, his fingers lightly stroking her face. 'You deserve more than a quick fuck up against the bathroom wall.'

'Maybe it's for the best,' she whispered, taking his hand and holding onto it. 'This was never meant to happen, Ryan. Me and you, we were over.'

'Were?'

'You're with Ellen now.'

He threw back his head, sighing heavily. 'No, Amber. No, I'm not. I was never really *with* Ellen.'

'Then you need to tell her that, before you break her heart. And you should tell her before tomorrow. How you've managed to keep all this a secret from her when she works in the PR Department is beyond me…'

'She organises the press conferences, Amber. She doesn't always know what they're going to be about.'

'And you've made sure that's the case with this one, huh?'

He looked at her, smiling slightly. 'You're killing my hard-on with this conversation, do you know that?'

'Well, like I said, maybe that's for the best.' She smiled back, letting go of his hand and walking away, out into the bedroom.

He watched her, scared to turn away in case she covered that naked body up, which was the last thing he wanted her to do. She looked hot; so fucking hot with that lightly tanned skin, those super-sexy hips, those long, toned legs. And she'd kept those heels on, just like he'd wanted her to, making this whole situation one he couldn't walk away from as he felt those urges, that never-gone need to have her rising up again. Talking about Ellen may have dampened his ardour slightly, but it hadn't got rid of it altogether. How could it? When the most beautiful woman in football was here, with him, naked and there for the taking. No matter what else she thought was going to happen tonight, he was going to make love to her one last time. That was a given.

'Amber?'

She turned around, running her hands through her hair as she looked at him, her legs slightly apart, which only made his need for her grow even more.

'I meant what I said.'

'You've said a lot of things tonight, Ryan, so you're gonna have to elaborate on that one I'm afraid.'

'I'm still in love with you.'

She looked away, reaching over to the bed to pick up a towel she'd thrown on there after her earlier shower, but he was quicker than her, grabbing her wrist to stop her from taking it. 'I don't want to hear you say that anymore, Ryan.' Her eyes met his, boring right into them. 'Do you hear me?'

'I can't change the way I feel, Amber. I've tried, don't think I haven't tried. But I can't switch those feelings off, and I can't walk away without knowing what you feel like just one more time.'

'That isn't fair. On either of us.'

'Who said life was fair? We spend most of the time dodging the shit and hoping that, somewhere along the line, we end up with something worth wading through the crap for.'

'Have you any idea how selfish that sounds? Coming from someone like you? Someone with a dream career, the world at his feet; more money than he could ever need...'

'Money doesn't buy you happiness, Amber. And that's one cliché I truly fucking believe.'

She stared at him. 'What do you want, Ryan? What do you *really* want?'

'I think you already know the answer to that.'

She couldn't break the stare, even though she wanted to. 'Well, we can't always have what we want, can we?'

Still her eyes bored into his, his hand gripping her wrist, an energy fizzing between them that neither of them could explain, but they felt it. Both of them. They felt it.

'What happens in this room, Amber, it stays in this room.'

'Because it's *that* easy, isn't it?' Amber said, finally pulling her wrist free from his grip.

He shook his head, sticking his hands back in his pockets. 'Nobody said any of this was going to be easy.'

'Any of *what*, Ryan? I don't even know what we're doing in

here, where any of this came from…' She grabbed the towel off the bed and wrapped it around herself. 'You really need to go.'

'I can't,' he said, his voice so quiet Amber had to strain to hear it. 'I can't leave it like this, Amber. If I walk out of this room, leaving things the way they are now, I'm never going to be able to get my head straight…'

'No. No, don't you *dare* stand there and blame *me* for the fact you still can't sort yourself out. That isn't fair. This has got nothing to do with me now, Ryan. Nothing. I can't be there to hold your hand, not this time. And you will not make me feel responsible for the fact *you* think the only way you can sort yourself out is to leave the fucking country.' She turned away from him, grabbing her make-up wipes from the bedside table and pushing past him, back into the bathroom. 'You really need to go.'

He hung his head, his hands still in his pockets. 'Is that what you really want?'

She looked at him, waiting until he lifted his head, their eyes meeting again. 'What I *want*, Ryan, is to get some normality back into my life. I want my husband back, I want my home back…' She trailed off, placing her hands on the edge of the sink as she looked down, a sudden feeling of loss for something she'd never actually had sweeping over her. A familiar feeling. A feeling she'd experienced so many times over the past few months. 'I want a baby, Ryan. That's all I really want. I want my husband, and I want his baby.' She looked back up, his eyes still on her, the expression on his face changing as he saw the pain in her eyes. 'I want Jim's baby. And it's the one thing I can't fucking have.'

'Oh, Jesus, Amber…' He ran over to her and she fell into his arms, both of them sinking to the floor. The tears came out of nowhere, streaming down her face like a never-ending waterfall, a rush of emotions so strong overwhelming her she couldn't breathe. The intensity of the sobs racking her body was making her breathless, something so raw washing over her in waves of pain so brutal she just wanted to curl up into a ball and lock herself away from the world until it all subsided. Because it would. This had happened before, and it would happen again, she just had to ride the wave and wait for it to pass.

She pulled away from him and sat back against the bathroom wall, looking up at the ceiling, wiping her eyes with the back of her hand. 'I'm sorry. I'm sorry, it's just… it comes and goes, you know? These feelings. And the drink doesn't help.'

Ryan sat back next to her, pulling his knees up. 'I don't suppose I've helped much either. Have I?'

She didn't reply, just looked down at her hands that were balled into tight fists. 'It's like there's this huge, empty space inside me that'll never be filled. I've learnt to put it away at the back of my mind, learnt to live with it…' She looked at him, and neither of them could help smiling. 'I haven't really, though, have I?'

'I never thought you wanted to be a mum that bad,' Ryan said, reaching out to take her hand. An almost involuntary action, but one she didn't seem to mind as she let him wrap his fingers around hers. And it felt good – just holding her hand.

Amber shrugged. 'I don't suppose I did. Not in the past, anyway.'

'Did you ever think me and you…? I mean…'

She smiled again, squeezing his hand. 'No. Not really. You don't strike me as daddy material.'

'Gee, thanks, babe,' he laughed.

Amber rested her head on his shoulder, giving in to the spinning room and the tears that were still falling silently down her face. 'We were never really in a position to even think about that kind of shift in our relationship, Ryan. I'm not saying you won't be a great dad, though. One day.'

'Yeah,' he sighed. 'Maybe.'

She looked up at him, letting him wipe away her tears with his thumb. 'You never know, if you and Ellen can make a go of things…'

'There *is* no me and Ellen, Amber. And I know I've messed up yet another relationship, but…'

'If you're going to end it with her just because of me, then don't, Ryan. Please. Give it a go with her, see what happens.'

'I can't. I can't do that. It wouldn't be fair on her.'

'And you think you've been fair on her so far?'

He squeezed her hand again, his eyes looking deep into hers. 'I can't be with anyone right now, Amber. I'm not strong enough. I don't want the responsibility. That's why I need to get away from here.'

'To run away, you mean. Isn't that what you're really doing?'

He shrugged. 'I don't know. Maybe. But maybe that's what I *need* to do. And anyway, isn't that what *you're* doing? Aren't you running away from things, too?'

She looked down at their joined hands, uncurling her fingers from around his but he stopped her, clinging onto her tighter, refusing to let her go.

'Let's make a promise, Amber. Let's promise ourselves that we'll have tonight – we'll stay with each other, we'll talk to each other, and tomorrow we'll start putting our lives in some kind of order. How does that sound?'

She looked at him, her eyes searching his handsome face, the heat of his body warm against hers, and every alarm bell inside of her was ringing out as loud as it possibly could. But still she felt herself giving in, against all her better judgement, she could feel it happening.

'I need to make love to you, Amber. I need that like you wouldn't believe. But tomorrow… tomorrow we start again. I'll be moving abroad for a while, and you'll be here, getting on with your life.' His fingers lightly stroked her cheek, his mouth close to hers as he spoke, and she hadn't even realised that he'd pulled the towel she'd had wrapped around her away from her body. She was naked again, and way too close to a man who'd caused her nothing but trouble in the past. But then, couldn't the same be said about Jim? And he was still causing her trouble now.

Pushing all thoughts of Jim to the back of her mind, she

reached out and gently touched Ryan's slightly open mouth, her eyes following her fingertips as they traced his perfect lips, putting up no fight as he pulled her astride him.

'One more night, Amber,' he whispered, lifting her up slightly so he could free himself, before gently lowering her back down. 'That's all I want. Just one more night.'

She closed her eyes, burying her face in his dark, messed-up hair as she felt him slowly push into her. And she accepted him, pushing herself down onto him, throwing her head back as he hit that spot that told her he was deep inside her now. There really was no going back.

His legs were still pulled up slightly, and she rested against them, arching her back, keeping her eyes closed – to ease the guilt? – as he covered her breasts in tiny kisses, his tongue flicking over her nipples, sending her whole body into spasms of something she couldn't even explain, all she knew was that it felt incredible. Why did everything that was so wrong feel so good?

'I want to look at you,' he whispered, gently pushing her head down so her mouth was on his. 'All of you. Inside and out, I want to look at it all.'

'Ryan…'

He slowly pulled out of her, pushing himself up onto his feet before lifting her up, and she clung onto him, her arms around his neck, her legs wrapped around his waist as he carried her over to the bed. He lay her down gently, and she closed her eyes again, throwing her arms up above her head, stretching out and drawing her legs up, opening them wide.

'Shit, Amber… I was one fucking idiot for letting you go.'

She couldn't help smiling. All of a sudden that sexy side of her she'd only just discovered came rushing forward. Or maybe it was still the effect of too much alcohol. But whatever it was, all her inhibitions seemed to have disappeared. Along with any common sense she might have had left. 'You wanted to look at me.' She kept her eyes closed, although she badly wanted to see his expression.

'So, come on. Look at me.'

'Jesus Christ…' he groaned.

He could feel his heart hammering so hard inside him it was almost distracting. He'd wanted this for so long, this chance to be with her again, to see her like this, to touch her in all those places he missed so much. And now she was here, naked and beautiful with her legs wide open, inviting him back into heaven – a brief visit, maybe, but he was going to make the most of it. He had to. Because it could be his last chance.

Grabbing a pillow, he slid it underneath her hips, raising her up slightly, giving him better access, and a better view, of somewhere he dreamed of constantly. Placing his hands on her knees, he pushed her legs even wider apart, kneeling between them, bending his head and closing his eyes as his mouth took a much-needed taste of her. Something else he'd missed – the taste of her. And she was so wet, so ready for whatever this turned out to be that he knew he had a few minutes maximum down there or he was going to come so fast he'd lose that chance to feel her properly, to live inside a woman he was still completely in love with. And inside her was the only place he wanted to be right now.

Pulling the pillow out from underneath her, he moved so he was leaning over her, his fingers slipping in between hers as he gently pushed into her, and he was staying there this time. No more false starts.

'Ryan…' she moaned, her fingers holding tightly onto his as her body gripped him hard, holding him there, keeping him there.

'It's okay,' he whispered, his mouth touching hers as he spoke, her legs wrapping around him. 'It's okay.'

But was it? Was it really? One night, he'd said. One more night of being with her, of touching her, making love to her, having her want him like he constantly wanted her. One more night. But as he felt her body buck up beneath him, felt that wave of sweet release begin to wash over him, was one night really going to be enough?

Chapter Twenty

Tynebridge was packed with waiting press and media, and Amber couldn't help but wonder how many of them actually had an inkling as to what this press conference was really about. As far as she was aware, nobody except a handful of people knew anything about Ryan Fisher's request to be loaned out to a foreign club. And, right now, she wasn't entirely sure how she felt about it all. Part of her thought it was for the best. Being around him hadn't been a great idea before, but now it was positively reckless. But there was another part of her that didn't want him to go anywhere, for reasons she didn't even want to think about.

'How's your head?'

She turned quickly to see Ronnie standing beside her, looking handsome and smart in a black suit, white shirt and red tie, his short dark hair slightly spiked. He looked good, but then, he always did. 'My head's fine, thank you.'

'So, did you sleep with him?'

She narrowed her eyes as she stared at Ronnie, looking around to see if anyone was within earshot. The amount of people milling about in the main entrance was huge, and considering most of them were press, she really didn't want to give them anything they could twist into something she didn't want the world to know about. 'Who?'

'Oh, you know who, Amber. Don't play dumb.'

'I didn't see you leave the party last night.'

'You're changing the subject.'

'Because I don't want to talk about it.'

'Nobody saw *him* leave either.'

'There were a lot of people there, Ronnie. It would have been pretty difficult to keep track of everyone's entrance and exit.'

He laughed, looking down at the ground, his hands in his pockets. 'Yeah. You really know how to try and detract from a conversation, don't you?'

'I told you. I don't want to talk about it, especially not here.'

'Why? In case your husband gets wind of the fact you fucked your ex-boyfriend the night before the press conference to announce his departure from Newcastle Red Star? That abstinence from sex didn't last long, did it?'

'He isn't leaving permanently.'

'There you go again!'

'What?'

'Veering off the real reason I'm trying to have this conversation with you. Did you sleep with him?'

'Yes. Is that what you want to hear?'

'No, Amber. Of course it isn't what I want to fucking hear. For Christ's sake… what the hell were you thinking?'

'I wasn't thinking anything, Ronnie. I was drunk.'

'So he took advantage of you?'

'No…'

'Well what then? You were drunk… so…?'

She turned away, sitting down on the edge of a nearby sofa. 'It was a mistake.'

Ronnie gave that laugh again, pushing a hand through his hair. 'You're telling me. After I told him…'

Amber looked up. 'After you told him what, Ronnie?'

'I told him to leave you alone.'

'And you think you had a right to do that, do you?'

'I'm your best friend, Amber. I care about you, and if I think you're about to do something stupid…'

'Like what happened between us?'

He looked at her. 'That was different.'

'How? How the hell was that different?'

'I would never, ever hurt you,' Ronnie hissed, moving closer to Amber so as not to make their conversation too obvious. 'I genuinely care about you, and okay, what we did was a mistake, I accept that. But we do that sometimes, kiddo, me and you. We make that mistake, we do it and then we walk away, and even though we shouldn't have done it at all now you're married, it isn't the same as you letting Ryan Fisher back into your life.'

'That speech was so full of double standards it's unbelievable,' Amber gasped, shaking her head. 'So it's okay for *you* to sleep with me because *you* really care for me, but it's not okay for Ryan to do the same?'

Ronnie pushed a hand through his hair, messing it up slightly as he turned away from her for a second. 'Jesus, you really are one fucking frustrating woman at times.' He turned back to face her. 'Have you forgotten what you went through with him? How much he hurt you? The crap you had to deal with? Have you forgotten all of that?'

'For Christ's sake, Ronnie. It was a drunken fuck, we weren't planning a life together.'

'Well, *you* might not have been.'

She stared at him. 'What's *that* supposed to mean?'

Ronnie said nothing, his eyes never leaving hers as she stood up.

'It's a mess, Ronnie. I get that. But I am *not* planning on letting Ryan Fisher back into my life, okay?'

'You sure about that?'

'Jesus… What do you want me to say?'

'I don't know, Amber. I'm just so disappointed that you let that happen last night.'

'You're not my fucking father, Ronnie, so back off.'

'Everything okay here?'

Both Amber and Ronnie swung round at the sound of Jim's voice. He stood a small distance away from them, dressed in his trademark dark suit, white shirt and no tie, his grey-flecked hair pushed back off his face, his expression stoic.

'Everything's fine,' Ronnie said, backing away from Amber slightly.

Jim raised a questioning eyebrow, but said nothing.

Amber felt her heart start to beat faster, an overwhelming feeling of guilt washing over her as she looked at her estranged husband. How had it come to this? This huge mess that stretched out in front of them. How had it got this bad?

'Can I have a word, Amber?' Jim looked her straight in the eye, and she felt a shiver run right through her, her skin breaking out in thousands of tiny goose bumps.

'Now?' she asked, slightly surprised at his timing. 'Isn't the press conference...?'

'We're running a bit late. Still waiting for a few people to turn up. So can I have that word? Please?'

She looked at him, trying to read his almost blank expression. He was too good at hiding his real feelings sometimes, and it was never something she felt comfortable with as far as he was concerned.

Ronnie just shrugged before turning and walking away.

'Come on.' Jim smiled, something which threw Amber slightly, given his demeanour. 'We'll go to my office. It's a bit more private in there.'

She fell into step beside him as they walked the short distance from the main entrance to his office beside the dressing rooms, just a few metres away from the Press Lounge.

'You and Ronnie – was that some kind of disagreement happening there?' Jim opened the door, standing aside to let her through.

'No.' Amber walked over to his desk, leaning back against it as he closed the door behind him.

'Well, you could have fooled me, honey. Because it certainly didn't look like one of your usual friendly conversations from where *I* was standing.'

'It was nothing, Jim. Okay?' Amber pushed a hand through her long hair, not really wanting to get into this conversation. 'Anyway, this press conference. I'm assuming it's to announce Ryan Fisher's imminent departure from Newcastle Red Star? Am I right?'

'He'll be leaving us for a while, yes.'

'You've managed to keep it very quiet.'

'I haven't really been in the mood to court publicity lately, Amber. Despite you doing your level best to make sure I attract it anyway.' He slipped his jacket off and threw it over the back of the sofa.

'Is there something you want to say to me, Jim?'

He moved closer to her, reaching out to gently tuck a strand of hair behind her ear. 'When my wife – my exceptionally beautiful wife – is all over one of the country's most popular men's magazines, naked for all the world to see, in photographs taken in various locations around *my* club's stadium, that's going to guarantee publicity. Wouldn't you agree? Especially as everyone knows we're not together right now.'

'You could have been there, Jim,' she whispered, that brief touch of his fingers on her skin sending a tiny electric shock coursing through her. 'Despite our situation, you still could have been there.'

'I know, baby. I know. But how could I stand there, watching you lie naked across the benches in the home team dressing room, and not want to fuck you so hard they'd hear you screaming all the way over at the training ground?'

His mouth was almost touching hers now, and she felt her resistance weakening by the second. Suddenly, all thoughts of Ryan and what had happened last night were washed away by her need for this man in front of her. Her husband. Jim Allen. The love of her life.

'I've got a copy of that magazine right here, in my drawer.' He smiled, lightly running his thumb over her slightly parted lips, '… so I can look at those pictures any time I like.'

'I thought you weren't happy with me doing that shoot.' She could feel her stomach flipping over, her heart leaping about like an over-excited jack-in-the-box as his mouth gently brushed over hers.

'I wasn't. At the time. I mean, we'd just split up, meaning you were back out there in the big wide world, looking like that… What husband could possibly be happy with that scenario?'

'You wanted a word, Jim,' Amber said, trying to keep her emotions under control, because, to be fair, they were a bit all over the place right now.

'I wanted to see you, that's all. I miss you.'

'Yeah,' she whispered, tipping her head back slightly, his hand resting on the back of her neck. 'I miss you, too.'

'So why don't we use this opportunity to make the most of the fact we've got a bit of time together, huh?'

She closed her eyes, trying not to let the confusion take over as his mouth touched hers, kissing her so gently she literally melted in his arms, her whole body falling against his.

'I want to fuck you,' he said quietly, his mouth resting against hers as he spoke. 'Now. Here.'

She quickly tried to get her head around what he was saying, because, from where she was standing, it sounded very much like he was trying to take control of things, which is what Jim Allen did best. From the second they'd met, all those years ago, he'd taken control of her life, and whether she'd realised that or not, that's what he'd done. But now – now she couldn't help but think what a really bad idea it would be to allow him to continue to do that, given their circumstances. But then again, despite everything that had happened with Ryan, she wanted him. She wanted her husband. She wanted him so much. So she put up no fight, keeping her eyes closed as he slowly unfastened her shirt, his lips on her neck as he pushed it back off her shoulders, and she said nothing as he slid her skirt down over her legs, throwing it aside, running his fingers back up her thighs as his mouth fell onto hers again, the kiss deepening this time, his tongue slipping inside her mouth, tracing the back of her teeth, making it feel like the thousands of tiny shivers she was experiencing had just merged together to make one huge, body-tingling spasm.

'Come here.' He took her hand, leading her over to a full-length mirror he kept in the corner of his office. 'I want to watch everything I'm about to do to you.'

Amber felt another shiver run through her, something deep inside her telling her this didn't feel right, but there was also a level of excitement rising up that she couldn't ignore.

'See how beautiful you are?' Jim whispered, standing behind her, his mouth close to her ear, his hands on her hips.

Amber briefly closed her eyes before looking at their reflection, her body naked and exposed – except for her knee-high boots – against his fully-clothed one, and she was surprised at how much that turned her on, looking at herself, knowing what he was about to do to her.

'For over twenty years all I ever wanted was you.' His hands moved towards her inner thighs, pushing her legs slightly apart. 'You were my beautiful baby girl, Amber. My teenage dream, my fantasy… and now you're this incredible woman. This beautiful, sexy, vibrant woman, and I don't even know when you became that person. When you became someone that every man I know wants to sleep with. When the only man you should be sleeping with is me.'

She bit down on her lip as his hands travelled back up her body, over the curve of her waist until they reached her breasts, his fingers running over them so lightly she couldn't breathe. For a few seconds she literally couldn't breathe as his thumbs flicked over her nipples, stroking them until they were hard, and all the time she watched him do it, as those butterflies in her stomach continued to fly wildly round and round, making her breathless.

She wanted him to touch her so badly, so much it hurt, but when he finally slipped a hand down there, touching her briefly before pulling away again, she felt something shift inside her. Something that told her she couldn't let him do this. No matter how much she wanted him – and she *did* want him. She really wanted him. No matter how strong those feelings were, something was telling her to stop this, now.

'No, Jim.' She walked away, grabbing her clothes up off the floor, pulling them back on as quickly as she could.

'I thought you wanted this as much as I do,' Jim said, watching her as she pulled her hair back into a loose ponytail.

'I want normality, Jim. That's what I want. And this – this isn't normal. Sex isn't going to put right everything that's gone wrong with our marriage. It goes deeper than that, don't you see? We need to talk, that's what we need to do. We don't need this.'

He pushed a hand through his hair, turning his head away from her for a second or two. 'Yeah. You're right.' He looked at her, right at her, his eyes staring deep into hers. 'You're right, Amber. We *do* need to talk. I just wanted… I just…'

She continued to stare at him, even though he'd looked away again. 'You just wanted what, Jim?'

'Nothing.' He smiled at her, but Amber didn't return it. 'It doesn't matter.' Checking his watch, he retrieved his jacket and slipped it back on. Amber could see his mood changing right in front of her eyes, shifting instantly into professional mode. 'I'd better go and make sure everything's ready for the press conference.'

'Jim?'

He turned round to face her, his hands firmly in his pockets.

'This *is* about Ryan, isn't it? The press conference. It really is happening?'

He looked at her for a few seconds, saying nothing.

'Jim…?'

'How does that make you feel, Amber?'

She frowned, but she didn't break the stare. 'What… what do you mean?'

'About Ryan leaving Newcastle Red Star. About him leaving the country. How does that make you feel?'

'I don't… It doesn't… It doesn't affect me in the slightest, Jim. Why would it?'

He raised an eyebrow before walking out of the office, leaving Amber wondering where everything went from here.

'Shouldn't you be somewhere else?'

Ryan looked up, realising he'd just bumped straight into Amber coming out of Jim's office.

'Well?' she asked, staring straight at him. Jesus, she was hot. Even now, in the cold light of day, dressed all business-like with her hair pulled back off her face, she was managing to turn him on as memories of last night came rushing back, flooding his head, which wasn't a great idea just before one of the most important press conferences of his life. Especially as he'd be sitting right next to her husband. But how could he forget what had happened between them? All the things they'd talked about, the incredible sex they'd had.

'You weren't there. When I woke up this morning, you weren't there.'

Amber leaned back against the wall, folding her arms in a way that told him in no uncertain terms to come no closer. That would be a really bad idea. 'I was up and out of there before 5 o'clock, Ryan. I had to get ready for this, didn't I? Maybe *you* should've got up a bit earlier, too. You look rough as hell.'

'Amber, last night…'

'You need to go and find Jim.'

'Isn't he in his office?'

Amber shook her head. 'He's gone to the Press Lounge. And I'm guessing that's where you should be, too.'

Ryan said nothing for a second, staring down at his feet before facing her again. 'What happened last night…?'

'Shouldn't have happened at all, Ryan. And I'm sorry, for giving in to feelings I really should have pushed aside.'

'But you didn't. You didn't push them aside. Doesn't that tell you something?'

'Yes, Ryan. It tells me that what's happening here, this morning – you leaving the North East, it's for the best.'

He stared at her, looking right into her eyes. 'You really believe that, do you?'

She nodded, pulling her folded arms tighter against her. 'Yeah. I do.'

'Well, this looks cosy. My two favourite clients, together.'

They both looked up to see Max standing there, looking very much the power magnate he was. Dressed in a dark grey suit, red and white tie, dark glasses covering his eyes, and the most highly polished pair of shoes Amber had ever seen, he looked every inch the famous football agent that he was.

'Shouldn't you be somewhere else?' he asked, directing his question at Ryan.

'That's what *I* said,' Amber muttered, looking down at the ground, her eyes focusing on the red carpet.

'Okay, I'm going,' Ryan sighed, pushing a hand through his dishevelled hair. 'Amber?'

'I'll see you in there, Ryan.' She didn't look up when she spoke and that frustrated the hell out of him. Shit! That could have been his last chance to get her alone before those wheels that had now officially been set in motion began turning too fast for him to concentrate on anything else. Why hadn't he said anything last night? When they'd had all that time alone? Because they'd both been drinking, that's why. Which should have given him the confidence he'd needed, in reality. But even if he'd had that confidence to ask her, she wouldn't have taken him seriously anyway. She would have put it down to the drink talking. But she would have been wrong. Because he still felt that way, and he was stone-cold sober now.

'You heard the lady.' Max threw Ryan a look that told him to get out of there. 'People are waiting for you. Go on. I'll be there in a minute.'

Reluctantly, Ryan walked away, heading off to the Press Lounge. Within the next hour, a guaranteed media frenzy would once more surround him, and he wasn't altogether sure he was ready for it now.

'Something you've forgotten to tell me, Ryan?'

Ryan looked up as Ellen materialised beside him, looking more than a touch sexy in a tight black pencil skirt and white blouse, her long blonde hair piled up on top of her head. Her expression, however, was anything but that of a woman who was pleased to see her boyfriend. Then it hit him – like a massive kick in the stomach. He hadn't had a chance to tell her, had he? About his move to Tenerife. He hadn't told her. He'd meant to – he'd had every intention of going home last night, so he'd be there, waiting to see her when she came home in the morning. He'd been going to tell her then, and yes, okay, he'd done a great job of making sure he'd left it all to the last possible minute, which had been a massively stupid risk in the first place, but he *had* been going to tell her. Before the press conference. But then last night had happened. Amber had happened. And all thoughts of Ellen had gone straight out of the window, when she really should have been the first thing on his mind.

'Ellen, please...'

'Forget it, Ryan. I think it's quite obvious where I stand in your life now.'

'Ellen, wait! Come on...' He followed her out of the Press Lounge, across the corridor to the empty Players' Lounge, shutting the door behind them. 'Ellen, babe...'

'Don't "*Ellen, babe*" me, Ryan. How dare you! How dare you ask people to keep this from me, how dare you make people lie for you...'

'I wasn't... That wasn't what I was doing, Ellen. I swear. It's just that... this has all been so up in the fucking air for so long, and I never knew one way or the other what was going to happen, whether the club was going to loan me out or not, and I... I just didn't see the need to tell you anything until I knew for sure.'

'And how long *have* you known?'

He looked down at the ground, keeping his hands firmly in his pockets. 'A couple of days.'

'A couple of days,' she repeated, turning away from him. 'You've known a couple of days...' She swung back round to face him, her expression now a mixture of anger and hurt. 'I thought we were a couple, Ryan. I actually thought that, I believed that. I was stupid enough to believe that you cared about me, that we could talk to each other, but it seems I'm so wrong on that score. So, so wrong.'

'Please, Ellen... I really didn't want it to be like this...'

'What *did* you want it to be like, Ryan? Huh? Because... because I just don't get it. I don't understand why you'd keep something like this from me, I really don't... I mean, I don't even understand why you'd *want* to be loaned out when things are going so well here...' She stopped talking and looked at him, the penny slowly dropping. 'Oh no. No. Please tell me I'm wrong... I'm wrong, Ryan, aren't I? Please tell me you're not leaving because of... because of her. Because of Amber?'

He looked down at the floor again, his hands in his pockets.

'Ryan? Please?'

What could he say? Another lie? On top of the pile he'd already told her? She wasn't that stupid.

'You... you're putting your whole career in jeopardy because you're still in love with *her*? Jesus... I don't believe this.' She backed away, sitting down on the arm of a nearby sofa, throwing down the clipboard she'd been holding. 'What was I, Ryan? Huh?'

Her eyes met his, and he couldn't help but flinch at the pain in there, the hurt he'd caused to someone who really didn't deserve it. But that's what he seemed to be an expert at these days – hurting people who didn't deserve it; messing up his life because he couldn't handle something like the adult he was supposed to be.

'Was I just some replacement, some stand-in you could use while you tried to forget her? Is that what I was?'

'No, Ellen…'

'And then, when you realised you couldn't forget her… Did I mean so little to you, Ryan, that you could treat me like this? That you could keep something so important from me? We were living together, for Christ's sake. We were a couple, and yet you treat me like some outsider who didn't deserve to know the truth.'

'I never meant for that to happen, Ellen. I promise you. I was going to tell you, I was…'

'When, Ryan? When? There, in the doorway of the Press Lounge? Hmm? Just minutes before the rest of the world finds out?'

'I thought you had a day off today…'

'Oh, so what does that mean, then? You were just going to let me find out along with everyone else? While I was eating my cornflakes watching Cloud Sports News? Is that how you wanted it to play out?'

'No. You're blowing this all out of proportion…'

She couldn't help laughing, standing up and pacing the floor, crossing her arms against her chest. 'Sorry. I'm blowing this all out of proportion, am I?' She stopped pacing and turned to face him. 'I came home last night, Ryan. I know I told you I was staying out, sleeping over at Dina's, but I didn't. I thought I'd come home and surprise you because I miss you. Do you know that? When you're not around I miss you. But I came home to an empty house, which was fine, for a while, because I knew you were at Gary's and I know how late his parties can run. But once it got to 4.30 this morning even *I* had to admit that would have been one hell of a late party, even for him. Especially considering his wife is pregnant.'

'So I stayed over. What's so strange about that?'

'Were you on your own?'

'No. Gary and Debbie were there.'

'Were you alone?'

'Jesus, Ellen, what the fuck *is* this? What gives you the right to fucking interrogate me like some deranged frigging detective? Get off my fucking back!'

'Guilt. I can see it, right there, all over your cheating, lying face, Ryan. I can see it.'

Ryan stayed silent. She'd caught him off guard and she knew it.

'That pause says it all,' she whispered, shaking her head. 'You were with *her*, weren't you?'

'Ellen…'

'No! No more lies, Ryan. No more. Look, it's fine, okay? It's fine. If this is how you want it to end then that's fine. You obviously never wanted me…'

'That isn't true. You have to believe me, Ellen, that isn't true. In the beginning… in the beginning I really thought we could make a go of things. I did. I really did…'

'Really?' Her tone carried more than a touch of sarcasm. 'Forgive me if I struggle to believe that.'

He leaned back against the wall, staring down at the floor again, letting the silence take over for a few seconds, before he finally broke it. 'I'm sorry, Ellen. I really am sorry.'

'Just tell me one thing, Ryan.'

He looked up, their eyes locking.

'Was there ever – even just one, fleeting second – when you considered asking me to come with you? To Tenerife?'

Another pause.

'I think we've said everything we need to say,' she said quietly, picking up her clipboard and walking towards the door. 'You know…' she turned around, once again looking him straight in the eye, '… you really are throwing it all away over someone you can't have. And yet, you could have had me. And I could have given you so much more than she ever could.'

He watched her walk out the door, and for the first time in

weeks he wondered if she might just be right.

'Everything okay between you and the boy wonder?' Max asked, keeping his eyes fixed on a quite nervous-looking Amber.

'Any reason why it shouldn't be?' Amber lifted her head to look at him.

Max shrugged. 'Don't know. You tell me. It looked like there was something going on between the pair of you just then, that's all.'

'We were talking… Look, it's a bit of a strange day, Max, so forgive me if I'm not firing on all cylinders.'

'Well, you'd better start, kiddo. You're at work now. Nobody cares that you've split from your husband, or that you'll soon be saying goodbye to your ex-boyfriend as he boards a plane for the Canary Islands.'

Amber narrowed her eyes as she looked at her agent. 'I'm not sure I like what you're insinuating there, Max.'

He looked at her, raising surprised eyebrows. 'I'm not insinuating anything, Amber. I'll see you in there, all right? Don't be long.'

Amber leaned back against the wall and closed her eyes, sliding her hands round the back of her neck, groaning quietly at the tenseness she could already feel beneath her fingers.

'Where've *you* been?'

She opened her eyes and looked at Ronnie.

'You know where I've been. I've been talking to Jim.' She rubbed the bridge of her nose with her thumb and forefinger.

'That was ages ago. Come on, let's get in there.'

She sighed heavily, following him the short distance to the Press Lounge, where things looked as though they were ready to get started any second now. The room was a hive of activity, people huddled together in several small groups, all of them speculating as to what this press conference was going to involve, but seeing as Ryan had now been spotted, rumours were rife and the Chinese whispers had already started. At least they wouldn't have long to wait before they found out who'd guessed right.

'What was *that* for?' Ronnie asked, watching as Ellen pushed her way through the crowd of journalists and cameramen towards the back of the room, but not without first throwing Amber a look that could have curdled milk.

'Beats me,' Amber mumbled. 'Is this thing getting started soon or what?'

Ronnie looked around the room, mouthing something at the Cloud Sports cameraman who was over by the long desk behind which Jim, Ryan and a handful of club officials would be sitting in just a few minutes' time.

'Looks like they want us all to take our seats now,' Ronnie said. 'Come on. I want to be front row for this.'

Amber wasn't so sure. But she was at work now, so any personal feelings she still had kicking about had to be shoved quite firmly to the back of her mind, for the time being. She had to be professional about this.

'You all right?' Ronnie asked, giving her hand a quick squeeze as they both sat down.

Amber smiled at him, not entirely sure the smile had reached her eyes. 'I'm fine. Just shouldn't have stayed out as late as I did last night.'

'What did Jim want? Just now, I mean.'

Amber shuffled about in her seat, looking over towards the back of the room where a small crowd of people had gathered, waiting for Jim to finally take his seat and let everyone know if their hurriedly guessed rumours were, indeed, true.

'Nothing, really.'

'Nothing?' Ronnie asked, raising a questioning eyebrow.

'Not now, Ronnie, okay?' Amber hissed, turning her attention towards the long, slightly elevated table at the back of the room as the flash of camera bulbs and the shouting out of questions signalled the arrival of Jim, Ryan, and two club officials.

She watched as Jim sat down beside his star striker, watched as Ryan clasped his hands together in front of him, staring down at them rather than up at the crowd of waiting journalists and reporters. She watched as Jim also clasped his hands in front of him, but he was quite happy to meet the eyes of the waiting media. In fact, it was him who silenced them all without having to say a word, so strong was his presence. She watched and listened to her estranged husband as he explained just why everyone had been called to Tynebridge that morning, looking down at her redundant notepad as the room erupted into a cacophony of mutters and gasps. She listened as some fabricated story about giving Ryan the chance to play over in La Liga was cited as a reason for this surprise loan to CD Adeje when, in reality, it all sounded so lame to Amber. Because she knew the truth. Yet, when Jim spoke, even *she* felt as though everything he said made perfect sense, he was that good at spinning things, no matter how complicated or outlandish the subject. And if he could make even *her* believe that what he was saying was true, then surely everyone else would be well and truly sucked in.

She looked up, glancing briefly over at Ryan who was now giving his undivided attention to the rest of the room as Jim finished speaking and called for questions from the media. Of which there were plenty of takers, but she let Ronnie do the talking for Cloud Sports. She didn't think she'd be that great an actress, especially as she knew the *real* reason behind Ryan leaving Red Star, even if it was just a temporary thing.

Jim's eyes met hers for a second, and she felt her heart skip that familiar beat as he smiled at her, just a small smile. A very brief smile. A smile she couldn't return because her stomach was too tied up in knots for her to concentrate fully on what was going on. But she had to get her head together, she had to start thinking straight, because when she interviewed Ryan later, in front of the camera, she was going to have to look as surprised as everyone else about this shock decision of his. But even she was fast beginning to wonder whether everyone would stay as convinced as they seemed to be now about his reasons for going. Or maybe she was just being paranoid.

'Well,' Ronnie sighed, sitting back down after making sure Cloud Sports had had their say on the matter, '... it's all official now. Looks like Ryan Fisher's leaving Newcastle Red Star.'

Amber looked over at the table again, watching as Ryan tried to answer as best he could all the questions being thrown at him, most of which were being fielded towards Jim to answer on his behalf. 'Yeah. It looks like he is.'

Chapter Twenty-One

The crowd outside the main entrance to Tynebridge was growing by the second as news of Ryan's shock loan filtered through to the fans. No one had expected it, and none of the fans who'd already gathered at the bottom of the steps leading up to the glass-fronted entrance seemed to be turning cartwheels at the prospect of losing their best striker in years to a foreign club, even if it was just for a few months.

'Could have a riot on their hands here,' Ronnie said, joining Amber as she looked out at the sea of people down below. 'I can't see one fan out there who's going to understand what's just happened.'

Amber folded her arms, suddenly wishing she was somewhere else. She just didn't know where. 'They'll come round.'

Ronnie raised his eyebrows, looking at her with more than a hint of surprise. 'You reckon? Amber, you grew up around North East football, you know how passionate these fans are about their club. And you know how gutted – not to mention confused – they're going to be at this news.'

'Yeah. I know,' she sighed, rummaging round in her bag for her car keys. 'But there's not a lot we can do about it now, is there?'

Ronnie leaned back against the huge floor-to-ceiling windows that lined the front of the main entrance. 'You sure you're okay?'

'It's just been a weird day, Ronnie, that's all. And it's not even 10 a.m.'

'Are you going straight to the airport?'

They were both due to fly down to London later, as another weekend in the Cloud Sports studios beckoned. And Amber could only guess what the main topic of conversation was going to be.

'No. I've got to nip home first, throw a few things into a holdall. I didn't have time to pack this morning.'

'Late night, huh?' Ronnie said, with more than a hint of sarcasm.

Amber just looked at him. 'I'll meet you there.'

But he was looking over her shoulder, indicating that someone was behind her, and she swung round to see Jim standing there. Her hot, handsome, American husband.

'We need to talk, Amber.'

She turned back around to face Ronnie.

'All right. I'm going,' he sighed, pulling himself away from the window. 'I'll call you in a bit, okay? See you later.'

Amber watched as Jim's eyes followed Ronnie's exit from Tynebridge, waiting until he was well away from the entrance before he turned his attention back to her.

'Come on. We'll go back to my office.'

Amber checked her watch. 'I haven't got a lot of time, Jim. I've got to get home and pack, I'm flying down to London in a couple of hours.'

'This won't take long.'

She frowned slightly as she followed him through the still-packed main lobby, back into the corridor that led to his office, and all the while a little voice at the back of her mind kept nagging away, telling her this didn't feel right. Something didn't feel right.

Walking into his office, she watched as he shut the door but stayed with his back to her for a few seconds, which made that nervous feeling in the pit of her stomach intensify. But it was only when he turned around that she really felt something she could only describe as fear sweep over her from out of nowhere.

'I want a divorce, Amber.'

She wasn't entirely sure she'd heard him properly, which was why she couldn't say anything. No words would come out, nothing was there, except this weird, empty feeling of shock, and sadness.

She looked up at him as he walked over to her, his hands in his pockets, his eyes fixed firmly on hers, but again no words were coming. They weren't even close. Her throat was dry, her stomach tying itself up in knots and pulling them tight, leaving her almost struggling to catch her breath.

'I could cope with you and Ronnie,' Jim said, reaching out to gently touch her cheek. 'For some reason, the thought of you sleeping with him wasn't something that kept me awake at night. Oh, I'm not saying I was okay with the fact you were fucking around behind my back…' His thumb was now stroking her jaw, his fingers running lightly down over her neck, '… but Ronnie… well, he's Ronnie, isn't he? Ryan, on the other hand, he's a different matter altogether.'

Amber quickly dragged herself out of the almost zoned-out state she'd drifted into, pushing his hand away and stepping back slightly.

'Knowing you've slept with Ryan, that's something I *can't* ignore, honey.'

She looked at him, narrowing her eyes, trying to make sense in her mixed-up mind of just what it was he was saying. 'Ryan? I…'

'Last night, Amber. You were with him last night.'

She felt her stomach pull tighter, that mess of knots pulled so taut now she felt nauseated.

'I asked Brandon to keep an eye on you, at the party.'

All of a sudden she found that voice she'd thought she'd temporarily lost, her eyes fixed on his. 'You got your son to *spy* on me?'

'That isn't what I said, Amber. I asked him to keep an eye on you…'

'And that's different, is it?'

He said nothing, just continued to stare her down.

'I don't believe you…' She finally broke that stare, turning away from him, her head spinning at the rapid change of events these past few months seemed to be throwing at her.

'He saw you with him, Amber. Last night, he saw you with Ryan…'

'I don't even want to get into this,' she said, pushing past him, but he grabbed her wrist, swinging her back round to face him.

'Okay, so he only saw you talking to him, but given your history, Amber, you can't blame me for reading something into what would, under normal circumstances, be a pretty ordinary situation. But I can't believe that's all it was with you two. I can't. Knowing what I know, and… I know I'm right. I trust my instincts. Given the history between you and Ryan Fisher, and the fact that all this shit is happening today… I've had to give up my star striker because he can't cope being around you, Amber. He can't do that, because he's still in love with you. Have you any idea how hard that is for me to deal with? And I can usually deal with anything, but this…'

'It was a mistake,' she whispered, pulling her wrist free as she tried to ignore the ache in her chest, the pain of realisation – that her marriage to the one man she loved more than anything, a man who'd been such a huge part of her life for such a long time, it could be over. And, despite the separation and the living apart, despite all of that, she'd never really thought it would come to this. She'd always thought – naively so, it would seem – that they'd eventually sort things out. It might have taken time, but she'd honestly believed they'd get there. One day. 'Last night, it was a mistake.'

He hung his head, running a hand through his hair. 'So you *did* sleep with him, then?'

'I never meant it to happen, Jim.' There were no excuses she could make, nothing she could say that would make this right, and all that did was make the pain she was already feeling hurt all the more.

'But it did,' he whispered, finally lifting his head to look at her, and she was horrified to see he had tears in his eyes. Is this what their messed-up marriage had come down to? Was it really going to end like this? 'It happened, Amber.' He shrugged. 'It happened.'

She shook her head, herself now blinking back unexpected tears that had started to spill rapidly down her cheeks. 'I'm so sorry, Jim.'

All she'd ever wanted was this man – this one man. He was all she'd ever wanted, and for a few blissful months she'd had him, in a way she'd been dreaming of since she was sixteen years old. But she'd let a need for some kind of perfection they could never achieve get in the way. She'd allowed herself to dwell too much on the things they couldn't have, rather than concentrate on the things they already had. And they'd had each other, hadn't they? Why hadn't that been enough? When, for almost two decades, it had been all she'd ever wanted. Him. That's all she'd ever really wanted.

'So am I, Amber. So am I.'

She didn't know what to do. Should she just turn and walk away, leave him behind without any kind of fight? Did he even *want* her to fight for him, for their marriage?

'I'll speak to my solicitor, see what happens next...'

She looked at him, her heart beating hard, hammering against her ribs as though it was desperate to break free from its cage. 'Can't we talk about this, Jim? Please?' Her voice was barely a whisper, her words stilted and slow to come out. But she now felt as if her life was running in slow motion, like she was being made to watch as all the stupid mistakes she'd made were played out in front of her like some kind of visual torture.

'There's no point, Amber.'

'You're willing to give up? On everything we had? Just because of one night?'

'But is it just going to stay one night? You see, that's what I have the problem with, that's... that's what I can't... I saw your reaction out there today, Amber. I saw the look on your face when it was finally made public that he was going. I saw that. I saw the face of a woman who doesn't really want him to go anywhere.'

'But he *is* going, isn't he? He's leaving, he's going to be miles away, in another country, out…'

'Out of temptation's reach, is that what you were going to say?'

She stopped talking, leaning back against his desk. 'No, Jim. That wasn't what I was going to say.'

He walked over to her, tilting her chin up with his thumb and forefinger. 'Maybe we were never really meant to be together.'

Her eyes searched his face, trying to find something that would make her feel any better about what was happening here, but there was nothing there. Nothing but a heart-breaking reality that her dream come true was about to come tumbling down, shattering into a million pieces on the way.

'What we had, it was amazing. And I know I will never, ever stop loving you, Amber. Ever. I know that.'

'Then why are we doing this? Why are *you* doing this, Jim? I don't understand, because… because an hour ago you wanted to make love to me, and I…'

'I wanted to be with you one last time, that's all I wanted. I wanted that so much you have no idea, baby. No idea.' His mouth was almost touching hers now and she could feel that ache in her chest, those knots in her stomach tightening, pulling so hard it was like the breath was being squeezed out of her. 'But I can't do this anymore. I can't. I'm tired, Amber. My work's been slipping, I haven't been able to concentrate and… and I can't afford to let that happen. I've got a reputation to keep, a club to run. And I need to be on my A-game for that. So we need to end this. Now. Before it destroys us both.'

She just let the tears fall now, let them stream down her face, running into her mouth, the salty taste of them making her cry even more. 'Why… why a divorce, Jim? Why something that drastic?'

'I need closure, Amber. I need to make that break, sever those ties…'

'Sever those ties? You… you're making it sound like you don't ever want to see me again.'

He looked down, his hand still resting against her cheek, but he couldn't meet her eyes. He couldn't look at her. And that in itself made Amber's heart break into even more tiny pieces.

'Jim? No… I can't… No. Please, don't do this…'

'We'll have to wait a few more months, before any divorce can be made final, but, as long as we're both in agreement, once those proceedings are in place it should all be pretty quick and straightforward. We've got no kids…'

He stopped himself, his eyes finally meeting hers again, and even she could see him visibly flinch at the words he'd just spoken.

'Amber, baby, I'm so sorry. Honey, I am so, so sorry…'

She just shook her head, pushing his hand away from her face before making her way over to the door. 'I think we've said everything there is to be said now, don't you?'

'Amber, please, wait… don't leave like this. I shouldn't have said… I should have been more tactful.'

'It's true, though, isn't it? What you said. No kids equals a much more straightforward divorce. Less mess all round, huh?'

'That isn't what I meant. It isn't…'

'I'm sorry, Jim. Okay? Please believe me when I say that – I'm sorry. Because, despite what you may think, I love you. So much. And I always will. Always.'

Chapter Twenty-Two

'Feeling any better?' Ronnie asked, sliding onto the banquette opposite Amber. 'Or shall I go get us another bottle?'

She smiled, laying the beer mat she'd been fiddling with down on the table. 'It's been a fortnight, Ronnie. I'm fine now.'

'Really?' He raised a sceptical eyebrow. 'Despite the fact there's been all that stuff in the press about your marriage breakdown? All those rumours about you and Ryan and his real reasons for leaving Newcastle Red Star? You're okay with all of that, are you?'

'I didn't say that, did I? No. Of course I'm not okay with all of that. But, in reality, it was inevitable, wasn't it? Inevitable that they'd put two and two together and come up with…'

'Something not too far from the truth?'

She looked at Ronnie, picking up her glass and taking a sip of wine. 'Ryan isn't to blame for my marriage breaking down.'

'He is, indirectly. Sort of.'

Amber sat back, sighing heavily as she pushed both hands through her hair. 'You see? What you've just said there, that just shows what a huge fucking mess this all is.'

'You're handling it extremely well, though, I have to say.'

She took another sip of wine, willing the alcohol to take effect soon. She was quite looking forward to the numbness it might bring if she drank enough. 'I'm not the type to sit wallowing over something I can't control, Ronnie. You know that. I'll put my game face on and deal with things like a grown-up. What's the point of collapsing into a heap and sobbing myself to sleep every night? It won't make him change his mind.'

'But you haven't been back to Newcastle since it happened, babe.'

'So? There's no point in me going back up there if I don't really need to. There's nothing there for me now, is there? Most of my work is down here, so…'

'What about your dad? *He's* still up there. And he's really worried about you.'

'I'm sure my dad's fine. Freddie Sullivan brought his daughter up to be as tough as he is. He knows I'm okay.'

'Well, maybe Freddie Sullivan's daughter isn't quite as tough as she thinks she is.'

Amber just threw him a look, finished the last of her wine, and refilled her glass.

'You sure you don't want me to get another bottle?' Ronnie asked, smiling slightly.

'We make a right pair, don't we?' she sighed, sitting back against the wall of the booth they were sitting in at the bar in the Cloud Sports complex. They'd just finished presenting an episode of *Scoreline* together and were taking the opportunity to wind down after another long day. 'Both of our marriages, over within months.' She looked at her best friend, who was staring down into his drink, fiddling with the stem of his wine glass. 'But you weren't to blame for the way yours ended, were you? I was.'

Ronnie looked up at her, reaching out to take her hand. 'Hey, come on.' He sat forward, clasping both his hands around hers, smiling a smile that was designed to try and get her to smile back. 'Look, why don't you take a trip back up north? Talk to Jim. If that's what you really want.'

'Do you think I should?'

'You know my feelings on Jim Allen, kiddo, but please don't let that cloud your judgement. You've got to do what *you* want to do, not what you think anyone else *wants* you to do. If that makes any sense.'

'There's no point,' Amber sighed. 'I mean, he hasn't contacted me in all that time, has he? Two weeks, and he hasn't called, hasn't texted… he hasn't even emailed me. Nothing. Surely I've got to take something from that, haven't I?'

'You're giving up, then? Just like that?'

'Maybe he's right, Ronnie.'

'About what?'

'About us being together, how it wasn't good for us. We got carried away, getting married as quickly as we did. We let our hearts rule our heads, and we didn't even stop to think about the reality of it all. He'd only just walked back into my life and I was confused and overwhelmed, but I knew from the second I saw him again, I knew I was still so in love with him… or in love with the memory of him. Because sometimes – sometimes I wasn't sure if I really knew him at all. Maybe it was the younger Jim I was still in love with, not the one who came back to me sixteen years later… Oh, I don't know. I don't know, Ronnie.'

He squeezed her hand, bringing it up to his mouth and kissing it gently, his eyes meeting hers. 'You know, maybe we really should have listened to your dad when he said we would have made the perfect couple.'

She couldn't help smiling at him, so glad he was there. So glad he could be with her to keep her sane and stop her from wallowing in that self-pity she knew she would have quite happily sunk into if she'd been left alone, despite what she'd just said before. 'Yeah. Maybe.'

Their eyes stayed locked together for a few seconds longer, a loaded silence hanging in the air, a silence that Ronnie was about to break when they were interrupted by a rise in the noise level near the entrance to the bar. And the moment was broken.

'What's going on over there?' Amber asked, pulling her hand away from Ronnie's, standing up to get a better view.

'Dunno,' Ronnie muttered, sitting back and topping up his own wine, finishing his drink in one mouthful before grabbing the empty bottle from the middle of the table. 'I'll go get us a refill. Something tells me we're gonna need it.'

Amber sat back down and frowned as she watched him walk over to the bar, forgetting all about the sudden activity over by the entrance.

'You on your own?'

She looked up sharply at the sound of that familiar voice, her heart involuntarily jumping slightly. He was the last person she'd expected to see, but there he stood, all cocky and handsome in scruffy jeans that probably cost more than she earned in a week, his dark hair falling over his eyes. He'd let it grow a bit longer recently, and the beard he'd once had was now just heavy stubble. He looked hot, sexy – everything she wished he didn't. 'You've had a shave I see.'

He grinned, sliding into the seat Ronnie had just vacated.

'And no, I'm not on my own,' Amber went on, just a tiny bit irritated by his sudden appearance. 'Ronnie's getting the drinks in over at the bar.'

'Yeah, I know. He's getting me one, too.'

'Aren't you supposed to be on a plane heading towards the Canary Islands?'

'Not leaving until tomorrow morning. First thing. We're flying from Gatwick instead of Newcastle. Me and Max had a few things to sort out down here first. But, all being well, by tomorrow afternoon I should be settled in a bar somewhere sipping on a cold lager and thinking how great it is to have left the British weather behind.'

She looked at him, hoping he was joking.

'Jesus, Amber, come on. I'm kidding. As soon as I land I'm heading straight to CD Adeje's ground for a follow-up medical and a proper look around the place. Then I've got to move into the villa the club have sorted out for me somewhere in La Caleta… Haven't got a clue where that is…'

'It's a small fishing village just a short walk away from Costa Adeje. Jim and I visited it when we were over in Tenerife pre-season.'

Ryan didn't miss the way her expression changed the second she'd mentioned Jim's name. 'You okay?'

'Not really.' She looked up at him, those dark, almost navy-blue eyes of his looking straight into hers. 'My marriage is over, I can't face going back up north because I can't deal with the memories, and you're sitting here in front of me for a reason I've yet to fathom.'

He sat back, looking over at Ronnie as he approached the table. Ronnie looked from Amber to Ryan, his expression carrying more than a hint of warning. Aimed at both of them.

'I'll be fine.' She smiled at Ronnie, answering his silent question, taking the bottle of wine he held out for her. 'I promise.'

He paused for a second, hoping she'd change her mind and tell Ryan to leave. But she didn't. So he did the only thing he could do, and conceded defeat. 'Well, I'll only be over there, if you need me. And if you don't, I'll see you in a bit, okay?'

She nodded, still smiling. 'Okay.' Amber waited until Ronnie had gone back over to the bar – but not without throwing Ryan a look first – before she turned her attention back to her surprise visitor. 'I wasn't expecting to see you again before you left.'

'Was that a conscious decision?'

'Don't start, Ryan. I'm really not in the mood.' She so badly wanted to ask him how Jim was, but something inside her was far too stubborn to let the question out. And show Ryan how vulnerable and upset she still was? Yeah. That'd be a great idea.

He sat forward, clasping his hands together on the table in front of him. 'I couldn't leave, Amber. Not without seeing you first.'

'I thought we'd already said our goodbyes.'

'Then call me greedy, because I want the chance to say another one. Although, if I'm gonna be totally honest about why I'm here, I don't really want to say goodbye at all.'

Amber looked at him, narrowing her eyes slightly. 'Like I said, Ryan. I'm really not in the mood for games so just get to the point, okay?'

'Come with me. To Tenerife.'

She couldn't break the stare as she tried to digest what he'd just said. 'What the hell are you talking about? Are you out of your fucking mind? Have you forgotten why you're out on loan in the first place?'

Ryan shrugged, sitting back and making himself comfortable. 'Things have changed.'

'Things have… I don't believe you… Is this just some kind of game to you?'

'Your marriage is, by all accounts, finished, Amber. And the world and its mother seems to think that's because of me and you anyway, so why not just go with it?'

Amber was still staring at him, almost speechless. Almost. 'Why not…? I'm not hearing this. You really do have to be taking the piss… Get out of here, Ryan. Go back to your hotel, get a good night's sleep, then get on that plane tomorrow and start that new life. Okay? Get your head together, get it sorted, and come back a grown-up.'

She took one last gulp of wine as she stood up, grabbing her bag from the banquette beside her.

'I'm serious, Amber.'

She looked at him again, still unable to get her head around the fact he'd had the nerve to come here and do this to her.

'Two weeks, Ryan. It's been two weeks since my husband told me he wanted a divorce and I've had to go through it all with the eyes of the media on me constantly. And as well as that, I've had to put up with rumours that my marriage broke up because me and you were having some kind of affair, which couldn't be further from the truth…'

'I still love you, Amber.' He stood up, too, reaching for her hand, but she pulled it away, shaking her head as she quickly made her way out of the bar, pushing past the growing crowd of people in there, almost running across the car park.

'Amber, wait!'

She really wanted to jump into her car and drive off, away from this ridiculous situation, but something – some feeling she hadn't encouraged and didn't welcome – was causing her to stay rooted to the spot.

'We need to talk.'

'Do you know how sick I am of hearing people say that to me lately, Ryan?'

'I still love you.'

'Which is why you're going away.'

'And I want you to come with me.'

'Which then renders this whole loan period a pointless waste of bloody time! Don't you get it, Ryan? Are you listening to yourself?'

'Amber, it's over. You and Jim, it's over. And I'm still here. *I'm* still in love with you, still waiting for you to come back…'

She shook her head again, blinking back tears that she was so angry had appeared in the first place. She was trying to be strong again, trying to work out in her own mixed-up, messed-up head how she was going to get through these next few months, and the one thing she'd been more than relieved about was the fact Ryan would be far away. He wouldn't be around to confuse her or make her think she wanted something she really, really didn't. And yet he was here, doing exactly that, saying things she really didn't want to hear.

'You have no right, Ryan… no right to come here and do this. It isn't fair.'

'Okay…' He pushed a hand through his hair, looking away for a second. 'Okay. Maybe I've played this completely the wrong way…'

'You think?' Amber asked, raising a sarcastic eyebrow.

'Maybe I've played it all wrong. There's no way you're just going to up and leave everything you've got here to be with me in a different country, I see that.'

'Oh, *now* he's finally talking some sense.'

'It's a mess, right?'

'Understatement, Ryan.'

'But maybe, at the same time, it's fate guiding us in the direction we should have been going all along.'

She frowned as she stared at him, still feeling as if she was in the middle of some surreal dream. 'And now you've stopped. Talking sense, I mean. Fate doesn't come into this, Ryan. Not anymore.'

'You used to believe in it.'

'I used to believe in a lot of things.'

'Do you blame me?'

She looked at him, right into those dark blue eyes, just staring at him for what felt like ages but was really only a few seconds. 'Blame you for what?'

'For your marriage breaking up. I mean, it all happened just after me and you…'

'Go back to the hotel, Ryan.' She turned away from him, opening the driver's side door, but he quickly grabbed her arm before she had a chance to climb into the car.

'Come with me, Amber. Please.'

She swung round to look at him, laughing slightly. 'You *are* joking, aren't you?'

'He's left you, your marriage is over, what's stopping you…'

'No, Ryan.' She shook her head, wishing he hadn't turned up here. Wishing a lot of things.

He carefully pulled the car keys from her grip, sliding them into his pocket, which was met with another incredulous look from Amber.

'What are you doing?'

'You've been drinking, Amber. Remember? And I suspect, even though we may just be talking slightly here, that you're over the limit. So I can't really be seen to condone you getting behind the wheel of that car now, can I?'

'Saint Ryan. How ironic is that, huh?'

He just smiled, his hand still gripping her wrist. 'The last thing you need is any more headlines.'

'Yeah. Thanks for your concern.'

'We'll get a cab, okay?'

'Okay… Hang on. What's with the *we*? *We* aren't doing anything. *I'll* call for a cab, thanks. Go on. You can go now. Just give me my keys back first.'

He let go of her, shaking his head, smiling as he shoved his hands in his pockets, along with her keys. 'You're not getting those back until the cab gets here and you're safely in it. With or without me.'

'Without. Definitely without. And you really are quite irritating, do you know that?'

He was still smirking, leaning back beside her against her car. 'Well, from one irritating person to another, I'll take that insult with a pinch of salt.'

She just looked at him before turning away, scrolling down the contact list on her phone to find the cab firm Cloud Sports used. Just a few more minutes and she'd be safely on her way home to her little house – her quiet, empty, little house…

'Is this really what you want, Dad?'

Jim looked up, placing his fork down on his half-eaten plate of food. 'It's what I've got to do, Brandon.'

'Why? You see, I don't get it. I don't get why… If you love her so much, why do you need to do this? I mean, a divorce? I know what she did was wrong, but you were no saint either. By your own admission.'

'I didn't sleep with anyone else while we were together.'

Brandon looked at his dad from across the table. 'Not this time around, maybe, no.'

Jim held his son's gaze for a minute before turning his attention to the glass of whisky by his side.

'You kept secrets from her, Dad. Big secrets. Things you probably should have told her about and…'

'Are you saying I drove her to sleep with Ryan Fisher?'

'No. Of course I'm not saying that. What I'm trying to say is…'

Jim scraped his chair back and got up from the table, throwing his napkin down beside his unfinished food. 'It was a mess, Brandon. From the start it was a mess and we should never have tried to go back there. Too much had happened already, too many things had been said that couldn't be taken back. We were naive to think we could make a marriage work.'

'You said you loved her like you'd never loved anyone before.'

Jim looked at Brandon, picking up his glass of whisky and taking a sip. 'I did. I do. But sometimes that isn't enough, when other things get in the way.'

'What things?' Brandon asked, following his father into the living room.

'Things that you don't need to know about, Brandon.' He sat down on the arm of the sofa, finishing his drink in one mouthful. 'I love her, yes, okay. I love her. And she probably still loves me, but that doesn't mean we should be together.'

Brandon leaned back against the wall, confused by everything his father was telling him. He didn't understand any of it. Surely, if you loved someone, and you knew they loved you, too, you'd do anything to make it work. Even if mistakes had been made. Surely, if the love was still there, then there was no mistake that couldn't be rectified, somehow. In time.

'It's not like you to quit anything, Dad.'

Jim got up and walked over to the sideboard, pouring himself another drink. 'I've got my career to think of, Brandon. I've got a club to run and a title to defend.' He turned around, sipping his fresh whisky. 'And I need to have my wits about me in order to do all of that. I've got people relying on me.'

'So you'd rather put your career ahead of the woman you love?'

'She slept with Ryan Fisher. Now he's on his way to Spain, and she's got her own career to keep her busy, meaning I can finally concentrate on what needs to be done here.'

Brandon narrowed his eyes as he stared at his father. Did he really mean everything he was saying? His expression was almost stoic, so it was difficult to tell. Jim Allen had always been a man who never really showed his feelings, if he could help it, so knowing whether everything he was telling him was the truth or not was difficult to work out.

'You're really not even going to *try* and fight? Really?'

'I don't want to talk about it anymore, Brandon.' Jim walked over to the fireplace, taking a long sip of whisky as he looked at a photograph of him and Amber, taken in the back garden not long after their whirlwind wedding. 'It's over. It's time to move on. Amber and I had some good times, but that's all they should have stayed – good times. It should never have turned into marriage.'

'And what if doing this – if you refusing to fight for your marriage, what if that sends her running straight back to Ryan Fisher? What if that happens, huh? What if his plan to leave Newcastle Red Star actually backfires and instead of it being like some kind of therapy for him in order to forget what he thinks he can't have; what if, instead, it turns out to be the one thing that actually pushes him and Amber back together? What happens then?'

Jim took another sip of whisky, his eyes on Brandon's all the time, never wavering, never flinching. 'Then Ryan Fisher will never play football in the U.K. again, Brandon. That's what happens.'

Chapter Twenty-Three

Amber closed the front door behind her, leaning back against it and closing her eyes, taking a long, deep breath. It had been a tiring day, and in hindsight she wished she hadn't let Ronnie talk her into going for that drink after work. She should have just come straight home, ran herself a bath and gone to bed early with a hot drink and the movie channels. Maybe then she could've avoided Ryan – who was *she* kidding? He would have tracked her down somehow. She knew him too well. When Ryan Fisher wanted something, he usually found a way to get it.

She threw her bag down on the chair next to the door and walked into the kitchen, filling the kettle. For the past couple of weeks she'd felt as though she was operating on some kind of autopilot – she was going through the motions but not always feeling everything that was happening. And all of a sudden it was a feeling she didn't like, one she didn't want to feel anymore. She wanted some control back in her life. But the only way she could do that was to do the one thing she'd avoided doing up until now.

Grabbing the phone, she tapped in a number, hoping the person she was calling would answer before she had time to change her mind and hang up. They answered after just three rings, and as soon as Amber heard his voice she felt her stomach dip, as if someone had just pushed her over the top of the biggest roller coaster there was.

'Amber?'

Just the sound of his voice caused tears to well up and she blinked rapidly to try and stop them from falling. 'We need to talk, Jim. Please. What's happening here, it isn't fair…'

'You sleeping around behind my back wasn't fair, Amber.'

Could he really be that cold? His voice certainly didn't sound as though it had any warmth to it. 'We… we just didn't handle things properly, Jim. We didn't… we didn't talk about anything, and we should have done, we should have talked to each other but instead we…'

'It's too late.'

She closed her eyes, swallowing hard, not wanting this conversation to be happening, but, at the same time, knowing it had to. She had to do this, to know where she stood with a man who had never really made her feel safe or settled – but he was a man she loved so much. Too much. She always had, and she always would. No matter what. He was under her skin, embedded there like a permanent tattoo, and there was nothing she could do about that. Nothing. 'You really believe that?' she asked, her voice quiet, shaking slightly, those tears now streaming down her face so fast her cheeks were soaked within seconds.

She kept her eyes closed as he stayed silent, her question hanging in the air, and she couldn't stop a fleeting glimmer of hope bubble up inside her. Maybe he didn't believe it. Maybe it had taken her calling him to realise that what they were doing was stupid, throwing everything they could still have together away just because they'd let things get out of control for a while.

'I do, Amber. I believe that. It's too late.'

She took a deep breath, squeezing her eyes tight shut as though doing that would change his answer, make this whole situation miraculously better. 'I… I know I didn't handle things well, Jim. I know that. But finding out about Brandon, finding out I couldn't have a baby, it… it all happened at once, it all hit me too hard, all in one go, and I know I didn't handle it well…'

'Neither of us handled anything well, honey. We're both to blame. We both did things we shouldn't have done, and I'm sorry. I'm so, so sorry…'

She didn't want to beg, but she could feel him slowly slipping from her grasp, like the cruellest case of history repeating itself, and she felt powerless to do anything about it. Was this just the way things were always meant to be between her and Jim Allen? Together for such short periods, each of them filled with emotions so intense it was draining, only for it to end in heartbreak all over again?

'I wanted too much,' she whispered, keeping her eyes closed, placing a hand on her stomach and clenching it into a tight fist. 'When all I really wanted was you.'

'Amber… Baby, don't do this. Please. Don't do this.'

'I love you, Jim. I love you so much.'

'And I love you, too. Believe me, I love you, too…'

'Then why are you doing this? Why? I don't understand…'

'I have to, Amber. I just… I have to. It isn't fair on either of us to carry on the way we have been doing. It's too destructive, too tiring.'

She finally opened her eyes, wiping away tears that were still falling in a steady stream down her damp cheeks.

'You survived without me before, baby.' His voice was quieter now, more gentle, the coldness replaced by a warmth that only made Amber cry even more. 'You can do it again. Your life will be so much better without me in it, believe me.'

What if she didn't want to believe him? What if she was quite willing to take her chances? She could cope with anything now, she was sure of it, given what they'd already been through.

'Shouldn't what's happened have made us stronger, Jim?' She was trying desperately to stop the emotion she was feeling from spilling over into her voice, but it was hard. It was so hard.

'Amber, honey, please don't cry. Please. Don't cry. Baby, I know this is hard, I know it is. And I didn't take this decision lightly, I really need you to know that. But we can't keep doing this to ourselves. Years and years of wanting each other, loving each other, hurting each other… I can't do it anymore. I can't. I can't do it anymore.'

She threw her head back, staring at the ceiling, those tears she'd been crying falling back into her eyes, stinging them, but she didn't care. Nothing could be more painful than what was happening now.

'Amber?'

Taking one last deep breath she tried to compose herself, tried to claw some clarity back. But still nothing felt right. None of it felt right. 'I… I'll need to come back to the house. There are still some things I need to collect.'

'You don't have to ask my permission, Amber. You can come round any time to pick up your stuff. I'm at work most days, so… You've got your key, haven't you?'

'Yeah.' Her voice was almost a whisper now, the enormity of what this whole conversation meant overwhelming her. 'I've got my key.'

There was a pause for a few, heart-breaking seconds, nothing between them but a painful silence and an air of finality that was almost gut-wrenching.

'You're gonna be okay, Amber.'

She closed her eyes again as he spoke those same words to her that he'd spoken twice before – each time heralding the end of their relationship. The end of her dream. And this was no different.

'Yeah.' She kept her eyes closed, gripping the phone tight as she felt her stomach lurch so heavily she felt physically sick. 'Yeah. I know I will.'

She had no other choice.

Jim slowly replaced the phone in its cradle and sat forward, his head falling into his hands as hot, uninvited tears began to trickle slowly down his face. Nobody had said it would be easy, saying goodbye to her a third time, especially given the line of work they were both in – it was obvious they were going to constantly be around each other more than either of them needed to be. But he knew it was the right thing to do. Their relationship was too intense, too destructive to survive. There was so much they wanted, and most of it was out of reach, so how could they ever have made this marriage work?

Sighing heavily, he sat up, slamming his head back against the cushions of the sofa, pushing both hands through his hair. He was never going to stop loving her – that was a given. Amber was a part of him, a permanent fixture; she was the love of his life. But now it was time to move on. Time to break those ties and forge ahead with everything he hoped would take his mind off what his life had become.

Jim Allen was alone again – and that was the way it had to be.

The doorbell ringing saved Amber from sinking into a well of self-pity and she almost ran out into the hall, knowing it would be Ronnie, and for once she was glad of his almost psychic tendencies to know just when she needed him.

But flinging open the door gave her a surprise she wasn't ready for, but one she should have expected, if that phone call to Jim hadn't distracted her so much.

'You all right?' Ryan asked, standing on the doorstep, his hands in the pockets of his jeans.

She shook her head, standing aside to let him through. She didn't have the energy to fight him anymore, not tonight, anyway.

'Do you want to talk about it?'

Amber closed the door behind her, pushing a hand through her hair, sighing rather a touch heavier than she'd intended, but all of a sudden she was exhausted. 'No, Ryan. I don't want to talk about it. I'm tired of talking about it.'

He wasn't Ronnie, and she didn't feel like going over everything again, least of all with him. That just seemed like a really bad idea.

'You sure?'

She threw him a look and he stepped back, holding his hands up in surrender. 'Okay, okay. I get it. You don't want to talk about it.'

'What are you doing here?' She pushed past him and walked back into the kitchen.

'What do you think I'm doing here? Look, it's my last night here in the U.K. for a while, and I just want to…'

She leaned back against the counter, folding her arms and fixing him with a questioning look. 'You just want to, what?'

He looked slightly nervous, and for a fleeting second Amber actually felt sorry for him. There were times when this cocky, arrogant man could actually appear quite vulnerable, although those times were few and far between. But she knew they existed.

'I just want to be with you, Amber. Is that such a bad thing?'

'When things are this crazy and fucked up, yes. It is.' She sighed, again rather heavier than intended, throwing her head back and letting out a frustrated cry. 'Shit!' Shaking her hair out in the hope that would help rid her of any lingering frustration, she looked at Ryan, cocking her head. 'You tired?'

'Who? *Me*? Tired?'

'Yeah, you. It's getting late, and I know you've got a flight first thing in the morning, but… I've had a really crap night, Ryan. I mean, *really* crap. And if tomorrow *does* have to be the first day of the rest of my life – even if I'd rather it wasn't – then I might as well say goodbye to it all in style.'

Ryan frowned as he stared back at her. Something had obviously happened between leaving her at the Cloud Sports studios and him turning up here, and he suspected it had everything to do with Jim. But if she needed a little bit of respite, some kind of brief escape, who was he to argue? He was saying goodbye to a few things himself tonight, and even though he'd rather not be saying goodbye at all, maybe she was right. Things were way too complicated to begin anything they might regret, but there was nothing stopping them from giving all the crap in their lives a send-off to remember. Or to forget. Depending on the way the night went. And there was only one way Ryan intended it to go.

Amber watched Ryan as he flirted outrageously at the bar with a group of young women dressed in short skirts and the highest of heels, their long hair extensions hanging loose down their tanned backs, their faces fixed in expressions of star-struck awe as this famous footballer paid them the attention they'd been looking for all night. There'd once been a time in her life, not all that long ago, when this kind of behaviour from Ryan would have filled her with a stomach-churning sense of dread. But now all it did was make her smile. This was who he was, what he needed to be. It still wasn't out of his system, no matter how much he protested it was. Deep down inside he was still that slightly arrogant, over-paid footballer with the expensive clothes and the sexy smile who could make women fall at his feet with just one flash of that cocky grin. And even though it had taken quite a bit more than that for Amber to succumb to him, there had been times when his smile had floored her, when she'd been unable to keep her hands off him.

She felt a tiny shiver run up her spine and she shook herself inwardly, trying to get rid of the delicious tingle it had created. It was the alcohol that was making her feel that way, that was all. Champagne always went straight to her head and tonight was no exception. But, oh, she'd needed this. She'd needed to get out of the house because to sit and dwell on how that conversation with Jim had made her feel, that wouldn't have been good. She'd needed to get out and forget, and even if drowning all the bad stuff out with alcohol wasn't the most sensible of decisions, at least it would numb the pain for a few hours.

'You've got that look on your face again,' Ryan said, throwing himself back down beside her.

She looked at him, smiling slightly. 'Has your fan club gone home? Mind you, it's probably way past their bedtime.'

He just grinned at her, and she couldn't help but notice the way his hair fell slightly over his eyes. Those beautiful blue eyes. 'You jealous?'

'As if.'

He took a long swig of beer straight from the bottle, looking away briefly before meeting her eyes again. 'Bit young for me, really.'

'Oh, now I *know* you're talking crap,' Amber laughed.

He shrugged, taking another swig of beer. 'I like my women that little bit older.'

She couldn't help laughing again. 'Yeah. Of course you do.'

'Okay. Maybe not *all* my women... But I know one woman in particular I wouldn't have any other way.'

She looked at him, still smiling slightly. 'Oh, really?'

'Really.'

She felt her head start to spin, and a feeling of déjà vu washed over her – the last time she'd been this close to Ryan she'd been buoyed up by alcohol, too. The only difference being, this time, she felt more in control. And this time, she was beginning to realise that she didn't care what the consequences were. Last time she'd been with Ryan in circumstances very similar, she'd still thought her and Jim had a chance. But now things were different. And so was she. Gone was the Amber who'd wanted to settle down with the only man she'd ever loved, and in her place was a woman Amber wasn't sure she recognised just yet. But she would. In time. She'd get to know her, she was sure of it. She might even like her, given half a chance.

'I could do with another drink,' Amber muttered, polishing off the last of her champagne.

'Is that a good idea? You've had quite a few and… and given my past history, I know better than anyone that that one last drink can sometimes lead to trouble you really don't need.'

Amber stared at him, letting the irony of the situation sink in for a second. 'I'm not drunk, Ryan. And I've got a long way to go before I hit the heady heights of *your* past.'

'I didn't say you were drunk, Amber, I just… I don't want you to be so wasted that you end up doing something you might regret, that's all.'

'Like what? Like sleeping with you, again?'

Ryan's stare matched hers, his deep blue eyes boring right into her with an intensity she was sure was magnified by the alcohol. 'You'd regret that, would you?'

She felt as though she was temporarily hypnotised because she just couldn't break the stare, even though quite a big part of her wanted to. Which answered his question, really. 'Yeah. I think I would.'

He arched an eyebrow, giving her that look of his that said he didn't totally believe her. And, much to her surprise, she found herself laughing, at what, she wasn't quite sure. She'd drank enough champagne for it to dull her senses just a touch, she knew that much.

'I would!' she laughed, throwing herself back against the sofa they were sitting on, placing a hand on her forehead because, all of a sudden, she felt quite hot. That exhaustion she'd felt a couple of hours ago, and then pushed to one side, had returned, and now all she could think about was her bed. Playing out all night wasn't something she was used to. It was going to take a lot more practise if this was the way her life was heading now, but she'd work on it. It had to be more fun than sitting home alone dwelling on all those things she'd lost. All those things she couldn't have yet still wanted so much it hurt.

'You all right?' Ryan asked, gently placing a hand over Amber's as it rested on her knee.

Amber looked down at his hand, watched as his fingers slowly curled around hers, not ignoring the tiny frisson of electricity that one small action seemed to create. Although, that could be purely down to the alcohol, too.

'I'm fine,' she whispered, raising her eyes to meet his, and this time that tiny frisson of electricity increased to a voltage strong enough to actually make her flinch slightly.

They stayed there, just looking at each other, for what felt like an eternity, until he took the lead, pulling her up out of her seat, his hand still holding tightly onto hers as he almost dragged her through the VIP area of the club, and out of a back entrance reserved for those celebrities who didn't want to be papped on their exit, because, right now, Ryan didn't think that being photographed together on the eve of his temporary departure from English football would be such a great idea.

'Ryan! Where are we going?' Amber groaned, the fresh air she'd just been pulled out into hitting her head-on, sobering her up just a tiny bit.

He stopped walking, pushing her gently back against the wall, checking quickly to make sure nobody else was about before he kissed her. A kiss she hadn't seen coming, but a kiss she fell into as though it was the most natural thing in the world. His hand was on her hip, hers snaking round the back of his neck, keeping him right where he was, their bodies moulding together in the cold night air so that neither of them felt the almost freezing temperatures.

'Now, I can either reach up under that dress of yours, yank off your underwear and fuck you right here, right now, or we can jump in a cab and get the hell back to your place where we can have a lot more dirty sex in the comfort of your own home. But, either way, Amber, I'm coming inside you tonight. You got a problem with that?'

She felt the most incredible shiver run all the way up her spine and down again, repeating itself two or three times before she felt the ability to speak return, her whole body tingling with an anticipation she hadn't expected, nor asked for. But now it was here she welcomed it with open arms.

She closed her eyes and kissed him back, burying her fingers in his dark hair, pushing herself against him, all of a sudden wanting him so much it was actually creating an ache deep inside her – or maybe she just needed *some*one, anyone, and he was there. He was right there. And he wanted her. Which was more than her husband did right now.

Pulling away slightly, she ran her fingers lightly over his rough chin, her eyes following their every move until they finally fell back on his, those deep, dark eyes of his that seemed to have the ability to totally mesmerise her tonight. Or maybe that was just the alcohol, too. Either way, she knew how this night was going to end just as much as he did. And she couldn't find a reason to stop it from happening.

'No.' She smiled, moving her mouth closer to his until they were almost touching. 'No. I don't have a problem with that. I don't have a problem at all.'

Ronnie threw the phone down on the table and sat back in his chair, sighing heavily. Brandon Palmer had needed to talk to someone, and with no real close friends with which to share his feelings yet, he'd turned to Ronnie. He'd been the obvious choice, as someone who knew both Amber and his father well. And Ronnie had been only too happy to provide a much-needed sounding board on which to let a very confused young man vent those feelings.

He'd listened as Brandon had voiced his concerns about the way his father was handling his marriage break-up, how he still felt – in some way – responsible for what was happening, and even though Ronnie couldn't really sit there and truthfully tell him that Jim keeping his existence a secret from Amber *wasn't* to blame, in part, for their marriage breaking down, Amber and Jim Allen's relationship was a crazy, fucked-up situation, and there were so many reasons why it wasn't working. So many complicated, messed-up reasons. And if neither Amber nor Jim could get their heads around it, no wonder poor Brandon was having trouble dealing with it all.

All he'd wanted to do was talk, but it had been a conversation that had made Ronnie realise just how much Amber and Jim's problems affected everyone around them. Their relationship was almost toxic, reaching out to pull others into a situation that nobody could fully understand. And Ronnie hoped that, this time, it really was the beginning of the end of whatever it was those two had. Amber didn't need it, and Jim had other things to concentrate on, like the son who just wanted to get to know his father.

He reached out for the remote control lying beside him on the arm of the chair and switched on the TV, leaving it on the news channel that popped up on the screen. He wasn't in the mood to concentrate on anything, he just wanted something to take away the silence. Something to stop him from worrying about what Amber was doing.

He hadn't seen her leave the bar at Cloud Sports, but someone had mentioned they'd seen Ryan heading out just seconds after she'd left. Ronnie had gone straight round to her house because he'd needed to know she was okay. It wasn't like her to leave without saying goodbye, and anyway, he'd thought they were going home together, to share a takeaway, grab a nightcap – talk some more. But the place had been in darkness when he'd got there, and even though he'd tried calling her from the doorstep, he'd still got no answer. He'd assumed she was either sleeping and wasn't hearing the phone, or she just didn't want to see him, but he refused to believe that. Amber wouldn't ignore him, she wouldn't do that. She needed him more than ever now, and he wanted to be there for her, but something was going on tonight. Something had happened, and all he wanted to do was talk to her, make sure she was all right. And although Ronnie really hoped Amber had more sense than to let it happen, he couldn't help feeling that she was on some kind of downward spiral that he needed to put a stop to – now. Because if that downward spiral involved Ryan Fisher, then that could only spell trouble. For both of them.

Amber splashed cold water over her face and stared into the mirror. She didn't look tired. She didn't even feel tired anymore, even though it was coming up to 1.30 in the morning. She just felt as though she was going through the motions, even though she was more than aware of what was going on.

Pushing both hands through her hair, she closed her eyes, breathing in deep and exhaling slowly, opening her eyes suddenly when she felt him come up behind her.

'Jesus, Ryan. You gave me a fright!'

'You've been gone a while. I just wanted to make sure you were okay.' He slipped his arms around her from behind, gently moving her hair away from her shoulder so he could kiss it, his mouth travelling so lightly over her skin it made every inch of her tingle. Why was she doing this? Because the rejection from Jim was just too much to take all on her own? Probably. But, right now, she was going to stop thinking about that and concentrate on what they'd come here to do – fuck, and forget. If that was at all possible.

She turned round in his arms, pleased to see he was almost naked, bar a pair of Newcastle Red Star shorts. And just seeing him in his football kit – albeit only part of it – reminded her of how much of a turn-on that could be. She loved seeing him in his 'work gear', as she used to call it, because he was, without any shadow of a doubt, one of the sexiest players ever to grace a football pitch. And that was an opinion shared by more than just her.

'I really wish people would stop wanting to make sure I was okay,' she said, running her fingers lightly over his chest. He was toned and hard, his skin warm and welcoming to the touch, and a sudden overwhelming need to be in his arms had taken over all her rational thinking. That had long gone. Now all she wanted to do was lose herself in something that didn't matter, something that didn't mean anything. Something that would take her mind off the things that did.

'Well, maybe the people who are wanting to do that are doing it because they care about you.' He caught her hand in his, bringing it up to his mouth and kissing it gently, causing her stomach to dip as low as it could go.

'And you care about me, do you?' she whispered. She wanted to be naked now. She wanted to play games with this man, dirty, dangerous games, because tomorrow he was out of there. He'd be gone, out of her life, and she just wanted to wake up with memories of something other than the searing pain losing Jim was making her feel. Anything was better than that – guilt, anger, frustration at herself for being so weak, it was better than those feelings she needed to rid herself of before they took over and consumed her totally.

'I've always cared about you, Amber. From the second you walked into that Press Lounge last year, all tough talk and attitude, I've done nothing but want you. And now is no exception.'

She smiled, pulling her hand away from his so she could loosen the short robe she was wearing, letting it fall open. She didn't care anymore. She didn't care what he did to her, she just wanted him to take her any way he wanted to, anything to give her the relief and the escapism she needed tonight.

Keeping her eyes on his, she took a couple of steps back, opening her legs slightly, smiling as his gaze lowered, following her hand as it moved down, watching as she began to touch herself.

'Jesus, Amber...'

She continued to move her hand slowly, very slowly, back and forth, enjoying the almost liberating feeling it was giving her, knowing she had him completely where she wanted him now. She was in control, and that was the way it was going to stay. 'We should really get some sleep, Ryan. You've got a big day tomorrow.'

'You have got to be fucking kidding me,' he groaned, watching as her fingers disappeared into a place he was desperate to go, his hard-on now straining against the material of his shorts, so desperate was he to revisit old haunts.

Amber let out a tiny sigh, closing her eyes and throwing her head back as she gently slipped two fingers inside herself, wondering whether it would just be safer to bring herself to climax and rid herself of this growing frustration without even involving him, but that wouldn't really be fair, would it? She'd brought him here, she'd promised him something. So she had to give him that, didn't she? She had to give him something. But, oh, it felt good, being completely in control.

Suddenly, she felt him take hold of her wrist, gently pulling her hand away from herself and replacing it with his own, his mouth pressing down on hers in a kiss that literally took her breath away. He was touching her, playing with her, his tongue running over the roof of her mouth, his fingers pushing inside her – two, or three, she didn't know, all she knew was that it was sending her stomach into spasms of pure pleasure, her body slowly weakening with every touch, every kiss he was giving her.

'When did you get so fucking hot, Ms. Sullivan?'

He'd called her by her maiden name, and, for some reason, that made her heart start to race harder, her head start to spin faster – it was as though he'd finally made her realise she was back to where she'd been before; that forthright and feisty woman who could take on the world, if she wanted to. And maybe she would, at some point in the future. Just, not yet. Not yet.

'You okay with this?' he whispered, his mouth resting on hers, his fingers still deep inside her, a feeling she liked. It felt good; safe. Even though it was anything but.

She nodded, gasping quietly as he withdrew those fingers, and he watched as she pushed past him, walking over to the bath, sitting down on the edge, opening her legs so wide he could see it all.

Sinking to his knees he touched her again, slowly exploring every inch of her, probing harder, pushing deeper, the sound of her moans and the tiny gasps escaping from her parted lips taking him almost to the point of no return. She was so wet, so turned on and he knew he wasn't going to be able to hold out much longer, which was why he hadn't set his quite obviously frustrated erection free just yet. If he kept it confined for just a little while longer then it might make the release he was going to inevitably feel just that little bit sweeter.

Amber gripped the side of the bath tight as she felt him pull her wider apart, his fingers back inside her, playing games that were making her crazy. He knew just where to touch her, where to go that would guarantee she'd be crying out loud and wanting him more, and it felt incredible. Sometimes it hurt, but it was a beautiful pain, and once again it was helping to mask the real pain she felt underneath all this. The real feelings she was trying to dispel, trying to get rid of in the only way she could think of right now. A weak, almost cowardly way, but what did she have to lose? Nothing. She'd already lost him.

'Oh, Jesus…' she groaned, leaning back as far as she could go, biting down on her lip as he pulled out of her, pulling her to her feet and into his arms, tilting her chin up with his thumb.

'Feel good?' He smiled, and she nodded, smiling back, her whole body suddenly feeling as though it had just undergone the most intense, the most erotic massage ever. She was tingling all over, and ready for more.

'Oh yes. Christ, yes, it feels good. *You* feel good.'

His smile grew wider, and when he smiled she felt those tingles intensify, the anticipation growing stronger as this night got ready to reach its final act. 'Then let's go finish this job, huh?'

She shrugged off the robe that hung loosely from her shoulders, taking his hand and leading him back out into the bedroom. Time for her to take control again.

Sitting down on the edge of the bed, she put her hands on his hips, pulling him between her open legs, slowly slipping his shorts down, watching as the rest of his incredible body was revealed. She wanted him inside her so badly, and as she ran her fingers over his erection, feeling it hard and throbbing in her hand, that need only got stronger. Just a few minutes more, that was all. A few more minutes and she'd have him, but he deserved a little something extra first.

Leaning forward, she took him in her mouth, her fingers stroking him as her tongue teased him, causing him to cry out loud. He buried his fingers in her hair, pushing her against him, wanting to feel her take him totally, every inch of him, and she accepted the invitation. For a few incredible seconds he was in the kind of heaven he'd waited all his life for, and even when she pulled away, setting him free, he knew there was still more to come.

She stood up, one hand still holding him, gripping him tight, her fingers in his dark, messed-up hair, her mouth almost touching his as they looked at each other, the electricity sparking between them almost visible, it was so strong. And then she just turned and pushed him back on the bed, standing with her hands on her hips, smiling at his expression of total surprise.

'Oh, so *you're* in charge now, then?' He grinned, propping himself up on his elbows, watching as she knelt up on the bed, leaning forward to slowly crawl towards him and he honestly felt as though he'd been thrust straight into some kind of perfect wet dream. 'But, hey, do you know what? I don't have a problem with that.'

'You don't get a choice,' she said as she straddled him, pushing both hands through her dark red hair, arching her back and pushing her breasts out, which only served to make Ryan's aching erection all the more painful. He was verging on desperate now, yet, at the same time, he knew the quicker it happened, the sooner it would be over. And then what? Back to a reality he wasn't even sure he wanted anymore?

'Amber…'

She shook her head, leaning over to shut him up with a kiss, his fingers entwining with hers as the heat between them intensified so much he could literally feel himself burning up. 'No more talking, okay?' she whispered, sitting back up and once more taking him in her hand, her eyes locked on his as she carefully guided him inside her, and all he could do was lie back and let it happen.

Amber finally closed her eyes, leaning back and pushing down onto him, his hands on her hips keeping her right where she needed to be because this wasn't going to take long. That was a given. But she wasn't sure either of them wanted it to be over. This was nothing but a smokescreen, for both of them, she knew that. And she was certain he knew that, too, and when it was over they were both still going to have to face up to everything they were trying to ignore right now. So to feel him there, a part of her again, like he used to be not that long ago, it was a beautiful escape. A distraction she needed. A mistake. But one they couldn't reverse, so when she finally felt him come inside her with a force so hard it almost rocked her backwards, the cries that forced out of her weren't just because it felt incredible, they were also cries of frustration and pain and anger that the life she'd dreamed of had come crashing down around her. She'd lost control. Of everything.

With him still inside her, she turned over onto her back, wrapping her legs around him, keeping her eyes closed until she reached her own climax, stretching out as that blanket of hot pins and needles crept its way up her body. His hands were holding hers, his breath warm on her skin as her hips bucked up against him, that wave of intense pleasure now hitting her full-on, making her scream out loud again, giving her another opportunity to get every ounce of pent-up frustration she had left inside of her out, until there was nothing more to give. Nothing.

He collapsed on top of her, his breathing heavy and ragged, and she could feel his heart beating against her own chest as he lay there. Ryan Fisher. Her big mistake.

'Jesus, Amber, you're killing me, babe.' He finally rolled off her, onto his back, as he tried to slow his breathing down.

'Says the man who's eleven years younger than me.' She turned onto her side, propping herself up on one elbow. 'Your fitness levels down then, mister?'

He smirked, reaching out to touch her breasts, letting his fingers trail slowly over them. 'My fitness levels are fine, thanks.' He moved his hand to her hip, quickly pulling her down over him. 'In fact, give me five minutes and I'll be more than ready to show you just how much stamina I've got.'

'Five minutes, huh?' She raised an eyebrow. 'That long?'

He laughed, his hand resting in the small of her back, and just the feel of her skin beneath his fingers made him feel more safe, more relaxed than he had done in months. 'Impatience isn't a trait I'd associate with you, Ms. Sullivan.'

Once again he was using her maiden name – was it his way of trying to make her realise a chapter of her life was coming to an end? Whether she wanted it to or not.

'I need to pee,' she sighed, climbing off him and walking into the en-suite.

Ryan lay back, closing his eyes, letting himself drift off into that place in his head that always wondered what their life would have been like if he hadn't thrown it all away just weeks before their wedding. Would they have been happy? Would the sex always have been this great? Would Jim Allen have been the same distraction he still was now? He couldn't answer any of those questions. He only knew what he felt now – and that was regret, for losing the chance to even see where their life together could have gone.

'You okay?'

He opened his eyes to find her sitting cross-legged beside him, now wearing his shirt, her hair piled up messily on top of her head. 'You always did look better in my clothes than I did.' He smiled. She returned it – for a brief second, anyway, before her expression became more serious.

'Ryan... Look, I...'

'We could make a go of this, Amber.' He had to try, didn't he? He had to. Even if he didn't get the answer he really wanted.

'No,' she whispered, shaking her head, her fingers fiddling with the wedding ring she still wore. She wasn't all that sure that she'd ever be able to take it off. 'No, Ryan.' Her eyes met his, and there was still something there, still that spark she felt with an intensity she wished didn't exist. But everything was just way too confusing right now to make sense of anything – to know what was real and what she was feeling only because she was trying to blank other things out. 'We couldn't.'

He hung his head, breaking the stare, because he felt it, too. That spark. He felt it with a heart-breaking force that almost physically winded him.

'You going away for a while, it really is the best thing,' she said, although he was fighting against agreeing with that now. 'For both of us.'

'You really think so?' he asked.

'I really think so. We have to move on, Ryan. As much as I…' She stopped talking, and he felt a ridiculous feeling of hope sweep over him that he couldn't stop. 'It's for the best.'

That feeling of hope was crushed as she got off the bed, walking over to the window. He got up, too, quickly pulling on his shorts before walking up behind her, gently pulling her against him. She leaned back, resting her head on his shoulder, that feeling of closeness making her feel safe, for a little while, at least.

'So, this really is goodbye?' he asked, her fingers entwining with his as they rested on her stomach.

'I hate that word – goodbye,' she whispered. 'It's so final.' She turned round in his arms, sliding a hand round the back of his neck. 'I mean, it's not like I'm never going to see you again, is it?'

Once more he was filled with a ridiculous feeling of hope as he read a million and one things into that last sentence of hers. 'Of course you'll see me again. Amber, baby, you could see me every day if you…'

She stopped him from talking by placing her fingertips over his mouth, shaking her head again. 'No, Ryan. Please. No.' She stared up into his eyes – her handsome Geordie boy. But he didn't need her; he needed that new start, that new adventure – he needed time to sort his head out, and she wasn't helping. She wasn't good for him. He wasn't good for her. But tonight, they'd needed each other. 'I really want you to stay with me tonight, Ryan. I want you to stay, but if you…'

'I'm not going anywhere.' He smiled, stroking the hair from her eyes, kissing her so gently she felt those stupid tears reappear, but she was determined they weren't going to escape. Not this time.

'No more talking, okay? We've done enough of that, and I'm tired. I'm tired of it all.' She looked up at him, a fleeting moment of something she couldn't explain hitting her somewhere deep in the pit of her stomach that was quickly pushed aside to let reality start to creep its way back. 'I just don't want you to go yet, that's all.'

He pulled her close, resting his chin on the top of her head as he held her tight, his own eyes filling with tears as the harsh realisation of what was happening tomorrow hit him head-on. But it had been his choice. His decision. Nobody else's. And maybe it *was* for the best. He could only hope the day when he finally started to believe that came quickly, because, right now, he couldn't see it happening at all.

Chapter Twenty-Four

The sound of the doorbell being rung continuously, followed by a round of knocking loud enough to wake the neighbours almost made Amber drop the mug she'd just lifted from the dishwasher.

'Okay, okay. I'm coming!' she shouted as she ran from the kitchen out into the hall, flinging open the door, not really sure what or who she was expecting to see. But finding Ronnie standing there on the doorstep wasn't a huge surprise.

'Oh, you're in, then,' he said dryly as he leaned against the porch frame.

'Of course I'm in. Where did you think I'd be?'

'Well, you see, Amber, I had absolutely no fucking idea because you haven't been answering your fucking phone, have you?'

'All right. Calm down. I'm sorry, okay? I didn't think…'

'No. You didn't.'

'I'm fine.'

'Yeah, but *I* didn't know that, did I? Where were you last night anyway?'

She looked down at the tea towel she had in her hands, aware that she was wringing it to within an inch of its life. 'Nowhere.'

'Nowhere,' Ronnie repeated, looking at her with an expression that said he didn't believe a word she was saying. 'You gonna let me in or what?'

She quickly looked over her shoulder. She couldn't hear the shower anymore, which probably meant Ryan was out of the bathroom and likely to come downstairs any second now, and the last thing she needed was Ronnie knowing he'd stayed the night. Just the thought of the lectures *that* scenario would invite was giving her a headache already.

'You lost something?'

She quickly turned back to Ronnie. 'No. No, I'm just... I'm busy.'

He raised a questioning eyebrow, giving her that look again. 'You're busy. Doing what, exactly?'

'Nothing, it's...'

Ronnie sighed, walking into the hall before Amber could stop him, just as Ryan came jogging down the stairs. And even in the midst of this rather awkward situation Amber couldn't help but notice how hot and handsome he looked in jeans, army boots, and a t-shirt that showed off those toned and tattooed arms, his dark hair falling over his eyes, that familiar stubble still making him look all the more sexy. No wonder her stomach couldn't stop flipping over.

Ronnie stopped dead in his tracks and stared at Ryan, before turning to Amber, shaking his head. 'No. Don't tell me... not again, Amber. Please tell me you didn't...'

Ryan stood at the bottom of the stairs, looking at Amber, who once again had decided to focus on the tea towel that was wound tightly between her fingers.

'What do you *think* happened, Ronnie?' She pushed past both of them, going back into the kitchen.

'For fuck's sake... What the hell are the pair of you playing at? Huh? I mean, if this was a mess before, then you've both just upgraded it to fucking chaos!'

'You don't know anything, Ronnie,' Amber said quietly, watching as Ryan followed them into the kitchen, leaning back against the wall and folding his arms.

'I know that you and him shouldn't be doing *this. He's* supposed to be on a plane to frigging Tenerife and *you're* supposed to be sorting your marriage out...'

'My marriage is finished, Ronnie, and you know that,' Amber hissed, finally ridding herself of the tea towel. 'It's over, and if I wanted – if I *needed* – just a few hours to forget that fact, a few hours where my fucking heart isn't breaking because the man I love with every inch of my being doesn't want to be with me, then I'll take those few hours. I'll take them, and what's more, I enjoyed them.'

'You should have called *me*,' Ronnie said, his voice quieter but still with an edge that displayed more than a hint of anger and frustration. 'I'm your friend. That's what I do, I help you, Amber. *I'm* supposed to be the one you turn to; *I'm* the one who's supposed to be there for you.'

'I needed more than just a chat, Ronnie.'

'And I could have given you that, too. Don't you see? Have you fucking forgotten what happened just a few months ago?'

'I needed him.' Amber's voice was raised now, tired of trying to explain something she couldn't really explain herself. And then the anger suddenly faded, leaving her words quiet and only just audible. 'I needed *him*.'

Ronnie leaned back against the counter, pushing a hand through his hair. 'You didn't need him, Amber. You just needed someone.'

Amber turned away, her eyes meeting Ryan's, and whilst last night she may have agreed with what Ronnie had just said, now she wasn't quite so sure.

'You really need to make sure you lock your front door, Amber. Anyone could walk in.'

She broke away from Ryan's stare to see Max standing in the kitchen doorway, hands in pockets, dark glasses pushed up into his salt-and-pepper hair.

'Something either of you two want to tell me?' he asked, indicating first her then Ryan.

'Shit! Sorry, Max,' Ryan sighed, throwing his head back. 'I should have called you.'

'Yeah. You should have.'

Ronnie looked at Amber, raising that cynical eyebrow again. She ignored him.

'Doing a disappearing act the night before you're due to begin a pretty high-profile, not to mention controversial, loan period abroad wasn't the smartest of moves, Ryan,' Max said, helping himself to coffee. 'So I can only hope that you were careful enough not to have allowed any unnecessary publicity to rear its head.' He looked straight at Ryan, fixing him with a look that said the answer he was expecting was yes.

Ryan's eyes met Amber's again, and neither Max nor Ronnie missed the look that passed between them.

'So,' Max went on, taking a sip of coffee in his usual calm and controlled manner. There was no situation that could faze Max Mandell. He'd seen it all, and more, in his years as a top football agent. There was nothing he couldn't handle. 'You two got anything you want to share with the rest of us? Or can we just assume that this was your way of saying goodbye?'

Amber looked down at her hands, unsure of what to do with them now that she'd discarded the tea towel. 'It was just a night out,' she said, wishing her stomach would unravel itself from the mass of knots it was tied up in. It was making her feel sick again.

'Ryan?' Max turned his attention to his unpredictable client.

Ryan said nothing for a second, pushing a hand through his hair as he turned his head to look out of the window. 'Like Amber said, it was just a night out.'

Amber didn't miss the slightly sarcastic laugh that came from Ronnie, but again she ignored him.

'Right. Well, in that case, you'd better finish saying your good-byes, Ryan, because we have a plane to catch. Five minutes, then I want you outside and in that car, you listening to me?'

Ryan nodded, once more looking over at Amber, who seemed more interested in what was happening out in the garden.

'Everything all right, princess?'

She turned to see Max standing right beside her, his voice a little softer than it had been before. She smiled, folding her arms against her chest. 'Everything's fine.'

'You sure?'

'It's a crazy time, Max. That's all.'

He reached out to gently squeeze her shoulder. 'Yeah. I know it is, kiddo. So you call me if you need me, okay?'

She smiled again, not sure if it had reached her eyes, but she didn't really care. Suddenly she was too exhausted to worry about things like that.

'Do you want to say goodbye to Romeo over there on your own?'

She looked up, surprised that he'd asked that. But glad. Because she didn't want Ryan to walk out like this, not like this. It would leave things way too open-ended and she needed some kind of closure if she was ever going to deal with moving forward.

'Yeah.' Her voice was quiet again, almost a whisper. 'Thanks.'

'Max…' Ronnie objected, looking at him with an expression of disbelief.

'Come on, Ronnie. Let them say goodbye. A couple of minutes, that's all.' Max looked at Amber again, and she nodded, all of a sudden loving this man in front of her for giving her this chance she hadn't even realised she'd needed. She'd thought she'd said every goodbye there could be to Ryan Fisher a long time ago, but it seemed she'd been wrong. It seemed that she'd never really said goodbye at all.

'Jesus Christ,' Ronnie sighed, walking out of the kitchen, closely followed by Max.

Amber waited until the door closed behind them before she looked up, watching as Ryan walked over to her.

'Thank you,' he said, his hands still stuck in his pockets as he stood in front of her. 'For last night.'

'You make it sound so impersonal when you put it like that.' Amber was finding it hard to even look at him as every confusing feeling she'd been experiencing for hours now seemed to whirl round faster and faster inside her head.

He looked down at his boots for a second before raising his head to finally meet her gaze, their eyes locking together in a stare so intense she felt a bolt of something sharp and shocking shoot right through her.

'You take care of yourself,' he whispered, stepping forward, reaching out to gently touch her face, cradling her cheek in the palm of his hand. 'You hear me?'

She closed her eyes as his mouth met hers, her body pressing against his, and it was an automatic reaction to slide her arms around his neck, to hold him tight and lose herself in that kiss.

His hands slid up under her shirt, the touch of his fingers on her skin making her gasp out loud before the kiss deepened even more, their tongues entwining, dancing round each other. He tasted so good, and he'd been there for her at a time – and this was where Ronnie had been right – when she'd needed somebody. But not just anybody, because, deep down inside, Amber knew she'd needed *him*. For those few hours she'd needed *him*. But now it really was time to say goodbye, to move on and let him start that new life he was moving abroad to begin.

He pulled away slightly, looking at her, playing with the open collar of her shirt, letting his hand slide down slightly, skimming the curve of her breasts with his fingertips.

'Go on, get out of here,' she said, trying to force a smile as a hundred and one memories of her time with this man – good and bad – flooded her already crowded brain. She really had loved him. Once.

'You trying to get rid of me?' He smiled, too, tucking a strand of her hair behind her ear as he leaned forward to kiss her again. 'Because I'm sure Max said I had five minutes, and I may not be the best mathematician there ever was, but I'm positive I've still got a couple of those left.'

This time the smile came naturally. He was making her feel like a teenager saying goodbye to the boyfriend she'd been forbidden to see, rather than a thirty-eight-year-old woman who should know better than to let this get to her.

'Then shut up and kiss me some more, before you waste what little time you have left.'

She closed her eyes again as his mouth rested on hers, moving slowly against it until they had that perfect rhythm going, and for a final few seconds she lost herself in him, in this crazy, complicated man who'd stolen a piece of her heart she would never get back, she knew that now. She knew that. And that was all she was sure of right now.

'You could still come with me,' Ryan whispered, his hand holding tightly onto hers, clinging onto her as though he was scared to let go.

'No, Ryan, come on, baby. We've been through this. You know where my head is at the minute – it's all over the place. And I think yours is, too, which is why you're going away in the first place, you need to remember that.'

He rested his forehead against hers, kissing her quickly, still reluctant to let go of her hand. 'It's all so fucked up, Amber. All of it. I don't even know what I'm doing anymore.'

'Hey, come on.' She placed a hand on his face, stroking his cheek with her thumb. 'Listen to me, okay? You're gonna be fine. You're gonna get out there and show the Spanish how it's done, do you hear me? Yes, things are confusing and fucked up and what we've done here hasn't exactly helped matters, but once you get out there, Ryan, you'll see that this really is the best decision. For all of us.'

He squeezed her hand, suddenly aware that he had tears in his eyes, but he didn't care. He didn't. Right now he felt like someone had just kicked him hard in the solar plexus, knocking every breath he had clean out of him. And he was scared. Yeah, he was scared. Scared of what he was doing, and sad for the things he hadn't done.

'And the next time I see you I expect you to at least be able to say a few words of Spanish. Okay?'

'Amber…'

'You'd better go.' She smiled, letting go of him and turning away, focusing on the garden outside and not him, because to focus on him would be dangerous. She'd said her goodbyes, and now he needed to leave.

'I love you, Amber. I want you to know that. I love you. And I don't think I ever stopped.'

She closed her eyes as she heard him walk away, heard the sound of muffled voices out in the hall before the sound of the front door banging shut heralded in a fresh bout of tears that she quickly blinked away. She was determined that today was the day she became stronger and stopped letting weakness take hold at a time when showing weakness just wasn't going to work. It wasn't going to get her anywhere. It wasn't going to help.

'You okay?'

She swung round to see Ronnie standing there, his expression softer now, his voice more understanding. 'Not really.'

'It's for the best, Amber. You know that.'

'Yeah.' She sniffed, turning away from him for the briefest of seconds to wipe away a stray tear that had escaped. 'Yeah, I know.'

He walked over to her, reaching out to take her hand, but she pulled it away, folding her arms against her. Right now, she didn't want his sympathy. She didn't want to be comforted by him or sit down and have one of those 'chats' that were supposed to make her feel better. She wasn't even sure she *wanted* to feel better. Maybe she deserved to feel this miserable and confused. Maybe it was some kind of payback for displaying so much weakness. She was a different woman to the one she'd been a year ago, and she wasn't altogether sure she liked this version of her.

'Amber, sweetheart…'

'No, Ronnie. I don't want to talk, okay? I just want to be on my own.'

'Don't be stupid, kiddo. I can't leave you on your own when you're like this.'

'Like what? I'm fine, okay? I'm just tired of always having people around, confusing me…'

'How the hell am *I* confusing you? Come on, Amber. I just want to be there for you, I want to help you…'

'Then leave me alone.' She looked at him, right into eyes that had never hurt her, never lied to her, and she knew they never would. But she didn't need him right now. She didn't need anyone. 'If you really want to help me, just leave me alone. Please.'

'I don't want to do that,' Ronnie whispered.

'Please, Ronnie.'

He stared back at her, knowing exactly what was going on inside her head. And knowing he shouldn't be going anywhere. 'You don't have to pretend to be strong with me, Amber.'

'I'm not pretending to be anything. I just want to be alone.'

He shook his head, taking a couple more steps forward, his eyes still on hers. 'No, you don't. Not really.'

'Please don't tell me what you think I'm feeling, because you have no idea.'

'Why are you pushing me away, Amber?'

'I'm not pushing you away.'

'Yes, you are. I'm trying to be there for you and you're just…'

'I don't want you to be there for me, Ronnie. I don't need that from you, okay? I don't need that anymore. I'm a big girl now. I can handle all this crap on my own. So just go. Please.'

He stared at her for a few more seconds, willing her to look at him, too, but she'd turned away from him. A clear message that the conversation had been shut down.

'What's happening here, Amber?' Ronnie asked, his voice quiet, his tone confused.

'I don't know,' she whispered, pulling her arms tighter against her chest as she focused on nothing in particular outside in the garden. 'I really don't know anymore.'

Chapter Twenty-Five

Amber took Debbie's hand as she lowered herself down onto the sofa in the Players' Lounge. Her baby bump seemed to be growing bigger by the day, and with just a few weeks left until baby put in an appearance, even Amber was starting to get just a little bit excited.

'So how was your Christmas?' she asked, smiling slightly as she watched Debbie grab a cushion and shove it behind her back, her hands resting on her rapidly growing bump.

'Alcohol-free, unfortunately,' Debbie replied. 'And I could do without having to come here today. I don't know why Gary suddenly feels the need to have me around as support when it didn't seem to bother him before.'

'He was never this close to becoming a daddy before, was he?' Amber smiled. 'All of this has really changed him, don't you think?'

Debbie looked at Amber out of the corner of her eye, smiling slightly. 'Yeah. And I'm not altogether sure it's for the better, actually. I've never been fussed over so much in my entire life. Every time I turn around he's there, making sure I'm all right, that I've got everything I need… Sometimes I think I preferred him when he was out every night chatting up wannabe WAGs and rolling home at all hours.'

Amber leaned forward, resting her elbows on her knees. 'Well, he's lost his partner-in-crime now, hasn't he?'

Debbie paused for a second before speaking. 'Do you know how he's getting on over there?'

Amber stared down at the floor, focusing on the red carpet. 'I can't avoid knowing, can I?' She looked back up at Debbie, smiling a small smile. 'It's my job, isn't it? To know what's going on in the world of football. Especially when it involves a name as big as Ryan Fisher's.'

'So he's doing okay, then?'

'He's doing fine. He's already made his mark in the first few weeks of him being there; he's scoring goals, drawing the crowds in, and by all accounts he's settled right into his new life.'

Debbie gave a small snort of derision, causing Amber to stare at her.

'What was *that* for?'

'Ryan Fisher, settling into a new life on a holiday island frequented by tourists fifty-two weeks of the year? He'll be like a kid in a candy store. Of course he's settled in. Why wouldn't he have?'

Amber stared back down at the floor. 'I don't think he's like that anymore, Debbie.'

'Really? You truly believe he's one leopard who can change his spots? You thought that before and look what happened.'

Amber said nothing, she just continued to stare down at the floor. 'Look, I'd better go. I'm supposed to be over in the press area…'

'I know what happened between you and Ryan, Amber. The night of Gary's birthday party. I know you spent the night together, so I know there's still something there between you two, but…'

Amber stood up, shaking out her hair, which had started to become a bit of a habit of hers when she felt as though she needed to rid herself of something she didn't want to think about. 'There's nothing going on between Ryan and me, Debbie. Not anymore.'

'And what about you and Jim?'

Amber pushed both hands through her hair – another habit

of hers that seemed to occur when she was nervous, or trying to avoid talking about subjects she didn't want to discuss. 'There *is* no me and Jim. Remember?'

'Did you see him? Over Christmas, I mean.'

'No. No, I didn't. As far as I was aware he spent it with Brandon. I've really got to go, Debs…'

'Amber, hang on.' Debbie slowly hauled herself up off the sofa. 'Wait a minute… Are you okay?'

Amber cocked her head, frowning slightly. 'Why wouldn't I be?'

'I don't know. You tell me, chick. All I know is we didn't see much of you over Christmas and New Year, and…'

'I was working. You know as well as I do that the football season doesn't stop for Christmas.'

'I know. I know that, I just thought…'

'I'm fine, Debbie. Really. I'm fine.' She smiled. 'I'll speak to you later, okay?'

'You're not fooling me, Amber,' Debbie shouted after her as she tried to lower herself back down onto the sofa. But Amber just threw her another smile over her shoulder as she left the Players' Lounge, bumping straight into someone on her way out.

'Oh, Jesus, I'm sorry…' She stopped dead in her tracks as she looked up at the recipient of her shoulder-bump, her heart almost thudding to a halt as their eyes met. For the first time in weeks.

'Don't be.' He smiled, and Amber wished with all her heart that he hadn't done that. She'd known there was a good chance she'd have to see him at some point today, seeing as this was the big game between Newcastle Red Star and Wearside Spartans at Tynebridge. She'd just hoped she'd have been better prepared for the moment, that was all. 'You look… you look incredible, Amber.'

She looked away, taking a second to compose herself because he still had the ability to turn her world upside down in a split second. 'I've got to go and find Ronnie…'

He gently grabbed her wrist, stopping her from going anywhere. 'Amber, hang on, honey.'

She swung round to look at him, digging deep to find the strength she needed to get through this confrontation. 'Why, Jim? I thought we'd said all there was to say to each other.'

'I thought I would've seen more of you over Christmas. I tried to call you...'

'I was busy. I spent Christmas in London. Cloud Sports wanted me to do a lot of studio work over the holiday period and...'

'I know. I saw you on TV. I just thought you might have come home, to see your dad.'

'He came to me, Jim. We spent Christmas together, along with Ronnie.'

'How cosy.'

She narrowed her eyes, not entirely sure what he'd meant by that comment. 'Have you named the team for this afternoon's game?' she asked, changing the subject, bringing everything back round to the professional level she was far more comfortable with now, as far as Jim was concerned. It was the way it had to be, or she knew she'd be in danger of losing any composure she had left.

'I'll be releasing the details in about ten minutes.' He shoved both hands in his pockets, his eyes never leaving hers. 'Amber, baby, it really doesn't have to be this way.'

She couldn't help but stare back at him, every memory she spent every minute of every day pushing to the back of her mind flooding forward in an unwelcome torrent. 'Yes, Jim. It does.'

He said nothing, both of them standing there feeling, for one confusing second, that they were the only two people there in that crowded, noisy stadium.

'How's Brandon doing?' Amber asked, swallowing hard to stop any more unwanted emotions from showing themselves. She needed to be strong now. She needed to be very, very strong.

'He's doing good. He's all fired up for this afternoon's game, and, to be honest, he could be the biggest threat to Red Star. My own son, huh?' He gave a small laugh, looking down at the ground before meeting her eyes once more. 'He's one hell of a player.'

'Yeah. He is,' Amber said. 'Guess he got that talent from you.'

Jim smiled again, and it made her heart bounce around inside her chest so much she felt breathless. How could she feel so distant from a man who was once her entire world? 'Yeah. Maybe. Anyway, I'd better go talk to the team. Make sure my defence are on their A-game if they want to stop my son from taking those three points away from us.'

Amber watched him walk away, off in the direction of the dressing rooms. That meeting had been almost surreal in her eyes. After weeks of never being this close to him – seeing him only on a TV screen – she now felt as though all the breath had been knocked out of her.

'You all right?'

She swung round to see Ronnie standing there. The expression on his face told her he'd seen most of that encounter, and in a way she was glad. At least it would mean she wouldn't have to explain what had just happened.

'I'm fine. It was going to happen at some point today, wasn't it? Might as well get it over with sooner rather than later.'

'Was everything…? Was he okay? With you, I mean?'

'Why wouldn't he be? We don't hate each other, Ronnie. It isn't like that. Things just… things just didn't work out, that's all. Come on. Let's go. We've got work to do.' Whether she felt like it or not.

The sun beat down on the terrace of Ryan's new Spanish home, a cool sea breeze taking the edge off the heat, which was extremely welcome given that, even in January, the temperature was still almost 30 degrees in the shade.

He hadn't expected to settle into his temporary life on this Spanish island quite as fast as he had done, but everyone was going out of their way to make him feel welcome. In a team made up of British, German, Spanish, and even Australian players, he thanked God the main language was English, and all the guys in the CD Adeje squad were friendlier than he could have hoped for.

Maybe it was the fact they all lived here, on this beautiful island with its abundance of sunshine and constant flow of women on tap, that made everyone so happy all the time, he didn't know. All he knew was that he was enjoying it. There were even times when he actually did believe that asking for this loan period had been the right thing to do, because his head was beginning to feel clearer than it had done in a long time. And, despite the fact he was just a stone's throw away from the main tourist resorts and all the temptations *they* could bring, he was behaving himself as far as the partying was concerned. He couldn't claim to be a saint, or even anything close to that, but he knew his limitations. He knew when to stop, go home, and save some for another night.

'You coming back inside, Ryan?'

Having said that, when he *did* come home, he didn't always make that journey alone. But, hey, if the perks were there, he was going to take them. He was Ryan Fisher. And he still had a reputation to uphold, even if, at times, it was somewhat watered down.

He turned around and smiled at the young woman standing by the open patio doors that led out onto the terrace from the living room. All messed-up blonde hair and a pretty face, she was on holiday from Liverpool with three of her friends, but even he'd resisted the temptation to bring them *all* home. That would have just been stupid.

'Give me five minutes, babe. Just getting my breath back.'

She giggled, shaking her hair out, and for a second he felt a twisting in his stomach as he was reminded of Amber, and the way she'd used to do that. He waited until the patio doors were closed behind her before he let out a deep breath. He could do this. He had to. He didn't really have much choice.

Checking his watch, he smiled to himself as he saw the time. It was almost kick-off back home in Newcastle – the big match between the two rival local teams. And a little part of him wished he was there, getting caught up in the unique atmosphere those derby games created. The competitive spirit seemed to take hold stronger than any other match, as pride, as well as points, came into play. And with Brandon Palmer now a key player in the Wearside Spartans squad, this wasn't going to be an easy match for Newcastle Red Star. Especially as their star striker was now languishing abroad, playing an altogether different kind of game.

Walking back inside, he was grateful for the cool of the air conditioning as he quickly found the remote control and flicked through the on-screen TV guide until he came to the Cloud Sports News channel. No way was he living without his sports channels, even in a foreign country. He needed to keep up to date with what was going on back home. He needed to still be able to see Amber.

His stomach fell as he realised she wasn't in the studio that afternoon, which could only mean one thing – she was actually at the match itself. She was at Tynebridge. With Ronnie. With Jim. With everyone who was close to her. He lowered the sound down on the TV and threw the remote onto the glass-topped coffee table, pushing a hand through his hair as he walked over to the open-plan kitchen at the other end of the room. Maybe he should have resisted that urge to have the satellite dish fitted. Maybe he should have tried to live without that link to her. But it was never really going to go away, was it? This burning confusion that had wrapped itself around his heart and seemed in no hurry to loosen its grip.

Grabbing a bottle of water from the fridge, he turned round suddenly as he heard his guest walk into the room. She was naked, having now disposed of the sheet she'd had wrapped around her before. Jesus, not even a stirring! What was wrong with him? He had a young, naked woman right there in front of him and all he wanted to do was lie on the sofa and watch the football results come rolling in.

'Ryan. I'm waiting, come on. I thought we were spending the day together.'

He took a drink, looking her up and down, trying desperately to feel something that would make him want to take her back to bed and fuck away the frustration. But nothing was happening.

'Something's come up, sweetheart.' And it wasn't what *she* wanted.

'Huh?' She looked at him with an expression of utter confusion. 'What does *that* mean?'

'It means, I need you to get dressed and get out of here.'

She pouted at him, fluttering her false eyelashes as though that would change everything. 'Right now?'

'Right now.' She was hot, there was no denying it, and he'd enjoyed last night. What he could remember of it. But he hadn't promised her anything more than the chance to fuck a famous footballer, and a bed for the night. Nothing else. And he was absolutely sure he hadn't promised her they'd be spending the day together. He had training later that afternoon, and tomorrow's match to prepare for – there'd been nothing else on the agenda as far as he'd been concerned.

She walked over to him, twirling her hair around her finger, still pouting, still fluttering, and still it had no effect on Ryan. It was almost as if he'd just thrown up barriers that were deflecting any kind of advances, even those from stunning, naked blondes. 'Are you sure you can't spare just five little minutes?'

He reached out and ran his fingers over her breasts – fake, of course. Unlike Amber's – they were perfect and rounded and felt incredible when he touched them… Shit! He really had to get rid of this one.

'Come on, babe. That's enough, okay?' He gently pushed her away. 'I'm really busy this afternoon and… I just need you to leave, all right? It was fun, you're a beautiful girl, but I've got things to do.'

She threw him a look that said she was far from happy before making her way back to the bedroom with a toss of her hair and a wiggle that, under normal circumstances, would have made him follow her. But now he felt nothing but relief that she was finally on her way out of there.

She reappeared just minutes later, dressed and ready to leave.

But she wasn't going without a fight. 'Will I see you again?' she asked, moving in for one last kiss, but Ryan was too quick for her, turning his head so she caught his cheek.

'If you come to the game tomorrow, yeah. You'll see me there, won't you?'

'That's not what I meant!' she huffed, reaching out to stroke his shoulder, running her fingers lightly down his arm. Once upon a time this would have worked like a dream. Having a woman like this want him so badly, practically offering herself to him on a fucking plate; back in the day he would've been ready for action before you could say *penalty*. But now – now there was nothing. He just wanted her gone.

'I know what you meant.' He smiled, trying to ease the atmosphere. It wasn't *her* fault he was feeling like this. But she'd got what she'd wanted – and those were the rules in this game. No promises, no ties, just sex. 'Look, I might see you around, it depends. When do you fly home?'

'Next Tuesday. Do you want my number?'

'Like I said, babe, I might see you around. Okay?'

She gave him one more look from beneath those long lashes of hers, but even she was beginning to realise it wasn't getting her anywhere. 'I'll see you later, Ryan.'

'Yeah. Later.'

He watched her walk out into the hall, waiting until he heard the front door bang shut before he opened one of the kitchen drawers and pulled out a copy of Ice Magazine. The one with Amber on the cover wearing nothing but a smile and a strategically placed Newcastle Red Star scarf. A real-life naked woman right there in the room with him hadn't managed to stir anything, yet one quick look at Amber staring at him from the cover of a magazine and he was already standing to attention, his super-fast hard-on straining to be set free.

Taking the magazine into the bedroom, he got naked and sat down on the bed, flicking through the pages until he got to Amber's photos. There she was, lying across the benches in the Red Star home team dressing room, naked and beautiful, with her back arched and that incredible body of hers almost totally on show, but he didn't mind that those breasts were covered by her arm or that her legs were positioned so that only a hint of what lay between them could be seen. He knew what she looked like, knew what she felt like. And was it a sign – hadn't anyone noticed that she was lying right underneath his space in the dressing room? His number 9 strip was hanging right there, above her. *Was* that a sign? Or was he just reading way too much into what was nothing but a coincidence?

Moving his hand down to touch himself, he flicked the page over to another set of photos – she was wearing a pair of Newcastle Red Star shorts, pulled right down as low as they could go without letting the world see that part of her he loved living in. She'd left little to the imagination as far as those photos were concerned, and his imagination was certainly running wild right now as his hand started to move faster, up and down, taking him to where he wanted to be, that place in his head he'd never really left behind. And he wasn't sure he ever could.

Despite the best efforts of a full-strength Wearside Spartans, they couldn't quite get past Newcastle Red Star, even without Ryan Fisher. The final score was a 2-2 draw, so this time the points were shared in a game that had, as was usual with these derby matches, been littered with rougher tackles, harsher challenges, and more than the usual amount of bookings, on both sides. But, on the whole, it had been a friendly meeting. Even the fans had been on their best behaviour, although it hadn't escaped Amber's notice that some of them were still quite happy to voice their obvious annoyance at the fact Ryan Fisher wasn't there. To some extent he *had* been missed, and even Amber had to admit there'd been times when his presence could have quite easily grabbed Red Star the full three points. But his temporary replacement – a seasoned

French player the club had managed to secure on a rolling monthly contract from one of the big Italian clubs – had more than proved himself, netting both of Red Star's goals, which had gone some way to placating the fans.

'You did good today,' Ronnie said, leaning back against the bench at the back of the Press Lounge, watching as Amber packed away her things.

'I'm not five, Ronnie. I *can* handle being here, you know. It's my job. And, if nothing else, I'm a professional.'

Ronnie shoved his hands in his pockets, looking down at his feet for a second. 'You've got that defensive tone turned up full today, haven't you?'

'That's because I feel guilty.'

'About what?'

'About Ryan not being here. I'm not stupid, and I know more than a few of those fans out there blame me for his temporary departure. I've heard some of the things they've been saying.'

'Take no notice.'

'That's easier said than done.'

'Look, it isn't your fault he can't control his feelings, Amber.'

'I know,' she sighed. 'I know that. But it still feels like I'm partly to blame, somehow.'

'In what way?'

'I shouldn't have slept with him for starters.'

'What? Ever? Or recently?'

'You know what I mean.'

Ronnie looked down at the floor, shoving his hands in his pockets. 'You could have offered to stay down in London. Instead of being here, I mean. You know they love it when you do the studio stuff.' He looked up at her, smiling slightly. 'It gets them way more viewers than usual. Especially since you did the Ice Magazine shoot.'

'You're such a sexist pig,' she said, unable to stop herself from smiling back as she zipped up her laptop bag.

'Anyway, it's over now, isn't it?'

'Yeah,' she sighed, lying her bag down on the floor and leaning back against the bench beside Ronnie. 'Yeah. It's over.' She looked at her best friend, squeezing his arm and standing up on tiptoe to kiss him on the cheek. 'And thanks for doing the post-match interview with Jim. I wasn't sure I could hack it today.'

'I thought you said you were a professional.' But he'd said that with a smile, pulling her in for a hug, kissing the top of her head. 'I'd better get going. I said I'd meet a few of the guys from Tyne Star Radio over in the pub across the road. You coming?'

She shook her head. 'No. Don't really feel like it. I said I'd meet Dad back at his place after the game, then I might go see Debbie this evening.'

'Okay, well, I'll call you later. You gonna be all right?'

'Ronnie! Like I said before, I'm not five.' She smiled, pushing him gently in the direction of the door. 'Go on. Get out of here.'

She turned to gather the rest of her things together, but the sound of someone coming into the room distracted her.

'What did you forget?' She turned around, expecting to see Ronnie standing there. But instead she saw Ellen. Ryan's ex. 'Can I do something for you?' Amber asked, folding her arms against her in a slightly defensive manner. Although, she was only mirroring the stance of the woman in front of her.

'You could leave Ryan alone,' Ellen replied, her voice almost a whisper but still carrying a hard-edged tone to it.

'I'm sorry,' Amber laughed, totally confused by this sudden encounter.

'Leave him alone. We were happy. We'd moved in together, we were actually a couple, and then, all of a sudden, he decides he wants to leave all that behind and move to Spain because, apparently, he can't forget *you*.'

'And that's *my* fault?'

'Of course it fucking is! If it wasn't for you, he'd still be here, we'd still be together…'

Amber couldn't help another slightly sarcastic and cynical laugh from escaping. 'You really think that? Listen, sweetheart, Ryan Fisher is a long way off settling down, believe me.'

'He almost married *you*.'

'The clue is in the word "*almost*", Ellen. And that's about as close as Ryan Fisher is going to get to settling down right now.'

'You know that, do you?'

'Yes, I know that.' Amber was more than a touch agitated by this conversation, because it was one she really didn't feel like having. 'I know that better than anybody because I was there, I was right there when it all fell apart. I saw him broken and battered, unable to cope with situations he just isn't ready for. Jesus, Ellen, he's like a big kid! If he sees something he wants, he thinks all it takes is one click of the fingers and it's his, whether he's fully prepared for it or not. He doesn't think ahead, doesn't consider what the future might bring…'

'You think you know it all, don't you?' Ellen sneered, moving a step closer, whilst Amber stood her ground, staying put. She was going nowhere.

'I don't even know why I'm having this conversation.'

'But you don't, okay? You might think you're this beautiful, popular TV presenter with the celebrity lifestyle and the perfect existence, but just because your husband doesn't want you anymore, it doesn't give you the right to go running back to Ryan.'

This time Amber did move, her face up close to the pretty PR girl's, her temper simmering but still under control. She could do without this, but she could also handle it. 'Okay, sweetheart. I think you've said enough. One more word from you and I'll consider it a line crossed that you can't come back from. So I suggest you get out of here and forget this happened, all right?'

'He'd still be with me, if it wasn't for you.' Ellen wasn't giving up without a fight, and Amber couldn't help but admire her tenacity, in a strange kind of way. It was wasted, though. On Ryan. 'It should be *you* who's moved away. Not him.'

'You can do better than Ryan Fisher,' Amber said, her voice quieter, because she meant it. Ellen *could* do better than Ryan. He'd only hurt her, in the end. More than he already had.

'I love him.'

'Oh Jesus, Ellen…' Amber sighed, taking a couple of steps back, pushing a hand through her hair. 'Don't fall in love with him, please.'

'Why? Because you want him for yourself? You talk about *him* clicking his fingers and getting what he wants, but isn't that all you have to do with him? If you shout loud enough does he not come running?'

'Leave it, Ellen. Just, leave it.'

'Have you slept with him? Recently, I mean? Is that why he's run away?'

'He hasn't run away…'

'Yes, he has. He has. There is no need for him to be over there, he should be here, but everybody – *everybody*, even your husband – knows he's only gone because he's still in love with you. That's why he's left, Amber. To get away from you.'

'I'm warning you, Ellen. We're shutting this conversation down, right now.'

'No wonder Jim left you. Why would a man like that want to stay with a cheating bitch like you?'

'Okay, Ms. Taylor, I think you've said enough.'

They both looked round to see Jim standing in the doorway, hands in his pockets, his expression, as usual, stoic.

'Mr. Allen… I'm sorry, I…'

'I'm sure you've got something far more important you should be getting on with,' he said, although his eyes were fixed firmly on Amber. He waited until Ellen had left the room before he said anything else. 'You all right?'

'I can handle Ryan's ex-girlfriends, Jim.'

He walked slowly over to her, his eyes still locked on hers. 'It was good to see the old Amber back for a second there. The woman I fell in love with. The strong, feisty one that quite obviously doesn't need me.'

She felt her stomach flip as he said those words. He thought she didn't need him? How wrong could he be?

'She's just another poor cow who got sucked under Ryan Fisher's spell.'

'And you'd know all about that, wouldn't you?'

He was still staring into her eyes, and it was unnerving her. It was unfair of him, to be this close when this was as far as it was going to go.

'He's gone, Jim.'

'For now, yes. But he'll be back. We both know that, don't we?'

'What's that supposed to mean?'

'It means nothing, Amber. Nothing. I'm sorry.' It was almost as if he'd suddenly broken free from his own trance as he finally tore his eyes away from hers, stepping backwards. 'As long as you're okay. I'll make sure that doesn't happen again.'

'Jim, please. I don't need you to fight my battles... Shit! This is crazy!'

He raised his head to look at her, pushing a hand through his hair.

'I need to go. I promised my dad I'd...'

She tried to push past him but he gently grabbed her wrist, stopping her dead in her tracks. 'Come home with me, Amber.'

She stared at him, trying to read his expression, to find out why he was doing this. 'Why, Jim? To talk?'

'We've talked enough, don't you think? Baby, I need you like you wouldn't believe. Just seeing you here today, watching you at work... It's been a hell of a day, kiddo. And things aren't so bad between us that we can't use each other for a bit of company now and again, surely?'

She continued to stare at him, pulling her wrist free of his grip. 'You're serious, aren't you?'

But she didn't stop him from sliding an arm around her waist, resting his hand on her hip as he pulled her closer, so close their mouths were almost touching, and all Amber was aware of now was the sound of her heart beating so hard and so fast she was sure he could hear it. 'We may not be able to live together, Amber, but I see no reason why we can't enjoy each other whenever the mood takes us.'

She closed her eyes as a moment of utter weakness took over, blinding her to everything else that was happening, everything he was saying, drowning it out in a rush of emotion so strong she couldn't breathe. And as his mouth touched hers, pressing gently against it, moving slowly, tongues touching, entwining in the most beautiful, deep kiss, she knew she didn't need to. He was breathing for her, he was giving her everything she needed, because that's what he did.

Slipping a hand around the back of his neck, she pushed him down harder onto her, the kiss getting faster and longer, his hand sliding under her shirt to touch her naked skin, cupping her breast, sending shivers up and down her spine so strong she literally felt herself shudder in his arms.

But then, almost as fast as that sudden rush of feelings had arrived, a sense of reality hit home like a punch to the stomach and she pushed him away, stepping back, shaking her head.

'No. No, Jim. No. This isn't happening again, I won't let it. I won't let this happen again.' She looked at him, all handsome and strong, a powerful man with a reputation for always winning. For always getting his own way. Was that what was happening here? Was she letting him win this crazy, complicated game they seemed to be playing? 'I can't do that kind of relationship again, and I can't believe you'd let me go through that. I can't... I... I really thought you'd changed, but you haven't, have you? You still want this all *your* way, don't you?'

'Amber, baby...'

'No, Jim, please. Please don't do this.'

'I love you, angel... I love you so much...'

'And I love you, too. Jesus… I love you so much it still fucking hurts – right here.' She punched herself hard in the chest, but she felt nothing. She didn't seem to feel anything anymore as far as this relationship was concerned. Nothing except a painful, confusing kind of love. 'We can't do this, Jim. Not again. I mean, what was it, huh? Was I just a bit too demanding? Did my desperation for a family scare you away? Or couldn't you cope with a wife who wasn't the full package? A wife who couldn't give you kids; a damaged wife, a wife from the bargain basement where slight seconds are the order of the day…'

'Amber, come on, please. Don't do this to yourself. Will you just listen…'

'But you don't want me back, do you? As your wife. You don't want me back.' Her voice was so quiet even she could only just make out what she was saying, and as she looked at him, his head down, his hands in his pockets, she felt her heart break all over again.

'I can't, Amber. I just… I can't.'

'And I can't do *this*, Jim. This running to you whenever you need me, only for you to walk away when you've had enough. I can't do that again. No matter how much I love you. I don't even understand how we got here, how it came to this. I don't… I don't understand.'

He came over to her, reaching out to gently stroke her cheek, and as much as she wanted to push him away, she didn't.

'I don't understand it either, baby.'

Her eyes locked onto his again. 'Do you know how weak I'm feeling right now? Right at this very second? Even after all of this, I just want you to make love to me. I need to feel you inside me, Jim, and it's a feeling that won't go away.'

'Then let me go there.' His lips were almost touching hers again, her heart resuming that frantic, erratic beating as it hammered hard against her ribs. 'Just forget everything else and let me go there.'

She shook her head again, but it was futile. She was already giving into him, she could feel that weakness, that uninvited resistance taking over as those familiar tingles washed over her. After everything she'd just said, she was about to cancel it all out by letting this happen. But she couldn't stop it – wouldn't stop it.

They were in the middle of a football stadium that was still bustling with players and press, the noise evident as it echoed around them from the empty Press Lounge. But all of a sudden she didn't care. She didn't care where they were, because if she started to care then it wouldn't happen. She'd pull away again, let doubt take over and she wasn't willing to give doubt an opportunity to put in an appearance.

So she closed her eyes, pushed everything else to the back of her mind and concentrated only on what was happening now – on his hands unfastening her jeans, sliding them down her legs until she had no other option but to step out of them. She concentrated on his mouth as he kissed that space just above her pubic bone, his breath warm on her skin, sending those tingles into overdrive as he slipped his fingers into the sides of her panties, dragging them down over her thighs.

She knew she was ready for him – she could feel it, that familiar anticipation between her legs, and it took just seconds for him to find out for himself just how ready she was as he rested his hand there, touching her as he stared so deep into her eyes she felt as though she was physically falling into him. Nothing else mattered. The whole room could fill up with people and she didn't think she'd care. As long as he didn't stop what he was doing to her. As long as he didn't stop.

In one swift movement he'd lifted her up onto the table behind them, quickly freeing himself before pushing into her so hard and so fast she completely lost her breath, but the pain was one she welcomed, one she craved. With her hands placed palm-down behind her, she arched her back, gasping out loud as he loosened her shirt, unclipping her bra and exposing her breasts, bending his head to cover them in kisses so light and beautiful she could barely stop herself from crying out. It felt so good, his tongue flicking over her skin as his body merged with hers. She hadn't made love to this man in months, and it was crazy how much she'd needed to feel him there. It was like she'd suddenly been given a dose of a drug she just couldn't do without. She'd gone cold turkey, and as long as she didn't see him, wasn't close to him, then she could manage. If the temptation wasn't there she could cope. But the second she was near him that addiction kicked in all over again and she needed this. She needed that hit.

Wrapping her legs around his hips, she threw her head back as he thrust harder, pushing in and out of her so fast, then slowing down, knowing that if he kept that pace up he was going to come way too soon. And she wasn't sure either of them really wanted that, despite the dangerous situation they were in. If they were caught fucking in the Press Lounge, then every newspaper in the country would want some sort of pictorial evidence. They couldn't have picked a worse place to do this. But sometimes you just didn't have the option of choosing the perfect setting.

She bit down on her lip, stifling another cry as she felt him flood out into her, felt every spasm, every thrust, felt him stiffen as the inevitable climax happened; felt his fingers touch her down there to help her along, and it took just seconds for her to reach her own endgame as those white-hot tingles washed over her, causing her to buck her hips, her breasts pushed right out as he held her tight. Her handsome husband. The man she knew now she could never really have. She just had no idea why.

'We should get out of here,' he whispered, pulling out of her and quickly straightening his clothes. It was like a switch had just been flicked, his mood had changed so fast. 'If anyone catches us…'

He left that last sentence hanging in the air, watching as she dressed, his expression one she really couldn't read.

'Say hi to your dad for me,' he said, his hands back in his pockets as he turned to go. 'I'm sure he's ecstatic at the news of our separation.'

'Is that it?' Amber asked, ignoring his comment about her father, although he wasn't wrong in his assumption of Freddie Sullivan's feelings towards Amber's impending divorce from Jim. His one-time close friend. But the way he was now, his whole demeanour – part of her wasn't at all surprised at the way he was acting, but another part of her felt almost destroyed by his sudden coldness.

He turned around, looking straight at her. 'What do you want, Amber?'

'I want to understand what the hell is going on, Jim. Because I don't. I don't understand any of it and it's killing me.'

He said nothing for a few seconds, just stood there, holding her gaze. 'I can't help you to understand something I don't understand myself.'

And then he was gone, out of the room, leaving her more confused than ever before.

Grabbing her things, she almost ran out of the Press Lounge, making her way back outside. She just needed some air, but for some reason she didn't feel like leaving this place just yet.

Venturing out into the stands, she stopped for a second, looking around the now almost deserted stadium. It was so strange how one place could carry such contrasting atmospheres, depending on how many people were there at the time. When it was full it felt like the most incredible carnival was happening with all the noise and the shouting and the cheering. But when it was empty it could feel like the most eerie and lonely place on earth as the silence echoed around the ground.

She walked slowly down the stone steps, choosing a seat close to the pitch, sitting down and staring out ahead of her. She didn't even care that it was freezing outside, she just needed some air.

'You look like a woman with something on her mind.'

She looked up sharply as someone sat down beside her. 'Brandon! Hi.'

He smiled that smile at her, that smile that was so like his dad's. 'Hi. So – what you thinking about?'

She looked out ahead of her again, clasping her hands together between her knees. 'You don't want to know,' she sighed.

'Maybe I should be the judge of that.' He paused before speaking again. 'Is it my dad?'

She looked at him, knowing her expression had probably told him everything he needed to know.

'I want to hate him, you know? I want to hate him so much, Brandon, I really do. Because if I hated him, then maybe all this shit wouldn't hurt so much.'

'He still seems to love you like crazy, Amber, and you're obviously still in love with him, so… I just don't get it. What *is* it with you two?'

'I wish I knew, Brandon. I don't know how it happened, and I certainly don't know how it got so fucking confusing. All I know is we're here, and there doesn't seem to be a thing we can do about it.'

'Maybe you shouldn't let him… maybe you shouldn't let him do some of the things he does to you.'

She frowned slightly. 'What do you mean? What things?'

He looked down at his hands, fiddling with the leather bands round his wrist. 'You shouldn't let him have sex with you whenever he demands it.'

She was still frowning as she looked at him. 'What…? Did you *see* what was…?'

'I closed the door, Amber. Anyone could have looked inside, you were lucky no press happened to be walking past at the time. I made sure nobody else was getting in there, that's all.'

'Jesus, Brandon… You were outside…? Shit! I'm sorry, I'm so sorry, I… Shit!' She sat back, pushing both hands through her hair.

'It's like he has some kind of hold over you, Amber. I don't understand how someone as strong as you can let him do what he does. I don't understand how you can be so…' He stopped talking, looking down at his hands again.

'How I can be so weak? Is that what you're trying to say? Listen, Brandon, if *I* can't understand the way I feel about your dad, then I can't really expect anyone else to understand, can I? All I know is he walked into my life when I was sixteen years old, and he never left. I doubt he ever will.'

'Is he really that controlling? I mean, is it true what everyone's saying about Ryan's loan to CD Adeje? Did my dad only agree to that because he wanted Ryan away from you? And… and if that's the case then why are you two separating when Ryan isn't even around anymore? Jesus, Amber, it's crazy! None of it makes any sense.'

'Welcome to my life,' she sighed, sitting forward again. 'And what they're saying about your dad and the circumstances surrounding Ryan's loan, yeah, I suppose it *is* true. Partly, anyway. But he'll come back a much stronger person because of it. Ryan, I mean. This is what he needs, to get away from here. Some time over in Spain… it'll be good for him.'

'And what about you? Don't you feel like *you* need some time away, too?'

She smiled at him, thinking how unlike his father he really was. He might look the image of a young Jim Allen, but as far as personality and temperament were concerned they couldn't be further apart, father and son. 'I don't really have the option right now, Brandon.'

'Too busy, huh?'

'Something like that, yeah.'

Neither of them said anything for a minute or two, both of them just staring out at the groundsmen who'd come out onto the pitch, kneeling down in the goalmouth at the other end of the ground.

'I really wanted you to be a part of our family,' Brandon said, finally breaking the silence.

She turned to look at him, smiling warmly at this beautiful, handsome young man beside her. Just twenty years old, yet he seemed to have such a wise head on his shoulders.

'Yeah. I wanted that, too.'

He looked down at his hands again, his dark hair falling loosely over his eyes as he hung his head. 'I'd better get going. Got a few things to do before I go out tonight.'

'You going into town?'

Brandon nodded, looking up at her. It was so difficult for Amber to meet his eyes sometimes, because of his resemblance to a young Jim.

'Yeah. A few of the guys are heading out to a new bar. We've got VIP passes, apparently. Should be a good night. And, hey, it's legal for me to drink in this country.'

Amber couldn't help laughing. 'The life of a professional footballer, huh?'

Brandon grinned back at her, and another reminder of a young and beautiful Jim Allen hit her like a punch to the stomach, past memories and recent pain merging together in one huge mess of mixed emotions. 'Got to grab the perks while I can.'

She managed a small smile back, looking down at her wedding ring. It was still there. Maybe she'd never take it off. She didn't know just yet. 'Yeah, well, you just take care. I've seen what all those perks can do to someone.'

Brandon said nothing, but they both knew she was talking about Ryan.

'I'll see you soon, Amber.'

She watched him as he stood up, running up the stone steps that led back inside. And then he stopped, turning back around to look at her. 'You take care, too, okay?'

She couldn't help smiling as he turned away again, and she watched as he ran back up those steps, finally disappearing inside. And that was the moment when Amber realised she'd never felt so alone.

Chapter Twenty-Six

'You were on frigging fire, mate!'

Ryan couldn't help but grin at his CD Adeje teammate Callum Henderson's friendly shoulder-slap as they walked down the tunnel back to the dressing room. They'd just bagged an unexpected 4-3 win over a team from the mainland that had, so far that particular season, remained unbeaten. But, thanks to a hat-trick from Ryan, and a late injury-time winner from Callum, they'd pulled off a win that now saw CD Adeje climb to their highest position in the league for a number of years.

Callum Henderson had become Ryan's closest friend since his arrival on the island. A twenty-three-year-old Australian, originally from Melbourne, he was on loan to CD Adeje from English club Grantham Town, so he and Ryan weren't exactly strangers. They'd played against each other several times in the past back home. But now they'd also found out they had quite a bit in common off the pitch, too, which had thrown them together in what was a new experience for both of them.

'Yeah, well, you helped seal the deal,' Ryan said, pulling off his strip. Even though it had been an evening match the heat outside was still quite oppressive. The island was currently going through a bit of a winter heat wave, which meant that temperatures were way up on what they usually were at that time of year, but Ryan wasn't complaining. He loved the all-year-round sun and heat Tenerife offered. Yeah, he was really loving his new temporary home.

'So, you coming out to Las Americas later?' Callum asked, following Ryan into the dressing room. 'We've got to celebrate this win, mate. We killed it out there tonight.'

Ryan sat down, pushing both hands through his messed-up hair before leaning forward, resting his elbows on his knees. 'I don't know, Callum. I don't know if I'm in the mood.'

He and Callum had been out quite a bit recently, hitting the bars most nights, and when there was a long enough break between games they'd even tried out a couple of the clubs. And whilst Ryan had made the most of being young, free, famous and single again, knocking back very few of the offers that were made to him any time he set foot outside, he'd now reached a point where he felt like he needed a break. A sign that he really was trying to leave the old Ryan behind.

Callum looked at him, raising a questioning eyebrow, and for one split second it reminded Ryan of the way Gary had used to look at him. He missed Gary. He missed a lot of things about back home, but on the other hand he was glad he'd made the decision to leave. Just for a little while. Because he hated the thought of never going back.

'Okay,' Ryan sighed, sitting back and smiling. 'Okay. I'll come. You happy now?'

'Hey, listen, mate, we need you with us when we hit those places. You're the one that attracts all the women. The ones you don't want come running to the rest of us, remember?'

Now he *really* reminded Ryan of Gary. 'Have you listened to yourself?' Ryan laughed. 'You make it sound like some kind of meat market out there.'

'And it isn't?' Callum asked, raising that eyebrow again. 'You know as well as I do that most of those girls make a beeline for you because of who you are, although, to be honest, you're one hot-looking son-of-a-bitch regardless of the fact you're famous and loaded. They'd probably come running anyway. I fucking hate you, Fisher.'

Ryan laughed again, looking down at his clasped hands. Callum was a breath of fresh air, the kind of friend he needed right now. Someone to help him take his mind off things while he tried to sort his head out. But it was taking a lot longer than Ryan had ever thought it would. Maybe he was still too close to home. Maybe there were still too many links to the U.K., too many chances to be reminded of the things he was trying hard to deal with.

'You okay?' Callum asked, kicking off his football boots.

'Hmm?' Ryan looked up. He'd been deep in thought there for a second. 'Sorry, did you say something?'

'You okay? Only, you look a bit distracted.'

'I'm fine.' He stood up, sliding his shorts off and stripping naked, ready for one of those cold showers that were so popular due to the heat over there. 'Come on. We'd better get moving if we want to make the most of what's left of this night.'

'That's my boy,' Callum grinned, slapping Ryan on the back again before running off into the showers.

It was going to be another one of those nights on the beautiful island of Tenerife. And that suited Ryan just fine.

Amber felt sick. She felt physically sick as she scrolled down the page she'd just logged onto, reading information she didn't really want to read, but she knew she had to. She had to know.

'What you looking at?'

She hurriedly closed the lid of the laptop as Ronnie wandered back onto the studio floor. She'd thought he'd left with the rest of her fellow *Scoreline* presenters for a quick post-show drink with a couple of that evening's guests – a popular manager of a team already in the midst of a relegation battle, and an injured player from one of the top flight clubs who'd been giving his opinions on the current race for the title. A race which Newcastle Red Star was winning, at the moment, despite the absence of Ryan Fisher.

'I'm not looking at anything,' Amber said, resting her arms on the closed laptop lid.

Ronnie stopped in front of the desk and looked at her, raising an eyebrow, which told her he wasn't convinced. With good reason. 'So why the guilty look, then?'

'I don't look guilty.'

'Yeah. You do.'

'What you doing here anyway? I thought I'd told you I'd meet you in the bar.'

'That was half an hour ago, Amber. I got tired of waiting, so I decided to come looking for you. So, what you up to?'

'Nothing. Jesus, stop with the Spanish Inquisition, will you?'

He walked round the back of the desk, behind her chair, resting his hands on her shoulders as he began to rub them, causing Amber to close her eyes and moan quietly.

'Oh, that feels *good*,' she groaned, leaning back in her chair, not realising she'd just been duped. The second she took her arms off the laptop lid, Ronnie dived over and opened it, and Amber's reflexes just weren't quick enough to stop it from happening.

'Hang on…' Ronnie frowned, his eyes scanning the page Amber had been reading. She said nothing, she just waited for him to finish as her stomach tied itself up in a million knots that seemed to get tighter by the second. And she still felt sick.

Ronnie finally turned away from the laptop and leaned back against the desk, folding his arms, his eyes meeting hers. And it was a look that told Amber he wanted the truth. No lies. No trying to avoid the subject.

'Something you want to talk about?' he asked.

Amber broke the stare, looking down at her wedding ring. She still couldn't bear to take it off. The thought of doing that made her feel a sense of finality she wasn't ready to face just yet. Even though she knew her life would be so much easier if she could do that. Especially now. 'I just needed to find out… I needed…' She looked back up at him. 'I don't know what's going on, Ronnie. I don't know.'

'Are you late?'

It was Amber's turn to frown. 'Late?'

'Your period, Amber. Jesus, do I have to spell this out for you?'

'I haven't had a period for weeks now, but I just put it down to the stress of what's been happening, and the extra workload, I mean...'

'Have you done a test?'

'A test?'

'Christ, it's like trying to get blood out of a frigging stone... A pregnancy test. Have you done one?'

'No. No, why would I? I can't get pregnant, Ronnie, you know that.'

'No, Amber, you were told you *probably* wouldn't be able to get pregnant, not that you *definitely* couldn't. It isn't the same thing.'

'As good as.'

'You need to do a test.'

'Why?'

'Because you need to rule it out, Amber. I take it you're experiencing other symptoms, too?'

She nodded, feeling her head start to spin. She'd been feeling like this for a while now – sick, tired, headaches that wouldn't go away. But she'd put it all down to stress. What else could it possibly be?

'I can't do it, Ronnie,' she whispered, standing up and walking round the front of the desk.

'So what's your next move, then? Just sweep it under the carpet like you always do and pretend it isn't happening?'

'I'm just tired. I need a break.'

'Yes, you do. I think you *do* need a break because you've been working yourself into the ground instead of facing up to certain things. And, yes, it's quite possible that everything you're feeling *is* linked to nothing but stress. But what if it isn't, Amber?'

'I'm scared, Ronnie. I'm scared that if I do a test and it's negative then it's just going to bring back all the pain and the hurt I felt before. I'd just started to accept the fact that I was never going to be a mum, and I don't know how I'm going to feel if I have to go through all that again. I can't let myself believe that it might actually be happening. I can't do that.'

'But what if it *is* happening?'

She leaned back against the desk, dropping her head into her hands.

'Amber?'

'I'm still scared,' she whispered.

'Of what, sweetheart? What are you scared of? I mean, isn't this what you've wanted? Huh? Couldn't this, potentially, be great news?'

She closed her eyes, keeping her head in her hands as she took a long, deep breath.

'Come on,' Ronnie said, pulling her hands away from her face, keeping tight hold of one of them.

'Where are we going?' she asked, managing to grab her bag before he almost dragged her out of the studio.

'We're going to get this sorted, one way or another.'

'Now *she* is one hot woman!' Callum whistled, watching as a tall and beautiful blonde sauntered over to the bar, throwing him a look that said he could quite easily be onto something, if he played his cards right. 'You stay where you are, Fisher. She gets one look at you and she'll probably decide to ditch me in favour of the good-looking one.'

'You're selling yourself short, mate.' Ryan grinned. 'You were hardly last in the queue when they were giving out looks.'

Which was true. Callum was just as good-looking as Ryan, in a taller, slightly more pretty-boy kind of way. He wasn't quite as rough around the edges as Ryan was, but he still had his fair share of wannabe WAGs hanging around him.

'Yeah, I know, but all the girls love a bad boy, don't they?' Callum said, keeping his eyes fixed firmly on the blonde at the bar. He wasn't letting her out of his sight.

'Not all of them,' Ryan muttered, leaning back against the wall as he checked out the view around him – a seething mass of people in a bar made up mainly of tourists.

Callum looked at his teammate, briefly averting his gaze from his intended conquest. 'You need a woman,' he said, turning his attention back to the blonde, who was now making her way over to them. 'So go and find one. Go on. Before *she* gets over here and realises who you are.'

'Has it ever occurred to you that not everybody cares who we are? Or even *knows* who we are?'

'Not really.' Callum smirked. 'See you later.'

He didn't wait for the blonde to reach them, making his move before she had time to check Ryan out, and Ryan couldn't help shaking his head and smiling as he watched Callum go in for the kill, snaking his arm around the pretty blonde's waist as she giggled at something he said. One of his famous Aussie chat-up lines, no doubt, Ryan assumed. They were his trademark.

Sighing rather too loudly, Ryan picked up his drink and drained the glass, checking his watch. It was after midnight, and all of a sudden a wave of tiredness hit him from out of nowhere. Maybe it was time to call it a night. He hadn't really been in the mood for all of this, and it would appear those were the vibes he was giving off because the women weren't exactly flocking around him tonight.

'You going somewhere?'

He swung round at the sound of a familiar voice, squinting slightly in the dim light of the bar as he tried to focus on the person in front of him.

'Ellen?'

She smiled, shaking out her hair and giving him a look that told Ryan she was ready for business. Even if he wasn't.

'What... what are you doing here?'

'Well, seeing as you so rudely ran out on me without really

giving me a chance to show you how much you mean to me, I thought I'd make use of my few days off to come and see you.' She walked over to him, reaching out to touch his arm, running her fingers up and down it as she moved closer. 'You see, I've been doing a lot of thinking since you left, Ryan. And I don't think you realised just how good we could be together, you and me. You didn't really give us a chance. I understand why you had to go, but I don't think you needed to lose *me* in the process. I mean, I could actually help you to forget… to forget *her*, if that's what you want…'

He'd heard enough, and she'd only been there a matter of minutes. 'How did you find me, Ellen?' His voice was tinged with a coldness that Ellen chose to ignore.

'Well, it wasn't easy, but I went round to your villa…'

'You went to my villa? Who the hell told you where I lived?'

'Someone at the club… I was at the match tonight…'

'For fuck's sake! What happened to privacy? And how did you know I'd be here? In Las Americas?'

'Your neighbour told me you'd gone out in a taxi, and I assumed, because you'd won your match tonight, that you'd be out celebrating. So all I had to do was ask around a few of the bars along the strip here to see if a group of footballers were out and about…'

'Jesus. You're verging on stalker material now, sweetheart. I really need *this*, don't I?' He pushed a hand though his hair, turning away from her. He'd thought this part of his life was over, done. He'd thought he'd left her behind in Newcastle, to get on with her life, and let *him* get on with his. He'd thought the message had been clear enough.

'I could be good for you, Ryan.'

He turned to look at her. She was so pretty, so, so pretty, and when he'd first met her she'd seemed so innocent – a complete contrast to the ice-queen image that Amber sometimes gave off. But it would seem that the innocence had quickly faded, to be replaced by a manipulative, almost scheming side to her. He just hoped it wasn't verging on the obsessive. He could do without *that* hassle.

But whatever he felt for this woman who'd flown all the way over there to try her best to win him back – a futile act that had no chance of working – he didn't want to see her hurt. He didn't want to do that to her again, but she was leaving him with no other option. So what was his next move supposed to be now?

Amber squeezed her eyes tight shut as she sat on the closed lid of the toilet, holding the small white stick in her hand. Ronnie was perched on the side of the bath, watching the clock as the seconds ticked by.

'Give it here,' he said, realising they were now way past the time the box had said it would take for the test to be complete.

Amber shook her head, her eyes still closed. 'No. It was bad enough you being in here while I peed on the bloody thing without you telling me what the outcome is.'

'So you're just gonna sit there holding it with your eyes shut? For how long? Jesus, just give it here…' He leaned over and took it out of her hand, an action which caused her to finally open her eyes.

Her heart was beating so hard it hurt, those knots in her stomach tightening, pulling and pulling until she had no breath left, because she really didn't want to know what that test said. After everything she'd been through, she didn't want to know. Whatever the result, she didn't know if she was ready to hear it. Or ready to deal with it.

She looked at Ronnie, watching as he stared down at the little white stick before looking back up at her. But he said nothing, just held it out for her to take, keeping his arm outstretched until she took it from him.

'Look at it, Amber.'

'I can't.' Her hand was shaking, and all she wanted to do was throw that stick in the bin and forget this was happening.

'Amber, please. Just look at it.'

She closed her eyes for a few more seconds before opening them again, finally looking down at her hands. Her heart continued to hammer against her ribs, her head spinning faster and faster as she stared at the result, hardly able to dare believe what it was telling her.

'I'm pregnant,' she whispered, her voice steady and calm, belying everything she was actually feeling. 'How…?' She looked up at Ronnie, a feeling of utter confusion washing over her, mixed with a realisation she now had to face up to.

'According to that, it says date of conception occurred 3+ weeks ago,' Ronnie said. 'Have you and Jim…?'

She shook her head. 'I said I was scared, Ronnie. Remember?'

Her eyes met Ronnie's again and he frowned, that expression of confusion taking over *his* face now, too. 'Yeah, but…'

'It's Ryan's,' she said, her voice now beginning to lose that calm edge it had managed to hang onto for so long. 'Ronnie, if this is right, if this test is right… this baby, it's Ryan's.'

Chapter Twenty-Seven

'You shouldn't be here,' Ryan said, watching as Ellen brushed her hair and applied a coat of pale pink lip gloss, smiling at her reflection.

'*You* were the one who brought me back last night,' she said, fluffing out her hair. 'And you didn't exactly push me away when it came to bedtime, did you?' She turned around, directing her smile at him.

No, he hadn't. But it had taken a good few drinks and another couple of hours in three more bars before he'd been drunk enough to not care what was happening anymore. Last night hadn't been the time or the place to have the conversation he needed to have with her, even though he couldn't help feeling it was a conversation he'd already had. Repeating himself wasn't something he was a fan of doing.

'Yeah, well, we'd both had a bit to drink, hadn't we?' He got out of bed, pulling on a pair of combats and running his fingers through his hair.

'Are you saying you only slept with me because you were drunk?' Ellen asked, still smiling, wrapping her arms around him from behind.

'No, I'm not saying that,' Ryan said, unwrapping her arms from around his waist before walking into the bathroom, closing the door behind him, leaving her standing on the other side. 'I'm just saying that the circumstances were… they were…' He stopped talking, taking a few blissful seconds on his own to pee. 'Last night was last night,' he said, opening the door and leaning against the frame. 'And now we move on.'

Ellen frowned. 'Move on? Are you dumping me?'

Ryan couldn't help laughing, folding his arms as he stared at her. Was she for real? 'Ellen, babe, how can I dump you when we're not even together? We were finished before I came out here, remember? Just because you turn up out of the blue claiming that you could be "*good for me*", that doesn't mean we're suddenly an item again. I never agreed to anything, sweetheart.'

She looked at him, pouting like some teenager who was trying anything to get her own way. 'No, I know that. And I don't expect you to do anything straightaway, I'm here for a while…'

He raised an eyebrow. 'A while?'

'A few more days. And a lot can happen in a few days, can't it?'

He continued to stare at her, saying nothing. He hadn't been prepared for this, and he wasn't enjoying the fact it was happening. But he had training to go to, and right now wasn't the time to carry on this conversation.

'You'd better go back to your hotel.' Ryan pushed past her, out into the main living area of his Tenerife villa. 'I'll call you later, okay? I've got a busy day ahead, so I'm assuming you can amuse yourself while I'm away?'

'Of course I can. Ryan…?'

He turned to look at her. She really was one beautiful woman, but she just wasn't Amber. And that was the problem. She wasn't Amber.

'I *will* see you later, won't I?'

He sighed, hanging his head before looking up and out of the patio doors at the view of the Atlantic. It was another gloriously sunny day in paradise – so why did he feel like he'd just been handed a prison sentence?

'Yeah. You'll see me later.'

What other choice did he have?

'Miracles do happen, Amber.' Dr. Lowry smiled at her from across his desk. 'And you, it would appear, are carrying one.'

'And… and the dates?' she asked, her fingers fiddling frantically with the hem of her t-shirt. 'They're right, are they?'

'You appear to be around eleven weeks pregnant, so that would mean conception took place sometime around mid-November last year. You're looking at an August birth, Amber.'

She felt her stomach tighten again. The dates were right. Which meant *she* was, too. This baby, it wasn't Jim's. It couldn't be Jim's. It was Ryan's. She was having Ryan Fisher's baby.

'Is everything okay?' Dr. Lowry asked, aware of Amber's almost sombre mood. 'If there's something you need to talk about…'

'No.' She shook her head, fixing him with a smile she could only hope reached her eyes. 'No. Everything's fine. I'm just a bit shocked, that's all. I mean, after everything I was told before, and then for this to happen…'

Dr. Lowry returned her smile. 'Well, like I said, miracles *can* happen. And sometimes, when the pressure is off, nature just takes its course. Now, I'll be taking care of you during this pregnancy myself, so make sure you stop by reception for your next appointment, okay? And don't worry. We'll do everything we can to make sure it all runs as smoothly as possible. You're a very special patient, Amber Allen. And this will be one very special baby.'

She felt quite dazed as she made her way out of Dr. Lowry's rather prestigious Jesmond clinic, and over to the bar across the road where Ronnie was waiting. She needed a drink like she'd never needed one before, but alcohol was now strictly off limits. Even though she would have done anything to dull the feelings she was experiencing right now. Feelings she couldn't really explain – a strange mixture of excitement tinged with a raw pain and a crushing disappointment she just couldn't shake. Because this baby wasn't Jim's. It wasn't Jim's.

Ronnie looked up as she sat down next to him, her eyes meeting his – telling him everything he needed to know.

'It's Ryan's,' she whispered. The last thing she needed was for *this* little piece of information to get out. Even though it was going to, at some point, she knew that. And how she handled it all when that finally happened was something she didn't even want to think about at the minute. She had enough to get her head around as it was.

'Definitely?'

She nodded. 'Definitely. The dates… they coincide with that time we slept together at Gary's party back in November last year. Me and Jim, we hadn't had sex in ages back then, and we didn't have sex again until months after that…'

'Hang on,' Ronnie interrupted. 'You've slept with Jim since he told you he wanted a divorce?'

She looked at Ronnie as though he should already know this, before realising that only Brandon was aware of that last encounter. She hadn't told anyone else it had happened. And now she knew why. 'Yeah. After the derby match, a few weeks ago. It was a mistake.' Her whole life was one long mistake right now. But this – this one topped the lot. 'What do I do, Ronnie?'

'I don't know, kiddo,' he sighed, reaching out to take her hand, squeezing it gently. 'But we'll work something out.'

'I mean, this is what I wanted, right? I wanted a baby. I wanted to be a mum. I wanted that more than anything.' She felt dazed, her head spinning as she looked at Ronnie again. 'But I wanted it all with Jim. I wanted *his* baby.' Tears started to prick the back of her eyes as she stared up at the ceiling, blinking desperately to try and stop them from falling. 'It's such a fucking mess, Ronnie. All of it. It's such a fucking mess.'

Ronnie squeezed her hand again. He couldn't really argue with that. A mess didn't even begin to describe it.

'I'm pregnant. Can you believe that?' She took a deep breath, sitting back in her seat, a feeling of resignation sweeping over her. 'I'm pregnant. But it's with the wrong man, Ronnie. This baby – it's the wrong man's.'

'Amber, listen. Listen to me, sweetheart…'

She looked at him – her best friend, and the one man she could trust over anybody. Why couldn't she feel for him what she felt for Jim? What she felt for Ryan.

'We can sort this out, the two of us. We can…'

'No, Ronnie, please. I know what you're going to say and I can't let you do that. I can't, it isn't fair.'

'And seeing you like this isn't fair either, Amber. Come on, we can do this, me and you. We can do this.'

She shook her head, pulling her hand away from his. 'I can't deal with this right now. I need some time on my own, I need to get my head around it all before it drives me insane.'

'Amber…'

'Ronnie, I'll be fine. Really.' She smiled at him, even though smiling was the last thing she felt like doing. 'I just need to get used to the idea, okay? I need to be alone. Just for a little while.'

'You'll call me if you need me?'

She nodded, pushing her sunglasses down over her eyes.

'You promise?'

'I promise.' She leaned over and kissed him quickly, giving his hand one last squeeze. 'I'll talk to you later. And Ronnie? Thank you. For being here. For being the best friend I really need right now.'

He smiled, too, reluctant to let her go anywhere on her own after the news she'd just had. 'I'll always be there for you, kiddo, you know that. Always.'

'Sounds like you've got yourself a bit of a bunny boiler there, mate,' Callum said, squirting water over his head and shaking it out. The temperature down on the training pitch was around 32 degrees, and even though they had cloud cover that morning, the heat was still stifling.

'I mean, she just flew over here, without telling me. Again.'

'Again? You mean, she's done this before?'

Ryan sat down on the touchline, pulling his knees up to his chest. 'When Newcastle Red Star were here pre-season she flew out to see me. We've been in this kind of on/off relationship since I came out of rehab. I thought she was what I needed, you know?'

Callum sat down next to him, drinking his water this time, staring out ahead of him as the rest of their teammates carried on with training against the backdrop of Mount Teide that loomed large in the distance.

'And she isn't, I take it?'

Ryan hung his head, saying nothing.

'Listen, mate. I know the official line about you going out on loan from Newcastle Red Star was because you wanted some experience of playing in the Spanish League, but... the rumours that are still going around... Did Jim Allen want you out of the picture for a while, because you and his missus...?'

Ryan looked up, surprised it had taken someone this long to actually ask that question out loud. 'That's not strictly true, no. I mean, if that was the case, then why aren't him and Amber together anymore?'

'Yeah,' Callum sighed. 'What's *that* all about?' He looked at Ryan, who still had his head bowed, staring down at his football boots. 'Was it because of you? That Jim Allen and Amber split up?'

'I don't know.' Ryan shrugged, still looking down. 'Maybe. I don't know.' He threw his head back, sighing heavily. 'We slept together, me and Amber, just before I came out here and... and I think he might have found out, so...' He finally met Callum's gaze. 'I really don't know. I always thought nothing could break those two apart, given their history, but...' He hung his head again, leaving that sentence unfinished.

'Maybe you and her... maybe you and Amber have history, too, mate.'

Ryan couldn't help smiling slightly, keeping his head down. 'I love her, Cal. I love her so fucking much, and when we… when I was with her it felt so right. It felt like I had her back; she was where I wanted her to be, with me. With *me*. Where she should be right now.' He looked at Callum, trying to ignore the thumping headache that had started banging away behind his eyes. 'I'm here to forget her, Cal. I came here to try and forget her, but it's a waste of time. It isn't going to work because I can't stop thinking about her. Every second of every fucking day she's there, in my fucking head, reminding me of what I threw away because I couldn't fucking grow up in time to realise she was the best thing that ever happened to me. And I lost her.'

'Jesus, mate, you've got it bad.'

'This isn't some stupid crush, Callum. She isn't just some older woman who came into my life and showed me things I'd never experienced before. I fell in love with her, but I just couldn't cope with those feelings. I'd never felt anything like it before, that need to be with just one woman, and it scared the shit out of me. It wasn't what I did, I couldn't be with just one woman, and that's what I kept telling myself. Even when I was with her I'd pretend that everything I was feeling was only because I wanted to sleep with her, and once the sex was finished those feelings would be gone. But they weren't, and that's when I got scared. That's when I started to push her away by going back to being a grade-A prick.'

'Have you told *her* this?'

'I tried to explain it to her, before I went into rehab. We talked, you know? But I wasn't in the right frame of mind to tell her how I really felt. She was about to marry Jim Allen, and what was I supposed to do? I was in a state, Callum. I'd hit rock bottom and I couldn't expect her to deal with that.' He sighed again, pushing both hands through his dark hair. 'All I know is, I thought coming out here would ease those feelings, make me finally realise she isn't coming back to me, but the day her and Jim separated, that was the day my world changed. The day I let hope back in; the day

I knew I was still in love with her. And I can't shake that. Being here, it isn't going to get rid of those feelings.'

Callum let out a low whistle, handing Ryan his water bottle. 'Jesus, mate. I had no idea you felt that way about her.'

Ryan took a long, much-needed sip of water, throwing his head back again. 'I've got to talk to Ellen. It isn't fair to lead her on, to let her think there's even the tiniest chance that I'm going back to her. I just wish I'd been strong enough to tell her that last night.'

'We all make mistakes, Ryan,' Callum said, gently squeezing his shoulder. 'But, yeah. You do need to talk to her. She needs to know how you feel – about her, anyway.'

'How do I manage to make my life so frigging complicated? Huh?' Ryan sighed.

Callum smiled at him, taking his water bottle back. 'You're Ryan Fisher, mate. You don't do anything by halves.'

And wasn't *that* the truth?

Chapter Twenty-Eight

'You're very quiet,' Debbie said, sipping her coffee before looking at it with an expression of pure hatred. 'I'm beginning to really dislike this stuff. I'd kill for a long, cold glass of champagne, wouldn't you?'

'Hmm? Sorry?' Amber asked, dragging herself back to the here and now.

'I said, you're very quiet. You got something on your mind?'

'No. No, I'm fine. I'm fine. Anyway, how are *you* doing? Not long now until Baby Blandford makes an appearance. You must be really excited.'

Debbie couldn't help smiling, placing both hands over her now quite large baby bump. 'Do you know what? I fought so hard against becoming a mum. I mean, it wasn't something I'd ever intended to do – have kids, I mean. Especially being married to someone like Gary. But impending parenthood really does seem to have changed him. I'm even getting used to being fussed over continuously. However...' She shifted slightly in her seat as she tried to make herself more comfortable, '... I can't say I won't be sorry when this little one finally makes his or her appearance. I'm getting just a tiny bit tired of lugging this bump around with me everywhere. It can really interfere with shopping sometimes.' She smiled a wide, beaming smile, and Amber couldn't help but smile back. 'But, yeah. We're both so excited to see him or her, Amber. This baby. We can't wait.'

'You're gonna be a fabulous mum.' Amber returned Debbie's smile, reaching out to take her friend's hand. 'That's one very lucky baby in there.'

'Well, we'll see. I hope so. But I'm actually quite terrified if the truth be told, chick. I'm even thinking of asking my mum to come and stay with us for a few months to help out, so that shows you how terrified I am… Anyway, enough about me. How are things with you? And why are you still down here instead of back up north where you belong? We miss you.'

Debbie was in London with Gary and the rest of the Red Star squad for their match against one of the big north London clubs. And Amber was so glad she'd decided to fly down and see her, because she'd missed her, too. Missed that shoulder to lean on, that person to confide in. She had a lot to tell her. And she'd tell her it all – soon. But not yet. There were others who needed to know first.

'Work's really busy now,' Amber said, taking a sip of her own coffee, more as a distraction, really. Something to stop her from having to talk too much.

'Yeah. I know work's really busy. You're never off the TV, and me and the girls are sick of seeing your face splashed all over the front of magazines.'

She'd said that with a glint in her eye and a big smile on her face, which really was quite infectious because Amber couldn't stop herself from smiling, too. Despite the way she was really feeling inside.

'Are you not taking on more than you need to, though?' Debbie asked, her tone a little more serious now.

Amber shrugged, her eyes going back to her still-present wedding ring. 'I *want* to do it all. Nobody's making me work that hard. It keeps me busy, and I need that.'

'Keeps you distracted, you mean.'

'You're beginning to sound like Ronnie now.'

'You seen Jim since he's been down here?'

'No. Why would I have done?'

'He was on *Scoreline* last night. I know you weren't presenting it, but I thought you might have been around at the time. You know, in the studio or something.'

Amber shook her head. She'd deliberately stayed away, taking on another photo shoot just so she could avoid him. Seeing him right now wasn't something she felt strong enough to do, under the circumstances.

'And what about the match tomorrow? You covering that?'

She shook her head again. 'No. I'm in the studio with Ronnie.'

'Was that deliberate?'

Amber looked at Debbie. 'It's over, Debs. Me and Jim. It's over, okay?'

'Really?'

'Look, I don't want to get into this right now. I'm meeting Max in a few minutes and the last thing I need is to be distracted by anything to do with Jim Allen.'

'He's not seeing anyone you know.'

Amber looked at Debbie again, narrowing her eyes. 'So? What business is it of mine whether he is or he isn't seeing anyone?' But just the thought of it made her feel sick.

'Because you still love him?'

'Leave it, Debbie. Please. Things are so complicated right now they'd...'

She quickly shut up, realising that if she said much more then Debbie was going to start asking questions she really didn't want to answer just yet.

'They'd what, Amber? Come on, chick. Things are so complicated right now they'd what?'

'They'd make your head spin, believe me.' She was saved from saying anything else by the arrival of a text message. 'That's Max. I'd better get going. He hasn't got long, he's flying out to see

Ryan this afternoon.' Just saying Ryan's name made her stomach flip over in a way she wasn't entirely sure she understood. So she tried to ignore it.

'Everything all right with Ryan?' Debbie asked, fixing Amber with a look that told her she knew she was hiding something. And she'd get it out of her one day – soon.

'Ryan's fine, as I'm sure you're well aware, him being Gary's best friend. In fact, you probably know how he's getting on better than I do. I only know the stuff that's being reported from Tenerife.'

'Ellen's flown over to see him, did you know that?'

Amber felt her heart almost stop dead. For another reason she couldn't quite understand. 'Ellen? But I… I thought it was all over between those two?'

'So did Ryan,' Debbie sighed, running a hand along the small of her back. 'Jesus, this baby can kick!'

'So why is she out there with him?' Amber was confused now. Ryan had all but told her that he didn't love Ellen – that he never had done. So why would he encourage her to go and see him?

'It wasn't his idea,' Debbie said, pulling her phone out of her bag. 'She just turned up, out of the blue, apparently. Told Ryan she wanted him back, that she could be good for him, all that kind of crap.'

'And… I mean… *are* they back together?'

Debbie fixed Amber with another one of her looks. 'Do you care?'

Amber rummaged round in her bag for nothing in particular just so she could avoid Debbie's eyes. 'Just curious, that's all. I had a run-in with her – with Ellen – after the derby game, and…'

'A run-in? Really? You never told me. Did she have a go at you?'

Amber nodded. 'You could say that. Blamed me for the fact Ryan's out on loan…'

'Well, she's right, really, isn't she?'

'Jesus… thanks for that, Debs.'

'I'm sorry, chick. I didn't mean it like that, but… Look, from what I can gather from Gary – and you know how crap he is at conveying any kind of gossip – Ryan is trying to let her down gently. Again.' She rolled her eyes, and Amber smiled. She loved Debbie, she really did. 'Hey, you know he's become all pally with Callum Henderson, don't you?' Debbie went on. 'And, although he isn't saying anything, I think Gary's just a tiny bit jealous.'

Amber couldn't help laughing. 'Does it feel like his best friend's cheating on him?'

'Something like that, yeah.' Debbie smiled, briefly, before another baby-kick made her wince slightly. 'I swear this baby's a boy. He's already kicking like a frigging footballer.'

'They're quite similar, really, I suppose,' Amber went on, quickly banging out a text to Max before throwing her phone back into her bag. 'Ryan and Callum, I mean… Look, I've really got to go.' She leaned over and kissed Debbie on the cheek. 'You take care of yourself, and baby. And I'll see you soon, okay?'

'Do you want me to pass a message on to Jim for you?'

'Stop it, Debbie.' Amber half-smiled at her, throwing her a look over her shoulder before she ran out of the café, quickly hailing a cab to take her to Max's offices in Covent Garden.

It took a while to get there, thanks to the Friday afternoon London traffic, but it was a meeting she needed to have. To help her decide just what it was she was supposed to do next. Max needed to know what was going on – Max needed to help her.

'You look a bit flustered,' Max said, kissing her lightly on the cheek as he closed his office door behind her.

'Well, you can thank London on a Friday afternoon for that,' Amber sighed, taking a look around a room that couldn't really be described as an office – it was more like a suite, it was so big. Painted almost entirely in white, bar one wall that was a deep, dark red, floor-to-ceiling plate-glass windows lined one entire wall, making the room feel incredibly bright and airy. A TV the size of a small cinema screen took over another wall directly opposite Max's ridiculously over-sized desk, and two huge black leather sofas were placed at opposite ends of the room, amidst an array of furniture that seemed to be a mixture of classic retro and Ikea's finest. Pictures of a multitude of famous footballers, past and present, took pride of place on the dark red wall behind one of the sofas, all of which had been, or still were, clients of Max's, and Amber couldn't help but notice the picture of Ryan, her eyes going straight to it. He was in his Newcastle Red Star kit, all handsome and hot with his tattoos and his stubble, down on his haunches in front of a football bearing the name of one of his biggest sponsors, those dark blue eyes of his staring right back at her. She felt her stomach take another dive into nowhere, making her swallow hard before she took a deep breath and turned away, walking over to the chair in front of Max's desk.

'Everything all right?' Max asked, frowning slightly as he leaned back against the front of his desk, folding his arms as he looked at Amber.

'I'm pregnant.' There was no point in beating about the bush. Max didn't have long, and she couldn't be bothered to skirt around the issue. It had to be dealt with.

'I'm… I'm sorry. You're *what*?'

She'd never seen Max lost for words before, and it was actually quite amusing, for a few seconds.

'Now who's flustered?' she smirked, crossing her legs and clasping her hands together, her eyes never leaving Max's.

'But, I thought…? I thought you couldn't…?'

'Well, I'm not going to go over my entire appointment with Dr. Lowry, suffice to say, I'm what you might call extremely lucky. I beat the odds.' She shrugged. 'I beat them.'

Max frowned again. 'You don't sound too happy about it, if you don't mind me saying.'

'It isn't Jim's.' Her voice had wavered way more than she'd wanted it to when she'd said those words. But Max needed to know the truth.

'Jesus, Amber…' Max pushed a hand through his hair, letting

out a deep breath. Before realisation took over. 'It's Ryan's. Am I right?'

She looked down at her clasped hands, a strange kind of relief washing over her – relief that she'd taken that first step towards sorting this whole mess out. Although they were a long way off making any kind of sense out of it. 'You're right.' She looked back up at Max. 'There's no doubt, Max. This baby was conceived at a time when Jim and I hadn't slept together for weeks, so there's absolutely no chance it could be his.' She closed her eyes for a second, silently willing the tears to stay away. She should be experiencing the happiest time of her life, yet all she felt was overwhelming confusion and a pain so deep it hurt in a way she couldn't explain. 'The dates, they…' She swallowed hard before exhaling deep, desperately trying to keep her composure. 'It's Ryan's.'

Max stayed silent for a few more seconds, taking in a bombshell he just hadn't been prepared for. How could he ever have seen *this* one coming?

'I knew something had gone on between you and Ryan, but…'

'It was sex, that's all.'

'It's never as simple as that with you two,' Max sighed.

'Well, it certainly isn't now.'

Max looked at her again, all hard-edged ice queen with a determination not to let her true feelings show. But he didn't think even *she'd* be able to keep that up for much longer, given everything she'd been through, and everything she was about to go through now.

'Does anybody else know?'

'Just Ronnie.'

'You haven't told anyone at work?'

'There's no need for anyone else to know anything. I'm not showing yet, I can pass off morning sickness as something stress-related, and… Oh, I don't know, Max. I really don't know what I'm supposed to do next.'

'I take it you haven't told Ryan?'

She looked back down at her hands, shaking her head. 'But I

think I need to do that.' She looked up at him, her eyes meeting his. 'Don't I?'

Max sighed again, walking over to the window. 'I have no idea how he's going to take this news.'

Amber continued to stare at her hands, the confusion she was already feeling doubling in intensity. 'I've really messed up, haven't I?'

Max turned around to face her, shoving his hands in his pockets. 'It takes two, kiddo.'

'He's over there in Tenerife for no reason other than to try and get his head straight, and I'm about to drop *this* on him? So what was the point, huh? What was the point of him going over there if all this shit is about to kick off? How is any of this going to help him sort himself out?'

'Okay, okay. Don't get hysterical. Look, in a way, it's probably best he *is* over there. It'll give him some space to get his head around everything. If he was back here, I think there'd be a far greater chance of him going off the rails.'

'You reckon?'

'I know him.'

'Yeah. So do I, remember?' Amber threw her head back, running her hands through her hair. 'That's it. Decision made. I'm going to see him.' She sat up, looking straight at her agent. 'This afternoon. I'm coming with you. To Tenerife.'

'Are you out of your fucking mind, Amber? You can't just up and leave on the spur of the moment. What about work?'

'I'll tell them I need some time off. Surely you can sort something out for me, it's what you're good at, isn't it? Come on, Max. Please. I don't think I can go through the entire weekend with this hanging over me, avoiding conversations with people because I know they can tell something's wrong, but I can't say what. Not yet. Because I need to see Ryan first.'

'Jesus, you kill me. You and Ryan, the pair of you – you fucking kill me.'

Amber stood up, walking over to Max, her hands in the pockets of her black trouser suit. 'You know I need to do this, Max. I need to speak to him first. Before it all goes public. He deserves that at least.'

He looked at her. 'You're avoiding Jim, that's what you're doing. Come on, Amber. I know he's down here this weekend…'

'You have no idea what's going on in my head right now, Max. The man I love with every inch of my heart doesn't want me anymore, and I'm pregnant by a man I slept with purely to forget that fact. It's so fucked up it's unbelievable! So, yes. Yes. Maybe I *am* avoiding Jim – for now. Because, until I've spoken to Ryan, I really have no idea what to say to him. I don't know how to handle this, Max. And I'm scared. I'm really, really scared. So, please, just get me on that flight with you to Tenerife, and let's try and begin to sort this mess out.'

Chapter Twenty-Nine

'Thanks for doing this.' Amber smiled at Max as she joined him outside in the hotel's terrace restaurant for breakfast. Although she wasn't in the mood to eat. Food was the last thing she felt like. 'It means a lot.'

'Well, you're right, kiddo. This *is* a mess, but at least you came to me first, which means we can at least try and keep a lid on things until we work out exactly what's happening. I take it you *are* keeping the baby?'

Amber just looked at him as she poured herself a cup of tea. She thought she might just be able to keep that down.

'Okay. Point taken. Sorry.'

She sat back in the comfortable padded chair and pushed her dark glasses down over her eyes, staring out at the view of the Atlantic, the sound of jet skis already piercing the morning's peace. It was the middle of February, the sky was the most incredible blue, and the sun was beating down on her bare shoulders, yet all Amber felt was a cold, fierce pain in the pit of her stomach.

'Maybe coming here wasn't such a good idea,' she said quietly as a million memories of her visit to this beautiful island with Jim and the Red Star squad just a few months ago invaded her brain. She'd been happy then. *They'd* been happy then. It had felt as though nothing could have pulled them apart after all those years of wanting nothing but each other. Yet now look at them. Torn apart by – by what? By anything? Or by so many things it was impossible to separate them out?

Max turned to look at her. 'Things happen for a reason, Amber. I'm a real believer in that.'

She said nothing. She'd long given up believing in fate.

'Do you want me to come with you? When you tell him?' Max asked, trying to direct the subject away from whatever she was thinking about, because, whatever it was, it wasn't making her happy.

'No. No, I think I'd rather tell him on my own, if that's all right?'

'That's fine with me,' Max sighed, placing his hands behind his head and stretching his legs out in front of him. 'You know where I am when the pieces need picking up.'

She looked at him, not really knowing what he meant by that. Not that it mattered. Nothing mattered anymore except trying to get a situation she couldn't quite believe she was in under some sort of control, to a point where they could at least begin to start making some sense out of it, anyway.

'Do you… do you think it's best if I just go round to his villa or… or should I ring him first? Shit! This is ridiculous, Max. I'm thirty-eight years old yet I'm acting like some teenager who's got herself into trouble with the school's most popular boy.'

Max looked at her out the corner of his eye, unable to stop a slight smirk from twitching at the corner of his mouth. 'Just go and see him, Amber. Sitting here talking about it is only delaying the inevitable.'

She let out a quiet, frustrated cry, throwing her head back. 'I want to run away. I really just want to run away, curl up into a ball and hide from all of this.'

'No you don't.' Max sat up, leaning forward slightly. 'Look, kiddo. You can tackle most shit, because I've seen you do it. You've got a reputation as this beautiful, smart, intelligent woman…'

Amber raised an eyebrow at the word *'intelligent'*. She wasn't so intelligent now, was she?

'You're a smart, intelligent woman,' Max went on, ignoring her expression. 'Successful, talented, stunning to look at...'

'All right, Max, you can stop laying it on quite so thick. What's your point?'

'You can handle this, too. You just need to make a start, because it won't go away. And the longer you leave it, the worse it's going to be. Do you want the press to get hold of the news first? Is that how you want people to find out about it? You can't hide a pregnancy forever you know.'

'Jesus, don't even talk about the press.' Amber shuddered at the thought of what was going to happen the day the media got wind of this little gem of a story and, given her line of work, surrounded by media constantly, she knew that day wouldn't be too far away. And that's why, all of a sudden, she knew she'd give up every single second of her success if she could just go back to being Amber Sullivan, local North East Sports Editor and a woman nobody cared all that much about. 'My dad is gonna flip, big time... I sound about fourteen again, don't I?'

Max smiled, reaching out to take her hand, squeezing it gently. 'You can handle this. Okay? Now go, go on. Go see him. He's not training till this evening and he doesn't have a match until Monday night, so at least your timing is pretty good. Sort of.'

Amber couldn't help but smile back, leaning over to kiss her agent. Her lifeline. How she'd ever survived without him before, she had no idea. 'Thanks, Max. I really love you for this.'

'Yeah, well, don't tell everyone I'm such a soft touch. I've got a reputation to keep up you know... Shit! Is that my phone?'

She left him to his calls and made her way back up to her room, her head still spinning with everything that had happened. Maybe if she closed her eyes and pinched herself she'd wake up and realise she was still on that blissful pre-season tour, she was still with Jim, and everything was the way she wanted it to be. Because she didn't want it to be like this.

The cool of the air conditioning hit her head-on as soon as she walked into the room and she leaned back against the door for a few seconds, letting it wash over her.

'I can do this,' she whispered to herself, trying to push to the back of her mind her dad's reaction to this news, Debbie's reaction to this news – but thinking about Jim's reaction was what hurt the most, what caused a wave of pain so raw to rush through her at such speed it knocked the breath right out of her.

Her phone ringing stopped her from sinking into another unnecessary pit of self-pity and she grabbed it from the bed, answering it immediately. Because she knew exactly who it'd be.

'Where the fuck are you?'

'Hey, Ronnie.'

'Hey, Ronnie? Is that all you've got to say? Where are you, Amber, because if you're where I think you are...'

'He needs to know, Ronnie. Before any of this comes out, he needs to know.'

'Jesus fucking Christ... Why didn't you talk to *me* first?'

'Because you'd have stopped me from coming here. You'd have tried to talk me out of it, tried to make me do...'

'Amber, sweetheart, you've got me all wrong. I'm not stupid. I *know* you've got to talk to Ryan, I know that. I just... did you have to do it right now?'

'Yes, Ronnie. Because I can't even begin to work this whole mess out until he knows what's going on.'

There was a brief silence from Ronnie, and even Amber couldn't think of anything to say to break it as she walked over to the full-length mirror by the window, lifting her top up to reveal her still-flat stomach. Funny. She didn't think she'd actually believe she was pregnant until that bump started to show. But right now there wasn't even a hint.

'We should have talked about this some more, Amber,' Ronnie said quietly.

She closed her eyes, resting her hand on her non-existent baby bump. 'Me telling Ryan I'm having his baby doesn't mean me and him are suddenly going to live happily ever after. I just need him to know, that's all. What happens after that is so up in the frigging air it's lost gravity. So don't go on about it, okay? We'll talk about everything when I get home.'

'And when *are* you coming home? Only, everyone here at Cloud Sports seems to think you're on holiday for a week to deal with some urgent family problems.'

'Well, that's kind of true, isn't it?'

Ronnie didn't reply.

'I don't know how long I'm going to be here in Tenerife,' Amber continued, finally letting her top drop back down. 'Could be a couple of days, might be a bit longer. I just don't know.'

'You're with Max, right?'

'Yeah.'

'And everything's okay?'

'So far.'

'You told him yet? Ryan, I mean.'

'I'm just on my way over to his place now. Shit, Ronnie, I'm so fucking scared.'

'Do you want me to come out there?'

'I *am* a grown-up you know.'

'Really? Only, you don't act like one sometimes.'

'Piss off.'

'I love you, too.'

'I'll see you tomorrow?'

'I'm booking my flight online as we speak.'

'Ronnie?'

'Yeah?'

'I *do* love you. You know that, don't you?'

'I know, kiddo. I know.'

'And I'm sorry. For being such a major pain in the arse.'

'Don't be stupid. And I love you, too.'

She ended the call, throwing her phone back down on the bed

before turning to look in the mirror again. She tried pushing her stomach out in an attempt to try and imagine what she was going to look like when this bump finally did start to show, but it wasn't really helping. She'd lost so much weight after Jim had left her that she couldn't even push out the tiniest of pot bellies.

'Well, baby,' she whispered, laying a hand on her stomach anyway, stroking it gently, 'I can't put this off for much longer, can I? Looks like it's time to go tell your daddy everything.'

Ryan pulled open the blinds and looked outside, smiling to himself as he took in a view he was fast falling in love with. It was so calming, so peaceful, looking out to see nothing but that huge expanse of water stretching way out in front of him.

He loved the little fishing village he'd been living in since his arrival in Tenerife three months ago. He loved the fact he could walk down the small, narrow streets and nobody knew who he was. He loved the fact he could wander down to his favourite harbour-front restaurant and eat fresh sardines for lunch, or take a late dinner outside and watch the bright lights of Costa Adeje and Playa de las Americas out in the distance, reminding him of where he was, and the temptation that lay out there that he just didn't want to take anymore. He was quite happy to sit on his own with a bottle of wine and the passing conversation of other diners, or the restaurant owners who'd often sit down and chat with him about his day. It was so different to the life he'd left behind in Newcastle. But whether it was one he could live forever, he didn't know. He was happy here, and he was enjoying this unexpected but self-enforced loan period. He was enjoying the experience of playing in another country, of doing things a slightly different way. But he was also looking forward to going home. At some point.

Turning away from the window, he walked over to the kitchen, flicking on the TV on his way over, taking a brief second or two to check out the headlines on the British news channel. But a knock at the door broke his attention, and a sinking feeling in the pit of his stomach took over. Surely it couldn't be Ellen. He hadn't exactly told her to sling her hook, or anything even close, but he was hoping that his indifferent attitude towards her over the past couple of days was telling her, in no uncertain terms, that their relationship had no chance of being rekindled.

Sighing a touch too heavily, he walked out into the bright white hallway, slowly opening the door, that sinking feeling in his stomach quickly replaced by that of his heart almost stopping dead when he saw who was standing there.

'Amber, I… what are you…?'

'Can I come in?'

He couldn't believe how ridiculously happy he felt just seeing her standing there; how much hope it filled him with. Even if he *was* slightly confused at her sudden appearance. 'Jesus, yes. Of course, yes.' He stood aside to let her through, following her back into the main living area.

'This is nice,' she said, looking around her. 'And, oh, Ryan, what an amazing view!'

'Yeah. I kind of like it.' He smiled, sticking his hands in the pockets of his three-quarter-length combats. 'Beats looking out at the River Tyne, huh?'

She walked over to the patio doors, looking out at that amazing view, focusing on a catamaran way out in the distance. 'Ellen not here?'

'Ellen? How did you know…?'

She turned around to face him. 'Debbie told me you'd been talking to Gary. You told him she'd come out here to see you. To try and patch things up.'

'It's over, Amber. Me and Ellen. It's over. I mean, yeah, she's still here, in Tenerife, and she's tried everything she can to… to convince me that…' He stopped talking, pushing a hand through his hair. Why the hell did he feel so nervous all of a sudden?

'I don't want to know the whole story, Ryan. It's really none of my business what your relationship status with Ellen is. I just wondered if she was here now, in your villa. Because I really need to talk to you – alone.'

He still felt slightly confused, but that feeling of hope was also beginning to bubble up inside him again. She needed to talk to him. In private. Surely that was a good thing?

'No. She's… she's not here. She's at her hotel. Or she's out somewhere, I don't…'

'So, you're on your own?' Amber asked, trying to batter down that feeling of nausea that was threatening to spill out of her.

Ryan nodded, his hands still in his pockets as he looked at her. She was so beautiful, so unbelievably beautiful. Dressed in a short white skirt and top, her dark red hair piled messily on top of her head, her face carrying only the minimum of make-up, she looked stunning. And there was nothing Ryan could do to stop every feeling he still had for this woman from flooding his brain.

'Okay. Well…' She stopped talking, folding her arms as she looked out of the window again, trying desperately to think of a way to say what she had to tell him. She hadn't realised it would be this hard.

'Amber?' He frowned as he watched her standing there. Her stance was one of a person who was trying to avoid telling him something, and he couldn't help but feel slightly nervous, although he had absolutely no idea why. 'Is… is something wrong? Only, you've come all this way, and, to be honest, you're the last person I expected to ever see turning up on my doorstep voluntarily. Did you come over with Max? I know I've got a meeting with him later and…'

'I'm pregnant.'

He stared at her, blinking rapidly as a way of trying to take in what he'd just heard. 'You… you're… you're pregnant? I… I don't…'

'It's… Jesus, why is this so fucking hard?' She pushed both hands through her hair, shaking it free from the grips that had been holding it up, throwing her head back before looking at him.

'It's yours, Ryan.' Her eyes locked onto his. 'This baby. It's yours.'

He still couldn't quite get his head around what she'd just told him. She was pregnant. With his baby. He was sure that's what she'd just said. She was pregnant with *his* baby. 'But… how…? I don't… I thought you couldn't…'

'Well, so did I,' she whispered, her arms still folded tight across her chest. 'I really thought that ship had sailed. But it looks like I was wrong.' She reached into her pocket and pulled out a piece of paper – a copy of the test results from her visit to Dr. Lowry. Confirmation that everything she was telling him was the truth. 'Miracles do happen, Ryan. That's what I was told.'

He reached out and took the piece of paper from her, scanning the words, but it took a few reads before everything sunk in. 'You're… you're three months gone,' he said, raising his head to look at her. 'That means… when we were at Gary's party? That night…?'

She nodded, taking the paper from him and shoving it back into her pocket.

'Jesus, Amber…' He felt like he'd just been hit head-on with something hard and solid. He'd had no idea why she'd come all this way to see him, but whatever the reason, he certainly hadn't expected it to be this. This was off the scale. 'I don't know… I don't know what to say.'

She looked out of the window again. There was something about that view of the sea that made her wish she was somewhere out there, floating away, out of reach of all the shit that was about to hit the fan.

'It's my dream come true, you know? To actually have this miracle happen. But it's… it's…'

He didn't know what to say. All he could do was stand there as everything slowly started to sink in that little bit more. 'It's with the wrong man,' he whispered, the words falling out of his mouth without him actually realising.

She turned sharply to look at him, her expression telling him everything he needed to know. And that realisation didn't help matters.

'I don't know what to do, Ryan.' And that was the truth. In fact, ever since she'd arrived at his villa, from the second she'd seen him standing there in his combats and his white t-shirt, those sexy-as-hell tattoos and that ever-present stubble making him look so incredibly hot, she was more confused than ever. She still had so many feelings for this man, it was just that she couldn't explain them, couldn't quite understand them. And now her hormones were shot to pieces that wasn't going to make anything any easier. 'Ryan... What are we going to do?'

He didn't know. How was he supposed to know? Ten minutes ago he'd been a twenty-seven-year-old footballer enjoying his temporary but carefree new life in the sun, and now he'd just been told he was going to be a dad. Him. Ryan Fisher. A dad.

A feeling of utter panic suddenly washed right over him like an unexpected tidal wave, sending his head spinning and his stomach turning over so fast he actually felt sick. What the hell was he supposed to do with this news? What was he supposed to do now?

'I need to get my head around this,' he said quietly, sitting down on the arm of a chair, resting his hands on his knees.

Amber watched him, watched his panic-stricken expression and the way his body stiffened, his eyes filled with the same kind of confusion she was feeling. Of course he needed to get his head around this. Of course he did.

'I'll leave you alone for a while, okay?' she said, making her way back out into the hall, but as she passed him he reached out and took her hand, an action that sent her stomach flipping over and over, her heart almost jumping into her mouth.

'I don't want you to go,' he whispered, making no attempt to loosen the grip he had on her.

'You need some time, Ryan. You said it yourself. Time to get your head around this.'

'I've got my head around it.'

'What? Just like that?'

He stood up, his eyes meeting hers. And it was almost as if someone had quickly flicked a switch somewhere inside him, changing his mood in an instant. 'That night, at Gary's party – you were so broken, Amber. At one point. So broken and damaged and crying for the fact you couldn't have that baby you wanted so much, I can still remember it, as clear as yesterday. I can remember the expression on your face, the pain in your eyes… You said… you said all you wanted was Jim. All you wanted was his baby…'

'But it's not his, is it? That night was just the beginning of a mess we couldn't possibly have known was going to be created. But look what it's done.'

'It's given you that baby you wanted so much, Amber.'

'But it isn't Jim's,' she whispered, glad he was still holding her hand, but angry at herself for letting the tears she'd promised not to cry today fall freely down her cheeks. 'It's yours.'

Ryan felt his own heart break as he remembered that conversation they'd had on the bathroom floor at Gary's. The night he'd made love to her in the most beautiful way; how she'd gone from sad to super-sexy in a matter of minutes, replacing that sadness with sex he couldn't forget. Sex that had created something she'd wanted so much. Even if he wasn't the man she'd wanted to create it with.

'You also… you also said… do you remember? You also said that… that you thought I'd make a great dad, one day…'

'One day, Ryan.'

'That day's here, Amber. Whether we like it or not. It might not be the way either of us would have planned this, but that day is here. And now we've got to start dealing with it.'

She looked down, closing her eyes as more tears fell onto the white tiled floor. He was right. Whatever the circumstances, it had happened, and they couldn't change that. As much as she wanted to go to sleep, wake up and find that this baby was Jim's, that wasn't going to happen. It was never going to happen.

'Amber?'

He tilted her chin up, and when she finally opened her eyes he was smiling at her. He had such a beautiful smile, a smile that made his whole face light up. A smile that made him seem so much younger than he actually was, and that only made Amber feel even worse. He was twenty-seven, she was thirty-eight. Eleven years didn't seem all that much in reality, but sometimes when they'd been together, it had felt like a gulf so wide she just hadn't been able to bridge it.

'I love you, Amber. I love you...'

'I told you I didn't want to hear you say that, Ryan.'

She tried turning her face away but he stopped her, placing a hand on her cheek, making her look at him. 'I don't care what you do or don't want to hear me say, Amber. I'm sick of hiding the way I feel, I'm sick of lying to myself, sick of pretending that being here, away from Newcastle... I'm sick of pretending it's going to make a difference, when it isn't. It isn't. I love you, and this... this just... Maybe it's fate. This baby. Maybe it's been given to us to show us that we really should be together. You and Jim...'

'Don't talk about me and Jim,' Amber said, pulling away from him and walking back over to the patio doors, resuming that defensive stance of folding her arms as she stared out at the sun glinting off the bright blue sea. And once again she wished she was out there, in the middle of nowhere, drifting away from a situation she didn't want to handle. She didn't want to have to do this. Because she didn't know if she could. 'You don't know anything about me and Jim. Not really.'

'I'm sorry.' Ryan didn't make a move to go over to her. He just stood there, his hands in his pockets, watching her. 'I didn't mean... I just...'

She turned around to face him, her folded arms still signalling that she didn't want him to come any closer. 'I just don't want to talk about Jim, okay? This doesn't... it doesn't involve him. Not yet, anyway.' She took a deep breath, pushing a hand through her hair. 'I'm so scared, Ryan.' Her eyes met his again. The tears had dried up now, but he could still see a sadness in them that he wished he could erase. 'I'm so fucking scared.'

He walked over to her, slipping an arm around her waist, pulling her closer, gently kissing her forehead. 'So am I, babe. Believe me, so am I.' He looked at her, smiling that smile again and Amber couldn't help but smile back. Even if she didn't exactly know why. 'But together… together we can do this. Me and you. We can give it a damn good try, anyway.'

She looked down again, avoiding his eyes. This wasn't why she'd come here. Telling him about the baby wasn't meant to signal the restart of their relationship. That had never been her intention. 'I can't… Ryan, I… I'm just so confused right now, and I don't want to…' She looked at him, right into those beautiful dark blue eyes. 'I don't want you to feel trapped by this. You're young, you've got this incredible career, you've got the world at your feet and I… I just wanted you to know, that's all. You needed to know.'

'Will you look at me, Amber? Please.'

She didn't want to, and she knew why. She knew that if she looked at him all those hidden feelings she still kept locked away, all those things she still felt for this man, they'd come flooding forward, as they always did when she was looking for some kind of barrier to deflect everything she was trying to forget. They'd all come flooding forward, confusing her even more, turning Ryan Fisher into the one thing she didn't need him to be right now – her favourite mistake. The one she needed to stop making when everything else looked like it was turning to crap.

'I can't pretend this isn't fucking with my head, Amber. Because it is. Big time. You have no idea…' He tilted her chin up again, once more giving her no other option but to look right into his eyes. 'But I love you so frigging much that I know… I know I want to do this. I know I *can* do this.'

She stared at him for a few seconds, cocking her head slightly as she tried to get her mixed-up emotions into some kind of order.

'You can't possibly know that yet, Ryan.'

'I know that's how it feels.'

'You could change your mind.'

'This baby, he or she, they're going to be in my life forever now, Amber. They're going to become the focus I need to get myself sorted, really sorted this time. Do you see that? They're going to be in my life forever, and I want you to be in it, too. Believe me, I want that more than anything.'

'I will be,' she whispered, looking away again, back out of the window. 'I'll be the baby's mum. I'm always going to be a part of your life now.'

'That isn't what I meant and you know that. Jesus, will you stop trying to put barriers up where there doesn't need to be any.'

She turned to look at him, a wave of anger washing over her now. 'I'm not putting up barriers, Ryan.'

'You and Jim, it's over. It's over, baby. He wants a divorce, and that's pretty final, don't you think? So maybe it's time you tried to move on...'

'Because it's *that* easy, isn't it?'

He threw his head back and sighed, pushing a hand through his hair. 'Jesus fucking Christ... Okay. Okay, I'll back off, if that's what you want. If you want to spend the rest of your life praying that he'll come back to you, then you go and do that. Go on. You do that. And he probably will – he probably *will* come back to you, now and again. He'll sleep with you and then toss you aside, because that's what he does, Amber. That's what he does, and that's what he's been doing to you since you were sixteen fucking years old. Since you were sixteen, Amber. He walks into your life, stays for a little while, takes everything you've got to give him, then he just walks out and leaves you to pick up the pieces. Until the next time. So you carry on doing that, if that's what makes you happy. If the occasional fuck and the chance to be close to a man that nobody truly understands is what you want, then you go right ahead and save yourself for him.'

She shut him up with a slap so hard he literally reeled backwards, his hand immediately flying to his face as he stared back at her.

'You deserve more than that, Amber. You deserve more than him.'

She could feel her heart breaking, the pain so intense it felt like someone dragging a jagged shard of glass across her chest. 'I love him, Ryan. I love him so much it hurts. And this – this is killing me…' She couldn't keep it inside any longer; all the pain and the anger and the frustration that this baby she was carrying wasn't Jim's. It all came flooding out of her in uncontrollable sobs as she sank to the floor, pulling her knees to her chest as she cried like she'd never cried before – for all the things she'd thought she could never have, for the impossible dream that was still so out of her reach it ripped her apart; for all those things that Ryan had said, because he was right. He was right.

'Jesus…' Ryan ran over to her, sinking down beside her, pulling her into his arms, holding her as she cried it all out, rocking her slowly, kissing her tears away and wishing everything was different. He wished Jim Allen had never walked back into her life, wished she'd been strong enough not to let him back in; he wished for a happily-ever-after that may never come. Not while she still felt so much for a man he could never really compete with.

'I'm sorry,' she sniffed, pulling away from him, wiping her eyes with the back of her hand. 'My hormones are all over the place right now.'

'Amber…'

She pulled herself to her feet and went into the kitchen, taking a glass from the draining board and filling it with water. 'I should go. You need to have some time to yourself now. You need to think about this.'

'I don't need to think about anything.' Ryan walked over to her, taking the glass from her hand. 'I love you, Amber. And when I say I want you in my life, I don't mean as just a mum to my child. I want you *in* my life, right there beside me.' He rested a hand on her hip, his mouth moving closer to hers. 'I want you in my bed…' He kissed her slowly, her lips automatically parting to let his tongue slide inside, '… I want to make love to you before I go to sleep at night, and I want to feel you wrapped around me every morning, taking me deeper, letting me love you – the way you deserve to be loved.'

She felt her stomach dip, her heart start to race, her skin break out in a million goose bumps. All familiar feelings, and every single one of them a warning sign. But he did things to her she couldn't deny. He wasn't Jim, and he never would be. But Jim didn't want her. He didn't want her. And he never would, not now. Not when he heard she was pregnant with Ryan Fisher's baby. She knew that would be the final nail in the coffin of their complicated, crazy relationship. And that's when she knew she'd have to let him go, even if it was the last thing she wanted to do.

'I'm trying to be so grown-up about this, Ryan.'

He was kissing her neck now, his hand sliding up under her skirt, his fingers already hooked under the sides of her panties.

'We can be grown-up later,' he whispered, his hand now sliding round to cup her bottom, pushing her against him.

'No, Ryan…' she groaned, but it was useless. She was too weak to resist, and a part of her didn't even want to. Being here, talking to him, it had made her realise so many things. Things that hurt, things she'd never really wanted to face up to before, but now she knew she had to. Whether she wanted to or not. This was real life, and she had to start living it. In a minute. Soon.

'What more damage can we do?' Ryan said, gently stroking her cheek with the palm of his hand, his eyes boring deep into hers again. 'I think we've just about knocked the damage radar right up to full now, don't you?'

She couldn't help smiling, covering his hand with hers. 'I didn't come here to do this, I didn't… I don't even know if this is what I want.'

'Then let me try and convince you.' He smiled, too, taking her hand in his and leading her into the bedroom.

She wasn't going to put up a fight. She was too tired, too confused. And being close to him might actually be a good idea – it might make her start realising that this whole scenario was actually happening, because, right now, she still felt somewhat of an outside spectator looking in on something she wasn't really a part of.

'It's not going to be pretty, when all of this comes out.' She watched as Ryan pulled off his t-shirt, once more revealing that toned stomach and those tattoos that were such a turn-on. There was still something there, something that fluttered away deep inside her every time she saw this man – which was why she'd spent so long trying to avoid him. And with good reason it would seem, because look what had happened the second she'd let him get close to her again.

'We've dealt with worse.'

She raised an eyebrow, more than aware of the stirring between her legs, that ache that had started up and wouldn't go away until it had been eased. She hadn't invited it, hadn't wanted to feel it, especially not right now. But it was there, whether she liked it or not. 'You think?'

He grinned, edging closer to her, sliding his fingers under the waistband of her skirt, slowly pushing it down. 'We'll deal with it when it happens, okay? Right now… right now I just want to feel you, fuck you… taste you. I don't want to think about anything else.'

She felt her stomach almost rise up into her chest, like she'd just gone over the precipice of the wildest big dipper there was. She was completely aware that she was now stepping out of her skirt, kicking it away; she was aware that he was removing her panties, that she was kicking those away, too. She was aware of everything she was about to do next, and she wanted it to happen. Now. Maybe she hadn't before – maybe she had. All she knew was that she wanted a reprieve from the confusion and the reality. Even if this wasn't the most sensible way of getting that respite.

Holding her arms up, she closed her eyes as he pulled off her top, the coolness of the air conditioning immediately hitting her naked skin, and the strangest feeling of freedom suddenly washed over her. She didn't know why, as everything that had happened lately meant she was anything but free. But, right now, she felt as though nothing could touch her; like the world was hers. Hers and Ryan's.

'No bump yet?' Ryan smiled, his fingers entwining with hers, her arms still up above her head.

She smiled, too, staring into his eyes, every nerve ending in her body on red alert as they waited in anticipation of his first touch. 'I guess I'm lucky, so far.'

'You look fucking incredible,' he groaned, letting go of one of her hands so he could finally make that first move, running a thumb gently over her nipples until they were hard. 'Jesus, Amber…' He lowered his head, his tongue replacing his thumb, circling her nipple lightly, the warmth and the heat of his mouth turning her on to the point of agonising frustration. So much so that she was halfway to touching herself, to bringing herself to a climax she now desperately needed.

But he could sense that, and he pulled away, taking a couple of steps back to just take her in, to look at her, that Ryan Fisher grin lighting up his face again as his eyes scanned her naked body. And it was a grin that made Amber laugh, she couldn't help it. Her beautiful boy was here to make everything better, and whether he really could do that, she didn't know. She doubted it. This whole situation was only going to get worse before anything felt like it was making any kind of sense, but, for now, he was here, and he was smiling. Handsome, hot, sexy and dangerous. Everything she could do without. But everything she was going to take.

And then the mood changed, in a split second, as the smiles disappeared and the air was filled with an intensity so charged it almost crackled. Within seconds he had her pressed up against the wall, his hand between her legs, his mouth on hers as the heat rose, and he did, too, his erection digging into her thigh so hard she almost cried out with the pain.

He lifted her up, her legs wrapping themselves around him as he carried her over to the bed, gently laying her down, positioning himself between those incredible legs of hers so he had the best view, and easy access into that place he'd been aching to visit ever since he'd left the U.K.

He could see how wet she was, he could see how ready she was, and as he reached out and touched her, let his fingers lose themselves in that warm, wet heaven, he almost lost control, almost came there and then, spectacularly early, because that's what she did to him. When she was lying there, with those legs wide open and everything on show, she was his obsession.

'Ryan…' she groaned, arching her back as he gently and carefully pushed his fingers inside her, moving slowly, making every inch of her shiver. It was the most beautiful feeling, an almost exquisite feeling of frustration mixed with pure lust as his mouth kissed its way up her body, lingering on her hips, his other hand in the small of her back, keeping her pushed up against him.

She felt young again, she felt free and alive and everything she really wasn't, but the fact he was making her feel that way was enough for now; it was enough to keep her hoping that everything might just work out, that this fucked-up situation could actually end up with some kind of conclusion. It was just that, right now, she couldn't see it. She couldn't.

'You're thinking,' Ryan said, slowly pulling his fingers out of her, his body moving slightly, his knee gently pushing her legs a touch wider apart. 'Don't. Don't think about anything except what we're doing here. You can't change it, Amber, you can't do anything. You can't…' She closed her eyes as his mouth touched hers, '… do anything.' His tongue danced around hers, sending her head spinning as he slowly pushed into her, filling her with that brief feeling of hope again, and she embraced that. She took it and she ran with it, throwing her arms above her head as his fingers slipped between hers, her legs now wrapped around him as their bodies moved together in a gentle, slow rhythm. A familiar rhythm. A rhythm that built up, bit by bit, with every push, every thrust, every buck of her hips, until they both shuddered to a simultaneous climax that was both understated, yet, at the same time, quietly brutal in its intensity.

She didn't want to open her eyes when it was over. Opening her eyes meant stepping back into reality and she knew that's what she was scared of. What she was trying to avoid. She'd taken the first step by coming here, by telling Ryan. And she'd taken one huge step backwards by letting this happen.

'I'm not walking away,' Ryan whispered, stroking strands of hair from Amber's eyes. 'I can't do that. Not now.'

She looked up at him, her chest still rising and falling quite rapidly as her breathing tried its best to return to normal. 'I know.'

'So, what do we do now?'

She didn't know. She still couldn't answer that question. It was way too early to be deciding on any kind of future. 'I don't know, Ryan.'

She let go of his hand, turning over onto her stomach. He lay next to her, propping himself up on one elbow.

'I know how we can make a start,' he said, gently running his fingers along her arm until they reached her left hand, and she didn't do a thing to stop him as she felt him slowly start to slip off her wedding ring, sliding it over her finger until it fell into his hand. 'We can start by getting rid of that.'

She turned to look at him, watching as he balled his hand into a fist, enclosing her wedding ring inside it.

'Do you want it back?' he asked, stretching out his arm and letting the ring fall out onto the bedside table.

'I… I…' She didn't know. She really didn't know.

'You can have it back, if you really want it,' he whispered, slowly running his fingers over her hip, stroking it gently, moving down over her thigh. 'If you really, really want it.' His eyes were boring deep into hers again, turning everything on its head, complicating an already complicated situation even further.

'I don't…' She couldn't even string a sentence together, and she hated feeling like this. She wanted to be strong, she wanted to put those barriers back up and let nothing and no one get past them again, because this is what happened when they did. And she didn't know how to cope with these feelings anymore.

'It's pointless looking back, Amber,' he said, pulling her against him. 'I mean, after what's happened, you can't really *go* back now, can you? Everything's changed.'

And that's what worried her more than anything. Everything *had* changed. Everything. And the problem with that was, she didn't want it to.

Chapter Thirty

'I'm experiencing a slight feeling of déjà vu here,' Ronnie said as Amber drove out of the car park at Reina Sofia Airport. 'And you're not saying much. Everything all right?'

'I'm just concentrating, Ronnie. If I miss this turn off I've got to drive miles before I get a chance to double back. Roundabouts aren't as frequently placed here as they are back home.'

'How did Ryan take the news of impending fatherhood, then?'

'You really want to have this conversation now?' she asked as she finally turned off onto the TF1 motorway to begin the short journey towards Costa Adeje. 'I'm driving.'

'And when did you suddenly lose the ability to multitask? Surely pregnancy hasn't turned your brain to mush already.'

'Ronnie, please…'

'Okay, okay… You had dinner yet?'

She shook her head. 'Not yet, no. Can't say that eating is high on my list of important things to do at the minute.'

'You're eating for two now, missy, remember?'

'That's such a fallacy.'

'Yeah, well, keeping yourself healthy isn't. So let's go eat.'

'Who died and made you my dad?'

'Talking of your dad…'

Amber sighed heavily, throwing Ronnie a quick sideways look.

'He's worried about you. He hasn't heard from you in days, every time he sees you, you look miserable…'

'He knows I'm busy. And he knows I'm… he knows I'm missing Jim.' She swallowed hard, trying not to let the mention of her estranged husband's name get to her, but it was something she still had to work at.

'He should know you're carrying his grandchild.'

'Jesus Christ…'

'All right, okay. I'm sorry. I'm sorry.'

'But you're not, though, are you? And I really hope you haven't come all the way here just to nag me into the ground.'

'As if.'

She couldn't help smiling. 'I really hate you sometimes.'

'The feeling's mutual,' he grinned, and she laughed, suddenly feeling incredibly happy that her best friend was here. Because she needed him.

'Okay, you win. Let's go eat.'

Jim flicked through the pages of the paper, his head resting in his hand as he looked at the pictures of Amber over in Tenerife. She was walking along the seafront with Max, who Jim was well aware had gone out there because Ryan was doing a photo shoot with one of his sponsors. He was also aware that Amber had taken a bit of time off from Cloud Sports, which bothered him. She didn't take time off, not just like that. Not Amber. He knew her too well, knew that she didn't like to let people down, but he should have known something was wrong when she'd suddenly pulled out of hosting *Scoreline* the evening he'd been interviewed. He should have known.

'Well, that's the dishwasher loaded.' Brandon smiled, coming back into the dining room from the kitchen, a tea towel slung over one shoulder, a bottle of beer in his hand. 'Thanks for dinner, Dad. It was good to spend some time with you.'

Jim sat back in his chair, rubbing the bridge of his nose. 'Yeah, it was.' He smiled at his son. 'We need to do it more often.'

'Dad...'

Jim looked back at the paper, once again staring down at that picture of Amber in a black bikini, a short sarong tied low around her hips, that beautiful dark red hair of hers piled messily up on top of her head so that loose strands fell over her bare, tanned shoulders. And he was divorcing her. Why? Only he knew the answer to that one. Nobody else needed to know. And, as painful as it was, it was the way it had to be.

'What?' Jim asked, not looking up. Not wanting to, because he really wasn't in the mood for any kind of deep conversation.

'When you were... when you were my age everyone said you had a bit of a reputation. Some even say you clash with Ryan Fisher so much because you're actually quite similar. Or you were. Once upon a time.'

Jim looked up, narrowing his eyes slightly as he looked at his son. 'A lot of my life at that age is a bit of a blur.'

'So there *are* comparisons between you and him, then?' Brandon smirked, but that smirk was soon wiped from his face when he saw his father's expression change.

'There are no similarities between myself and Ryan Fisher, Brandon. None.'

'Okay, but you must have had lots of girlfriends. Everyone says you were a real hit with the women, you were good-looking and...'

Jim looked up from the paper again, pushing his reading glasses up onto his head. 'Do we have to talk about this?'

'I'm just curious.' Brandon shrugged, taking a long drink of beer. 'Curious to know what your life was like before me. Before Amber.'

Jim said nothing for a second or two, sitting back and rubbing the bridge of his nose again. He could feel another headache starting to form. This was something he really didn't want to get into with Brandon. With anyone.

'Before Amber... before Amber there was nothing, okay?'

Brandon frowned. 'Nothing? Come on, Dad. You must have had

other girlfriends before you met Amber. You were twenty-seven when it all started with her, so… there must have been others before that.'

Jim looked down again, pushing his reading glasses back down over his eyes. 'Nobody that meant anything. Now, can we leave this alone, please?'

'Do you miss her?'

Jim took off his glasses, throwing them down on the arm of his chair. 'What the hell *is* this, Brandon?'

'I just don't understand why you're divorcing her. I can't get my head around it. She still loves you, because she told me so, she said those words. And you quite obviously still feel something for her, otherwise you wouldn't get so worked up over all of this.'

'The only reason I'm getting worked up over anything, Brandon, is because you're pushing a subject I really don't want to talk about. And shouldn't you be getting home? It's late.'

'Thought I'd stay the night, if that's okay.'

'I don't need looking after, thank you.'

'I didn't say that was the reason I was staying, did I? If anyone doesn't need looking after it's you. You seem to like being on your own, the way you push people who love you away.'

'I really don't need this, Brandon, and if you *are* going to stay then quit with the questions, okay? And any conversation concerning Amber is over now. Do you hear me?'

'So why are you staring at pictures of her in the paper?'

'I'm not…'

'You are. I know what you're doing, I can see. She's over there, and it's killing you to know why.'

Jim closed the paper, standing up and throwing it aside. 'I'm going up to bed.'

'You might just have pushed them together again, that's what's bothering you, isn't it?'

'I've told you, Brandon. I'm not talking about this.'

'But you still love her. You're still *in* love with her, aren't you?'

Jim remained silent.

'Aren't you, Dad?'

'Yes, okay. Yes. Is that what you want to hear? Yes, I'm still in love with her.'

'So why the fuck are you divorcing her?'

'Jesus Christ... what is the matter with you?'

'Why, Dad?'

'Because I have to, Brandon. I have to. And don't... please don't make me talk about this anymore. Please. This conversation – it's over. You got that? It's over.'

'So, what are you going to do now?' Ronnie asked, watching Amber as she lay down on the sun lounger next to him, the black bikini she was wearing leaving little to the imagination. It was hard to believe she was pregnant to look at her.

'That question is really starting to give me a headache, Ronnie.' She propped herself up on her elbows, sliding her sunglasses up onto her head. 'Honest answer? I don't know. In a perfect world I'd like to think that Jim would try and forgive what's happened and tell me we can try and work something out, but...'

'Hang on. Why is Jim the only one forgiving here? Have you forgotten what he's done to you?'

'Keeping a few secrets isn't quite the same as sleeping with one of his players behind his back and getting pregnant, is it?'

'Keeping a few...? I don't believe you. You're talking like some lovesick teenager, have you heard yourself? He's no saint, Amber. And the sooner you wise up to that the better off you're going to be.'

'He's my husband, Ronnie.'

'And he's told you he wants a divorce. He wants to end the marriage, Amber. Have you got that yet?'

'Because I betrayed him.' Amber's voice was quiet as she stared out ahead of her at the stunning view of blue sea and cloudless sky, the palm trees swaying gently in the wonderfully warm yet cooling breeze.

'You betrayed him,' Ronnie repeated. 'And he's never done that to you before, huh?'

She turned her head sharply to look at her friend. 'Once upon a time, yes, okay. He did. But since he… since he came back… Look, what do you want me to do, Ronnie? Forget Jim, just like that, and let Ryan back into my life just because he's the baby's dad?'

'I didn't say that, did I? And I don't want you to do anything you don't want to do, but I *am* going to try and make sure you don't make the same mistakes twice.'

'I think we're over making mistakes, Ronnie. Don't you?'

Ronnie sat forward, looking straight at her. His beautiful best friend. He'd do anything to make sure she was happy. Anything. But what he didn't want was for her to repeat the past. He wanted her to move forwards, not backwards. Repeating the past wasn't going to solve anything. 'When are you going to tell Jim about the baby?'

She pushed her sunglasses down over her eyes, lying back on her lounger. 'As soon as I get home. He needs to know before it becomes obvious. Before the press get hold of it.'

'And you think it was wise coming out here? With the possibility of being seen with Ryan? You know how the papers love to put two and two together where you two are concerned. You're probably giving them all the ammunition they need right now.'

'They can think what they like, Ronnie, because I'm still living in a time when they weren't on my back 24/7. I didn't invite them to stalk my every move.'

'Then you should be more careful who you hang out with, shouldn't you?'

She lifted up her sunglasses and threw him a warning look. 'I had to come here. It wasn't fair to tell Ryan something like this over the phone. The least I could do was tell him in person.'

'Speak of the devil…' Ronnie sighed, hanging his head, knowing this conversation was finished now. But it was far from over.

Amber sat up, removing her sunglasses as she watched Ryan

stride through the pool area of her hotel, handsome, hot and sexy as hell in three-quarter-length cargo pants and a black t-shirt, his dark hair all ruffled and messed up by the breeze. He had a wide smile on his face, and he looked happy. Happier than Amber had seen him look in a long time. She didn't know whether that was a good thing or not. She couldn't ignore the little flutter inside her, though. As much as she wanted to.

'Hey, beautiful.' He grinned, sitting down on the edge of her lounger. 'You okay this morning?'

'I'm fine,' she replied, not missing the look Ronnie gave her. 'Good win for Adeje the other night, by the way. And a couple of great goals from you.'

'Yeah. It wasn't a bad game. Did you watch it?'

'We saw it on TV in a bar down on the seafront, didn't we, Ronnie?'

Ronnie just looked at her, saying nothing.

'I'm impressed,' Amber went on, knowing full well she was only talking about football to avoid having to talk about anything else. 'You've slotted into the team really well.'

She threw Ronnie a look as he let out a snort of derision that Ryan must have heard.

'You all right, Ronnie?' Ryan asked, not managing to hide the fact he wasn't entirely happy to see Amber's close friend here on the island. He was all too aware that *she* probably needed him right now, but Ryan could well do without his presence.

'Yeah, I'm fine. How are *you* feeling? After hearing Amber's news, I mean?'

Ryan let out a small laugh, looking down at his hands clasped between his knees. 'I'm good, thanks.' He looked back up, still speaking to Ronnie, but directing his gaze at Amber. 'It was a shock, I can't lie, but…' He smiled, and Amber couldn't help but smile back. Why was that smile of his so infectious? Was it something to do with the sun? With the change in atmosphere a different setting could create? 'Yeah. I'm excited. It's like I've been given that new start I've been looking for.'

'Jesus Christ...' Ronnie sighed, pushing a hand through his hair as he stood up, leaning over to kiss Amber quickly on the mouth. 'You take care, all right? And remember what I said. About being seen with him.' He cocked his head in Ryan's direction, without looking at him. 'I'll see you later.'

'Yeah. Later,' Amber said quietly, watching Ronnie walk back across the pool area towards the hotel.

'What's he mean? About being seen with me? What's he talking about?'

Amber sat up, twisting her hair into a loose knot and pinning it up on top of her head. 'He thinks that if I'm seen here with you it's only going to cause more tabloid gossip back home.'

'Okay. Well, it doesn't have to, does it?'

She looked at him, arching a sceptical eyebrow. 'You know, for someone who's a veteran of the gossip columns you can still be incredibly naive sometimes. Me and Jim split up, and then all of a sudden I'm spotted hanging around with you – and you don't think people are going to start talking? You don't think rumours are going to start flying around?'

'So why did you come here, then? If you knew that's what was going to happen?'

'To tell you about the baby... Jesus, Ryan, come on. Would you rather I'd sent you an email? A text? Stuck a message on Facebook? I wanted to tell you in person, that's all. It's the least you deserve.'

'And what if those rumours were true?'

She looked at him, pausing for a second before saying anything else. 'But they're not, are they?'

He looked down at his clasped hands again, and for a brief second Amber saw a glimpse of the ordinary young man he could be – underneath that famous footballer façade was the man she wanted to have as a dad to this baby, if that was the only choice she had. And it was. She could lie there, night after night, crying herself to sleep, wishing this baby was Jim's, but nothing could change the fact it wasn't. And she had to begin accepting that.

'Ryan… Things are just… they're so complicated right now, you understand that, don't you? And what's to come… we both need to be ready to face Christ knows what once news of this baby gets out and… and I need you, all right? We're going to need each other.'

'I want to be there for you every step of the way, Amber.' He looked up at her, those beautiful dark blue eyes staring deep into hers. 'I meant what I said the other night, about wanting you in my life – permanently. I know I don't deserve any second chances…' He noticed the look she gave him, and he smiled slightly. 'Okay. Third, fourth, whatever. I don't deserve another opportunity to show you how much I regret throwing away what we had before. I know I don't deserve that. But ever since the day I lost you I've wanted you back. I've wanted that life we could have had…'

'Ryan, baby, it was never going to happen. The circumstances, the fact Jim was back… that life you think we could have had, it was never going to happen.'

'But it could – now.' His eyes were still fixed on her, boring right into her, sending a small shiver running up and down her spine. 'Circumstances have changed, haven't they?'

'Jim's still there, Ryan. He's still in my life.' Her voice was quiet, a slow realisation sinking in. 'He's still in my life.' And, if she was completely honest with herself, that's where she wanted him to stay.

'He doesn't want you anymore, Amber. Please, babe, you have to start realising that.'

She was. She *was* beginning to realise that, but it didn't make any of it any easier to deal with. 'None of that means I've stopped loving him, Ryan. I can't just switch those feelings off, feelings I've carried with me for over twenty years… I can't…'

He reached out and touched her cheek, gently stroking it with his thumb. 'I know. I know you can't. So you'll understand when I tell you *I* can't just switch off what I feel for you either. You'll know what I'm going through, how fucked up my head is, how I can't stop thinking about you, about how much I want you. And it was bad before, Amber. It was bad before I knew about the baby, but now it's just got a hundred times worse because all those feelings have just intensified tenfold. Have you any idea how much what you've told me has affected me? How it's changed the way I think, changed the way I want to live my life?'

Amber shook her head, pulling away from him, aware that he was now way too close to her in a very public place. Ronnie was right. She did need to be careful.

'Not here, Ryan.'

He watched as she covered up with a short, thin, black kaftan, her eyes doing all they could to avoid his.

'Come with me this afternoon.'

'Come with you, where?' Amber asked, slipping her sunglasses into her bag.

'I'm doing a photo shoot for one of my sponsors, down on the beach in Adeje. Come with me.'

She looked at him. 'You think that's a good idea, do you? Given what we've just talked about?'

'Max'll be there. Come on, Amber. He's *your* agent, too…'

'I shouldn't really be anywhere near you, Ryan.'

'Jesus, Amber… Fuck all of that shit, okay? Just, fuck it! It's all going to come out eventually, that we're expecting a baby together…'

'Except that, we're not together, are we?'

The way she looked at him almost broke his heart. Her eyes had developed a sudden coldness; she was pushing him away. He could almost see those barriers flying right back up around her again.

'He'll keep on doing this to you, Amber. And if that's the way you want to live your life then I can't do a thing to stop you. But, like it or not, I'm a part of your life now, and I'm going to be there for a very long time. That baby in there connects us, it means I'll never go away. Ever.' He held her gaze, desperate for her to see the truth in his eyes. 'Can you say the same about Jim?'

Chapter Thirty-One

'Maybe he's right,' Amber said, kicking her heels against the low wall she was sitting on as she watched Ryan get ready for his photo shoot down on Costa Adeje's white-sand beach, one of the few amongst the more familiar black sand that was more common on the island. A group of tourists and assorted passers-by had gathered to see what all the fuss was about, and Amber hoped she'd disguised herself well enough so that nobody would recognise her in oversized dark glasses and a huge sun hat. She figured she'd be safe. She wasn't *that* well-known. She just wasn't in the mood for small talk that was all.

'Maybe he's right about what?' Ronnie asked, taking a sip from the bottle of beer he was holding.

'About us. Me and him.'

Ronnie looked at her. 'What do you mean? Oh, hang on. Come on, Amber. Don't rush into something just because you *think* it's the right thing to do.'

'Well, maybe it is. I mean, I loved him once, didn't I? And there's still something there. Still something that… that makes me want him. I wouldn't have slept with him the other day if…' She stopped talking, looking down at her naked left hand, now devoid of the wedding ring she'd, so far, declined to put back on. What was the point? The marriage was over. And every second it sunk in that little bit more, it hurt like a fresh dagger to her heart.

'You had *sex* with him? Here? Jesus, Amber…' Ronnie closed his eyes, letting out a loud sigh. He couldn't even begin to describe the frustration he was feeling now. 'Before or after you told him about the baby?'

'After,' Amber whispered, looking back up at Ryan. He'd finally noticed her, the smile on his face widening the second their eyes met.

'You really know how to complicate a situation, don't you, kiddo?'

'Yeah, 'cause it wasn't complicated enough already.' Amber continued to watch Ryan as he talked to one of the models who was taking part in the shoot with him, a beautiful blonde girl who couldn't have been more than twenty-five. The kind of girl Ryan usually went for. The kind of girl that scared Amber when they were that close to a man she – what? A man she still had feelings for? Well, she knew that already. She'd just told Ronnie that, hadn't she? A man she still loved? She felt a shiver run all the way through her body as he turned to look at her again, that smile back on his handsome face, and all she wanted to do was run.

'I shouldn't have come here,' she said quietly, looking down at the sand.

'Well, I told you it wasn't a good idea.' Ronnie sighed again, reaching out to take her hand, squeezing it gently.

She looked at him, smiling slightly. 'Don't start with the lectures.'

'I'll keep my mouth shut, I promise.' He smiled, too, squeezing her hand again. 'Doesn't mean to say I can't think these things, though.'

'Everything okay?'

Amber looked up to see Max standing in front of her, as suave and sophisticated as ever, looking cool and relaxed – even in 85 degree heat – in light chinos, a white linen shirt and dark, undoubt-edly very expensive, glasses pushed up onto his head.

'Everything's fine,' Amber replied, still clinging onto Ronnie's hand.

'Ryan said you might be passing by.'

'I told him I wasn't coming, actually,' Amber corrected, taking another furtive look in Ryan's direction. He was doing what Ryan Fisher did best – flirting outrageously with the two female models he was working with – and that's what sent the warning signals racing to Amber's brain. It really did seem as though he'd changed after everything that had happened, but had he? Really? Deep down inside?

'I told her being seen with Ryan wasn't the best idea right now,' Ronnie said, taking one last swig of beer, '... given the circumstances.'

'It'll be fine,' Max sighed, leaning back against the wall beside Amber, his hands in his pockets. 'I've got it all under control. We'll keep everything under wraps until it needs to come out. Until those that need to know first have been told.'

Amber said nothing. She just stared down at her naked left hand again.

'I'll go get us some more drinks.' Ronnie smiled, squeezing Amber's other hand one last time before sliding down from the wall and making his way over to the bar a few yards away.

'You sure you're okay?' Max asked, his tone now less business-like.

Amber nodded, raising a small smile. 'Yeah. It's strange, you know? Even my morning sickness has disappeared since I arrived here.'

'And you and Striker over there... He seems quite relaxed about this whole situation.'

'That's because he's only looking at the rose-tinted version. Over here, away from all the reality, the complications don't seem so real. Not in *his* head, anyway.'

'And in yours?'

Amber shrugged, still staring down at her left hand. 'I've got to tell Jim, haven't I? I've got to put that final nail in the coffin of my short-lived marriage. Because he isn't going to want to take me back after he hears this, is he?'

'So I'm assuming that if he asked you to come back to him, you'd go?'

She looked up at her agent. 'In a heartbeat.'

Max looked down at his feet, kicking away at the sand. 'Amber…'

'But that isn't going to happen, I know that. I know that, Max. But when I close my eyes at night it doesn't stop me from dreaming about it. It doesn't stop me from wanting him, or loving him so much I don't know how I get through most days without him.'

'You got through almost sixteen years, kiddo.'

'Because I had to. Back then, I had to. But now he's here, right there in front of me, and it isn't going to get any easier, is it? Now that I'm having his star striker's baby. Jesus, it couldn't *get* any messier!'

'What's Ryan think about all this?' Max really didn't want to upset her any further, but he needed to know what was going on, so he could deal with it all.

'He wants us to be together,' Amber replied, wringing her hands, and then stopping herself from doing it by gripping the wall either side of her. 'He wants us to be a family – me, him and the baby.'

'And you don't want that?'

She looked at him again. 'No… I don't know. Shit, Max, I really don't know what to do.'

'Do you still have feelings for him? For Ryan?'

She looked over at her ex-fiancé. He was being photographed now, his arm firmly around the waist of one of the models, her bikini-clad body pressed against his half-naked one as he stared into her eyes, and Amber felt something in the pit of her stomach she couldn't explain. He was so young, so handsome, but was that enough? She'd been there before, and she'd been badly burned. There was a baby to think about now, and she needed more than just a young, hot footballer with an oversized ego. She needed someone she could rely on.

'He was a distraction from Jim, Max. I mean, I loved him, I did.

I really did. At times. When he wasn't pissing me off or making me hate him. There was a time when I loved him so much. But never as much as I loved Jim. Never in the same way. I'm not sure I'll ever love anyone the way I love Jim, so he was a distraction. And that wasn't entirely fair on him.'

'Do you still have feelings for him, Amber?'

'I don't want to do that to him again, Max. I don't want him to be nothing but a distraction from Jim, because I know that's all he could be. Right now, I can't promise him anything more than that.'

'You're still not answering my question, kiddo.'

She looked at Max, her fingers gripping the wall tightly. 'Yeah. I've still got feelings for him. I don't think I ever stopped caring about him. We went through too much together for me to push it all aside like it never happened. But I don't know if I love him. I don't know if I can.'

'He's grown up a lot, you know? Since all that shit happened.'

'I know.'

'And this baby – well, I know it isn't exactly an ideal situation, and the crap it's going to cause is something we really need to control, but I think it'll be the making of that kid. He needs something like this, something to shock him into the real world and realise that life isn't one long party.'

'I'm glad it'll help with his therapy,' Amber said, her voice tinged with more than a hint of sarcasm.

'I didn't mean it like that, Amber.'

'I know,' she sighed, pushing a hand through her hair. 'I know. I'm just extra sensitive right now, I'm sorry.'

'Hormones?'

She looked at Max, returning his smile. 'You really want to go down that road?'

Max sat down on the wall next to her. 'Listen, sweetheart. I know this is a really tough time for you right now, and I'll help you to get through it – I'll help you both get through it the best I can, I mean that. That's what I'm here for. Okay? So I don't want you to worry about the press or the media or…'

'That's easy for you to say.'

'Trust me, all right? I just want you to know that, whatever happens, people are there for you. And Ryan – just give him a chance to prove himself. I'm sure he'll make a great dad.'

'You think?' she asked, unable to stop another small smile escaping.

Max smiled, too, quickly squeezing her knee. 'This is what you wanted, Amber. This baby.'

'I wanted Jim's baby,' she whispered, suddenly realising that that statement was now making her sound like some selfish, spoilt kid who'd been given something beautiful and precious, but she was ungrateful because it wasn't *exactly* what she'd wanted. It was just as special, just as welcomed, it just wasn't that thing – that one, perfect thing she'd dreamed of. And she had to get over that. She'd been given a chance she'd never thought she was going to get, and she should be so grateful for that. Even if it wasn't working out quite the way she'd wanted it to. 'But…' She took a deep breath, exhaling slowly, '… I wanted a baby. And now that it's finally happened I've got to put this little one first, because it's a miracle I didn't think I'd ever see. And I know how lucky I am to have been given this chance.'

Max smiled, taking her hand and squeezing it tight. 'I'd better go see how he's doing. You gonna be okay?'

'Yeah. Ronnie'll be back in a sec… Max? Thank you. For being here. For being so understanding and… and for doing whatever it is you're going to do to get us through all of this. I really am grateful to have you on my side.'

'You'll be fine.' He winked at her, walking backwards towards Ryan and the photo shoot. 'You can deal with anything, kid, remember that.'

She only wished that were true.

'I'm going home tomorrow.' Amber twirled the straw in her

mocktail round and round the glass as she stared out ahead of her. The sun was just beginning to set behind the island of La Gomera way out in the distance, the sky a myriad of colours as it got ready to welcome darkness in. They were at Ryan's favourite harbour side restaurant, the perfect setting in which to spend a relaxing couple of hours, just taking in the view. Except that, despite the idyllic setting, Amber was anything but relaxed.

'Tomorrow?' Ryan looked at her, shocked at how depressed he felt at the thought of her leaving so soon. 'But… you've only been here a few days.'

'If I don't go tomorrow, Ryan, there won't be another flight until Friday, and I don't think I can wait that long. I need to tell people now, do you understand? I need to tell my dad.' She looked out to sea again, taking a moment to let the peace and tranquillity of the setting wash over her. 'I need to tell Jim.'

Ryan sat back in his seat, staring down into his pint of lager. What had he expected? That she'd come here, tell him this news, and then never want to leave his side? Maybe that's what happened in his dreams, but reality was much more of a kick in the teeth.

'I don't want you to go, Amber. Not yet.'

'Yeah, well, I don't want to be in this position, Ryan, but we can't always have what we want, can we?'

He looked at her, but her eyes were looking down, into her drink.

'I'm glad you came tonight. Or did you just come here to tell me you were leaving?'

She looked up, their eyes finally meeting. 'I could have told you that over the phone.'

'So you wanted to see me?'

'I thought another chance to talk about things wouldn't hurt.'

'Things?'

'Don't start, Ryan. You know what I mean. Like you said the other night, circumstances have changed now. Everything's different, and that's what we need to talk about.'

'What hasn't changed are my feelings for you.'

'Ryan, please, can we not talk about this right now?'

'Then what *do* you want to talk about, Amber? Monthly child-care payments? A rota for when I can see my kid? What? Come on, I'm all ears.'

'You can still be so childish at times.'

'And you're not exactly great at playing the grown-up yourself, sweetheart.'

Amber sat back, looking out across at the calm expanse of water in front of them. Darkness was almost upon the island now and out in the distance the lights of Costa Adeje and Playa de las Americas twinkled away, like tiny candles lighting up the shoreline.

'You know, there's almost a part of me that doesn't want to go back,' she said quietly, still staring out ahead of her. 'It's all just beginning to feel real, now that you know.' She turned to face him, her heart beating hard as his eyes met hers.

'So stay. Stay here, with me. You know that's what I want, you and me back together, trying again.'

She shook her head, looking down at the table, fiddling with a stray beer mat because she didn't know what else to do with her hands. 'That's not the way to deal with this, Ryan. I need to go home and face up to what's happened.'

'You got pregnant, Amber. Something you never thought would happen. We should be celebrating.'

'I know I make it sound like the worst thing in the world sometimes, and I don't mean to do that, I really don't, it's just...' She looked back up at him. 'It's just hard. Knowing this baby isn't Jim's. And I've still got to tell him that.'

It was Ryan's turn to look down at the table. 'I know it won't be easy...'

'You have to go back to Newcastle Red Star at some point, Ryan. The baby's due in August, just as the new football season is getting ready to begin, and you'll be back there, back home in the North East... and you'll be a dad. To your manager's ex-wife's baby. Christ, it sounds like something straight off the Jeremy Kyle show.'

Ryan couldn't help smiling, which, in turn, made Amber smile, too.

'It's not funny, Ryan. This is people's lives we're affecting here.'

'He doesn't want you, Amber.'

'I know. You don't need to keep reminding me. But it doesn't mean he's just going to shrug his shoulders and be fine about it all.'

'And how do you *think* he'll react?'

'I have no idea,' Amber sighed. 'It's hard to say how Jim'll react to anything. All I know is… it's going to be one of the hardest things I've ever done, telling him this.'

'Telling him about us?'

She looked at him, holding his stare. 'There is no *us*, Ryan.'

'Not yet.'

'You're so sure of yourself, aren't you?'

'I believe in fate, Amber.'

'Really?' she asked, raising that sceptical eyebrow again.

'Really. I believe that everything that happened before, all that crap, it was meant to happen. We were meant to go through all of that so that by the time we got here, to where we are now, we'd know it was the right thing to do. It was meant to be.'

'Now you're sounding like something straight off the pages of a romance novel.'

He paused for a few seconds, still staring deep into her eyes, making her stomach jump about and her heart hammer even harder against her ribs. 'This. Me and you. It's fate, Amber. This baby, it was never meant to be Jim's…'

She turned away, her eyes filling up with tears she really didn't want to cry. She'd thought she was over all that. 'I'm so tired, Ryan. I just want to feel happy again. And I *should* be happy, I mean, I'm pregnant, aren't I? I'm pregnant.'

'Then let me try and *make* you happy, Amber. Let me try. Give me that chance.'

She looked at him again, and she couldn't help smiling. Her beautiful boy. Maybe she hadn't been able to shut down all those feelings she'd once had for him, but was it wise to bring them back to the surface now? When she really had no idea whether what she was feeling was real, or whether she felt those things simply as a smokescreen to forget that the man she'd loved for so long didn't want her anymore. If he ever really had. 'You make it sound so easy, Ryan.'

'Why can't it be? Why *can't* it be easy? Who's making it difficult? Certainly not me...'

'It isn't that simple.'

'Really?'

She stared at him again. He really was incredibly hot; one handsome, dangerous, unpredictable young man. And she wanted him. She couldn't deny that. She wanted him. But she didn't know why. And if she wanted him only because Jim was pushing her away then that wasn't fair, and she didn't want to do this for all the wrong reasons. She didn't want to hurt him. 'Somewhere, deep inside, I do still love you, Ryan.'

'And I love you, too, you know that...'

'But...'

His expression changed the second she said that one word.

'But I need time. And so do you. We both need time.'

'I don't,' he said, shaking his head, his fingers absentmindedly ripping apart the beer mat Amber had been fiddling with before. 'I don't need time, Amber. I know what I'm getting into.'

'I said those exact same words when I first got involved with you, Ryan. Remember? I know exactly what I'm getting into... but I didn't, did I? Not really. I didn't have a clue.'

'You're making this so much harder than it needs to be.'

It was her turn to shake her head, her dark red waves bouncing over her bare, tanned shoulders. 'No, I'm not, Ryan. I'm just being realistic. What's happened here, me telling you about the baby, that's just the first step in sorting this whole mess out.'

'You keep calling it a mess, Amber. How's it a mess? You're expecting a baby, that isn't a mess.'

'It is when it's under these circumstances, Ryan. Will you please just grow up and think about things? Think about the circumstances. You have to go back to Newcastle Red Star as the father of this baby, and you will have to play for a club managed by my husband. You don't think that's a mess?'

'He doesn't want you.'

'And I don't think he wants me pregnant with your baby either, Ryan, but it's happened.'

'Jesus, what else do I have to do to make you realise how good we could be together?'

'I need time, Ryan. That's all. I just need time.'

He leaned forward, dropping his head into his hands.

'I'm sorry,' Amber whispered, reaching over the table to take his hand, her fingers closing around his, stroking them gently. Just the touch of him made her skin tingle and her heart race, all of it making her slightly breathless.

He looked at her, clinging onto her hand, his eyes full of something Amber couldn't quite place – desperation? No. It wasn't that. It was honesty. There was something there, something inside this man that hadn't been there before, and she couldn't help but feel something in the pit of her stomach that was telling her chances were there to be taken. Life was one, long risk, and maybe now she had to take one. Another one. But could she really trust him again? After everything that had happened? Had he really changed enough to make her feel like it could work this time?

'I'm not over Jim,' she said quietly, her eyes watching her thumb as it stroked the back of his wrist. 'And I don't know if I ever will be. And that isn't fair on you, Ryan.' She looked at him. 'It isn't fair.'

'I can deal with it, Amber. I can.'

'Baby, this isn't a game. This is real. And it isn't just you and me and Jim anymore. There's a baby to consider now, and they don't deserve to be dragged into all this. They're going to need stability.'

'And I can give them that. I can give you *both* that, believe me. I'll work so hard to make sure...'

She leaned forward, kissing him gently, stopping him from saying anything else. She didn't want to hear it, didn't want to have to think about it anymore. Not yet. It was far too early to be jumping into new relationships and playing happy families with a man she still didn't know if she could trust – no matter how much he seemed to have changed. And he did seem different. He *had* grown up. But was that enough?

'Take me home, and take me to bed.' She smiled, pulling away from him slightly. 'We can't sort this out tonight, and I think we've done all the talking we can do for now, don't you?'

He smiled, too, running his fingers lightly up and down her forearm. 'You sure?'

'I'm sure. I'm going home tomorrow, and I don't know when I'm going to see you again, so… I kind of like the way you say goodbye.'

He didn't need to be asked twice.

The windows were open, a light, cool breeze blowing in from the sea, and Amber stretched out on Ryan's huge bed, sighing contentedly as that breeze washed over her naked body.

Maybe it was wrong, to be here, about to do what they were going to do, but she needed him. Ryan. Spending this time with him, being here, in this warm and heavenly atmosphere, it felt good. Because it was a million miles away from the reality that awaited her back home. So, no, it wasn't wrong to make the most of that escape. That's what she kept telling herself, anyway.

'Do that again.'

She opened her eyes, smiling as she saw him standing there, naked and beautiful, hard, hot and sexy as hell with that tanned skin, those tattoos that never failed to turn her on, and that grin that had made her fall in love with him in the first place. Was it possible he could do it again? Or were her feelings for Jim so far engrained into her soul that she could never really let herself love another man the way she loved him?

'Do what again?' she asked, trying to push all thoughts of Jim to the back of her mind. That was tomorrow's mess, and she'd deal with it then. Tonight, well – tonight she still had some time left to play.

'The way you stretch, pushing those incredible tits right out… I could look at you forever.'

'Well, you wouldn't get much training done if you did that, would you?'

He grinned, lying next to her, running his fingers lightly over her stomach. 'I can't believe there's a baby in there. Our baby.'

'I'm sure he or she will make themselves known soon enough,' Amber sighed, closing her eyes as his fingers dipped lower, his lips kissing her shoulder as a million mixed emotions played kick-about in her head. He felt so good, but he wasn't Jim. He wanted her, but he wasn't Jim. She needed him, but she wanted Jim. 'Make love to me, Ryan. Now. Please.'

'What's the hurry?' he whispered, gently pushing her legs apart with his hand, eliciting a small moan from her as he touched her down there, resting his hand against her. 'You're not ready yet.'

'Then make me ready.' She smiled, arching her back and pushing down on his hand, rubbing herself against it, closing her eyes again as he pressed harder.

'I think you're doing a pretty good job on your own,' he groaned, sinking his fingers into a warm, wet piece of heaven, his own erection telling him this wasn't going to be a long, drawn-out game this time. She wanted him inside her, and that's exactly where he was going.

Moving so he was lying over her, he placed his hands on her knees and pushed her legs farther apart, taking a second to look at where he was going, which did nothing to ease his throbbing hard-on, the anticipation almost killing him. All those women he could have had; a never-ending stream of beautiful, sexy girls all wanting him so much, willing to give him anything he wanted – anything. And yet now – especially now – all he wanted was Amber.

Kneeling up between her legs, he took one last look at her, at the open invitation she was giving him, before he pushed inside her; carefully, gently, taking his time. He wanted to make every second count, every touch last as long as it could, because once she was back home, he couldn't predict what was going to happen next. He didn't know what Jim was going to say or how he was going to react. So he wanted this night to last as long as it could. He wanted to make the most of her while she was there. Because he didn't know when he'd be with her again, like this. Or even if he ever would be. He didn't know.

Closing his eyes, he leaned forward, falling deeper into her, his hands holding onto her hips as his mouth brushed over her breasts, his tongue flicking over her hot, hard nipples, the small, quiet moans that escaped from her slightly parted lips causing his stomach to flip over and over, his heart beating like crazy inside him. Because *he* was inside *her.* His favourite place.

'Okay?' he whispered, his hands moving up to join with hers either side of her head, their fingers entwining as he pushed a little deeper, her legs wrapping themselves around him, accepting him fully.

She nodded, gripping his fingers tight, biting down on her lip as her back arched and her hips bucked up. Feeling him there, a part of her, knowing what they'd made together, it gave her a feeling of something she'd tried not to feel before, something she'd dared not feel – hope. Hope that something could be salvaged from what she still considered to be one big mess. Hope that she could do the right thing by this baby and make sure it got the love and security it needed, because she came second now. She wasn't the most important person in this scenario. Her, Jim, Ryan, even Ronnie – none of them mattered, *she* didn't matter. But this baby did. She owed her tiny miracle the chance of having a life that made them feel safe. She owed them a life with their father. Didn't she?

As she began to feel those familiar pins and needles creep up her body, that tingling between her legs start to intensify, she pushed everything else to the back of her mind as she clung onto this man inside of her. She wanted to feel every heart-breaking, confusing second of what he was about to give her, and as a white-hot pain shot through her, filling her with a beautiful, burning sensation that wiped everything else clean out of her mind, she cried out his name, her fingers tightening around his as he gave that one, last, final thrust. She felt him come, felt him give himself completely to her, and as the last of those wonderfully prickly tingles eased off, she felt him relax, his body falling gently onto hers, his head buried in her shoulder as he tried to catch his breath.

She ran her fingers through his dark hair, the roughness of his stubble tickling her skin, but she loved it – loved lying there with him, remembering the days when this was unheard of in Ryan Fisher's world. The days when they'd have sex and he'd be up and out of bed before she'd had time to blink. And she smiled as she remembered the morning all that had changed – when he'd stayed with her, beside her, his hand slipping into hers. Was that the day she'd fallen in love with this man? Had she *ever* fallen in love with this man? She'd felt something, she knew that much. And she was feeling it again, despite Jim. Despite everything.

Closing her eyes, she felt him leave her body, rolling over beside her, propping himself up on one elbow. 'Stay with me,' he whispered, letting his fingers trail lazily over her breasts, which were still rising and falling quite heavily, the recent exertion not yet giving way to steady breathing. 'Tonight. Stay with me.'

She turned her head to smile at him, reaching out to gently touch his cheek. Those stomach flips she was feeling, were they just because her hormones were all over the place right now? Because she was confused and cocooned in this perfect little world, so far away from reality? A reality that still waited for her back home, and it was only a matter of hours away now. 'I've got an early flight, Ryan. I really do need to go back to my hotel, or Max is going to come looking for me.'

'Not Ronnie?' Ryan asked, knowing that the second she was

back in her best friend's company he was going to try and talk her out of anything she might be considering, if it included him.

'I don't have to go just yet,' she said, ignoring his intentional dig at Ronnie. 'Unless you want me to.'

'Jesus, Amber, come on. I don't want you to go at all, I…' He stopped talking. Was there any point in telling her what he wanted? She already knew. It was up to her now. The ball was very much in her court. 'I don't want you to go.'

'Good.' She smiled, turning onto her side to face him, kissing him slowly, burying her fingers in his hair as he pulled her against him. 'Because I'm not ready to go anywhere yet.'

Maybe she never would be. Only time would tell.

Chapter Thirty-Two

Jim opened the door, not missing the way her eyes had dipped down the second she'd seen him. She looked beautiful, with her lightly tanned skin and that crazy red hair falling over her shoulders.

'Can I come in?' she asked, her eyes finally meeting his. 'It's freezing out here.'

'Oh God, sorry, yes. Yes.' He stood aside to let her through, closing the door behind her, shutting out the sub-zero February temperatures. 'I forgot you've been used to the more tropical temperatures of Tenerife lately.'

Amber looked at him, as usual unable to read his expression. 'Hardly tropical, Jim. But warmer than north-east England, that's for sure.'

'Go on through to the living room,' he said, forgetting, for a second, that this had once been her home. And not all that long ago. Now he was acting as though she was some stranger who wasn't familiar with the place. 'I'm sorry. You know where it is.'

Amber looked at him again, frowning slightly before leading the way into the living room. 'You haven't redecorated, then?'

'Why would I?' Jim asked, slightly confused by that comment.

She turned to face him, her hands in the pockets of her black, three-quarter-length winter coat. 'Well, you seem to want to erase anything that alludes to us ever being together.'

'That's not what I'm trying to do, Amber.'

'It's what it feels like, sometimes.' She was finding it quite hard to look at him, and not just because of what it was she'd come here to tell him. He was still that man who'd been in her life since she was a teenager. The man who'd taken her youth, invaded her world and refused to disappear. Even when he wasn't around he was still there, under her skin, ever-present – whether she wanted him there or not. But she usually did. For over twenty years she had.

'Then I'm sorry,' Jim said, turning his head away for a second, focusing on the view of the cold, grey North Sea over the road, the wind whipping up white-tipped waves that made it seem almost sinister. Threatening, even. 'I never meant it to feel that way.'

'How did we get to this?' Amber asked, her voice quiet, her hands burrowing deeper into her pockets.

He turned to face her. 'I don't know.'

'But we can't ever go back, can we?' Back to what, though? Back to a relationship that had always been confusing and never felt safe? Is that how she really wanted to spend the rest of her life? Always wondering whether, this time, it really was for keeps, or whether she was going to lose him again. Just like she always seemed to do. But this time – this time it was partly her fault.

'I don't know,' he whispered, his eyes fixed on hers now. And she knew she had to tell him, sooner rather than later. Standing there and avoiding the subject wasn't going to make it any easier.

She took a deep breath, looking down at the ground for a second before meeting his eyes again. 'Something's happened, Jim.'

He frowned, and she felt her stomach tighten as she got ready to say the words – words she'd dreamed of saying to him, but under very different circumstances.

'I'm…' She couldn't get the words out. It was like someone had pressed mute on some invisible remote control, rendering her speechless. She felt breathless all of a sudden, the nausea that had seemed to disappear when she'd been over in Tenerife returning with a vengeance. 'I'm pregnant.'

Jim looked at her, his expression one of disbelief. 'You… how? I mean, I thought…'

She shrugged, trying desperately to summon up the courage to tell him the most important part. The part that she knew was going to shatter her heart into a million tiny pieces and hurt like hell, but he had to know. 'I guess someone was looking down on me,' she whispered, folding her arms – a defence mechanism? Probably.

'Jesus, Amber… how – how far…?'

'Three months.'

That was when his expression changed, his mind quickly ticking over past events, adding up dates, remembering when…

'It's Ryan's.' There was no other way to tell him a truth she didn't want to believe herself, but no amount of wishing or hoping was going to change anything. 'The baby – it's Ryan's.'

Jim just looked at her, his handsome face now expressionless, and with each second that passed, she felt her heart break even more, the pain becoming almost unbearable.

'I wish… I wish things were different, Jim, I really do. But they're not.' She looked right at him, every single memory she had of this man crashing together inside her head to make one mixed-up, emotional montage of a life she wanted so much but was never going to have. 'They're not.'

'I don't know what to say.' His voice was steady, calm, and Amber didn't know whether to feel relieved that he was taking it so well, or nervous that this was nothing but a calm before a storm that had yet to hit. 'That's why you went out to Tenerife?'

She nodded, folding her arms tighter against her. 'He had to know.'

'And how did he take it?'

His tone was almost business-like now, something which saddened Amber but didn't really surprise her. She'd just hoped he'd have been more – more, what? Receptive? Interested? Who was *she* kidding? She'd just told him she was expecting a baby by one of his players, how did she expect him to react?

'He's okay about it. He's fine. I mean, it was a shock, but… but I think he's getting used to the idea.'

Jim said nothing, turning away from her and walking over to the French doors at the back of the large living room, staring out into the garden. 'The baby'll be here in August.' He turned to face her again. 'Am I right?'

She nodded, unable to relax her arms. She knew she'd feel too vulnerable if she let them fall.

'Just as the new season is about to start,' Jim went on, looking back outside. 'And by that time Ryan will be home, back at Newcastle Red Star.' He turned round again, his hands in his pockets, his expression still one she couldn't read. He was a man who was too good at hiding how he really felt, and that confused her. Did he really care so little about what was happening here? '*If* he comes back to Newcastle Red Star.'

Amber looked up sharply, her eyes narrowing as she stared at her estranged husband. 'What do you mean, *if* he comes back?'

'You're having his baby, Amber. How does that look, huh?'

'I don't…'

'How does that make *me* look? Did you think about that when you were fucking him behind my back?'

'I didn't… I couldn't… Shit!' She finally uncrossed her arms, pushing both hands through her hair. 'I didn't plan any of this, Jim. I didn't plan for you to keep yet more secrets from me, I didn't plan for me to be told I might never be a mum; I didn't plan to handle it all so fucking badly. But the one thing I certainly didn't plan on was getting pregnant. I had no idea there was even the slightest possibility that that could happen, and I'm sorry, I really am, because if I could turn back time then I would change it all. Everything. I'd even miss out on having this baby if it meant I could be with you, do you understand? Do you understand how much I still love you, how I would do anything to change this situation? Have you any idea how heart-breaking this all is? How fucking confusing and painful it is?'

'That doesn't change the fact that when this comes out, I'm the one who's going to look like they've been humiliated...'

'Is that all you care about? Your reputation?'

'It's very important to me, Amber. In this business I need that respect.'

'You can't control his life, Jim.'

'He crossed a line, Amber.'

'We *both* crossed that line. He didn't do this alone.'

'How's it going to look to the rest of the players? He swans back into the dressing room after a few months abroad, a father to my wife's baby? Think about it, Amber.'

'I've done nothing but, Jim. Believe me.'

He turned away again, staring back outside, his head spinning with news he'd never expected to hear. And once again he was faced with a situation he wasn't sure he could control.

'Don't play with his life, Jim. Please. Not now.'

'You almost sound like you care about him?'

'I *do* care about him.'

He swung round to look at her. 'Are you and him...?'

She shook her head, folding her arms again, re-erecting those barriers between them. 'Everything's so confusing right now. I don't know what to do.'

'Are you even considering it?'

'Jim, please. I don't know, okay? I don't know anything. All I know is that I need to concentrate on this baby, and everything else I'll deal with later.'

'Are you all right? I mean, you've seen a doctor...?'

'Dr. Lowry's looking after me. Everything's fine. I've got my twelve-week scan next week and...' She stopped talking. He didn't need to know that. 'It's fine. I'm fine, the baby's fine.'

'Have you told Freddie?'

She looked away for a second, remembering her dad's reaction when she'd broken the news to him that morning, less than an hour and a half after arriving home from Tenerife. To say he wasn't best pleased was an understatement. Of course he was over the moon that Amber was pregnant, that wasn't the issue. It was the circumstances in which it had happened that were the problem. All Freddie Sullivan wanted for his daughter was for her to be happy, and he wasn't entirely sure that she was as happy as she should be, despite Amber trying to convince him otherwise.

'I feel as though I'm continually disappointing him,' she said quietly.

'Freddie loves you, Amber. And he knows how much you wanted this baby.'

'I wanted *your* baby, Jim.' Once again she quickly realised how selfish that made her sound and she sighed, pushing her hands through her hair again. 'I wanted this to be *our* dream.'

He looked at her. For so long she'd been all he'd wanted, but he'd never really deserved her. He'd treated her so badly over the years and still she'd come back to him, whenever he wanted her. Until now. Now he felt as though he'd lost control and that's why things had to be the way they were. He had his reasons, and now those reasons were more important than ever.

'Maybe it's for the best, Amber.'

She looked at him. 'For the…?'

'That this baby isn't mine. Given the way things are between us at the minute. Maybe it's best Ryan's the father.'

Her expression must have conveyed nothing but pure confusion as she continued to stare at him, because that's how she felt. Confused. 'I… what… what do you mean?'

'Well, we're not together, are we?'

'Brandon's turned out okay, and you weren't exactly a 24/7 kind of father to him, were you?'

'The baby isn't mine, Amber. And I'm relieved about that.'

'Relieved?' The coldness in his voice shocked her to the core. Is that how he really felt? 'Did I ever mean anything to you?' she asked, suddenly wishing she was back in Tenerife. Back with Ryan.

Jim nodded. 'Yes. You did.'

She couldn't help flinching at his use of the past tense, her already shattered heart fragmenting even more as she looked at him. 'I did,' she repeated, walking backwards towards the door. 'The thing is, though, Jim – you still *do*.'

And then she turned and left. Just like that. How could she stay now? What good would it do to stand there and watch her marriage disintegrate right in front of her?

Jim closed his eyes briefly as he heard the door slam shut behind her. He walked over to the bay window, watching as she ran down the path to her car, and that's when he felt it hit; a pain so raw he couldn't hold it in, no matter how much he wanted to. And as he sank to his knees, his head in his hands, loud, howling sobs erupted from his body as he tried to set that pain free. But it hurt, like someone twisting a blunt, rusty knife right into his heart, ramming it home until he couldn't take it anymore. It was like he was in the middle of some surreal, unreal dream; this cruel twist of fate that had finally taken her away from him. She was having the one thing he hadn't been able to give her – a baby. The one thing that could have kept them together because, despite what he'd just told her, if she'd stood there and told him that baby was his, then he would have taken her back in a heartbeat.

He breathed deep, trying to stop the tears from falling as anger and frustration began their climb, taking the place of the tears, filling him with a rage he couldn't control. It was unbearable, knowing how close she was to another man, and as memories of a past before Amber flooded his head, he felt that rage build even further, until he couldn't hold it in any longer.

Pulling himself up off the floor, he replaced the sobs with frustrated cries, slamming his hands down on the sideboard, swiping them through the bottles and glasses that sat there, sending them crashing to the floor. He didn't even feel the pain from the cut on his forearm as a brandy glass sliced through it, blood spilling down over his white shirt, because he didn't care. He wanted to end this frustration, to take it out on things that couldn't fight back, but even as he continued to send pictures and ornaments flying, the sound of glass shattering and china smashing on the hardwood floor echoing round the room, it wasn't making him feel any better. Punching the wall, he felt a sharp pain reverberate up his arm, but still he felt nothing, except that feeling of emptiness, and a fierce frustration that he hadn't been the one to give her the one thing she'd wanted most. The one thing Ryan had given her. Maybe Brandon had been right – in a way he *had* pushed them closer together, and that realisation set off another wave of destruction as he slammed doors, kicked chairs, shouted out every darkest, deepest thing he was feeling as the kitchen became the next target for his own personal cleansing therapy, until he could do no more. Until there was nothing left to destroy.

His head was hurting and his heart was breaking, but he was Jim Allen. He could deal with this. He could deal with it. And he would. Eventually. He'd find a way to ease the pain, and when he did, he wouldn't be the one feeling like this. It wouldn't be him. He'd make sure of that.

'How did he take it?'

'How do you think, Ronnie?'

'Okay. Don't start on me, I was only asking.'

Amber let out a loud sigh that was tinged with more than a hint of frustration. 'He was surprisingly fine, at first, then his whole mood just seemed to change in an instant. He started going on about his reputation, how I'd made him look... then he said something about... about...'

'About what?' Ronnie asked, leaning forward.

'He worked out the baby's due in August, and by that time Ryan will definitely be back at Newcastle Red Star... *if* Ryan comes back to Newcastle Red Star. That's what he said. *If* Ryan comes back.'

Ronnie frowned, clasping his hands together between his knees. 'He can't do that, Amber. He can't make those decisions on a whim.'

'Oh, Jim can do anything he wants, Ronnie. It was down to Jim that Ryan had his emergency loan request granted in the first place, remember? So he can do what he wants. He's got that fucking power.'

'Look, babe, he was probably just saying things in the heat of the moment. You did spring one hell of a shock on him.'

'I could see the look in his eyes, Ronnie. He knew exactly what he was saying.'

'It isn't that simple though, Amber. Jim Allen is not in sole control of what goes on at Newcastle Red Star. He can't just pick and choose who plays for the club and who doesn't.'

Amber sat up and looked at Ronnie, raising an eyebrow. 'You think?'

'Come on, Amber. I'm not denying he isn't a powerful man with just as powerful connections, but it isn't up to him whether Ryan comes back to Newcastle Red Star or not. He has a contract, and if he was to leave Red Star before the end of that contract then the club'll have to pay out a small fortune in release fees – we're talking about a big name player here. And Jim Allen knows that. He's just throwing words about, that's all.'

'I don't know,' Amber sighed. 'You didn't see the look in his eyes.'

'He's bluffing.'

'I hope you're right. The last thing anyone needs is him playing more games… Is that my phone?' She reached into her bag, digging out her phone from the bottom. 'It's Gary.' She frowned as she looked at the caller display. Then her eyes suddenly widened as realisation hit her. 'The baby… Gary? Is Debbie okay? Is something wrong?'

'No, nothing's wrong,' Gary said, his voice carrying an almost excited tone to it. 'I just thought you might like to know that your goddaughter's just arrived. Do you want to come and meet her?'

Amber couldn't stop the smile from spreading across her face as she cradled baby Jodi Cassidy Blandford in her arms, bending over to kiss her tiny forehead.

'She's beautiful, Debbie.'

'Yeah, well, she obviously gets that from my side of the family,' Debbie grinned. Her hair was all over the place, her face devoid of make-up, all very different to the image Amber was so used to seeing Debbie radiate. But she'd never seen her friend look happier.

'So, how was it?' Amber asked, handing the baby back to her mum.

'Fucking painful.' Debbie grimaced, kissing her new daughter gently, smiling down at her as though she was the most precious thing in the world. Which she probably was. 'She wasn't due for another couple of weeks, so it was a bit of a shock when my waters broke right in the middle of me trying to choose a handbag for the end-of-season party, but, thankfully, she didn't want to hang around. It was painful, but she only took a couple of hours to get here, didn't you, poppet? My tiny little surprise.'

'Was Gary with you? For the birth, I mean.'

'They had to drag him out of training, but he got here just in time. Not sure it'll be something he wants to repeat, but he had his uses.'

Amber looked at Debbie, and they both burst out laughing.

'Anyway, chick, you're looking well.'

Amber frowned, because she didn't exactly feel it. 'You think so?'

'The tan suits you. I take it Tenerife was hot?'

In more ways than one, at times, Amber thought. 'Not bad, for the time of year.'

'And Ryan?' Debbie asked, with a tone to her voice that told Amber she wanted to know everything. But Amber reckoned even Debbie wasn't ready to hear just what it was she had yet to tell her. 'You know the rumours about why you went over there are rife, don't you? Everyone thinks you and him are rekindling your relationship now you and Jim…' Debbie stopped talking the second she noticed Amber's expression change. 'Oh, chick, I'm sorry. I didn't mean to…'

'The rumours aren't exactly true, Debbie.'

It was Debbie's turn to frown. 'What do you mean, aren't *exactly* true?'

Amber sighed. She was going to have to tell her at some point. She was going to have to tell everyone. It wasn't something she could hide forever. 'Debbie, you're not gonna believe this, but… I'm pregnant.'

Debbie let out the beginnings of what would have been a huge squeal, but she stopped herself for fear of terrifying her two-hour-old child. 'You're *what*? Christ, I knew Dr. Lowry was pretty good at his job but I didn't have him down as a miracle worker.'

'It was a surprise, I'll give you that.'

Debbie looked at Amber, cradling her daughter close to her chest. 'You don't exactly look ecstatic, hon. Is everything okay?'

Amber stared down at her hands as she fiddled with the cuff of her shirt. 'Physically, I'm fine. The baby's fine, I've got a scan next week and…'

'And, what? Amber, chick, what is it? What's wrong?'

Amber looked at Debbie, more than aware that she was slowly putting the pieces of the jigsaw together all by herself.

'Hang on… your trip to Tenerife…'

'The baby's Ryan's.' Amber saved her the job of stating what was fast becoming obvious to everyone close to her. 'I'm almost three months gone, which means the date of conception could only have been around the time of Gary's birthday party.'

'The night Ryan stayed over in your room…' Debbie said, reaching out for Amber's hand. 'Your wedding ring. You've taken it off.'

'Ryan took it off for me. When I was over in Tenerife.'

'Amber… oh, babe, I don't know what to say. Should I be happy for you? You look so sad…'

'Oh, God, yes. Be pleased for me – I *am* happy, really. I am. I think I'm still just a bit in shock, that's all. And I wish with all of my heart that things could have been different, but they're not.

And now I've just got to deal with it.'

'Have you told Jim?'

Amber nodded, smiling as baby Jodi made the cutest gurgling sound, stretching her tiny arms out. 'That was… that was hard.'

'How did he take it?'

Amber shrugged. 'It's hard to say, Debs. You know how he is. He appears calm, emotionless, almost, on the surface, but I know him. He deals with things in a way others don't normally do.'

Debbie frowned again. 'What do you mean?'

'Oh, I don't know. He said things about… about how humiliating this could all be for him, about how this could damage his reputation. He mentioned something about Ryan's return to Newcastle Red Star – *if* he returns to Newcastle Red Star. That's what he said.'

'Jim said that?' Debbie gasped, her eyes wide.

'Ronnie says he's just bluffing, that he's throwing threats around that don't mean anything, but I'm not so sure, Debbie. Like I said, I know Jim. I know what he's capable of.'

'Oh, sweetheart. I'm sure it's just his way of getting his head around something that's come completely out of left field.'

'Maybe,' Amber sighed, reaching out to Jodi, who grabbed her finger, wrapping her tiny hand around it. 'I just wish the news had been different, that's all.'

'And… and you know it's definitely Ryan's, do you?'

Amber nodded. 'There's absolutely no doubt, Debs. None.'

Debbie let out a low whistle, lying back against the pillows of her hospital bed. 'Okay. Well, I have to admit, this is pretty big news, chick. So how did the daddy-to-be take it?'

'Shocked, at first. Like you'd expect. But then he starts going to the other extreme, talking about getting back together, being a family… and I can't think about all of that just yet, not when I'm still trying to get my head around everything.'

'So you only went over there to tell him about the baby?'

'He deserved to find out news like that in person. It was the least I could do, only now… now I'm kind of regretting it because all it's done is start the rumour mill working overtime again. And Ronnie did warn me.'

'Listen, chick, I know how much you wanted this baby…'

'I wanted Jim's baby, Debbie. I wanted Jim's baby.'

'Hey, come on. Don't start crying, okay? I'm an emotional wreck myself right now. Have you any idea how much this whole process fucks with your hormones?'

'I guess I'm going to find out, aren't I?'

Debbie smiled, squeezing her hand. 'Yeah. You are. Look, things might not have worked out quite the way you wanted them to, in an ideal world, but… you and Jim…'

'It's over,' Amber whispered, looking over at the door as Gary walked in. He looked tired, dishevelled, but incredibly happy.

'Definitely?' Debbie asked, letting go of Amber's hand as baby Jodi started to grizzle.

'Definitely.' Amber took a deep breath, because saying that word gave everything she still wanted so much an air of finality she really didn't want to have to face. 'So now I've just got to move on and make the best of the situation, for this baby's sake.'

'Hey, you're gonna be a mum now, chick. Remember that. Even if that kid *is* gonna have Ryan Fisher for a father.'

Gary sat down on the edge of the bed, immediately taking his daughter from Debbie, cuddling her close. It was a sight Amber had never thought she'd see, but it was a sight that gave her some hope for the unexpected future that had suddenly been thrust upon her.

'Sorry, have I missed something here?' Gary frowned, his expression more than a touch confused. 'Amber's gonna be a mum? How? I mean…?'

'I'll explain later, babe,' Debbie said, running her fingers through her hair. 'Ugh. I so need to wash this!'

'Yeah, okay, but… did you just say Ryan's the father?'

'I said, I'd explain it all later,' Debbie sighed, reaching over to the bedside table to retrieve her make-up bag, which made Amber smile. She'd had a feeling it wouldn't be long before the old Debbie returned. Motherhood wasn't going to change her *that* much.

'No, hang on. Amber, is that true? You're pregnant? And Ryan's the dad?'

Amber looked at Gary, and for the first time since she'd heard the news herself she felt a glimmer of happiness start to push its way through the confusion. A miracle had happened, despite the one flaw she couldn't change. But if that was the price she had to pay in order for her dream to come true, then she'd pay it. She had no choice.

'Yeah, it's true. Who the hell would have thought, huh?'

Chapter Thirty-Three

'You okay, Dad?' Brandon stood in his father's office, arms folded as he leaned back against the wall, watching Jim at work.

'I'm fine, Brandon.' He threw down his pen and looked at his son. 'Look, it's for the best, okay? I can't say I'm happy at the way things have turned out, because I'm far from that, believe me. But I can't change it, can I? Not all of it, anyway.'

Brandon narrowed his eyes as Jim turned back to his laptop. 'What do you mean, not all of it?'

'Nothing, Brandon. I didn't mean anything.'

Brandon wasn't so sure, but he'd quickly learned not to question his dad on certain things, and his relationship with Amber was one of them.

'You finished training early today,' Jim commented, without looking up from his laptop.

'We're flying down to London later for the match on Sunday.'

'You're on TV.' It wasn't a question. Why would it be? Jim knew full well his son's match against one of the big London clubs was being televised Sunday teatime. Red Star's home game against West Midlands club Langdon Rovers was also being televised on Saturday afternoon. And it was a big game, an important one for Newcastle Red Star – if they won the match, taking all three points, then it would give them an extremely high chance of regaining the league title. Something Jim was determined to do. If he could prove to everyone that Newcastle Red Star didn't need Ryan Fisher, then his life would be a whole lot easier.

'Yeah. We're on TV. Dad...'

Jim looked up at him, sliding his reading glasses down onto the end of his nose.

'What's happened with Amber...?' So much for his not pushing the subject. Sometimes he just couldn't help himself.

'I don't want to talk about it, Brandon.' Jim dismissed the subject immediately, turning away, back to whatever it was he'd been doing before.

'But you're acting like it doesn't matter, Dad. And I think it does. I mean, does it *really* have to spell the end for you and Amber? Couldn't you just...'

'That's enough, Brandon. Do you hear me?' Jim looked straight at his son, his expression stern and deadly serious. 'There are things you don't understand...' He let the words trail off, not wanting to get into this conversation. It was nobody else's business.

'Then explain them to me.'

'There are things you don't understand. Things that happened, things that... It's over, Brandon. What Amber and I had, it's over. It has to be.'

'Yeah, you keep saying that, but I don't get it.'

'You don't need to, because it's got nothing to do with you. It's got nothing to do with anyone.' Jim fixed him with another serious look. 'So drop it. Right now.'

'Do you love her?'

'We've already been over this, Brandon, so just drop it, okay?'

Brandon sighed, pushing both hands through his hair. 'I'm outta here.'

'Good. I've got work to do.'

'You're burying your head in the sand, Dad. So she's having Ryan Fisher's baby...'

Jim looked up sharply, his eyes narrow, his expression hard.

'Can you leave now, Brandon? Please.'

'If you love someone, Dad; if you really, truly love someone, then you can get over anything. That's what Mom always says, and I believe that. I believe that if you really can't live without that person, no matter what they've done, there isn't anything that can't be resolved. Don't you believe that, too?'

Jim said nothing, he just turned away, instantly dismissing Brandon's question.

'Jesus, Dad!' But it was pointless trying to get through to him, that was becoming increasingly obvious. If Jim didn't want to help himself be happy, then why should *he* bust his balls trying to get through to him? He'd leave him to it.

'You okay?'

Brandon turned round as he closed the door of Jim's office behind him, a smile forming on his face the second he saw her. 'I am now I've seen you.'

She returned his smile, leaning back against the wall, clutching the pile of files she was holding against her chest. 'I've got my lunch break in ten minutes. You busy?'

Brandon grinned, moving a couple of steps closer to her, reaching out to gently tuck a strand of hair behind her ear. 'Not at the moment, no. Is that an invitation?'

'An invitation? You need an invite now? I thought we were past all that.'

He leaned forward, kissing her gently, sliding an arm around her slim waist, pulling her against him. 'Oh, I think we are, don't you? It's just that, I'm a nice guy. And I don't want to sound too – pushy.'

'You can be as pushy as you like,' she breathed, looking up into his dark eyes. He had to be the most incredibly handsome man she'd ever laid eyes on. Even sexier than Ryan Fisher, and that was saying something, because he could get her hot just by looking at her. Until he'd turned into the biggest bastard there was. He didn't deserve her, but she'd still drop everything if he told her he wanted her back. She'd still go running. 'And if you come back to my flat for lunch, you can push me until I cry out loud.'

'Jesus, baby, what are you trying to do to me?'

'I'm trying to convince you that a naked lunch is the best kind.'

He grinned again. 'I don't need all that much convincing.'

'You're coming, then?'

'Not yet,' he whispered, moving his mouth close to hers until they were almost touching. 'But I sure plan to. I'll wait for you outside.'

She smiled, hugging her files closer to her chest as she watched him walk down the corridor. He had a swagger to him that was gaining him one hell of a fan club amongst female football fans, and he was hers. For now. He was all hers. She'd made sure of that. She might not have Ryan Fisher anymore, but she had the next best thing.

'Ms. Taylor… Is there something I can do for you?' Jim asked, coming out of his office and standing in the doorway, his hands in his pockets, his expression cold.

Ellen shivered. She hoped Brandon wouldn't turn out to be like his father, although, in the looks department she wouldn't complain. For an older man Jim Allen was still sexy as hell, in a George Clooney kind of way.

'No. I'm sorry, Mr. Allen, I was just… I was just on my way over to the admin block.'

'Well, I'm sure they'll be wondering where you are.'

She nodded, making her way down the corridor as fast as her four-inch heels would carry her.

'Oh, and Ellen?'

She stopped, turning round to face Jim.

'You be careful with my boy. He's very precious to me.'

She waited until he was back inside his office before she continued her escape back into the main reception area. Of course she was going to be careful with Brandon. He was very precious to her, too. She didn't hurt people. Unlike Ryan. She didn't hurt people. And, when the time came, she was going to try very hard not to hurt Brandon.

Jim closed the office door behind him and leaned back against it, closing his eyes and breathing in deep. Ever since news of Amber's pregnancy had hit the headlines he'd slowly felt as though, as each day went by, he was losing more and more control. And it wasn't a feeling he liked. It didn't make him feel comfortable. But he was dealing with it. In his own way.

The one thing it *had* done was bring him and Freddie Sullivan closer again. Their shared mistrust of Ryan Fisher had become the main topic of conversation between them over the past few days, and it had made Jim realise how much he'd missed his one-time best friend. Jim Allen didn't have many friends, he didn't like to get too close to people in case – well, he just didn't. It wasn't his style to let emotions take over. He'd let that happen with Amber and look at the outcome. So it was best to steer clear of all that now. Even if it wasn't the easiest thing to do when Amber's face was everywhere, stories of her and Ryan's rumoured romance in every paper he picked up.

Walking over to the sideboard, he poured himself a large whisky. It had only just gone midday but he needed it. He needed to get his head straight. His beautiful wife was having another man's baby. That still cut through him like the sharpest of knives, slicing away at his heart in the cruellest of ways. It wasn't something he was dealing with all that easily, even though the image he gave off to the public was one of a man completely in control and getting on with his life.

But he knew that if this baby had been anyone else's – if it had been Ronnie White's – he could have dealt with that way better than he was dealing with this. But Amber was carrying Ryan Fisher's baby. And that was a whole different ballgame.

His phone ringing pulled him back from the brink of darker thoughts, and he walked over to his desk, sitting on the edge of it as he answered the call.

'Jim Allen?' He sipped his whisky and listened as the voice on the other end spoke. 'And you're sure about that?' He took another sip of whisky, a smile slowly starting to creep across his face as he listened. 'Okay. Thanks. I'll be in touch.'

Placing the receiver back down on his desk, he finished his whisky, clutching the empty glass tight in his fist, that smile still there. Because his day had suddenly just got a whole lot better…

Chapter Thirty-Four

'It's rumours, Ronnie. That's all.'

'You sure?' Ronnie asked, pulling into a car parking space at Tynebridge.

'Of course I'm sure. I haven't seen Ryan since we were in Tenerife, and that was weeks ago, so how could we possibly have had a chance to *"rekindle our relationship"* as the press are so nicely putting it?'

'There's such a thing as the telephone now, you know. And the internet. Have you heard of email, or Skype?'

'Yeah, you're funny,' Amber said dryly, climbing out of the car and slamming the door shut behind her. 'There's nothing going on, okay?'

'You've spoken to him though, surely. To let him know about the scans.'

Amber nodded, walking alongside Ronnie as they climbed the steps up to the main entrance, the sound of a match-day crowd already filling the air. 'I've emailed him photos. There's no reason why he shouldn't be as much a part of all this as he possibly can, even if he *is* thousands of miles away.'

'And are you doing all of this because you think it's what you *should* be doing? Or is it because you *want* him to be a part of it all?'

'He's the father, Ronnie.'

'That's not answering my question.'

'You're digging for information, and I don't have any to give you. I'm only doing what anyone else would do under the same circumstances.'

'I doubt anyone's circumstances are anything like yours, kiddo.'

'You're not helping, do you know that?'

'Sorry.' Ronnie grinned, kissing her quickly on the cheek as they stepped inside the huge and airy entrance to Tynebridge. 'I'm off to ring the guys back in the studio, see what's happening back at base.'

They were there to report on the televised game between Newcastle Red Star and Langdon Rovers, or rather, Ronnie was. Amber was having a weekend off for hospital appointments, and to come home and see her dad. Their relationship was slowly getting back to some sort of normality, and Amber was glad of that, because she needed Freddie. He was the only real family she had, and she missed her dad, more than anybody, since she'd started to spend more time down in London.

'Amber!'

Amber swung round to see Debbie standing there waving wildly at her, her new hair extensions immaculate, her make-up perfect, and her heels just as high as they had been pre-pregnancy.

'You look amazing!' Amber smiled, walking over to her friend, enveloping her in a huge hug.

'I should do,' Debbie said, flicking her hair back over her shoulder. 'All this cost me a small fortune. Gary thinks it was well worth all the money, though.'

'Yeah, well, I have to agree with him,' Amber laughed. 'You really do look incredible. But where's Jodi?'

'My mum's got her. She just adores her new granddaughter, even if the idea of being called Nana isn't one she's particularly happy with. She still thinks she's far too young to be a grandma, but one day she'll wake up and realise you can only keep knocking years off your age for so long. People are already starting to question the fact it would appear she had me when she was nine.'

Amber smiled again, absentmindedly placing a hand on her slightly swollen stomach. At four months pregnant she had the tiniest hint of a baby bump, and she was growing to love it. In fact, she couldn't wait for it to grow bigger so she could finally start to believe this was really happening.

Debbie looked down at Amber's tummy, not missing the tiny bump just visible beneath Amber's hand as it pressed lightly against her dress. 'Oh, hello, baby! Finally starting to make an appearance I see.'

'Just.' Amber smiled, something she couldn't really seem to stop doing lately – smiling. Despite everything she was still feeling. Despite the nights she still cried herself to sleep, and those quiet hours when she had far too much time to think. Those hours when she'd still allow herself to briefly imagine what all this would have been like if the baby had been Jim's. But she really was trying to do that less and less. For the good of the baby. She really was trying to move forward, even if being around Jim still hurt with a pain she sometimes found unable to bear.

'Do you know the sex yet?' Debbie asked, wide-eyed and hopeful.

Amber looked down at her hand on her tummy, the smile still there on her face.

'Amber? Come on, chick! Do you know what you're having?'

Amber looked up, nodding. And then her smile grew even wider as she realised she had to tell someone, even if she *had* been trying to hang on until this evening, when she was going to call Ryan to tell him the news. But she was too excited to keep it all to herself.

'Well?' Debbie persisted, gripping Amber's hand tight.

'It's a boy,' Amber whispered, shushing Debbie immediately as she looked set to screech out loud. 'And don't tell anyone else, do you promise me? I was trying to let Ryan be the first to know, I haven't even told Ronnie yet. But I couldn't keep it to myself any longer.'

'A little Ryan Fisher…' Debbie grinned, linking her arm through

Amber's as they headed off to the Players' Lounge. 'Do you think he'll be happy? That it's a boy?'

'I think we both just want a healthy baby, Debs. But, yeah. I think he'll be over the moon that he's getting a son.'

'And you're still feeling okay? No problems?'

'Dr. Lowry is keeping me under very strict observation, Debbie, believe me. I hate to use the term "older mum", but, like it or not, that's exactly what I am, and given the problems I've had in the past, well… he just wants to keep an eye on me.'

'And so he should. I told you he was an angel, didn't I?'

Amber smiled, squeezing her friend's arm as they both grabbed bottles of water from the bar. 'I'm just grateful you've been through it all before,' Amber sighed, leaning back against the wall as she looked around the room, trying to see if she could spot her dad anywhere. 'I'd be terrified otherwise.'

'It's easy.' Debbie grinned, running her fingers through her platinum blonde hair.

'Not sure that's how I remember you describing it when I saw you straight after Jodi's arrival,' Amber said, giving her friend a sideways smile. 'Oh, look, there's my dad. I'd better go say hello. See you later.'

'Yeah, see you, hon. Tell Freddie I said hi!'

Amber pushed her way through the growing crowd of people gathered in the Players' Lounge before finally reaching her father.

'Hey, kiddo.' Freddie Sullivan smiled at his daughter, slipping an arm around her waist and pulling her in for a hug. 'You look well. You been to see Dr. Lowry today?'

Amber nodded, kissing her father's cheek. 'This morning.'

'And? Is everything all right with my grandchild?'

'He's fine…' She stopped talking, wincing slightly as she realised what she'd just said.

Freddie's smile turned into a grin and Amber knew she might as well just tell him, too. It was pointless trying to hide it now. 'I'm getting a grandson?'

'You're getting a grandson. But don't go shouting about it, okay? I've only told Debbie, and I shouldn't even have told her, not before I told Ryan. It doesn't seem fair that he isn't the first to know the sex of his own child.'

Freddie just gave a derisory snort. 'Well, you know my feelings on Ryan Fisher. Still, if this baby inherits just half of his errant father's talent, he could be one very special little boy. It's what else he inherits from him that concerns me.'

'I really wish you'd give him a chance, Dad. I honestly believe he's changed from what he used to be. He's curbed that playboy image, tried so hard to put all that shit behind him, and since he heard about the baby... It could be just what he needs, you know? This kind of responsibility. This chance to prove he really has grown up.'

'If you're so sure of him, why aren't you willing to give him another chance? Not that I'm condoning you doing that, in fact, I'd really rather you didn't. But you seem so certain he's changed...'

Amber's focus was suddenly distracted by the door opening and Jim appearing, which was strange in itself. Most managers, and especially Jim, very rarely showed their faces in the Players' Lounge before a game. But just the sight of him was enough to make her heart race and her stomach sink, all at the same time. Her handsome soon-to-be-ex-husband.

'Are you two okay?' Freddie asked, squeezing his daughter's waist.

'We're on speaking terms, if that's what you mean. But only in passing. We've got to try and keep a professional relationship going, to some extent, given our jobs. But I think you talk to him more than I do these days. And how ironic is that, huh?'

'Hey, come on. Who said life was going to be an easy ride?'

Amber looked at her dad, so happy they were finally getting back on track. 'It still hurts, Dad. I know you never really approved of my relationship with Jim, but... I don't think anyone will ever understand how I really feel about him. Not even me.'

Freddie gently kissed her forehead, pulling her in for another hug. 'I know, sweetheart. But you've just got to try and move on. Easier said than done, I know, but you've got that little one to think of now, so maybe you should concentrate on doing what's best for him. Okay? And you know I'll always be here for you.' He kissed her forehead again, hugging her tighter. 'Always.'

Amber smiled, snuggling into her dad, placing a hand on her stomach again as a slight commotion over by the door to the lounge struck up. She looked over, craning her neck to see what was going on, finally catching a glimpse of just what was causing all the fuss. Or that should be, *who* was causing all the fuss.

'What's *he* doing back?' Freddie asked, his grip on his daughter's waist tightening slightly.

'I don't know,' Amber said quietly, confusion now joining the mixture of emotions that were slowly gathering inside her head.

'Well, he's with Jim, so…' Freddie stopped talking and looked at Amber, but her eyes were fixed firmly on the group of people at the door. 'You didn't know he'd be here?'

She shook her head. 'As far as I was aware he wasn't due back for another month or so. Maybe he's just over for a visit.' But Amber didn't think that was really the case. There were far too many people with him, too much attention and fuss being generated for this to be just a quick trip home.

'I'll go have a word with Jim. Find out what's happening. You gonna be okay?'

She smiled at her father. 'I'm thirty-eight, Dad.'

'You'll always be my little girl, Amber, and right now you need looking after. Why you and Ronnie couldn't…'

'Go and speak to Jim, Dad. Go on.'

She watched him head over to the group gathered by the doorway before finally catching sight of Max. If anyone knew what was going on he would, because he'd probably orchestrated it.

'You all right, kiddo?' Max smiled, walking over to her and leaning in to kiss her cheek.

'I'm fine. And I'm pregnant, not ill. What's *he* doing back here? Because the fact he seems to have an entourage with him tells me this isn't just a flying visit.'

'No. It isn't. Hasn't Jim told you?'

'Told me what? And in case you hadn't realised, me and my husband aren't exactly close at the minute.'

'Ryan's back.'

'Back? Back, where?'

'Back at Newcastle Red Star. He was only on a rolling monthly contract, Amber, remember?'

'Yeah, but that contract was still supposed to run until the end of the season, wasn't it?'

Max shrugged. 'Technically, yes.'

'Technically?' Amber frowned.

'Circumstances have changed, Amber.' Max looked briefly down at Amber's stomach. 'Ryan wanted to come home a little earlier than planned, for reasons I'm sure you can understand, and that contract meant it was easier for that to happen. You know how these things work.'

Amber looked back over to where the gathering crowd had thinned out slightly. But she couldn't see Ryan anywhere.

Max followed her gaze. 'Jim's called an emergency pre-match press conference to explain everything. Speaking of which, I'd better get in there.'

'Max…'

'I'll talk to you later, kiddo.'

Amber stood there, rooted to the spot, trying to let the brief details of what Max had told her sink in. Didn't anyone think she'd had a right to know about this before now?

Pushing her way out of the lounge, she headed straight to Jim's office opposite the home team dressing room, barging in without even attempting to knock. He was still talking to Freddie, both of them turning round sharply to see just who it was who'd decided to make such an uninvited entrance.

'It was nice of you to tell me, Jim.'

'I was assuming Ryan would have had the decency to do that,' Jim replied, leaning back against his desk, his hands in his pockets. Freddie walked over to Amber, reaching out to touch her arm but she shook him off, too angry to respond to him any other way. Even though none of this was his fault.

'Amber, sweetheart, I'm sure Jim'll explain everything after the press conference… in fact, why don't you…'

'It's okay, Freddie,' Jim said, not moving from his position at the desk. 'I've got time. I'll talk to her now.'

'You sure?' Freddie asked, finally managing to give Amber's hand a quick squeeze before she pulled it away.

Jim nodded.

'Okay. Well, I'll be outside,' Freddie said, looking at Amber, but her eyes were still very much on Jim.

She waited until her father was back outside before she spoke again. 'Was this Ryan's idea?'

'He wanted to come home, Amber. He wanted to be with you.'

'Why? I mean, it's not like we're even a couple, we're not together…'

'He's the father of your baby. Surely he deserves to be a part of that? Doesn't he?'

She narrowed her eyes as she looked at him. 'None of this makes any sense, Jim. Why would you pull yet more questionable strings to bring him home early? I don't get it.'

'Are you casting aspersions on my integrity?'

'Jesus, Jim, come on! I thought you would have done your utmost to prevent him from having anything his own way. Again. Especially now. I just don't understand…'

'We all need to move on, Amber.'

For some reason, the second he'd said those words she felt a pain akin to someone sliding a sharp blade through her heart, her breath catching in her throat. 'Yeah. I suppose we do.'

'He wanted to come home, so I brought him home. And CD

Adeje were very understanding, under the circumstances. But they're very big on family, aren't they? The Spanish. You more than anyone should know that, Amber. So they completely understood Ryan's reasons for wanting to come back to the U.K.'

'Family…? Jesus… Why didn't you tell me this was happening, Jim?'

'Like I said before, I assumed Ryan would have told you. It's not up to me to keep you informed of his comings and goings anymore, is it? I would have thought, in your line of work, you'd know more than me.'

'You're not being fair,' she whispered, shaking her head. 'This… all of this is confusing enough without you making it any worse.'

Jim said nothing for a few seconds, his eyes looking straight into hers, and as much as Amber wanted to turn away, she couldn't. She couldn't seem to move.

'I'm sorry,' he said, his voice quiet, the tone of it more friendly now, less cold. 'Look…' He finally moved away from the desk, walking slowly over to her. 'This has been one hell of a few months, and even though I might not show it, Amber, I still care about you. I always will, and I want you to know that.'

'Then why do you play these games, Jim?'

He looked down at the ground, his hands still in his pockets, before his eyes met hers again. 'If it was me… if I was in Ryan's shoes, I'd want to be here, too. I'd want to be with you.'

She couldn't tear her eyes away from his, every painful feeling she still carried for this man hitting her head-on.

'You're looking good,' he went on, reaching out to gently touch her cheek, but she found herself backing away. What was the point in letting him get too close when she couldn't do anything about it? It was painful enough without adding any more confusing feelings to the mix.

'I'd better go,' she said, her hand finding the door handle, a strange feeling of breathlessness taking over until she was back out in the corridor. Only then could she breathe again.

If he was Ryan he'd want to be with her, too – but he wasn't, was he? And that's what hurt the most.

Jim watched her walk out the door, closing his eyes as it slammed shut behind her, the smell of her perfume lingering in the air. His chest felt tight and his heart was beating so fast he had to quickly sit down on the arm of the sofa, pushing both hands through his hair as he threw his head back, sighing heavily.

That had been hard – that had been so hard. He hadn't seen her in person for so long, his only glimpses of her being on the TV, and even that was difficult to cope with, seeing her there, smiling and laughing, blossoming into the popular presenter she was fast turning into.

Of course he'd pulled strings to have Ryan brought back to the North East early. But it wasn't because he really cared about how his star striker was feeling; Amber was right on that score. He didn't see why he should be so keen to let Ryan Fisher have his own way when *his* feelings were the last thing Jim was concerned about. But having him close was what Jim needed right now.

His plans had changed, his options had suddenly become clearer. It was easier to have Ryan right under his nose rather than fight to make sure he never returned to Newcastle Red Star. That would only have attracted more unwanted attention and ruined any chances Jim had of showing his young player just who was winning this game. And it certainly wasn't Ryan.

'Well, who'd have thought?' Ronnie sighed, leaning back against the wall outside the main entrance of Tynebridge as he and Amber grabbed a few minutes of fresh air, away from all the commotion Ryan Fisher's sudden reappearance back at the club was causing. 'Can't believe not one reporter out there had any idea he was coming home.' He looked at Amber. 'And you didn't know a thing about this?'

'I'm as surprised as you are,' Amber said, closing her eyes and letting the unusually warm early spring sunshine wash over her face. 'Although, right now, pissed off would describe my mood better.'

'You haven't told me what Jim said.'

'That's because I don't want to talk about it.'

'Is he still being a cold bastard?'

She opened one eye and looked at Ronnie out the corner of it. 'I said I didn't want to talk about it.'

He stared straight ahead again, watching the growing crowd of people outside, all waiting for Ryan to make his first official appearance on the steps; all of them waiting to welcome him back home.

'I take it you haven't seen daddy-to-be yet, then?'

'Not to speak to, no.'

'He looked happy. At the press conference.'

Amber said nothing. She hadn't gone into the press conference. Her hormones were way too fragile for her to sit there and watch Ryan and Jim together; she hadn't been sure, given the surprise events of the day, if she'd have been able to cope with that.

'He mentioned you,' Ronnie said, turning to look at her again.

'I know. You told me.'

'He looked happy because he was back home, to be with you, Amber.'

'Will people stop saying he's come home to be with me. That isn't what's happening. He wants to be close to his baby, Ronnie. Not me.'

Ronnie said nothing at first, watching her reaction, the way she couldn't hold his gaze, her eyes darting this way and that. 'Whatever. He's just happy to be home, that's all I know. And Newcastle Red Star are certainly glad to have him back. So it seems I was right about Jim Allen. He *was* just bluffing when he mentioned Ryan never coming back here.'

'You think so?' Amber raised a cynical eyebrow. 'Never take Jim Allen at face value, Ronnie. You should know that by now.'

'You think he's got some kind of ulterior motive for bringing

Ryan home early?'

'I don't know,' she sighed, closing her eyes for another brief second, summoning up the energy to go back inside and see if she could finally find Ryan. 'All I know is this all seems a bit weird. It doesn't feel right.'

'You're just being paranoid. Maybe Jim really is just trying to move on, trying to do the right thing.'

'I'm going back inside,' she said, shutting that conversation down. She really wasn't in the mood to pursue it any longer.

'Want me to come with you?'

She couldn't help smiling, leaning over to kiss his cheek. 'No. You're all right. I think I can manage.'

Walking back inside, Amber still couldn't see any sign of Ryan. So, feeling like she still needed some time alone before facing him, she headed off upstairs to see if her father was still in the hospitality box he used for entertaining at Tynebridge – when he had visitors he was trying to impress, or fellow managers he wanted to get on the right side of when he needed to talk transfers. Or when he just fancied bringing some of the staff from his own club over to watch one of the big games, which is what he'd done today. But it was empty now. Everyone had obviously moved on to one of the bars within the stadium to carry on the post-match socialising there. In fact, everywhere seemed quieter, now the fuss of Ryan's return and the match itself was over.

She walked into the box, enjoying the peace and quiet, the tranquillity being on her own brought. She hadn't realised quite how much she'd needed these few minutes to herself, to get her head straight and think about the consequences of Ryan's early return home.

'Hey, beautiful.'

She swung round. 'It's taken you this long to find me?'

'Things have been a bit hectic, babe. I've only been back in the country four hours.'

'Forget it, Ryan. I'm too tired, and right now all I want to do is go home, have a bath, and think about an early night.'

He gently grabbed her wrist as she tried to push past him, giving her little option but to look at him. 'I needed to be here, Amber. With you. That's why I came back. Why I pushed for an early return.'

'You're not *with* me, though, are you?'

'I want to be.'

'You should have told me this was on the cards, Ryan. I really don't need surprises like this. Not today.'

'Is something wrong?'

'Jesus…' She couldn't help but let out a cynical laugh. 'Yes, something's wrong. You, turning up here unannounced like the return of the prodigal fucking son… and shouldn't you be outside, getting a hero's welcome?'

'I wanted to see *you*.'

'That's big of you. Three hours later than everyone else.'

'That wasn't my fault, Amber. You saw how crazy it was down there. I couldn't get away, couldn't… You weren't in the press conference.'

'I'm not at work, Ryan. Not today. Ronnie was covering all of that.'

'You look… you look incredible.'

'Well, I feel like crap.'

'Debbie said you had an appointment with Dr. Lowry this morning.'

Amber looked up sharply, her eyes meeting his. 'What else did she say?'

'Nothing. Why? Has something…?'

'No…' She quickly tried to stub out the panic in his voice. 'No, nothing's wrong. I just wanted to… there's some news, that's all.' This wasn't really the way she'd wanted to tell him, but it looked like she had no other choice but to let him know about his baby boy, right here, right now. 'I had another scan today and…' Her eyes met his again. 'Do you want to know the sex, Ryan? Of this baby.'

He laughed a slightly nervous laugh, pushing a hand through his dark, messed-up hair. 'Oh, Jesus… yes. Yes, shit! Of course I do!'

Amber couldn't help smiling. He seemed so animated all of a sudden, excited, almost. 'We're having a boy.'

His face broke into the widest smile, those beautiful dark blue eyes of his crinkling up at the edges, and all of a sudden Amber felt a rush of something she couldn't explain sweep right over her.

'A boy,' he whispered, reaching out to touch her face, resting the palm of his hand on her cheek. 'We're having a boy.'

'You're pleased, then?' Amber smiled, looking up into his eyes, that feeling she still couldn't explain in no hurry to leave. And all of a sudden, neither was she.

'Shit, Amber… I still can't believe this is happening, but…' He laughed again, throwing his head back and letting out a cry of excitement that was almost infectious. 'I'm gonna be a fucking dad!'

Amber watched him, a man who, less than a year ago, had been a mess, in danger of losing it all. Was he really strong enough to cope with everything that lay ahead? Was she really ready to trust him again?

He grinned at her, and it was like some sort of invisible string was pulling her closer to him, whether she wanted to go there or not, but she put up no fight as he slipped an arm around her waist, pulling her against him. 'You really do look incredible.'

'You're jetlagged.'

He raised an eyebrow. 'From Tenerife?'

She smiled, reaching up to run her fingers through his hair, a reflex action she'd been unable to stop. 'You don't look all that bad yourself.' And he didn't. Dressed in dark jeans, a Bruce Springsteen t-shirt and black army boots, his tanned skin and those incredibly sexy tattoos on show, he looked hot as hell. And Amber couldn't stop a stirring deep inside her, a feeling that made her stomach flip and her heart start beating way faster than she wanted it to. But did she really want him to do this to her again? Could she really go back there?

He moved closer still, his breath now warm against her cheek, his mouth almost touching hers. 'Do you know how long I've waited to kiss you again?'

She rested her forehead against his, her fingers still in his hair, his hand in the small of her back, keeping her close. 'I'm so scared, Ryan. Of all this… of you…'

'You're scared of me?' he asked, letting his hand slide down, slipping it up and under her short dress, touching skin, making her break out in goose bumps. A nice, familiar feeling.

'I'm scared of what this is. Of what's happening. Of *why* it's happening…'

His mouth was on hers before she had a chance to say anything else, his lips moving so slowly and gently against her own it sent her stomach dipping so high then low then back again that she almost lost all sense of reality. It was a kiss so deep and dirty, so unbelievably sexy that she couldn't break away – she didn't want to. He'd walked back into her world and given her no option but to sit up and take notice.

She slid a hand round the back of his neck, fanning her fingers out as she pushed him down, keeping the kiss going, and loving the way it felt. Tongues touching, breathing heavy, bodies moulded together as though they were the perfect fit, his erection digging into her hip; it all spelled out what Amber had feared – Ryan Fisher was back in her life, and there was nothing she could do about it. They had a connection now that could never be broken. A connection that was pushing her back towards him. Back towards a man she'd vowed never to go near again, but that's what you got when you played with fire. She'd played just a little too close, and now she had to deal with the consequences. Whatever they turned out to be.

All she knew was that, right now, she wanted him. And all of a sudden she didn't care where they were, that they were about to have sex in front of a huge glass window that overlooked the pitch – what did it matter? The place was empty now. All she cared about was feeling him close to her, inside her, helping her once more to forget everything Jim Allen was to her. Everything he would always be.

Lifting her up onto the table at the back of the hospitality box, Ryan slipped his hands up and under her dress, his eyes on hers as he slowly slid his fingers underneath the thin material of her panties. She raised herself up slightly, letting him slowly pull them down, throwing them aside as she pulled her dress up over her head, leaving her naked and vulnerable, but, Jesus, she felt incredibly hot! She felt like the sexiest woman alive as she spread her legs, letting him look at her first before she wrapped them around his hips, throwing her head back as he leaned over to kiss her breasts, his fingers running lightly over her nipples until they were hard and ready and waiting for his mouth to cover them. And when it did, his tongue flicking and circling, sending her stomach into spasms of never-ending somersaults, she wanted to cry out in pure ecstasy. But, instead, she bit down on her lip, stifling the pleasure she desperately wanted to voice out loud so as not to attract any unwanted attention. In a place full of media this was the last thing they needed to see.

She kept her eyes closed as he continued to touch her, kiss her, and she enjoyed every sensual second as he suddenly pulled her legs away from him, spreading them even wider as he sank to his haunches, his hands on her ankles keeping her legs apart. The almost painful anticipation of what he was about to do made her physically shiver, and her fingers gripped the edge of the table behind her tightly, just waiting for that second – that beautiful, sweet second – when he touched her in the most intimate way there was. And when it happened she couldn't help but let out a moan of excruciating frustration as his tongue touched her so lightly, teasing her, his hands still gripping her ankles, keeping her legs wide apart and open, enabling him to go anywhere he wanted. And she wanted him everywhere.

'Jesus, Ryan...' she groaned, arching her back and pushing

herself against him, her legs aching because he had them pushed so far apart, but she didn't care, because what he was doing to her was incredible. Her skin was tingling, her thighs were on fire and her stomach was flipping about like it was on some kind of elastic bungee rope as his tongue pushed harder, deeper, his stubble tickling her, but it only intensified everything. He was close, so close to making her come, and although she didn't want him to stop, because she'd never experienced anything like this before, she wanted to feel him inside her, properly inside her, so deep it would feel like he was taking her over. That's what she wanted, what she needed. And he seemed to get the message, pulling away from her and standing back up, finally freeing himself so she could see his impressive erection for herself. And just the sight of it made her stomach flip over another dozen or so times, so fast she almost felt dizzy. 'Where the hell did you learn to do that?' Amber breathed, wrapping her legs around him again, pulling him against her.

He gave her that famous Fisher grin, wiping his mouth with the back of his hand. 'You don't want to know.' Placing a hand in the small of her back, he pushed her onto him, slipping inside her as though it was the most natural thing in the world to be doing right now.

'Yeah.' She smiled, running her fingertips over his rough chin as she felt him push deeper, rocking her body back with each gentle thrust. 'You're right. I don't.'

'You taste fucking amazing,' he whispered, his mouth so close to hers now. 'Do you know that?' And then he was kissing her, and she could taste herself on his lips, something which only served to turn her on even more, and she ached for the coming climax, for those sweet and sensual shockwaves to invade her body and send her reeling. 'See?' He grinned again, his thumb gently stroking her cheek. 'See how good you taste?'

'You are so bad, Ryan Fisher.'

'But you know how good I can make you feel,' he whispered, his mouth resting on hers.

Her breathing was getting heavier now, speeding up as he continued to push in and out of her, and she wrapped her arms around him, clinging onto him as the wave began to rise, growing closer, getting nearer, because he was touching her now, too. He was touching her as he pushed inside her, sending her whole body into some kind of erotic overdrive until she didn't know if she could control it any longer. She certainly knew she couldn't hold back anymore as everything seemed to hit her all at once, all those incredible feelings and that white hot pain, it all seemed to come surging forward in some epic tidal wave of emotions and she couldn't stop the cries of pure pleasure from escaping. She could feel him come, too, his body stiffening and jerking with the effort, that one last thrust that was so hard and final before that moment of silence, that tiny time frame of peace that always came before the reality returned.

'I want to be a proper dad to our son, Amber,' Ryan breathed, his body still inside hers, his arms holding onto her, not wanting to let her go just yet, and she was fine with that. She really was. Because she wasn't ashamed or regretful of what they'd done. Not anymore. Her dad was right – she had to start thinking about what was best for this baby now. Her son.

'You will be,' Amber said, her voice quiet as she looked right into his eyes, almost falling into them because that's where she wanted to be. Right at this second that was where she wanted to be.

'Do you understand what I mean by a proper dad?'

'As long as you're around, Ryan, and not acting like the first-rate prick you used to be, then you *will* be a proper dad. I have no doubt about that.'

'Move in with me.'

She felt her stomach jolt as he spoke those words to her a second time, but this time under completely different circumstances. And she'd made the mistake once, hadn't she? By doing exactly that – moving in with him. Something which had been an unmitigated disaster. But who was to say this would end the same way? Things were so very different this time.

She shook her head, common sense and reality suddenly kicking in big time. 'It's too soon, Ryan. And anyway, until we know exactly what's happening here...'

He stopped her from talking by kissing her, long and slow and deep, holding her close as his tongue danced around hers, his arms still holding her close as he finally left her body. 'We're having a baby, Amber. That's what's happening here.'

She looked at him, not really knowing what she should do next. 'I need to get dressed,' she said, gently pushing him away and sliding down from the table, quickly retrieving her clothes from the floor.

'Amber, please, come on... We need to talk.'

'And you think here is the best place to do that?' she asked, running her hands through her hair and shaking it out.

'I don't know what to do, babe. I really don't. All I want is to be with you, and I know it's hard to believe that I mean that this time, after everything...'

'Let's not go over old ground, Ryan.' She turned to look at him, walking over to him, sliding a hand round the back of his neck and pulling him down for another slow kiss. Because she liked it, kissing him. She'd almost forgotten how good he was, how wonderful he felt; the way that stubble of his tickled her skin, giving her no doubt that it was him she was kissing. It was him she was with. And it was then that she realised, for the first time in a long time, that she hadn't been thinking about Jim. All the time she'd been with Ryan, even when they'd been having sex, he hadn't crossed her mind once, not even fleetingly. He just hadn't been there. Whether that was a good thing or not, she had yet to work out, all she knew was that it felt like progress. Of some kind.

'You still love Jim, right?' Ryan asked, his hand slipping into hers, pulling her closer.

'I don't know.' She shrugged, an action which surprised her more than anything. 'I don't know whether I'm willing to waste yet more energy loving someone who really can't love me back. I spent over twenty years doing that – do I really want to waste another twenty?'

He gently tucked a strand of hair behind her ear, leaning in for a quick but still incredibly sexy kiss. Her hot, young ex-fiancé. The father of her baby boy. What exactly did she do with *that* scenario?

'I'm still in love with you, Amber. And you can choose to believe that or not, but I am.'

'Are you sure those feelings aren't just there because of the baby, Ryan?'

'Come on, Amber. I laid my fucking heart open to you before we knew about the baby. I told you how I felt back then, so, no, this isn't just because of the baby. It's because I still regret, every single day, the shit I put you through. The way I treated you, I wouldn't blame you if you didn't want to come near me anymore…'

'Well, I think we can safely say *that* isn't going to happen.' Amber smiled, playing with the hair at the back of his neck.

He smiled, too, gently stroking the small of her back. 'Give me another chance, Amber. Please.'

She looked up into his eyes again, still smiling, still wondering if this was the right thing to do, or whether it could turn out to be the biggest mistake of her life. 'Maybe. And that's all I can say for now, Ryan. Maybe.'

'Then I'll take that.'

'Good. 'Cause that's all you're getting. Anyway, come on. You'd better get out there before everyone gives up and leaves, and you wouldn't want to miss your hero's welcome home, would you? I can't believe Ryan Fisher's changed *that* much.'

'No. I guess he hasn't,' he whispered, lowering his mouth down onto hers again in one last kiss that still had the ability to rock her all-over-the-place world. Suddenly all she wanted was to feel his lips on hers and his arms holding her close. Because it didn't feel wrong anymore. It didn't feel right, but it didn't feel all that wrong, either. 'I'll see you later. Okay?'

He looked at her with wide, hopeful eyes and she folded her arms against her, a small smile still there on her face. 'Yeah. Okay.'

And as she watched him run out of the room, her young, hot, handsome footballer, she knew this was just the beginning of another new chapter in a life that was already reading like some 80s soap opera. And how it was all going to end was still anybody's guess.

Chapter Thirty-Five

'What are you doing?' Ellen asked, slipping her arms around Brandon's neck as she stood behind him, leaning over his shoulder to see what he was up to.

'I'm doing some digging,' Brandon replied, swinging round in his chair and pulling her down onto his lap.

'Digging?' Ellen frowned as she sat astride him, her arms circling his neck again.

'For information. About my dad.'

'Your dad? Why? Is something wrong? Or are you just trying to get some kind of heads-up on the local competition?'

Brandon smiled, pulling her down for a quick kiss. 'I wish it was that simple.'

'I don't understand.'

He sighed, throwing his head back, keeping his hands on her hips to hold her steady. He didn't want her to go anywhere just yet. It was about time he had a break, and the kind of escapism she could give him was exactly what he needed right now. 'It doesn't matter.'

'Well, it looks like it does. Do you want to talk about it? Is it something to do with him and Amber?'

'Yes… No… look, it really doesn't matter. It isn't important.'

'You sure? Because when I get back from work tonight we can

have dinner and you can talk all you like. I'm a great listener.'

He smiled, pulling her down for another kiss. 'It's fine, really.'

'Okay. If you're sure.'

'Where are you going?' Brandon asked as she climbed off him, slipping on her jacket and grabbing her bag from the table.

'Work.'

'Now?'

'We don't all have the luxury of footballer hours.' She winked at him, running back over to give him one last kiss.

'Jesus…' he groaned, swinging round and round on his chair. 'I was really hoping you could give me some light relief before I head off to training.'

'And you think that's a good idea, do you?' she asked, raising a questioning eyebrow.

He grinned, reaching out to grab her, quickly pulling her back down onto his lap.

'Brandon!' she squealed, putting up no real fight to stop him from keeping her there. 'I'm gonna be late, babe.'

'Just five minutes, I promise. I'll be quick.'

She shook her head, untangling herself from his grip and climbing off him again. She really didn't want to be late today. She was working over at Newcastle Red Star's training ground all morning, and with it being Ryan Fisher's first official day back with the Red Star squad, being late wasn't an option.

'Well, I don't want you to be quick.' She smiled, slinging her handbag over her shoulder. 'I want you to take your time, so we'll save this for later. Okay?'

'If we have to,' he groaned. 'Have a nice day!'

She threw him one last wink and a smile over her shoulder before running out the door.

Brandon swung his chair back round to face his laptop, tapping something new into the search engine. He didn't know all that much about his father's private life, but he was now on a mission to find out everything he possibly could. Whether his father wanted him to, or not.

'I can't get me head around you being a dad,' Gary said, throwing the ball back to Ryan from the touchline as they trained together for the first time in months.

'I could say the same about you.' Ryan smirked, kicking the ball over to another team-mate.

'Yeah, well, kids change you. Believe me. I'm not saying I want to spend every night sat on the sofa with Debbie watching *Coronation Street* while she feeds the baby and goes on and on about the search for the perfect high-chair, but sometimes it's nice, you know?'

Ryan stood still, his hands on his hips as he looked at his best friend. 'Well, not yet I don't, but I guess I'll find out soon enough.'

'So, you and Amber getting back together then or what?' Gary asked, sitting down behind the touchline.

Ryan sat down next to him, pulling his knees up to his chest as he stared out ahead at the familiar view of fields and trees and houses, so different from the training ground at CD Adeje with its view of palm trees, the sea, and Mount Teide looming large in the distance.

'You tell me, mate. I have no idea what's happening. All I know is we're getting closer, and that can only be a good thing.'

'You're fucking her again, you mean.'

'Jesus, Gary, come on.' He looked at his friend, trying to keep his stare stern, but he couldn't help smiling. 'Yeah, okay, I am. And I can't tell you how good it feels to be that close to her again, but…'

'But what?' Gary asked, twisting the cap off a fresh bottle of water.

'I dunno.' Ryan shrugged, taking the bottle when Gary offered it, swigging a large mouthful of water down.

'Is it the right thing to do?'

Ryan looked at Gary again. 'What do you mean?'

'You're not just doing this because of the baby, are you?'

'No. And I wish people would stop accusing me of that, that

isn't what's happening. I'm not doing anything *because* of the baby.'

'You cut your loan period short because of the baby.'

'That's different, Gaz, and you know it is. Of course I want to be a part of this pregnancy. I want to be there every step of the way, I want to feel as close to this baby as I possibly can, in case…'

'In case that's as close as you get?' Gary asked, taking a swig of water himself.

'No. No, that isn't gonna happen, Amber isn't like that. She'll let me be a part of that little boy's life, that isn't what I mean. I just… I just want more, Gary. I want to be there all the time. I don't want to be a part-time dad.'

'Have you told *her* that?'

'I've tried. But I think it's just too soon to be pushing her on relationships, considering her divorce from the boss is due any day now.'

'Oh, yeah. I'd forgotten about that.'

'I wish *I* could,' Ryan sighed. 'He's forever gonna be this fucking cloud hanging over us, and there's nothing I can do to change that.'

Gary nudged him gently, smiling. 'Hey, come on. It'll all work out, you'll see. Amber's a sensible girl. She'll do what's best for that baby.'

'Yeah. I know. I know that…'

'You might want to lose that *mañana* attitude, Fisher. You're back home now, and we've a title race to win. I haven't brought you back here to sit on your ass and chat to your friends.'

Ryan quickly pulled himself to his feet as Jim Allen stood over him, hands in the pockets of his suit trousers, his white shirtsleeves rolled up to his elbows.

'Yeah, sorry, boss. I was just taking a break.'

'I wasn't aware Colin had called one.' Jim fixed Ryan with a look that unnerved him slightly. 'And what are you still doing here, Gary?'

Gary pulled a face behind Jim's back and ran off to join the others.

'You settling in back home okay?' Jim asked, his expression softening slightly, which didn't actually make Ryan feel any better.

'Yeah. Yeah, I am. It's good to be back.'

'Well, I imagine Amber's pleased to have you home.'

Ryan narrowed his eyes as he looked at his manager. Where was this conversation going, exactly? 'I don't... I don't know that she is, actually.'

Ryan kept his eyes fixed firmly on Jim when he said that, but his boss showed no change in expression or emotion. His face stayed stoic, almost, giving nothing away.

'Is she okay?' Jim asked, his stare never wavering from Ryan.

'Why don't you ask her yourself? We're not together like everyone seems to think we are. There's no relationship there, except for the fact we're both going to be parents to this baby.'

'I see... Listen, Ryan, everything *is* okay, isn't it?'

Ryan held his arms out, laughing a slightly confused laugh at this almost surreal conversation. 'Listen, boss, I don't know what you're trying to ask me here, but...'

'Do you love her, Ryan?'

Ryan laughed again, confusion well and truly setting in now. 'I... this is crazy...'

'Do you love her?'

Ryan stared at Jim, not knowing what to say next. What was it he wanted to hear?

'I can't be there for her, Ryan,' Jim went on, and as Ryan stared at his boss, he saw something in his eyes that he'd never seen in Jim Allen before – vulnerability.

'I don't... *why*?' Ryan just couldn't shake the confusion, and even though he didn't want to be saying the words that were about to come out of his mouth, he knew he had to say them. 'You know she still loves you.'

Jim looked down at the ground, pulling his aviator shades out of his pocket and slipping them on, covering his eyes, hiding away any more emotion he didn't want anyone else to see. But Ryan had already seen it.

'I can't be there for her, Ryan,' Jim repeated, ignoring Ryan's comment. 'So I need you to…' He looked up, but his eyes were hidden behind those sunglasses now. 'I need you to step up and look after her. Do you hear me?'

'Is this…?' It was just getting more and more surreal the longer the conversation went on, and Ryan wasn't comfortable. Something just didn't feel right. 'I really don't understand what you're saying, boss.'

'I brought you back early, Ryan, not because the team necessarily needs you. As you may have noticed we've been doing pretty well without you. Although, to be fair to you, we probably could have done better if you'd been here. But… I brought you home early to be with Amber. She thinks she can do this on her own, but I think she needs you there with her.'

'You do?'

'This isn't a trick, Ryan. I'm not trying to fool you into anything, believe me. I just think it's time we all moved on and got on with our lives, don't you? But I still care about Amber. I always will, even if I can't be the one to…' He trailed off, looking away for a second, almost as if he was deep in some kind of private thought, and Ryan felt the uneasiness return. 'The divorce will be final soon,' Jim said, regaining his composure as he turned to face Ryan again. 'Time for us all move on, don't you think?'

Ryan narrowed his eyes again as he looked at Jim. 'This isn't making a whole lot of sense to me…'

'You're home, Ryan. Be grateful for that. Now just… just step up and look after Amber. I really need you to do that for me, okay?'

'But what if she…? For Christ's sake, she doesn't even *want* me like that.'

'Look after her, Ryan. In any way you can. That's all I'm asking you to do. Now, get back out there and do what we're paying you to do. With you back in the squad we might just be able to regain that league champions title a little easier than we first thought.'

Ryan held Jim's stare for a few seconds longer before turning away, not really feeling as if he understood anything any better after that conversation, but it was quite obvious it was over. For now.

Jim watched as Ryan ran back out onto the training pitch, a small smile forming as he removed his sunglasses and slid them back into his pocket. He had Ryan Fisher right where he wanted him. And a new game had just begun.

'What's the matter?' Ronnie asked, looking over at Amber, who was suspiciously quiet.

'Hmm? Sorry? Did you say something?' Amber looked up at the ceiling. 'Do you think that needs painting?'

'What's wrong?' Ronnie asked again, leaning back against the wall, putting the colour charts he was holding down on the chest of drawers beside him.

'Nothing's wrong. And if one more person asks me that question, I swear I'll scream.'

'Well, forgive us all for caring,' Ronnie sighed, turning his head to look out of the window.

Amber looked at him. 'It's too early to be doing all of this, isn't it? I mean, I've still got about twenty weeks to go, anything could happen in that time…' She stopped talking, turning her attention back to the bedroom wall.

'Amber, sweetheart, you need to stop that.'

'Stop what? Stop worrying? Stop thinking that something bad could happen? Stop being so superstitious?'

'Yeah. All of those things. It isn't doing you or the baby any good.'

She turned round to face him again, smiling slightly. 'Sorry. I can't help it. I just keep thinking…'

'Well, don't. For once in your life stop with the thinking and just get on with your life.'

'That's easier said than done,' Amber muttered, throwing herself down into the big, blue comfortable armchair by the door. 'My divorce is due any day now, I have no idea what's happening with Ryan, and we're supposed to be back down in London in a couple of days.'

'Which is probably a good thing.' Ronnie smiled, sitting down on the arm of her chair, playfully ruffling her hair. 'It might take your mind off everything.'

'You think?'

'Well, okay. Maybe not *everything*, but at least it gives you a bit of distance, a bit of time to get a clearer view of things, maybe?'

She looked up at him, returning his smile. 'Yeah. Maybe.'

Ronnie took the paint colour chart she was holding out of her hand and flicked through it. 'So, are we going with the stereotypical blue for this room, or a more neutral yellow?'

Amber pulled her knees up to her chest, resting her chin on them. 'What if all of this is a waste of time?'

'Huh? What do you mean?'

She crossed her legs up underneath her and looked up at Ronnie again. 'What if I… if I do decide to give things another go with Ryan?'

'And by that do you mean moving back in with him? So decorating this place is pointless, then?'

'Oh, I don't know, Ronnie. I don't know what the hell to do. I suppose, at the back of my mind, I haven't stopped wishing for the impossible, for Jim to tell me he could cope with the fact this baby isn't his…' She stopped talking, not really wanting to go over something she was tired of replaying over and over in her mind – the perfect scenario. Because it was never going to happen.

'Are you seriously considering that? Giving it another go with Ryan?'

'There's still something there, Ronnie. And no, before you ask, it isn't just because of the baby. It was still there before; I'm not even sure it ever went away. At Gary's party, when I saw him, when I let myself get close to him again, I could still feel it – that attraction, that chemistry…'

'You were drunk at Gary's party, Amber.'

'Not so much that I didn't know what I was doing, thanks.'

'You're just confused, after all this shit with Jim. So don't go rushing into anything you're not 100 per cent sure of.'

She pulled her knees up again, hugging them tight as she stared straight ahead. 'Am I ever going to be 100 per cent sure of anything, Ronnie? I thought I was 100 per cent sure of my relationship with Jim, but if I'd been as happy as I thought I was, would I have even gone near Ryan?'

'I still think you should take things slowly, Amber. Ryan Fisher, he's… Can you trust him? After everything he put you through?'

'I'm not going over this again… He's changed, all right? He's not the same man he was this time last year. Back then he was some arrogant, egotistical idiot who thought he could have anything he wanted and fuck the consequences. Now he's… he's different. He's grown up.'

'You reckon?' Ronnie asked, raising a cynical eyebrow.

'I know.'

The doorbell ringing interrupted the conversation. 'I'll get it,' Ronnie said, giving Amber back the paint colour chart. 'You stay where you are. And no, by the way. I don't think the ceiling needs painting.'

Amber smiled as he ran down to answer the door. She got up and walked over to the window, opening it slightly to grab a breath of fresh air. Peering down onto the street below, she recognised the car immediately, the voice she could hear talking to Ronnie down in the hall confirming it, and she felt her stomach jolt up into her throat as she heard footsteps running back up the stairs.

She turned to face Ronnie as he came back into the bedroom.

'Do you want to talk to him?' he asked. 'Because if you don't, I can always tell him to come back…'

'It's okay,' Amber said, giving Ronnie a small smile, folding her arms across her chest as she leaned back against the windowsill. 'Tell him to come up.'

'Do you want me to stick around?'

She shook her head. 'No. I'll be fine. I'll see you tonight, okay?'

He looked at her for a few seconds, trying to gauge whether she really was all right, or whether she was just putting on that brave face again. 'Okay. Well, call me if you need me. You know where I am.'

She closed her eyes as Ronnie left, waiting the few seconds it took for more footsteps to be heard coming up the stairs, her stomach tying itself up in knots as she waited for him to get there.

'Since when did he become your bodyguard?'

She opened her eyes and looked at Jim, her heart picking up speed as it began hammering away, hard and fast. 'He's just looking out for me, whether I like it or not. Is something wrong?'

He shook his head, standing a few feet away from her, his hands in his pockets. 'No. Well, not really. I just… the divorce. It's… it's final. I know your own lawyer will let you know officially, but I… I wanted to tell you myself.' His eyes met hers, and she felt a pain so raw cut right through her that it took her breath away. 'I'm sorry, Amber. I never wanted this to happen, I really didn't…'

'It's okay.' She interrupted him before he could say anything else. She didn't want to stand there and analyse everything, she was over that. It had happened, and now it was over. They were finished. Done. And she really didn't have the strength to fight it anymore. 'It's just one of those things.'

'You were never just *one of those things*", Amber.'

She looked down at the floor, at her tanned bare feet with their bright pink nails standing out against the light beige carpet. 'Thanks for letting me know.' She looked up at him again, trying to force a smile onto her face. 'It'll be less of a shock now, won't it? When the confirmation arrives in the post.'

'I'm sorry all this had to happen now, with the baby and…' His eyes met hers again, staring right into them. 'I really am sorry, Amber. For everything.'

'Don't be,' she whispered. 'Please. Don't be. Neither of us were blame-free in all of this.'

'You take care of yourself, and that baby, okay?'

She nodded, knowing that if she tried to speak she was going to start crying, and she was so tired of crying. So, so tired.

'Well, I'd… I'd better get going. We've got this charity dinner to get ready for tonight and… you *are* still coming to that, aren't you? Only, I know Cloud Sports are involved and…'

'I'm still coming,' she whispered, her voice not willing to go any higher.

'Okay. Good. I'll… I'll see you there.'

She smiled at him, nodding again, willing him to leave now because she didn't know how long she was going to be able to stand there and pretend she was feeling all right about all of this. Because she wasn't. Her head was hurting and her heart was breaking but she knew that was a reaction that she'd never have been able to avoid, no matter how much she'd told herself she was going to be fine about this when the time came. That time was now, and she wasn't really fine with it at all.

'I'll see myself out,' Jim said, pausing for a second, as though he was thinking about coming closer but then thought better of it. And she watched as he left the room, closing her eyes as she heard the front door shut. She was finally alone.

Keeping her eyes closed, she sank to the floor, her hand on her tiny baby bump as those silent tears began falling.

'Did you know she was seeing Brandon Palmer?' Gary asked Ryan as they made their way across the car park at Red Star's training ground.

Ryan shrugged. 'Got nothing to do with me anymore who she sees, mate.'

'You're not bothered, then?'

'Why would I be? It's not like I haven't got a hundred and one more important things to think about, is it?'

Gary slung his bag onto the roof of his Range Rover as he

opened the driver's door. 'Okay. I can tell you don't want to talk about your ex-girlfriend's new conquest.'

'You got that right.'

'You coming to this charity event on your own tonight?'

'Got no choice. As far as I know Amber's going with Ronnie, and why wouldn't she? It's not like we're a couple or anything. To be honest, I could do without it. I'm not really in the mood.'

'Yeah, well, the boss wants us all there, doesn't he? He keeps banging on about how we're a community club and should be showing our faces more at events like this one tonight. Anyway, Debs is looking forward to it. It'll be the first real chance she's had to get dressed up and venture out for an evening without the baby. And if *she's* happy…' He rolled his eyes and Ryan laughed.

'Yeah, well, you've probably got a point there. See you later, mate.'

Ryan turned to walk over to his own car, hitting the key fob to unlock it, when he heard someone walk up behind him.

'Looking good, Mr. Fisher.'

He swung round to see Ellen standing there, all sexy secretary in a tight black pencil skirt, close-fitting white top and skyscraper heels, her blonde hair tied back in a high ponytail.

'You don't look too bad yourself.' He smiled, he couldn't help it. She *did* look like a walking fantasy. All she needed were the glasses so she could whip them off, let her hair down, and make a man's wet dream come true.

'Tenerife suited you. That tan makes you look even sexier.' She moved closer, reaching out to trail her fingertips over his upper arm.

'I hear you're shacked up with the boss's son now,' Ryan said, quickly steering the subject onto something else.

'Well, what did you expect me to do? Sit wailing in a corner because God's gift to football didn't want me anymore?'

'It wasn't like that, Ellen.'

'What was it like, then?'

'I'm not getting into this.' He turned to go but she grabbed his wrist, stopping him from walking away.

'I'm sorry, okay? I didn't mean to sound all bitter. You just look really hot, that's all. Even after a morning's training. You kind of caught me a bit off guard.'

'Brandon Palmer wasn't exactly last in the queue when it came to giving out looks, Ellen. As long as he hasn't inherited any of his dad's less attractive qualities, you might have found yourself your perfect man there.'

'I doubt it,' Ellen muttered under her breath, too quietly for Ryan to catch exactly what she'd said. 'Anyway, will you be at this charity event tonight?'

'Got no choice, have I? Jim Allen's got us all under orders to be there.'

'Yeah,' she sighed, hitching her bag back up onto her shoulder. 'He's been a bit like a bear with a sore head today, hasn't he?'

'Has he?' Ryan frowned. 'He seemed okay this morning.'

'Well, there's a rumour going round that his divorce became final today. So he's not in the best of moods.' Ellen's eyes met Ryan's. 'I would have thought that was good news, as far as you're concerned. It means Amber's a free woman again.'

'You trying to make some kind of point here, Ellen?'

'You can pick up where you left off now, can't you? Especially now Ms. Wonderful's having your baby.'

She almost spat the words out and Ryan narrowed his eyes as he looked at her. 'I thought you didn't want to come across as bitter?'

She tossed her ponytail back over her shoulder. 'I'm *not* bitter,' she sniffed.

Ryan raised an eyebrow. 'Really?'

'Really. Why would I be? Brandon Palmer is ten times the man you'll ever be, Ryan. So you've probably done me a favour.'

Ryan laughed, he couldn't help it. Today was throwing up one surreal conversation after another. 'Glad I've been able to help you in some small way, Ellen. You have a nice day now.'

She watched him walk over to his car, silently berating herself for letting her true feelings show more than she'd intended them to. He didn't seem to be in the least bit bothered that she was now with another man, and someone younger, just as handsome, and just as talented as he was. He should be seeing Brandon Palmer as a threat, not as someone who'd taken her off his hands.

Still, she shouldn't be expecting the earth just yet. He was bound to be a bit distant right now, with everything that was going on. But Ryan Fisher wasn't cut out to be a dad. He wasn't the type. He wasn't ready to be tied down or trapped by a life of domesticity. Ellen knew exactly what he wanted, and what he didn't want. She just had to sit and wait it out until the time was right. Until she could make him see just what it was he needed. But, until then, she had Brandon. And who said waiting around had to be boring?

Ryan closed the car door and leaned forward, resting his forehead on the steering wheel, breathing in deep.

Amber was free. And even though he knew she wouldn't exactly be celebrating the news, he couldn't help that feeling of hope from swelling up inside him. There was nothing holding her back now – oh, who was *he* trying to kid? She was never going to forget Jim Allen, and how could she? When he was still a big part of both their lives. If he wanted to turn this around; if he wanted to chase that future he'd thrown away before and now had a second chance to grasp with both hands, he had a tough job ahead of him. He wasn't naive enough to think otherwise. But they had a special bond now, him and Amber. They had something no one could take from them – they had their baby. And that had to mean something.

He sat back, opening his eyes, breathing out slowly. He could do this. He could make her love him again, he knew he could. Hadn't he already shown her how much he'd changed? So he could do this.

He wanted Amber Sullivan. And he knew Amber Sullivan wanted him. He just had to make her see that. And tonight, he would.

Chapter Thirty-Six

'It's crap, isn't it?' Debbie said, straightening the top of her bright white tube dress. Now she was getting her figure back she wanted to flaunt it.

'What is?' Amber asked, leaning back against the bar in one of Tynebridge's bigger function suites, which was host to the evening's charity dinner in aid of a local hospital.

'Not being able to drink champagne.'

Amber grinned. 'Because you knock it back like water, huh?'

Debbie smiled. 'How many happy pills have *you* taken tonight? For a woman who's just been told her divorce is final, you seem overly cheerful.'

'I'm sick of being miserable, Debbie. I seem to have spent most of the past few months being bloody miserable and I haven't got the energy to waste any more time on that emotion. It's exhausting!'

'So, you're over him, then? Jim, I mean.'

'I'll never be over him, Debbie. I'd be stupid to think that could happen. But, I'm learning to deal with the fact that we just can't be together. It doesn't work, does it? As much as I want it to… We tried, and it failed. It's time to move on.'

Debbie looked at her out the corner of her eye. 'You sure you're okay? You're not just putting on some kind of brave face because you think that's what we all want to see?'

'I'm fine. Really.' She smiled, taking a sip of her non-alcoholic wine. 'I guess seeing Jim today, it knocked me into a reality I've as yet been unwilling to face.'

'So, what does that mean for you and Ryan?'

'It doesn't mean anything. As far as me and Ryan are concerned, things are exactly the same as they were before – he's the father of this baby, and that's the only connection we have.'

Debbie looked over towards the door as it opened, heralding a fresh intake of guests. 'Speak of the devil…'

Amber followed Debbie's gaze, her heart skipping those proverbial beats as she saw him walk into the room. Dressed in dark trousers, a beige shirt with the sleeves rolled up to the elbow, his dark hair all mussed up and sexy, he was quite obviously, without a shadow of a doubt, the most beautiful man in the entire room. Heads turned the second he walked in, and she was sure she could hear audible gasps from a group of women standing behind her.

'So, you don't care one iota that the father of your baby looks *hot* tonight?' Debbie asked, smirking slightly.

'Hot as hell,' Amber groaned, unable to stop herself from blushing. Where the hell had *that* come from? What was she – fifteen?

'Ha! So you *do* care, then?'

'Just because I agreed that he looks hot tonight doesn't mean to say I've suddenly decided to pack my bags and move in with him. And even if that *was* the case, which it isn't, I'm talking purely hypothetically here, that apartment of his is totally unsuitable for a baby.'

'Tell him to move in with you.'

'Do you really think he'd move into my house? It isn't really private enough, is it? And, to be honest, I'd rather we found somewhere…' She suddenly stopped talking, noticing Debbie's grin growing wider. 'No. No, you aren't going to make me do this, Debbie. Not tonight. It's way too soon. I just got carried away, that's all. No. I've got my own little house and that'll do me and my son just fine.'

'That baby's due in less than twenty weeks, Amber. Do you really want to be house-hunting with a new born? Wouldn't you rather you found somewhere *before* he arrives?' Debbie turned to face Amber, suddenly warming to this subject of Amber moving. 'Listen, there's a fabulous house for sale right beside mine and Gary's – the one with the triple garage, that amazing indoor pool, and the cinema in the basement, do you remember? I was telling you about it the night of Gary's party, about how it belonged to a Wearside Spartans player who's moved over to Spain to play in Madrid? The sale's in the hands of his solicitor now, and I know for a fact they're taking stupid offers on it because they really need to sell. You could snap it up for a bargain. And don't you think it's fate? That I told you about that house the night you and Ryan... the night baby Fisher was conceived?'

Amber frowned before giving Debbie a small, sideways smile. 'How did this suddenly become about me moving? I've got no intention of moving anywhere, but I love the way your mind works, Debbie. Anyway, even if I *was* thinking about moving, which I'm not, there's no way I could afford that house. I suspect even the stupid offers are way above my price range. I know I'm earning more than I used to, but...'

'Ryan can afford it.'

Amber looked at Debbie again. 'Okay. Let's stop this conversation now. I'm staying where I am. Ryan can do what he wants.'

'Amber!' Debbie moaned, stamping her foot like a petulant child. 'It would be so much fun if we were neighbours. Our nannies could take the babies out on play dates while we go to the spa, it would be perfect!'

'This is getting ridiculous now... Debbie, I won't have time to go to the bloody spa, I have a job.'

'You'll get maternity leave.'

'If I want it.'

'You *are* kidding, aren't you?'

'I don't know, do I? I don't know how the hell I'm going to feel until it all starts happening. And who mentioned nannies?'

'Come on, Amber. Be realistic. You are going to need a nanny, believe me.'

'I've got a bloody headache now.'

'Just come and take a look around the house. Please. I *really* think you'll like it.'

Amber eyed Debbie suspiciously. 'How do *you* know? Have you been inside?'

'Just once or twice.'

'You're incorrigible, Mrs. Blandford,' Amber laughed. 'And, for the last time, I'm not buying any house. I don't need to move, and I don't remember saying anything about me and Ryan living together. We aren't even a couple.'

'I didn't say *buy* the house, Amber. I said come and have a look *around* it, that's all.'

'It would appear there's no such thing as *"that's all"* with you, Debbie.'

'That's why you love me, chick.' Debbie winked, and Amber laughed again.

'What are you two conspiring to get up to?' Gary asked, wandering over to them.

'Nothing for you to worry your handsome head about, babe.' Debbie smiled, kissing him quickly. 'Where's Ryan disappeared to?'

'How should *I* know? I'm not his frigging bodyguard. You rang your mam yet? To see if Jodi's okay?'

'Aaah, he is *so* sweet!' Debbie grinned, pinching Gary's cheek. 'He's worried about our gorgeous little girl, who is absolutely fine, by the way. I rang mum just a few minutes ago and Jodi's been fed, had cuddles, and is now fast asleep. So chill out and enjoy yourself.'

'Get off, woman,' Gary said, playfully pushing Debbie away. 'I can't help it if I'm concerned, can I? It's the first time we've left her for a night out.'

'It's the first time *I've* left her, Gary. You've been out more than once since she arrived.'

'Yeah, but she was with you, then, wasn't she?'

'And who's my mum? Hannibal Lecter? Have a drink and stop worrying.'

Amber couldn't help smiling as she watched Debbie and Gary, two people who really had changed over the past year. Which was why she was sure Ryan could do the same. It was the one thing that was still giving her some hope.

'I'll see you two in a bit,' Amber said, putting her empty glass down on the bar.

'Where you going?' Debbie asked. 'I haven't finished with you yet.'

'Yeah, you have,' Amber laughed.

'We'll see about that, missy. I'll catch up with you later.'

Amber began winding her way through the growing crowd of people gathering in the function suite, stopping to say a quick hello and exchange a few words with those she knew, and even those she didn't. She may not be officially at work, but she was still an ambassador for Cloud Sports, who were covering the event for a slot on *Scoreline* the following week focusing on football clubs and their involvement in the local community.

'Looking good!'

She swung round at the sound of that voice, her face breaking into a smile the second she saw him. 'Looking good yourself, mister.'

Ryan grinned at her, that famous Fisher charm turned up full pelt as he stood there with his hands in his pockets, his feet slightly apart, a stance Amber found incredibly sexy, for some reason, and she shuddered inwardly as she looked right at him, her stomach fluttering about as though a million tiny butterflies had just been let loose in there. She'd put it down to the baby, but it was a touch too early for her to be feeling him move just yet.

'That dress, it suits you. And our bump.'

When he said those words she felt her stomach flip over, which, along with those butterflies, was now making her feel slightly unsteady on her feet.

'It's new,' she whispered, laying a hand gently over her tiny bump, which was just visible underneath the close-fitting dress.

'It's nice,' Ryan said, his eyes not moving away from hers. 'You look amazing.'

She couldn't help smiling, a sudden and ridiculous shyness coming over her, causing her to look down at her black and silver heels.

'Amber…'

She looked up at him, noticing his expression had suddenly got a touch more serious.

'I… I heard about your divorce.'

'Yeah. It seems the grapevine moves a hell of a lot faster round here these days.'

'It's all over, then.' It wasn't a question. And even though she'd all but accepted it, hearing the words still cut a little deeper than she wanted them to.

She nodded, looking down again, until he tilted her chin up, forcing her to look back into his eyes.

'I'm sorry. I didn't mean to bring it up, I shouldn't have said anything.'

'No. It's okay. Really.' She smiled, letting his hand slide into hers, their fingers entwining in an almost involuntary action.

'It must've been a hard day,' Ryan said quietly, his stare growing more intense as he looked deeper into her eyes.

'In some ways,' Amber replied. 'But I've still got a lot to be grateful for. A lot to be happy about.'

It was his turn to smile. 'I've got to go and circulate – on the orders of your ex-husband…' Ryan threw his head back and sighed heavily. 'Jesus, I'm sorry, Amber.'

'You don't have to walk on eggshells around me, Ryan.' She let go of his hand. That last reference to Jim had broken the moment somewhat. 'I think we're past all that, don't you?'

He ran a hand through his hair, pushing it back off his

handsome face. 'I'll see you later, okay?'

'Yeah.' She smiled again, allowing her heart to skip another little beat. 'You will.' She watched him walk away, engaging in conversation with everyone who stopped him, bringing out the Ryan Fisher charm offensive with all guns blazing.

'Everything all right?'

She turned around to see Ronnie standing there, himself handsome and smart, as always, in a dark suit and white shirt. 'Everything's fine.'

'What did *he* want?'

'Ryan? Nothing in particular. Just saying hello.'

Ronnie raised an eyebrow, falling into step beside Amber as they walked over to their table. 'Just saying hello?'

Amber shrugged, slipping her arm through Ronnie's as they walked. 'You know Ryan.'

'Yeah. I do.'

'Out of everyone, Ronnie, I'm really counting on you to give him a chance. Please. For me. For this baby, who's going to be your godson, remember?'

Ronnie stopped walking, turning to face her. 'You're serious, then? About taking him back?'

She shrugged again, looking away for a second. 'I didn't say that. I just want you to give him a chance, stop thinking of him as the same person he was before. And I don't think making a decision to jump straight back into another relationship is wise on the day I've officially become a divorcée, do you?'

'I hadn't really thought about it. I mean, it's not like you and Jim have been an item for a while now, is it?'

'Yeah, thanks for reminding me about my short-lived marriage.'

'Hey, come on. Come here.' He pulled her into his arms, hugging her tight. 'Me and my mouth. I knew it was a bad idea to have a whisky before dinner.'

She looked up at him, quickly kissing his mouth. 'I do love you, Ronnie White.'

'Just not in that way, huh?' He smiled, and she returned it.

'You couldn't handle me. We're too similar. We're both too stubborn for starters.'

'You got that right,' Freddie Sullivan said, joining them at the table.

Amber smiled at her father, letting go of Ronnie and turning to hug Freddie.

'You okay?' Freddie asked quietly, and Amber nodded. He squeezed her waist and hugged her again. 'Good. I hear Jim came to see you. This afternoon.'

'Yeah. He did.'

'And it went all right?'

'Can we not talk about this tonight, Dad? Please? I'm trying really hard to put that chapter of my life behind me now because, in case you hadn't noticed, there's a new one just beginning.'

'How could I forget my new grandson?' Freddie grinned.

'Have you seen the stuff he's already bought for him?' Ronnie said, pulling out Amber's chair for her at the large round table they were seated at for this charity dinner. 'That's gonna be one spoilt little boy, I'm telling you.'

'Ever the gentleman.' Amber smiled at Ronnie as she sat down, him on one side of her, her father on the other. 'And I've told you, Dad, I don't want anyone buying anything for him yet. It's too early.'

'She's gone all superstitious,' Ronnie said, pouring Amber a glass of water.

'No, I haven't, I'm just being wary. He's one very special baby, and I don't want anything to go wrong with this pregnancy, that's all.'

'The only thing going wrong with this pregnancy is you constantly panicking over everything.'

'I'm not panicking, Ronnie. I'm just being careful. And is this as exciting as it gets?'

'What?'

'Water. Is that all I'm allowed?'

'You just said you were being careful.'

She stuck her tongue out at him, but he just grinned at her, quickly retrieving his phone as it rang from inside his jacket pocket. 'Sorry, kiddo, got to get this. It's the boss. Back in a bit.'

Amber turned to her dad, looking at him with wide eyes. 'What?'

'Can you not see how perfect you two are together?'

'I'm not getting into this, Dad. Me and Ronnie are friends, and that's all we'll ever be.'

'He could look after you and this baby, you know that, don't you? And God knows I'd feel a whole lot better about everything if you two were together.'

'Since when did I need looking after?'

'You've been through a lot these past few months, Amber.'

'And people have been through far worse.'

Freddie took a sip of wine, taking his daughter's hand in his. 'Are you and Ryan…? Are you getting back together?'

'I don't know, Dad. And that's the honest truth. I feel something for him, I can't deny that. And no, it isn't just because of the baby, before you ask. There's still something there, some attraction…' She trailed off, sitting back and looking around the room. 'I don't know. I don't know what I'm doing yet. Let's just get today out of the way and then maybe I can start to think straight again.'

'I just want you to be happy, Amber.'

She smiled at her dad. 'I *am* happy. I can't say I don't wish things had been slightly different, but this little one in here has given me everything I need to be able to push my life forward. He's going to change everything, and that can only be a good thing.'

'Amber?'

She swung round in her seat to see Ryan standing behind her. 'Oh, hi. We were just talking about you.'

He looked from Amber to Freddie, a slight smirk on his face. 'Anything good? Or just the usual?'

Freddie looked at Ryan, ignoring his rather flippant remark. 'You settling back in okay?'

'It's like I've never been away.'

'Well, now you're back, Newcastle Red Star have got a real chance of retaining that Premiership title. And that's all that matters.'

Amber frowned at her father. Getting him to accept that Ryan was back in her life – in whatever capacity that turned out to be – was quite obviously going to be one hell of an uphill struggle, she could see that now.

'Can I have a word, Amber?' Ryan asked, his eyes looking right into hers.

'Erm, yeah. Have we got time before dinner?'

'It won't take long.' He held out his hand and Amber took it, letting him pull her up out of her seat. 'Somewhere more private, if that's okay?'

'Yeah. Okay. I won't be long, Dad.'

Freddie Sullivan just sniffed his disapproval and turned his attention to another ex-Red Star player who was sitting next to him.

'Family parties are gonna be fun,' Ryan muttered, gripping Amber's hand as they wound their way through the tables and those people still hanging around by the bar.

'Family parties…? Ryan, where are we going?'

'I told you, somewhere more private. I need to talk to you.'

'You pick your moments.'

'Yeah well, time waits for no man and all that. Come on. We're going down to the dressing room.'

'The dressing room? Ryan…'

He stopped, still holding onto her hand, his eyes boring deep into hers again. 'Or we can just do it right here. If you want everyone to watch me fucking you, that is. Your choice.'

He threw her that smile again, and she felt her stomach dip, her heart suddenly starting that run of faster beats, banging away inside her like some out-of-control drum. 'Oh, Jesus… Who told you to come back into my life and fuck it up all over again?'

'I've never really done as I'm told, Amber. I thought you would've known that by now.'

She couldn't help smiling, too, falling into step beside him as they quickened their pace, slipping – hopefully – unnoticed out of the function suite, almost running down the corridor and back out into the main entrance of Tynebridge.

'You're serious, aren't you?' Amber said, holding tightly onto his hand as they crossed the atrium, past the bemused security guy manning the reception desk, out into the corridor that led to the dressing rooms.

'Of course I'm serious. One look at you tonight and I knew I wouldn't be able to settle until I'd got you on your own.'

'What if we get caught?'

'I don't care, Amber. Right now, all I care about is you.' He pulled her into the empty home team dressing room, making sure no one else was about before closing the door behind them.

'Don't you even want to know how *I* feel?' Amber asked, already feeling that familiar stirring between her thighs.

He flashed her the famous Fisher grin, pushing her back against the wall, placing a hand beside her head as he leaned in closer to her. 'I know how you feel.'

'Oh, you do, do you?'

'I think you want me just as much as I want you.'

'I see the cocky, self-assured Ryan is back. That's nice.'

He laughed, a low, deep, sexy laugh, and Amber thought her heart was going to leap out of her chest, so hard was it beating now.

'You said this wouldn't take long. So what are we looking at here, Mr. Footballer? A quick in and out job? Or were you just lying to me back there?'

He moved his mouth closer to hers, his breath warm on her face, his aftershave overwhelming her. He smelt fantastic, and she knew this was a battle she wasn't going to win. So she might as well just wave the white flag and surrender. Everything.

'I don't lie anymore, Amber. Those days are over. But if this takes a little longer than we first thought it might, then – well, sometimes you can't rush these things, can you?'

She reached up and ran her fingertips lightly over his mouth, desperate to kiss it, to taste him again, but she was enjoying the build-up too much to go straight in for the kill. 'You'll ruin this dress.'

'Take it off, then. Take everything off and let me look at that incredible body… just let me look at it…' His mouth was on hers now, resting lightly against it, sending her head spinning, and she was glad of the wall behind her to keep her steady because she could feel her knees starting to give way already. '… Before I come inside you all over again.'

'Jesus, Ryan…' Amber groaned, closing her eyes as he began covering her neck in tiny, feather-light kisses, his lips brushing over her skin, sending a million tingling electric shocks shooting right through her with every touch. She didn't want to feel this way, not today. But he wasn't giving her much choice.

She slipped her hand up and under her dress, tugging down her own panties, desperate to feel him now. And when he took over, slipping her dress up over her thighs, crouching down to slide her panties off, she felt as though she was going to explode with the sudden rush of excitement he'd created within seconds, turning her from calm and collected into a helpless wreck with only one thing on her mind. Him.

Pulling her dress off over her head, she reached out and hung it on one of the pegs that lined the dressing room wall, all the time her eyes never leaving Ryan's as he unclipped her bra, throwing it aside, leaving her completely naked. She was the vulnerable one now. He was the one very much in control, and that kind of excited her. So much so that she could feel that shiver between her legs, the one she always got when she knew something good was about to happen. And it was about to happen now.

He slid a hand into the small of her back, his other hand gently stroking the curve of her waist, her hip, his mouth moving closer to hers, and the heat between them was almost unbearable now. She felt breathless, her heart still beating away to that super-fast rhythm, her stomach leaping about like an inane jack-in-the-box. She wanted him to kiss her, but at the same time she was totally overwhelmed by the incredibly erotic overtones he was creating by keeping just that tiniest of spaces between them, playing with her, teasing her; silently telling her what was coming, but holding back from giving it to her too soon.

She was aching for him now, physically aching. It was a pain so beautiful she could take it, but she didn't want it to go on forever, she wanted it to end at some point, to feel him where she wanted him to be, so much she couldn't explain. And maybe tomorrow she wouldn't feel that ache quite so much, when reality rolled back into her life, but right now – right now she needed him. She wanted him. And she was going to have him.

Pushing his shirt back off his shoulders, he shrugged it off, letting it fall to the floor, and Amber felt her stomach leap around all over again at the sight of him – his tanned, toned chest, so smooth she just wanted to reach out and touch it, and when he finally pulled her against him, her naked breasts touching his skin, it felt like hundreds of tiny fireworks all going off at once. Every cliché she could think of was happening, right there, as he lifted her up, pushing her back against the wall, and as she wrapped her legs around his hips, she could hear those fireworks shooting off in all directions, her head spinning faster and faster as his mouth finally touched hers. At the same time, he pushed into her so gently, easing that pain and intensifying those tingles, making her entire body shiver as he held her close. It was the most beautiful, most incredible feeling; the sense of danger that still hung in the air, the fact they could be caught at any given moment, it all added to the excitement Ryan Fisher could give her. He'd given it to her before, and she'd felt just as she was feeling now – alive and free and on top of the world.

Burying her face in his hair, stifling the screams she so wanted to let loose, she clung onto him as his thrusts speeded up, going from gentle to hard, slamming into her, touching her right where she needed to be touched to make sure her own climax wasn't far off. And although she didn't want this to end, she also wanted to feel that burning, white hot pain he caused when he finally came, which he did within minutes, spilling out into her in a barrage of fast and furious thrusts, causing her own body to convulse in a serious of incredible spasms, both of them trying hard to stay quiet when all they wanted to do was cry out loud.

'Jesus – fucking – Christ!' Ryan breathed, keeping his hands underneath her bottom, holding her against him as he stayed inside her. He wasn't ready to leave just yet. 'You okay, babe?'

She nodded, her arms still wrapped around him, her face still buried in his hair. She wanted to stay this close to him for just a little while longer, just the two of them. She wanted a few minutes more to think about things. To think about a future she hadn't wanted to have to think about, but circumstances had seen to it that she didn't have any other choice.

'Amber...'

She finally looked at him, her mouth gently touching his as he lowered her back down, keeping his hands on her hips. 'I really don't know what's happening here, Ryan. And I'm scared.'

He smiled, a small smile, but one that was still capable of making her heart start up with that rhythm once again, that rhythm that sent her stomach reeling and made her breath catch in her throat. 'Sometimes being scared is good.'

'You think so?' She smiled, too, running her fingers lightly over his naked chest, his skin warm and soft beneath her fingers.

'What kind of life would it be if we didn't take risks?'

'A more secure one?'

He laughed, that low, deep, sexy laugh that only served to send Amber's heart into overdrive. Shit! Talk about history repeating itself. Is this what her life had become? A constant cycle of feeling scared and falling in love, only to get hurt and then begin that whole cycle all over again?

'I just want to be with you, Amber,' Ryan whispered, his lips so close to hers she could feel every defence she'd been about to put right back up come crashing down around her. 'That's all.'

'It isn't that simple, Ryan.'

'It is to me.' He was kissing her now, slowly and gently, his mouth moving against hers, his tongue sliding inside, tracing the roof of her mouth, the back of her teeth, and she had to cling onto him to stop her knees from giving way. She felt like a teenager who'd just got to kiss the best looking guy in school, that was what Ryan Fisher did to her.

'I need time, baby,' she whispered, pulling away slightly, gently stroking his cheek with the palm of her hand before letting go of him, trying to move away, but he gently took hold of her wrist, stopping her from going anywhere.

'Can I look at you, Amber? Please? I just want to look at you…'

She leaned back against the wall, her eyes locked onto his, and what he could do to her with just one look was like something out of a book of magic. It was as though someone else had completely taken over her body as she stretched her arms up above her head, moving her legs slightly apart, closing her eyes as his hand ran lightly over her tiny baby bump.

'We did that,' he said quietly, leaving his hand there, causing her stomach to flip over and over in a barrage of super-fast somersaults. 'We made him.'

She bit down on her lip, keeping her eyes closed as his hand moved lower, slipping between her legs, and she couldn't help but let out a small moan of pure pleasure as he touched her just that little bit harder. It was one of the most erotic experiences of her life, standing there, naked, wanting him to look at her, to touch her, to do whatever he wanted to her. And she knew, right there and then, that fighting this was going to be a waste of time. She'd raised that white flag again, and that new chapter really was about to begin.

Dinner was over, the formalities of the evening all done and dusted and all that was left to do now was a bit more mingling before the time was right to politely leave. And for that, Amber was grateful. She was tired. The events of the day had finally caught up with her and all she really wanted to do was go home, slip into bed, and sleep. She was due back in London in a day or so and she didn't want to go back down there exhausted and worn out. She wanted her head straight and her life back on track, although, maybe hoping for the impossible was a step too far, for now.

Taking the opportunity to grab a few minutes alone, and some much-needed fresh air before she said her goodbyes, she leaned back against the wall outside Tynebridge's main entrance and looked out over the floodlit car park below. The stadium looked quite spectacular when it was all lit up the way it was tonight. She loved this club, because she had so many connections to it. Her dad had been a player here, along with Jim. She'd spent many a happy time at matches back when she'd been a child, watching her father play, before Jim had come on the scene and changed her life forever. And even though all of those times had happened at the old ground, before Tynebridge had been built to accommodate all those new facilities that Premiership clubs needed to offer these days, she knew there would always be a place in her heart for Newcastle Red Star. Her life was too connected to this club, and the people involved with it, for it to be any other way.

'You look deep in thought.'

She quickly looked up to see Jim standing there, and if it really was possible for a heart to stop beating, just for a fraction of a second, then that's what hers had just done. 'It's that time of the night, isn't it? When you start thinking about things just a little too much.'

He leaned back against the wall next to her, sticking his hands in his pockets as he stared straight ahead. 'Well, that usually happens when you've had a few too many drinks. And I'm assuming you haven't touched a drop of alcohol all night.'

She looked down at the ground for a second, part of her wishing he would just go away. She didn't want him this close to her anymore. She didn't want to have to deal with the feelings that alone threw up.

'You got something on your mind?' he asked, and she turned to look at him, a little surprised he even had to ask that question, given their circumstances.

'Sorry,' he said, finally realising what he'd just asked her. 'That was a bit of a stupid question, really.'

She said nothing, just turned away again, looking back out at the car park, a small stream of people now starting to leave, saying their goodbyes before setting off in search of their ride home for the night.

'I didn't want any of this to happen, Amber.'

'Neither did I, Jim.'

'But I… it's just the way it has to be.'

She turned to look at him again. 'Why? Why does it have to be this way? I still don't understand…' She stopped herself from saying any more. She didn't want to sound as though she was begging him for some explanation that he probably couldn't give her. If he did have his reasons, then maybe it was better she didn't know. Maybe those people who'd told her everything happened for a reason were right – and maybe she just had to wait that little bit longer before she found out the reason why this had happened. Why she'd lost the one man she'd loved for most of her life.

'I don't want to upset you, Amber, or…'

'Then maybe it's best you leave.' She was surprised at how steady her voice was, because, deep down inside, she didn't really want him to leave. She didn't want him to go anywhere. She wanted him to tell her he'd been wrong, that divorcing her had been a huge mistake; that he wanted her back because there wasn't anything they couldn't work out, as long as they were together. But how could you work out something you didn't understand?

He moved so he was standing in front of her, looking down at her slightly swollen belly. 'You're beginning to show.'

'A bit,' she whispered, automatically placing a hand on her bump.

'I hope it all goes well for you, Amber. This baby... I know how much you wanted it – wanted *him*.'

Amber didn't know whether he meant the baby or Ryan when he'd said that. And she wasn't really in the mood to analyse it.

'You're so beautiful,' he whispered, moving closer to her, reaching out and resting the palm of his hand against her cheek. 'My beautiful baby girl.'

She closed her eyes, and for a second she allowed herself to wonder what it would have felt like if things had worked out how she'd really wanted them to, opening them only when she felt his lips touch hers.

'Jim...'

She closed her eyes again, resisting every urge to push him away, falling against him, letting him hold her, wanting to feel that kiss for the last time, to remember what he felt like, how he tasted. She hadn't realised how much she'd needed that until now. Until his mouth had touched hers in a way that was making her cry silent tears, tearing her apart inside with every movement of his lips against hers, his fingers stroking her cheek, wiping away those tears that wouldn't change anything, she knew that. But she couldn't stop them. And maybe she needed to cry them, to finally get him out of her system. Maybe...

'I will *always* love you, Amber. Remember that.' He pulled away from her, and all of a sudden she felt a pain so deep, so intense it literally took her breath away. It was as if panic had numbed every single one of her senses, allowing total helplessness to take over.

'I don't want you to go, Jim. I don't... I don't want you to go...'

'Baby, I can't do this, I can't... Don't make me do this...'

'I love you so much, Jim. And you know... you know that is *never* going to stop. It's...'

He pulled her back into his arms, holding her close, rocking her gently as she cried tears she really hadn't wanted to cry, but then, she hadn't banked on this happening, had she? She'd thought she was just beginning to get her crazy emotions under some kind of control. It would seem she was still a long way off that happening.

'Amber, baby, look at me. Look at me, honey, please.'

She didn't know if she could. She didn't know if she could stand there and look into those eyes and not want to leave here. He was her world, her whole reason for living, she knew that now. Despite everything, despite Ryan and whatever feelings she thought she might still have for him, it was quite evident that she was never going to be free of Jim Allen. Because she didn't want to be. But, as she eventually looked up, into eyes that had lied to her, betrayed her; eyes that had loved her, once, she saw eyes that were still hiding something. And she doubted very much whether she'd ever find out what that was.

'I love you, I do, and you have to believe that. You have to, but… this. I can't do it. I'm too weak, I can't… I… I just can't, Amber. Okay? I can't do it anymore.'

'If I wasn't having Ryan's baby…?'

He stopped her from asking that question by kissing her, by holding her close and breaking her heart all over again, and she clung onto him for those last, few, precious seconds, banking every memory, every touch, every sound of his voice, every move of his lips against hers.

'There are reasons, Amber, but I… It's just the way it has to be. It's the way it has to be.'

He let his hand run down over her collarbone, gently skimming her breasts until it rested briefly on her bump. And that was an action that tore her apart, an action that made her feel as though someone was physically hacking away at her heart. This was a future she'd wanted, but it was one she couldn't have. She couldn't have it. She couldn't have *him* – her beautiful American man.

'You take care now. Okay?' he whispered, his mouth so close to hers she just wanted to close her eyes and feel him kiss her until she fell asleep in his arms, desperate to wake up tomorrow and find out that these past few months had been nothing but one long nightmare.

But, instead, she could do nothing but watch him walk away, breathing in deep as she fought to regain her composure, determined not to break down again. She was never going to be free of Jim Allen, she'd already accepted that, but she had to learn to live without him now. She had no other choice. She'd done that before and succeeded, hadn't she? She could do it again. And this time she had something far more important to help her move on with a life that didn't have to have him at the forefront. Someone far more special was about to take his place as the main man in her life. Her son. *He* was her world now. *He* was her reason for living. *He* was the one who was going to get her through this.

'You okay, kiddo?'

She looked up as Ronnie joined her. 'I'm fine.'

'Just checking you haven't come out here to indulge in a sneaky cigarette.'

'I gave those up a long time ago,' she said, snuggling into him as he slid an arm around her shoulders.

'Yeah, I know you did. I was just trying to avoid having to mention Jim, that's all. I saw him leave just now and… you've been crying. What's happened? Has he upset you?'

'We were just saying goodbye, that's all… Look, can we not talk about him, Ronnie, please? Today was… it was the end of that part of my life, okay? That's how I have to look at it now. I have to.'

Ronnie hugged her close, gently kissing the top of her head. 'I know, babe. I'm sorry. I just want to make sure you're all right, that's all. It's been a strange day for you. I can totally understand how confused you must be feeling.'

She pulled away from him slightly, looking right into his eyes, determination slowly starting to fight its way through the pain she still felt at losing Jim. But that was a pain that would never go away; she just had to learn to deal with it a lot better than she had been doing. 'You know, I'm not sure I've got time to be confused anymore. I've just got to suck it all up now and start getting my head together before this little one arrives. God knows he's going to be thrust into a complicated enough scenario as it is, the last thing he needs is his mother falling apart. No. I've got to pull myself together, put Jim to the back of my mind and start concentrating on my baby.'

'And what about Ryan?'

'What about him?'

Ronnie shrugged. 'I dunno. I mean, what's happening with you two?'

'It's a work in progress,' Amber sighed, pushing both hands through her hair, closing her eyes briefly in the hope that it would rid her of any final thoughts of Jim. Because he was still there, filling her head with memories she couldn't forget.

Ronnie frowned. 'What do you mean?'

'I mean, I don't know what's happening with me and Ryan. We see each other, we have sex, it's a vicious cycle, really, but…' She leaned back against the wall, closing her eyes again, taking another of those deep breaths she was so used to taking these days. 'There's something there, and I don't know what that is, because… because he isn't Jim.' She opened her eyes and looked at Ronnie. 'And he never will be. But he's the father of this baby, and he's doing all he can to prove to me that he's going to be the best dad he can be.'

'To be fair, Amber, he hasn't got a clue what that job entails just yet.'

'No, but then, neither do I. And I'm scared out of my wits about how I'm going to cope, so…' She stopped talking, staring straight ahead again.

'So, what?' Ronnie asked.

She shrugged, shaking her head. 'Nothing. It doesn't matter.'

Ronnie put his arm back around her, pulling her closer, her arms circling his waist as she snuggled in against him, neither of them saying anything, letting the noise of the growing crowd of people now leaving the stadium after the charity dinner fill the silence for a few minutes.

'You know, I actually think, for the first time since all of this happened – since Jim and I split up, since this surprise pregnancy… since Ryan crash-landed back into my life…' Amber pulled away from Ronnie again, suddenly feeling something click inside her, something that told her the time had come to step up and take control of this situation, before it was too late. 'For the first time since all of this happened, I actually feel as though I know what I need to do now.'

'You do? Care to share?'

She smiled, leaning forward to plant a quick kiss on his unsuspecting mouth. 'Not yet. I'll let you know.' She quickly winked at him before almost running back inside, bumping straight into Ryan. Literally.

'Hey! Steady on there, beautiful,' he laughed, gently grabbing hold of her arms. 'I was just coming to look for you.'

'Well, looks like you found me.' She smiled, and for the first time in days she began to feel a confidence she'd lost somewhere along the way slowly start to return.

'Something up?' He let go of her arms, resting one hand on her hip and pushing a strand of hair behind her ear with the other.

'No. Nothing's up. Everything's fine.' Well, maybe fine was pushing it a bit, but things were slowly starting to become clearer.

He frowned slightly, before letting that frown give way to a small smile, but even that managed to light up his beautiful face. Her hot, handsome footballer.

She reached out to stroke his rough chin with her fingertips, leaning forward to lightly kiss his slightly open mouth. But with Jim's kisses still tingling on her lips, she didn't linger, pulling away after just a few seconds.

'You sure everything's okay?' Ryan asked, that frown reappearing.

Amber cocked her head slightly, taking a couple of steps back. 'Everything's fine, I told you.' And maybe she was right. Maybe one day everything *would* be okay. If she let it. Nobody said it was going to be easy, but it didn't have to be impossible.

'Amber, listen…'

She looked at him, right into those deep, dark blue eyes of his, the memory of that night's incredible sex still very fresh in her mind, and although the idea of a replay was something she briefly considered – anything to make her forget Jim, to help her push him further and further away, back into the recesses of her mind where she didn't have to think about him too much or wish for that life she just couldn't have – she let the sensible part of her brain take over. For once.

'You and me…'

She may not be living the life she'd dreamed of, but she still had a great life. A life she should be more than grateful for, whether Jim was a part of it or not. She was just going to have to learn to let go. Finally.

'I can't make any promises, Ryan. I told you that.'

'I know. I know you did.'

'I said maybe. And I said I couldn't give you any more than that, not yet. It wouldn't be fair on you.'

'Shouldn't *I* be the judge of that?'

She moved closer to him, reaching out to gently touch his cheek, kissing him quickly. He really did have the softest lips.

'You still need time, don't you?' His voice had a resigned tone to it. And there was a part of her that just wanted to throw all caution to the wind and see where this new journey with Ryan could take her. But there was also another part of her that didn't want to hurt him. He wanted more than she could give him right now, so the last thing she wanted was for him to believe that their relationship was anything close to being back on track.

'And so do you,' she whispered, putting up no fight as his arm circled her waist, pulling her closer against him. 'But, if you're up for some fun… I mean, there's no harm in mummy and daddy-to-be spending some time together, is there? If that's okay with you?'

His face broke into a wider smile, that slightly cocky edge to him now shining through. 'Oh, that's absolutely fine with me, babe.'

'There's a lot to do before this little one gets here, so we may have to see quite a bit of each other.'

'I'm sure we'll work something out,' he said quietly, his mouth almost resting on hers now.

Ryan Fisher was back in her life, whether she wanted him there or not. But, as far as their relationship was concerned, whatever happened there was still a long way off being decided. Right now, though, she was willing to see what the future had in store for her. For both of them. For all three of them.

'So, beautiful, where do we go from here?'

She smiled, she couldn't help it. Her heart was still breaking, but this man here in front of her could help to ease that pain, help her to at least put some of her past behind her. If she let him.

'Watch this space, Mr. Footballer. Just, watch this space.'

It was impossible to be 100 per cent sure of anything anymore, but there was one thing she was certain of – Amber Allen may be history, but Amber Sullivan was making a comeback...

The game continues...

Turn over for an exclusive sneak peek at the final book in the series,

Final Score

Final Score

Chapter One

'You gonna let me in or what?'

Amber folded her arms and leaned back against the doorpost, her eyes fixed upon Ryan – Ryan Fisher, famous footballer, local north east hero; a man who'd crashed into her life just a couple of years ago. Even though she'd done everything in her power, at the time, to stop that from happening.

She had a slight smile on her face. She couldn't help it. Sometimes he just had the ability to make her smile, whether she felt like it or not.

'You don't have to bring him something *every* time you call round, you know.' She stood aside to let him through into the hall.

'I know. But I want to. Where is my beautiful boy anyway?'

'He's in the living room, and he's asleep. Which is how I'd like him to stay for the time being. And I'm sure *you'd* like him to stay that way, too, seeing as you're looking after him this afternoon.'

Ryan turned to look at her, his handsome face lit up by the widest smile, and Amber felt her heart dance around in her chest, followed by a succession of feelings she couldn't explain, and didn't really want. But sometimes, just the sound of his voice – that beautiful, soft Geordie accent of his – it could set off waves of confusion she didn't always welcome.

For months, she'd tried so hard to fight against everything

she was feeling for this man, because she'd never really been sure how much of it was real, and how much of it had to do with the fact she'd been pregnant, and therefore probably slightly more emotionally unstable than usual. But she'd given birth three months ago. And she still couldn't shake those feelings Ryan Fisher could stir up inside her. He'd been there for her after her split from Jim – the love of her life. Her ex-husband. Ryan's manager at top-flight football club Newcastle Red Star. He'd helped her deal with everything that came with that, in ways that probably hadn't been the most sensible course of action. Sex never had been the best form of therapy as far as Amber was concerned. It only led to more trouble. So why did she seem to turn to it so readily these days? But just having him around, well, she'd needed that. She'd needed to have him with her, and not just because she'd been carrying his baby. She'd needed him. Simple as that.

'You got a bit of time to spare?' Ryan grinned, placing the tiny t-shirt emblazoned with the words *"I Love my Daddy"* on the table behind him.

'Seriously?' Amber arched an eyebrow as Ryan pulled her towards him, circling her waist with his arm. 'Do you know how much sleep I've had lately? Or how much sleep I *haven't* had, that should be.'

'Well,' Ryan began, gently nuzzling her neck, his fingers playing with her long, dark red hair, 'if we moved in together then I could help you, couldn't I? I could take some of the load off your shoulders.'

'Don't start, Ryan, please. We've been over this.'

'I'm serious, Amber.' He stroked a strand of hair from her pale blue eyes, kissing her lightly on her slightly open mouth. 'It seems crazy, you and the baby living here and me all on my own in that huge new house of mine. I mean, I'm over here most of the time anyway, when you're not in London that is, so surely it'd make more sense if we...'

Amber shook her head, but she still let him push her back

against the wall. She didn't put up much of a fight, despite the constant wave of tiredness that seemed to inhabit her body these days, as he sneakily ran a hand up her thigh before sliding it up and under her t-shirt.

'Jesus, Ryan, do you ever stop?'

'I'm dying here, babe. All I can think about is fucking you, which is hardly surprising, considering we haven't done much of that lately.'

Amber looked at him, shaking her head again. 'I don't believe you...'

'What?' Ryan shrugged as she pushed past him and walked into the living room. 'Come on! What have I done now?'

But she wasn't listening any more. She was looking down at their beautiful baby boy. Rico Alejandro Fisher had been born three months ago, just two days before the start of the new football season back in August. With Ryan by her side – although, only just – and a labour so short she figured she must have done something really good in a past life to have deserved that, she'd given birth just after 11am and been home by tea-time, back to a house full of people and all the help she'd so desperately needed in those early days. Days when she'd missed her mum so much, with a pain so physical it almost wore her down. So she'd had no hesitation in giving her son a Spanish name, as a nod to her Mediterranean heritage – Rico, because she liked it, and Alejandro after her Spanish grandfather.

He was the most beautiful baby, and she was all too aware that everybody said that about their own children, but he really was. She could spend hours just looking at him, and there were times when she did just that. When her busy schedule allowed. Because every second she spent with her son was precious.

'Amber?'

She turned around, folding her arms as she looked at Ryan. 'You think I don't want a little bit of relief, too, huh? A little bit of time to feel sexy again because, God knows, it's the last thing

I feel these days.'

She pushed a hand through her hair as Ryan came closer, reaching out to take her hand. 'You're always sexy to me. Even with baby sick down the front of your t-shirt and your hair all over the place.'

She couldn't help laughing, looking down at the floor as he gave her hand a quick squeeze before bringing it up to his lips and kissing it gently. 'Yeah. Thanks for that.'

'And I still don't understand why you haven't taken up the option of maternity leave. Cloud Sports are quite willing to let you have the time off, aren't they?'

'Yes,' Amber sighed, letting go of Ryan's hand, folding her arms against her once more. 'But it's just not for me, Ryan. And we've already been over this. In fact, I've been over this countless times – with you, my dad, Ronnie… I'm tired of explaining it. It's just the way I am, okay? Rico isn't suffering; he comes with me whenever he can, and between you, my dad, and my wonderful family we're managing just fine, aren't we?'

'Yeah. I suppose we are. But you've been working yourself into the ground for months now. I mean, come on, you were back at work two days after giving birth! Isn't it about time you gave yourself a break?'

'I don't want a break. Breaks give you far too much time to think about things.'

She walked over to the dining table at the back of the room and started folding a pile of baby clothes that was lying on it.

'Like what?' Ryan asked, sitting down on the arm of the chair next to Rico's carry cot.

Amber said nothing for a few seconds. She wasn't in the mood for some deep conversation; she was way too tired for that. 'Nothing.'

'I hate it when you say that,' Ryan sighed, throwing himself down into the chair. 'There's quite obviously *something* wrong, I can tell. You're in one of those moods.'

'One of those…? Jesus, Ryan.'

'Okay, okay. I'm sorry.'

She couldn't help smiling, throwing a babygro at him.

He grinned, flinging his legs over the arm of the chair as he held the babygro up in the air. 'I can't believe how small he is.'

'Yeah, well, one day he'll be as big as his daddy. I'm just hoping that doesn't apply to his head, too.'

Ryan looked at her, still grinning. 'You got something to say there, Ms. Sullivan?'

She just smiled at him, nudging his legs down. 'Right, I've got to be somewhere.'

'What? Already?'

'Yes, Ryan. Unlike you my working day is only just starting. You gonna be okay looking after him for the afternoon?'

'I'm his dad, Amber.'

She fixed him with a look. 'Alright. I'll be at Tynebridge if you need me.'

Ryan sat up straight. 'You're going to Tynebridge?'

She looked down into Rico's carry cot, smiling at her son as his eyes flickered open. 'Hey there, baby. You gonna be a good boy for daddy while I'm out earning us some pennies?'

'Amber. Why are you going to Tynebridge?'

She reached into the cot and carefully picked up Rico, cuddling him to her, kissing the top of his head as she gently ruffled his mass of dark hair. 'Because, unless it's slipped your notice, it's the derby weekend. And Cloud Sports are showing the game live, as you well know. Me and Ronnie are going over there to set things up. He's one of the pundits, and I'm presenting… Ryan, you know all of this.'

'Is Jim gonna be there?'

She nestled Rico in the crook of her arm as she fixed Ryan with another look. 'I have absolutely no idea. Would it be a problem if he was?'

Ryan shrugged, his manner verging on the petulant. 'I've got to be at the ground myself by six. The boss wants us ready to leave for the hotel by half past. You gonna be back by then?'

'I'll let you know. If I'm not gonna make it you can just bring Rico down there. He can stay with me. Ryan, will you quit acting like a sulky teenager? Please? Me and Jim, it's over. You know that. But I can't avoid him forever; it's impossible. So just grow up and deal with it. You know, sometimes it's like having two kids…' She kissed Rico again, reluctant to let him go. He was so warm and soft, and he smelt of baby talc, and all of a sudden Amber had an overwhelming urge to just stay there and cuddle him all afternoon. Just one mention of Jim's name had done what it usually did – change her mood entirely. 'Okay, poppet. Daddy's taking charge now, so, you keep an eye on him and make sure he behaves himself.'

'Yeah, you're funny,' Ryan said, standing up and carefully taking Rico from Amber, holding him up in the air and bringing him back down for a huge kiss. 'Hey there, little fella. We're gonna have some fun, me and you.'

'Wear him out, will you?' Amber half-smiled, grabbing her jacket from the back of the sofa. 'It's a busy weekend this weekend and I could do with a few more hours sleep. I'll call you later, but you know where I am if you need me.'

She was about to run out of the door when Ryan stopped her. 'Amber?'

She turned around. 'Yeah?'

'Come here. Please.'

She walked back over to him, watching as he lay Rico back down in his cot. 'What do you want, Ryan?'

He moved closer to her, resting his hand lightly against her cheek. 'I want *you*, Amber. And you know that.'

'Ryan…' His mouth was on hers before she had a chance to say anything else, and she gave in to his kiss, she couldn't help it. Despite everything they'd been through in the past; despite the kind of man he'd used to be, he was giving her a sense of calm she really needed right now.

She pulled him closer by his t-shirt, slipping a hand around the back of his neck, and for a few, beautiful seconds she lost herself in that kiss; lost herself in something she could have, if she wanted it. A wonderful life with a man who'd finally grown up, and he loved her. Ryan Fisher truly did love her. So she could have this, all of it. If she wanted it.

He pulled away slightly, running his thumb lightly over her parted lips. 'Things are crazy right now, Amber, I know that, but…'

She backed away, grabbing her bag and jacket as she headed for the door. 'I'm gonna be late. Call me if you need me, okay?'

'Jesus… Amber!'

She turned around again, but she had no intention of going back this time. 'I've really got to go.'

He looked at her, his hands in his pockets, his eyes locked onto hers. 'Me and you… what's really happening here?'

She stared back at him, not really knowing what to say. 'You know what's happening, Ryan.'

She knew as well as he did that that was no kind of answer. But it was the only one she had.

*

'Well, if it isn't Superwoman herself.'

'Don't you start,' Amber sighed, throwing her bag down onto the couch in the Players' Lounge before going over to quickly kiss Ronnie's cheek.

'Trouble in paradise?' Ronnie grinned, leaning back against the wall and folding his arms.

Amber threw him a look out the corner of her eye but said nothing in reply.

'Everything's okay, though, isn't it?' Ronnie asked, dropping the flippancy.

'Everything's fine, thank you. I'm just really busy.'

'Yeah, I'm aware of that, Amber. I work with you.'

She sat down, pushing her hands through her long, tousled hair. 'It's been good, you know? Having him around. And since we found out I was having Rico he's changed, he really has.'

'I take it we're talking about Ryan?'

She nodded, fiddling with the bracelet hanging on her left wrist.

'Am I waiting for a "but" here?' Ronnie asked, narrowing his eyes slightly.

Amber sat back, letting out a small sigh. 'No. Things just feel a bit weird, that's all.'

'Weird?' Ronnie frowned.

'I'm still getting used to being a mum, Ronnie. Something I never thought I'd be. I'm a mum. And every day I worry about whether I'm doing it right and if Rico's okay and... it's hard, sometimes. Especially when Ryan's going on at me constantly.'

'About what?'

'Sex.'

'Okay.'

She looked up at him. 'It's not that I don't want it, Ronnie... Are you uncomfortable talking about this?'

He shook his head. 'Too tired, huh?'

'You could say that.'

'You sure that's not just an excuse?'

It was her turn to narrow her eyes as she looked at her best friend. 'What's that supposed to mean?'

Ronnie looked down at the ground, his hands in his pockets. 'I don't know, Amber. It's just that, sometimes, I wonder whether you going back to Ryan... I wonder whether it was the right thing to do.'

'He's Rico's dad, Ronnie.'

'That doesn't mean you actually have to be *with* him. Not if you don't want to be.'

'Who said I don't want to be with him?'

'Well, that's the impression you're giving off here, kiddo.'

'Is it?'

'Yeah.'

Amber sat forward, pushing her hands through her hair again. 'I never said we were love's young dream or anything.'

'No. I know you didn't.'

'But, I needed him, you know? I was pregnant, going through a divorce,' She trailed off, absent-mindedly looking at her naked left hand. She still couldn't get used to not wearing her rings. Even though they'd only really been there for the shortest of times.

'And now Rico's here?'

'Hmm? Sorry?' She looked back at Ronnie.

'Now that Rico's here, do you still need him? Ryan, I mean.'

'Of course I do.'

'You paused for a second there.'

'I didn't.'

'You did.'

'Jesus. I'd forgotten how irritating you could be.'

'He's here, you know.'

She sighed again, throwing herself back against the couch. 'Who?' As if she didn't know.

'Manager of the Month, two months running.'

She eyed Ronnie with a look of something verging on suspicion. 'Shouldn't we be doing something other than sitting here?'

'Probably. But I quite like watching you squirm.'

'You're such a bastard.'

He smiled, walking over to her and holding out his hand, pulling her up off the couch. 'You need to sort out what you really want, Amber.'

'I just want to get on with my life, Ronnie. As simple as that.'

'There's nothing simple when it comes to you getting on with your life, kiddo.'

'Yeah. Thanks for reminding me. What about you, anyway? Any sign of a new romance on the cards?'

'You've got to be kidding me! No time for any of that.'

She couldn't help smiling as she looked at him, cocking her head slightly. 'Surely you've got women falling at your feet, Ronnie White. Good looking bloke like you. You've still got it, even at your age.'

'Yeah, okay, enough with the smart remarks. Come on. We've got work to do.'

Work. The only thing that was keeping Amber's mind off the one thing she couldn't stop thinking about.

*

Jim Allen sat back in his chair, his eyes scanning the computer screen, but he was taking nothing in. His mind was on way too many other things, and for a man who was usually so focused and in control it was a feeling that didn't sit well with him. But these past few months had been nothing short of crazy. Unpredictable. Painful.

A knock on his office door broke into his thoughts and he looked up from his laptop. 'Come in.'

'Hey, Dad!'

Jim smiled at the sight of his son. Brandon Palmer. Twenty-one-years-old, tall and handsome, and a player with the region's rival top-flight team, Wearside Spartans.

'Hey back. What you doing here? Spartans sent you over enemy lines to spy on what we're up to before the big game?'

'Well, if I'd wanted to do that I could have sneaked over to the training ground this morning, couldn't I? No, I just came over to see how you're doing.'

Jim eyed Brandon warily, smiling slightly as his son perched himself on the edge of his desk. 'I'm doing just fine. Why wouldn't I be?'

Brandon shrugged. 'Dunno. You just seem to have been throwing yourself into your work a lot lately, that's all.'

'I'm the manager of a top-flight football club, Brandon. It isn't

575

exactly a nine-to-five kinda thing.'

'You don't take any time off?'

'I don't want to take any time off. Manager of the Month awards aren't given out to just anybody, you know. You've got to put the work in.'

'Is that all that matters to you?'

Jim narrowed his eyes as he looked at his son. 'Have you come here for any particular reason, Brandon? Apart from to give me a headache I don't need.'

'I worry about you.'

'Why?'

'I mean, Ellen and me, we asked you over for dinner the other night and you refused to come. You won't even take a night off to spend a bit of quality time with your own son.'

'I'm fine, okay? I've just got a lot on.'

'Yeah. You seem to have had a lot on for a while now.'

Jim fixed Brandon with a hard stare, which Brandon returned.

'Ever since Amber became pregnant. Ever since she took up with Ryan Fisher. Again.'

'She hasn't "taken up" with Ryan Fisher, as you put it.' Jim got up and walked over to the sideboard, pouring himself a small measure of whiskey.

'So, you're not bothered, then?'

'About what?'

'About Amber and Ryan.'

'There *is* no Amber and Ryan.'

'Oh, really?'

Jim turned around, leaning back against the sideboard, his eyes once more locking with Brandon's. 'Really.'

Brandon gave another shrug, sliding down from the desk and heading back towards the door, his hands in his pockets. 'Okay. Whatever. Anyway, I just thought I'd drop by and say hi, see how you were. But you still look like the same old Jim Allen to me.'

Jim said nothing to that, he just took a sip of his drink and remained silent.

'Look, Dad…' Brandon turned around and faced his father. 'Have you thought about getting out more? Maybe meeting someone else, you know, to take your mind off…'

'I'll see you later, Brandon.'

Brandon held up his hands as he turned to go. 'I'm outta here.'

Jim waited until he'd closed the door behind him before he took the letter from his inside jacket pocket, opening it up and reading it through. One more piece of proof. Another piece of a jigsaw he'd been trying to put together. But he had all he needed now. The ball was very much in his court. And it was up to him whether he chose to hit out or not.